# Praise for
# JAYNE ANN KRENTZ
## and

## *THE GOLDEN CHANCE*

"*THE GOLDEN CHANCE* is Jayne Ann Krentz at her very best. Pure entertainment."

—Susan Elizabeth Phillips

"A breezy, funny tale of love conquering all. . . ."

—*Publishers Weekly*

"Vastly entertaining, completely delightful. . . ."

—Dorothy Garlock

"Jayne Ann Krentz has taken the powerful themes of family loyalty, the struggle for power, and sex, and drawn them into a suspenseful and satisfying story that strikes a deep, human chord."

—Patricia Matthews

## *SILVER LININGS*

"An action-packed plot and a charming heroine."

—*Publishers Weekly*

"Jayne Ann Krentz entertains to the hilt in *SILVER LININGS*. . . . The excitement and adventure don't stop."

—Catherine Coulter

This book is a work of fiction. Names, characters, places and incidents are products of the author's imagination or are used fictitiously. Any resemblance to actual events or locales or persons living or dead is entirely coincidental.

An *Original* Publication of POCKET BOOKS

POCKET BOOKS, a division of Simon & Schuster, Inc.
1230 Avenue of the Americas, New York, NY 10020

ISBN: 0-7434-2295-3

First Pocket Books trade paperback printing January 2001

10 9 8 7 6 5 4 3 2 1

POCKET and colophon are registered trademarks of
Simon & Schuster, Inc.

Cover design by Jim Lebbad

Printed in the U.S.A.

# CONTENTS

❧

THE GOLDEN CHANCE

SILVER LININGS

# THE
# GOLDEN CHANCE

# 1

᠅

Something in Nicodemus Lightfoot understood and respected small towns and the kind of people who lived in them. He did not wax nostalgic about them, nor did he believe in the myth that small towns were somehow best at incubating American values and right thinking. He did not even particularly like small towns, especially small farm towns in the summer. They tended to be hot and slow. Every kid who had just graduated from the local high school was probably desperate to get out of town as soon as possible, and Nick understood their desire.

He was afraid that his intuitive knowledge of towns such as Holloway, Washington, was in his blood. Nick himself was only one generation away from jobs like working cattle or driving a combine, and he knew it. He accepted it. He had no problem with it. And that was what gave him the edge over everyone else in the families. The other members of the Lightfoot and Castleton clans were still trying to forget how close their roots ran to towns such as this one in eastern Washington.

Nick took another swallow of beer and shifted into a more comfortable position. He was leaning against the trunk of an aging apple tree that dominated the front yard of a little white clapboard house. The grass in the yard was rapidly turning brown. By August it would be dead.

Nick had been sitting in the shade of the tree for almost an hour. The beer was warm, the street of small, neat houses was empty and Nick was getting bored. That took some doing, because he was good at waiting.

Hearing a clatter in the distance, Nick turned to watch two lanky youngsters hurtle down the street on beat-up skateboards. Faithful dogs, tongues lolling, jogged behind. The boys seemed oblivious, as only kids can be, of the late June heat. Nick watched the foursome until they disappeared around the corner, and then he finished the beer.

None of the neighbors had come out to ask him what he was doing sitting under the apple tree, although Nick had seen a few curtains twitch in the houses across the street.

Earlier a couple of teenagers had checked out his Porsche with shining eyes. One of them had worked up the courage to ask if the car was Nick's. He'd admitted it was and tossed them the keys so that they could sit in the front seat and dream for a while. They'd finally left reluctantly when a curly-haired woman down the street had waved them home. That had been the end of Nick's social interaction with the neighbors of Miss Philadelphia Fox.

He was beginning to wonder if the Fox was ever going to return to her lair when the insistent whine of a small-car engine made him glance down the street.

A candy-apple-red mosquito-sized compact darted around the corner and homed in on the one open space left at the curb. With the unerring instinct of a small, annoying insect spotting bare skin, the little red car zipped around a battered pickup truck and dove headfirst into the parking space behind the Porsche.

Nick watched in fascination as the driver of the mosquito realized she was not going to be able to wedge the vehicle into the limited space from such an angle. The compact whined furiously, jerking back and forth in several short, convulsive movements before abandoning its attack.

Nick held his breath as the thwarted mosquito maneuvered its way back out of the parking space and reluctantly pulled forward alongside the Porsche so that it could back properly into the slot. The Porsche survived unscathed, but Nick had the impression the mosquito was defiant in defeat.

He guessed then that the driver of the red insect was Philadelphia Fox. He watched her turn off the engine and climb out of the car holding two paper bags of groceries that were so full they effectively blocked her vision.

His first impression was that he was watching an entity of condensed, restless energy. Her movements were quick, sharp, impulsive. With a flash of insight Nick realized that he was looking at a woman who did not wait for things to fall into place in their own time and in their own way. She pushed them into place.

So this was his ticket home. He did not know whether to be dismayed or delighted.

He had been in exile for three long years and was not yet certain what to make of Philadelphia Fox, but if he played his cards right he might be able to use her to do what had to be done. It wasn't as if he had a lot of choice, he reminded himself. It was Phila Fox or nothing. He had no other options, and time was running out.

The real question, of course, was whether he really wanted to go home. He told himself he was still ambivalent, but he knew that in his heart he had already made the decision. He would not be sitting in the heat and boredom of Holloway, Washington, if he didn't know what he wanted to do.

Nick smiled faintly as he watched Philadelphia struggle with the grocery bags and her keys. From this distance she looked neither sufficiently powerful nor beautiful enough to be capable of tearing the families apart. But that only went to show that dynamite could be packaged in raspberry-pink jeans and an orange, green and black jungle-print camp shirt.

*Fox.* She suited her name, Nick decided. There was something vixenish about her, something that was both keen and delicate. Her eyes were large in her triangularly shaped face, and they tilted slightly upward at the corners. They were watchful, wary eyes.

She was not very tall, probably only about five-four, and she was slender, with small, high breasts and a narrow waist. Her tawny brown hair was cut in a smooth, shining bob that hugged her jawline. He knew she was twenty-six years old and that she was unmarried. That and the fact that she had apparently had close ties to Crissie Masters was about all he knew.

Yesterday morning's phone call from Eleanor Castleton replayed itself in his head.

"She's a problem, Nick. A terrible problem."

"Yeah, I can see that. But she's not my problem."

"That's not true and you know it, dear. She's a serious threat to the families, and you're family. What happened three years ago doesn't change that fact, and deep down inside I'm sure you realize it."

"Eleanor, I don't give a damn what happens to the families."

"I don't believe that for one minute, dear. You're a Lightfoot. You would never abandon your heritage when the chips are down. Go and see her, Nick. Talk to her. Someone has to deal with her."

"Send Darren. He's the one with charm, remember?"

"Hilary and Darren both tried to talk to her. She refused to listen to either of them. She's biding her time, looking for a way to turn the situation to her advantage. I know that's what she's doing. What can you expect from someone of her background? She's just another mischief-making little tramp like that Masters creature who descended on us last fall. That horrid little tart started all this. If it hadn't been for her—"

"What makes you think this, uh, other little tart will talk to me?"

"You'll find a way to deal with her, dear." Eleanor Castleton spoke with serene confidence. "I know you will. I have complete faith in you. And you're family, dear. You simply must do something about Philadelphia Fox."

"I'll think about it, Eleanor."

"I knew you wouldn't let us down. Family is family when all is said and done, isn't it?"

To his chagrin, Nick had discovered Eleanor was right. When all was said and done, family *was* family. So here he sat under an apple tree contemplating possible methods of manipulating a mischief-making little tramp.

Philadelphia Fox walked right past him up the sidewalk to the front door of the little white house. The screen door banged as she opened it, caught it with her toe and shoved her key into the lock of the main door. The paper bags wobbled.

Nick got slowly to his feet, removing his glasses to rub the bridge of his nose as he strolled up the cracked walk behind her.

The key seemed to have gotten stuck in the old lock and refused to turn. The grocery bags jiggled precariously. The screen door escaped the restraining toe, and Nick heard a softly uttered curse as Philadelphia tried to force the issue.

Nick nodded to himself and replaced his glasses on his nose, satisfied with this confirmation of his suspicion that Miss Fox did everything the fast way and, therefore, sometimes wound up doing things the hard way. This was the kind of woman who, once she made up her mind, would charge straight toward her goal. The eager, zealous, reckless type. Nick contemplated that tantalizing tidbit of information. One didn't run across eager, zealous, reckless, mischief-making little tramps every day.

He wondered suddenly if the little Fox made love at a hundred miles an hour, the way she appeared to do everything else.

Nick scowled at that errant thought and slid his glasses back onto his nose. It was not like him to let such thoughts get in the way of business. Besides, Philadelphia Fox was not his type. At least, he didn't think she was.

Still, perhaps he shouldn't blame himself for the brief fancy. After all, he had never had a woman make love to him at a hundred miles an hour. It sounded exciting.

But maybe that was because it had been so damned long since he had had a woman make love to him at all.

Moving up very close behind the struggling Phila, he asked politely, "Can I give you a hand with those bags?"

He had expected to startle her. He was not expecting the truly frightened gasp and the flash of raw terror in her huge eyes when she swung around to face him. He barely managed to catch one of the grocery bags as it fell from her arms. The other hit the steps, spilling out a loaf of bread, a can of tuna fish and a bunch of carrots.

"Who the hell are you?" Philadelphia Fox demanded.

"Nicodemus Lightfoot."

The fear vanished from her gaze, replaced first by an odd relief and then by disgust. She glanced morosely down at the spilled groceries and then looked up again, her eyes narrowed.

"So you're a Lightfoot. I wondered what one would look like. Tell me, are the Castletons any better-looking? They must be or Crissie wouldn't have turned out so lovely." She crouched and began to retrieve her groceries.

"The Castletons got the looks and charm. The Lightfoots got the brains. It's been a profitable partnership." Nick scooped up the tuna fish and reached out to jiggle the key in the frozen lock. He maneuvered it gently, and a second later the door popped open.

"Funny," Philadelphia Fox said, her face grim as she got to her feet and glared at the open door. "That's what Crissie and I used to tell each other. She got the looks and I got the brains. It was supposed to be a profitable partnership for us, too, but it didn't quite work out that way. I expect you want to come inside and browbeat me, right?"

Nick gazed thoughtfully into the colorful, plant-filled interior of the little house. Bare wood floors gleamed beneath red and black throw rugs, and the walls were painted a brilliant sunshine yellow. The sofa was as red as the little car parked out front. Somehow all the vivid hues combined to look very cheerful and welcoming. Apparently Miss Fox's sense of interior design was similar to her taste in clothing. He smiled again.

"Yes," Nick said. "I would very much like to come inside and talk to you."

"Come on, then," Philadelphia muttered as she pushed past him into the house. "We might as well get this over with. I've got some iced tea in the refrigerator."

Nick smiled again with satisfaction as he watched her precede him into the house. "That sounds just fine."

There was a word for what was wrong with her, Phila knew. Several words, in fact. As she slapped the groceries down on the counter and went to the refrigerator, she considered those words. *Burnout* was one. *Stress* was another.

Her grandmother would have brushed aside such contemporary jargon, of course, and gotten right to the point.

*Stop feeling sorry for yourself. The trouble with you, my girl, is that you've let yourself wallow around in your own emotions long enough. It's time to pull yourself up by your bootstraps. Get hold of yourself, child. Get up and get going. The world is waiting for you to fix it. If you don't do it, who will?*

Matilda Fox had seen everything as a challenge. The prospect of righting the wrongs of the world was what had kept her going, she had frequently claimed. It gave life purpose. Her son, Alan, Phila's father, had followed in his mother's footsteps. He had been passionate about his causes and in due course had married another passionate world-fixer named Linda. The two of them must have shared a few passions other than the political sort because eventually they had produced Phila.

Phila had no real recollection of her parents. They had died when she was very young. She had a picture of them, a faded color photograph of two people dressed in jeans and plaid shirts standing beside a jeep. Behind them was a cluster of huts, a brown river and a wall of jungle. Phila carried the photo in her wallet along with a picture of Crissie Masters and one of her grandmother.

Although she had no clear memory of them, Phila's parents had bequeathed her more than her hazel eyes and tawny brown hair. They had left within her their philosophy of life, which Matilda Fox had in turn nourished into full flower. From the cradle Phila had been inculcated with a healthy dose of skepticism toward established authority, conservative thinking and right-wing institutions. It was an independent, decidedly liberal philosophy. Some might have called it radical. It was the sort of philosophy that thrived on challenge.

But, Phila reflected, lately it had been very hard to get interested in a new challenge. Everything seemed increasingly unimportant. She now felt her parents and grandmother had been wrong. One person could not save the world. In fact, one person could only get hurt trying to fix things.

It was tough trying to carry on the family tradition when there was no family left to support it. She had been doing it alone for years and now she seemed to have run out of steam.

Crissie Master's philosophy of life, on the other hand, was finally beginning to make more sense to Phila. It could be summed up in five words: *Look out for number one.*

But now Crissie was dead, too. The big difference was that, while they had died young, her parents had died for a cause in which they had believed and to which they had been committed. Matilda Fox had died at her desk. She had been busily penning yet another article for one of the score of strident left-wing newsletters which printed her work. She had been eighty-two years old.

Crissie Masters, however, had died behind the wheel of a car that had plunged off a Washington coast road and buried itself in a deep ravine. She had been twenty-six years old. Her epitaph could have been, *Am I having fun yet?*

Phila dropped ice into two tall glasses and poured the cold tea. She felt no overpowering need to be courteous to a Lightfoot, especially not to one as big as the specimen out in her living room, but it was awkward to drink tea in front of someone else without at least offering a glass. It was, after all, very hot outside and the Lightfoot looked as if he had been sitting under her apple tree for some time.

She picked up the tray of drinks and headed for the living room. An echo of fear rippled through her as she recalled how close he had gotten to her a few minutes before without her even having been aware of him. *That's how it could happen*, she thought uneasily. No warning, no intuitive sense of danger; just *wham*. Someday she would simply turn around and find herself in trouble.

Phila forced herself to relax as she set the tray down on the glass coffee table. Surreptitiously she studied the intruder. He looked big and dark sitting on her bright red sofa. His eyeglasses did nothing to soften the effect.

He really was a large man, she realized, and that alone made her feel hostile. She did not like large males.

"Thanks for the tea. I've been getting by on warm beer for the past hour." Nicodemus Lightfoot reached for a frosty glass.

The vibration of his voice sent a distant, whispered warning through Phila's nerve endings. She told herself she was imagining things. Her nerves had been more than a little frayed lately. But she had always relied on her instincts, and now she couldn't ignore the way his voice disturbed her senses.

Everything about this man was too calm, too still and watchful, as if he could spend hours waiting in darkness.

"Nobody asked you to sit out in front of my house for an hour, Nicodemus Lightfoot." Phila sat down in a yellow canvas director's chair and picked up her own glass of tea.

"Call me Nick."

She didn't respond immediately. Instead she examined him for a few seconds, noting the gold-and-steel watch, the blue oxford-cloth button-down that he wore open at the throat, and the snug, faded jeans. The jeans looked like standard-issue Levi's, but she guessed that the casual shirt had cost a hundred bucks or more. His type would wear hundred-dollar shirts with old jeans.

"Why on earth should I call you Nick?" She took a swallow of cold tea.

Nick Lightfoot didn't rise to the bait. Instead, he studied her in turn, his eyes thoughtful behind the lenses of his glasses. The window air conditioner hummed in the silence.

"You're going to be difficult, aren't you?" he finally observed.

"It's what I'm good at. I've had a lot of practice."

His eyes swept over the glass coffee table, spotted the stack of travel brochures. "Going on a trip?"

"Thinking about it."

"California?" He flipped through a couple of the folders with their scenes of endless beaches and Disneyland.

"Crissie used to say Southern California would be good for me. She always claimed I needed a taste of life in the fast lane."

Lightfoot said nothing for a few minutes, and Phila watched him out of the corner of her eye. He was a predator, she decided. His light gray eyes reflected little . . . only perhaps an unending search for prey and a cold intelligence. The thin lips, bold, aggressive nose and the high, blunt cheekbones made her think of a large animal. The heavy pelt of his dark hair was lightly iced with silver. He was somewhere in his mid-thirties, she guessed. And he'd done some hunting in his time.

There was an unconscious arrogance in the set of his shoulders and a lean but powerful strength in his body. She knew that his must be a smooth, prowling stride that ate up ground as he moved. He could stalk a victim all day if necessary and still have plenty of energy left for making the kill at the end of the hunt.

"You aren't quite what I expected," Nick said finally, looking up from the brochures.

"What did you expect?"

"I don't know. You just aren't it."

"I've had phone calls from someone named Hilary Lightfoot who sounds like she runs around in an English riding habit most of the time. Also, some from a man named Darren Castleton. He sounds like he's running for office. Where do you fit into the scenario, Mr. Lightfoot? Crissie never mentioned you. Frankly, you look like hired muscle."

"I never met Crissie Masters. I moved from Washington to California three years ago."

"How did you find me?"

"It wasn't hard. I made a few phone calls. Your ex-boss gave me your address."

"Thelma told you where I was?" Phila asked sharply.

"Yeah."

"What did you do to her to make her tell?"

"I didn't do anything to her. I just talked to her."

"I'll bet. You say that a little too easily for my taste."

"No accounting for taste."

"You're accustomed to people answering questions when you ask them, aren't you?"

"Why shouldn't she have been willing to cooperate?" he asked with the mildest possible expression of surprise.

"I asked her not to give out my address."

"She did say something about you wanting to dodge reporters but when she found out I wasn't interested in doing an interview, she opened up."

"You mean you applied pressure and she caved in." Phila sighed. "So you *are* the muscle for your families. Poor Thelma. She tries, but she isn't very good at resisting pressure. She's been a bureaucrat too long."

"You, I take it, are better at it?" Nick's brows rose skeptically.

"I'm a pro. And I'll save you a lot of time by telling you now that there's nothing you can say that will convince me to change my mind. I'm not about to sell back the shares in Castleton & Lightfoot that Crissie left to me. Not for a while, at any rate. I have some serious thinking to do about those shares. I may have some questions I want answered."

He nodded, looking neither annoyed nor startled. He just looked disturbingly patient.

"What questions do you have, Phila?"

She hesitated. The truth was, she did not really have any questions. Not yet. She hadn't been able to think clearly enough to come up with any. She was still trying to adjust to the trauma she had been through lately.

First there had been the trial, which had dragged on for weeks, and then had come the shock of Crissie's death. Phila thought she would have been able to handle the trial if that had been all there was to deal with at the time. But the news about Crissie had been more than she could handle.

Beautiful, bold, flashy Crissie with her California looks and her vow to get what was coming to her. The night of the vow came back to Phila now, a clear, strong image in her mind. It had been the first time she had tried more than a sip of alcohol.

Crissie, looking a worldly twenty-one at the age of fifteen, had talked the clerk of an all-night convenience store into selling the teenage girls the cheap wine. Crissie could talk any man into anything. It was one of her survival skills.

She and Phila had gone to the small town park near the river and drunk their illicit booze out behind the women's rest rooms. Then Crissie had outlined her plans for the future.

*There are people out there who owe me, Phila. I'm going to find them, and I'm going to make them give me what's mine. Don't worry. When I do, I'll cut you in for a piece of the action. You and me, we're like sisters, aren't we? We're family and family sticks together.*

Crissie had learned the truth of her own words the hard way. She had found the people she felt owed her and when she had tried to make them accept her, she had discovered the real meaning of a family sticking together. They had formed a solid wall against her and her claims of kinship.

"I don't know if I'm ready to ask my questions yet," Phila told Nick. "I think I'll wait and ask them at the annual C&L stockholder's meeting in August."

"The stockholders of Castleton & Lightfoot are all family."

"Not anymore." Phila smiled, really smiled, for the first time in weeks.

Nick Lightfoot appeared amused. "Planning to make trouble?"

"I don't know yet. Possibly. Crissie deserves that much, at least. Don't you think? She loved to stir up trouble. It was her way of taking revenge on the world. Making a little trouble on her behalf would be a fitting memorial."

"Why was Crissie Masters important to you?" Nick asked. "Were you related?"

"Not by blood or marriage, and that's probably the only kind of relationship you would understand."

"I understand friendship. Was Crissie your friend?"

"She was much more than a friend. She was the closest thing to a sister I ever had."

He looked politely quizzical. "I never met the woman, but I've heard a lot about her. From what I've heard, the two of you don't appear to have had much in common."

"Which only goes to show how little you know about either Crissie or myself."

"I'm willing to learn."

Phila thought about that, and she did not like the direction her mind was taking. "You're different from the other two who called me."

"How am I different?"

"Smarter. More dangerous. You think before you choose your tactics." She spoke carefully, giving him the truth. She was accustomed to relying on her instincts when it came to judging people, and she was rarely wrong. She had developed survival skills, too, just as Crissie had. But she had not been born with Crissie's looks, so those skills had taken a different twist.

"Are you complimenting me?" Nick asked curiously.

"No. Just stating obvious facts. Tell me, who will the Castletons and Lightfoots send if you screw up your assignment to browbeat me out of the shares?"

"I will try very hard not to screw up."

"How's your track record in that department?" she taunted, although she suspected it was excellent.

"Not perfect. I've been known to screw up very badly on occasion."

"When was the last time?"

"Three years ago."

The apparently honest answer surprised her, and thereby threw her off guard. "What happened?" she asked, with somewhat too obvious curiosity.

He gave her a slow, remote smile. "We both know that what happened to me three years ago doesn't matter a damn right now. Let's stick with the issue at hand."

She shrugged. "You can stick with it if you like. I've got better things to do."

He studied the brochures on the table again. "Are you sure you want to go to California?"

"I think so. I feel the need to get away, and it would be a sort of memorial trip in honor of Crissie. She loved Southern California. We were both born and raised in Washington, but she always said California was her spiritual home. She went down there to work as a model after she graduated from high school. It seems fitting somehow to spend some time there. She would have wanted me to have some fun."

"Alone?"

Phila smiled, showing her teeth. "Yes. Alone."

Nick appeared to consider that for a moment, and then he switched back to the only topic that really mattered to him. "Are you going to fight the Castletons and Lightfoots every inch of the way, or is the word *cooperation* a part of your vocabulary?"

"The word is there, but I use it only when it suits me."

"And right now it doesn't suit you to cooperate by selling those shares back to the families?"

"No, I don't think so."

"Not even for a great deal of money?"

"I'm not interested in money right now."

He nodded, as if she had verified a personal conclusion he had already reached. "Yeah, well, that settles that."

Phila was instantly wary. "What does it settle?"

"My job is done. I was asked to approach you about the shares. I've done that, and I'm convinced you aren't about to cooperate with the families. I'll report my failure, and that will be the end of it."

She did not believe what he said for a moment. "You said you were going to try very hard not to screw up."

"I gave it my best shot." He looked hurt that she would think otherwise.

Phila grew more alarmed. His best shot, she sensed, would never be this ineffectual. "You never answered my question about who they'll send next."

"I don't know what they'll do. That's their problem."

She put her glass down on the table and eyed him narrowly. "That's the end of it as far as you're concerned?"

He shrugged. "I don't see that I have much option. You've made it clear you don't even want to talk about the shares."

"You're not the type to give up this quickly," Phila stated.

His eyes widened. "How do you know what type I am?"

"Never mind. I just do and you're not acting true to form at the moment."

"Disappointed?"

"No, but I am very curious about what you're up to."

"Yeah." His smile came and went again. "I'll bet you are. And I'm equally curious about what you're planning to do. But I guess we'll both find out all the results eventually, won't we? I'll look forward to hearing about whatever trouble you manage to stir up, Phila. Should make for an interesting annual meeting. Too bad I won't be there to watch you in action."

"Why won't you be there? You're a Lightfoot. Don't you hold stock?"

"I still have the shares I was given when I was born and the shares I inherited from my mother, but they're a long way from constituting a controlling interest. I haven't paid much attention to them lately, anyway. For the past three years I've let my father vote my shares."

"Why?"

"It's a long story. Let's just say I've lost interest in Castleton & Lightfoot. I've got other things to do with my life these days."

Phila's fingernails drummed a quick staccato on the arm of her chair. Mentally she flipped through a variety of possibilities she had not yet considered.

Crissie had never mentioned this particular member of the clan. Maybe that was because he was estranged from the families for some obscure reason. He was certainly implying as much when he claimed he no longer voted his shares at the annual meeting. If that was the case, Phila told herself with a sudden rush of interest, she might find him very useful.

"If you're no longer involved with Castleton & Lightfoot, just what are you doing with your life these days?" she asked bluntly. Almost immediately she sensed she had made a tactical error. The last thing she should do was show any interest in him. She should have been more subtle. But it was too late to take back her words.

Nick seemed unaware of any blunder on her part. "I'm running my own business in Santa Barbara—Lightfoot Consulting Services. I just agreed to get in touch with you as a favor to the families. But the bottom line is that I'm not really sure I give a damn how much trouble you cause Castleton & Lightfoot. Have fun, Phila."

But he did not rise from the sofa and head back out into the heat, Phila noticed.

"What does Lightfoot Consulting Services consult about?" she asked.

He gave her an unreadable look. "We provide advice and information to firms trying to open overseas markets. A lot of companies want a cut of the world pie, but they don't have the vaguest idea of how to do business in Europe or the Pacific Rim countries."

"And you do?"

"Some."

"Would you still be working in the family firm if you hadn't shot yourself in the foot three years ago?" Phila demanded.

"I didn't exactly shoot myself in the foot three years ago."

"You said you screwed up badly."

"It was more like a family quarrel. But to answer your question, yeah, I'd probably still be with the firm if things hadn't happened the way they did. In fact, I'd still be running Castleton & Lightfoot if I'd stayed."

"You were running it?" She frowned.

"I'd just gotten myself appointed CEO the year before I walked out."

"This is getting more and more weird. Why did you walk out if you'd just gotten appointed chief executive officer? What are you doing down there in California? Why did you do anybody the favor of contacting me? What is this all about?"

A slight, oddly tantalizing light appeared in his eyes. "I've told you what this is all about, Miss Fox. I am no longer with the family firm. I got a phone call from the one person connected with Castleton &

Lightfoot who still speaks to me on occasion, and I agreed to talk to you as a favor to her. I've talked to you. End of favor."

"And that's the end of the matter as far as you're concerned?"

"Yeah."

"I don't believe you." Something was very wrong here.

"That's your prerogative, Phila. Have dinner with me tonight?"

It took a minute for the invitation to penetrate. She looked up at him blankly, aware that her mouth had fallen open. "I beg your pardon?"

"You heard me. It's too late to start for California this evening. I'm going to be spending the night here in town. I just thought we could have dinner. After all, I sure as hell don't know anyone else in Holloway. Unless you have other plans?"

She shook her head slowly as the light dawned. "I don't believe this."

"What don't you believe?"

"You aren't really going to try to seduce me in order to get back those shares, are you? I mean, it would be such a trite, old-fashioned, dipstick dumb sort of approach. Also a useless one."

He thought about that for a while, meditatively studying the ivy growing from a red pot on a nearby table. When his eyes came back to Phila's, she did not like the cool intensity she saw in his gaze. She had the impression he had made a major decision.

"Miss Fox," Nick said with a disconcerting air of formality, "just for the record, I would like you to know that if I tried to seduce you it would be because I wanted to sleep with you, not because I wanted to get my hands on those C&L shares."

She stared at him with narrowed eyes, trying to analyze, assess and categorize him. She had thought she had known precisely what to expect from any member of the wealthy, powerful Lightfoot and Castleton clans. But Nicodemus Lightfoot was refusing to fit into the mold she had prepared for him. That just made him all the more dangerous, she reminded herself.

But she couldn't get the idea out of her head that it might also make him all the more useful.

"If I had dinner with you, would you spill any juicy family secrets?" she asked.

"Probably not."

"Then what would be the point?"

"The point would be that neither of us would be forced to eat alone."

"I don't mind eating alone. I often eat alone."

"You know something, Miss Fox? That does not surprise me. I eat alone a lot myself. Too often." He got to his feet. "I'll pick you up at six. You know the local places. I'll let you make the reservations."

He walked to the front door and let himself out into the late-afternoon sun. He did not look back once.

Phila took that as another danger signal. It was a minor point, that business about not looking back to see if she was watching him, but it was significant. Any other man could not have resisted one small glance over his shoulder to see how she was reacting to his sudden departure.

She knew that his having failed to do so was not a reflection of unconcern on his part; it was a matter of self-discipline. The man was obviously in complete control of himself and was accustomed to being in equal command of the situation around him.

The soft, husky roar of the silver-gray Porsche filled the empty street outside the house. Phila listened to the powerful car as it drove off and decided that Nicodemus Lightfoot was going to be a problem.

Maybe that was what she really needed, Phila thought suddenly. Maybe she needed a problem she could sink her teeth into. It might do a lot more for this vague sense of depression than a trip to California.

Foxes thrived on exercising their cunning, she reminded herself.

# 2

❧

"I thought you'd better know, Hilary, that I phoned Nick and asked him to contact that Fox woman." Eleanor Castleton did not look up from her plants as she spoke. She moved around the heavily laden tables of the greenhouse, her gloved fingers working with assurance amidst the deceptively delicate blooms and leaves.

"You called him?"

"Oh, yes, dear. I do call him occasionally, you know. I don't want him to think he's totally out of touch with the families. He is a Lightfoot, after all."

"Did he agree to meet with Philadelphia Fox?" Hilary Lightfoot examined a small cream-colored flower. The bloom was amazingly inno-cent-looking, she thought, rather like Eleanor Castleton.

"Yes, dear, he agreed. Why shouldn't he?" Eleanor asked in the faintly astonished, slightly vague way that never failed to irritate Hilary.

Eleanor Castleton was in her sixties, but Hilary was certain she'd had that sweet, distracted, charmingly flighty air since the cradle. It went well with the faint traces of an aristocratic Southern accent.

"Nick hasn't been interested in family business for some time. I'm a little surprised he would get involved now," Hilary Lightfoot said. It was warm and humid in the greenhouse and Hilary hoped she could get out before her clothes began to stick to her. She intended to drive into the village as soon as she finished this annoying little chat with Eleanor.

She was dressed in a cream-colored silk blouse and fawn-colored pants. A row of narrow wooden bracelets clinked lightly on her wrist. Her dark red hair was drawn straight back from her face and caught at the nape of her neck in a classic knot that revealed her patrician features to fine advantage.

The only ring she wore was her wedding ring, a simple band of gold. A woman who was thirty-five years younger than her husband had to be careful about appearances. Hilary had always felt a gaudy-looking diamond would have been tacky under the circumstances. Besides, she was not the gaudy type.

"Nick is family," Eleanor said as she clipped a small, bowl-shaped leaf and discarded it. "He might have walked out three years ago, but that doesn't mean he doesn't care about something as serious as this situation with Philadelphia Fox."

"I doubt if there is anything Nick can do," Hilary said. "I tried to call her and got nowhere. Darren has also tried. She refused to even meet with him. I don't know what you think Nick can do. Frankly, if she were susceptible to masculine charm, your son would have had those shares back by now, Eleanor."

"You never know what will work with that sort of woman."

Hilary smiled. No one could convey subtle contempt for the lower classes quite the way Eleanor Castleton could. "True, I suppose. But our best bet will probably be to let her come to the annual meeting and then offer to buy her out."

Eleanor gave a small shudder. "I can't bear to think of an outsider at a C&L meeting. I'd much rather clear this up beforehand, wouldn't you? We'll see if Nick can accomplish anything."

"You really believe Nick can accomplish what Darren and I couldn't?" Hilary asked, forcing herself to keep her voice at a smooth, polite level.

"Nick has his own way of doing things," Eleanor said vaguely. "Hand me that watering can, will you, dear?"

Hilary picked up the metal vessel and handed it to the older woman. For a moment their eyes met. Hilary looked down into Eleanor's slightly vague pale blue gaze and thought she caught a glimpse of something that could have been steel. It wasn't the first time she had seen that expression, and it never failed to disturb her. But in the next instant it was gone, replaced by Eleanor's relentlessly distracted air.

"Thank you, dear." Eleanor maneuvered the spout of the watering can along a row of pots. "Mustn't let these new Nepenthes get dry. They're coming along so nicely. See how well the little pitchers are starting to form? Where's Reed today?"

"Playing golf." Hilary examined the delicately shaped leaves at the base of the plant Eleanor was watering. They were as innocent-looking as the fragile flowers.

"It seems he's always playing golf these days, or else he and Tec are busy fiddling with their guns out on the firing range. He wouldn't even talk to Darren about the Fox woman."

"My husband is enjoying retirement," Hilary said coolly. "He's earned it."

"I suppose so," Eleanor said softly. "But you know, dear, I never thought Reed would ever stop taking an interest in the firm the way he has. Castleton & Lightfoot was his whole life for so many years. He and Burke put everything they had into the company. It just doesn't seem right that Reed shows so little concern with company business these days."

"Reed trusts me to look after things for him," Hilary said coolly.

"Yes, of course he does, dear. And rightly so. You're doing an excellent job as CEO. An excellent job, indeed. Would you hand me that little trowel? No, not that one, the other one. Going into town?"

"I've agreed to have lunch with the new chairwoman of the Port Claxton Summer Theater Guild."

"Oh, dear. I suppose the guild will be wanting more money from C&L this year."

"Undoubtedly."

"I do think we've given enough to that group over the years, don't you? I was very disappointed in that production they put on last summer."

"*War Toys?*"

"It painted the military in a rather uncomplimentary light, didn't you think? Not to mention the business interests that are connected to the military establishment. We don't need that sort of theater here in Port Claxton."

Nor were the good people of Port Claxton likely to be treated to another play with a strong antimilitary theme in the near future, Hilary thought wryly. The Castletons and Lightfoots had made no secret of their reaction to *War Toys.*

Last year's guild chairman must have been temporarily insane to have authorized the production of the play in the first place. Then again, perhaps it hadn't been insanity, Hilary decided. Perhaps it had been a final, defiant stab at artistic freedom by the outgoing bureaucrat.

Hilary hoped the chairman had enjoyed thumbing his nose at the guild's largest contributor, because Port Claxton's struggling summer theater program would be paying the price for a long time to come. The new chairwoman would no doubt be scrambling today to apologize for the mistakes of her predecessor. Hilary did not look forward to lunch.

"I believe I'd better ask Tec to run out to the nursery for me,"

Eleanor said as she frowned over a tray of greenery. "I need some more sphagnum moss for my *Dionaea* leaf cuttings."

"I'll tell him you want to see him." Hilary turned toward the greenhouse door just as it burst open.

"I've got one! I've got one! I've got one!" An excited five-year-old boy dressed in a striped polo shirt and jeans came rushing into the greenhouse. His light brown hair was cut cute and short and his small face already showed the promise of the chiseled good looks he had inherited from his father.

Eleanor Castleton smiled down at her grandson. "What have you got, Jordan?"

"A dead fly." Jordan opened his palm to reveal a plump, moribund housefly. "Can I feed one of the plants? Can I? Can I? Can I?"

"*May* I," Eleanor corrected gently. "Yes, dear, I think we can find one hungry enough to eat your fly. Let's see, what about this little *Dionaea?* It hasn't eaten in ages."

Hilary watched in reluctant fascination as Jordan carefully dropped the now-dead insect into the open leaves of the Venus's-flytrap. The small carcass rolled across the trigger hairs and, with a speed that made all three on-lookers blink, the spined leaves snapped shut. The fly was locked inside.

"Wow," said Jordan. "Wow, wow, wow. Did you see that, Hilary?"

"Yes, Jordan, I saw it." Hilary took one last glance around at the lush-looking plants that filled the greenhouse. Some were in hanging baskets, a few aquatic species floated in aquariums, others were planted in rows of boxes that covered the workbenches.

Eleanor Castleton had developed a very interesting collection of pitcher plants, flytraps, sundews, butterworts and bladderworts. They all had one thing in common: they were carnivorous.

Nick walked into the brightly lit diner behind Phila and took in the surroundings with a sense of resignation. The place was classic: red vinyl seats in the booths, wood-grained plastic-laminated tables with chrome legs and a long counter with stools that appeared to be a size too small for the people sitting on them. Loud waitresses in grease-stained uniforms that were also a size too small scurried between the tables. The open doorway to the kitchen revealed a smoky, sizzling grill filled with meat that dripped fat into the flames. The classic decor was capped by a stunning view of the parking lot.

"This is the best you could do?" Nick asked Phila politely as he followed her to a booth.

"This is it," she answered cheerfully. "Best place in town. Everyone eats here on Saturday night."

"This is Friday night."

"Which explains why we didn't have to wait for a table," she concluded smoothly. "I recommend either the chicken or the steak. Anything else is liable to entail a certain risk."

"I'll bear that in mind." Nick gazed idly around the room again before bringing his attention back to the woman sitting across from him. He smiled. Being with Phila was like sitting in a lot full of parked cars and finding himself next to the one vehicle that had its key turned on in the ignition.

Tonight Phila was dressed in a pumpkin-colored silk blouse and a pair of jeans belted with a sliver-and-turquoise-studded strip of leather. He was learning that Miss Fox favored bold colors. They went well with her air of restless energy.

A waitress came by to take their order for drinks. Nick asked for scotch and was not unduly surprised when Phila ordered a prim white wine. The drinks came immediately. He gazed around the busy restaurant for a moment, thinking.

"What's the matter, Mr. Lightfoot," Phila purred as she examined her menu. "Not accustomed to such fancy surroundings?"

"I've eaten in worse." He opened his menu. "I've also eaten in better. Tell me, Phila, what made you decide to accept my invitation for dinner this evening?"

"I figured we might as well get it over with. The suspense was killing me."

"Get what over with?"

"Whatever approach you plan to use to convince me to give back the shares." She studied the menu with a small frown, as if having a tough time choosing between a baked potato or fries.

"I told you, I've already given it my best shot."

"Hah. I don't buy that for a minute." She glanced up. "What are you having?"

"The special."

"You don't even know what it is yet. You're supposed to ask the waitress."

Nick shrugged, unconcerned. "I'll take my chances."

"I told you it would be risky."

He smiled faintly. "I'm good at taking risks."

Phila scowled and snapped her menu shut. "Suit yourself. I'll have the chicken. As usual." She put her elbows on the table, folded her hands together and rested her chin on her interlaced fingers. Her hazel eyes regarded him broodingly. "So tell me, Nicodemus Lightfoot, how long have the Lightfoots and the Castletons been in the business of building death machines for the government?"

"Since before you were born, little girl."

She blinked. "You're not even going to deny it?"

"Well, technically they're electronics and instrumentation products, not death machines. Some people think of them as a kind of technological insurance, a way to balance power in the world. In fact some people might even say C&L is a very patriotic company. But I suspect the definition of a death machine is in the mind of the beholder."

"Castleton & Lightfoot makes the kind of electronics and instrumentation used in fighter planes and command posts, from what I've been able to determine. It designs to order for the military establishment. That means you build death machines. It also means that C&L is intimately involved in some cozy financial arrangements with the Pentagon."

Nick nodded. Things were falling into place quickly. "I get it," he said gently. "You're one of those."

"One of what?"

"You're," he paused delicately, "shall we say, of the liberal persuasion."

Her answering smile was grim. "If you think I'm bad, you should have met my grandmother."

"A flaming-pink, radical left-wing anarchist, right?"

"Let's just say she didn't care for the idea of the world being run by your kind."

"My kind?"

"Aristocrats with everything but the title. Too much money and too much power. She felt very strongly that having both power and money corrupts."

"So does a lack of either. Show me ten people who don't have enough money and power to control their own lives, and I'll show you nine dangerous human beings. The tenth is probably a wimp."

The vibration in the air around Phila was almost palpable now, and there were sparks in her eyes. Her engine was definitely shifting into gear.

Having all that feminine energy focused on him was doing things to his groin region, Nick discovered—things that hadn't been done in quite a while. He could tell that Phila had no concept of how she was turning him on, and that was as amusing as it was frustrating.

"Is that how you justify having been born into a privileged class? You pretend you're more noble than those who aren't as wealthy as you are? That you wouldn't stoop to some of the things a poor person might have to do in order to survive?"

"There seems to be some misunderstanding here. The Castletons and Lightfoots are not Rockefellers or Du Ponts. When you look at me you're only looking at second-generation money and I, personally, haven't even had that for the past three years."

"Now I'm supposed to feel sorry for you?"

"Look, Phila, I don't know what Crissie told you, but the fact is my father, Reed Lightfoot, and his buddy, Burke Castleton, were a couple of shitkickers who got an education in the Army when it turned out they showed an aptitude for electronics. When they got out of the service they had some big plans and big ambitions and the advantage of an inside view of the way the military works. They built C&L from the ground up. They were lucky. Their timing was good, and they turned out to be as shrewd about business matters as they were about electronic design."

"And they were smart enough to get into the death machine business," Phila finished with satisfaction.

Nick discovered he was enjoying the new enthusiastic gleam in Phila's eyes. He wondered if the expression was anything like the one she would have when she was lying naked under a man.

The prospect made him feel a little light-headed while the rest of him began to feel heavy and tight. He realized just how long it had been since he had genuinely anticipated going to bed with a woman. He could remember the date clearly: September twenty-fifth, four and a half years ago. It had been his wedding night. Things had gone downhill from there until the divorce eighteen months later.

There had been one woman since his marriage had ended, another shell-shocked veteran of the divorce wars who had been as terrified of the singles scene as Nick. They had consoled each other for several months in what had become a safe and comfortable, if totally uninspired, relationship.

It had been a healing time for both of them. Neither had been looking for or expecting to find a great love. Five months ago Jeannie had put an end to the affair, saying she was ready to search for something more substantial and meaningful. Nick had been vegetating in peaceful celibacy ever since.

Until tonight. Tonight everything was changing. Tonight he was relearning the simple masculine joy of sexual anticipation.

With an effort, he pushed his sensual feelings aside and concentrated on looking for the key to Philadelphia Fox.

"To be perfectly truthful," Nick said, swirling the scotch in his glass, "I used to have a few questions myself about all the military contracts Castleton & Lightfoot handled. That was back when I was involved with the firm, of course."

"Really?" Phila looked skeptical. "What happened when you asked those questions?"

"I was told I was in serious danger of becoming a left-wing liberal establishment dupe," he said dryly. "I was also called a coward and potential traitor to my country. Among other things."

Phila's shocked expression was priceless. It warmed Nick to the core because it told him he was on the right track. To catch a wary little liberal Fox, one used bait that was bleeding from the heart.

"How dare they call you that just because you stood up to them?" Phila demanded, instantly indignant on his behalf. "Is that when you left Castleton & Lightfoot?"

"Yeah. Right about then."

"You had a falling-out with the families over the business of making death machines?"

"That wasn't the only problem," he felt obliged to confess. "There were other things going on at the time."

"What other things?"

"Do you always get this personal this fast in a relationship?"

She immediately settled back against the vinyl seat and put her hands in her lap. "We're not talking about a relationship. We're talking about business."

"I don't want to talk about business tonight, Phila. Not unless you want to discuss those shares."

"I don't."

"Then we're left with a relationship discussion."

She looked him straight in the eye. "Are you going to try to seduce me after all?"

"Are you in a mood to be seduced?"

"No. Absolutely not, so don't get any ideas." She waited a beat and then, drawn inevitably back to the bait, asked, "Did you really walk away from Castleton & Lightfoot because they make military electronics?"

"As I said, there were a lot of things going on at the time besides that argument." He had her now. He was certain of it. The pleasurable sense of anticipation increased. The bright, glittering little Fox was hooked. It would take skill and subtlety to close the trap, but Nick looked forward to the challenge. "Let's talk about something else."

"I'd rather talk about what made you decide you wanted Castleton & Lightfoot to get out of the death machine business," she said.

He took a firm grip on his patience and chose his words carefully.

"Let's just say that military contracts are often more trouble than they're worth from a business point of view. It's a damned nuisance having to get security clearances for so many employees, there's too much paperwork involved in tracking costs and there's too much interference from bureaucrats trying to make brownie points by playing the role of government watchdog."

Disappointment dawned immediately in her expressive eyes. "Those are the reasons you wanted your firm to stop working for the government? You didn't like the paperwork?"

His lips curved slightly. "You want me to tell you that I suffered a liberal conversion and saw the light?"

"I'd like to think that there was some vague form of ethics involved in your decision, yes."

"Well, there may have been a few other reasons besides the paperwork problems, but as I recall they didn't carry much weight with the other members of the families."

"What reasons?" Phila demanded, on the scent again.

"I don't think this is a good time to go into them," Nick said smoothly. "Let's talk about you for a while. Tell me why you quit your job. You were a social worker or welfare worker or something, I take it?"

"I was a caseworker for CPS," she said, her voice cooling.

He tried to place the initials and failed. "CPS?"

"Child Protective Services."

"Foster homes? Abused kids? That kind of thing?"

"Yes," Phila said, her voice growing even colder. "That kind of thing."

"Your ex-supervisor said something about your trying to avoid interviews. What was that all about?"

"There was a trial involving a foster parent. I had to testify. After the trial a lot of people wanted interviews."

The more reticent she became, the more curious Nick grew. "You decided to quit your job after the trial ended?"

"People in my line of work have a high rate of burnout." She smiled gratefully at the waitress who arrived to take their order. "Oh, good," she told him. "I'm starving."

Nick watched her make a major production out of ordering the chicken and sensed he wasn't going to get her back on the topic of her former job.

"I'll have the special," Nick told the waitress.

The woman looked up from her order pad. "It's macaroni and cheese," she said in a warning tone.

"Fine."

"Macaroni and cheese?" Phila murmured in deep wonder as the waitress left.

"I happen to like macaroni and cheese. I'm a man of simple tastes."

"Sure. That's why you drive a Porsche and drink scotch."

"Having simple tastes does not imply a lack of standards," Nick said blandly. "I also like beer. Now, where were we?"

"I'm not sure. I think you were trying to get the story of my life so you could figure out how to use it to convince me to turn over the shares. That's your way, isn't it? You're sneaky."

"You flatter me."

Phila tilted her chin aggressively. "Not likely. I wouldn't go out of my way to flatter a Lightfoot or a Castleton. In fact, I think it's time we put our cards on the table."

"What makes you think I'm holding any cards?"

"Because you're the type who always keeps an ace up his sleeve. Now, then, why don't you just be straightforward with me, Mr. Lightfoot? And whatever it is you're going to offer or threaten, you can rest assured I'll give you a straightforward answer in return."

"And that answer will be no, right?"

"Right." Phila's eyes were alight again with the promise of battle. She started to say something else but stopped abruptly, her gaze going to the door behind Nick. The gleam went out of her eyes instantly, to be replaced by a wary, almost nervous expression. "Oh, damn," she said very softly.

Curious, Nick glanced over his shoulder, wondering if he was about to encounter an irate boyfriend of Phila's. What he saw was a thickly built woman in a faded, tie-dyed cotton dress. She must have been around forty but she was wearing her thin, graying hair in braids that hung to her waist. Her face was singularly lacking in character, showing no signs of maturity or past beauty. She wore no makeup to compensate for the unusual lack of color in her skin and lips. Her small eyes took in the crowd in one glance and alighted on Phila. She started down the aisle of booths.

"Friend of yours?" Nick asked, turning back to Phila.

"No."

"Trouble?"

"Probably." Her fingers were clenched around the edge of the table.

Nick wasn't sure what to expect of the coming confrontation. The last thing he wanted to get into was a cat fight between two women. Nor did he want to see Phila get hurt. "Does this by any chance involve a man?" he asked.

Phila's gaze met his. Her eyes were bitter. "In a way. Her name is Ruth Spalding. Feel free to leave."

"Not yet. I'm hungry, and here come our salads." He glanced at the waitress who was bearing down on the booth at the same rate of speed as the woman with the braids. With any luck the salads would get to the table first.

They did—or rather, Phila's did. Ruth Spalding spotted the tray and leaped for it with a muffled cry of rage. She seized one of the platefuls of iceburg lettuce, swept it off the tray and hurled it straight at Phila.

Nick managed to reach out and intercept the heavy plate before it struck Phila but the lettuce, together with its blue-cheese dressing and cherry tomatoes, cascaded down over her bright pumpkin blouse. Phila did not move. She simply sat staring at Ruth Spalding with an expression of resigned sorrow in her eyes.

"*Bitch*. Lying, scheming bitch." There was an ugly mottling of red in the Spalding woman's thick face now as she screamed at Phila. Her eyes were feverish with hatred. "You lied, damn you. You lied and they came and took the children away. Those kids were all we had. He loved those children. And now they're gone. Now my husband's gone. And it's all your fault, you rotten, lying whore!"

Phila was shaking as she slowly got to her feet. Nick saw the fine trembling in her fingers and he slid out of the booth to stand beside her. He was startled by the fierce, protective instincts that were suddenly surging through him. Nobody else in the restaurant had moved, but all eyes were on the scene taking place in front of them.

"I'm sorry, Mrs. Spalding." Phila spoke with a calm gentleness that amazed Nick. She took a step toward the heavy woman. "More sorry than I can say."

"You're not sorry, you meddling bitch," Ruth Spalding hissed through her teeth. "You did it on purpose. You ruined everything. *Everything*, damn you!" She swung a huge hand in a wide arc.

Phila did not even try to duck the blow. Ruth Spalding's palm cracked against the side of her face with enough force to make Phila stagger backward a step.

"Jesus. That's enough." Nick spoke very softly. If a man had acted this way toward Phila he knew he would have thrown a punch by now. He moved in front of the Spalding woman, looming directly in her path. She did not appear even to see him. She was staring rigidly over his shoulder, her entire attention focused on Phila.

"It's all right, Nick. Please. I'll handle this."

Phila stepped around Nick, reaching out to the other woman. Nick watched in amazement as Phila put a hand on Spalding's plump shoulder. Spalding flinched as if she had been struck.

*"Don't you dare touch me, you bitch."*

"I'm sorry, Ruth. I know you're hurting."

Huge tears formed in Ruth Spalding's tiny eyes and coursed down her cheeks. "Bitch," Spalding whispered again, her large body shaking with barely stifled sobs. "He was doing okay. We were gonna make it. He was doing good until you came along and messed it all up."

"I know. I know." Phila moved closer, putting both arms around the big woman. "I'm sorry, Ruth. So sorry."

For a few seconds Ruth Spalding simply stood there, her head against Phila's shoulder as she sobbed heavily. Then she jerked herself back a step, as if ashamed to find herself taking comfort from the enemy. She pushed Phila away and wiped the back of her hand across her eyes.

"You'll pay for what you did," Spalding said as she backed slowly away down the aisle. "I swear to God you'll pay for ruining everything." Then she turned and lumbered awkwardly out of the diner.

Nick took one look at Phila, who was standing very still as she watched Ruth Spalding leave the diner, and he pulled out his wallet and threw enough cash on the table to cover the tab.

"Let's go." He took Phila's arm and steered her firmly toward the door.

She did not resist. Every eye in the restaurant was on them, but she appeared oblivious as Nick urged her out into the warm night. He helped her gently into the Porsche and leaned down to study her face in the harsh neon light of the diner sign. She looked exhausted. All traces of the battle flags that had been flying earlier were gone. Without a word he closed the car door and went around to the driver's side.

Phila said nothing until he parked the Porsche in front of the little white house. Then she seemed to come slowly back from some distant place as she realized she was home.

Nick turned off the engine and shifted slightly in his seat. "You want to tell me what that was all about?"

"Not particularly. It's none of your business."

"Somehow I had a hunch you'd say that. You okay?"

"Just tired." She massaged her temples. "I've been feeling very tired lately."

"Who was that woman?" Nick persisted gently.

She hesitated, her eyes drifting to the front steps of her house which were illuminated by a pale light. "Ruth Spalding. She and her husband used to run a foster home on their farm outside of town. I . . . didn't like the way things were going for the kids. I was responsible for taking the children away and putting them in other homes. She hasn't forgiven me, as you can see."

"What I saw was you trying to comfort a woman who obviously hates your guts. You do that kind of thing a lot? If so, I can see why you got burned out. Sort of a thankless job, isn't it?"

"It gets to you." Phila shook herself like a small terrier throwing off water after falling into a cold stream. She blinked twice and opened the door. "Guess I really do need a vacation." She climbed out of the car.

Nick immediately slid out from behind the wheel and followed Phila up the path to her door. "Phila, wait."

She was fumbling in her shoulder bag for her keys. "I don't feel like talking any more tonight, Mr. Lightfoot."

"I do." He removed the keys from her hand, deliberately taking advantage of her distracted state. He was good at taking advantage. He shoved the key into the door and stood aside.

"Are you always this obnoxious?" Phila asked as she stepped into the hall and turned on a light.

"Yeah. So I've been told. Sit down and I'll fix us a tuna-fish sandwich." He headed for the kitchen without waiting for permission.

Phila trailed after him and sat down in one of the small kitchen chairs. She scowled. "You think this is amusing?"

"No. I think I'm hungry and I think I've got a few more questions. That's all." He opened a cupboard door and located a bowl. Tried another drawer and discovered a can opener. He was on a roll.

Phila's eyes followed him without much enthusiasm, but her shoulders had already relaxed a bit from the hunch of tension and depression she'd been sitting with in the car. "What questions?"

"Let's see. How about we start with how long did you know Crissie Masters?" he asked casually.

The vibration she'd emanated earlier abruptly returned. He was not even touching her, but he could feel her immediate reaction. She was on the alert again; the exhaustion cleared from her eyes.

"I met Crissie when I was thirteen."

"You know she raised hell when she descended on the families last year, don't you?" he said quietly, spooning mayonnaise out of a jar. He remembered the barely concealed despair in Eleanor's gracefully accented voice when she had phoned to tell him of the trauma the family was experiencing at the hands of Crissie Masters. No one had suffered as much as Eleanor Castleton during the time Crissie was on the scene.

"I know she raised hell, but I'm sure they deserved it. She only wanted what she felt was rightfully hers. After all, she was Burke Castleton's daughter."

"A daughter he never knew he had."

"Hardly Crissie's fault. Did you know she spent years looking for him? She used to fantasize about him all the time when she was a teenager. I remember lying awake in bed at night listening to her make up elaborate tales of how he must be searching for her and how he would find her someday. He lived in a mansion, she would say. And he was handsome and rich and dynamic."

"She wasn't far off," Nick admitted.

"I know." Phila smiled wistfully. "Except for the part about his actively searching for her. He never bothered to look, did he? I still remember the day she phoned to tell me that she had finally traced her father and that he had turned out to be everything she had fantasized he would be. Wealthy, attractive and dynamic. And to top it all off, he welcomed her with open arms."

"He was the only one who did, from what I hear. What did you say when she told you the good news?"

Phila's mouth tightened. "I pointed out that since he hadn't even been aware of her existence, he was probably an irresponsible bastard by nature. Any man who goes around fathering children and not being aware of it has a serious character flaw."

"I can hear the lecture now."

"Then I asked her how she could be certain he hadn't known about her or even suspected she existed. In which case he was even more of a bastard because it meant he'd deliberately ignored her all those years."

Nick took a deep breath, remembering an aesthetically lean, good-looking, charismatic man whose sensual appetites had apparently been inexhaustible. He had rarely been without a cigarette in his long-fingered hands. Burke Castleton had been larger than life, with a beguilingly wicked grin and the kind of eyes that made women catch their breath. *The Castletons got the looks and the charm.*

"The bastard, as you call him, is dead, Phila."

"I know. Crissie was stunned when she got word of Burke's heart attack a few months ago."

"And was she just as stunned when she found out he'd left her a big chunk of his shares in Castleton & Lightfoot?" Nick asked blandly.

"No. By the time he died, Crissie had gotten to know him well enough to believe he wouldn't leave her out of his will. She was right about that at least, wasn't she?"

"Yeah. But Burke Castleton rarely did anything out of the kindness of his heart. He always had a motive, and sometimes that motive was nothing more than a desire to stir up trouble."

"Sounds like that might have been a family trait," Phila murmured. "One Crissie inherited." She watched as Nick spread tuna-fish salad on slices of bread.

"Apparently so."

"Tell me something, Nick. Just how badly did the families hate Crissie?"

He hesitated, thinking of what he had learned from Eleanor. "She didn't go out of her way to make herself lovable, from what I understand. Why did she leave the shares to you?"

"I was the sole beneficiary of her will, just as she was in mine."

"The two of you made out wills? Isn't that a little unusual under the circumstances? How old were you when you did that?" Nick was amazed.

"We made them out the day we turned twenty-one. It wasn't that we had much to leave to each other, you understand. It was sort of a symbolic gesture. But the wills exist, and I am Crissie's legal heir."

"Okay, okay, I believe you. What were you implying with that question about how much the families hated Crissie?" Nick asked quietly as he served the tray of sandwiches. He sat down at the small table and helped himself to one of his own creations. "You're not crazy enough to think someone might had tried to kill her, are you?"

Phila made no move to touch the sandwiches. "The thought crossed my mind, so I hired a private detective to look into it. His report says it was clearly an accident. She was driving too fast that night, and she'd had a few drinks. She took a turn too quickly, went through a guard rail and landed in a ravine. There was no evidence of foul play. Just tragedy. Lots of evidence of tragedy."

Nick stopped chewing. "I don't believe I'm hearing this. You actually checked out the possibility of foul play?"

"Of course. I told you. Crissie was like a sister to me. Do you think I'd take a Castleton's or Lightfoot's word that her death had been an accident?"

"What about the word of the cops who investigated the scene of the accident?" Nick asked with set teeth. He was suddenly feeling angry.

"Cops can be bought. Especially by people as powerful as your precious families."

"Jesus." Nick forced himself to breathe slowly. "Who the hell do you think you are to hurl those kinds of accusations?"

"Me? I'm the only real friend the deceased had, remember? Who else has a better right to hurl accusations? Besides, I'm not hurling them. Not any more. I already checked them out. The families are technically off the hook—technically, at least."

"Technically? What the hell does that mean?" Nick was having a hard time controlling his rage now.

"I mean that as far as I'm concerned the Lightfoots and the Castletons bear some moral responsibility for what happened to Crissie."

*"Moral responsibility."*

"Oh, nothing that would ever hold up in court, I'll grant you that."

"Thank you very much." He wanted to pick her up and shake her. "You've got a lot of nerve, Philadelphia Fox."

"Why? Because I dare impugn the honor of the noble clans of Lightfoot and Castleton? Let me tell you something, Nicodemus Lightfoot, there are plenty of ways to ruin a person's life short of murdering her. Believe me, in my line of work I've seen a whole lot of examples of just how it can be done."

"You can't blame us for what happened to Crissie Masters."

"No? The fact that she even came into this world was Burke Castleton's fault. And he didn't stick around to help raise her, did he? Who knows how she might have turned out if she'd had a loving home and a father who cared? What's more, when she did find her roots, no one tried to make her welcome. None of you accepted her. She knew you all hated her. What do you think that does to a person? None of you even gave a damn when she died until you found out she had left the shares to someone outside the families."

Nick almost lost it then. He forced himself to put down the remainder of his sandwich very carefully. "When you're drawing up your list of people you believe hated Crissie Masters, don't include me. I never met her, remember?"

"So what? You probably wouldn't have been any kinder to her than the others were. She was an outsider."

"You know what you are? You're a bigoted, narrow-minded, totally biased little fool who is automatically against anyone who makes more money than you do."

"Is that right?"

"Yeah. And you know what else?"

"What?"

"You're making me lose my temper, and I haven't done that in a long time."

"Don't worry, it's just a right-wing, knee-jerk reaction to what you perceive as a threat to the privileged upper classes. And don't get any ideas about getting out of that chair and coming over here to manhandle me. I'll call the cops. I've been abused enough this evening." But Phila didn't look like the victim of abuse; she looked as if she was almost enjoying the blazing light of battle in her eyes.

"What's the matter, Phila?" he challenged softly. "Aren't you going to put your arms around me and offer me a bit of comfort and understanding the way you did Ruth Spalding when she attacked you?"

"I feel sorry for Ruth Spalding. I don't feel any pity at all for you. You're a Lightfoot. You don't need any of my comfort and understanding."

Nick bit back an oath and watched in amazement as Phila reached for a sandwich. The battle with him had obviously whetted her appetite. He watched her take a huge bite and wondered what the hell he was going to do next. Things were spinning out of his control and that he was unaccustomed to.

"Phila, let's take this from the top. One way or another, you're going to have to make some decisions about those C&L shares you inherited."

"One way or another," she agreed, reaching for another sandwich. "But I'll make my own decisions. I've been doing that for a long time, Lightfoot. I'm real good at it."

"You are really irritating is what you are."

She smiled, showing a lot of little white teeth. "You haven't seen anything yet. Good night, Mr. Lightfoot."

He drummed his fingers on the table, caught himself and stopped immediately. "We need to talk."

"Not tonight. I'm tired. We've talked more than enough this evening. Go."

He knew there was no point forcing the issue further now. She was too wired from the aftereffects of the confrontation with Ruth Spalding and the short battle she had just conducted with him. Nick knew when to stage a strategic retreat. He got to his feet without a word and started for the door.

"Thank you for the sandwich, Mr. Lightfoot," she called after him, her tone sarcastic.

"Anytime," he said dryly, his hand on the front doorknob.

"And thanks for trying to fend off Ruth Spalding," Phila added softly, no longer sarcastic.

He said nothing, stepping out into the night and closing the door quietly behind him. He had the feeling Phila wasn't accustomed to anyone trying to fight her battles for her.

It was then he realized there probably was no man in her life, at least not at the moment.

That thought cheered him up for some reason as he climbed into the Porsche and headed back toward the Holloway Park Motel.

# 3

❖

Nick stalked into his motel room, then turned around and stalked back out again when he realized that he was in no mood to sleep or watch television. He headed for the flashing promise of a neon sign that signaled a tavern across the street.

Five minutes later, ensconced in a booth with a beer and a hamburger, he gave himself over to brooding.

He could not seem to get a handle on Philadelphia Fox, and that worried him. What worried him even more was the fact that he was attracted to her.

It made no sense. She was definitely not his type, although after the fiasco of his marriage he had never been quite sure what his type was.

But his father had taught him to admire courage and his mother had taught him a grudging respect for compassion, and Nick had to admit Phila had shown both tonight when she had dealt with the Spalding woman. On top of that, he automatically gave a few points to anyone who had the guts to defy the combined forces of the Castletons and the Lightfoots. There was definitely more to Phila than met the eye.

Still, he did not normally get turned on by feisty, mouthy, left-wing types who had the arrogance to lecture others on matters of moral responsibility. Nick grimaced and pushed aside his personal reaction to the Fox. He knew he had to think with his head, not his balls. Too much was riding on his next move with Phila.

Unfortunately for all concerned, Phila was not the simple, straightforward opportunist Eleanor Castleton wanted to believe she was, that much was for certain. There appeared to be a steel core of something that looked suspiciously like integrity running through Phila's spine. Integrity combined with the bleeding-heart compassion of a true liberal always made for a volatile combination: warrior and saint.

Such people tended to be quite zealous in their approach to problem solving.

Such people were never really happy until they felt justice had been done on behalf of the weak and wretched of the earth.

Such people hired independent investigators to verify the true nature of what everyone else considered an accident.

Nick concentrated, seeking the right method for dealing with his quarry. He knew there had to be a way to get to Phila. It was just a matter of pulling the right strings.

Quickly he summarized the basic facts. The woman had no job at present, she had just been through a courtroom trial, and she had lost her best friend. All in all, that added up to a lot of stress.

He remembered his initial impression of her, an idling engine that normally moved through life at full speed.

Maybe what she needed was a fresh focus, something to fill up the void in her life that had been left by the loss of her job and friend; something that would galvanize her natural sense of integrity and tap into the fire of both the warrior and the saint.

Nick sat for a long time, worrying the problem like a dog with a bone. The beer went down slowly and the hamburger disappeared bite by methodical bite.

When he had finished the hamburger he sat turning the empty beer bottle slowly between his palms. Philadelphia Fox was his ticket home, and he was not about to lose her at this stage.

It wasn't until he reached for his wallet to pay for the meal that he acknowledged the whole truth. He needed a way to keep Phila within reach not only because of the C&L shares she possessed, but also because some part of him was never going to be satisfied until he had gotten the Fox into bed.

Phila's fingers touched cold metal the next morning while she was rooting around in her drawer for a pair of panties. She paused, pushed back a spare nightgown and stared at the 9-mm automatic pistol she had bought the week before.

She hated the sight of the handgun. Talk about a death machine. She had a lot of gall hurling accusations at Nick Lightfoot because of the products his family manufactured when she herself was carrying a thing like this around. Owning the weapon violated every principle she had ever been taught about gun control.

But she was scared, and Phila was discovering that fear changed a few things. It hurt, though, to remember her grandmother telling her that her parents had never carried guns, not even into the terrible jungle where they had died.

Phila sighed. She was angry and depressed because she had given in to the fear and bought the gun, but she knew she wasn't going to take it back. She covered up the pistol with the nightgown and several pairs of pantyhose.

Aside from her natural dislike of the thing, she was very uncomfortable with the automatic. The salesman at the sporting-goods store had shown her how to load the magazine, and she understood the necessity of removing the safety before firing. But she had never been able to bring herself actually to practice shooting the gun. It felt obscene and ugly in her hand.

Every time she looked at the automatic Phila could almost hear her grandmother's outrage. *This country is running amok with guns. Every Tom, Dick and Harry has one. It's because of all that nonsense about winning the West. People act as if they've got to keep on winning it! They say they're protecting themselves against crime. What a ridiculous argument. The surest way to cut back on crime in this country is to get rid of handguns.*

Matilda Fox had strongly supported gun-control measures. She had waged a personal, one-woman, ongoing war with the National Rifle Association as well as every congressman who had ever dared come out against gun control.

Her grandmother wasn't the only one Phila heard scolding her in her imagination when she looked at the lethal automatic. She could also hear Crissie Masters. *If you're going to carry one, Phila, for God's sake, learn how to use it.* Crissie had had a pragmatic approach to most things.

The knock on her front door distracted Phila from her reveries. She found the underpants she had been searching for, pulled them on and reached for a pair of gauzy cotton pants. It was going to be hot again today. It would get hotter here in Holloway as the summer wore on. Another depressing thought.

The knock sounded again, more demanding this time. Phila decided that since the gauze pants were turquoise, her yellow T-shirt would go nicely. She slipped into it as she called out to whoever was making the racket.

"Who is it?" These days she thought twice about throwing open a door without first checking to see who was on the other side. The scene with Ruth Spalding last night had increased her wariness.

"It's Nick."

Phila didn't think twice about opening the door; she thought three times. Then, with a muttered groan, she went down the tiny hall into the living room and flipped the dead bolt.

Something told her that Nick Lightfoot was the kind who would either stand out there on the steps all day waiting for her to emerge or go fetch a cop and claim something was seriously wrong inside her house. Either way he would see her today. She braced herself as she opened the door, not certain how to handle him.

She stood blinking up at him in the bright morning sunlight. He was wearing a khaki shirt and a pair of jeans, and his hair was still damp from his shower. He looked good, she thought with some surprise. He was still much too large, of course, but there was something very appealing about him, nevertheless.

"Good morning." His gray gaze moved over her with a delight that made her self-conscious.

"What do you want?" Phila did not particularly care if she sounded ungracious.

Nick held up a hand, palm outward. "I come in peace bearing gifts." He waved a white paper bag in front of her.

"What's in there?" Phila asked suspiciously.

"After watching you devour my tuna sandwiches last night, I decided that food was the way to your hard little heart. I stopped at the fast-food joint next to my motel and picked up some breakfast. I figured the least you could do was make the coffee."

"Why?"

"So that we can have something bracing to drink while we eat my food and discuss your summer vacation." He flattened his palm against the door and pushed slowly, steadily inward.

With a groan of resignation, Phila fell back. "All right, you're in. What about my summer vacation?" She led the way into the kitchen and turned on the drip coffee machine.

"Sit down, Phila, I have a proposition to make, and I would very much appreciate it if you could manage to sit through my entire presentation before jumping on top of it with both feet." He dropped into one of the kitchen chairs and began unpacking the egg-and-muffin sandwiches.

"Let's hear it." Phila sat down in the other chair, unable to ignore the food any longer. She realized with some surprise that she actually was hungry this morning, just as she had been last night. That was a nice change. Her appetite had been off lately. The only meal she had been eating on a regular basis was dinner, and she usually had to down a couple of glasses of wine to work up enough enthusiasm for that.

"You are going to have to make decisions soon that will affect a number of people."

"Castletons and Lightfoots."

Nick's eyebrows rose behind his glasses. "This may come as a shock to you, Phila, but Castletons and Lightfoots are people, just like Ruth Spalding and the kids you put into foster care."

"Do me a favor, okay? Don't try to make me feel charitable toward Castletons and Lightfoots. The thought of it nauseates me." She picked up one of the breakfast sandwiches and sniffed appreciatively.

"You don't look nauseated." Nick eyed her narrowly for a moment before continuing. "I think you should get to know us before you decide what you're going to do about the shares, Phila. I think you could put your mind at ease if you spent some time with the families. You'd realize we're all human, just like everyone else."

"What are you suggesting I do? Hold a party and invite them to it?"

"I'm serious about this. Everyone's in Port Claxton now, and they'll be there for a few weeks. Sort of a summer tradition. Castletons and Lightfoots are very big on tradition. You could go over to the coast, too. You'd have a chance to get to know the families, ask questions and make an informed decision about what to do with your shares. You hold a lot of power. Don't you want to use it intelligently?"

"I already know a lot about the families. More than I really want to know, in fact."

Nick's mouth turned grim. "You've judged us all and found us wanting, haven't you? And you've never even met any of us except me."

The truth of his words made Phila feel uneasy. She concentrated on the second egg sandwich. "I just don't think I'd get any satisfactory answers by spending time in Port Claxton."

"The Castletons and Lightfoots have their problems, Phila, and one or two family skeletons in the closet, but none of us are monsters. I think if you got to know us, you'd realize that. And you should realize it before you make any permanent decisions regarding your inheritance."

She stared at him intently. "You know something? I tend to forget sometimes that you're one of 'them.' Probably because Crissie never mentioned you. You told me yourself you walked away from the clans three years ago. But it's beginning to dawn on me that every time you mention the families you include yourself in the group. You always say 'us.' "

"What do you expect me to do? Deny I'm related to the Lightfoots? I can't do that. I've got the nose, you see." He tapped it with an air of importance.

"Phila surveyed his nose gravely. "Did the women in your family also get that nose?"

"We never found out. I was the only kid my parents had. The nose is from my father's side of the family."

"And your mother?" Phila asked carefully.

"My mother was very lovely," Nick said quietly. "She died seven years ago."

"I see. I'm sorry." Phila wished she'd kept her mouth shut.

"You've mentioned a grandmother, but what happened to your parents, Phila?" he asked after a moment.

"They died when I was very young."

"Who raised you? Your grandmother?"

Phila nodded. "Until I was thirteen. Then she died."

"Who raised you after that?"

"I went into foster care."

Nick frowned. "Jesus, Phila. You went into one of those places? You didn't have any other family? No one who would take you in?"

His genuine shock was almost humorous. "Don't look so horrified, Nick. Lots of people wind up in 'those places,' as you call them. There are some very good, kind people running them. It's not so bad, given the alternative."

"But wasn't there *anyone?*" he persisted.

"I think there are a couple of distant relations out there somewhere. But they didn't bother to come forward when they heard of my grandmother's death. My caseworker tracked down one of them, an aunt on my mother's side, but she said she couldn't possibly afford to take me in. She had her hands full with her own three kids, and her husband had just walked out on her."

"Jesus," Nick said again, making it sound halfway between a prayer and an oath.

Phila shook her head, smiling thinly. "You say that as if you can't imagine a world in which you would have been sent into foster care."

"I can't," he admitted. "As long as I can remember there's always been family around, Lightfoots and Castletons both. If something had happened to my parents when I was younger, the Castletons would have taken me in and raised me as their own. My folks would have done the same for Darren. There would have been no question about it. Hell, if anything happened to Darren and his wife tomorrow, I'd take their little boy." He shrugged. "It's just understood."

"Not everyone has an extended family clan like that, much less the financial resources to raise a relative's orphaned kid."

"You think I'm a little naive on the subject, don't you?" he asked wryly.

"Not any more than I was when I first went into foster care." Phila closed her eyes briefly. "I was so scared in the beginning. Then I met Crissie. She was the same age I was, but years older in some ways. She'd been through the wars. In and out of foster care most of her life.

She preferred it to living with her mother, who tended to have the kind of boyfriends who abused helpless little girls."

"Things must have been bad at home if she actually preferred foster care," Nick said quietly.

"They were. At any rate, for some reason neither of us ever fully understood, she took me under her wing and helped me find my feet that first year; helped me to survive, in fact. I owe her, Nick."

He got up to pour coffee from the pot into two mugs. "And that's why you feel you can't let go of her now that she's dead? You feel some sense of obligation?"

"We were a team. As close as sisters. She was all I had for a long time. And now she's gone." Phila felt the familiar burning sensation at the back of her eyes. She seemed to cry on the slightest pretext lately. She found this new tendency extremely annoying. This morning she refused to let the tears fall.

There was a long silence before Nick spoke again. "Come to Port Claxton this summer, Phila. Find out what the families are like and what really happened while Crissie was with them."

"What if no one in the families will talk to me, let alone answer questions?"

"They'll talk to you."

"How do you know?"

"Because you'll be with me. They'll have to be polite to you. Besides, you said yourself, you need a vacation. The coast will make a nice change from Holloway, I guarantee it."

Phila wondered if he was even remotely aware of the arrogance in his words. She downed the last of the egg sandwich and brushed crumbs off her turquoise pants while she tried to think.

There were several advantages to the strange, unexpected offer. Going to Port Claxton would get her out of Holloway, and after last night's meeting with Ruth Spalding that seemed more desirable than ever. And Nick was right. It would give her a chance to meet the people Crissie had thrust herself upon last year. It would give her a chance to learn what she could about the long-lost family Crissie had discovered. Phila knew she would be better equipped then to make her decision about what to do with the C&L shares.

But with her usual perception she sensed that Nicodemus Lightfoot rarely did things for altruistic reasons. He had an angle. She wondered what it was.

"Why are you doing this, Nick?"

"I told you."

"You mean that garbage about allowing me to put my mind at

ease? I don't buy that for one minute. You're looking for a way to get those shares back, aren't you? Until you find one you figure it might be a good idea to keep an eye on me."

"It's your decision, Phila."

"It would be impossible to get a summer place on the coast at this late date," Phila said slowly, still thinking it through.

"You could stay at my family's cottage. Plenty of room."

"Not a chance," Phila answered instantly. She knew he was right about the room. Crissie had described the "cottages" the Lightfoots and Castletons had built side by side in Port Claxton, Washington. From all accounts they qualified as mini-mansions by most standards. Still, she had no intention of taking up residence in either of them.

Nick paid no attention to her response. He just reached for the phone on the wall. He got directory assistance, obtained the number he requested and then he dialed it.

"Harry, it's Nick Lightfoot. Yeah. A long time. Listen, Harry, I'm coming to Port Clax for a while and I've got a friend who needs a place to stay. What have you got available?"

Phila glowered as the conversation continued for a few more minutes. Nick saw her expression, and his brows rose in polite inquiry.

"The old Gilmarten place sounds fine, Harry. We'll be there on July fourth. Any problem? I didn't think so. Thanks, Harry. See you on the Fourth." Nick tossed the receiver back into the cradle. "That settles it. You've got a nice little place near the beach. Not far from the family cottages, in fact. Fully furnished. How does that sound?"

"It sounds too good to be true. What poor soul got evicted?"

Nick shrugged. "Some couple from Seattle will be given another place when they arrive next week. They'll never know the difference."

"I take it good old Harry owed the families a couple of favors?"

"I've known Harry for years. Dad and I used to go fishing with him."

"Sure. So now you can casually pick up the phone, and Harry rearranges his whole schedule of summer rentals. Just like that."

Nick smiled blandly. "Not much point in being a Lightfoot if you can't throw your weight around once in a while."

" 'Evenin', sir. I just finished building the martinis. How was the golf game?" There was more than a shade of deepest, darkest Texas in Tec Sherman's accent, but after years of self-discipline it had become overlaid with standard military drawl.

"Not bad. Won fifty bucks off Fortman." Reed Lightfoot sauntered over to the small bar where Tec Sherman was using a swizzle stick with crisp authority. A row of large green olives stuffed with pimientos was arranged nearby. Reed tossed ice into a glass and helped himself from the pitcher of martinis. "The poor, benighted fool landed in the goddamn trap on the sixteenth hole, and by the time he got out he was dead meat."

"Congratulations, sir." Tec Sherman paused expectantly.

Reed took a healthy swallow of his martini and eyed the other man. William Tecumseh Sherman was built like a slab of beef. He was an ex-Marine who managed to give the impression he was still in uniform, even though he habitually dressed in garishly patterned aloha shirts and loose cotton slacks. Sherman was in his mid-forties, bald as a billiard ball, with huge, bushy brows and a chronically pinched expression around the mouth. He had worked for the Lightfoots for years and he was as loyal as the rottweilers that guarded the front gate. Reed would have trusted Tec Sherman with his life.

"Something wrong, Tec?" Reed finally inquired.

"No, sir. Just heard the good news, sir. Wanted to tell you I was damned glad. It's about time."

Reed wandered over to the window and gazed out toward the sea. Through the trees he could see the Pacific. It was steel blue today under a sun still high in the early evening sky. "You know something I don't know, Tec?"

Tec cleared his throat and clasped his hands behind his back in a parade-rest stance. "I heard about Nick, sir. That's all. Saw Harry in town today. He told me about it, sir."

Reed went still. "What the devil are you talking about, Tec?" he asked very softly.

Sherman coughed slightly. "Sorry, sir. Assumed you knew. Harry said he talked to Nick on the phone the other day. Nick told him he was comin' home on the Fourth. Bringin' a friend with him. A lady friend, sir. Needed a place for her to stay. Harry's lettin' 'er have the Gilmarten place down the road."

Reed's martini sloshed perilously close to the rim of the glass. "Nick's coming home?" He turned his head to pin Tec Sherman with a piercing gaze. "He told Harry he was coming here to Port Clax?"

"Yes, sir. Like I said, thought you knew."

"No, I did not know." He wondered if Hilary did. It would be just like her to keep the information a secret until the last minute. Hilary liked games of one-upsmanship, and she was very good at them. "Nick hasn't seen fit to notify his family yet."

Sherman turned a dull red. "I'm sure he will real soon, sir. Probably wanted to line up the Gilmarten place for his, uh, lady friend first before he made his plans."

"This lady friend. Is she by any chance named Fox?" Hilary, Darren and Eleanor had been nagging him about Philadelphia Fox for weeks. So far he'd been ignoring them.

"I believe so, sir."

"Philadelphia Fox ?"

"I believe that's what Harry said, sir."

"Goddamn it, what is Nick up to now?" Reed asked under his breath. "Sir?"

"Never mind, Tec. I was just wondering what the devil is going on."

"Beggin' your pardon, sir, but sounds to me like Nick got word the families had gotten themselves in a bind and he decided to do somethin' about it. It's just what you'd expect of him, sir."

"You have a lot of faith in my son, Tec."

"Known him a long time, sir, under some interestin' conditions. He's a Lightfoot. When the chips are down no Lightfoot is gonna stand by and let the families get into trouble."

*Nick was coming home.* Something that had been frozen for a long time began to thaw inside Reed. The sensation was almost painful. He looked out toward the distant horizon, and for the first time in nearly three years he permitted himself to think seriously about the future.

Until three years ago a sense of the future had been the guiding force in Reed Lightfoot's life. The need to create something substantial that could be handed down through the generations had kept him going during the lean years when Castleton & Lightfoot had struggled to survive and gain a foothold in the competitive world of high-tech electronics. It had sustained him even in the dark time seven years ago, after his first wife's death.

But Reed's passion for the future had begun to wither and die in him the day Nick had walked out. It had vanished altogether when Hilary had lost the baby.

But now, with a few simple words, he could feel the embers rekindling within him.

Nick was coming home.

He warned himself not to put too much stock in the event. Nothing had really changed. The past could not be altered. Everything that had occurred three years ago still stood locked in time. They all had to live with it.

But no matter how hard he tried to maintain a realistic view of his son's return, Reed could not prevent an overwhelming sense of relief from surging through his veins. *Nick was coming home.*

It looked as though he owed that fact to that brassy blond troublemaker who'd landed like a bomb in the Castletons' laps last year. Reed wondered if the Fox woman was going to prove equally explosive.

No need to worry, he told himself with gathering satisfaction. It sounded as if Nick already had her under control. When Nick bothered to exert himself, he could handle anything. He was a Lightfoot.

"Hello, Reed, I suppose you've heard the news? It's all over town."

Reed turned at the sound of the cool, beautifully modulated voice. His wife was gliding through the doorway, dressed in flowing silk trousers and an artfully draped blouse that framed her elegant throat. As always, his eyes went once, briefly, to the gold band he had put on her finger.

"Tec just told me." He kept his voice perfectly neutral. He found himself doing that a lot around Hilary. It was as if he took some petty pleasure in not giving her whatever reaction she wanted or anticipated.

"Trust Nick to make his reappearance in a suitably spectacular fashion. He'll probably parachute onto the lawn in a blaze of fireworks. Pour me a drink, please, Tec."

"Yes, ma'am. The usual?" Tec's voice was more clipped than before. It was always that way when he spoke to Reed's second wife.

"Of course, Tec." Hilary did not look at him. She concentrated on her husband while Tec prepared a martini straight-up for her. "I suppose Nick's return has something to do with those shares?"

"Sounds like it," Reed said quietly.

"I wonder what he thinks he can do." Hilary picked up her martini and toyed with the spear holding the olive. "Harry referred to the Fox woman as Nick's *lady* friend. You don't suppose Nick is trying his hand at seducing those shares out of her, do you?"

"Beats me." Reed wasn't about to give her the satisfaction of speculating aloud about his son's intentions, although privately he was wondering the same thing. He sighed inwardly at his own pettiness. This was what it had come down to between himself and his beautiful, young wife. A grim, silent battlefield had been carved out between them, a battlefield where the fighting was done not with words but with a chilling display of courtesy and a total lack of outward emotion.

"Harry says Nick made it clear the Fox woman was staying alone at the Gilmarten place. How quaint. Imagine Nick worrying about the proprieties. Oh, well, I suppose that means we'd better prepare a room for him here."

"Goddamn right," Reed muttered, some of his control slipping for an instant. "Of course he'll be staying here. This is his home." He swallowed the rest of the martini in a single, numbing gulp.

The small towns of eastern Washington all had a certain similarity about them, Phila had often thought. Her job had taken her to a number of them. Hardworking and unpretentious, they were generally oriented toward the farms and ranches that surrounded them.

Holloway was no different. There were more pickup trucks than anything else on the main street. The downtown shopping district consisted of three banks, a couple of gas stations, two fast-food places—including an old-fashioned drive-in hamburger joint—and a variety of small shops.

The shops sold such things as yarn, hardware, work clothes and real estate. Most of the stores looked vaguely depressed, and with good reason. The new mall in the next town had siphoned off the majority of Holloway's downtown business.

The landscape around Holloway was also typical of this part of the state. The endless vista of arid desert, which always astonished visitors who thought of Washington as a rain forest, were broken by acres of lush farmland. At certain times of the year hot, dry winds cut a swath through the area, raising dust that hung suspended for hours in the air. When the wind blew, the effect was similar to a snowstorm. Traffic came to a halt and people stayed indoors.

But today the air was still. The sky was clear, cloudless and free of dust, a vast blue bowl that stretched over the desert to the jagged peaks of the distant mountains.

There was nothing wrong with Holloway, Phila thought. She had been raised in towns just like it. She knew them intimately. But she realized suddenly that she would be very glad to leave this place.

She sat at a table that was sheathed in chipped, gray Formica in Emerson's Four Star Café, a cracked mug full of coffee in front of her. Outside on the hot sidewalk a few people hurried from their cars to the nearest air-conditioned business establishments.

"Going to be a hot one today," Thelma Anderson announced as she slid into the seat across from Phila.

Phila smiled faintly at her friend and former supervisor. "You've been living here too long, Thelma."

"What makes you say that?" the older woman demanded, her dark eyes snapping.

"It's a sure sign you've been in Holloway too long when the first thing you mention is the weather."

"This is farming country," Thelma pointed out casually. "Farmers always talk about the weather. I'm just trying to blend in. How's the coffee?"

"As bad as ever."

"Good. I'll have a cup." She signaled to the waitress, who nodded to her from the other side of the counter. Then Thelma turned back to Phila with an assessing eye. "So you're really going to do it, huh? You're going to quit for good? I can't talk you into coming back to your old job?"

Phila shook her head. "No. But I'm going to miss you, Thelma." And she meant it. She would miss her friend's short, no-nonsense haircut, her functional navy-blue skirts and white blouses and serviceable walking shoes. Thelma, who knew all the secret methods of shoving paperwork through an overburdened system that periodically tried to choke itself to death on forms and multiple copies and reports done in triplicate.

Thelma was dedicated and she was good at what she did, but somewhere along the line she had learned the trick of detaching herself enough emotionally from her work to ensure her own survival. Phila knew after the Spalding trial that she herself would never be able to develop that detachment. She was finished as a social worker.

"I have to get out, Thelma. I need a change."

Thelma regarded her soberly. "Yes, I think you do," she said finally. "You've been through hell. It takes awhile to recover. Feeling any better?"

"Some." Phila smiled again, realizing it was the truth. She had been feeling better, more *focused*, since she had made her decision to go to Port Claxton.

"A summer on the coast will be good for you. You always did like the ocean. Can you handle it financially?"

"Yes, thanks to Crissie's insurance policy. It wasn't much but together with my savings, it will keep me going for a while."

"How did you manage to get a place near the beach at this time of year?" Thelma demanded. "Port Claxton summer houses are always booked months in advance. I know. I've tried to get in once or twice, myself."

"Someone I know pulled a few strings for me."

Thelma grinned. "A man?"

"Uh huh."

"Well, good for you. Just what you need to take your mind off that trial and your friend's death. It's time you put it all behind you, Phila."

Phila shrugged. She did not want to explain to Thelma that Crissie's death was still very much on her mind and that she was far from letting it go. "You'll keep in touch, won't you, Thelma?"

"You know I will. We won't be forgetting you around here anytime soon, Philadelphia Fox. If it hadn't been for you we never would have nailed Elijah Spalding. You're a heroine in the office."

"You'd have gotten him sooner or later."

"Later, maybe." Thelma sounded skeptical. "After a lot more kids had been abused and psychologically scarred for life. Later would have been too late for a lot of them." She shook her head. "Cases like that are so blasted frustrating. Everyone in the office knew what was going on, and no one could prove a thing. Every time we sent the sheriff out to the Spalding farm things were in apple-pie order. The kids were too frightened to talk, and Spalding's wife was useless."

"Ruth was as frightened of him as the children were. She was also desperate to hold on to him. In her own way, she loved him."

"A sick kind of love, if you ask me."

"We see that kind of love a lot in this business, don't we, Thelma? The sick kind."

"Well, Spalding's in prison now, and he'll be there another year and a half. Thanks to you. Too bad it had to happen the way it did, though. You could have been seriously hurt or even killed. I shudder every time I think about how close it all was."

"So do I," Phila admitted. And sometimes she did more than shudder. Sometimes she dreamed about it. And woke up in a cold sweat.

"I heard you had a run-in with Mrs. Spalding last night at the diner. True?"

"It's true. She's hurting, Thelma."

"I think she could be dangerous, Phila. Watch yourself around her, okay?"

"Maybe it's just as well I'm leaving town." But Phila's instincts told her Ruth Spalding was not the real threat.

"I agree. Go off to the coast, friend, and see if you can't get that old gleam back in your eye."

"I didn't know I had an old gleam to recover." Phila smiled.

"You do, you know. In fact, I think I detect a few returning sparks already. You look a lot better than you did a couple of weeks ago."

"Thanks. I think." Phila drew a deep breath. "Thelma, I'm a little scared."

"Leaving a career is always a little scary," Thelma said gently.

"I feel I'm changing more than just a career. I think I'm changing my whole life, and I can't see what the new direction is going to be."

"You're strong, kiddo. Don't ever forget that. Want some advice, though?"

"Sure. You're one of the few people whose advice I trust and you know it."

"Choose carefully when you choose your next line of work. You were a good caseworker, one of the best, but you were a maverick. An urban guerrilla trying to work within the system. You were always twisting, bending and pushing the rules. That can be very frustrating after a while."

Phila wrinkled her nose. "I hadn't realized you noticed."

Thelma shrugged. "I let most of it go by because I wanted the results I knew you could get. But that's a hard way to work. Hard on you. I don't think you were really cut out to work in a bureaucratic system of any kind, let alone one like ours where you can see your failures in a string of little ruined lives. But you're a born crusader. A rescuer of others. it's your nature, Phila. It's one of your strengths. It's also your greatest weakness. Take that into consideration when you go job hunting again."

Later that evening Phila finished packing the last of her things and stood surveying the little house she had been renting for the past two years. It had been the closest thing to a home she'd had since the day her grandmother died. It hurt now to see her once cozy retreat looking empty and lifeless.

There would be another house, she told herself. That was one of the things you learned in foster care. There was always another house. And one of these days she would have one that really belonged to her; a real home. For keeps.

She was taking very little with her, just her personal belongings and the books she could not bear to give away. Most of the furniture and kitchenware had been put into storage. The phone would be disconnected in the morning.

Phila realized she did not even know where she would be living a month or two from now. She felt as though she were starting over from scratch, and she knew that was the way it had to be.

She had closed the door on her career as a social worker the day she had testified at the Spalding trial. She could no longer lay claim to being a professional, and she knew it. Everything for which she had trained and worked was over.

The stupid tears started to burn in her eyes again. She dashed them away with the back of her hand just as the phone rang. Grateful for the interruption, she snatched up the receiver.

"Hello?"

"Hello." Nick Lightfoot's voice was as calm and quiet over the phone as it was in person. "I called to see how the packing was going."

"It's done. I'll be leaving tomorrow." Phila sank down onto a suitcase, clutching the receiver. For some silly reason she no longer felt like crying. "Don't worry, I'll be in Port Claxton on the Fourth."

"Got a pen? I'll give you directions to the cottages."

"Yes. Yes, I've got one here somewhere." She fumbled for a pen and a pad of paper in her purse, hoping it would take him a long time to give her the directions. She wanted companionship tonight, any companionship, even that of a Lightfoot. "All right, go ahead."

Nick gave her directions in a crisp, well-organized fashion that made her realize he was, by nature, a very methodical, organized man. She would have to keep that in mind, she told herself. Methodical, organized, conservative thinkers rarely did things without specific reasons. Definitely not impulsive types.

When he was finished, she dropped the pad back into her purse and tried to think of some way to keep the conversation going. There was a long silence on the other end of the line.

"What are you doing?" she finally asked, somewhat inanely.

"Right now? Taking care of some things here at the office in Santa Barbara so I can leave town for a few weeks without worrying too much about Lightfoot Consulting Services falling apart."

"Oh."

"Yeah. Not too exciting."

"About on a par with packing."

"Yeah. What did you have for dinner?"

"Nothing. There's nothing left in the house to eat."

Nick muttered something that sounded like an oath. "Why don't you go into town and have a burger or something?"

"I'm not hungry."

"Promise me you'll have breakfast before you start the drive to Port Claxton tomorrow, okay?"

"Why should I promise you that?"

"Humor me. I get the feeling you don't eat properly."

She was not up to arguing. "All right, all right, I'll have breakfast. Satisfied?"

"For now. I'll see you soon, Phila. Good night."

"Good night." Reluctantly she put the phone back in the cradle. Her stomach rumbled. It occurred to her that she was a little hungry, after all. Maybe she would run into town and grab a burger.

Phila was still sitting on her suitcase, feeling bemused and confused and wondering how hungry she really was, when the phone rang again. She jumped and picked up the receiver, ruefully aware that she was half hoping Nick had thought of some small twist in his directions that needed to be explained in greater detail.

"Hello?"

"It's not over, you bitch, just because you're leaving. It's not over. *You lied.* You lied about my husband. He's in prison because you lied. They took away the children. All the children are gone and my man is in prison because of your lies. You've ruined everything—"

Phila cringed and gently lowered the phone back into its cradle, cutting off Ruth Spalding's sobbing accusations.

# 4

It was not the first time Phila had stood at the gate and stared through the bars at a large family party that didn't include her. She and Crissie had spent most of their teenage years knowing what it was to be on the outside looking in.

But Phila had to admit this was the first time she'd stood outside such an elegant gate or observed such a huge bash. When the Lightfoots and Castletons celebrated the Fourth of July, they went all out. It looked to Phila as if the entire town of Port Claxton had been invited.

She curled her fingers around the wrought-iron bars and stared at the festive scene. The sweeping expanse of incredibly green lawn was filled with people in shorts, halter tops, short-sleeved shirts and jeans. Four long barbecue pits had been set up, manned by a team of professional-looking chefs. The fragrance of broiling steaks and hamburgers wafted through the air. Ears of corn on the cob wrapped in aluminum foil were sunk deep into hot coals. Massive bowls of potato salad, pickles and relish were arranged on side tables. Beer and soft drinks were being dispensed under a striped awning.

All very patriotic and traditional and, done on this scale, very expensive.

Two stately homes with long, graceful porticos dominated the crest of the hill above the lawn. Behind them was a sloping, wooded hillside that fronted the wide expanse of beach.

The Lightfoot and Castleton *beach cottages* were each two stories high and painted a fresh, crisp, classic white. The charming, multi-paned windows had dark green shutters. Phila could see green porch swings behind the columns of the porticos. She just knew there wouldn't be a stick of furniture inside that dated from any later than 1850.

For a minute she thought she must have taken a wrong turn and wound up in the wrong place and the wrong year. Virginia, say. Or Maryland, sometime in the early eighteen-hundreds.

The biggest American flag Phila had ever seen waved from the top of a tall flagpole set in front of the two homes.

"May I help you, ma'am?"

It wasn't a polite inquiry; it was a direct challenge. Phila jumped as the masculine voice cracked behind her. She whirled around, half expecting to find herself facing a uniformed guard armed with a high-powered rifle and a big dog.

What she saw was a heavily built bald man in a truly spectacular aloha shirt. The shirt, colorful though it was, did not reassure her. All her ingrained animosity toward people who thought they could tell her what to do rose to the fore.

"Help me?" she repeated sweetly. "I doubt it. You don't look like the helpful type." She swung around to continue staring through the bars at the Castleton-Lightfoot Fourth of July picnic.

"This party isn't open to tourists, just local residents, and I sure don't recognize you, ma'am. You'll have to be on your way."

"It's all right, General, I'm here at the request of his lordship." Phila didn't turn around again.

"What's this lordship crap? Cut the comedy, sister, and move your little ass on out of here. This is private property. No one goes through those gates unless they're local residents or friends of the families."

A palm the size and weight of a steer carcass closed around her shoulder.

Phila lost her temper. She tried to shrug off the heavy palm and failed. That only made her angrier. "Take your hand off me, you big ape. I told you, I've got an engraved invitation."

"Is that right? Then suppose you show it to me?"

Phila looked up into a face dominated by a nose that had obviously been broken more than once. A thin, severe little mustache crowned the man's tight lips. There was something in his painfully upright posture that clued her in.

"Ex-Marine, right?" she hazarded.

"For your information, ma'am, there ain't no such thing as an ex-Marine. A Marine's a Marine till the day he dies."

"How unfortunate for you," Phila retorted. "That will certainly be a terrible burden for you to carry the rest of your life."

A dark red flush rose beneath the man's leathery tan. The severe little mustache twitched, and the beady eyes bulged with outrage. "Why you smart-mouthed little—"

"Take your hands off me this instant or I'll get myself an ACLU lawyer and sue you from here to the shores of Tripoli!"

"Is that right? Well, I might as well give you something to sue about." Without any warning, he put his huge hands around her waist and tossed her over one massive shoulder.

Phila screeched at the top of her lungs, but apparently no one on the lush green lawn heard her above the general laughter and chatter. "Put me down or so help me I'll see you in jail." She started pounding his back furiously with her fists. It was like hitting an elephant. He was not crushing her so she did not panic, but she fiercely resented the man-handling. "You're a perfect example of the sort of imbecile produced by this country's military mentality. Where did you come from? Some secret government breeding program that's run amok? *Put me down.*"

"Hello, Tec. I see she got to you real fast. She's good at that."

"Nick!" Phila raised her head at the sound of the familiar—and in-furiatingly calm—voice. "Thank heavens you're here. Do something quick. This jerk is crazy."

"*Sir.* It's you, sir." The ape sounded thrilled, Phila thought in disgust. "Welcome home, sir. We're damn glad to have you back again."

Phila twisted frantically. "Nick, do something. Tell this monster to put me down. Then call the cops. This man is extremely dangerous. I want him arrested for assault."

"Tec wouldn't hurt a fly unless he was really provoked," Nick said casually. "Of course, if you're going to go around provoking people, you've got to expect some response, Phila."

"I was not provoking him. I was standing on my constitutional rights, damn it. Make him put me down this instant or I'll sue Castleton & Lightfoot as well as this creep. I'm sure a good lawyer could prove that anybody who hired this guy was guilty of extremely bad judgment."

"Holy shit, sir, this isn't her, is it? Is this that lady friend you told Harry you were bringin' with you?"

"I'm afraid so. Philadelphia Fox, allow me to present William Tecumseh Sherman. An old friend of the family. He's worked for the Lightfoots for years. Ever since he got out of the service, in fact."

"Fire him," Phila answered.

"You'd better give her to me, Tec. She gets a bit temperamental at times."

"Sure thing, sir. Real sorry about the mistake." Tec began to shift his burden. His hands went around Phila's waist and he lifted her off his shoulder. "I asked her who she was, and she just gave me some sass."

"That sounds like her."

"I was supposed to keep an eye on everyone who tried to get through the gates this year. Last year a couple of bikers tried to crash the party. Caused a little trouble before I could get rid of 'em."

"Do I look like some kind of motorcycle mama, you idiot?" Phila closed her eyes as the sky spun overhead. She waited impatiently for her feet to touch the ground. She kept talking while she was in midair. "This is absolutely intolerable. I can't believe this man has kept a position with your family all these years, Nick. Do you people booby-trap your front lawn, too? Put alligators in swamps around the front door maybe? Are there any more military robots like this one hanging around? Uzi machine guns in the hall . . . Ooof! *Nick!*"

A second pair of large hands caught her around the waist, and the next thing Phila knew she was hanging over Nick's broad shoulder.

"I'm going to use my shares in Castleton & Lightfoot to drive both families into bankruptcy," Phila swore.

"Take it easy, Phila. I'll handle it from here, Tec. See you a little later?"

"Yes, sir. You better believe it, sir. Sure is good to have you back."

"Thank you, Tec. I wonder if the others will feel the same way."

"I'm sure they will, sir. Not much doubt about it."

From her upside-down position Phila caught the expression on Tec Sherman's face. He was grinning widely at Nick. This was one member of the clan who was apparently happy to see the prodigal son. Of course, she reminded herself, Tec wasn't exactly family. Just hired help.

"Put me down, Nick. The joke has gone far enough." She saw the wrought-iron gates slip past her field of vision as Nick strode through them. When she looked down she saw a sea of deep, verdant green under his feet.

"This is the Fourth of July, Phila," he explained. "You're supposed to have a little fun on the Fourth."

"This is a Lightfoot's way of having fun? Manhandling innocent women?"

"I've never tried it before," Nick said thoughtfully. His palm slid higher up along her jean-clad thigh. He squeezed gently. "It's not half bad."

Before he could continue, another male voice interrupted. This voice was vaguely familiar. Rich, well modulated, very smooth. An excellent speaking voice that could make the listener believe anything. She had heard it once on the telephone. It belonged to Darren Castleton.

"Hey, Nick. What the hell have you got there? Your technique with the ladies undergone a few changes during the past three years?"

"I never did have your finesse, Darren."

"That goes without saying. You're a Lightfoot, not a Castleton. But you sure as hell never used to go in for the kind you had to bring home over your shoulder. This one must be interesting."

"She is."

"Good to see you, Nick." Darren's voice turned earnest. "Damn good. It's been too long."

"I just hope it's been long enough."

Phila felt Nick's right arm move from across the back of her thighs and she realized he was shaking hands with Darren. "If you two have finished the grand reunion, I would appreciate it if someone would let me stand on my own two feet."

"I think she's irritated, Nick."

"Not my fault. She had a small altercation with Tec down at the front gate." With an easy movement, Nick put Phila down and watched, grinning, as she pushed hair out of her eyes and straightened her fuch-sia-and-green-print camp shirt. "Darren, meet Miss Philadelphia Fox."

Phila glowered at the remarkably handsome man in front of her. He looked to be about the same age as Nick, but that was where the re-semblance stopped. While Nick was big and solid and blunt of feature, Darren Castleton was graceful, lean and aristocratic.

There were just enough craggy edges on his fine features to save him from being pretty, Phila decided. He had the kind of teeth that would grace any campaign poster. His light brown hair and clear, blue eyes gave him the sort of all-American look that people tended to trust on sight.

There was, she had to admit, something quite attractive about Darren Castleton, something beyond the nice features and the charm. The word *charisma* came to mind when she realized she was smiling up at him. When he held out his hand, she took it.

"Hello, Mr. Castleton."

"Darren," he corrected instantly. His handshake was solid. "Glad to meet you, Phila. Sorry about whatever happened down at the gate. Tec tends to take his duties seriously."

"It's probably the military mentality," Phila explained. "It's a severe handicap."

"You may be right." Darren exchanged a quick grin with Nick.

"I guess the Castletons and Lightfoots suffer a lot from that sort of thing," Phila murmured.

"Some of us endeavor to rise above it," Darren said, still smiling.

Crissie had had little respect for males in general and had not dwelt on them in her correspondence or phone calls. Men were just creatures to be maniuplated when it was useful to do so. But she had made one or two observations about Darren Castleton that Phila remembered. *They're talking about a political career for him*, she had remarked. *He'll probably be good at it. Endless teeth and a wife Eleanor handpicked especially for the job of being a politician's wife. Hilary says she's willing to have the families finance Darren's campaigns. Running for office takes a ton of money, she says, and lots of clout. The Lightfoots and Castletons have both.*

"Let's get you two something to eat. Reed's supervising things at the barbecue as usual. You know how he loves it." Darren looked at Nick. "Your dad's looking forward to seeing you again, Nick."

"Is he?" Nick threw a casual arm around Phila's shoulders and started walking toward the barbecue pits.

"Give him a chance, okay?" Darren suggested softly.

"Think he'll give me one?"

"I think things are going to work out just fine if everyone gives them a chance to do so," Darren said. "Are you hungry, Phila?"

She inhaled the aromas coming from the direction of the barbecue pits and was again surprised to find herself anticipating food. "Yes, I think I am."

"Good. Plenty for everyone."

Phila glanced at him. "Do you people put on a Fourth of July party every year?"

"Every year for as long as Nick or I can remember. It's a C&L tradition. People around here count on it."

Phila nodded, aware of the weight of Nick's arm around her shoulders. She wondered at it. His casual air of possessiveness disconcerted her, but it also intrigued her. This was the first time she had seen him since he had left Holloway, and she was startled at the strange little leap of excitement that had shot through her a moment ago when he had put her over his shoulder.

Halfway to the barbecue pits two large, muscular-looking dogs came bounding through the crowd. They clustered around Nick, who played with their ears for a few minutes and spoke to them quietly.

"Looks like they remember you," Darren observed.

"What kind of dogs are they?" Phila asked warily as the black-and-tan dogs turned their broad heads in her direction.

"Rottweilers," Nick said.

"I knew it," Phila muttered. "Killer dogs." She tried to step back when the animals thrust their inquisitive noses into her hands, but she wasn't quick enough. With a sigh of resignation she gingerly patted their heads. They seemed overjoyed at the attention and eagerly demanded more.

"How about that?" Darren said. "They're taking to you right off,

Phila. They don't usually do that. Normally it takes them awhile to accept a stranger."

"They're probably just sizing me up for dinner," Phila said. "Figuring the easiest, quickest way to tear out my throat. What are their names? Bruno and Devil?"

"Cupcake and Fifi," Nick told her.

"Oh, sure."

"It's true. My father bought them just before I left. He named them." Nick pushed his glasses higher on his nose and smiled faintly as he watched the dogs' antics. "Darren's right. You've got them eating out of the palm of your hand. Very unusual."

"I can't tell you how thrilled I am," Phila said. The rottweilers laughed up at her, tongues lolling, as if she had said something very funny. "They remind me of you."

"Crissie Masters hated the dogs," Darren said quietly.

"Crissie was terrified of dogs," Phila explained coldly. She gave the rottweilers a last pat and tried to step back.

"Come on, let's get that food we were talking about," Darren said, leading the way. "How about a beer, Nick?"

"Sounds good."

The dogs danced around Phila's heels all the way to the barbecue pits. She finally gave up trying to discourage their attention. It was not the first time she'd found herself in this position. Animals and kids frequently reacted this way around her.

People were standing three-deep near the barbecue pits, but the crowd parted almost magically as Nick, Phila and Darren approached. When the last hungry guest stepped aside, a big, broad-shouldered man in his mid-sixties was revealed. He held a spatula in his right hand as he supervised the half dozen other men dressed in chef's aprons.

Phila recognized the nose immediately as the silver-haired man turned to glance in her direction. She also recognized the cool gray eyes and the high, blunt cheekbones. Reed Lightfoot. She felt Nick's arm tighten around her shoulders, but his voice was as calm as ever when he spoke.

"Hello, Dad."

Reed nodded once casually but there was an intensity in his hooded gaze as he examined his son. "Heard you were coming back. Glad you could make it to the picnic this year." The words sounded stilted but genuine. "This is Miss Fox, I take it?"

"Phila, this is Reed Lightfoot. My father."

"How do you do?" Phila said, carefully polite. She wasn't sure what to expect. Crissie had said very little about Reed Lightfoot. *He's always out on the golf course. Stays out of Hilary's way.*

"Nice to meet you, Phila," Reed said, flipping a meat patty with a deft movement. There was an awkward silence before he added, "You two want a burger?"

The question seemed to be directed at Nick, but when he failed to respond to it Phila automatically stepped in to answer. "That sounds great," she said.

Reed nodded, obviously glad to have something constructive to do. "We'll get you fixed up here. Eleanor, where are you? We need more buns over here."

"I'll have one of the caterer's people bring out some more, Reed."

Phila glanced around to see a polished-looking woman in her early sixties approaching them through the crowd. She had a clever little nautical cap perched atop her discreetly tinted beige-blond hair, and she was wearing a red-white-and-blue silk top over a pleated white silk skirt. Her smile was vague, but polite. Her pale blue eyes went immediately to Nick.

"Nick, dear! You're here. It's so good to see you, darling. We heard you were due to arrive today, and we're all so delighted."

Nick released Phila to accept Eleanor Castleton's hug. "Hi, Eleanor. Good to see you again. Meet Philadelphia Fox."

Eleanor turned to Phila, her smile still gracious but her eyes cold. "Of course. Miss Fox. You were a friend of Crissie Masters, I believe?"

"That's right. She was my best friend. Like a sister, in fact." Might as well get the cards on the table at the start of the game, Phila decided. She already knew how Eleanor Castleton felt about Crissie. *She hates my guts. But that's okay. I'm not real fond of her, either,* Crissie had said once.

"Such a dreadful accident," Eleanor said dismissively. She turned toward an attractive, slim, black-haired woman whose striking dark eyes were on Phila. "Vicky, dear, meet Phila Fox. Crissie's friend."

"How do you do, Miss Fox? I'm Victoria Castleton, Darren's wife."

"How do you do?" Phila said quietly as she held out her hand and silently remembered Crissie's description of this clan member: *Handpicked by dear Eleanor to be an asset to her son's political career.*

Victoria Castleton looked at Nick and smiled warily. "Hello, Nick. Good to see you again."

"Hello, Vicky." Nick nodded toward her. "Where's Jordan?"

"I'm here," announced a small boy as he stepped out from behind the shelter of his mother's legs. "Who're you?"

Nick went down on his haunches. "I'm Nick. You don't remember me, but I remember you. The last time I saw you, though, you were only about two years old and only about that high." He held his palm out about a foot above the grass.

"I'm big now." Jordan grinned proudly, standing beside Nick's hand to demonstrate the difference in height. He looked up at Phila. "Hi."

"Hi, yourself. My name is Phila." The boy's self-confidence spoke for itself, she thought. This was a child who had always received a great deal of love and attention; a boy who was sure of his place in his family and therefore sure of his welcome from others. The children she usually worked with rarely demonstrated this kind of comfortable confidence. She caught herself on that last thought. She would not be working with such children in the future. Her career was finished.

"D'you like seaweed?" Jordan asked.

"Yes, as a matter of fact, I do," Phila answered readily. "I like seaweed a lot."

"I got some in my room. Wanna see it?"

"Some other time, Jordan." Victoria took her son's hand and tugged him back a step from Phila. "Phila and Nick want to eat now."

"I believe the hamburgers are ready," Eleanor Castleton said smoothly. She picked up two plates and handed them to Nick and Phila. "Do help yourselves to salad and all the trimmings."

"Thanks, Eleanor." Nick took his plate and steered Phila toward the potato salad table.

"Lots of real genuine regret over Crissie's death there," Phila muttered. "Such a *dreadful* accident." She added, mimicking Eleanor Castleton's dismissive tone.

Nick scooped potato salad onto Phila's plate. "You'd better get realistic about this business, Phila. You can't expect her to feel a lot of sorrow over Crissie's death. Your friend made Eleanor's life hell while she was here."

"It's wasn't Crissie's fault Burke Castleton cheated on his wife twenty-six years ago."

"You're absolutely right, of course," said a new voice from behind Phila. The newcomer spoke with a hint of a New England accent. "It was not her fault at all. But don't expect Eleanor Castleton to ever admit it. She's put a lot of effort into polishing the Castleton image."

Phila knew who the speaker was without being told. When she turned around she was not surprised to see a sleek thoroughbred of a woman with chestnut-red hair and emerald-green eyes. She was dressed in beautifully cut camel-colored trousers that emphasized her long legs and an off-white silk blouse, an elegant outfit that perfectly complemented her features. She wore a gold wedding ring on her left hand.

"Hello," Phila said.

"Hello, Phila. I'm Hilary Lightfoot." Hilary put out a perfectly manicured hand. "I want to tell you how sorry I am about Crissie. She was a fascinating creature, bright and full of life. I miss her."

Phila accepted the long-fingered, long-nailed hand. "Thank you, Mrs. Lightfoot. It's a pleasure to meet you. Crissie liked you." This was the only member of the clan Crissie had liked, Phila recalled, and because Crissie had liked her, Phila was prepared to like Hilary Lightfoot, also.

"Call me Hilary." She withdrew her hand from Phila's and turned to Nick, who was munching potato salad. Her expression was serene but oddly unreadable. "Hello, Nick."

Nick nodded once. He did not offer his hand. "Hilary."

"I was surprised to hear you had decided to return."

"Were you?" Nick bit into a pickle and glanced out over the throng. "Quite a crowd this year."

"It gets bigger every year. One of these days we may have to start limiting the invitations to just friends of the families." Hilary followed his gaze. "This business of inviting the whole town is getting awkward, not to mention expensive."

"Castleton & Lightfoot can afford it." Nick's voice was neutral, but Phila thought she detected an undertone of annoyance.

"True, but it's hardly worthwhile."

"The Fourth of July picnic is a Castleton & Lightfoot tradition. I don't see Dad ever giving it up." Nick took a sizable bite out of his hamburger, his eyes still on the crowd.

"Reed is leaving more and more of the important decisions in my hands these days," Hilary told him quietly. "In fact, you might be interested to know that at last year's annual meeting he turned both his shares and yours over to me to vote. He trusts me to do what's best for the firm."

"He's always trusted you, hasn't he, Hilary?"

"Why shouldn't he trust me? I've always had the best interests of C&L at heart, unlike you."

Phila edged closer to the relish tray and concentrated on slathering her hamburger bun with mustard and pickles. She could feel the eerie crackle of emotional tension around these two and it sent shivers down her spine. It also raised a few interesting questions. She wondered just what Nick's relationship with Hilary had been. It was obvious he hadn't wasted any money on Mother's Day cards for his father's wife during the past few years.

Darren wandered over, a couple of cans of beer in his hands. He handed one to Nick as Hilary nodded at Phila and moved off into the crowd.

"Here," Darren said. "Figured you could use one of these."

"You figured right." Nick took the can and popped the tab.

"Since you're here," Darren said easily, "you can give us a hand with the fireworks later."

"Sure. Why not?"

"I knew there would be fireworks," Phila said under her breath.

Nick looked at her. "I've got a feeling the ones tonight are only the beginning."

The first crackling display of pyrotechnics lit up the evening sky at precisely ten o'clock that night. Phila sat cross-legged on the lawn in front of one of the colonnaded porticos to watch. She was surrounded by the women of the Lightfoot and Castleton clans. The only male in the group was young Jordan, who was so excited he could not sit still.

The townspeople sprawled across the wide lawn. Some were drinking a final can of beer, and others were trying to put away one more slice of apple pie. The dogs had stuffed themselves and were laying supine nearby. Somehow one of them, the one called Fifi, Phila thought, had managed to get her head lodged on Phila's lap.

Nick had vanished along with his father, Tec Sherman and Darren.

"Do all the Castleton and Lightfoot males get involved with the fireworks?" Phila asked Vicky, who was sitting next to her.

"It's a tradition," Vicky explained, her tone brusque. She looked at her bouncing son. "In a few years Jordan will get to help stage the fireworks display."

"Next year, next year, next year," Jordan chanted and then shrieked as another flash of color filled the night sky.

"Fireworks are dangerous," Phila said with a frown. "Basically, they're explosive devices. Small bombs. They're supposed to be handled by experts."

"Reed and Darren and Nick are experts. So was Burke."

"Is that right? Where did they all get this expertise?" Phila glanced up again as a starburst of red exploded overhead.

"Oh, every Castleton and Lightfoot male does his military service," Vicky said. "I suppose when Jordan is out of college he'll go into the Marines or the Air Force for a while."

"Another tradition?" Phila asked dryly.

"You wouldn't believe how many traditions these families have established in just two generations. My people have lived in Virginia since the seventeen-hundreds and we don't have as many rites and rituals as the Castletons and the Lightfoots."

"Nick and Darren went into the service?"

"Their fathers would have kicked them out of the business if they hadn't done their military duty. Don't worry. They all know what they're doing around explosives and firearms."

"How reassuring."

Hilary spoke softly out of the darkness to the right of Phila. "I'm going to get something to drink. Anyone want anything?"

Phila shook her head. "No, thanks."

"Nothing for me, Hilary," Victoria murmured.

"I'll come with you, Hilary, dear." Eleanor Castleton got out of the porch swing and followed Hilary into the house.

Victoria and Phila sat in silence for a few minutes as fireworks shrieked overhead. Phila absently played with Fifi's ears. The dog shuddered with pleasure.

"Are you going to pick up where Crissie left off?" Victoria finally asked quietly.

Phila had been wondering about the woman's tense tone, and she was glad the reason for her unfriendliness was finally out in the open.

"What do you mean?"

"Are you going to cause trouble for us?"

"Do you think I can?"

"Crissie certainly did."

"I'm not Crissie."

"No, you're different. Very different. I knew that the minute I saw you. But you're in a position to cause all kinds of trouble. You've got the shares now. Why did Nick bring you to Port Claxton?"

"To let me find out for myself what happened while Crissie was here. I want to know what you people did to her, Vicky."

"It's more a case of what she did to us," Victoria snapped. "I'm sorry for your sake that she's dead, but she did a lot of damage during the short time she was around, Phila. I hope you won't do more of the same. The families have been through enough."

"What, exactly, have the families been through?"

"Never mind. It doesn't concern you. I just thought you ought to know that what happened between the families and Crissie wasn't all one-sided."

"Perhaps."

They were silent again for several minutes before Victoria Castleton spoke. "Nick came back today because of you, didn't he? You have no idea what a shock that was to everyone, except maybe Eleanor. She always believed he'd return sooner or later. I wonder what he's planning?"

"He's planning to get his hands on my shares, just like everyone else." And if she were smart, Phila thought, she would not forget that simple fact for one minute.

Another brilliant display crackled overhead, and in the faint glow of the explosion Victoria eyed Phila with cool interest. "I saw that little scene down by the gate this afternoon. We all did. Quite an entrance."

Phila winced. "It certainly wasn't my idea of a grand entrance."

"I'd have said it wasn't Nick's idea, either. At least, not the Nick I knew three years ago. I'd have bet my last dollar Nicodemus Lightfoot was not the kind of man who would ever throw a woman over his shoulder and carry her through a crowd of people."

"Maybe he's been living in California too long."

"Whatever the reason, it certainly revealed a new side of him. And it's a side Hilary never saw, that's for sure. I can't imagine Nick throwing her over his shoulder. Never in a million years."

"Hilary?" Phila went still. "Why would he want to toss her over his shoulder?"

Victoria studied her for a moment in the flare of another explosion. "Don't you know?"

"Know what?"

"I'm sorry. I shouldn't have said anything. I just assumed Nick would have told you by now."

"Told me what, for heaven's sake?"

"Hilary is Nick's ex-wife. They were divorced three years ago. She married Reed the day after the divorce was final."

# 5

⭇⭍

The silence in the library was oppressive. Nick lounged in one of the mahogany cabriole chairs, his legs stretched out in front of him, and watched his father pour brandy at the early-nineteenth-century butler's tray. Old crystal clinked melodically. Nick wondered what Phila was doing at that moment.

He decided she was probably sound asleep. He had walked her back to the Gilmarten place half an hour before. She had been suspiciously silent. He had thought about attempting a kiss and decided not to risk it. Her mood had been a dangerous cross between thoughtful and volatile.

As Reed fixed the brandies Nick shifted his gaze to the familiar book-lined walls of the high-ceilinged room. He knew the library was a fine example of the Federal period. Eleanor Castleton had designed it and overseen the selection of furnishings here as in every other room in the beach cottages and the main homes on Bainbridge Island. He had it on the best authority that if Eleanor said this room was decorated in the Federal style, then it undoubtedly was.

*I'm sure it's perfect, Nick,* his mother had once said with a wry smile. *Eleanor knows how to do everything perfectly. She was raised to be a lady.*

The books lining the shelves ranged from *Moby Dick* to a recent exposé of the inner workings of a beleagured CIA. They resided in glass-paned Duncan Phyfe–style bookcases made of mahogany and poplar and pine. In one obscure corner of a particular bookcase, stuffed behind a three-part series on nineteenth-century American history, was an aging copy of *Playboy* magazine. Nick assumed it was still there. He had shoved it there himself, a long time ago when he thought he'd heard his mother's step in the hall. He'd never gotten around to retrieving it.

To the best of his recollection the women featured in it were top-heavy in the extreme. Not at all like Phila, who had delicate, pert little breasts and a neat, lush rear he was pretty sure he could cup in both palms.

His gaze moved on around the room to the girandole mirror with its American eagle decoration. The antique crewelwork fire screen was still in front of the fireplace. The circular library table covered in green baize was positioned as usual near his chair.

There were echoes of Nick's childhood as well as his more recent past in every corner of this room. He had not been here in a long time. He did not feel comfortable now.

"Goddamn fireworks get trickier every year, don't they?" Reed remarked in a determinedly conversational tone as he handed Nick a glass. He sat down in a blue wing-backed armchair across from his son.

A truce had apparently been declared. Nick sought to hold up his end of it. "It was a good show tonight. The kids got a kick out of it."

"They always do." Reed sipped his brandy. "So how's business? Much demand for this consulting work of yours?"

"Enough." That seemed a little brusque. Nick tried to expand his answer. "California's full of fast-food geniuses who think the time has come to open a chicken-fried grapefruit outlet in downtown Tokyo or Milan. They're all willing to pay for advice."

"What do you know about chicken-fried grapefruit?"

"Nothing," Nick said, forcing himself to ignore Reed's skeptical tone. "But I know a lot about doing business in places like Tokyo or Milan."

"Thanks to having been raised a Lightfoot."

"Yeah. Thanks to that. No substitute for a good, well-rounded background, is there, Dad?"

"Didn't think you bothered to remember your background these days."

"I get reminded of it every once in a while." Nick heard the belligerence in Reed's voice, but he had questions of his own. "Speaking of the old family background, how are things going with Castleton & Lightfoot?"

Reed regarded him with hooded eyes. "Fine."

"That tells me a lot."

"If you cared about getting more details, you'd come to the annual meetings."

"I think that would be a little uncomfortable for everyone, don't you?"

Reed got to his feet and walked to the end of the room without speaking. He stood looking out the window into the darkness for a long moment. "If you weren't so goddamned stubborn, none of it would have happened."

"Be reasonable, Dad. You can't blame me for the stubbornness. It runs in the family."

"We could have worked things out."

"The business about getting C&L out of government contract work? Maybe. But we both now we couldn't have worked out the other glitch."

"Damn it, Nick . . ."

"You didn't have to marry her, Dad. I'm a big boy now. I can clean up my own messes."

"Well, you sure as hell didn't bother to clean this one up, did you? You just left it for someone else to fix."

Nick felt his temper flare. "I knew what I was doing. You could have shown a little faith in me."

"Goddamn it, I had to do something. I couldn't just turn my back on her. It wasn't right. If you hadn't . . ." Reed made an obviously heroic effort to swallow the remainder of the sentence. "Let's change the subject."

"Yeah. Let's."

Reed swung around abruptly. "All right, what the hell's going on between you and that Fox woman?"

"Not much. Yet." The brandy glass dangled from Nick's fingers.

"You can at least tell me what you're planning."

"I'm not sure."

"Why did you bring her here?"

"She's got some questions she wants answered."

"Questions about what? Castleton & Lightfoot?"

"No, she already knows the firm makes death machines." Nick smiled slightly.

"*Death machines.* Oh, hell, she's not one of those, is she?"

"I'm afraid so."

"I was hoping she'd be more like her friend, the Masters woman. Out for what she can get."

"Sorry. It's not going to be that simple."

"You said she had some questions she wants answered."

"About us and about what happened to her friend, Crissie Masters."

Reed looked exasperated. "What about her?"

"She wants to know how the families treated her and whether they bear some moral responsibility for what happened to Miss Masters. What she decides about us will determine what she does with the C&L shares, I think."

"*Moral responsibility.* For Crissie Masters's death? Is she crazy? Masters got drunk and got into a car. End of story. No one else is involved, and we sure as hell don't bear any *moral responsibility* for what happened. It's just like some muddle-brained liberal type to try to put responsibility on everyone else except the one person who really was responsible."

"What can I say?" Nick shrugged. "Phila's an ex–social worker or something. That's the way that type thinks."

"For Crissake." Reed's brows beetled threateningly. "You don't believe any of that moral responsibility nonsense, do you?"

"No. I haven't been living down in California long enough to start thinking like that."

"Well, that's something at least."

"Thanks."

Reed paid no attention to his son's dry tone. "What's the point of bringing her here?"

"I thought if she had a chance to meet the families and ask her questions, it would put her mind at ease. Phila's been through a lot lately, from what I can tell. She needs something to focus on, something to help her get her feet back on the ground. Crissie Masters was more than her best friend; she was like family to Phila. I thought if she had a chance to satisfy herself that the Castletons and Lightfoots aren't a couple of demon clans, she might be inclined to be reasonable about the shares."

Reed nodded slowly. "I see your point. Might work. Unless she's too much like Crissie."

"What do you know about Crissie Masters?" Nick asked.

"Not much. Hilary got to know her better than I did. All I know is that she landed on Burke's doorstep a year ago and proceeded to set everyone's back teeth on edge, except Burke's. Christ, I felt sorry for Eleanor. Whole thing was such a goddamn shock to her. It can't have been easy having to accept Burke's bastard daughter."

"Especially after having spent nearly forty years turning a blind eye to Burke's running around," Nick agreed.

"Eleanor's no fool. She knew what was going on. But she was too much of a lady to acknowledge it."

"Unlike mother?" Nick asked with a small smile.

"Nora would have had my scalp on a silver platter if I'd tried chasing outside tail." Reed smiled reminiscently. Then he shook his head. "But Eleanor was different. Nora always said you could put Eleanor to work shoveling shit and she'd find a way to make it look as if she were planting tea roses. As long as Burke didn't parade his conquests in front of her, Eleanor could pretend everything was all right."

"But when Crissie appeared with proof she was Burke's daughter, there was no way to pretend any longer, was there?"

Reed shook his head. "No, although I'll give Eleanor credit for trying goddamn hard to ignore her. Treated Crissie as though the gal was just some shade tree relative instead of Darren's half sister.

"But there was never any doubt Crissie was Burke's daughter and Eleanor knew it. Even if the girl hadn't spent a fortune on private detectives to trace her father, you'd have known who she was the minute you saw her. Crissie had the Castleton looks."

"What about Burke?"

"Burke took to Crissie right from the start. Made it clear he was pleased as all get-out with her. Called her a chip off the old block. Kept saying she was the one who had inherited his guts and nerve."

"Must have made Darren feel like a real second-class citizen."

"You know Burke. He made a big production out of Crissie. It gave him a chance to hold center stage. He always liked to be the center of attention."

"Yeah," Nick agreed. "He did. And he was good at it."

Reed scowled. "No getting around the fact that Crissie Masters caused a lot of trouble while she was here and, besides Burke—really because of Burke's behavior—no one went out of their way to make her feel like one of the family, that's for sure. But the shit flew both ways."

"I know that."

"Think you can convince the Fox woman we're not 'morally' responsible for Masters's death?"

"It's not up to me to convince her, is it? It's up to the rest of you."

"Bullshit. You've obviously got a handle on her. Use it."

"A handle?"

Reed went back to his chair and sat down. "Come on, Nick. I'm your father, remember? I know you better than anyone now that Nora's gone. I saw that scene down at the gate when Phila arrived and I saw the way you watched the woman all afternoon. If you're not sleeping with her already, you soon will be. Is that your scheme? Are you going to get those shares back by talking her out of them in bed?"

"An interesting thought. Think I could?"

Reed studied the ceiling for a moment. "Don't know. She strikes me as a sharp little cookie. Gutsy, too, or she wouldn't be here waving those shares in our faces."

"You could be right."

Reed's eyebrows rose, revealing a gleam of humor in his eyes. "Better be careful, son. She may be too goddamned smart to let you climb into bed with her."

"Yeah. After all, as far as she's concerned, I'm one of the enemy."

"She's goddamn right. You are the enemy. Don't let yourself forget it for one minute. You're a Lightfoot. If you do wind up in bed with her, you'd better watch your ass."

"I'll do that."

Reed's grin came and went. "She sure set Tec off today."

"Yeah."

"Got to say I've never seen you throw a woman over your shoulder before, either."

"Not my style," Nick agreed.

"What did you say this Phila did for a living?"

"She was a social worker."

"Sounds like a real bleeding-heart type."

"The kind of bleeding hearts who practice what they preach are always the most difficult ones to deal with, aren't they?" Nick offered his father a wry smile.

Reed's gaze sharpened perceptively. "You're finding this really funny, aren't you?"

"Let's just say I think it will prove interesting."

Reed stared at him. "Interesting," he repeated thoughtfully. "You may be right."

"Why did you let Hilary vote my shares and yours at the last annual meeting?" Nick regretted the question as soon as the words left his mouth, but he also knew he could not avoid asking it. It had been gnawing at him all afternoon.

Reed's face went taut. "If you give a damn about who votes your shares, come home and vote 'em yourself."

"You've made a mistake turning things over to her, Dad."

"Have I? She's devoted to Castleton & Lightfoot. It's all she cares about."

"Unlike me? You're only partially right. Hilary is devoted to herself, not C&L and if you ever forget that, you're in real trouble."

Reed's expression turned cold. "You've said enough, Nick. Goddamn it, Hilary is my wife now. You'll show her the proper respect or you'll get your ass out of this house."

"She's a piranha. Haven't you realized that yet?"

"Shut up, Nick. *Now.* Before I have to do something about it."

"How did it happen?"

"How did what happen?"

"How did it get to the point where you turned over complete control of the Lightfoot half of the company to her?" Nick insisted coldly.

"You want to know how it happened?" Reed leaned forward, his face taut and angry. "I'll tell you how it happened, goddamn it. She was devastated after she lost the baby. She was on the edge of a nervous breakdown. I thought it might help if she had something to do, something else to think about besides the miscarriage. I let her start getting involved with the company. She took to it like a duck to water."

"Yeah. I'll bet she did."

"It's true. The woman's got a real talent for management. And she cares about what happens to Castleton & Lightfoot."

"And you don't anymore?"

"I'm discovering the joys of retirement." Reed sat back in his chair and gulped his brandy. "Golf game's better than it's been in years."

"Don't give me that crap. Running Castleton & Lightfoot was the only game you ever really liked."

"The whole point of building up a firm like Castleton & Lightfoot is to create something worth leaving behind. I don't have anyone to leave my half of the firm to, now do I? When you walked out you made it goddamnn clear you weren't coming back."

Nick exhaled slowly and closed his eyes for a moment. "You could try for another baby."

"That would be a little tricky, given the fact that Hilary and I have separate bedrooms," Reed shot back bitterly.

Nick opened his eyes and stared at his father. "Don't tell me you found out the truth."

"What truth?"

"That going to bed with her is like bedding an ice sculpture."

Reed slammed his fist against the arm of the chair. "Goddamn it, Nick, I told you to keep your mouth shut and I meant it. She's my wife, and I won't let anyone talk about her, not even you. Especially not you. Not after what you did to her."

"Shit. I knew this was going to happen."

"If you hadn't walked out on your responsibilities three years ago none of us would be in this situation. You've got real balls to sit there and talk about Hilary and me having babies." Reed set the brandy glass down on the table with a violent snap. The fragile crystal shattered.

Nick watched the shards sparkle in the light from the table lamp for a long moment. Then he got to his feet. "So much for the big reunion scene. Thanks for the brandy. I think it's time I went to bed."

Reed looked up instantly. "Your room's the one across from mine. Hilary had it made up for you."

Nick nodded and walked to the door.

"Nick."

"What?"

"About those shares the Fox woman owns."

Nick glanced back over his shoulder. "What about them?"

"They belong in the family," Reed said bluntly. "Stop playing your goddamnn games with me. Give it to me straight. Are you going to get those shares back for us?"

Yeah," Nick said as he turned the doorknob. "I'll get them back for you."

He stepped out into the hall and closed the door behind him. There was no noise at the top of the stairs, but something made him glance up. Hilary stood on the landing, her hair a gleaming mass of dark fire around her shoulders. Her emerald eyes blazed at him, and he could see the outline of her slim body through the fabric of her flowing robe. He remembered that body all too well. A beautifully molded alabaster statue he had never been able to bring to life.

"I won't have you upsetting Reed."

"I've got news for you, Hilary. My father can take care of himself. Be careful or one of these days he might show you just how well he can do it."

Hilary glided one step down from the landing. The silky peignoir flowed around her ankles. "What game are you playing, Nick? Why are you here? Why did you bring that woman here?"

"You don't really expect me to tell you, do you?" He started toward the front door.

"Where are you going?"

"To find a warm place to sleep." He let himself out into the cool night air.

It was a ten-minute walk to Phila's cottage.

The loud knock on the cottage door brought Phila up out of a surprisingly sound sleep. Fear lanced through her. She sat bolt upright in bed, orienting herself to the cheerfully shabby surroundings of her new bedroom.

The knock came again, harsh and demanding. Automatically Phila swung her legs over the edge of the bed and reached for her purple velour robe. She was almost to the bedroom door when she remembered the gun.

*The gun.* This was what it was for, she thought wildly. She rushed back to the nightstand and yanked open the drawer. She fumbled for the weapon in the darkness, her fingers closing around the awkward, square grip.

The knock sounded once more, and this time it was accompanied by a familiar masculine voice.

"Phila. It's Nick. Open the door."

Relief poured through Phila. She dropped the gun back into the drawer and whipped around. She took a few deep breaths on the way to the front door. Her pulse was almost back to normal by the time she opened it.

"What are you doing here?" she demanded, opening the door and peering up at Nick. He looked larger than ever standing there in the shadows.

"Mind if I come in?" he asked impatiently. It wasn't a request. He was already halfway through the door.

"You can come in, but what do you want?" She stepped back and flipped on the light switch. "For heaven's sake, Nick, it's nearly one o'clock in the morning."

"I know what time it is. I've got a two-thousand-dollar watch that tells the time with absolute accuracy." He strode past her, crossing the comfortably shabby living room with its sagging furniture and bare board floors. He went straight into the kitchen and began opening and closing cupboard doors in a methodical fashion.

"Is that right? Who gave you the watch?"

"My father. He gave it to me the day I took over the reins for Castleton & Lightfoot. I thought for sure he'd ask for it back along with my sword and brass buttons the day I walked out, but he didn't. Probably forgot about it."

Phila hurried after him. "Nick, what is going on here?"

"Questions. All I get are questions. Haven't you got anything to drink?"

"You mean something strong like scotch or bourbon? No. I just got into town this morning, remember? I picked up enough groceries for breakfast, and that's all. Nick, what are you doing here at this time of night?"

He turned around and leaned back against the chipped tile counter top, his arms folded across his chest. "I'm looking for a place to spend the night."

That stopped her for a few short seconds. "I thought you were going to spend the night up at Tara West."

"I changed my mind."

"Why?"

"Let's just say that I had an unpleasant father-son chat with Reed Lightfoot, and by the time it was over I felt I'd worn out my welcome."

"Already?"

"I can do it really fast when I put my mind to it. Are you sure you don't have anything to drink?"

Phila sighed. "Warm milk."

"What?" He looked startled.

"You heard me. I can heat some milk for you."

"That sounds disgusting."

"Well, there's tea."

"I don't drink tea."

Phila started to lose her temper. "I'm sorry, *sir*, but that's all I've got in the place. If I'd known you were going to be dropping by in the middle of the night I'd have picked up some brandy to sedate you, sir."

"I've already had enough brandy. That's what I was drinking with Dad when I decided I was going to have to spend the night somewhere else."

"What brought you to that conclusion?"

"We got into an argument. It was a totally predictable scene, and I'll give us both credit for trying to avoid it. We both started out with good intentions. To be perfectly honest, I broke first."

"What did you argue about?" Phila asked cautiously.

"A number of things."

"Hilary, for instance?"

Nick's eyes narrowed behind the lenses of his glasses. "Now, what makes you say that?"

Phila folded her arms under her breasts, tucking her hands into the sleeves of her robe. She noticed her feet were getting cold. "I know she's your ex-wife, Nick."

"You pick up information fast, don't you?"

"That's what I'm here for, remember? To find out things."

"Who told you about Hilary and me?"

"Vicky."

"Yeah, that figures." Nick nodded as if confirming something to himself. "I didn't think it was Eleanor. Eleanor's committed to keeping family secrets locked in the closet where they belong."

"You must feel the same way, or you would have told me about Hilary being your ex-wife."

That seemed to surprise him. "Why would I have told you about her? She's not important one way or the other."

"Women look at these things a little differently."

"Only a woman who was seriously thinking of getting involved with me would look at it differently. Are you thinking about getting involved with me, Phila?"

She flushed but refused to be drawn. "It must be a little awkward for you," she offered hesitantly. "I mean Hilary being your ex-wife and all."

"Yeah, sure. Awkward. Just to set the record straight, Dad and I did touch briefly on the subject of Hilary this evening, but our chief argument concerning her had nothing to do with any father-son rivalry. Dad's welcome to her, although from what I can gather his bed's as cold as mine used to be when she was married to me."

"She's a beautiful woman."

"That's something you tend to notice right off, isn't it? Coldest bitch this side of the Arctic Circle, though. But what the hell. Maybe that was as much my fault as hers. God knows I'm no Casanova."

"Nick . . ."

"Maybe you've got something to drink in the refrigerator." He opened the door and stood scanning the empty shelves. His face looked harsh in the glare of the appliance light. After a moment he swore softly in resignation and gave up the search. He reluctantly slammed the door.

"I told you there was nothing to drink except milk. How did you meet her?"

"Who? Hilary?" Nick went back to leaning against the counter. "Eleanor introduced us. Hilary's the daughter of some old friends of Eleanor's family. They all go way back together."

"The original boat people, hmmm? An awful lot of upper-class East Coast folks seem to think they came over on the *Mayflower*. Must have been a crowded ship." So that's what it was, Phila thought. Hilary had been another of Eleanor's handpicked brides.

"Skip the lecture on inbreeding among the upper classes, will you? I'm not in the mood for it tonight."

"The bit about Hilary marrying your father after being married to you does sound a bit incestuous."

"Well it's not, so don't try to make it sound that way."

"I've heard that in some old, established East Coast families it's almost traditional to pass girlfriends around from brother to brother or father to son," Phila asked.

"Jesus, Phila."

"It's true. I've read about it."

"If the girlfriend happens to be a movie star and the family is tilted to the extreme left, I suppose it's a possibility," Nick growled. "Trust me, Phila, no one in my family holds liberal views."

"Was Hilary the only thing you and Reed argued about?"

"We talked about a few other things," Nick answered casually.

"Such as?"

"Your shares in Castleton & Lightfoot."

"Hah! I knew it. I just knew it."

"What did you expect us to talk about? Your shares are the reason I've returned to the bosom of my family, remember?"

"It's not a joke, Nick."

"Who's laughing?"

Phila studied him intently. "Your father wanted to know if you would be able to get your hands on my shares, I suppose?"

"Yeah. That's what he wanted to know, all right."

She lifted her chin. "Well? What did you tell him?"

Nick shrugged. His eyes met hers in a level look. "I told him I'd get the shares back."

Phila's feet felt colder than ever. "Yes, of course you did," she whispered, almost to herself. She went back out into the living room, heading for the bedroom. Nick followed.

"Phila?"

"Yes?"

"About the little matter of where I'm going to spend the night." His voice was rough around the edges, but otherwise as calm as ever.

"Use your Lightfoot pull to get yourself a motel room in town."

"I'd rather stay here."

She spun around to confront him and discovered he was practically on top of her. Instinctively she backed up. She wondered how he'd gotten so close without her realizing it. "Why do you want to stay here?"

He reached out and gently caught hold of the lapels of her robe, drawing her close. "You know the answer to that."

Phila tried to tamp down the energy that was beginning to sizzle through her. "Going to bed with you would be a very stupid thing for me to do."

"You think I'm one of the enemy."

"Aren't you?"

"No, Phila. I'm not."

"You want my shares."

"That's a side issue. The shares belong in the family, and sooner or later I'll get them back. But the fact has got nothing to do with you and me. It doesn't make me your enemy."

"How can you say that?" She searched his face. "Damn it, Nick, how can you *say* that?"

"It's easy because it's the truth. I can say it loud or soft or anywhere in between." His thumb moved along the angle of her jaw. "Take your pick."

"I could never really trust you," she pointed out, feeling desperate. A heady sense of awareness, a feeling of being gloriously, recklessly alive was kicking in for the first time in months.

"Yes you can. You can trust me, Phila." His thumb moved across her lower lip, tugging it gently away from her teeth.

Phila shivered. "If push comes to shove, you'll side with your family."

"Will I?"

"You've already admitted as much."

"I've said I'll get back the shares. That's the only thing I've admitted. Don't read any more into it than that. What goes on between you and me has nothing to do with the families or those damn shares."

She thought he was going to kiss her, but he did not. He just stood there, holding her lightly by the lapels, and waited.

She fought herself for a long moment, holding herself stiff and proud, trying to step back from the brink.

"Will you kiss me?" Nick asked softly. "I've been going out of my head wondering what it would be like."

So had she. Phila finally admitted it to herself, moaned softly and surrendered to the unfamiliar driving force of passion.

She gripped his shoulders fiercely as the excitement raced through her. No man had ever sent her senses reeling this way, and she was frankly fascinated with her own responses.

Crissie had laughed at her in the past, telling Phila that her disappointment in sex was directly attributable to the fact that she'd never met the right mate. Crissie had encouraged greater experimentation, but Phila had shied away from that approach. It wasn't just her inbuilt sense of discretion that kept her from it. There was an old fear to contend with, a fear that made sex seem less that attractive. Because of what had happened to her, the thought of a man climbing on top of her was enough to awaken a primitive panic.

But tonight her sense of caution was a dim and distant voice. She ignored it in favor of the heat that was waiting for her in Nick's arms. Impulsively she brushed her mouth quickly, awkwardly against his, tasting brandy and desire.

"Yeah, that's it. That's what I want—" Nick's voice was growing thick. His hands framed her face. "Come on. Eat me up. A hundred miles an hour."

A firestorm was building inside Phila. She was shaking with need, longing to know more about the tantalizing feelings flowing through her. She grabbed Nick's head in both hands and held him still so that she could plunge her tongue between his teeth.

Her fingers twisted in his hair, and her nose bumped against his glasses. When her teeth grated against his, Nick chuckled softly.

"It's okay, honey. I'm not going anywhere tonight. I'm all yours." Nick caught her around the waist and lifted her high against him. "Why don't you try wrapping your legs around me," he suggested softly.

"Nick, wait. I . . . we shouldn't . . ."

"It's okay," he soothed gently. "Nothing to worry about. I'm healthy as a horse. Want to see my blood donor card?"

She shook her head frantically. "I'm healthy, too. That's not what I meant." But she could no longer think clearly.

"Put your legs around me," he urged again, his eyes brilliant with desire. "Do it, Phila."

She did so instantly, hugging his hips with her thighs as if he were a stallion she intended to ride. Her arms locked around his neck, and her mouth fastened onto his again. Teeth clinked once more. His glasses were in the way, she thought.

Nick carried her down the short hall to the darkened bedroom and fell with her onto the bed. He rolled onto his back, one leg drawn up. His eyes gleamed in the shadows.

"Nick?"

"I'm here."

Dazed and hungry, filled with emotions that left her shaking, Phila needed no further encouragement. She knelt beside him, fumbling with the buttons of his shirt. She was in such a hurry now that when one button got stuck she yanked at it. There was a soft plink as it flew across the room and bounced off the window. She looked up. There was just enough light to see the grin on Nick's face.

"So help me, if you're laughing at me, you son of a . . ."

He stopped the words with two fingers across her lips. "I'm not laughing. I want this more than you do."

Phila decided to take him at his word because in that moment she wanted desperately to believe him. She went back to work on his clothing, stripping the shirt from him with impatient, wrenching movements. Then she groped for the buckle of his belt.

Nick sucked in his breath as she unzipped his jeans. His manhood sprang free. He groaned heavily when she captured him in her hands.

For a short while Phila contented herself with exploring him intimately. She was enthralled with the fullness of him, captivated by the hard tension in his thighs. She laced her fingertips in the crisp curling hair of his groin and stroked the unbelievably hard length of his shaft.

"You're magnificent," she whispered, awed.

"Oh, Jesus," Nick's finger twisted in her hair.

The fire in her was very close to the surface now. She wanted to know what it would be like to quench it. Eagerly she pulled the last of Nick's clothing from his body. When he was lying naked on the bed, Phila knelt between his legs, drinking in the sight of him. He was a beautiful beast in the shadows.

"What about you?" he urged softly, toying with the hem of her robe.

"Oh, yes. Right." Phila stripped off her robe and nightgown, almost unaware of what she was doing. She was too excited to think clearly. Nick was a treasure she had discovered and unearthed all by herself. He was hers to do with as she pleased, and she was so excited by the prospect that she could not decide what to do first. Her hands slid over him in soft wonder.

"You look like a kid in a candy factory," Nick observed, his smile wicked and warm.

She heard the laughter in his voice but she no longer cared if he was amused. She could concentrate only on her own chaotic emotions. There was a liquid warmth between her thighs, an aching need that she knew Nick could satisfy.

"What are you waiting for?" Nick asked with a soft chuckle.

*What was she waiting for?* He was just lying there. He was not trying to climb all over her. He was not going to crush her beneath his heavy body. Phila hesitated briefly as the old memories and the primal fear they always brought with them surfaced. But an instant later the secret dread dissolved. He was offering himself for her pleasure, not forcing himself on her.

She moved upward, straddling him. With eager fingers, she guided him toward the center of her pulsating desire. Quickly she lowered herself, trying to impale herself on him.

"You're tight. Small and tight." His fingers slid up along her thighs to where she was fumbling with his manhood. He parted her softness gently. "You're hot but not quite ready for me. Give it awhile. There's no rush."

But she *was* in a rush. Phila had never felt like this, and she was very much afraid that if she did not take advantage of the sensations immediately she would never experience them again. It was imperative to hurry. Frantically she pushed herself downward.

"Not so fast. Take it easy," Nick murmured.

She paid no attention, forcing him into her snug sheath. It felt good, but it was not very comfortable. In fact it was almost painful. Phila gasped as her softness suddenly felt stretched beyond its limits. She eased herself carefully back up the length of him.

"I told you to slow down." Nick's voice sounded half-strangled.

But Phila wasn't listening. She began to glide up and down more quickly as her body adjusted rapidly to his. He was big, but she wanted him and she was determined to have all of him.

He still felt huge inside her, but the sensation was quickly becoming pleasurable again. She splayed her fingers across his chest, clinging to him, lost in the wonder of it all. She increased the tempo of her rising and falling movements, her knees pressing tightly against his hips.

"*Nick.*"

"Yes. Oh, God, yes," Nick muttered as she moved faster and faster on him. "I shouldn't let you run wild like this. Not yet. You're going too fast. A hundred miles an hour. But it feels so good. *So good.*"

And then he went taut beneath Phila, shouting hoarsely, shuddering heavily as he exploded deep within her.

# 6

❧

"Nick is sleeping with her." Victoria stabbed her grapefruit with her spoon.

Darren glanced up from the head of the table, frowning. "How do you know that? Nick was supposed to spend the night over at the Lightfoot cottage. Hilary told me she'd had her housekeeper prepare his old room."

"Well, I guess Hilary lied," Victoria said, taking some small pleasure from making the comment sound terribly casual.

"Vicky, really, dear. That's no way to talk." Eleanor, seated at the other end of the gleaming fruitwood dining table, glanced first at her daughter-in-law and then at her son. "Hilary certainly did not lie. Why on earth would she do a thing like that? I know Nick was expected to sleep at the Lightfoot cottage last night."

"Well, he didn't." It wasn't often she got the satisfaction of surprising both her husband and Eleanor. Castletons were notoriously difficult to startle. It took something on the order of an unknown illegitimate daughter's sudden appearance out of the blue to do that. "Jordan and I stopped by the Gilmarten place a while ago when we came back from our walk along the beach. I wanted to talk to her, so I thought I'd see if she was up. She wasn't. Nick was. He opened the door when I knocked."

"I see," Eleanor said blandly. "Darren, dear, would you please pass the cream? Thank you. Maybe Nick went for a walk this morning, too, and just decided to say good morning to Miss Fox."

"He was barefoot and he wasn't wearing a shirt. All he had on were the jeans he was wearing yesterday at the party. I asked if Phila was awake, and he said she wasn't but that when she woke up he would tell her I'd stopped by to say hello. Take my word for it, he spent the night there."

"It's hardly any of our business," Eleanor proclaimed primly.

"You don't think so?" Victoria looked at her.

"No, I do not. Really, dear, this is hardly a subject for the breakfast table."

"Don't fret, Eleanor. I think we're all adult enough to handle it," Victoria said. Jordan was safely out of earshot, having eaten breakfast earlier in the kitchen.

Darren ate a wedge of grapefruit. "I don't know why you're acting like it's a big deal, Vicky. It was pretty obvious yesterday Nick had something going with her."

"Maybe he's trying to seduce the shares out of her," Victoria suggested, thinking about it. "Or, maybe she's just a little tramp like Crissie was."

"Quite possible," Eleanor agreed with a sigh of resignation. "Probable, in fact. They both come from the same sort of background, I understand."

"You think she's a tramp?" Darren shook his head. "I doubt it. Not the type."

Victoria was irritated. "For heaven's sake, Darren. You're a man. That doesn't make you a good judge of women."

"No?" Darren regarded his wife with a level look.

Victoria flushed angrily and went back to work on her grapefruit. "Whatever the reason, Nick's sleeping with her and I'll bet Hilary is furious."

"Why should Hilary be upset?" Eleanor inquired politely.

"Because she probably figured she could manage Nick if he ever returned to the fold. It would be just like her to assume she could manipulate him the way she does everyone else around here. She's never really understood Nick. She doesn't know him."

"She was married to him for eighteen months," Eleanor pointed out. "I'd say that gives her some insight into the man. We all know what she went through because of him."

"Well, she was wrong about one thing. She thinks Nick left three years ago because he was weak. That was a stupid assumption. He left because he was sick of the whole mess. Who can blame him?"

"Vicky, I think you've said enough," Darren began warningly.

"But," Victoria continued, "the first night Nick's home, he goes off with another woman. Poor Hilary didn't even get a chance to sink her claws back into him."

"I said that's enough, Vicky." Darren did not raise his voice, but his tone was harsh.

Victoria slanted him a scornful glance. "I'm merely mentioning a few facts. Hilary is accustomed to having men make fools of themselves over her."

"Now, dear," Eleanor murmured, dabbing at her lips with a white linen napkin. "I really do think you've said enough."

"Damn it, Vicky, close your mouth. You don't know what you're talking about." Darren poured himself another cup of coffee from the silver pot.

Victoria smiled grimly. "You're wrong, Darren. I do know what I'm talking about. I'm not blind. Hilary's an expert. She knows how to make men jump through hoops."

"How can you say that after what she went through?" Darren demanded.

"It's easy to say because it's the truth."

"Would anyone like some more fruit?" Eleanor asked, picking up a heavily scrolled silver-plate tray that contained a selection of fresh strawberries and grapefruit.

Darren ignored his mother. "Let's close the subject."

"I don't feel like closing it," Victoria retorted. "Nick got free of her three years ago and from the look of him this morning, my guess is that he's in no danger of falling into Hilary's clutches a second time. But we all know the situation with Reed. During the past three years he's gradually turned over the entire Lightfoot half of the company to Hilary. He's given up. Now she's working on you, Darren."

"What the hell is that supposed to mean?" Darren snapped.

"She wants to run the Castleton side of things as well. And she's going to do that by offering you what you want most."

Darren pushed aside his grapefruit dish and folded his arms on the table. "What can she offer me that would make me give up running our half of the business?"

"Freedom. The freedom to devote all your time to your political career. And C&L money to wage your campaigns." Victoria glanced from one startled face to to the other. "Don't you see? She's already starting to do it. This past year she's graciously taken over more and more of the daily decision making so that Darren can be free to set up the foundations of his gubernatorial campaign. Little by little, Hilary's assuming full responsibility, and you two don't even see what's happening."

"Hilary is the current CEO. She's not *taking over*, she already has the day-to-day responsibility of running C&L," Eleanor said soothingly.

"I, for one, feel the firm is doing very well under her management. We can rely upon her."

"You don't understand, Eleanor. She's acting as if she really owns the business, not as if she's just been elected by the rest of us to run it."

"Hilary is family. She has the firm's best interests at heart, and that's all that really matters." Eleanor paused. "Actually, now that you mention it, I've been giving the whole matter some serious consideration. It could be an excellent arrangement, you know."

"What would be an excellent arrangement?" Victoria demanded. "Letting her handle C&L while Darren runs for office? Believe me, there would be a price to pay. One of these days we're all going to wake up and find out we're just puppets, totally dependent on her."

"Damn it, Vicky, you're acting like a spoiled brat," Darren said. "You know what's wrong with you? You're jealous. Hilary's worked hard to get involved with the business, and you're envious of her ability. That's what this is all about. She pulled herself together after Nick walked out and she lost the baby. She's made a career for herself, and you resent her for it."

"Maybe you're right." Victoria felt the angry, resentful tears welling up in her eyes. "After all, the only thing I've done during the past few years is bear your son and play the part of an up-and-coming politician's wife. Putting on dinners for a hundred potential backers and serving tea to fifty campaign workers is hardly a worthwhile career, is it?"

"Take it easy, Vicky. I didn't mean that the way it sounded," Darren said lightly.

"How did you mean it?"

Eleanor picked up the silver bell on the table and tinkled it loudly. When the door to the kitchen opened, she turned to smile at the housekeeper. "Oh, there you are, Mrs. Atkins. I believe we need more coffee."

"I'll bring it right out, Mrs. Castleton."

"Thank you." Eleanor looked from her son to her daughter-in-law as the housekeeper disappeared. For a moment the sweet, vague look disappeared from her eyes. "I really do feel it would be best for all of us if Hilary stays in charge of C&L. The most important consideration now is that Darren have the freedom and the financial backing to run for governor. We can only be assured of his having both if Hilary remains at the helm."

The queen had spoken. Victoria knew she had been given her orders. As always, she would follow them. She folded her napkin and placed it beside her coffee cup. Then she got to her feet and rose from the table. She was aware of Darren watching her in angry silence as she left the room.

Phila shifted drowsily under the covers. Something was missing, something she had grown accustomed to having next to her during the night. Something warm and comforting and male.

She came awake slowly. Memories trickled back; memories of strong, gentle hands guiding her; memories of a masculine voice laced with husky amusement, wicked and urgent and exciting as it commanded and cajoled and pleaded; memories of coming very close to a thrilling promise of release, a promise that had slipped out of her fingers at the last moment but one that she was sure she could capture the next time around. She just needed another shot at it, that's all.

At least she now knew for certain that there was, indeed, something to go after the next time. Crissie had been right, after all.

Phila opened her eyes and saw Nick sitting, legs spread wide, on a reversed ladder-back chair. He had his arms folded across the back of the chair and he was leaning forward, watching her intently. He had on his jeans and a shirt, although he hadn't bothered to fasten the buttons of the shirt. She could see the heavy mat of his chest hair through the opening.

The expression on his face was the one she remembered from the occasion of their first meeting: hard, remote, unreadable. A faint trickle of dread lanced through her. Then she saw the gun.

It lay on top of the nightstand, gleaming dully in the early light. The ammunition clip lay beside it. Too late she recalled she had carelessly left the drawer open last night in her rush to answer the door. Nick must have seen the gun the minute he opened his eyes.

Phila sat up slowly, her eyes going from Nick's cold, set face to the gun and back again. As the blankets fell away she remembered she was nude. Automatically, she pulled the sheet up to her chin.

"Nick? What's wrong?"

"You tell me."

"I don't understand."

"The hell you don't."

"You're wondering about the gun?" she hazarded.

"Yeah. Good guess. I'm wondering about the gun. You said you had some questions about what happened to Crissie Masters. You said you thought the Castletons and Ligthfoots might bear some 'moral responsibility' in the matter. But you forgot to mention you intended to play lady vigilante if you didn't like the answers you got."

She stilled, shocked by his interpretation of events. "Nick, you've got it all wrong."

"You really had me fooled, lady. I've got to hand it to you. What do you think you are? A hit woman? You put on a hell of an act. I went for it every step of the way, didn't I? Brought you right through the gate myself. Introduced you to all the Castletons and Lightfoots. Gave you free run of the place. And just to top it all off, I even let you seduce me."

"You can't possibly think I've come here to kill someone."

"What else am I supposed to think?" He nodded toward the gun. "That's an expensive 9-mm automatic pistol, not a squirt gun." He studied her with chilling detachment. "What the hell do you think you're doing? And what made you think I'd let you get away with it?"

Phila edged backward, taking the sheet with her. The look in his eyes frightened her as nothing else had since the Spalding trial. "You don't know what you're talking about. Please. Give me a chance to explain."

He reached out and snagged the sheet, tearing it from her grasp. "That's exactly what I'm going to do. You're going to explain the gun, your plans and what you think gives you the right to hunt my people."

"*Your people*," she repeated scathingly as she battled another jolt of fear. She felt horribly vulnerable. She was crouched naked in front of him, the wall at her back. She felt dizzy. Once before she had been in a position like this, and the old memories were starting to get tangled up with the present reality. "I suppose we're talking about your precious Lightfoots and Castletons?"

"Yeah, we're talking about Lightfoots and Castletons."

"I told you last night that when the crunch came, you'd side with them."

"Against a nut with an automatic? You'd better believe it."

She could not tolerate this position any longer. Fear was gnawing at her stomach now. It was as though a mask had been thrown aside and she was finally seeing the real Nicodemus Lightfoot. This was not the man she had felt so gloriously free with last night, the man whose body she had learned to enjoy with such wholehearted abandon. This was a very dangerous stranger.

Phila began to inch carefully toward the foot of the bed. She was trapped and defenseless as long as she was caught between Nick and the wall. The first thing she had to do was put some distance between herself and this large, threatening male.

Nick tracked her with his eyes. Phila lost her nerve. She gave up inching and launched herself full tilt toward the end of the bed, wildly seeking escape.

"Oh, no you don't—" He shot out an arm that caught her around the midsection.

It was like running into an iron railing. Phila fell back, gasping for breath. She twisted to one side, pulling herself into a ball and kicking out frantically.

Her foot struck Nick's thigh. He grunted in pain but he did not stop. He moved so fast Phila never stood a chance. He came down on top of her, pinning her wrists above her head and using the weight of his body to still her thrashing legs.

"Let me go, damn you!" Phila's head snapped around as she tried to find some vulnerable spot into which she could sink her teeth. Panic swamped her. She could not tolerate being held down like this. Old terror and fresh fear rampaged through her. She fought like a wild thing.

"Phila. Stop it."

Her hair lashed the pillow. He weighed a ton, she realized vaguely as she struggled to wriggle free. She had been on top of him last night. Last night she had been the one in control. She hadn't fully comprehended just how large and powerful Nick really was. Now she was crushed beneath him. She could hardly breathe. Her mouth opened on a scream.

"Stop it," Nick ordered again as he clamped a hand over her lips. "Just calm down, will you? Jesus, you're going crazy." He waited a moment and then slowly removed his hand from her mouth.

"Calm down? You're assaulting me! Let go of me and I'll calm down."

"Not a chance. Not until I get some answers. What did you plan to do with that pistol?"

"I have a right to own a gun."

"That depends. Don't tell me you really believe the Castletons and Lightfoots deserve a bullet just because they didn't welcome Crissie Masters with open arms?"

"I don't have to explain anything to you, damn it." The defiance was dangerous, Phila knew that. But in her anger and fear and outrage, it was also instinctive. It was the way she had always responded to that which threatened to control her. In that, she and Crissie had been very much alike.

"Don't be stupid, Phila. Tell me why you had that gun stashed in the bedside drawer."

Phila stopped struggling, exhausted. She inhaled deeply, trying to recover her strength. Frantically she tried to contain her fear so that she could keep talking. Words were all she had left at the moment. She knew how to use words.

"I don't owe you an explanation, but I'll give you one if you'll promise to get off of me," she said stiffly.

"I'm listening. Talk fast."

"Elijah Spalding."

Nick stared down into her face. His eyes glittered behind the lenses of his glasses. "Who?"

"Elijah Spalding. Ruth Spalding's husband. Remember her? I told you I testified at a trial a few weeks ago, remember?"

"I remember. You said the guy went to prison."

"The man was Spalding. And they sent him to one of those minimum-security places. When he gets out, he'll come after me."

"Why?"

"Because he said he would," Phila said fiercely. "He hates me. It was my testimony that sent him away. He'll never forget that. He's a dangerous man. He likes to hurt little kids and women."

Nick studied her for a moment longer, his eyes implacable as he searched her expression. "When did you buy the gun?"

"Right after the trial. Believe me, at the time I wasn't even thinking about Castletons and Lightfoots. Crissie was still alive."

"That would be easy enough to check out."

"Check it out. I don't give a damn."

Nick contemplated her for a long moment, seemingly unaware of the way her bare breasts were crushed beneath his chest. "I think," he said at last, "that you had better tell me a little more about this trial."

Phila held her breath, sensing that he was about to release her. She gathered herself. "Please," she whispered, hating herself for resorting to pleading.

"Please what?" Nick scowled.

"Please. Get. Off. Of. Me. I can't stand it."

He levered himself slowly away from her, watching her warily. "Phila? Are you all right? What the hell are you looking at me like that for? I didn't hurt you."

The instant she could move out from underneath him, Phila flung herself to the side of the bed and shot to her feet. She grabbed her brilliant purple robe, holding it in front of her like a shield as she backed as far away as she could get. She was brought up short by the closed door of the bathroom. She swallowed quickly a few times, trying to still her nervous stomach. Her fingers were white as they clutched the velour robe.

"Get out of here," she ordered tightly.

Nick sat on the edge of the bed, watching her. "I'm not going anywhere," he said quietly. "I think you're smart enough to realize that. Go take a shower, comb your hair, get dressed and calm down. I'll fix us some coffee and we'll talk."

"I don't want to talk to you."

"You don't have much choice." He stood up.

Phila flinched, her eyes widening. She fumbled with the bathroom doorknob. "Don't touch me."

"I'm not touching you. You're irrational."

"I'm not the irrational one around here. You're the one who was waiting for me with a gun this morning."

"I wasn't holding the gun on you." He raked his fingers through his hair in exasperation. "I just wanted some answers. I had a right to a few after I found that automatic." He took a step forward.

"No. Don't come any closer." Phila got the bathroom door open. She backed quickly into the small room.

"Take it easy, damn it. I'm not going to hurt you."

"You already have. I'm not going to give you a second chance."

He glanced over his shoulder at the bed where he had recently pinned her. "I didn't hurt you. I just held you down so you couldn't get away or do me any damage."

Technically, he was right, but Phila's emotions and memories weren't dealing in technicalities. Her chin lifted. "Will you get out of my bedroom?"

"Yeah. I'll get out of your bedroom." He paced to the door. "The coffee will be ready when you get out of the bathroom. Then we'll talk."

Phila slammed the bathroom door and locked it. The lock was a weak little device that probably would not last long against a determined assault, but it was all that was available.

Leaning back against the closed door, she listened carefully until she was satisfied that Nick had actually gone down the hall to the kitchen. Only then did the adrenaline begin to slow its wild rush through her bloodstream.

She stayed where she was for several minutes before she finally decided she could risk taking a shower. For the first time since she had awakened she began to pay attention to her body.

She wrinkled her nose at the hint of a faint, alien, musky scent. A man's scent. Something that had been damp and sticky a few hours ago had dried on the inside of her thighs. A new terror ripped through her. It was superseded almost instantly by raw fury. How could she have forgotten! How could he have— She vaguely remembered a short discussion on matters of health, but not one on the subject of birth control. Fury at her own appalling stupidity only served to fuel her anger at Nick.

Phila wrenched open the bathroom door, still clutching the robe in front of her. She flew down the hall, through the living room and came to a halt in the kitchen doorway.

"You didn't use anything last night, you bastard," she yelled.

Nick glanced up from where he was calmly measuring coffee into a drip machine. "No, I didn't. I didn't even think about it until it was too late. You mean you're not taking pills?"

"No, I'm not taking pills," she bit out furiously. "I haven't had any reason to take them. Do you go around doing this sort of thing a lot?"

"No." He finished spooning coffee and put down the container. He picked up the pot and started to run water into it. "You're a first. Normally, I'm the cautious type. Very cautious. But I went a little crazy last night when you swept me off my feet and carried me into the bedroom. Are you always that impulsive?"

"No. *Never.*" Phila was beside herself with fury. "Oh, my God, I might be pregnant, you big jerk."

"I'm sorry, but the truth is, you have a strange effect on me, honey. No one's ever dragged me off to bed before and made wild love to me until I couldn't think straight."

"This is not funny." Phila drew herself up ramrod straight. "Listen to me you son of a bitch and listen good. You wanted to know what I planned to do with that gun in the bedroom drawer? I'll tell you what I'll do with it. If I'm pregnant, I'll come after you with it. *Do you hear me?*"

"I hear you." Nick poured the water into the machine and flipped the switch.

Phila choked on a sob of helpless rage, whirled and ran back to the bathroom. Too late she recalled that she was holding her robe in front of her, not behind her. The image of Nick watching her bare derriere as she made her exit was almost too much to handle on top of everything else that had happened. She was on the edge of bursting into tears.

She dashed into the bathroom, slammed the door shut and turned on the shower full blast. She would not cry, she vowed. She would not cry this morning.

Twenty minutes later she felt calmer and more in control of herself. The long shower had helped. She had scrubbed herself thoroughly in an effort to get rid of any outward traces of Nick's lovemaking. She could only cross her fingers about inner traces. Every five minutes she asked herself how she could have been so stupid. Her whole life seemed to have become unbelievably muddled lately.

Stress. It had to be the result of too much stress. She was just not thinking clearly these days. It seemed to her that she hadn't been able to think clearly since the news of Crissie's death.

She pulled on a pair of green jeans and an orange-and-green striped T-shirt, stuffed her feet into a pair of soft leather moccasins and headed back toward the kitchen. The aroma of brewing coffee was an irresistible lure.

Nick was sitting at the table near the window scanning an old fishing magazine that had been left behind by a previous tenant. Two bowls of cold cereal, a carton of milk and and a couple of spoons were sitting on the table beside him. He looked up when Phila appeared in the doorway.

"I thought you might be planning to spend the day in the shower," he remarked.

"It was a tempting idea, but there wasn't enough hot water."

Phila went over to the coffee machine and poured herself a cup of the dark brew. She gazed out the window over the sink, trying to collect her thoughts. An early morning fog squatted above the ocean. Peering through the trees, she found it impossible to tell where water ended and the thick mist began. It was all just one solid wall of gray. The world looked as if it ended right there on the other side of the woods.

"Sit down and eat, Phila. You'll feel better."

"How do you know?"

"Call it a wild hunch. Eat some cereal and then we'll talk."

"I'm not hungry, and there isn't anything left to talk about. I told you the whole story."

"Not quite. Who is this Elijah Spalding?"

Phila swore under her breath, knowing she was going to have to explain everything to Nick before she could get rid of him. He was that kind of man. "Spalding and his wife, Ruth, have a large farm outside of Holloway. Two years ago they started taking in foster children. It looked like a great setup. To the authorities, the Spaldings seemed like a stable couple. Ruth was into organic gardening and health foods. Elijah came from a farming family and knew how to run that kind of business. He had served in the military for several years, including some time in Southeast Asia and Latin America."

"The Army?"

Phila's mouth twisted in disgust. "Not exactly. During the trial it came out that he hadn't been on active duty with U.S. forces during his time out of the country. But he had been waging war. Independently, you might say."

"A mercenary?"

"Yes. Nothing more than a hired killer. But no one knew about that part of his background when they started sending the kids to him. All they knew was that he and Ruth couldn't have kids of their own and they seemed to want to care for children. The farm they were running appeared to be prosperous, and it looked like a healthy environment for kids. Lots of fresh air, exercise, chores, wholesome routines. By the end of the first year there were five children living with the Spaldings."

"But there were problems?"

Phila wandered over to the table and sat down. She kept her eyes on the gray mist beyond the trees as she talked. "Thelma Anderson started to get suspicious because when she made her visits to the farm the kids were too well behaved. Too quiet. Too polite. They gave all the right answers to her questions. Every one of the children seemed to have adjusted perfectly to life on the Spalding farm."

"I don't know much about foster-home situations, but I do know that anything that looks too good to be true usually is."

"It was. Spalding is a huge, powerfully built man. He has a big, bushy beard and he wears overalls and plaid shirts. The picture-perfect image of a farmer." Phila sipped coffee. "He's got weird eyes, though."

"Weird eyes?"

"Like blue ice. Mesmerizing. Piercing. Maybe a little bit mad. Nobody seemed to notice his eyes except me. I didn't like the man the minute I met him."

"When was that?"

"About a year ago. I went to work in the region that included Holloway, and Thelma assigned me the job of keeping tabs on the Spalding farm kids. I knew she had her suspicions. After my first trip to the farm, I agreed with her. Something was very wrong. The difference between me and Thelma was that she only had an instinctive feeling things were bad. I'd had enough personal experience in foster homes to be certain things were bad. The hard part was proving it." Phila sighed. "That's always the hard part."

"The kids were still saying everything was fine?"

Phila nodded. "Oh, yes. They all claimed they liked living on the farm. But I could see the fear in their eyes, and I knew I had to act. Unfortunately, I had nothing concrete to go on. No obvious indications of abuse. No complaints. Nothing. I needed real evidence. But before I could figure out how to get it, one of the youngest kids was brought into the emergency room of the local hospital. Little Andy. He was unconscious. The Spaldings said he'd gone climbing against their orders and suffered a bad fall."

"What did the boy say?"

"He never regained consciousness. He died."

"Oh, Christ."

"Thelma was more suspicious than ever, and I was sure the boy had been beaten. I talked to the doctors who said the injuries could have been caused by a severe beating, although they were not inconsistent with a bad fall. Thelma and I sent the sheriff out to the ranch to see if he could turn up anything. Nothing."

"What happened next?"

"I went out to see Spalding myself, several times. I wanted him to know he was under close observation. I hoped he would watch his step while I bought myself some time to work with the kids. But the kids were better behaved than ever. So I went to work on Spalding's wife, Ruth. I thought she might be a weak link. But she was more terrified of Spalding than she was of me or the authorities."

Nick considered that. "What did you do?"

"I finally phoned Spalding and told him I wanted to talk to him away from the farm. Neutral territory, so to speak. He agreed to meet me at a diner in town."

"What did you think you were going to accomplish by getting him away from his farm?"

Phila fiddled with her coffee cup. "I just thought it would be easier to talk to him away from that environment. But I was wrong. He was angry and belligerent when he arrived in the parking lot. I was still in my car, waiting for him. I got out when I saw his truck pull in. He came over to me and starting yelling. Called me a lot of names and accused me of interfering with the sanctity of the American home."

"How did you respond?"

"I told him I was doing my job and I was very worried about the children in his care. He lost his temper."

"He threatened you?"

"He did more than that. He told me those children were his and he could do with them as he pleased. He told me he was going to teach me to keep my nose out of his business. Then he hit me."

Nick's fingers clenched around his coffee cup. "He hurt you?"

"Oh, yes, he hurt me." Phila smiled grimly. "He was used to hurting people and he was very good at it." She touched the side of her jaw, remembering the bruise she had worn for days after the assault. Her lawyer had taken photographs. "But then he made his big mistake. He tried to drag me to his truck."

"Did anyone see what was happening?"

"Not at that point. It was about ten-fifteen and the parking lot of the diner was empty. I started to scream, naturally, and he put his hand over my mouth. He was . . . very big." The memory of that huge palm smothering her made her stomach turn over. "He got me to the truck and opened the door. I was struggling, and I guess he thought he had better do something to make me keep quiet. He reached into the glove compartment and pulled out a gun."

"Jesus, Phila."

"That's when I got very lucky. That particular diner happens to be the spot where the local cops take their morning coffee break. A police car pulled into the parking lot just as Spalding tried to force me into the pickup. The cops saw what was happening and came to the rescue. They caught him with the gun, but that wasn't all. When they searched him, they found some heroin on him."

"He was carrying drugs?" Nick looked startled.

Phila nodded grimly. "The narcotics, together with the weapon and the obvious evidence of physical assault on me, were enough to get him put away for a while. More than enough to make certain he never qualified as a foster parent again."

"Which was the important thing as far as you were concerned," Nick concluded softly.

Phila glanced at him directly for the first time. His eyes were colder than she had ever seen them. It seemed to her she could feel the chill even sitting two feet away. Phila drew a deep breath.

"That's the whole story," she said. "They arrested Spalding for assault on me, not the kids. We never could prove he had done anything to the children. I'm the one who testified against him at the trial. I'm the one he intends to punish when he gets out."

# 7

❧

Nick walked back to the Lightfoot beach cottage twenty minutes after he'd heard Phila's tale. He was still burning with a cold rage against the unknown Elijah Spalding, but he was well aware he had more immediate problems. Spalding, at least, was safely tucked away for a while.

One of the things that was hammering at him now was the memory of the panic in Phila's eyes when she'd fought him this morning. There had been more to her fear than a simple desire to escape. She had struggled as if she had thought he might rape her or beat her.

Something had happened to her at some point in the past, Nick concluded. Something that made her fear a man's weight on top of her.

Nick allowed himself a brief, self-satisfied smile. Through a combination of sheer luck and brilliant male intuition he had stumbled onto the key to seducing Phila. She was as full of feminine fire as any man could want. The trick was to let her light her own fuse.

But he was definitely going to have to work on the problem of teaching her how to burn a little more slowly. When she finally got turned on, she approached sex the same way she did everything else—at Mach speed.

He thought fleetingly of all the long, cold months he had labored to find the right approach to use with Hilary. His failure with her had not totally crushed his masculine pride; he had been intelligent enough to understand that it was not all his fault. But it had left him with some serious qualms about his appeal to the opposite sex.

More specifically, it had made him wonder frequently how much of whatever attraction women did feel for him was induced by the name of Lightfoot. There was no denying he did not come equipped with the Castleton looks and charms. Business savvy only took a man so far in this world.

But right from the start he had not had to worry about Phila being interested in him because of the Lightfoot name. If anything, the name was a distinct turnoff for her.

Yet last night, even though she had tried to resist, she had gone crazy for him. He must have the magic touch with her, Nick told himself. His smile turned into a wide, laughing grin.

Contemplation of how he would proceed with Phila started doing invigorating things to his system. To get his mind off sex he switched his thoughts to the automatic he had found in the bedside drawer earlier. That sobered him immediately.

He was halfway up the long, curving drive when the white Mercedes convertible appeared from the back of the cottage and roared toward the gate. Reed Lightfoot was at the wheel. He was wearing his golfing clothes. The sleek car glided to a halt near Nick, and Reed scanned his son's rumpled shirt and unshaven face.

"You look like you just spent the night in some goddamned cathouse. Don't let Eleanor see you," Reed said.

"Eleanor's not that easily shocked. I wasn't planning on visiting her at this hour, anyway. It's only seven-thirty. You off to the golf course?"

"Got a game at eight." Reed's eyes narrowed. "I take it the status quo has changed? You're sleeping with her as of last night?"

"I'll make a deal with you, Dad. You don't pry into my love life and I won't make any more comments about yours, okay?"

"Suit yourself. As far as I'm concerned you can do anything you goddamn well please with Phila Fox as long as you get those shares back." Reed put his foot down on the accelerator, and the Mercedes roared through the open gate.

Nick watched for a moment until the car was out of sight and then resumed his walk toward the cottage. Phila was right. The Castleton and Lightfoot summer homes did look a little like some film-set version of a couple of plantation mansions.

Cupcake and Fifi spotted him as he drew close, and both bounded forth to greet him. He scratched their ears, and they fell into step beside him as he headed toward the colonnaded porch.

" 'Morning, sir," Tec Sherman said from the doorway. He was wearing a bilious-green aloha shirt. His bald head gleamed in the morning sunlight. "Breakfast is just about to hit the table. You interested?"

"No, thanks, Tec. All I want right now is a shower and a shave."

"No problem, sir. Your things are in your bedroom."

"I know." Nick took another look at the aloha shirt. "I think Phila has a shirt that color. The two of you would probably have fun shop-ping together."

"She may have good taste in clothes," Tec allowed magnanimously, "but she's sure got a mouth on her."

"You get used to it."

Tec cleared his throat. "Uh, we sort of wondered where you'd gone last night."

"Yeah?"

"Your dad figured you went to visit Miss Fox."

"Is that right?"

Nick went up the steps and into the house. Phila was not going to be thrilled when she found out their relationship was common knowl-edge. He probably should have warned her that it was inevitable everyone would figure out what had happened last night.

But, then, Phila was not going to be thrilled when she found out they still had a relationship, period. As far as she was concerned, the previous evening was going down as a deeply regretted one-night stand.

She had certainly done her best to kick him out of the Gilmarten place this morning. Nick had finally left when he came to the conclu-sion they both needed time to cool down.

He wondered if she would have been more relaxed about things if it had not hit her that, on top of everything else, she might be pregnant.

He made a mental note to pick up a package of condoms in town that afternoon. He also made a note to maintain more control the next time he took Phila to bed. Next time, he promised himself, he was going to make damn sure she had a climax. He desperately wanted her to associ-ate physical satisfaction with being in his arms. Nick shook his head, still unable to believe the effect she'd had on him last night. No other woman had ever broken through his iron-clad self-control the way Phila had. She had made him go wild, a totally unique experience for him.

Half an hour later, shaved, showered and dressed in jeans and a black pullover, Nick went back downstairs.

"If you manage to get those shares back by sleeping with her, I'll be very surprised." Hilary spoke almost idly from the breakfast-room doorway. "After all she was a friend of Crissie's and I can't see any friend of Crissie's being that stupid."

Nick swore to himself and halted in the middle of the hall. He turned halfway around to confront Hilary. She looked as stunning as ever this morning. Her dark red hair was tied at the nape of her neck, her wide-sleeved blouse flowed gracefully from the high-waisted, pleated trousers she wore.

"Good morning, Hilary. Beautiful day, isn't it?" Nick kept his voice perfectly bland.

"I think I've got this all figured out, Nick. You're going to try and buy your way back into Reed's good graces by prying those shares away from Phila, aren't you? Why bother? Or have you decided you want to be a part of Castleton & Lightfoot again, after all?"

"And if I have?" he asked softly.

Her green eyes glinted savagely. "If you think you can just walk back in here after three years and take over, you're out of your mind."

"It's my inheritance, Hilary. If you're smart, you won't forget that. One of these days I might just decide to take it back and if I do, your ass will be out the door."

She smiled coldly. "You really believe you could do that? After what you did to me? The families are on my side, Nick."

"If I decide I want to run the families and the company, I'll do it, Hilary." It was a statement of fact as far as Nick was concerned. But he knew from the confident expression in her eyes that Hilary did not believe him.

"Stop bluffing. I'm Reed's wife now. You can't touch me or the company. You shouldn't have come back, Nick. No one wants you here."

"Maybe no one wants me, but they all sure as hell want those shares, don't they? And right now I've got the best chance of getting them back into the family. So it looks as though everyone will just have to tolerate my presence."

"Do you really think anything's going to change if you do manage to get back the shares?"

Nick did some fast mental calculations and made an executive decision. It was time to rattle Hilary's cage. "Yeah, Hilary. I do think things are going to change. You see, I could do just about anything I want if I decide to have Phila give those shares to me instead of to Darren." He watched the anger form in her eyes as the full impact of what he was saying dawned on her.

"But those were Castleton shares. They belong to Darren now that Burke is dead, not you."

"They belong to whoever can get them out of Philadlephia Fox's hands."

"You bastard."

"Right, first time, Hilary. I think you're getting the point."

"Damn you, Nick."

"I told Dad I'd get the shares back into family hands, but I didn't say which family and I didn't specify whose hands. If I started voting my own shares again plus Phila's, I could begin to make some interesting waves in the moat around your little castle. Think about that when you sit in front of your mirror and tell yourself you're safe."

"I am safe," Hilary answered swiftly. "I'm family and I'm here to stay. No one is going to accept you back into the fold after what you did three years ago. You think about *that* while you screw your new girl-friend. You might also spend some time thinking about why she's will-ing to sleep with you in the first place. You aren't exactly hell on wheels in bed, as we both know. Better find out who's using whom." Hilary turned on one well-shod heel and walked back into the breakfast room.

Nick let himself out the front door. "Hey, Tec."

"Over here, sir." Tec came toward him, a garden hose looped around one burly shoulder. "What can I do for you, sir?"

"Let's hunt up Darren and see if he wants to get in a little target practice down at the range."

Tec's face lit up like a Christmas tree. "Great idea, sir. Your dad picked up a beautiful Ruger .44 a month ago that needs a workout. Let's hit the deck."

There was a storm coming in from the west. Phila stood barefoot in the gritty sand at the water's edge and watched the clouds boil toward shore. The wind was picking up, carrying a hint of rain. The sea was choppy with whitecaps cresting every small wave. Several hundred yards out an aging fishing boat was laboring toward port.

Phila had walked down to the beach with the hope of getting the morning's scene with Nick out of her mind. She was not having much luck. She was supposed to be gathering information on Castletons and Lightfoots in preparation for making an intelligent decision about what to do with Crissie's shares. She was supposed to be analyzing, judging, perhaps seeking some revenge for the way the families had ostracized poor Crissie.

Instead she had gotten herself tangled up in an affair with a Lightfoot.

Phila winced as she recalled the expression on Nick's face when she had awakened to find him watching her, the gun on the table beside him. But as hard as she tried to keep that memory firmly in mind, the one that kept pushing it aside was the one of last night.

Nick had been exactly what she had been looking for in a lover. Phila realized that now. He was perfect in every way except one: he was a Lightfoot. Crissie probably would have found the entire situa-tion vastly entertaining.

Phila had known she had some problems when it came to sex. She was realistic enough to have guessed that some, if not all, of those problems stemmed from what had happened to her when she was thirteen. But she had not known how to overcome the problem. The few halting attempts she had made to get involved physically with a man had usually ended in disaster. At best she had just managed to endure groping hands and a heavy, male body.

But last night with Nick, Phila had felt gloriously safe, secure and in control for the first time. That was obviously the way she needed to feel if she was to enjoy sex.

Nick was a big man, the kind she normally felt most uneasy with. But last night he had not used his strength against her. He had not tried to overwhelm her. He had let her set the pace. For the first time she had sensed she did have her share of normal responses. For the first time she had discovered she was capable of satisfying a man.

And she had loved the feeling.

It was too bad Nick had ruined everything this morning, she thought bitterly.

If she was pregnant, she was going to make good on her threat to use that gun on him, she vowed angrily. The thought of having possibly conceived threw her into a whole different realm of panic.

She was trying not to remember that she had been as irresponsible as Nick last night, when she realized she was not alone on the beach. She could hear nothing above the wind and the waves, but when she turned her head she saw Hilary approaching. Phila froze and waited.

"Crissie liked to walk on the beach in the mornings, too." Hilary said as she came to a halt next to Phila and gazed at the fishing boat in the distance.

Phila was silent for a moment before she said, "Crissie and I were both raised in eastern Washington. The sea always symbolized freedom to us. We used to talk about the day we would move to the coast."

"Crissie went to Southern California."

Phila smiled. "Marina Del Rey. She had an apartment overlooking the water. All chrome and white leather. Very flashy. Very beautiful."

"Like Crissie."

"Yes. Just like Crissie. California was her kind of place. She was a golden girl in a sunny, golden land."

Hilary put her long-nailed hands into the pockets of her pleated trousers. "She talked about you frequently."

"Did she?"

Hilary nodded. "She loved you, but she thought you were hopelessly naive about some things."

Phila laughed and realized it was the first time she had been amused by anything connected with Crissie since the day she'd learned of her death. "We were opposites. I'm sure if we hadn't been thrown together in a foster-home situation we would never have become friends. We had absolutely nothing in common."

"Maybe it was the fact that you were so different that drew you together. Maybe you needed each other in some ways."

"Maybe. Whatever it was, Crissie and I didn't question it too much. We were too young for that kind of introspection. We were friends, and that was all that mattered. We knew we could depend on each other."

"That's why you're here, isn't it? Because you were Crissie's friend and you need to know what happened during those last months with us." Hilary's voice was soft with understanding. "I'd feel the same way. Perhaps even more so. Because, unlike you, I did have a great deal in common with Crissie."

"You're as beautiful as she was," Phila observed.

"I wasn't talking about looks. I meant we had more important things in common. Crissie was a lot like me in some ways." When Phila gave her a sharp glance of surprise, Hilary smiled indulgently. "It's true, you know. We understood each other. Oh, I had private schooling and holidays abroad while I was growing up, but I didn't have any more love than Crissie did. My parents turned me over to nannies, tutors and boarding schools whenever possible. After they were divorced, I spent most of my time being shuttled from one place to another. I might as well have been raised in an institution."

"A nicely furnished institution," Phila said dryly.

"I won't argue that. But the result was the same, I think. Crissie realized that when she got to know me. We used to talk about what we wanted out of life, and it turned out that we both had very similar goals."

Phila chuckled. "Crissie always said her goal was to use her looks to get so rich she'd never have to worry about anything again as long as she lived. She wanted to be able to live in a big mansion and have lots of people at her beck and call. She wanted to be so powerful no one would ever dare try to hurt her or abuse her again."

"Umhmmm."

"Is that your goal?" Phila asked.

"Something very similar, I'm afraid."

"Would you do anything to achieve that goal?"

Hilary's mouth tightened. "Just about. I refuse to be prized only for my beauty and my background. I was forced to trade on those commodities for too much of my life. First while I was growing up and then in my marriage. From now on people will have to deal with me as a financially independent woman."

"Maybe you and Crissie did have a lot in common. She was certain money could buy her freedom."

"She could never understand why you chose to go into social work, you know. She said it was stupid and that you'd never last. You'd burn out, she said. You weren't hard enough for that kind of thing."

"She was right," Phila admitted. "I resigned my job a few weeks ago. I don't plan to ever go back into that field again."

"Crissie was shrewd when it came to knowing what made people tick. She could manipulate them."

"She had to learn how or she would never have survived her childhood," Phila explained.

"She certainly enjoyed herself pushing the families' buttons while she was around us. She used to think of it as a game. I was the only one she never played games with."

Phila wondered about that. "You do seem to be the only one who has anything kind to say about her."

"I told you, I liked her. Reed said something this morning at breakfast about your feeling the families bear some responsibility for Crissie's death. Is that true?"

"I don't know, Hilary," Phila said quietly. "I honestly don't know. I need to think about it, though, before I decide what to do with the shares."

Hilary nodded, as if in understanding. "I would just like to caution you about one thing. Don't get the idea that because Nick was not physically present during those last months when Crissie was here that he's somehow more trustworthy or innocent than any of the rest of us. Nick wouldn't be here now if he weren't working some angle."

"But he was estranged from the families during the time Crissie was involved with them."

"I've known Nick Lightfoot a long time, Phila. He's a very dangerous man. Be careful."

"Sure."

"Keep something else in mind about Nick. His reasoning processes don't always follow a normal, predictable pattern. He's hard to read, and his motives can be very obscure. Think about that if he tries to talk you into giving her shares to him instead of back to Darren."

Phila became lightheaded for an instant. She took a deep breath, and the world righted itself. "He's said nothing about having me turn the shares over to him."

"But he does plan to get the shares back into family hands. He told Reed that much last night."

"He told me the same thing. He was very up-front about it."

"Nick is at his most dangerous when he looks you right in the eye and tells you what he's going to do." Hilary paused for a moment, then asked, "What are you going to do, Phila?"

"I don't know," Phila answered honestly.

Hilary drew a deep breath. "I'd like to make you an offer for those shares."

Phila turned her head to look at Hilary's beautiful profile. "You want to buy them from me?"

"I'll give you an excellent price for them. More than enough cash to keep you from having to go back into social work. I'll give you what I would have given Crissie."

"Crissie was going to sell the shares to you?"

"Crissie wanted me to have those shares. But she was practical. She needed financial security," Hilary said. "I understood that. I was going to make sure she got it in exchange for the shares."

"I see."

"By the way," Hilary said easily, "I have an invitation to extend to you from Eleanor. She would like to have you join us for dinner tomorrow evening."

"A family affair?" Phila asked wryly.

Hilary smiled, showing perfect teeth. "Precisely. A family affair." She turned to walk back along the beach, pausing to say over her shoulder, "Think about my offer, Phila."

Port Claxton was a picturesque mixture of old Victorian homes, white picket fences and weathered seaside cottages. The small marina with its collection of sailing boats, fishing vessels and cruisers was the heart of the community.

Port Clax, as the locals called it, was typical of Washington's seaside towns in that it hibernated during the winter months and got rudely jolted wide awake during the summer when the tourists and vacationers descended on it.

But even at the peak of the season, it was still possible to park right in front of the entrance of either of the two small grocery stores. Phila chose the one at the north end of town.

Inside she went quickly down the short aisles, selecting salad makings, bread, cheese and other essentials. When she came to the wine shelves she remembered Nick going through her cupboards the previous night looking for something to drink. She picked up a bottle of northwest Cabernet Sauvignon, telling herself it was for her, not uninvited midnight visitors. When she got to the checkout counter a young man with curly blond hair and a shy smile greeted her.

"Hey, didn't I see you at the big Fourth of July party yesterday? You were with Nick Lightfoot, weren't you? You a new member of the family?"

"No. I am definitely not a new member of the family." Phila softened the curt response with a smile.

"Just wondered. Lotta folks did. Haven't seen Nick around for a long time. Thought when he showed up with you he might be bringing home a new wife or something."

"I take it the folks here in Port Claxton keep close tabs on the Castletons and Lightfoots?"

The young man grinned. "Sure do. Guess it's kind of a local pastime. They're big wheels around here. We've had Castletons and Lightfoots in this town since before I was born. My mom remembers when Reed and Burke built those fancy places out there near the beach. She always liked Reed's first wife, she said. A real down-to-earth person. Kind of looked after things here in town, Mom says."

"Looked after things?"

"You know what I mean. While Nora Lightfoot was alive, the Castletons and Lightfoots did lots of things for the town. Got a nice park built out by the marina. Got a theater group going. Gave a lot of money to local charities. Helped folks out when they needed it. Real nice lady, my mom says."

Phila was intrigued. "Don't the Castletons and Lightfoots still help out locally?"

"Well, when Nick Lightfoot was around we did get some new equipment for the hospital, I think, and there used to be a scholarship fund for local kids who went on to college. He kept that up for a while after the first Mrs. Lightfoot died. But it's different now."

"How are things different?"

"Don't get me wrong. The Castletons and the Lightfoots still make some local contributions occasionally, but it's not like in the old days. My dad says Eleanor Castleton and the others think people should stand on their own feet and not get used to handouts. Says it makes folks dependent."

"I can see how that philosophy would suit them."

"The Castletons and Lightfoots still put on one heck of a Fourth of July picnic, though, I'll say that for 'em. Everybody around here really looks forward to it. Sort of a local tradition."

"I take it people in town enjoy gossiping about them, too?"

The young man flushed. "I guess so." He brightened. "Way things are going, according to my dad, we may be voting for a Castleton for governor one of these days. Everyone says Darren's getting set to go into politics in a big way. Wouldn't that be somethin'?"

"Would everyone in town vote for him if he ran?"

"Are you kiddin'? Like a shot. He's one of us." The young man beamed with pride.

"Amazing," Phila muttered, picking up her bag of groceries. "You do realize that the Castleton and Lightfoot fortunes are founded on machines used for military purposes? That if Darren Caslteton got into public office he would probably hold extremely right-wing, militaristic views due to his background and family business? If he ever went into national office he would undoubtedly vote to increase the defense budget every chance he got."

The clerk gave her a puzzled look. "Castletons and Lightfoots are real patriotic. Proud to be Americans. They got a way of making everyone else proud of it, too."

"I give up." Phila headed for the door with her groceries.

The storm finally hit the coast later that evening. Phila closed the windows of her little house when the rain began pouring down. It was all very cozy, she told herself as she cleaned up after a simple dinner of soup and salad. She wondered what everyone was doing up at the family mansions. She had seen no sign of a Castleton or a Lightfoot all afternoon.

When she had washed the last of the small stack of dirty dishes she wandered into the living room and stood at the front window. For a while she toyed with the notion of going down to the beach in the storm. It would be a good place to think.

Lord knew, she needed to do some thinking.

She was going to have to make a decision about what to do with the shares by the date of the annual meeting of Castleton & Lightfoot. If she opted to keep them and vote them, she was going to be fighting an open war with the families, a war she could not win.

She did not own enough shares to outvote them on critical issues. All she could accomplish was to be a gadfly, a troublemaker in their midst. She would always be an outsider, just as Crissie had been.

But it seemed wrong just to return those shares to the families. They constituted Crissie's inheritance; the inheritance she had always fantasized would one day be hers. Any kind of inheritance meant a lot when you had grown up in foster homes. It symbolized something important, a sense of belonging, a sense of being part of a family, of having a place in the world.

But Crissie was dead and the inheritance was now hers, Phila reminded herself.

And soon she would have to make a decision.

Thunder partially masked the first knock on the front door, but Phila heard the second quite clearly. She recognized the blunt summons at once and gave serious thought to not answering. But she knew that would be a waste of time.

She went to the door and found Nick on the step. His dark hair was wet, and the black windbreaker he wore was soaked. His gray eyes gleamed as they moved over her.

"Do me a favor and don't go for the gun yet, okay? I've had a hard evening."

"Am I supposed to feel sorry for you?" Phila stepped back reluctantly, unable to think of a way to keep him out and not really certain she wanted to achieve that goal, anyway. "It's your family."

"You don't have to remind me." He moved over the threshold, shaking raindrops onto the scarred boards of the floor. He slipped off the windbreaker and hung it over the back of a chair. "I heard you went into town this afternoon. Can I assume you picked up something for me to drink?"

"We went through this routine last night. How did you know I went into town?"

He shrugged, heading for the kitchen. "Better get used to the reality of being associated with Lightfoots and Castletons. Everyone knows what you're doing, when you do it and who you do it with. I even know about the conversation with the Wilson kid in the grocery store."

He found the cabernet inside the first cupboard he opened. He started opening drawers, apparently looking for something he could use to pull the cork. "So you think Darren would be a hawk if he ever got into public office, huh?"

"Second drawer on the left," Phila volunteered when she realized he was going to go through each drawer systematically until he found what he wanted.

"Thanks." He went to work on the cork, removing it with a few swift, deft twists. "I don't suppose you have anything to eat with this? Some cheese, maybe?"

"Don't look so innocent. Your sources probably told you exactly what I bought in town today." She went to the refrigerator and withdrew the package of cheese. "Must be nice owning a whole town and everyone in it."

"We don't own it. We're just real neighborly and folks around here appreciate that."

"I'll bet they'd appreciate it even more if you went back to contributing heavily to scholarships and civic-improvement projects."

"The Wilson kid got real chatty, I take it?" Nick poured the wine into a water glass. "Don't worry, the families still give lots of money away."

"To whom?"

Nick gave her his slow, faint smile. "Mostly to the political campaigns of right-thinking politicians and a number of good, solid, all-American organizations."

"Such as the National Rifle Association?"

"You're hardly in a position to complain if it's on the list. The NRA is one of the reasons you can legally pack that automatic you've got stashed in the nightstand."

"The Constitution gives me that right, not the NRA."

"Odds are you would have lost the right years ago if the left-wing antigun lobbyists had had their way. I'll bet you held some pretty narrow views on the subject of gun control yourself until a few weeks ago."

Phila knew she was turning pink under his shrewd gaze. It was true. Until she had come to fear Elijah Spalding, she had been a staunch supporter of strict handgun legislation. "My views on gun control can hardly be of major interest to you," she said, her tone aloof.

"I've got news for you. Everything you do is of great interest to me. How much have you worked with that pistol, by the way?"

"Worked with it?"

"Fired it. Practiced with it."

"Oh. I've never had occasion to use it, thank God."

"You've never even fired the damn thing?"

"Well, no."

"You bought a fancy 9-mm automatic pistol and you don't know the first thing about it? How the hell do you expect to be able to use it in an emergency?"

"I read the manual."

"Jesus. You read the manual. That's just terrific, Phila. I'm really impressed. Did you figure out which end to point away from yourself?"

"I do not have to tolerate your sarcasm."

He sighed. "Yeah, you do, I'm afraid. I'm spending the night."

Phila stared at him. "Are you crazy? After the way you behaved last night and this morning? I'm not about to let you spend the night."

He took a sizable swallow of the cabernet and bit into a slice of cheese. "You were the one who dragged me into your bedroom last night. And as for what happened this morning, you know as well as I do that my reactions were understandable under the circumstances. When I came out of the bathroom and spotted that pistol in the drawer, I assumed I had just spent the night with a professional hit lady."

"You thought no such thing. Even you couldn't have been that stupid."

"Thank you, I think. In any event, I feel I am not entirely to blame for either the sex or the scene in the bedroom this morning and if you are half the logical, intelligent, fair-minded human being you claim to be, you'll agree with me."

She felt cornered. "If you stay here tonight, you'll sleep on the sofa."

"I'll take what I can get."

She couldn't believe it. "You want to spend the night on that lumpy monstrosity?"

"No, I'd rather spend the night in your bed, but as I said, I'll take what I can get. How much did Hilary offer you today?"

Phila blinked. "I beg your pardon?"

"I just wondered how much Hilary offered you for those shares of yours." Nick poured himself another glass of wine. "She did make an offer, didn't she?"

"She said something about paying me for the shares, yes," Phila admitted warily. "But how did you know? Did she tell you?"

"No. I just had a hunch she'd try something like that."

"What gave you the hunch?" Phila was now very suspicious.

Nick leaned back against the counter. "I set her up for it."

"You encouraged her to try to buy back the shares? But why?"

"Because I knew it would annoy you. I don't want you dealing with Hilary, and I figured the fastest way of cutting her off at the pass was to have her push you too far, too fast. Trying to buy you off is a surefire way to make you dig in your heels."

"My God." Phila felt winded.

"Money might work eventually, but this was the wrong time to make an offer to you. You're still feeling loyal to Crissie's memory. Those shares are a tie to that memory. You need a while to think through what you want to do, and you're bound to resent anyone trying to force your hand."

Phila stared at him. "So you pushed Hilary into doing just that. You must think you're a very clever man."

"Honey, when it comes to business, I'm as clever as they get."

# 8

❧

It was irrational and annoying, but Phila woke up the next morning with the realization that she had slept better the past two nights than she had at any time since Elijah Spalding had been arrested.

There was no denying that having Nicodemus Lightfoot sleeping nearby, whether in her bed or out in the living room, was a comfort.

She was so accustomed to having only herself to rely on that it had taken her awhile to understand just what was happening. The fact was that in spite of all the evidence to the contrary, in spite of all the obvious warnings, and against her better judgment, she was starting to trust Nick. The man was too big, too mysterious and a little too clever for her taste, but there was a steel core she found irresistibly comforting under all those troublesome traits.

A woman might not always have the comfort of knowing just what Nick Lightfoot was thinking, but she could be certain he would not bend once he had made up his mind. He could be relied on.

He had certainly been honest about his intentions regarding the shares, she reminded herself as she stepped into the shower. If she got burned in that department, she would have only herself to blame.

She was still lecturing herself about Nick Lightfoot when she emerged from the bedroom half an hour later to find him standing at the door talking to his father. A white Mercedes convertible was visible through the open door-way. Reed was dressed for golfing in a monogrammed polo shirt and plaid slacks.

Nick, on the other hand, was hardly dressed at all. He'd taken time to put on his jeans, but that was it. The couch, Phila noted, had already been made up and the blankets stowed. Nick had clearly taken time to do that before answering the door.

Apparently Nick did not want early-morning callers to know he'd been consigned to the living room. Simple male pride or something more devious? Phila wondered.

"Phila," Nick called over his shoulder, "Dad stopped by to ask you to play a round of golf with him this morning."

Phila raised her brows. "Sorry, I don't play."

"It's a great morning," Reed himself insisted. "A little nippy, but the sun's out. Why don't you walk the course with me while I hit a few balls?"

"Oh, I get it," Phila said yawning. "You want to get me off by myself so you can make your pitch for the shares. Hilary already offered me mucho bucks, and that didn't work. What have you got to offer?"

Reed shot a quick, questioning glance at his son. Nick just shrugged. Reed smiled broadly again at Phila. "I thought we'd spend some time talking. Get to know each other. Nick tells me you have some questions concerning what went on while Crissie Masters was here with us. Maybe I can answer a few of them."

"You don't look like the sort who volunteers answers."

Reed's smile vanished. "Well, I'm volunteering now, am I not? So go get a goddamned jacket and let's go."

"You don't have to go with him, Phila." Nick absently polished his glasses with a soft white handkerchief.

"I know. But I think I will," Phila decided. "If he'll guarantee to provide breakfast. I'm hungry."

"I'll buy you breakfast at the clubhouse," Reed promised.

The eighteen-hole course followed the cliffs along the ocean for half its length and then curved inland. The thick, carefully cropped grass stretched before Phila like a lush green carpet. It glistened with traces of the previous night's rain. Reed had been right. It was chilly this morning, but the sun was shining and it felt good to be outdoors.

"You don't use a cart?" Phila inquired as they approached the second green. Her yellow running shoes were already wet, and the cuffs of her pink-and-green pants were getting damp.

"Not unless the course is crowded. I like the exercise. Now keep quiet for a few minutes while I get this sucker on the green."

"Sorry."

"Umm." Reed selected an iron from his bag, stationed himself over the small white ball and took a slow, powerful swing.

The ball hit the green, bounced and rolled to within three feet of the cup.

"You missed," Phila observed.

Reed scowled at her, reminding her momentarily of his son. "That was a damn fine shot, young lady, if I do say so myself."

"Are all golfers this snappish?"

"Yes, ma'am, they are. Especially when they're getting a lot of unnecessary backchat from the gallery."

"You brought me out here to talk, remember?"

"About Crissie Masters and related family matters. Not about my golf game. What's all this crap about the Castletons and Lightfoots bearing some kind of responsibility for Masters's death, anyway?"

"I don't think she was treated very well while she was with the families, Mr. Lightfoot. I think that rejection could have been devastating for her after she'd spent so many years dreaming of finding her father. Indirectly it could have been a contributing factor in her death."

"No one drove her to her death. She drove herself. Literally," Reed's voice was rough.

"I've seen the cops' report of the accident, and I hired a private investigator to check it out. I know it really was an accident, but I'd like to hear what happened the night she died. Why did she have so much alcohol in her blood-stream? Crissie wasn't normally a heavy drinker."

Reed glared at her. "You hired a private investigator to double-check the accident report?"

"Of course." Phila shoved her hands into her pockets. "I never completely trust official reports. I've written too many myself. And I certainly had no reason to accept any assurances from the Castletons and Lightfoots, did I? Naturally I double-checked. It was the least I could do for Crissie."

"Christ almighty. No wonder Nick didn't know what to do with you. Who the hell do you think you are to question us, girl?"

Phila smiled grimly. "Your son asked me the same thing. I question everything all the time, Mr. Lightfoot. It's in the blood. Now why don't you tell me what happened the night Crissie died?"

"The hell with it. There's nothing much to tell. It was the night of Eleanor's birthday party," Reed said. "We'd all had a few drinks, including Crissie. There was a large crowd at the Castletons' cottage that night. No one saw her leave, but the accident report was clear. She had alcohol in her blood and the weather was bad. She had been driving a dangerous stretch of road. Put all that together and you have more than enough explanation for what happened to her."

"Did you dislike her, Reed?"

He considered that. "Didn't actively dislike her, but I can't say I took to her the way Burke did. But, then, Burke had his reasons for making a fuss over his long-lost daughter."

"What reasons?"

Reed pulled a putter out of the bag and walked over to where his ball lay on the green. "Burke Castleton was a man who admired nerve and gumption. Crissie had plenty of both. Take the pin out of the hole, will you?"

"What do you want me to do with it?"

"Just hold it, for crissake."

Phila obeyed and stood back while Reed lined up his putt. "Don't you think you should aim a little more to the right?" she asked just as he tapped the ball with the putter.

Reed swore as the ball rolled to within half an inch of the cup. "Are you this goddamned chatty with Nick at all the wrong moments?"

"Sorry."

"Huh. Put the pin back."

"The ball isn't in the cup yet. Isn't it supposed to go in?"

Reed glared at her and pushed the ball into the cup with the tip of his putter. "Satisfied?"

Phila smiled blandly. "This is certainly an interesting game. Do you play a lot?"

"Every day unless the weather is bad."

"Does Hilary play with you?"

Reed shook his head. "My wife prefers tennis."

"What about Nick?"

"Nick and I used to play together occasionally. But that was a long time ago. Haven't played with him for over three years." Reed picked up his bag of clubs and started for the next hole.

"You haven't played with him since Hilary and Nick got divorced and she married you?"

Reed spun around abruptly, his expression forbidding. "The circumstances surrounding my marriage are not something we discuss much in this family. I'm sure you've figured that out by now. Haven't you ever heard of tact, Philadelphia?"

"Tact doesn't always get the job done. My grandmother taught me that. She used to say that when your kind of people start getting extra polite you could pretty well figure they were up to something."

"My kind of people?"

"Yup."

Reed was grimly amused. "You might be interested to learn that I didn't know diddlysquat about genteel politeness until Eleanor married Burke thirty-six years ago."

"Eleanor taught you everything you know?"

"Goddamn right. Burke said we needed a real lady to get us all shaped up so we could mingle with the money crowd. We were raking in the dough, you see, but we didn't have the manners to go with it. Burke and me, we were just a couple of shitkickers with too much cash for our own good at that point."

"The money didn't buy you into the right crowd?"

"Money only takes you so far, even out here on the West Coast. Burke went looking for a genuine lady and when he found Eleanor, he married her."

"And Eleanor took you all in hand?"

"She did her best. Sometimes we don't all live up to her standards, but she keeps workin' on us. She's devoted to the project. Making Castletons and Lightfoots socially acceptable is her mission in life. I reckon if Darren gets to be governor, maybe she'll figure she's finally succeeded."

"Why did Eleanor marry Burke if he wasn't up to her standards to begin with?"

"You want to get real down and dirty, don't you?"

"I'm curious."

"Then you ask her why she married him. I'm not going to satisfy your goddamn curiosity, Philadelphia. I don't see that the answer is any of your business."

"You're probably right."

"I know I'm right. I'm always right. Now keep quiet while I tee off."

"No wonder you and Nick have a hard time communicating," Phila mused as Reed readied his swing. She waited until Reed's club started its descent before concluding, "You both seem to have developed the same nasty habit."

"*Goddamn* it, woman, can't you keep your mouth shut while I'm hitting the goddamn ball? Look what you made me do. I'm clear out in the rough. Jesus H. Christ." Reed slammed the wood into his bag. "What nasty habit?"

"Each of you thinks he's always right. You're both as stubborn as a couple of bricks." Unperturbed by Reed's furious glare, she started off in the direction in which his ball had disappeared. "I think it landed over there behind that bush."

"What kind of a fairy tale did Nick tell you about his divorce?" Reed demanded, overtaking Phila in four strides.

"We haven't discussed it in great detail but I'm sure we'll get around to it eventually."

"You're sleeping with my son and you haven't even bothered to find out why his marriage went on the rocks? If you don't know that, then there's sure as hell a lot more you probably don't know, either. I'd think a smart cookie like you would find out the details before she got too involved with a man like Nick. Which bush?"

"Over there." Phila pointed.

Reed shielded his eyes under his palm. "Goddamn. I'm going to lose two strokes on this hole thanks to your mouthiness."

"Do you always look for someone else to blame when things go wrong?"

"Take some advice. If you want to make it back to the clubhouse in one piece, you will keep your mouth shut while I get this goddamn ball back onto the fairway."

"Why don't you just pick it up and throw it back on the grass?"

Reed did not dignify that with an answer. In fact, he didn't speak again until he had shot the ball onto the green.

Phila decided to keep quiet for a while, at least until Reed lined up his tee shot on the next fairway. Then she said, "Are you hoping Nick will marry again?"

"Why should I care one way or the other if my son marries again?" Reed concentrated on the ball.

"I thought maybe you'd like some grandchildren, your kind being so family oriented and all. I mean, what's the good of founding an empire if you haven't got a dynasty to leave it to, right?"

"For Crissake, you're not thinking of trying that old trick, are you?"

"What old trick?"

"Trying to get a permanent piece of the action by marrying into the families. If that's your game, you're barking up the wrong tree. Don't think for one moment that if you get pregnant, Nick will feel obliged to marry you." Reed took a powerful swing at the ball and sent it sailing a good two hundred yards down the fairway.

"If I get pregnant," Phila said, her tone very even, "Nick will damn sure meet his responsibilities."

Reed's head came around abruptly, his eyes unreadable under the brim of his hat. "What makes you think so?"

"He feels as strongly about family as you do," Phila explained patiently. "He'd want his child. In fact, he'd demand it."

"You sound pretty goddamn sure of that."

"I am sure of it."

"Is that right?"

"The real question," Phila continued thoughtfully, "is whether I'd lower myself to marrying into this nest of ultraconservative right-wing pit vipers. Would you mind if I tried hitting the ball a couple of times?"

Reed looked momentarily baffled by the switch in topics. When he saw her enthusiastic expression, he finally nodded brusquely and handed her a club.

"No, no, you don't clutch it like a stick," he said as he stood over her. "Your thumb goes along the grip like this. That's it. Okay, take it back like this. Real easy. The back-swing is slow and controlled. Don't rush it. All right, bring it down nice and easy. I said, *easy*, damn it."

Phila ignored the last bit of advice and swung the club with all her might, eager to drive the ball as far as Reed had. There was a nice sensation of power, a satisfying whoosh and a loud, despairing groan from Reed.

She paid no attention to the groan, certain that she had hit the ball halfway down the fairway. When she couldn't spot it, she glanced down and saw that the little white ball had gone about three feet.

"Slow and easy, I said. Do you always rush into things that way?" Reed asked as he repositioned the ball.

"What way?" Phila planted her feet for another swing.

"Full speed ahead, no holds barred?"

"I guess so, why?"

"You're going to drive Nick crazy."

"Might be good for him. He needs to loosen up a bit. Now stand back. I'm going to try this again." She swung this time with even greater enthusiasm. The ball dribbled about four feet from the tee. "Well, damn."

"I told you, Phila. Slow and easy does it. You really believe my son would stand by you if you got pregnant?"

"Of course. After all, he is your son, isn't he? Would you walk out on a woman you'd gotten pregnant?"

"There's a word for people like you."

"Liberal? Left wing? Commie sympathizer?"

"No. *Naive.* I hate to shatter your illusions, Philadelphia, especially if Nick is playing on them in order to get the shares back from you. Hell, I want those shares back in the families, too. But the fact is, I think you would be very foolish to put too much stock in Nick's sense of obligation."

"Mr. Lightfoot, I may not play golf very well, but I've had a lot of experience dealing with different kinds of families. Many of them not very nice. Believe me, since the age of thirteen, I've been able to tell the good guys from the bad guys at a glance. It's one of the reasons I used to be very good at my job."

"Who taught you a neat trick like that when you were thirteen?" Reed asked, brows arching derisively.

"Crissie Masters." Phila smiled. "She always said I had a lot of natural ability, though. She claimed that all she did was fine-tune it a little for me."

Nick went to lounge in the Gilmarten doorway when he heard the Mercedes pull into the drive. Sending Phila off with his father had been a calculated risk. He was curious to find out the results.

As the convertible came to a halt, Phila waved and smiled at him. She looked good, he thought, cheerful and exhilarated. He had an overpowering urge to take her to bed right then and there and sample some of that sweet, sexy enthusiasm.

"How was the game?" he forced himself to ask politely as he opened the door for her.

"I nearly strangled her on the third, sixth and fifteenth greens," Reed said. "She's a mouthy little thing, isn't she?"

"Yeah. But you get used to it after a while."

"I resent that," Phila announced.

"I let her try a few shots," Reed said. "But she has a bad habit of rushing her swing. She'll have to learn to slow down a bit if she ever wants to be able to play."

"I'm working with her on the problem," Nick said calmly. *A hundred miles per hour.*

Reed's eyes were cool and curious. "She seems to think you're one of the good guys. Did you know that?"

"A good guy?"

"The kind of man who'd marry her if she got pregnant, for instance."

Nick glanced at Phila and saw the color staining her cheeks. "Did she tell you that?"

"Yup. Real sure of herself. Seems to think she can tell the sonsobitches a mile off."

"She's just bragging. Did she mention that she threatened to come after me with a gun if she gets pregnant?"

"No." Reed gave Nick a thin smile. "But she did say the real question wasn't whether you'd marry her, it was whether she'd lower her standards far enough to marry into our family."

Phila drew herself up to her full height, her eyes gleaming with irritation. "If either one of you continues to discuss me as if I were not present, I will hand over my shares in Castleton & Lightfoot to the Revolutionary Workers Brigade of America. I'm sure they'll make quite an impression at the annual meeting in August."

Reed glared at Nick. "Goddamn it. Do something about her. Fast."

"Yes, sir." Nick quickly removed his hand from the car door as the Mercedes shot forward.

"It's very tacky to discuss someone as if she weren't present," Phila announced as she turned to march into the cottage. "I'd have thought Eleanor would have taught you all better manners than that. By the way, your father certainly swears a lot, doesn't he? Eleanor should have cleaned up his language by now, too."

Nick followed her over the threshold. "You and Reed discussed the possibility that you might be pregnant?"

Phila was already in the kitchen, rummaging through the refrigerator. "He brought it up, not me. I think he felt he had a gentlemanly obligation to warn me not to use pregnancy as a means of getting a piece of the precious Lightfoot family pie. I wonder where he got the idea that the Great American Dream is to become a Lightfoot or a Castleton." She removed some carrots from the crisper. "Arrogant redneck."

"Dad?"

"Sure. He may drive that fancy Mercedes and dress in designer polo shirts, but deep down he's just a redneck cowboy. I'm surprised he doesn't wear a six-gun on the golf course." She went to the sink and began peeling the carrots.

"The holster would probably interfere with his golf swing. You told him you didn't think I'd walk out on you if you got pregnant?" Nick was fascinated with the way she wielded the peeler. Little strips of carrot flew into the chipped enamel sink.

"You're not the type to walk out."

"You know the type?"

"I'm an ex-social worker, remember? One who specialized in children? I've hunted down more deserters than the U.S. Army. If there's one thing I know, it's the type. Want a carrot?" She held one out to him. "Your cheap father only bought me a cup of coffee and a Danish at the clubhouse before we went out on the course. Said he had a scheduled tee-off time and we couldn't stand around eating."

Nick took the carrot and crunched down on one end, his eyes never leaving Phila's face. "If I'm not the type to walk out, what was that business about threatening me with the gun yesterday morning?"

"I said if you'd gotten me pregnant, I'd come after you with a gun. I didn't say I expected you to run."

Nick finished his carrot. It occurred to him that when a man took a calculated risk, he expected either success or failure. Having the whole business go off on some crazy, unforeseen tangent was a novelty. Nick was dumbfounded. "Sounds like you and my father had a very interesting morning."

"Uh huh. Why did you send me off with him, anyway?"

"I didn't send you off with him. It was your decision to go to the course."

"Come on, Nick, this is me, Phila, remember? Sell that bridge to someone else."

He smiled faintly. "All right, when he showed up at the door I figured it was a good opportunity for the two of you to get to know each other. You wanted to get to know Castletons and Lightfoots, remember?"

"There's more to it than that," Phila said. "Did you hope he'd bully me? Did you think he'd make me mad the way Hilary did when she offered to buy the shares?"

"It was a possibility," Nick admitted.

"I'll just bet it was. Why did you want him to try to push me around?"

"So you'd get really stubborn. I don't want you turning the shares over to him."

"Why not?"

"Because he's letting Hilary vote his shares these days, and I don't want her getting her hands on any more shares than she already controls."

"Got it."

"Speaking of not getting pregnant—" Nick continued and broke off as Phila began choking on the carrot. He slapped her helpfully on the back until she could swallow properly. "I picked up a package of condoms in town yesterday afternoon."

"Oh, fine. Why don't you just broadcast the fact on the local radio station? Buying condoms in a town the size of Port Claxton at a drugstore where the clerk has probably known you since you were born is real subtle, Lightfoot. What are you trying to do? Sink my reputation completely?"

"Everyone already assumes we're sleeping together," Nick pointed out gently.

"Well, everyone's wrong. You're sleeping on the couch, remember? A one-night stand does not constitute an affair or even a short-term shack-up."

"Does this mean you don't have any immediate plans to seduce me again in the near future?"

"My immediate plans are to take a book down to that little cove at the bottom of the hill. I've had it with Lightfoots this morning."

"That little cove is full of rocks, not nice, soft sand."

"Life is full of rocks. With a little practice you get used to sitting on them."

The book was good, a thriller in which the hero, an aging ex-hippie from the sixties, halted a fanatical, power-hungry, right-wing businessman who was secretly financing a band of guerrillas with the intention of taking over Texas.

Phila was halfway through the story when she realized she was concentrating on it in the old, familiar way. Reading had always been a secret pleasure for her, a treasured escape. But ever since the Spalding trial and Crissie's death, she'd had trouble keeping her attention on any book, even a very good one. It was a relief to sense she was getting back to normal in some areas of her life.

She squirmed a bit on the small patch of rough sand she had managed to find in the cove and resettled herself against a large, sun-warmed boulder. Gulls wheeled overhead and several long-legged wading birds darted back and forth in the foam of the retreating surf.

A high-pitched, childish screech of delight mingled with the cries of the birds, and Phila glanced up to see Jordan Castleton running across the wide beach toward the water at full speed. He was wearing a tiny pair of shorts and a shirt that flapped around his waist. His mother was right behind him.

"That's close enough, Jordan," Vicky called as her son showed every sign of charging straight into the waves. "We have to stay on the beach. That water is cold."

Jordan protested vociferously until his attention was caught by the sight of Phila sitting near the tumble of rocks in the cove. He stopped complaining to his mother and stared at Phila. Then he waved both arms excitedly and dashed toward her.

"Hi, Phila. Hi, Phila. Hi, Phila." He got sidetracked by a pile of wet seaweed. Seeing it, he halted immediately and squatted down to investigate.

Victoria turned to see what had first captured her son's attention. She hesitated when she saw Phila, then she started toward her.

"Good afternoon," Victoria said with restrained politeness as she came close to Phila. "I didn't realize you were down here on the beach."

"I had a hard morning playing golf with Reed. I decided to rest this afternoon."

Jordan now came running to join them, a long length of seaweed in his hands. "Look, Phila."

"Hi, Jordan. How's the world treating you today? Why, thank you. Just what I've always wanted," she added as he triumphantly placed the seaweed in her hand. She put it on display on the rock behind her. "There. How's that?"

Jordan cackled in delight. "Pretty."

"It's beautiful. Does wonders for that rock."

He nodded in ready agreement and started looking for more seaweed to add to the collection. Victoria hesitated and then put a towel down on a nearby rock. She sat on top of the towel.

"You went golfing with Reed?" Victoria finally asked.

"In a manner of speaking. I've never played before, and I'm afraid Reed was a tad impatient with my backswing."

"Hilary never plays with him."

"I'm sure he'd rather play with men."

"Eleanor says Nora, his first wife, learned. She used to go around with him sometimes in the evenings when the course was quiet."

"Reed was happy with his first wife?"

"According to everything I've ever heard. She died shortly before I was introduced to Darren. Eleanor says when she first met Nora, the poor woman didn't know where to shop for her clothes or which glass to set where at a formal dinner. But Reed was madly in love with her. It's too bad he got stuck with Hilary for a second wife, but I imagine he felt he didn't have a choice."

Phila decided to bite. "Why didn't he feel he had a choice?"

"He felt duty bound to marry her after she found out she was pregnant. Nick made it clear he wasn't going to take responsibility."

Phila's mind went totally blank for a split second. She accepted another bit of seaweed from Jordan and placed it carefully on the rock next to the first piece. "Hilary was pregnant when she married Reed?"

"Another family secret the Lightfoots haven't bothered to divulge, I gather? She was pregnant, all right. She made a major production out of it."

"But Nick denied the baby was his?"

Victoria nodded, her attention on the small stick Jordan was uncovering amid the rocks. "I heard he refused even to discuss it when his father called him and confronted him with the news. Reed was already feuding with Nick at the time, and he was angry about the divorce. The pregnancy pushed him over the edge. He rushed into marriage with Hilary. Felt sorry for her, I guess. Or maybe he felt duty bound to protect her. I don't know."

"Why was Reed feuding with Nick?"

"I'm not sure exactly. Something to do with the direction in which Nick wanted to take the firm. Darren explained it, but I don't remember all the details. I just recall that Nick and his father were battling tooth and nail over it while the divorce was in progress. Then came the announcement about Hilary being pregnant. Nick had already walked out by the time she realized she was carrying the baby."

"So Hilary became Mrs. Reed Lightfoot."

"She managed to lose the baby two months after Reed married her. Hilary's timing is usually very good."

"Why are you telling me this, Vicky?" Phila asked quietly.

Victoria flicked a quick glance at her and then looked away again. "I just thought you ought to know what you're up against. Hilary is a manipulator. And Nick is just as clever in his own way, if not more so."

"What are you afraid of? That I'll fall for Lightfoot lies or Lightfoot seduction techniques and decide to turn the shares over to a Lightfoot instead of a Castleton?"

"That's exactly what I'm afraid will happen." Victoria stood up and hugged her arms around herself as she looked down at Phila. Her fine dark eyes burned with resentment. "Those shares belong to the Castletons. By rights they should have gone to Darren when Burke died, not to that cheap little trollop who wandered into our lives and ruined everything!"

Phila was on her feet in an instant, rage heating her blood. "Don't you dare call Crissie names. I don't care what you think she did, she was my friend and I won't let anyone call her names. Apologize, damn it. Right now."

Victoria's eyes filled with hurt and anger. "Why should I bother? Crissie Masters came very close to wrecking my marriage. She enjoyed driving a wedge between me and Darren, and I hated her for that."

"How could she drive a wedge between the two of you unless there was one sitting around waiting to be driven?" Phila snapped.

"There are things you don't know. Private matters that concern only Darren and myself. I hoped they'd been buried three years ago, but your precious Crissie found out about them and brought them to the surface again. She took great delight in throwing them in our faces."

"You can't blame Crissie for everything, damn you."

"Believe what you want, but I'll tell you one thing, Philadelphia Fox. Those shares you got from her are my son's inheritance. I want them back in the Castleton family."

"Crissie had as much right to them as anyone in that family. They constituted *her* inheritance, not Jordan's. Burke was her father, remember?"

"She's dead."

"Right," Phila said tightly. "So now they're my inheritance, aren't they? Crissie was family to me, Vicky, the only family I had left in this world. No one insults her and gets away with it. Apologize for calling her a cheap trollop."

"All right, I apologize," Victoria said wretchedly. She dashed away the tears that had formed in her eyes. "But it changes nothing. She was a troublemaker while she was alive, and she's still making trouble even though she's dead. I'll never forgive her for turning Burke against Darren. And I'll never forgive her for leaving those shares to you. She gave away a portion of my son's future, and I want it back. If you don't give the shares to us, you're no better than she was."

Victoria whirled around, grabbed Jordan up into her arms and stood staring for an instant at a point just beyond Phila's left shoulder. Then she burst into more tears and hurried toward the cliff path with her small son.

"Well, well, well," Nick observed quietly from just behind Phila. "Aren't you a little ray of sunshine in everyone's life today?"

She swung around to see him leaning against a large boulder. He had one hand braced against the rock's surface, and his face was set in familiar, unreadable lines.

"How long have you been standing there?" Phila demanded, struggling to regain her self-control.

"A few minutes. You and Vicky were both so wrapped up in your girlish conversation you didn't hear me arrive."

Phila sank wearily back down onto her towel and picked up her book. Her fingers were trembling. She was fighting her own tears. "I didn't mean to upset her," she said. "But I won't let her or anyone else call Crissie names."

"Even if Crissie deserves them?"

Phila nodded resolutely. "Even if Crissie deserves them."

"I can understand that. Family is family." Nick sat down beside her and leaned back against the warm boulder. He drew up his jeaned legs and closed his eyes against the sun. "Ever made love on a beach?"

# 9

꧁⚜꧂

"No, I certainly have not made love on a beach and I don't intend to try it now, so don't get any ideas." Phila picked up her book and buried her nose in it.

Nick waited. While he waited he picked up a handful of small pebbles and tossed them idly into the waves. Two or three minutes passed.

"I suppose you have?" Phila eventually asked, sounding petulant. She did not remove her nose from the book.

Nick smiled to himself and picked up another handful of smooth, sea-washed pebbles. "No, can't say that I have. But I've always secretly wanted to do it."

That caught her attention. "Do you have a lot of weird unfulfilled desires?"

"As you get to know me better you'll find out, won't you?"

"I can't imagine why you would want to make love on a beach." She turned the page in her book. "It seems to me it would be extremely uncomfortable."

"Not for you."

"What do you mean, not for me?"

"The way I fantasize it, you'd be on your feet most of the time."

"On my feet!"

"Yeah. Kind of leaning over me. You'd have your legs wide apart and I'd . . ."

"Stop it. You're getting kinky." She flipped another page in her book.

"Thank you, Phila," he said gravely. "No one's ever said that to me before. It must be something you bring out in me." Nick was not concerned by her apparent interest in the book. It was obvious she had not read the last two pages. She was as aware of him physically as he was of her. The sense of primitive masculine power gave him a real rush. He was getting hard already.

"Don't blame me for your sexual fantasies," Phila muttered.

"How can I help but blame you? You're the subject of them. All of them."

"Will you please stop talking like that? I told you earlier, we are not having an affair. You're using my sofa, remember?"

"I'd like to have an affair with you," Nick said very humbly.

"Why? Because you think you could control me better if you were sleeping with me?" she retorted.

Nick heard the wariness in her voice and knew he had to move very carefully through this particular mine field. "I'm the one who should be worrying about being controlled by sex," he said softly. "I told you that you have a potent effect on me, Phila. No other woman does to me what you do to me."

"Hah."

"It's true." He paused a few seconds. "I'm thirty-five years old and I've never felt as good with anyone as I felt with you the other night when you made love to me . . ."

"That sounds like a line, Nick. An old, dumb, sappy line."

"It's not. That is, it may be a line, but it's certainly the first time I've ever used it. I like to think that I wouldn't use anything that sappy for a routine seduction. Would you at least kiss me here on the beach? My fantasies can take over from there if necessary."

Phila finally lifted her head and studied him cautiously. There was an urgent curiosity in her eyes as she searched his face. She was visibly torn by her own conflicting needs. She wanted him, he could tell. Even when she was doing her best to conceal the fact, it showed.

The knowledge made him feel great.

Nick dropped his handful of pebbles and touched the corner of her mouth.

"Kiss me, Phila. Please."

She hesitated, a dainty wild creature consumed by her own curiosity and a desire she did not yet know quite how to handle. Nick got even harder knowing he was the cause of her confusion. He vowed to himself he would satisfy both the curiosity and the sweet, hot desire.

"Are you laughing at me?" Phila demanded accusingly.

"No. You make me happy, Phila. Is that so terrible?" He traced the shape of her soft mouth. He felt the gathering excitement in her and knew she was practically his.

"Do I really make you happy?" she asked.

"Yeah." He smiled again, realizing how true that was. "Why does that surprise you?"

Her shoulder lifted in a small gesture of uncertainty. "I don't know." She looked down at the book in her lap. "I don't think of myself as a very sexy person, and I guess I just figured I'm not the type to turn a man on. The few times I've tried it things always went wrong."

Nick was fascinated by the tension in her. "What went wrong, Phila? You didn't find any satisfaction in it? Is that what you're trying to say? Don't worry about it. Some things just take practice."

She shook her head violently, not looking at him. "No, it's not that. I mean, what you just said is true, I don't . . . haven't ever experienced a . . . well, you know. But that's not the problem."

"What is the problem?"

"I get turned off as soon as some man starts pawing me," she said in a tight little voice. "It's hard to explain. I just get scared and I freeze. I can't stand to have some man on top of me, crushing me. That seems to be the way most men go at it."

"Probably because they're usually made to feel they're responsible for taking the initiative."

"Yes. I suppose so. And I didn't think to suggest reversing things. I just assumed I wasn't a very sensual person. But with you everything was different. You let me do what I wanted. I felt safe. I guess being in command like that, being on top is going to be the one way sex will work for me." She paused. "It was reassuring to know there's hope for me, if you want to know the truth."

"I'm glad," he said simply. "Why do you think you have the hang-up about the traditional missionary position?"

"It's probably because of something that happened to me when I was a teenager." She leaned her elbows on her knees and studied the sea.

"Tell me about it, Phila." His insides tightened. "Did some jerk force you?"

"He tried to rape me. He was the brother of a man who ran the foster home I was living in at the time. He used to visit a lot and help out around the place. He watched the girls all the time. I think he picked me because I was the most naive. I didn't like him; none of the girls did, but I didn't know how to handle him. He probably sensed that I was afraid of him and that's why he zeroed in on me."

"He attacked you?"

"He hung around the house until he found me alone one afternoon after school. He came into my room and started telling me how he was going to show me what women were made for. He said a lot of horrible things, mostly about how he knew that all the girls in the home were tramps and whores and how we'd all grow up to be prostitutes so I might as well get started learning my future profession." Phila shuddered. "I was so scared I was paralyzed with fear."

Nick touched her arm and she flinched. He started to withdraw his hand but changed his mind at the last minute. He let his fingers rest lightly on her skin and breathed a sigh of relief when she did not pull away. "You should have kicked the bastard in the balls."

"I know but at the time I was too frightened to try it. I was afraid I'd only make him more aggressive. I tried to get out of the room, instead. He let me get almost to the door and just when I thought I was safe, he grabbed me. He had just been playing with me, you see. He wanted me to try to escape. It made the game more fun for him."

"Oh, Phila."

"He caught me and threw me down on the bed. I kicked and scratched and struggled and he just kept crushing me into the bed. I thought I would go mad. I felt so helpless. He was so big and heavy. Like a mountain of meat. Whenever I think about it, that's the image that comes back to me; being crushed beneath a man. I can't stand the feeling."

Nick closed his eyes briefly. "What happened?"

"He had an arm across my throat and he was starting to tear off my clothes when Crissie came in."

Nick took a breath. "I should have known. Crissie Masters to the rescue again, hmmm? No wonder you're so devoted to her memory."

"She picked up a lamp that was on the bedside table and brought it down over his head," Phila said. "Crissie could always think fast in situations like that. I was safe, but then came the real problem."

Nick frowned. "What was that?"

"Explaining it to the foster parents and our caseworker. The man who ran the home claimed I must have led his brother on. The brother said that he hadn't done anything. He claimed he'd been fixing a light socket in the bedroom. He said Crissie and I set him up to make it look like attempted rape."

"Hell."

"There was no proof either way. But our caseworker was an old pro in the business, and she knew what had happened. She believed me. She pulled strings and called in a few favors and got me and Crissie and the other three kids out of the home within forty-eight hours. I think that was when I first considered social work as a career. I wanted to be able to rescue people the way she had rescued me and Crissie and the others."

That figured, Nick thought. Thus was a sweet little liberal do-gooder born. "I wish I knew where that jerk is now."

"The guy who attacked me? Why?" She gave him a puzzled look.

"Because I would like to tear him into small pieces."

Phila just stared at him. "You would? You don't even know him."

"Phila, I would want to tear anyone who hurt you into small pieces," Nick explained carefully. "Don't you understand?"

"No. I can see where you might feel that protective toward someone in your family, but I don't see why you should feel that way about me. You hardly know me."

"You know that's not a fair statement. You and I are getting to know each other very well."

"Is that right?" she challenged. "What do you really know about me?"

"For openers, I now understand why you like to be on top when we make love."

She flushed. "You make it sound as if we do it all the time."

"I'd like to."

"Forget it."

"Will you at least fulfill part of my beach fantasy?"

"What part?" she asked suspiciously.

He couldn't help himself. His mouth twitched in a smile he struggled manfully to conceal. "Just kiss me."

"If I do, will you stop pestering me about having an affair?"

"Just kiss me," he repeated softly, his fingers sliding up and down the length of her arm. "Please. You make me feel so damn good, honey."

For an instant he thought she was going to draw back. But just when he thought he'd miscalculated badly, she started leaning toward him, her arms going lightly around his neck. Nick exhaled in relief as her soft mouth brushed his.

"So sweet. You're so sweet." A shudder went through Nick.

Phila began to pull away but she made the mistake of dropping a small, warm kiss on his chin and after that she could not seem to resist running the tip of her tongue over his bottom lip.

Nick felt her tremble and knew everything was going to be all right. "Again, honey. You taste so good."

She crowded closer and her fingers began to clutch at him. "Nick," she whispered. "How do you do this to me?"

"I don't do anything to you, sweetheart. You do it all by yourself. I'm just lucky enough to get invited along for the ride."

"No, it's you. Something you do. I haven't figured it out yet, but I'm sure it's dangerous."

"No, Phila, it's not dangerous. Not as long as you're with me. You're safe with me. Remember that." He moved his hand soothingly down her back, tracking the sensual length of her spine. Her fragrance filled his head, triggering a flood of dazzling need throughout his body. She wasn't the only one who had to learn to slow down, he thought. Phila had the knack of catapulting him into a full state of arousal almost instantaneously.

She knelt in the coarse sand and began to nuzzle him hungrily, nipping at his earlobe, kissing his eyelashes. Nick groaned, leaned back against the warm rock and let her have her way with him.

Within a matter of minutes she had worked herself and him into a feverish state. He felt her fingers fumbling with the buttons of his shirt. He swore in frustration when she got everything tangled up, but he did not offer to help. He endured the sweet torture nobly until her palms at last flattened on his bare chest.

She found his lips again and drove her tongue boldly into his mouth, pressing herself against him. Nick gave himself up to the pure sensual joy of being a sex object until he realized that Phila, true to form, was once again charging full speed ahead. It wasn't going to happen that way this time. This time she would get it right.

"Slow down," he muttered into her ear.

She paid no attention. Her hands went to his belt buckle. She got it undone after several attempts and then she reached for his zipper.

"No," Nick said, although it nearly broke him. He gently caught her hand. "This time we're going to find out what you like."

"Please, Nick. I want to feel you again the way I did the other night. It was so good. I was so close."

"I know. The problem is you're rushing things."

She went still. "You don't like the way I do it? I thought you did."

He was exasperated by the uncertainty in her voice. "I go crazy and you know it. But as much as I like it, I think you need to give yourself more time." He guided her fingers to the snap of her jeans.

"More time?" She sounded confused. "But we must be doing it right. I've never felt like this with anyone else."

"Good." He kissed her forehead and then the tip of her nose and his hand rested on her thigh. "Now, if you'll just take it a little more slowly, you'll feel even better. Don't worry," he added, seeing the expression of concern on her face. "It's not going anywhere."

"You're laughing at me," she said with a resigned groan.

"Never." He urged her fingers to undo the snap of her jeans.

Slowly and then with increasing speed, she stripped off her jeans. Nick had to close his eyes and think of flag and country for a moment when he saw the dark triangle of hair showing through the sheer fabric of her panties. When he had control of himself again he opened his eyes and saw Phila watching him closely.

"Are you all right?" she asked. She paused in the act of unbuttoning her shirt.

Nick realized she was not wearing a bra. "If I were any better I'd go out of my mind."

She looked relieved and quickly finished undoing the last buttons of her shirt. She let the ends of the garment hang free. The soft curves of her breasts were barely visible, half-hidden in tantalizing shadow. "Then can we do it now? Please? Before this feeling goes away?"

"The feeling isn't going away. I told you that. Just give yourself a chance to experience it."

"That's what I'm trying to do," she replied impatiently. She grabbed his zipper again.

"No, not yet. Here." He held out his hand.

She stared down at his palm, mystified. "What am I supposed to do with it?"

"Use it any way you want," he instructed softly. "Show me what you need and how you like it. Teach me how to touch you."

Her head came up so swiftly she nearly cracked his chin. "You want me to show you how to touch me? Don't you want to get inside me?"

"Eventually," he promised through his teeth. "We'll definitely get to that part eventually. But let's try a little foreplay first."

"Oh. Foreplay." She leaned against him, nibbling his throat. "Okay. Do it."

"No, sweetheart, you're going to do it. You're the teacher, remember?"

She was quiet for a moment, and Nick began to worry. Then she gripped his hand and pulled his fingers toward her breasts. She shivered as she moved his palm over her nipples, and Nick experienced a few shudders of his own as he felt her harden beneath his touch.

"Look at you," he whispered, awed by her response. "Hard as little pebbles. Just the right size for my hand."

Phila made a small sound of pleasure and pushed her breast more tightly into his cupped palm. Nick carefully caught the nipple between thumb and forefinger and tugged gently.

"*Nick.*"

"Feel good?"

"It feels strange." Eagerly she adjusted herself so that she was sitting on his lap. "Do the other one."

He obeyed, kissing the nape of her neck as he gently prodded her other nipple erect. She felt tight and full.

"I'm ready," she informed him, clutching at him. "Let's do it now."

"Not yet."

"Damn it, Nick . . ."

"You haven't taught me all I want to learn."

"Now what?" she demanded.

"I don't know. Show me."

She moved on his legs. He felt the lush curve of her bare thigh pushing against his trapped manhood and thought he'd lose it all inside his jeans. He counted stars and stripes for a minute until he'd regained a portion of his control.

"Nick, please, I feel so hot. I want to do it."

He let his fingers curl invitingly in her palm. When he made no further move Phila grabbed his hand and plunged it down between her legs.

"There. Do something," she ordered.

"Yes, ma'am."

Nick allowed his fingertips to trace light designs over the silky material of her underwear. The soft stuff quickly grew damp under his touch. He could feel her growing plump and soft.

"You get wet so fast for me, baby. Know what that does to me?"

"Do that again," Phila said, moving against his hand with sudden urgency.

"Do what again?"

"Touch me like that." She grabbed his hand, held him steady and then slid along the length of his finger. "Yes, like that. Harder. No, here." She edged aside the elastic leg band of her panties and maneuvered his hand inside.

Nick sucked in his breath almost painfully as the full impact of her moist, welcoming warmth nearly overwhelmed him. "Show me exactly how you want it."

Phila was beyond protesting the torment. She fumbled with his hand, getting him thoroughly wet in the process. Nick felt so tight and hot he had to grit his teeth to maintain any kind of control.

He started to search out the little bud of feminine sensation but held off until she finally managed to find it for him. She cried out when he stroked her, cried out and clung to him with all her might, her face buried against his chest.

Then she moved against his finger with a woman's instinct.

"Oh, Nick, that feels so good."

"I told you it wasn't going anywhere. Just relax and enjoy."

Some of the frantic quality seemed to evaporate from her. A sexy, dreamy expression crossed her vivid features. She began to guide him with more certainty. Her tiny little sounds of increasing pleasure were muffled against his chest.

Nick was rigid with his own desire but he refused to ruin every-thing at this point by losing control. Nothing was more important in that moment than having Phila learn her first taste of satisfaction at his hands.

She shifted position after a few minutes, kneeling astride him and leaning over him. Then she started to move more and more aggres-sively against his finger. Her head tipped back as the excitement flowed through her.

Nick allowed one finger to slip slowly inside her slick, tight chan-nel. Phila's reaction was immediate. She went over the edge. She called out his name in a muffled shout. Her body went taut with sex-ual tension. Then she was convulsing gently around his fingers, clutching him fiercely.

For a long, wondrous moment she clung to him as her climax rip-pled through her. Nick knew he was more thrilled than she could ever be. He had never seen anything so glorious as Philadelphia Fox in the full flower of her womanly passion.

Slowly, slowly, she crumpled against him until she was sitting once more on his thighs. Her head rested against his chest and her whole body was filled with a gentle languor that was as sensual in its own way as her climax had been. Nick stroked her slowly, seeking the little aftershocks.

When his fingers drifted over the small button that was the chief focus of her recent pleasure, she flinched and mumbled a soft protest.

"Sensitive?" he asked.

"Um hmmm." She didn't open her eyes.

He grinned but he did not relax. He was still iron hard with his own need. He wanted to bury himself in her but he was reluctant to break the magic spell.

"Nick?" Her voice was drowsy.

"Yeah?"

"That was incredible. I've never felt anything like it. Fantastic. Thank you."

"You're fantastic. And don't thank me. You did it all by yourself."

She moved her head in a small negative gesture against his shoul-der. "No, it was you."

"Let's not argue about it." He opened his eyes and watched a gull soaring out over the sea. "The last thing I want to do right now is argue about anything."

"Okay." She shifted into a more comfortable position.

Chagrined, Nick realized she was about to go to sleep. "Phila?"

"Hmm?"

"You know that package I told you about? The one I bought at the pharmacy in town?"

Her eyes flew open. She looked up at him from under her lashes. "What about it?"

"Check my back pocket."

Shock filled her eyes. "Oh, Nick, I forgot about you. I'm so sorry. I didn't mean . . ."

"It's all right." He smiled heroically. "I understand. But now that you've remembered me do you suppose we might try it your way again?"

She giggled, reaching around behind him to withdraw the small package from his jeans pocket. She handed it to him. "Here you go."

He made no move to take the package from her hand. Instead, he looked at her. "You do it."

She blinked, a new gleam of interest in her eyes. "You want me to put it on you?"

"Apparently I'm a sucker for an aggressive, take-charge female."

A long while later Phila finally roused herself sufficiently to pay attention to her surroundings again. She was sitting across Nick's thighs and he had his eyes closed. He was still wearing his jeans but they were unfastened and unzipped. He looked wicked and sexy.

"Nick? We'd better get dressed. Anyone could come down here."

"Not likely. I checked before I came looking for you. Dad's gone into town with Tec, Eleanor's in her greenhouse and Hilary's working. Darren's having lunch with some of his local campaign staff. Vicky and Jordan have already been here and left. Trust me, we're safe."

"You're so thorough," she said, half in mockery and half in genuine respect for the care he'd taken. Leave it to Nick to orchestrate things behind the scenes so that nothing went wrong with a supposedly spontaneous sexual encounter. "You think you're so clever, don't you?"

Nick's eyes narrowed, but still glittered with amusement. "No, I just like things to work out the way I want them to work out. Which reminds me."

"About what?" She reached for her shirt which had somehow been abandoned, and slipped it on.

"We've done this twice now. That definitely takes our association out of the one-night-stand category."

She glanced at him out of the corner of her eye, wondering what he had up his sleeve now. "So?"

"So, I think it's time we agreed we're having an affair, don't you? Otherwise, what are we going to call this relationship of ours?"

Phila was feeling too pleasantly relaxed to argue. "Call it whatever you want," she said with an air of grand indifference.

"Fine. I'm calling it an affair. A full-time, monogamous, one-on-one affair."

Phila frowned in warning. "Just don't get the idea you can control me with sex."

"I wouldn't think of it."

"One of these days, Nick, I'm going to wipe that smug grin off your face."

"Why? You're the one who put it there in the first place."

Reed was at the wheel of the Mercedes with Tec Sherman sitting beside him as they drove back from town, when he spotted Nick and Phila. He saw the two figures in the distance as they came up the path from the cove and started toward the Gilmarten place. He knew from the casually possessive way his son's arm rested on Phila's shoulders that the pair had probably just made love down on the beach.

"That little gal's damn sure caught Nick's attention, hasn't she, sir?" Tec observed.

"That she has."

"Think it's serious?"

"I don't know. What do you think?" Reed knew Nick never did anything without a reason. That reason was not always fathomable to others, but it always existed. Had he truly fallen for little Miss Philadelphia Fox, or was he engineering some scheme to get back the shares?

"I don't know either, sir. Nick can be tough to figure out at times. But I'll tell you one thing. I've never seen him act like this around a female. It's like he's not real sure what to make of her, but he damn sure knows he can't let her out of his sight."

*What game are you playing, Nick?* Reed asked himself silently. "I know what you mean, Tec."

"Good havin' him back, ain't it, sir?"

*Goddamn right.* "About time he remembered he's got family."

The Mercedes came abreast of Nick and Phila a few moments later. Reed saw the faint flush in Phila's cheeks and the lazy, satiated look in his son's eyes. For a second he knew a flash of pure male envy. In the old days he and Nora had sneaked off to that cove a time or two and gone at it like a couple of mink.

"You two been for a walk on the beach?" Reed asked, slowing the car to a halt.

"Yeah." Nick put one hand on the frame of the windshield and leaned down. "Tec, I want to do some shooting with Phila this week."

"Sure thing, sir. Got a preference?"

"A .38, I think. Some nitwit sold her a spiffy little 9-mm automatic even though she's never used a handgun in her life. She's never even fired the damn thing."

"An automatic? Bad choice. Too complicated for a beginner," Tec said. "Unless she wants to put in a lot of work gettin' used to it."

"I think we can safely assume she's not going to become a handgun enthusiast. But I want her to be able to use something, so I think we'll educate her with a revolver."

"No problem."

"Wait a second," Phila interrupted. "I don't recall saying I wanted to practice shooting a gun."

Reed frowned at her. "Nick's right. An automatic is a poor choice for a novice. Too fancy. Takes practice to master. A revolver is simpler and easier to use in an emergency. Just point it and pull the trigger."

"But I . . ."

Reed turned to his son. "Make it the morning after tomorrow, and I'll join you. I've got a game tomorrow or I'd say make it then."

Nick stepped back from the car. "All right," he said. "We'll make it the day after tomorrow."

"Don't forget Eleanor's dinner party tomorrow night," Reed added as he put his foot down on the accelerator.

Ten minutes later Reed walked into the house and went in search of Hilary. He found her in the study that had once been his personal domain. As he walked into the room he realized that through the wide windows a person could see a portion of the cliff road. He wondered if Hilary had been watching Nick and Phila return from the beach.

"Hello, Reed." Hilary looked up from the file she was examining. She leaned back in her chair and smiled politely. "Did you want something?"

"Just wanted to let you know I've got a game at three o'clock."

"All right. I'll tell the housekeeper to plan dinner accordingly. Will Nick be eating with us tonight?"

"No, I don't think so." Reed looked at the beautiful, perfectly groomed woman who was his wife. Every hair was in place. Her makeup was flawless. She was the picture of elegant femininity.

Then he thought about Phila looking tousled and flushed, slightly embarrassed and happy. He could not imagine Hilary ever looking that way. He was pretty sure Nick wouldn't be able to imagine her looking that way, either.

His son had definitely missed out on something important during his disastrous marriage, something he appeared to be finding with Phila Fox.

# 10

❦

Eleanor presided over dinner the following evening with the elegant ease of one who has spent a lifetime cultivating the fine art of formal entertaining.

Phila eyed the array of cutlery and glassware in front of her and felt like a guerrilla heading into combat. She would not screw up, she vowed silently. She was a well-educated human being who, although she had not been raised amid upper-class surroundings, had learned somewhere along the line how to tell a seafood fork from a salad fork. *She would not screw up.*

She was not about to let Eleanor intimidate her, especially since she had a sneaking suspicion that that had been the purpose of the dinner party. Eleanor sat at the far end of the impossibly long table smiling vaguely out over a sea of Wedgwood creamware, Sheffield silver plate and Waterford crystal, and Phila just knew what she was thinking. Eleanor was taking the opportunity to demonstrate how out of place Crissie had been here and, by extension, how out of place Phila herself was.

Phila was very glad that Crissie had told her about the Wedgwood and the Sheffield and the Waterford. It made it easier to act casually when the stuff was plunked down in front of her. *I just pretend it's all plastic,* Crissie had said.

"I understand you're a social worker, dear," Eleanor said as she delicately separated a slice of fish from the halibut steak on her plate. "How did you meet Crissie?"

"I met her when I was sent to a foster home after my grandmother died."

"Your grandmother? Then you weren't an abandoned child?"

"You mean like Crissie?" Phila smiled brilliantly as she saw Eleanor's eyes flicker. "No, I was far more fortunate. My parents cared about me, but they were both killed when I was very young. My father's mother took me in and raised me until I was thirteen."

Reed looked up from his fish, his expression curious. "How did your folks die?"

"In a helicopter crash in South America. The 'copter was shot down."

"Shot down! What in blue blazes were they doing in South America?" Reed demanded, ignoring Eleanor's frown over the harsh language.

"They were involved in helping Indians who were being systematically hunted and shot by their own government. The local government always claimed it was Communist rebels who shot down the 'copter, but everyone knew it was the government's own forces that did it. It was an open secret."

Nick's eyes narrowed. "Did your parents do that kind of thing routinely?"

"You mean helping people like those Indians?" Phila picked up her water glass, aware of the diamond shapes of the cut crystal beneath her fingertips. "Oh, yes. They were devoted to doing what they could to help those less fortunate than themselves. They traveled all over the world on behalf of an organization called Freedom for the Future Foundation. Have you heard of it?"

Reed groaned aloud, and Nick's brows rose in amusement. Darren shook his head, and Victoria sighed. Hilary winced, and Eleanor made a tut-tutting sound and quickly passed a plate of asparagus.

Phila was pleased with the reaction. "Ah hah. You *have* heard of it."

"A troublemaking, anarchistic, radical left-wing fringe group that's always sticking its nose in where it doesn't belong," Reed declared, stabbing at his asparagus. "Financed by a bunch of hypocritical do-gooders who don't have the sense to know they're nothing but Communist dupes."

"Are you calling my parents hypocritical Communist dupes?" Phila asked very softly, more than ready for battle on this front.

Reed finally noticed the look in her eyes and muttered something under his breath. "I'm sorry about what happened to your folks, but you can't expect me to condone an outfit like that goddamned Freedom for the Future Foundation. They're all a bunch of wild-eyed crazies, and everyone with an ounce of common sense knows it."

"I don't expect you to condone the foundation. That would be asking too much, given your ridiculously narrow-minded views, but I do expect you to show some respect for my parents. They died working for something they believed in, and I would think even a Lightfoot could appreciate that."

"I'm sure Reed didn't mean to be unkind," Hilary said in a soothing tone.

"Of course he didn't," Eleanor confirmed. "Have some more asparagus, dear. Washington grown. It's excellent this time of year."

Darren regarded Phila thoughtfully. "Did you travel with your parents when you were a child?"

"No, I stayed behind with Grandmother. The places my parents had to go on behalf of the foundation were usually dangerous."

"I'm sure your parents meant well," Nick said seriously. "But as far as I'm concerned, they had no business risking their necks all over the world when they had a daughter to raise. You should have been their first priority."

Phila, who had often harbored similar disloyal thoughts in moments of great loneliness, began to get really angry. "They had a right to follow their consciences. If no one did, this world would be a much worse place to live in than it already is."

"I agree with Nick," Darren said unexpectedly. "Once you were born, your parents had an obligation to think of your future. Their first duty was to protect you, not a bunch of strangers."

Victoria nodded, her dark eyes shadowed. "I think it's very sad that you were left alone in the world because your parents were out trying to save other people."

"You're all speaking so piously on the subject because you don't happen to approve of the work my parents were doing. I'm sure if I'd said my father was in the armed forces and had got sent into dangerous trouble spots all over the world on behalf of the good old U.S. of A., you'd say it was his duty to go."

Reed scowled. "That's a different matter entirely."

"Talk about hypocritical reasoning." Phila smiled triumphantly and pointed her fork straight down the table at Reed. The asparagus stalk on the end of the fork wavered in the air. "Your logic is totally messed up. My parents were doing what they saw as their duty. Just as if they were in the military."

"There is one important difference," Nick pointed out. "If your father had been in the military, chances are your mother would have been at home with you. You wouldn't have lost both parents."

"Now you're saying that women shouldn't be allowed to serve in the military? I suppose you're one of those chauvinists who doesn't think women should serve in combat positions?" Phila made this point so emphatically that the piece of asparagus fell off the tines of her fork.

Phila glanced down at the green spear lying on the priceless an- tique lace and did the only thing she could think of to do. She snatched the stalk up off the tablecloth and popped it into her mouth. When she caught Nick's eye, she saw he was laughing silently at her. It was the same kind of laughter she saw in his eyes when she made love with him.

"I see no reason to put women into combat." Nick sank his strong white teeth into a large chunk of crusty sourdough bread. "They're not cut out for it."

"If you feel that way, I'm surprised you're so gung-ho about teach- ing me how to use a gun."

"I have nothing against a woman being able to take care of herself," Nick retorted.

Darren nodded soberly. "I taught Vicky to use a revolver a few years back. It's just common sense."

"Nick is an excellent teacher," Hilary murmured from the far end of the table. "He taught me how to use a gun the year we got married."

A lot of the wind went out of Phila's sails at that point. The thought of Nick teaching Hilary anything was depressing. Hilary's simple re- mark had the effect of forcibly reminding Phila that the other woman had once shared the most intimate of relationships with Nick. When she glanced across the table she saw that Nick's expression had re- verted to a hard, shuttered look. That irritated her.

She considered launching into a lecture on the evils of handguns but then remembered she was hardly in a position to make a fuss on the subject. But she couldn't resist one small comment, if only for the sake of form.

"If we had better gun-control legislation in this country, none of us would have to worry about learning how to use a gun for protection. There wouldn't be so many weapons floating around in the hands of criminals."

"The world is a dangerous place," Eleanor said serenely. "One must do what is necessary." When everyone turned to glance at her she quickly summoned up her distracted smile. She looked down the length of the table at Reed. "By the way, I wanted to remind everyone about Darren's fund-raiser in Seattle at the end of the month. Not long now, hmmm? I'm sure we'll get a substantial turnout. Just the sort of thing we need to kick off the gubernatorial campaign." She turned to look at Nick. "I do hope everyone will be there? So important to show a united family front, don't you think?"

There was a soft stillness around the table before Hilary said briskly, "I'm sure that whoever needs to be there will be there, Eleanor.

We all want to see Darren's campaign get off to a strong start. Isn't that right, Reed?"

"Sure." Reed did not look terribly interested, one way or the other.

Victoria looked anxiously at Nick. "What do you think about Darren's chances of being governor, Nick?"

"I think," said Nick, picking up his wineglass, "that the Castletons and Lightfoots are businessmen, not politicians."

There was a stark silence following that remark. Darren broke it with an easy smile. "I think you're definitely a businessman, Nick. And, to be truthful, a much better one than I am. But I think I can make a contribution in the realm of politics. I do have some ideas and some skills that can be useful in governing this state. Washington is one of the last frontiers and at the rate it's being discovered, we need to start managing our resources well. If we don't, we'll lose them the way California did."

"It takes money to run for office," Nick pointed out. "A lot of it."

Darren nodded, meeting Nick's eyes squarely. "No one makes it into public office these days without the backing of family money. Everyone knows that."

"That's certainly true," Phila interjected spiritedly. "Certainly makes politics a game for the wealthy upper classes, doesn't it? Not much chance for another Abe Lincoln these days."

Reed glowered at her. "If a man can't prove he can make a success of his own life, I don't want him running the country. How's he going to keep the economy strong if he doesn't even have any talent for managing his own finances?"

"Oh, for heaven's sake . . ." Phila began. But before she could continue, she realized that Nick and Darren were still contemplating each other very thoughtfully.

"In your case, Darren," Nick murmured, ignoring Phila, "it wouldn't just be Castleton family money involved, would it? It would be C&L money."

"Yes," Darren agreed. "It would, wouldn't it? I prefer to think of it as an investment in our future as well as the state's future. Castletons and Lightfoots have a major stake in Washington and the Northwest. Our destinies are linked."

"C&L will survive, regardless of what happens politically in this state," Nick stated.

Before Darren could argue, Victoria made a frantic stab at redirecting the conversation. "Well, I understand we're giving the townspeople a lot to talk about this summer," she observed with false brightness.

"People will always talk," Darren said with a shrug.

"You can't blame them for being curious under the circumstances," Victoria persisted, sliding a sidelong glance at Phila.

Phila smiled back benignly. "The least you can do is give the good people of Port Claxton something to talk about, since you've apparently cut off the scholarship money and most of the contributions to local charities and civic-improvement projects."

Everyone at the table turned to stare at her in astonishment.

"I believe we're ready for dessert," Eleanor announced quickly. "I'll ring for Mrs. Atkins." She picked up the silver bell beside her fork.

Bowls of fresh raspberries and cream arrived within minutes. In the subdued flurry of clearing dishes and serving dessert, Phila thought her last conversational gambit had been quashed. But she was wrong.

"What did you mean about cutting off scholarship and charity money?" Darren asked with a frown as Mrs. Atkins disappeared into the kitchen.

Phila swallowed a raspberry. "I recently had a very interesting chat with a nice young man who works in one of the grocery stores in town."

"The Wilson kid," Nick put in dryly, his eyes on Phila.

"He was complaining about a lack of charity handouts from us?" Hilary demanded.

Eleanor shook her head sadly. "People expect so much these days. There was a time when everyone had enough pride and gumption to stand on his own two feet."

"You misunderstand," Phila said smoothly. "He wasn't complaining. In fact, he admires you all tremendously. He even intends to vote for Darren, if he gets the chance. He merely commented on the fact that the Castletons and Lightfoots didn't seem to be taking as much of an interest in the town as they once did. I'm the one who's complaining about it."

"What the hell have you got to complain about?" Reed demanded.

"Reed, please," Eleanor said reprovingly.

"I think it's disgusting that people with as much money as you folks have don't pour a little of it back into the community," Phila declared.

"We pour a shitload of it into a whole bunch of causes and organizations," Reed retorted furiously. "Don't let anyone tell you otherwise."

"Really, Reed. Your language." Eleanor frowned at him.

"If you're talking about contributions to a lot of stupid ultraconservative lobbies and the campaigns of right-wing politicians, I've got news for you," Phila said. "They don't count. Helping people is what counts." She aimed her fork at Reed again. This time there was a raspberry on the end of it. "Scholarships for local kids who couldn't go on to college otherwise count. Books for libraries count. Educationalassistance programs for disadvantaged youngsters count. Food and housing programs for the homeless count."

"Jesus H. Christ," Reed exclaimed in exasperation. "She sounds like Nora. Nora was always having us give money to every fast-talking sharpie who showed up at the front gate with a sob story."

"That's an exaggeration, Dad, and you know it." Nick interrupted calmly. "Mom investigated each cause carefully. She only had us give to the ones she'd personally checked out."

"You know what they say about money," Phila murmured. "It's like manure. It doesn't do any good unless you spread it around."

Nick studied the fork she was waving in the air. "Phila, are you going to eat that raspberry or throw it at one of us?"

Phila blinked. "I don't know. It's a toss-up." But she redirected the fork toward her mouth and bit into the fruit. She glared across the table at Darren. "I suppose you're going to be one of those wrong-headed, right-wing, ultra-conservative Republican candidates?"

Darren grinned slowly, displaying the kind of charm that would undoubtedly carry him a long way on the campaign trail. "If I am, you can bet I'm not going to admit it here and now. I may be a Republican, but I'm not totally stupid."

Phila blinked again and then burst out laughing. Darren joined her. After a second's hesitation, Reed started to chuckle. The chuckle turned into a roar of laughter that filled the room.

When Phila glanced at Nick, she saw that he was smiling to himself, looking quietly pleased.

Eleanor rang for the cheese tray.

Much later that night Phila lay sprawled on Nick's chest, her chin resting on her folded arms. She was feeling delicious and powerful and happy, having just finished duplicating the marvelous sensation she had experienced earlier that day on the beach. Nick threaded his fingers through her hair, his eyes gleaming in the shadows. His skin still glistened with the sweat of their recent lovemaking.

"Did you have fun showing off tonight at the dinner table, foxy lady?" he asked.

"Was I showing off?" She toyed with a lock of his crisp, curling chest hair. "I thought I was just participating in the conversation as required by proper etiquette."

"You had Dad and Darren eating out of the palm of your hand by the end of the evening."

"I think they just like to argue. They get off on it."

"They certainly enjoyed arguing with you."

"Hilary and Vicky and Eleanor weren't so excited about it." Phila squirmed slightly, seeking a more comfortable position.

"They're not sure what to make of you yet. You're a threat. I think they understand that better than Dad and Darren."

Phila frowned. "I'm not a threat."

"Depends on your point of view. Stop wriggling like that. You're going to get me hard again and I'm too old to recuperate that fast Right now I want to talk."

Phila grinned, thoroughly delighted that she could make him react to her so quickly. "What do you want to talk about?"

"I have to go down to California for a couple of days."

"California." Phila stopped grinning. "Why?"

"I've got a business to run in Santa Barbara, remember? I've left a good man in charge, but there are some things only the boss can handle. I won't be gone long."

"Oh." It was funny how fast you could get used to having someone around, Phila thought bleakly. The little beach house was going to seem quite lonely without Nick.

"You sound disappointed," Nick said.

"Don't look so thrilled with yourself."

"Going to miss me?"

"Yes," Phila admitted starkly.

"Good. Now you can start wriggling again."

"She's a lot different from Crissie Masters, isn't she?" Darren observed as he came out of the bathroom. He was wearing only the bottom half of a pair of black silk pajamas. "Remember how Crissie used to raise everyone's hackles?"

"I remember." Victoria lay back against the pillows and studied her husband. "But I think Phila's a lot more dangerous than Crissie was."

"Why the hell do you say that?" Darren turned off the light and climbed into bed beside Victoria. He did not reach for her. Instead he folded his arms behind his head and stared up at the ceiling.

"It was easy to tell what Crissie was after. She wanted to cause trouble, to punish this family for abandoning her all those years ago. She wanted to make certain we all paid for what she had been through. Remember how she taunted all of us every chance she got? But I can't tell what Phila wants."

"I don't know what Phila wants, either, but I'll tell you one thing: Nick wants her. Bad."

"You mean he wants those shares. Nick's up to something," Victoria said quietly. "Eleanor thinks he'll get those shares back for us, but I wonder. Do you think he'd have the gall to seduce Phila into giving those shares to him instead of convincing her to give them back to you?"

"Nick's never been short of nerve."

Victoria was horrified. "For God's sake, Darren, we can't let him do that. Those are *Castleton* shares. They belong to us, and Nick knows that. Eleanor only called on him for help because she trusted him to do the right thing. She trusted him to get the shares back for *us*."

"Even if he were planning to have Phila turn the shares over to him instead of us, you're assuming he can get her to do it. You can't be sure he can manage that. Phila strikes me as a woman who has a mind of her own."

"Why else would he be sleeping with her unless he was seducing her into handing over the shares?" Victoria was impatient with Darren's lack of common sense. "Phila is not his type at all."

"You think Hilary is more his type?" Darren inquired.

"In a way, yes. Oh, maybe temperamentally they're not perfectly suited and God knows I'll never be fond of the woman, but you have to admit she's got breeding and background and poise and all the things Nick should have in a wife. You wouldn't catch Hilary dropping a stalk of asparagus on the dining table in the middle of an argument."

Darren grinned in the darkness. "No, probably not."

"Darren," Victoria said after a moment's thought, "if Nick did get those shares from Phila and if he used them together with the ones he inherited from his mother and his own block, would he have enough to take control of the company away from Hilary?"

Darren hesitated. "He'd need another large block."

"Reed's?"

"That would do it. Or mine together with yours."

"Nick will never get his hands on Reed's block," Victoria said with certainty. "Reed would never back him in a move to unseat Hilary. Not after what he thinks Nick did to her three years ago."

"What he thinks Nick did? You mean you don't believe the baby was Nick's?"

Victoria bit her lip, wishing she had not spoken. "Never mind. It doesn't matter now what happened. No point dredging up old news. It's the future we've got to think about. I'm worried, Darren. Your political chances depend on having the families back you both financially and by freeing you to run for office. Hilary's willing to do that on the Lightfoot side. Eleanor says we need her support."

"I know."

"You heard Nick tonight. He has the same attitude toward your going into politics that he had three years ago."

"I realize that."

"If you're going to make a successful run for governor, you've got to have the backing of C&L's chief executive officer. No, as much as I hate to admit it, Eleanor's right when she says we need Hilary in charge of the Lightfoot side of Castleton & Lightfoot. We have to support her."

"You're always so clear sighted and rational when we discuss my political future, Vicky. Sometimes I get the feeling my future is more important to you than it is to me."

Victoria caught her breath. "That's a terrible thing to say."

"Tell me something. I've always wondered how much my father offered you to stay with me three years ago when you were getting ready to file for divorce."

Victoria closed her eyes in silent anguish. They had been through this before. Twice. Once in the beginning and later when Crissie Masters had dredged it all back up again. "He didn't pay me a dime. I told you that three years ago and I told you that last year when Crissie found out about it from Burke and taunted you about it."

"Oh, come off it. You had an appointment with a lawyer three years ago. Something changed your mind. Dad always claimed he bought your loyalty. I figured he must have promised you a lot to compensate you for the trouble of being a politician's wife and your role as mother of his grandson. He had no intention of letting you walk off with Jordan. Dad must have made it worth your while."

"Stop it, Darren. I stayed because I wanted to be with you. I've told you that. Didn't I grovel enough the day I told you I wasn't going to get a divorce?"

"I just want to know what Dad promised you. A fortune in his will?"

"If he did, then the joke's on me," Victoria said bitterly. "Because he didn't leave anything extra to me, did he?"

"Maybe Crissie got what he had planned to leave to you. Crissie threw everyone's plans into the wringer."

"And Burke loved it. He loved watching her effect on all of us."

Darren exhaled heavily. "Nothing's been the same since she arrived last year."

"It wasn't Crissie who started changing things for all of us," Victoria muttered. "The real changes began three years ago when Nick left."

"Let's drop it. I'm sorry I brought up the subject."

"Not nearly as sorry as I am."

Darren sighed. "You know," he said softly, "when Reed laughed at Phila tonight, I realized it was the first time he's really laughed during the past three years."

"I know. God, I wish we knew what Nick was up to. Maybe Eleanor was wrong to bring him into this situation."

"She should have thought about the possible consequences before she called him."

"One's thing's for certain. We can't let Nick take control from Hilary," Victoria declared.

"It could complicate things. On the other hand . . ."

"No." Victoria stared at the ceiling. "It will ruin everything. Eleanor says we need Hilary at the helm while your career is getting started. Maybe sometime in the future Nick can come back, but not yet."

"The trouble with Nick is that he tends to make his own decisions in his own time and he doesn't always bother to inform everyone else until it's too late to stop him."

Eleanor sipped her late-night glass of sherry and stared out into the darkness. Too late she was beginning to wonder if she had made a serious mistake in bringing Nick back into the picture. She had realized as she watched him at dinner tonight that she was no longer certain she could depend on him to do exactly what she had wanted him to do.

She had pleaded with him to get the shares back from the little nobody to whom Crissie had left them, and Eleanor did not doubt that Nick would do exactly that. He would get them back. After all, he was family and he could work magic when it came to business. He had more of a talent for it than either his father or Reed or Darren.

But she was old enough now to know that magic never came cheap. What would this magician take as a fee for getting the shares out of Philadelphia Fox's hands? Perhaps, Eleanor, thought, the Castletons would lose them altogether. Perhaps Nick would get those shares for himself and use them.

She tried to imagine what he would do with them, and every option led back to one crucial point: Nick would have to get rid of Hilary if he came back to stay. The two of them could not coexist for long. The tensions between them were too violent.

But Nick would need more than the shares Phila now held if he wanted to wrest back control of the firm.

Eleanor knew she had to face the fact that if Nick succeeded in regaining control of C&L from Hilary, Darren's chances for a successful start in politics were going to be dimmed severely. Nick showed no indications of being enthusiastic about a gubernatorial campaign for Darren, and it would take combined family money to win an election. Money and the freedom to campaign actively.

Nothing must get in Darren's way.

"He's more of a man than you ever were, Burke, even though you could never admit it. But that's probably one of the reasons you were always so hard on him, always baiting him. You saw him as competition, didn't you? One of these days he'll have more power than you ever dreamed of having. He's going to be the next governor of this state."

Eleanor turned away from the window and gazed around the Federal-style bedroom with its fine old dressing table, high-post bedstead, and dimity hangings. She was so much happier here in this room these days. She had moved all Burke's things out, claiming it saddened her to be reminded of him. Everyone had accepted that explanation without questioning it.

But the truth was, she had experienced an enormous sense of relief the day Burke died. She had felt freed at last.

She was far from free, however. She knew that now. None of them was free.

"Did you plan it this way, Burke? You'd be happy if you knew that we're all still paying for your cruel games. I should have known you'd find a way to reach beyond the grave to hurt us."

She could envision him laughing as he watched those he had left behind struggle with the results of the disasters he had set in motion. Some people were destined to go through life wrecking the happiness of others. Burke Castleton had been an expert at doing exactly that, and his bastard daughter had inherited his talent.

But Darren was different. Darren was her son. He had inherited his father's looks and charm but not his callousness.

Eleanor's fingers tightened around the sherry glass. She refused to contemplate failure. She would not let her dead husband ruin her son's future.

"Did you enjoy the evening, Reed?" Hilary asked casually as she climbed the stairs ahead of her husband.

"Sure. Eleanor always puts on a good feed. If she weren't so hung up on proper wineglasses and forks we'd probably all enjoy ourselves more, but what the hell. The halibut was good." He tugged at his tie, amazed at how automatically he concealed his true feelings from Hilary these days. It was almost instinctive.

"Phila is an amusing character at times, isn't she?"

"She'll give Nick a run for his money, that's for sure."

"Did she really remind you of Nora?"

Reed wondered where all this was leading. He grew even more cautious. "Just once with that little lecture on charitable contributions. Nora was always after the rest of us to spread the money around a little. She used to quote the same bit about it being like manure, as I re-call."

"You know most charities are scams," Hilary said as she rounded the corner at the top of the stairs. "One has to be so careful. Much more effective to donate money to the conservative organizations and politi-cians who are working to keep the country on the right path. In the long run, everyone benefits that way, rich and poor alike."

"Goddamn right."

"Nick certainly seems taken with Phila."

"You can never tell with Nick," Reed heard himself say carefully.

"I know." Hilary walked into her room. "We all learned that the hard way three years ago, didn't we? Good night, Reed." She smiled wistfully before she closed the door.

Reed stood staring at the closed door for a long moment before moving slowly off down the hall to his bedroom. He walked inside and shut his own door. His gaze caught on the carved maple bed. He tried to visualize Hilary in that bed, her beautiful red hair cascading around her breasts, her fine body stretched out languorously beneath the sheets.

It was impossible. No matter how hard he worked at it, he could not summon up an image of Hilary in his bed. Nora was the only woman who had looked at home there.

In spite of everything, Reed realized he was glad that Nick was finding some happiness and satisfaction with Philadelphia Fox. Nora would have wanted her son to be happy.

# 11

❧

The revolver roared, the noise penetrating even the thick headgear Phila wore over her ears. The heavy gun jumped in her hand, and she struggled to bring it back in line with the target.

"Take it easy, Phila."

"What?" Phila shouted in return, squinting at the paper target in the distance to try and see if she had come remotely close.

"You're doing everything too fast. Slow down. This isn't a quick-draw contest."

"What?"

"I said," Nick repeated, lifting the muff-shaped headgear away from her ears, "this isn't a quick-draw contest. You want the whole operation to be smooth and easy. Try doing it in slow motion."

"I don't think I like this gun."

"You don't like guns, in general, so you're hardly a good judge."

"Why can't I practice with my own gun?"

"Because for someone who doesn't really like guns, someone like you who won't ever want to practice, a revolver is a much better option than an automatic. I've already explained that. You'd have to fire hundreds of rounds with your 9-mm to break it in and to get yourself familiar with it. Somehow I don't see you being willing to do that."

"This thing's hard to load."

"Stop bitching. You'll get used to it. Even if it is a little more awkward to load, a revolver is a lot less complicated to use. For your purposes you want something simple and direct, not fancy. Trust me, Phila, you're better off with a .38 than your 9-mm."

"This sucker's heavy. My arm's getting tired, and my hand is sore from pulling the trigger so many times."

Nick gave her an exasperated look. "You've been complaining since we got here this morning. Close your mouth and reload your gun, lady."

"You're getting impatient with me, Nick." She fumbled with the ammunition, feeling like some desperado in an old-time western movie. "You'll make me nervous if you start yelling."

"It was your idea to carry a gun. I'll be damned if I'll have you running around with something you can't handle. If you're going to keep a gun beside your bed, you're sure as hell going to know how to use it. That's final."

"You're starting to raise your voice, Nick."

"That's not all I'm going to do if you don't start paying attention. All right, step up to the firing line and for God's sake, try to remember what I just told you. Easy does it."

"Must be something about guns that brings out the macho in men, huh? Is that why you're talking so tough this morning?"

"Another five minutes and I won't be talking tough. I will be acting tough. Be interesting to see if that approach works any better." Nick shoved the muffs back down over her ears.

Phila groaned, took her stance and brought the revolver up with what she thought was a smooth, sweeping motion. She snapped off two shots in the general direction of the target and lowered the gun.

"Not bad," Tec said loudly behind her. "She's got a tendency to pull to the right and she's still trying to get the shot off too fast, but she's starting to hit the paper."

Phila removed the muffs and smiled loftily. "Why thank you, General Sherman. So kind of you to pass along some encouraging words to the troops. If I paid too much attention to Nick, I'd get very depressed. He hasn't said one nice thing to me all morning."

"Nick," said Nick, "is taking this seriously and you'd better do the same, Phila. Try it again."

Phila ignored him for a moment, eyeing Tec's orange-and-pink aloha shirt with some envy. "Nice shirt, General."

Tec beamed. "Thought you might like it."

"Get your little ass over to the firing line, Phila," ordered Nick, "or I will drag it over there, myself."

"Sheesh. What a way to spend a perfectly good morning." Phila grumbled and went through the motions once more. She didn't hear the Mercedes arrive but when she finished firing several more rounds and glanced around for approval, she saw that Reed had driven down from the house to join them at the outdoor firing range.

"She's rushing it," Reed announced as he strolled over to the small group near the firing line. "Just like she rushes her backswing."

"I know." Nick handed Phila more ammunition. "I'm working on the problem."

"I don't need any more of an audience," Phila said, annoyed. "It's hard enough doing this with Nick and Tec glaring at me."

"Why *are* you doing it, Phila?" Reed asked in a conversational tone as he picked up a .357 Magnum Tec had brought along. "It's fairly obvious you don't think much of handguns and you don't seem to approve of individuals owning them. Why are you so goddamned bent on carrying one?"

"I have my reasons," Phila muttered, not wanting to go into the whole story for the benefit of Reed and Tec.

"She had some trouble a while back with one of the operators of a foster home," Nick explained as he unpacked more ammunition. "The guy jumped her with a gun, roughed her up a bit and landed in jail. He made some threats about what he was going to do when he got out."

"Holy shit," said Tec, looking both reverent and awed. "Were you hurt?"

"No, just shaken up. The police arrived in the nick of time." Phila concentrated on the targets in the distance.

Reed frowned at Phila. "But the creep threatened to come after you when he got out of prison?"

"I know it sounds melodramatic," Phila said, examining the heavy weapon in her hand, "but the fact is, I'm scared of Elijah Spalding."

Reed looked at Nick over Phila's head. "Have you checked into this?"

"Not yet," Nick said. "But I intend to. All right, Phila, try it again and this time make it very slow and very smooth, understand?"

She stared at him, alarmed. "What do you mean, you're going to check into it? What's to check into?"

"Never mind. Stop arguing and for once in your life try following orders."

"I never follow orders if I can help it," Phila announced with fine hauteur.

"You'll learn," Nick replied, unconcerned.

"Who knows?" Tec added. "You might even get used to it."

"Not a chance," Phila retorted. "Antiauthoritarian, ultra-liberal, anarchistic tendencies are bred in my bones. Just ask Reed here."

"With all three of us yelling at her," Reed said equably, "she'll learn to follow a few orders."

"Make that four," Darren drawled as he strolled up to join the crowd. Phila surveyed the small circle of determined male faces and knew she was outnumbered. Feeling mutinous but temporarily subdued, she turned back toward the target.

It was an odd sensation to have all these people hovering over her, concerned with making certain she got this gun business right, she reflected as she lifted the .38.

It had been a very long time since anyone had worried about her personal safety and even longer since anyone had felt obliged to ensure it by teaching her how to take care of herself.

It made no sense, but for the first time since Crissie's death Phila didn't feel quite so alone in the world.

Nick arrived in Seattle at four o'clock that afternoon. The trip was another calculated risk, he acknowledged as he parked his Porsche in one of the company lots. But this whole project was dependent on a series of such risks. He had to keep things teetering on the brink until he was ready to send a few of them over the edge.

He turned off the engine and sat for a moment behind the wheel, examining the jumble of plain two- and three-story buildings that comprised the headquarters of Castleton & Lightfoot, Inc.

The company had grown in rapid spurts during the early years. Reed and Burke had paid scant attention to such niceties as coordinated office and manufacturing plant design. Business was booming and they'd had no time for frills.

They had acquired building space in the south end of Seattle and as needed erected the cheapest, most efficient structures they could find. The parking lots were scattered willy-nilly around the buildings. At some point in the distant past someone had planted a few scraggly bushes near the doorways in a futile attempt to soften the no-nonsense surroundings.

There was nothing about the Castleton & Lightfoot headquarters that would win any industrial-design awards, but that wasn't nearly as important to the work force as the fact that there had never been any layoffs in the entire history of the company. Jobs had been steady, even during the worst periods of the notoriously cyclical aerospace boom-and-bust industry.

The company had managed to tread water during the bad times and bounce back as strong as ever when the economy picked up again. Avoiding mass layoffs was just another Castleton & Lightfoot tradition.

There was no denying that C&L had done phenomenally well during the initial growth period when Reed and Burke had been at the helm. But for the past several years things had become comfortably staid as far as Nick was concerned. The company was set in its ways; it no longer responded quickly to the promise of new markets. Competitors nipped at its heels. When Nick had been given the CEO mandate, he'd immediately started making some changes.

He had contracted several relationships with new suppliers whose operations were more modern than some of the older companies C&L had always used. He had begun to expand the overseas markets, with a special emphasis on Pacific Rim countries. And he had started to expand product development so that it would be less necessary for C&L to depend on government contracts.

That was the area where he had found himself going toe-to-toe with both his father and Burke Castleton. They liked doing business the old-fashioned way, which meant the government way.

Nick felt strongly that sophisticated electronics and instrumentation had as many uses in industry and the home as they did in military hardware. To Reed and Burke the nongovernment market niches were afterthoughts, nothing more than casual sidelines in which Castleton & Lightfoot occasionally dabbled.

But Nick had seen the future of the company in those niches and had focused an increasing amount of Castleton & Lightfoot resources toward developing them. Darren had been receptive to the new ideas, but Nick had been forced to fight his father and Burke Castleton all the way.

It occurred to Nick as he parked the Porsche that if he'd had Phila on his side in those days when he'd been battling his father and Burke, he would probably have won the war.

He smiled briefly as he got out of the Porsche. It was obvious that once Phila gave her friendship or her love, she was fiercely loyal. She would have backed her husband to the hilt, unlike Hilary who had undermined Nick's position every chance she got. Nick had made few mistakes in his life, but he readily admitted that marrying Hilary had been a costly one.

He walked across the wide parking lot, cutting between rows of cars until he was on the sidewalk that led to the building that housed the corporate offices. He pushed open the glass doors and looked around with a sensation of possessiveness he could never quite suppress. It had been three years since he had walked into this lobby, but the feeling that he had a right to be here, that this was where he belonged, had never wavered during that time.

Over the years he had done everything in this business from emptying the wastebaskets to negotiating multimillion-dollar contracts. He knew C&L from the ground up, and half of it was his.

The Lightfoot portion of Castleton & Lightfoot constituted his rightful inheritance. Three years ago he had told himself to forget that inheritance, but he knew now as he walked through the front door again that one of these days he was going to reclaim it.

The receptionist at the front desk was new, thin and terrifyingly young. She looked as if she had done her apprenticeship behind a cosmetics counter—nothing but perfect skin, perfect hair, perfect makeup.

The nameplate read Rita Duckett. Nick wondered what had happened to Miss Oxberry, who had been thirty years older, gray haired and capable of fending off an entire battalion of nosy government bureaucrats.

"May I help you, sir?" Miss Duckett inquired with a smile that suggested Nick was probably in the wrong building.

"I'm Nick Lightfoot, and I'm going upstairs to the CEO's office."

Miss Duckett frowned over the name. "I'm sorry, sir, but Mrs. Lightfoot is not here. She's on vacation for a few weeks. I'm afraid her assistant, Mr. Vellacott, has already left for the day. You said your name was Lightfoot?"

"That's right. And you don't have to worry about my going upstairs. The office is mine. I just haven't been using it for a while." He headed for the elevators.

Miss Duckett leapt to her feet. "Mr. Lightfoot, wait a minute. I can't let you just barge upstairs."

Nick spotted the guard who was ambling forward to see what the fuss was about. "Hello, Boyd. How are the wife and kids?"

The guard's leathery face creased first in surprise and then in a wide grin. "Mr. Lightfoot. Good to see you again, sir. Been a long time."

"I know." Nick stepped into the waiting elevator. "Please tell Miss Duckett I belong here. She's a little nervous."

"Oh, sure. I'll let her know. She's new. You coming back to work here again, Mr. Lightfoot?"

"Soon," Nick promised as the elevator doors closed. "Very soon."

He stepped out of the elevator on the second floor and found himself facing another woman seated behind a desk. But this face was familiar.

"Mr. Lightfoot! So good to see you again, sir."

"Hello, Mrs. Gilford. How are you doing these days?"

"Just fine, just fine. But we've missed you around here, sir. Are you here to see your, uh, wife...I mean Mr. Lightfoot's wife?" Mrs. Gilford's competent, middle-aged face flushed with embarrassment. "I mean, are you here to see Mrs. Lightfoot?" she finally got out.

"It's confusing, isn't it?" Nick said. "The answer is no."

"Oh, good. Because she, I mean they, I mean everyone's at the place on the coast. Port Claxton, you know." She flushed a darker red. "Good grief, listen to me, as if you don't know where Port Claxton is."

"Don't worry about it, Mrs. Gilford," Nick said gently. "I'm here to do a little work while the families are off enjoying a hard-earned vacation."

"Work?" She stared at him in confusion. "You're coming back to work here at Castleton & Lightfoot?"

"That's right, Mrs. Gilford."

She smiled broadly. "That's wonderful, sir. But what about Mrs. Lightfoot? Excuse me, I didn't mean to pry. I was just wondering if there had been an official change in duties?"

"The change will occur officially in August at the annual meeting. But I thought I'd come in today and look things over. Sort of get the feel of the place again, if you know what I mean."

"Certainly, sir. Go right on in. If you have any questions, I might be able to contact Mr. Vellacott and have him return to the office. He left a little early but I'm sure I can reach him."

"Don't bother, Mrs. Gilford. I won't be needing Vellacott."

"Fine, sir. Uh, Mrs. Lightfoot has made a few changes in the office," Mrs. Gilford added on a note of warning.

"I'm not surprised."

Nor was he, but Nick winced anyway when he opened the door of the inner office. This had been his private kingdom when he had been the chief executive officer of Castleton & Lightfoot. The style he had maintained it in had been in keeping with the rest of the firm's physical plant: functional, unfussy and austere.

Now it was filled with exotic plants, lustrously polished Queen Anne–style furniture and an Oriental carpet on the floor. Hilary had moved right in and made herself at home. Probably with Eleanor's expert help.

Nick walked slowly around the office, opening desk drawers and examining the paintings on the wall. As far as he could tell, there was not a single Northwest artist represented in the collection of muted abstract works. Hilary had never really liked the Northwest, much less its art.

Nick paused beside the walnut desk, frowning at its delicate lines and curved, mincing little legs. Then he leaned forward and punched the button on the intercom. Time for another calculated risk.

"Mrs. Gilford, would you please bring me the Traynor file?"

"Certainly, sir. Just a minute."

Nick sat down at the desk and waited. Time passed.

Five minutes later, Mrs. Gilford's voice came over the intercom. She sounded worried. "I'm sorry, Mr. Lightfoot. Did you say Traynor?"

"That's right." He spelled it out for her, but he was already accepting the fact that this particular shot in the dark was not going to pan out. Hardly surprising. That would have been a little too easy.

"I can't seem to locate a file with that name on it. I'll take another look. Perhaps it's been misplaced."

"Don't worry about it, Mrs. Gilford. I think I know where it is."

"Very well, sir. Let me know if you want me to initiate a search."

"Thanks." He sat back and surveyed the room. Hilary had hung a subtly colored painting done in shades of mauve over the old wall safe. His father had always kept a portrait of a springer spaniel there. When Nick had moved in, he had left the spaniel in place. Something about the patient, mournful gaze had amused him.

He got up, went over to the painting and lifted it down from the wall. If Hilary had changed the combination on the safe, he would have to call in a professional locksmith. That would take time, but he didn't have much choice. He tried the old combination on the off chance that she had left it alone. Funny how he could still remember the numbers after three years.

The safe did not yield. Nick was about to get out the phone book to find a locksmith, when it occurred to him that Hilary had no talent for memorizing numbers. You couldn't help learning a few things about someone when you lived with her for eighteen months. Hilary could not even remember a telephone number. She always wrote down addresses, phone numbers and bank-card codes. She was very meticulous about that kind of thing.

Nick started going through the small drawers of the old desk, looking for a string of digits that might have been jotted down in a convenient location. Eventually he gave up on the desk and tried other places in the room. He finally got around to turning over the abstract painting that had covered the wall safe. He found the combination neatly lettered in Hilary's precise handwriting on the back. Very convenient.

Three minutes later he reached inside the safe and removed two thin files. Neither of them carried labels, but it did not take long to figure out which one was the Traynor file.

There was probably little new to be learned from the file, but the fact that it even existed confirmed what Nick had already concluded. The rumors he'd picked up in California had been true. Hilary was working a deal with Traynor. C&L was about to be slowly and quietly drawn and quartered. By the time the families realized what was happening, it would be too late.

Half an hour later Nick put the files back in the wall safe and re-hung the painting. He had been right, there wasn't much in the folder that was new but it had made fascinating reading, nevertheless.

He shook his head as he stepped back to be certain the painting was hung straight. He knew, because Eleanor had assured him of the fact, that Hilary had great taste. But there was no way he was ever going to learn to like mauve. He thought of Philadelphia in her bright plumage and smiled. Then he turned and walked out the door.

"Mrs. Gilford, I have one other project for you this afternoon."

"Of course."

"Would you contact whatever newspaper is published in Holloway and see if they've got anything in their files on the conviction or sentencing of an Elijah Spalding?"

Mrs. Gilford frowned as she jotted down the name. "Spalding?"

"That's right."

"I believe there's a Holloway in eastern Washington; is that the town you mean?"

"Yeah. If you turn up anything, see if they'll fax us a copy of the article. Thank you, Mrs. Gilford."

"Not at all." She smiled expectantly. "Will you be back on a permanent basis soon, Mr. Lightfoot?" Mrs. Gilford asked.

"Soon," Nick promised.

Out in the parking lot, he eased the Porsche from its slot and headed downtown. The cluster of high-rise buildings that dominated Seattle's central business area stretched upward into a cloudless July sky.

Elliott Bay looked like a blue mirror on which someone had artfully arranged a variety of long cargo ships and bright white ferryboats. There were very few pleasure craft on this part of the bay, however. This was a working port, and there was little room for frivolous vessels. The yachts and sailing boats stuck to Lake Union or Lake Washington or ventured out into Puget Sound to go island-hopping.

Nick took 99 into town, traveling the elevated viaduct along the waterfront. He glanced down once and saw the ferry from Bainbridge Island docking. The sight gave him an odd feeling. Bainbridge was where the Castletons and Lightfoots had built their main residences.

Nick turned off the viaduct on Seneca Street. He went left on First Avenue and drove past Pike Place Market to a concrete-and-glass condominium building that overlooked the bay.

He hadn't been in the condo for three years. On occasion he'd toyed with the idea of renting it out or even selling it, but he had always changed his mind at the last minute. Instead, he'd kept paying a cleaning and maintenance service to keep it in good condition even though he had not been certain until recently that he would ever come back to it.

Set near the year-round street fair that was the Market and equipped with a wall-to-wall view of Elliott Bay and the Olympics, the condo had been the one place he could be sure of being alone when he wished. Hilary hadn't liked the place. She preferred the Bainbridge Island home.

Even though she had not cared for downtown living, Hilary had managed to leave her mark on the condo. He had brought her here in the early days of their marriage, hoping that being away from the family home might help solve their problems.

No problems had been solved, but Hilary had immediately dedicated herself to redecorating the condo, and Nick walked in the door now to find things exactly as she had left them. The rooms were filled with dark mahogany, pine and walnut furnishings that could have come straight out of a New England colonial home.

Lightfoots, Nick reflected, appeared to be doomed to live in the past even though their business was strictly high-tech.

As he poured himself a glass of scotch from the bottle he'd left behind three years ago, Nick speculated idly on what Phila would do with the condo if she were given free rein. He'd probably wind up with fuschia walls and a lime-green carpet. He grinned at the thought.

The phone rang just as he was wondering where in the Market he would go for dinner.

"Mr. Lightfoot, I'm glad I caught you. We just got the article from the *Holloway Reporter*," Mrs. Gilford announced. "Will there be anything else?"

"No, thanks, Mrs. Gilford. You've been a great help. I'll pick up the fax sheet in the morning before I leave town."

His father had been right. It was time he checked into the story surrounding the trial that had put Elijah Spalding in jail. Nick realized he was beginning to feel a strong sense of responsibility toward one Philadelphia Fox.

On the morning after Nick had left to fly down to Santa Barbara, Phila found a pay phone at a gas station on the outskirts of Port Claxton. Her conversation was brief, and after she replaced the receiver she stood for a moment watching the gas-station attendant wash the windows of her car.

The words of Nick's secretary at Lightfoot Consulting Services in Santa Barbara rang in her ears.

"I'm sorry, but Mr. Lightfoot is not in the office and is not expected for some time. He's on vacation. Mr. Plummer is in charge. He'll be glad to talk to you. Whom shall I say is calling?"

Phila's response had been short and to the point. "Nobody."

She studied the gas-station attendant more closely as she stood mulling over what she had just learned. The grizzled, middle-aged man was on the scrawny side. He was wearing grease-stained coveralls and a cap that looked as if it had been run over by a car. He appeared to have made a career out of this line of work. Phila eased away from the pay phone and started toward her car.

So Nick had not flown down to California, or if he had, he hadn't bothered to check in with his office. That was nothing short of upsetting—even alarming—given the fact that he had said he was going down there on business.

No matter how you looked at it, Nick had lied to her.

She did not know precisely what had made her call. She had told herself she certainly was not checking up on him, but when you got right down to it that was just what she had done. She'd checked up, and Nick had not checked out. She wished she knew what to do with the unsettling information.

"Thanks for doing the windows," Phila said to the attendant as she climbed into the car. There was a twinge in her shoulder as she got behind the wheel. That heavy, ugly revolver she had been forced to practice with for two solid hours under the watchful eyes of Nick, his father, Darren and Tec Sherman yesterday had made itself felt. Her arms and shoulders were aching as if she'd been doing a lot of push-ups. She wrinkled her nose as she recalled that she was scheduled for another workout with Tec later in the afternoon.

"You're that lady who's stayin' out at the old Gilmarten place, ain't ya? The one who's shacked up—I mean, the one's who's here with Nick Lightfoot?" The attendant peered at Phila as he took the cash from her hand.

"Yes, I am staying at the Gilmarten place," Phila confirmed with a well-chilled smile. Small towns were all the same. Everyone felt a proprietorial interest in everyone else's business. "No, I am not with Nick Lightfoot. I am on my own."

The attendant did not seem to understand that he was displaying bad manners. He just looked puzzled. "But he's stayin' there with you, ain't he? I heard you and him were there together. Everyone wondered when he'd come back. Can't blame him for staying away so long, though. Not after his wife up and married his father. Kinda weird, you know? Maybe Nick thought it'd be easier to come back if he had another woman in tow. A man's got his pride."

Phila refused to respond to that. She turned on the compact's ignition and whipped the steering wheel to the right. Without more than a cursory glance to the left, she swung the little red car out onto the main street and headed back toward the Gilmarten place. The two-lane highway that followed the beach was clogged with campers, trailers and motor homes.

Nick had his pride, all right. Phila did not doubt that for a moment.

But somehow she did not think he would need to have a "woman in tow" before he felt he could face the families again.

He might, however, find a certain woman—one Philadelphia Fox, for example—extremely useful as a means of regaining a toehold in Castleton & Lightfoot.

Damn it, why had he lied to her about going to Santa Barbara? That hurt. But more importantly, it made no sense. Nick Lightfoot sometimes moved in mysterious ways. Dangerous ways.

She was pulling into the Gilmarten drive when she saw Tec Sherman coming toward her in the open jeep he used for running around. He peered out at her from under the brim of a fatigue cap. Today's aloha shirt was lavender, yellow and black. She had to admit that, obnoxious as he could be at times, the man did have excellent taste in clothes.

"Been lookin' for you, Phila," Tec called from the jeep. "Mrs. Castleton wants to see you. Can you come up to the house for a few minutes?"

"I suppose so. What does she want?"

"Damned if I know. Don't forget we have another session at the range scheduled today."

"You know, it had just about slipped my mind, Tec."

Tec grinned evilly. "I won't let you forget. Nick'd nail my hide to the nearest barn door if I let you get away without more practice."

"That's just an excuse. The truth is, you like the idea of having me under your thumb, don't you? You like giving me orders. Were you ever a drill sergeant, by any chance?"

"Spent a coupla years at Pendleton," Tec admitted, looking cheerful at the recollection.

"I'll bet you had fun beating up on new recruits."

"No fun in it. Just a job. But teachin' you to shoot straight is gonna be kind of fun, I think. Hop in the jeep. I'll drive you up to the house."

With a groan of resignation, Phila got into the vehicle. "Are you sure you don't know why Eleanor wants to see me?"

"No. But I reckon she'll tell you."

Five minutes later he brought the jeep to a halt in the Castleton drive. "She's around back in her greenhouse."

"Okay. Thanks for the lift. I guess. One never knows around here." A welcoming yip made her turn around, and she groaned in dismay. "Oh, no. The killer dogs."

Cupcake and Fifi came dashing around the side of the house, charging happily toward Phila. They were all over her in an instant, thrusting their noses into her palm and fidgeting with delight over her presence.

"Look at it this way," Tec said, "they make better friends than enemies. Same goes for Castletons and Lightfoots. I'll pick you up at three o'clock for target practice."

"I'll see if I can fit another practice session into my schedule."

But she could tell from the way Tec was grinning that she didn't have any choice. She followed the dogs around to the front portico of the Castleton beach cottage, wondering if her coming meeting with Eleanor Castleton would offer her any more leeway than Tec did.

# 12

❧

"There you are, dear. Do come in. I was just puttering." Eleanor looked up with her slightly distracted air as Phila appeared in the greenhouse doorway.

"This is quite a setup." Phila gazed around in wonder. The greenhouse was warm and humid and redolent of tropical smells. The curiously appealing scent of rich soil underlay the entire medley of odors. Water gurgled in a large aquarium. Phila's nose twitched appreciatively. "I've never been inside a private greenhouse. I think I'd like one of these myself."

Eleanor peered at her from under the brim of her denim gardening cap. She was busy snipping leaves from a plant that had a number of cup-shaped appendages. "You're interested in plants?"

"I like plants and flowers. I'd love to have a place where I could grow them year round." Phila leaned over to examine an oddly shaped red leaf that had a row of spines around its edge. "What is this? Some sort of cactus?"

"No, dear. That's a *Dionaea muscipula*. A Venus's-fly-trap."

Phila, who had been about to touch the unusual leaf, jerked her finger back out of reach. "A carnivorous plant?"

"Yes, dear."

"How interesting. I'm sort of into ivy and philodendron, myself." Phila looked around, frowning as she realized she did not recognize any of the abundant, healthy plant life that filled the greenhouse. "That plant you're pruning, the one with the little cups. What is it?"

"A variety of sarracenia. I'm working on developing a hybrid. Notice the nicely shaped pitchers?"

"Is that a pitcher plant? The kind unsuspecting bugs fall into and can't get back out of?"

Eleanor smiled fondly at the plant under her hands. "Yes, indeed, dear. The pitchers are modified leaves, of course. Quite fascinating to watch the insect discover the nectar and begin feeding on the lip of the leaf."

"I can imagine."

"The silly creature just keeps moving farther and farther into the pitcher until all of a sudden its little feet start sliding on the tiny little hairs inside the leaf. The insect slips and slides, trying to get its feet back under itself and then it reaches the waxy area where there's no footing at all. Before it knows what's happened, the little thing just falls straight down into the bottom of the pitcher."

Phila eyed the innocent-looking plant. "Then what?"

"Why then it gets eaten, dear." Eleanor smiled. "Once inside, it can't escape from the bowl of the pitcher, you see. It's trapped."

"How does the plant digest it?"

"The bottom of the pitcher has a set of special glands that secrete digestive enzymes," Eleanor explained. "A bacterial reaction is produced, too, which aids in the digestion of prey." She glanced around vaguely. "Jordan was playing with that row of sarracenia over there the other day. If you look inside some of the pitchers you might see some bits and pieces of ant chitin at the bottom."

"That's okay, I'm going to have lunch soon." The aquarium caught Phila's attention. "Are those plants in that tank carnivorous, too?"

"Oh, yes. A species of *Utricularia*. The common name is bladder-worts."

"Everything in this greenhouse is carnivorous, isn't it?" Phila looked straight at Eleanor, wondering if she would be insulted by her double meaning.

"Yes, dear. Carnivorous plants are my specialty." Eleanor snipped off another leaf.

Apparently the double entendre had been a bit too subtle. Either that or Eleanor was too much of a lady to rise to the bait. "How long have you been interested in these plants?" Phila asked.

"Let me see, how long has it been now? Over thirty years, I believe. I used to raise orchids before I became fascinated with carnivorous plants."

"Is that right?" Phila decided she'd had enough of the horticultural discussion. "Thank you for dinner last night, Eleanor. I had a very interesting time."

"You're quite welcome. I thought it might be nice for you to have an opportunity to spend an evening with all of us together."

"So I'd understand that I don't fit in with the Lightfoots and Castletons any more than Crissie did? What are you worried about, Eleanor? That I might be entertaining the notion of becoming part of this happy-go-lucky family group?"

Eleanor flinched at the blunt attack, but she rallied quickly. "I'm sure your background is considerably different from ours, just as Miss Masters's was."

"The amusing thing is that if Crissie's father had accepted his responsibilities, Crissie's background would have been exactly the same as Darren's. Makes one stop and think, doesn't it? Raises all sorts of interesting questions on the old subject of heredity versus environment."

Eleanor's pleasantly vague expression hardened as she took visible hold of herself. "I asked you to come here today because I wish to talk quite frankly to you about the shares in your possession."

"That doesn't surprise me. What's your pitch, Eleanor? Hilary tried to buy them back. Vicky cried and tried to put a guilt trip on me by telling me I was stealing her son's inheritance. I'll be interested to hear your approach."

"You're not so different from Crissie Masters, after all, are you? The others are beginning to think you might be, but I can see the truth. I've had a little more experience in detecting it, you see." Eleanor worked the garden shears with a small, violent movement. A handful of leaves cascaded to the table. "Oh, yes, I've seen the way the men in the families are starting to change toward you. Men are so blind, aren't they?"

"Are they, Eleanor?"

"You think you'll soon have them eating out of the palm of your hand, don't you? Reed was laughing at the table last night. Actually laughing. He hasn't done that in a long time. And Nick looks at you in a way he never looked at Hilary. Even Darren found you entertaining last night. Vicky told me this morning that he's not nearly as worried as he should be about you."

"You think your son should be worried?"

"Of course he should be worried. His whole future is in the hands of a hustling little opportunist who's obviously out for the best deal she can get. You're just like Crissie. Just as cruel and vicious as she was."

"If you're going to attack someone, attack me, not Crissie. She's dead, remember?"

The distracted expression vanished from Eleanor's eyes as her head came up sharply. Her gracious accent was taut with controlled fury. "Hilary tried to make an honest bargain with you, Miss Fox, but you turned her down. Vicky tried to reason with you. If you had been a decent person, you would have accepted the money and given back the shares. You did no such thing. You're out to cause pain and destruction, just as Crissie did."

Phila dug her nails into her palms. "This family caused Crissie a lot of pain. Eventually it destroyed her."

"That's not true."

"She's dead, Eleanor, and you're all still alive," Phila pointed out softly. "So don't talk to me about who caused the pain and destruction. The results speak for themselves."

Eleanor stopped clipping leaves. Her eyes were very bright with a mixture of anger and what looked like anguish. "Crissie Masters was cheap and spiteful. She caused trouble from the moment she appeared in our lives, always trying to set one of us against the other. Don't you dare try to make me feel sorry for her. I will never forgive her for what she did while she was here. She had no right to descend on us the way she did. No right at all."

"Crissie was not the one who originally caused the pain," Phila said. "She was another victim of the one who was responsible, just like you. Your husband caused your pain years ago when he had a tacky little one-night stand and got some poor young woman pregnant. Crissie is the result of your husband's indiscriminate womanizing."

"You have no right to talk about my husband that way. Burke Castleton was a fine man. A successful, influential businessman. A credit to his community. His son is going to be the next governor of this state, so you will do well to keep a civil tongue in your head, young woman."

"I'll admit it wasn't particularly charitable of Crissie to come crashing into your lives, but Crissie didn't know much about real charity. You learn things like that by example, Eleanor, and no one ever showed her any warmth or kindness while she was growing up."

"I don't have to listen to this."

"You started it. If you're going to insist on blaming Crissie for all the trauma your husband caused, I'm damn sure going to insist on setting the record straight. Put the blame where it belongs, on the man you married." Phila thought her nails were breaking the skin of her palms, but she was determined to keep a level tone to her voice.

"Stop it. Stop it. Stop it right now, do you hear me? The blame belongs on that cheap little tramp." Eleanor's voice was becoming shrill.

"No, Eleanor," Phila whispered through set teeth. "It belongs on a man who cheated on his wife all those years ago. And I'll tell you something else. If he did it once, chances are he did it several times.

Let's hope for your sake you don't have to deal with any more surprises from the past on your doorstep."

"Shut your foul mouth, you little slut."

"Ah, now I get it. That's the real source of your anguish, isn't it? You know deep down what kind of man your husband really was. I'll bet you knew it back then. You're a smart woman, Eleanor. Too smart not to know what Burke Castleton was like. Was that why you gave up growing orchids and started cultivating carnivorous plants? Is this how you started working out your frustration with a marriage you knew would never become what you wanted it to be?"

"You are a monstrous woman," Eleanor gasped. *"Monstrous."*

"I'm just spelling out a few facts." Phila could feel herself shaking.

"I will not let you talk to me like this." Eleanor gripped the workbench very tightly. "You're nothing but a no-account little whore, and I'm certain Nick realizes it. You've got no looks, no money and no background. Use your head, you fool. If you had any sense you'd see that Nick is only using you for his own ends. How could he possibly be interested in you except for some cheap sex? After all, he was once married to Hilary."

"You think Hilary is more his type?" Phila asked scathingly.

"Hilary is beautiful, well mannered and well bred. Her family goes back to the *Mayflower*. She's everything you're not, and Nick must know that. How can you possibly hope to compete with her?"

"I didn't notice there was a competition going on," Phila got out tightly. "Hilary's married to another man, or have you forgotten? I'm sure she's too much of a *lady* to go after one man when she's wearing another's ring. Besides, Nick doesn't show any signs of being interested in her. Don't get your hopes up about a grand reconciliation between those two, Eleanor. I know you handpicked her for Nick, but that doesn't mean you picked the right woman."

"You don't know anything, do you?" Eleanor's voice was as brittle as glass. "You silly little fool. You have no idea of what you're dealing with here. You're just standing on the outside looking in, trying to stir up trouble. But for your information, you're quite right. Hilary would not go out of her way to get Nick back. Why should she want him back after what he did to her?"

"Just what did he do to her, Eleanor?"

"Vicky said she told you about the baby."

"So what? You think the baby was Nick's?"

"I know the baby was Nick's." Eleanor's eyes had never appeared less vague. *"He raped her.* The next time you go to bed with him think about that, you little whore. You've got a lot of nerve calling my Burke a womanizer when you're sleeping with a man who raped his own wife."

"You don't know what you're talking about."

Eleanor smiled thinly. "Don't I? It's the truth. Nick forced himself on Hilary because he was furious with her for asking for a divorce. She got pregnant and nearly had a nervous breakdown."

"I don't believe you."

"Then you are a very stupid woman, Philadelphia Fox."

"Did Hilary tell you she was raped?"

"Yes, after she realized she had gotten pregnant. She took some tranquilizers and came to see me the next morning. Nick had already left a couple of weeks earlier. Hilary was rambling, almost incoherent. But she told me everything, including how she had been assaulted by Nick before he left. She didn't know what to do. I'm the one who called Reed."

"And Reed did the noble thing, of course?"

Eleanor drew herself up stiffly. "Reed is a good man. A bit rough in his ways still, even after all these years, but he's a good, decent man."

Phila forced herself to think through the swirl of emotions that threatened to blind her. "All right, I'll go along with you on that. I think he is a decent man. But so is Nick. And you know it."

"I don't wish to discuss Nick any further."

"Umm hmmm. Tell me, Eleanor, if you really believed he had treated Hilary so badly, why would you have bothered to keep in touch with him during the past three years?"

Eleanor tossed aside the clippers and picked up a small watering can. "Nick is family. I couldn't just let him be cut off completely," she whispered.

"Especially when you knew in your soul he'd gotten a bum rap?"

"You don't know what you're talking about."

"Maybe. Perhaps I'm being too charitable. I'm assuming that you kept in touch with Nick because you suspected he was innocent, but maybe the real reason was a lot more practical—a lot more mercenary. Did you keep in touch with him because you knew that someday the families would need him back to run Castleton & Lightfoot? Did you want to leave the door open in case you decided to recall him for active duty?"

The spout of the can trembled as Eleanor tried to water a plant. "I do not have to explain my actions to someone of your type."

"Fair enough. I don't have to stand around and explain myself to someone of your type." She turned toward the door.

*"Miss Fox."*

"Yes, Mrs. Castleton?"

"I demand that you tell me what you are going to do with those shares."

"When I decide, I'll be sure to let you know."

"Those shares belong to my son, damn you."

"Crissie had as much right to them as Darren did. She was Burke's daughter, remember?"

"No. No, damn you, no. *She was an outsider.*" Eleanor's eyes filled with tears, and her proud face began to crumple.

Phila went through the door and closed it behind her with shaking hands. Her legs felt weak. When the dogs danced over to greet her, she nearly collapsed beneath their assault.

But there was something very comforting about their cheerful, overflowing affection. Phila sank to the ground and hugged the animals close.

That afternoon on the firing range, Phila concentrated fiercely on Tec's instructions. He seemed to sense that her attitude toward the handgun lessons had undergone a major change. He gave his orders in a crisp, no-nonsense voice, and Phila did exactly as she was told. When she finally succeeded in putting a whole group of shots into the target, he nodded with satisfaction.

"Nick'll be pleased," Tec said. "Let's do it again."

She went through the routine over and over again. Time after time she gripped the revolver as she had been taught, found the trigger with her index finger, brought the weapon up in a sweeping motion and fired. Round after round went into the paper targets. The muffled roar of the .38 and Tec's harsh voice became the only sounds in the world.

"Don't worry about speed. It doesn't do any good to get off the first shot if it's a bad one. Just take it slow and easy for now."

When Tec finally signaled a halt, Phila had to yank herself back to reality. She pulled the hearing muffs off her head and rubbed her temples with thumb and forefinger.

"You're lookin' good," Tec said. "Damn good. Nick'll be real happy with the way you're comin' along."

"We must please Nick at all costs, mustn't we?" Phila said wearily.

Tec looked up from where he was packing away the .38. "Somethin' wrong? You sound kinda funny this afternoon."

"I'm fine, Tec. I think I'll walk back to my place."

"It's a long walk."

"I don't mind."

"I'll drop the .38 off at the Gilmarten place on my way back to the house. I've got a key."

"Thanks. You can leave it in a drawer in the kitchen."

"Right. But move it into your bedroom tonight, huh?"

"Yes, Tec."

Tec straightened and started for the jeep. Then he stopped. "This guy who jumped you. What's he look like?"

"Very big. Huge through the shoulders. Strange blue eyes. The last time I saw him, he had a beard and long hair, but that may be gone now."

"You're sure he didn't hurt you?"

"No, he didn't get the chance. The cops arrived just as he was trying to drag me into his pickup."

"Damn lucky for you."

Phila smiled fleetingly. "Yes. Very lucky. I'll see you later, Tec."

"Hey, you don't have to worry about that bastard, you know," Tec said gruffly. "Nick'll look after you."

"I've been looking after myself for a long time, Tec. I'm pretty good at it."

Hilary poured coffee from the early-nineteenth-century pot and handed a cup to Eleanor. The beautiful coffee service had been a wedding gift to Eleanor and Burke nearly forty years before, she knew. It had descended through Eleanor's family and had been used by generations of her female ancestors.

Hilary wondered if a loveless marriage was also a family tradition. How many of Eleanor's forebears had poured coffee from this lovely Georgian silver pot and secretly wondered if it and all the other things they had were worth the price they had paid?

"She upset you, didn't she?" Hilary asked quietly as she sat back on the sofa, her own cup and saucer in hand.

Eleanor took a fortifying sip of coffee. "She's a very difficult young woman."

"We knew that from the beginning. What did she say to you that disturbed you so much?"

"So many things. She made more of her vile accusations and refused to tell me what she's going to do with the shares."

Hilary sensed there was more to the story than that, but she also sensed this was not the time to find out what it was. "I think we can assume she's going to hand the shares over to Nick or at least vote them the way he tells her to vote them."

Eleanor sighed. "I was so certain Nick would do the right thing. I thought he could convince her to return the shares to us. Nick was always good at business matters. So good at making deals. I never dreamed it was going to get this messy."

"What made you think Nick would do the right thing in this matter when he didn't bother to do the right thing three years ago?"

Eleanor shook her head vaguely and looked away. "This is business. Family business. I thought surely . . ." She let the sentence trail off. "I was wrong."

"You thought that in a pinch he would come through for you? For the sake of the families?" Hilary smiled regretfully. "I know you did what you thought was best, Eleanor. But the net result is to make things infinitely more complicated than they were before you involved Nick."

"I know. I just wish I knew what that Fox woman wants from us."

Hilary looked at her pityingly. "Don't you know yet what Philadelphia Fox wants from us? It's rapidly becoming perfectly clear. She wants exactly what Crissie wanted. To be a part of the families."

Eleanor shuddered. "My God. Do you think she honestly believes she can get Nick to marry her?"

"Why not? Nick is obviously encouraging her to think precisely that." Hilary set her cup and saucer down on the table. "After all, he is sleeping with her."

"That means nothing. I warned her not to put too much stock in that kind of sordid maneuvering. She must realize she's far beneath him and that he's just using her."

"Perhaps. But she may be shrewd enough to put a price tag on those shares before she hands them over to him."

"Marriage being the price tag?" Eleanor shuddered. "Do you think he would pay that price, Hilary? She's such a little nobody."

"He wants those shares very badly," Hilary reasoned. "I think it's possible that, if he can't seduce them out of her, he might marry her for them. After all, he can always divorce her later."

"She'd make him pay heavily for a divorce."

Hilary lifted one shoulder negligently. "Her notion of a large settlement would probably be small change to Nick. He can afford it. Or perhaps I should say Castleton & Lightfoot can afford it."

"What are we going to do, Hilary?" Eleanor asked wearily. "Whatever are we going to do?"

Hilary ran her finger lightly along the delicate carving of the scroll-back sofa. "Nick can't do anything drastic at the annual meeting with just his shares and Phila's. He needs another large block to be able to control things."

"I know. But if he can talk Darren or Reed into going along with him, he could take control of the firm."

"Or you. He could do it if he had your block of shares, Eleanor."

"Don't say such things. I'm hardly likely to back him."

"It would certainly put Darren's future at risk, wouldn't it? If Nick regains control of C&L he's not going to make it easy for your son to go after the governor's mansion. You heard Nick the other night at dinner. He doesn't have any interest in financing a political campaign for Darren."

"No," Eleanor said uneasily. "It's obvious Nick's attitude toward a member of the families going into politics is as negative as it ever was."

"We must make certain no one in either family wavers."

Eleanor shot Hilary a searching look. "Do you think Reed might? He's starting to change toward Nick. I can feel it."

"Reed will do what he knows is right, regardless of how he feels about Nick. He might soften toward his son, but he would never back him to take control of Castleton & Lightfoot. He would never really trust Nick again." Hilary hoped she was right on that count. "But in any event, I think I will make another personal stab at getting the shares back from Phila."

"If she turned down your offer, what makes you think you have any chance of talking her out of them?"

"Crissie used to talk a great deal about Phila. I know more about her than she realizes."

"What's to know about that cheap little hustler?" Eleanor's cup rattled in the saucer. She set it down quickly. "She's just like Crissie."

"No," Hilary said thoughtfully, "she's not just like Crissie. And that's why I may be able to use another tactic."

Phila had intended to go straight back to the cottage from the firing range, but when she passed the path down to the beach, she changed her mind. The beach was empty. The promise of windswept solitude lured her. She started down the path.

She was halfway along the trail through the trees when a familiar yelp alerted her. She glanced back just as Cupcake and Fifi started to bound down the path. Darren Castleton followed more leisurely in their wake.

The dogs crowded around Phila for a moment. She patted them absently, her eyes on Darren. He was watching her with a thoughtful gaze.

"Hello, Phila. Tec said you were walking home from the range. Thought I'd meet you. I wanted to talk to you."

"What about? Or is that a dumb question under the circumstances."

"Not so dumb." He followed her down to the beach, his hands in the pockets of his windbreaker. "I'm not sure myself what I want to say."

Cupcake and Fifi raced to the water's edge and began chasing sea gulls.

"The dogs really love it down here, don't they?" Phila shoved her hands in her jeans pockets. "Look at them. Do they ever catch the gulls?"

"No. But, then, I'm not-sure how hard they really try. It's just a game to them. They're not serious about the hunt right now."

"What happens when they get serious?"

"Then they're dangerous. Just like some people I could mention."

"Is this a veiled warning about Nick's intentions?"

"I take it you've had a lot of such warnings?" Darren smiled and kicked idly at a small shell.

"From just about everyone, including his own father."

"Reed's got his reasons for warning you about Nick."

"Silly reasons."

Darren glanced at her. "What makes you say that?"

"We're talking about Hilary's famous baby, right?"

"So you know about that. You think Nick was right to let his father pick up the pieces after that disaster? Because that's exactly what Nick did. Reed felt obliged to step in and protect Hilary."

"Then he was a fool. Nick is perfectly capable of handling his own disasters. Reed should have known that."

"Wait a second. You do know the baby was Nick's, don't you?"

"I know that's what everyone thinks, including Reed, apparently,"

Darren frowned. "But you don't believe it?"

"Not for a minute."

"Well, I guess your viewpoint is bound to be a little biased. After all, you're having an affair with Nick. You want to believe the best of him."

"He's no angel," Phila muttered, thinking about the phone call to Santa Barbara that morning. "I know that. He's secretive, and I know for a fact he's deliberately misled me in some things. He's also quite mysterious, and I'm not sure how far to trust him when it comes to certain matters. But I do know he wouldn't have let his father step in and take responsibility for the baby if the baby had been his."

"You sound very sure of yourself. Why would Hilary have lied?"

"Good question. Perhaps because the marriage was falling apart and she didn't want to lose everything she'd gained by marrying into Castleton & Lightfoot?"

Darren was silent for a moment. "I thought of that possibility myself, once or twice three years ago," he finally admitted. "But my mother seemed so sure of her. She was convinced Hilary had been abused by Nick and that Reed as well as Castleton & Lightfoot owed her protection. She feels very protective toward her. How much do you know about Hilary?"

"Just the little Crissie told me."

"You can probably discard most of that," Darren said. "I know she was your friend, but Crissie Masters couldn't be trusted an inch."

"I could trust her."

Darren shrugged that aside. "Back to Hilary. Eleanor introduced her to Nick about five years ago. If it wasn't a case of love at first sight, it was definitely a case of satisfaction at first sight. They both seemed to want what the other was offering. Nick was ready to marry, and Hilary was a stunning woman who looked as though she would be a perfect wife for him."

"I know." Phila wrinkled her nose. "Good family background, good looks and lots of old money. The perfect combination. Too bad she didn't love him."

"He thought she did. Or at least he thought the potential for love was there. I don't believe he would have married her otherwise. He had been raised in a loving marriage, and I think he fully expected the same sort of relationship for himself when he married. But you're wrong about one thing. Hilary didn't have a lot of old money."

"No?"

Darren shook his head. "She had the family background, all right, and the looks, but that was about all that was left. She came from an old family that had been living on its expectations for the past couple of generations. Unfortunately, they hadn't produced anyone strong enough to keep the income flowing into the family coffers during the last forty years. They made the classic mistake of dipping into capital. They were on the verge of bankruptcy when Hilary married Nick."

Phila stumbled over a small piece of driftwood. "Did Nick know that?"

"Sure. He's not exactly stupid. At least not when it comes to money."

"Do you think he worried he was being married for his money?"

"Nick's a natural risk-taker. I think he just decided to take the risk in this case. After all, everything else looked good and Hilary certainly appeared to be in love with him."

"And your mother was pushing for the match?"

"Yes. She felt that after Nora died she had a duty to find a proper wife for Nick. She liked Hilary, and her family had known Hilary's family for generations."

Phila frowned. "Did she know Hilary's family was just about broke?"

"She probably did. But she understood that kind of situation. She didn't see it as a negative. Why do you think she married my father?"

"*What?*"

Darren smiled again, briefly. "I'm afraid so. A marriage of convenience, as they used to say. Her family was Southern aristocracy. Bloodlines all the way back to the Colonial era."

"But they were out of money?"

Darren nodded. "They had enough to put up a good front, but basically they were in deep trouble when Burke Castleton went east looking for a proper lady to marry."

"Poor Eleanor!"

"She knew what she was doing. It was expected of her. She may not have had money, but she had a strong sense of family honor and obligation. Who knows? Maybe in the beginning she actually cared for my father. God knows he had a way with women."

"She tolerated nearly forty years of marriage to a man she probably considered beneath her?"

"She did her best to elevate him and the rest of us. She's spent years polishing the image. I think she sees it as her life's work."

"In other words, she fulfilled her part of the bargain. She brought a little class to the Castletons and the Lightfoots." Phila grimaced. "And so it goes. Life among the rich and famous."

"Not that rich and certainly not that famous," Darren said. "Don't act so damn condescending."

"You don't have to lecture me. I'm already feeling bad enough for the way I talked to your mother this morning."

Darren's expression hardened. "What did you say to her?"

"She was accusing Crissie of having caused a lot of pain and anguish. I pointed out that the blame belonged on Burke. He was the one who played around all those years ago. I also pointed out that if he'd played around once, he'd undoubtedly done so many times."

"You said that to my mother?" Darren's voice was grim.

"I'm afraid so."

"You are a real little bitch, aren't you?"

# 13

⁂

A *real little bitch.*

*Just like Crissie.*

The words reverberated through Phila's mind as she fixed herself a salad that evening. They made her feel worn-out and depressed.

Phila took her plate over to the kitchen table and sat down. She'd lost her appetite again, she realized. She really didn't want to eat the salad. She didn't want to eat anything.

There was another storm moving inland. Rain was already striking the windows in big fat drops that sounded like small-weapons fire. She was becoming an expert on that particular sound.

The only thing she was accomplishing here on the coast was causing more trouble, Phila told herself, trying to face the situation clearly.

Crissie was dead. There was nothing to be done about it. There were no questions to ask. She had known that from the beginning. It was time to turn the shares back to their rightful owner and be done with it.

Strange how things had become so painfully clear this afternoon after that conversation with Eleanor. There was no point trying to punish the Castletons and Lightfoots. They had done a fine job of punishing themselves over the years.

On top of everything else, she was a fool to stick around and play dangerous games with Nick Lightfoot. There was no sense kidding herself. Everyone was right. Nick never did anything without a reason. He was using her. She knew it; they all knew it. Phila didn't blame him particularly. After all, she had been using him. But she was suddenly very tired of dealing with the situation.

She knew she had allowed Nick to persuade her to come to Port

Claxton because she had not known what else to do with herself. She had needed a focus for her burned-out emotions. She had needed something to revitalize herself. Creating trouble with the C&L shares had seemed a way to do that for a while. She could pretend she was somehow avenging Crissie. But the more Phila got mired in the quicksand of the emotional politics between the families, the less vengeful she felt.

It was time to call it quits and get out. Phila made her decision as she sat watching the storm come in. She would give the shares back to Darren in the morning, and then she would pack and head for Seattle.

Seattle seemed like a good place to start job hunting, and she had a life to put back together. It was time to get busy on that task.

Nick's Porsche pulled into the cottage drive just as Phila started on her salad. The sound of the powerful engine took her by surprise. She had not expected him back tonight. Slowly she got to her feet as Nick came through the front door. She went to meet him.

"I didn't think you'd get here until tomorrow," Phila said quietly as he set down his luggage.

He looked at her. "I finished my business and decided to come back early." He paused, eying her quizzically. "I think there's something wrong with this scene."

"Is there?"

"Shouldn't you be rushing into my arms? Climbing all over me? Ripping off my clothes?"

"Should I?"

"Oh, Christ. What happened?" He shrugged out of his jacket and tossed it across the nearest chair.

"Not much. I've decided to leave tomorrow, Nick."

He didn't move, but his eyes turned bleak and hard. "Is that right? What are you going to do with the shares?"

Phila turned back toward the kitchen with a humorless smile. "The first and foremost question, of course. What will I do with the shares. Well, you can all stop wondering. I'm going to give them back to Darren. They belong to him."

"For the past few days you've been claiming those shares were Crissie's inheritance." Nick followed her into the kitchen.

"Crissie's dead."

"That's not news. She's been dead for nearly three months."

"I guess I'm finally accepting that fact." Phila sat down at the table again and picked up her fork. "It was hard, you know. I think I was afraid to let go of her. There were times when she was all I had and it was hard to envision a world without her in it."

Nick opened a cupboard and found his bottle of scotch. "You want to tell me what happened while I was gone?"

"Not much, really. I had a talk with Eleanor today, and I felt like a piece of garbage afterward. It jolted me. It also put things into perspective."

"What did you say to her? Or was it something she said to you?" Nick watched her coolly as he poured his scotch.

"I said some nasty things to her. Afterward I felt as though I'd kicked a dog when it was down. She's obviously worked for years on shoring up an image of family unity. It was cruel of me to casually rip it apart."

"What exactly did you say?"

"I reminded her it was her husband who had caused the problem of Crissie."

"A logical deduction."

"But one Eleanor has chosen not to make. She doesn't want to admit that someone in the family, her own husband to be precise, had created the problem. She wanted to blame it all on an outsider. The family must remain inviolate at all costs."

"But you pointed out the truth?"

"A totally useless exercise in reality therapy. She won't ever acknowledge it, and why should she? She's built her life around the families. The image of the Castletons and Lightfoots is more important to her than anything else. What right do I have to mess with her little world?"

"I thought you wanted to avenge Crissie Masters. Represent her interests in the families. What about all that business about Castletons and Lightfoots bearing a moral responsibility for what happened?"

"I realized today that I'm tired of playing Lady Avenger. Crissie's dead and no one's responsible, not even Crissie. She was the victim of cosmic bad luck. The universe is full of it."

"I don't know if I can handle a Philadelphia Fox turned existentialist. I liked you better when you were paranoid about conspiracies."

She looked at him. "I'm glad you're still finding something amusing in all this. You really do enjoy playing your little games, don't you, Nick? You should. You're very good at them."

He scowled at her, swirling the scotch in his glass. "You really are in a hell of a mood, aren't you?"

"You want to talk conspiracies? All right, I'll talk conspiracies. Let's start with you telling me how your trip to Santa Barbara went?"

He winced around a swallow of scotch. "You were the one who called my office down there? Martha said the lady hadn't left her name. I thought it might have been Hilary."

"Maybe we both called," Phila suggested, annoyed.

"No. Martha said only one woman called asking for me by name. Had to be you or Hilary."

"Why did you check in with your Santa Barbara office in the first place? Worried someone might suspect you had lied about your little business jaunt?"

"It was one of the risks involved. Just out of curiosity, what made you suspicious?"

"I don't trust Castletons or Lightfoots any more than they trust me," she said.

"Ah, that's my old Philadelphia."

"I'm glad you find it all so damned funny."

"I went to Seattle, not Santa Barbara."

"Did you?"

"Do you care?" he retorted.

"Not particularly. Not any more. It's your business."

"Damn right." Nick set his glass down on the tiled countertop. "And I intend to get it back in August."

Phila nodded slowly, toying with the salad greens. "Everyone knows you're up to something. People keep warning me you're using me."

Nick leaned back against the counter, his eyes gleaming behind the lenses of his glasses. "What do you think?"

"That they're right, of course. You're using me."

"Any more than you're using me, Phila? You seemed to be having a great time in bed."

"Oh, I was. But the party's over. I'm tired and it's time to go home."

"Where's home? Holloway?"

She shook her head quickly. "No. Not there. Someplace new. Seattle, maybe."

He nodded. "I've got a place you can stay in while you hunt for an apartment and a job. A condo near the Market. You'd love it."

She was floored. "Why would you want to do me any favors? I've told you I'm going to give the shares back to Darren. You don't have to pay me off for returning them."

"I'm not trying to pay you off for them. I'm offering you a bribe so you'll hang on to them until the August meeting."

"Why should I do that?"

"I need them," Nick said softly. "More importantly, I need you."

She experienced a small rush of pleasure that she tried to suppress immediately. "How?"

"I want the others to know you're going to back me at the annual meeting. I want them to think you believe in me."

"I see." She clamped a lid on the surge of disappointment, just as she had damped down the initial hope. "But I think I'm losing this somewhere. Why do you want the families to think I'm going to back you?"

"Because if you continue to do so, there's a fair-to-even chance that the owner of one of the other large share blocks will throw his or her lot in with us."

"And if one of the others does decide to back you?"

Nick smiled slowly. "Then I get my old job back."

"You'll get control of Castleton & Lightfoot again?"

"Yeah. That's the scenario." He poured himself another glass of scotch.

Phila felt chilled. The rain was falling in heavy sheets against the old windows. "What makes you think that my backing you with Crissie's shares will encourage any of the others to do so?"

"You, my sweet, are shaping up as the Good Witch. You're annoying the hell out of the families, but some of the members are starting to think you may have a few good points."

"Such as?"

"Such as the primitive, rather naive qualities of honesty and integrity."

"Even if they do suspect me of having left-wing, antiestablishment tendencies?"

"Yeah. You're putting doubts in their minds about me, Phila. This wasn't quite the way I planned it, but I think things are going to work out. They're all starting to wonder if I really was the bad guy three years ago. I'm hoping that if you spread enough doubt around, it'll act like the manure you lectured us about at Eleanor's dinner. It'll do some good."

"You mean it will benefit you."

"Right."

"Who's the Wicked Witch in this story?"

"One guess."

"Hilary?"

"Yeah."

Phila shook her head. "I don't think I like it. Any of it. I'm tired of being used."

"You don't have much choice," Nick said. The steel core was showing again. "You haven't had any choice since the day you inherited the shares."

"I told you, I'm out of the vengeance business. If you're trying to get back at Hilary because she let everyone think you walked out on her and the baby three years ago, then you can do it on your own. You're a big boy. I want to get on with my own life." Phila looked down at the salad. She was never going to be able to eat it. She stood up and carried her dishes over to the sink.

Nick put out his hand and caught hold of her wrist. His eyes were the color of the rain outside. "I think we need to discuss this a little further."

"No. I've made up my mind. I'm leaving tomorrow."

"I want you to support me or at least pretend to support me until the August meeting."

"Why should I? What's in it for me?" Phila asked, suddenly feeling truly angry.

Nick stared at her for a long, considering moment. "What do you want out of it?"

She exhaled heavily. "Nothing. I can't think of anything I want from a Lightfoot, so I guess that means no deal."

"Phila, I need your help."

"I doubt it."

"Believe me, everything hinges on you. Things are at a very delicate stage. If you walk out on me now it could tip the balance of power back in Hilary's direction."

"I'm not interested in helping you get even with your ex-wife, damn it!"

"Jesus. You think I'm going through all of this just to get even?"

"Why else would you be doing it?"

"I'm doing it to save Castleton & Lightfoot, you little idiot. Which means I'm doing it for the families, whether they like it or not. My own personal problems with Hilary are the least of it."

Phila wriggled her captive wrist. "Let go of me."

Nick hesitated and then released her. He folded his arms across his chest. "Please help me, Phila."

She went over to the window. "What did you mean about trying to save Castleton & Lightfoot?"

"Before I tell you the story, you've got to give me your word you won't say anything to any of the others."

"If something is threatening the company, why shouldn't they be told?"

"Because at this stage Hilary could still cover her tracks and get away with what she has planned."

Phila hesitated, knowing he was shamelessly pushing her buttons and she was responding. She could already feel herself weakening. "All right, tell me about it."

"Your word of honor you'll keep quiet until the August meeting?"

"Yes."

"All right, here it is in a nutshell. About six months ago I started picking up rumors of secret negotiations that involved Castleton & Lightfoot. It was hard to tell what was going on at first. All I got were bits and pieces here and there. I had to be careful about checking out the gossip. I didn't want word to get back to Hilary that I was on to something."

"What did you learn?"

"With the help of a couple of friends who were in a position to check the rumors, I found out that Hilary was preparing to sell off a chunk of Castleton & Lightfoot to an outsider, a guy named Alex Traynor."

"Who's Traynor?"

"A fast-moving, very smooth Silicon Valley character. He's been walking a fine line down there in California for the past couple of years. Buys into high-tech firms, bleeds them dry and then sells out, leaving a carcass behind."

"Why would Hilary want to sell off part of the company she controls? It doesn't make sense."

Nick shoved his hand through his hair. "I don't know. I've asked myself that question a hundred times. Maybe Traynor has convinced her he can make Castleton & Lightfoot bigger and stronger than it already is. Or maybe she's got something else in mind. All I do know is that she's going to do it after she gets the backing she needs at the August meeting."

"The others won't back her in a move to sell off shares to outsiders. Good grief, Nick, that's the last thing they'd do. Look at how hard they're working to get Crissie's shares back."

"The others aren't going to know what's happened until it's all over. Hilary's not stupid. She's not going to put a simple motion before them to sell off some shares. She's just going to get them to vote her a greater range of powers."

"Why would they agree to give her more power?"

"Everyone on the board has his or her own reason. My father simply doesn't care enough to get involved anymore, apparently. He'd rather play golf. Darren wants more freedom to jump into politics in a big way. He'd rather turn the entire company over to someone else to run so long as that someone else promises to back his campaign. Vicky always votes the way Darren tells her to vote and she wants a political future for Darren, too."

"And Eleanor is also determined to give Darren his chance to run for office," Phila finished slowly. "Besides, she trusts Hilary. Feels she must support her. She'll give her whatever she asks for at the meeting."

"Yeah."

"But none of them would back her if they thought it meant hurting Castleton & Lightfoot. Why not just explain to them what's going on?"

"I told you, Hilary's still got time to cover her tracks. I've got no real proof, just rumors off the California network and a file on Traynor that's stored in the office safe in Seattle."

"What's in the file?"

"Nothing incriminating enough to prove my point, unfortunately. I went through it yesterday afternoon. Given the information I have from my contacts, I know it means Hilary is dealing with Traynor, but I can't prove she's going to sell off a chunk of C&L to him. I need to get control of Castleton & Lightfoot away from her long enough to smash the deal with Traynor. I can do that if I get my old job back in August."

"You intend to get yourself appointed CEO again. To do that you need a majority of the shareholders on your side."

"You've got the picture."

Phila stared out into the storm. "Do you really believe that with my backing you will convince one or more of the others to support you?"

"It's my only real chance. What it comes down to, Phila, is that I think you can convince at least one of them to trust me again."

"Which one? Your father?"

"Maybe," Nick swirled the last of the scotch in his glass. "Possibly Darren."

"What about Eleanor?"

"I think she's too convinced Hilary's the Benevolent Queen who can give Darren his shot at a political career. Also, Eleanor has the most to protect in terms of the past, as you found out today. She won't be able to trust you because you were involved with Crissie. She can't admit anything good could have come out of that mess with Crissie Masters."

"What if I can't get any of the others to go along with you?"

"Then I lose, and Castleton & Lightfoot goes under."

"You're taking a huge risk."

"A calculated risk," he corrected with a wry smile. "I'm good at those."

Of course he was. Phila swung around to confront him with a rush of tight fury. "Tell me something, Nick. When you came looking for me was it because Eleanor had asked you to get the shares back from me or had you already figured out a way to use me to retake control of the company?"

He shrugged. "When I learned about you, I realized I had been dealt a wild card. I wasn't sure at the time what I was going to do with it. I wasn't even sure what to make of you at first. You weren't what I expected so I just decided to play it by ear."

"What did you expect?"

"Someone who would have accepted a quick payoff for the shares.

I realized almost as soon as I met you that would be the wrong approach, though."

"So you offered me a chance to wallow in my anger and frustration over Crissie's death, instead. And I jumped at the opportunity." Phila shook her head. "Damn, but I hate being manipulated, Nick."

"I know. So do I. But don't you think that in this instance, we're both guilty of using each other? You were quick enough to take advantage of what I was offering."

"Don't try to make me feel guilty. I already feel stupid. That's bad enough."

"Why should you feel stupid?" he asked, his mouth hardening. "You got what you wanted out of the deal."

"A chance to torment Castletons and Lightfoots for the way they treated Crissie? That's a joke. They're already tormenting each other very nicely. They don't need me to add any more fuel to the fire."

"You weren't sure of that a few days ago. If your mind is more at ease about the whole thing now, if you've really been able to accept Crissie's death, then you've accomplished your goal. All I ask is that you let me accomplish mine."

Phila just looked at him, too weary even to cry. Then she turned and started to leave the kitchen. She got as far as the doorway before she lost her self-control. Rage boiled up within her, washing away the exhaustion. Her fist slammed against the door frame.

*"Why did you have to take it as far as sleeping with me?"* she got out in a choked voice, whirling around to confront him. "Why couldn't you have kept it on the level of a simple business deal?"

Nick didn't move, but there was tension in every line of his body. When he spoke his voice was soft. "I've told you from the beginning that our going to bed together has nothing to do with all this."

"That's pure bullshit, and you know it. You used the fact that I was attracted to you, just as you want to use my shares. Just as you want to use me as a Judas goat to lead one of the others over to your side in August."

"What about me?"

"What about you?" she said through her teeth.

"You've been happy enough to use me in bed. Just as you were happy enough to use me to gain entrée into the inner circle of the families."

Phila shut her eyes against the fury that was threatening to overwhelm her. "No. It wasn't like that."

"Wasn't it?"

Her eyes flew open. "I didn't sleep with you to get that entrée."

"I didn't sleep with you to get those shares."

Phila felt dazed and cornered. "I guess," she said slowly, "when you get right down to it, neither one of us can afford to trust the other. Not in bed, at any rate."

"Can't we?"

"No." She turned away again and went purposefully out into the living room. She came to a halt in the middle of the floor, realizing she had no particular destination in mind. She had just needed to escape the kitchen.

"Phila," Nick said quietly behind her, "don't run out on me. Help me. Please."

"Why should I, damn you?"

"I told you. I need you."

"To save Castleton & Lightfoot." She thought of Vicky and little Jordan and Reed and Darren and Eleanor. "It seems to me you should all be able to save yourselves."

"We can't do it without your help."

Thelma Anderson's words echoed in Phila's ears. *You're a born crusader. A rescuer of others. It's your nature, Phila.* Thelma was not the only one who understood her greatest weakness, Phila realized. Nick had caught on really fast.

"Tell me something, Nick. Why do you care what happens to Castleton & Lightfoot now after what the others did to you?"

Nick hesitated. "It's hard to explain. All I can say is that it's a family thing."

"The chips are down, and even though no one except Eleanor has spoken to you in three years you're going to try to save the family firm for everybody."

"That's a little heavy on the dramatics, isn't it?" he asked with a fleeting smile.

It may have sounded dramatic, but it also rang true. Phila realized she believed him. He was not asking this of her because he wanted revenge on Hilary, or if he did, that revenge was just a byproduct. His main goal was to save C&L for the families. She understood that need now. Family was family.

"All right," Phila said. "I'll do what I can. Just don't expect miracles."

"Thank you, Phila."

"Don't get maudlin about it, okay? Let's just keep this on a clean, businesslike basis." She started for the bedroom.

"Phila?"

"No," she said very firmly. "If you stay here again, you sleep on the couch. We're not going to get this situation any more confused than it already is."

\*   \*   \*

Three hours later Nick decided he'd had enough of the lumpy sofa. He kicked aside the blankets and got to his feet. Padding barefoot to the bedroom door, he opened it carefully and looked at the bed. He could just barely make out Phila's form curled up under the covers.

He eased the door open farther and stepped inside the room. She did not stir. He went to the bed and slowly pulled back the sheet. Then he slid in beside her.

Nick touched her lightly and, without waking, she immediately turned into his arms, snuggling close. One of her legs slipped between his. He heard her sigh softly against his chest, and a great tension seemed to evaporate from his body.

Phila was wrong when she said they could not trust each other in bed. It was in bed that she was at her most honest with him and he with her.

"Bastard," she muttered drowsily. But she did not pull away. The tip of her tongue touched his nipple.

"Do that again," he said, rolling onto his back and taking her with him.

She did, and a very pleasant tremor went through him. Then her tongue touched his other nipple, and he groaned softly. He stroked her sleek back down to her thigh, found the hem of her nightgown and pulled it up to her waist. His fingers moved lightly into the warm cleft between her buttocks. Nick felt the small shiver that rippled through her and he smiled in the darkness.

"Damn you, Nick. How do you do this to me?" But she wasn't waiting around for an answer.

She was starting to wriggle down under the sheet. Nick felt her bare teeth on the skin of his stomach. When he shifted his leg she moved lower. Her fingers blazed a trail ahead of her mouth, finding the base of his manhood and cupping him eagerly. He was already rock hard. He had been since he'd entered the room.

"Baby," he muttered. "Kiss me. Please. I want to feel your mouth on me."

She instantly started to crawl back up along the length of him, aiming for his lips. He halted her gently, his hands twining in her hair.

"Kiss me down there," he muttered thickly. "Where your hand is."

She trembled again and then she began to work her way back down his belly to the hard length of him. He felt her breath stirring the mat of hair above his thighs, and then he sucked in his breath as he felt her lips on his throbbing shaft.

"So good," Nick said. "So damn good." He lifted himself into her warm, soft mouth and she took him willingly. Her fingertips traced erratic little designs on the insides of his thighs. His whole body began to grow rigid.

"Now," he told her, reaching for a package in the bedside drawer. His fingers touched the revolver. He pushed it out of the way, scrabbling for the condom.

Phila released him as he quickly sheathed himself. Then she was flowing up and over him until she was lying on top of him. He reached down to guide himself into her, felt her tight, hot opening give way slowly as she pushed herself eagerly against him.

Then he was inside where he needed to be. Deep inside. He exhaled heavily, savoring the sweet heat that engulfed him. He slid his hands up Phila's soft, curving thighs and she cried out and clutched at his shoulders. He could feel her fingernails sinking into his skin, and he laughed silently in the shadows.

Within a few minutes she was rigid with shuddering pleasure, and he gave in to his own shattering climax. Phila collapsed on top of him.

A long time later he stirred sleepily and adjusted Phila more closely against him. He thought she was asleep, but her voice came softly out of the darkness.

"Whose baby was it?"

"Huh?" It took Nick a few seconds to orient himself to reality. He had been drifting in the pleasant aftermath and had been intending to glide straight into sleep.

She rested her chin on her folded arms and peered down at him with her big, questioning, wary eyes. "Hilary's baby. Whose was it?"

"That's a hell of a thing to bring up now."

"There was a baby. Everyone agrees on that. It wasn't yours, so whose was it?"

Nick rubbed the bridge of his nose, feeling weary. "My father's I guess. She probably started to work seducing him as soon as she realized I meant to end the marriage."

"Nah." Phila dismissed that impatiently. "Not Reed's."

Nick stopped rubbing his nose. "He was quick enough to marry her."

Phila eyed him thoughtfully. "You've been thinking all along that Reed slept with Hilary?"

"There's not much point speculating about it one way or the other. It's history."

"Wait a second. It's bad enough that Reed suspects you of walking out on your own kid, but I never realized you might have believed he was the one who got Hilary pregnant."

Nick was suddenly very tense. "You don't think that's the most logical explanation under the circumstances?"

"Good heavens, no. Reed would never have slept with your wife. Not while she was still technically married to you, at any rate. Besides, Eleanor says Hilary claims she was raped."

"Yes, I know."

"Reed would never use force on a woman any more than you would."

"No, but Hilary is quite capable of lying to Eleanor."

"Possible, but I still don't see Reed as the guilty party, either way. He only stepped into the situation because he was convinced he had to make up for what you had done. Honestly, Nick, how could you have been so dumb as to think your father had slept with your wife?"

Nick got angry. "He married her, for God's sake. The day after the divorce was final. What was I supposed to think?"

"What a pair of idiots. So smart in some ways but brick-dumb in others." Phila sat up, drew her legs up to her breasts and wrapped her arms around her knees. The puzzle was pulling at her again. "Let's think about this."

"Why bother?"

"Because I believe it may be important."

"It's old news, Phila."

She shook her head thoughtfully. "I'm not so sure about that."

"Damn it. It happened three years ago."

"It's still affecting the families."

"I'm not asking you to hang around until August so that you can play social worker. This is not a dysfunctional family situation that requires your professional counseling services. Just follow my lead, okay? Stick to the business side of things. I'll handle the details."

Phila was silent, but Nick could almost hear the wheels spinning in her head. Her engine was revving up again, and he had to admit it was a relief. She had given him a real scare earlier in the evening when he'd walked in and found her looking as though she had given up on all of them, including him.

Nick gave her a few more minutes of silent contemplation, but when she failed to stretch out beside him he grew impatient. "All right, maybe it was some outsider who got Hilary pregnant. Some man with whom she was having an affair."

"Not likely."

"Why not? She sure as hell wasn't in love with me. She could easily have had an affair, gotten pregnant at an opportune time and decided to use the pregnancy to her own advantage."

"I don't think that's the way it happened. Eleanor says she saw Hilary the morning after she found out she was pregnant. Hilary was very distraught. That's not the attitude of a mature, sophisticated woman who's simply having an affair and accidently gotten pregnant. A woman in that position would have taken care of the problem quietly."

"For crying out loud, Phila. I've told you Hilary is more than capable of lying."

"I believe you. But I don't think Eleanor was lying to me this morning. She genuinely believes Hilary was abused. She feels very protective toward her. I wonder why?"

"I've told you, Eleanor wants to keep Hilary in charge of things so that Darren's career can get launched. Naturally she feels protective toward her. Now stop looking for answers to old questions and go to sleep."

"Stop telling me what to do. You know I'm not good at taking orders."

"True. There are, fortunately, others things that you do very well, however, so I think I'll keep you around."

She looked at him, her eyes very large in the shadows. The eyes of a clever little fox, Nick thought. Even in the darkness he could tell Phila's gaze was full of energy once more.

"Just so long as you understand that this time around our relationship is strictly business," Phila declared.

He ran his thumb down the length of her graceful spine. "Lady, who are you trying to kid?"

# 14

❧

The knocking on the front door of the cottage awoke Phila the next morning. She opened her eyes slowly, aware that something heavy was weighing her down. Instinctively she shoved at the offending bulk, trying to push it aside. It didn't budge. Her fingers touched bare skin, skin with rough hair on it—masculine skin. She was suddenly, frantically, wide awake and struggling wildly.

"*Phila.* Phila, wait a second. Hold on. It's just me. Take it easy, honey."

"Get off of me," she hissed in muffled tones, shoving at Nick's broad shoulders.

"I am getting off of you. I'm sorry. I must have moved in my sleep." Nick rolled quickly to one side, disentangling his legs from hers. He had been lying half-sprawled over her, his heavy thigh anchoring her lower body, his arm across her breasts.

Phila sat up, breathing quickly, and pushed hair out of her eyes.

"Are you all right?" Nick said gently.

"There's someone at the door."

"I'll get it." Nick pushed aside the covers and stood up. He gazed down at her in concern. "Are you okay?"

She nodded rapidly, not meeting his eyes. "Yes. Yes, I'm fine. I just panicked for a minute, that's all. You know I can't stand having a man on top of me."

"It was an accident, honey."

"I know, I know. Go see who's at the door." She waved him out of the room.

Nick stepped into a pair of jeans and went reluctantly out of the bedroom. Phila took several deep breaths and pulled herself together.

It wasn't too bad this time, all things considered. The panic had been short-lived, and it was already fading.

Nick would never hurt her. He had just accidentally triggered some old reflexive fears.

She heard Reed Lightfoot's voice in the outer room. Phila got out of bed and pulled on her robe. When she opened the bedroom door she felt almost calm again.

"Well now, don't you look all bright eyed and bushy tailed this morning, Phila," Reed said cheerfully as he spotted her in the hall. "I was just telling Nick, here, that I thought you might like to take another stab at a golf ball today. What do you say?"

Phila blinked, her gaze going to Nick, who was standing barefoot near the front door. He had a watchful expression on his face, and she knew he was plotting again.

Phila yawned. "I don't think I'm up to it today, Reed. Why don't you go with him, Nick?"

There was a moment of awkward silence as both men assimilated her words. Reed cleared his throat. "It's short notice. You've probably got a lot of things to do, Nick."

"Yeah. And I don't have a set of clubs with me. Haven't played for quite a while," Nick said.

Phila's eyes narrowed. "Don't be ridiculous. The notice isn't any shorter for you, Nick, than it would have been for me. You don't have anything in particular to do this morning, and you can always rent a set of clubs at the course. Gee whiz, being Lightfoots, you could probably get the pro to loan you his personal set, if necessary."

"Course is probably crowded, anyway, this morning," Reed offered weakly. "Might be better to try it another time."

"Yeah."

Phila frowned at the two men. "Go on, both of you. I'm not used to having so many males standing around in my living room at this hour of the morning. Makes me nervous."

Reed inclined his head in an abrupt motion. "Suit yourself, Nick. Feel like a game?"

"You'd probably cream me."

Reed began to smile evilly. "Goddamn right. Especially if you're out of practice."

"I'm not that out of practice. Care to put a little money where your mouth is?"

Reed sighed. "Too much like taking candy from a baby."

"We'll see. Let me get some shoes on. I'll be right with you." Nick went down the hall to the bedroom with a long stride.

Reed looked at Phila. His brows rose. "Sure you don't want to come with us?"

"I'm sure. I want a real breakfast. Coffee and a Danish doesn't do it for me."

"We could have a real meal at the clubhouse restaurant before we go out on the course."

"Hah. I know you. You'd lure me out there with a promise of ham and eggs and then tell me we didn't have time to eat. Too many people waiting to tee off. You'd rush me out onto the course, and I'd have to walk eighteen holes with my stomach growling."

Reed glanced idly around the room. "Why did you push Nick into going with me?"

"I think it's time the two of you got to know each other again. I think somewhere along the line you've both forgotten a few important things about yourselves."

"Like what?"

"Figure it out. You're both reasonably smart. Not brilliant, mind you, but definitely above average for the male of the species. No telling what you might come up with if you try." Phila adjusted the sash of her purple robe.

Nick came out of the bedroom, his windbreaker slung over his shoulder. He walked over to Phila and kissed her squarely on the mouth. "You remember our deal, okay?"

Phila slitted her eyes. "Go on, get out of here."

"She always this grouchy in the morning?" Reed asked as he followed his son out the door.

"No. Sometimes she's worse. Don't worry, I'm working on the problem." The door closed behind him.

Phila rolled her eyes and went toward the kitchen to start the coffee. When she had it going she trooped back into the bedroom with the intention of taking her morning shower.

She was halfway down the hall when she noticed the closet door standing ajar. She opened it and saw that Nick had gathered up the bedding she had given him for the sofa last night and shoved it inside. He must have done it in a hurry on his way to answer the door.

This was the second time he'd scrambled to disguise the fact that he'd been relegated to the sofa. Had to be pure masculine ego. She found it oddly touching to realize that his male pride wouldn't allow him to let anyone think he might have had to spend the night in the living room. He was so cool and confident; so sure of himself in so many other ways.

It occurred to Phila that being married to Hilary might have been a difficult cross for a man like Nick to bear.

She opened the closet and began refolding the blankets he had tossed inside along with his clothing.

Something crackled in the pocket of the shirt he had been wearing when he arrived the previous evening. Phila glanced inside the pocket and saw the piece of paper that had been folded into fourths.

She almost talked herself out of looking at it, but some instinct made her go ahead and remove the sheet of paper from the pocket. She unfolded it carefully and saw that it was a fax copy of a newspaper article dated two and a half months earlier.

HOLLOWAY. A Holloway area man was convicted today on a variety of drug and assault charges stemming from an attack on a social worker earlier this year.

Elijah Joshua Spalding was given a total of eighteen months in prison.

The assault took place in the parking lot of the Holloway Grill. According to testimony at the trial, Spalding had agreed to meet Philadelphia Fox, a social worker, at the restaurant to discuss matters concerning the foster home run by himself and his wife, Ruth.

Spalding and Fox arrived in the parking lot at approximately the same time. There was an argument during which Spalding attacked the social worker and tried to drag her into his pickup truck. Fox fought back and Spalding got a gun out of the pickup. He was threatening her with it when police arrived on the scene.

When Spalding was searched at the time of the arrest, a quantity of heroin was found on him. Spalding pleaded guilty to the assault charges.

His wife maintained throughout the trial that her husband had never used drugs. The children who had been in the Spaldings' care have been sent to other homes.

Phila's fingers were shaking as she refolded the piece of paper. Nick had been digging into her past. She wondered frantically what he had been looking for or, worse, what he suspected.

He could not know anything more than what the newspaper story had covered, she told herself. There was no reason for him to think there was anything more to the tale.

She sank down onto the plump arm of the sofa, trying to think logically. There was absolutely nothing to worry about. He had merely been curious about Elijah Spalding. It made sense. After all, he knew she had a definite fear of the man, and he had taken care to see that she learned how to protect herself in the event Spalding showed up in her life.

That's all it was, she decided. Nick had just been indulging his curiosity. He had told his father he intended to check into the matter, so he'd gotten a copy of a clipping that covered the story.

Phila told herself she had enough things to worry about without getting paranoid over this.

"Looks like you owe me a beer, Nick, not to mention ten bucks." Reed Lightfoot was grinning broadly as he led the way off the eighteenth green toward the clubhouse. "Easiest goddamn money I've made in a long time. When was the last time you played?"

"Six months ago. I had a game with a client."

"You beat him?"

"Yeah. But he wasn't as good as you are. Of course, you've been practicing a lot lately."

Reed stopped smiling. "That's a fact."

"Come on, I'll buy you the beer."

"Don't forget the ten bucks."

They found a couple of chairs out on the clubhouse terrace. Nick leaned back, one foot cocked across his knee, a cold bottle of beer in his hand.

Reed took a big swallow of his Rainier straight from the can. "Good thing Eleanor isn't here. Look at us. We look like a couple of blue-collar working stiffs after a long day behind the wheel of a heavy rig. She thinks beer-drinking is low class."

"Eleanor always had a problem with class."

"Nora used to say it was because Eleanor secretly thought she'd married down." Reed was silent for a minute. "Nora used to be right a lot of the time."

"Yeah."

"That little gal of yours thinks she's right most of the time."

"She thinks she's right all of the time." Nick watched a foursome getting ready to go out on the course.

"Is she?"

"I don't know yet," Nick said slowly. "But I'm beginning to think her instincts are pretty good about most things."

"She's got goddamn screwy politics, but I guess that's only to be expected, given her upbringing," Reed noted charitably.

"Yeah. Only to be expected."

"She given up that wacko idea about us having some responsibility for Crissie Masters's death?"

"She's come to the conclusion it was a case of cosmic bad luck. I think that's how she described it."

Reed considered that. "There may be a grain of truth in that. Things were chaotic during the time Crissie was around. A lot of tension. A lot of anger. Burke was the only one enjoying himself. He was like a kid with a firecracker."

"Makes for an unstable situation."

"That it does." Reed swallowed some beer. "What are you going to do with Miss Philadelphia Fox?"

"I think I'll keep her around."

"Until you get the shares back from her?"

Nick smiled slowly. "Even after I get the shares back from her."

"Yeah, I was beginning to get that impression. When are you going to get those shares, Nick?"

"Soon."

Reed turned his head to look at his son with a level gaze. "What are you going to do with them when you get hold of them?"

Nick settled deeper into the chair, his eyes on the foursome that was now making its way up the first fairway. "Do you think it's possible one or both of us may have made a mistake three years ago, Dad?"

Reed exhaled slowly. "No need to ask where that notion came from, is there? The little Mouth put that idea in your head."

"Did she put it into yours?"

"Got to admit it, that little gal has a way of making you stop and think about a few things," Reed finally said carefully. "Nora used to be able to do that, too."

"Make you stop and think?"

"Uh huh." Reed swallowed more beer. "Had a way of seeing things a lot more clearly than I did sometimes. She was better with people than I ever was."

Nick decided that was as close as either of them was going to get for now. Maybe it was time to take another risk. "If you really want to know what I'm going to do with those shares of Phila's, I'll tell you."

Reed studied him expressionlessly for a long moment. "I'm listening."

"I'm going to have her back me at the August meeting."

"Why?" Reed's voice turned harsh. "The shares belong to Darren, and you goddamn well know it."

"I know it. But I can't be sure I can get Darren to back me. I need one of you besides Phila on my side, though."

"One of us?"

"You, Darren and Vicky or Eleanor."

"What the hell are you going for, Nick?"

"I'm going to try and pull Castleton & Lightfoot out of the water before it goes under."

Reed's hand flexed around his beer can. "Maybe you'd better tell me the whole story."

Nick took another swallow of beer and did exactly that.

Phila was wondering how the golf game was going and contemplating a walk on the beach, when Hilary arrived at the front door. The instant Phila saw who her visitor was, she wished she'd left for the beach five minutes earlier.

"Come on in," Phila said politely because it was the only thing she could say under the circumstances. "Would you like some coffee?"

"That would be nice, thank you." Hilary stood for a moment, looking elegantly out of place in the comfortably shabby room.

She was wearing a pair of slim black pants and an austerely cut russet shirt with wide cuffs. A handful of simple gold chains swung gracefully down the center of the shirt.

"Have a seat," Phila offered as she went into the kitchen.

When she returned she saw that Hilary had chosen the sofa. She was perched regally on the edge so as not to let herself get sucked back into the sagging depths of the old cushions. She examined Phila as she took her coffee.

"It's hard to believe you and Crissie were so close."

"Do you doubt it?"

"No. Crissie talked enough about you to make me realize you and she had a special relationship." Hilary paused. "Sometimes I was almost envious of that relationship."

"There was no need for you to be," Phila said gently as she took the chair across from her. "Hilary, if I ask you an honest question, will you answer it?"

"I don't know."

"Were you raped as Eleanor says?"

Hilary's head snapped around sharply. She fixed Phila with fierce eyes. "Yes."

Phila drew a deep breath as pity welled up in her. "I'm so sorry."

Almost immediately Hilary had control of herself. "I didn't realize Eleanor had told you so much. She's never told anyone else about that part of it."

"She was upset."

"You upset her," Hilary accused.

"Yes. I . . ." Phila swallowed. "I'm afraid I hurt her."

"You're hurting a lot of people just by being here. Don't you think it's time you handed over the shares and left?"

"Probably."

There was a long silence, and then Hilary said quietly, "He called me cold, you know. Told me I was only a beautiful shell of a woman. He could not tolerate the fact that I did not respond to him."

Phila put down her mug and clasped her hands together. "You don't have to tell me about it, Hilary."

"Why shouldn't I? You're thinking of becoming part of the family, aren't you? Maybe you'd better know a little more about the kind of family you're hoping to marry into. Maybe the truth will make you open your eyes."

"I don't think you want to tell me this."

Hilary eyed her sharply. "Perhaps you're right. It isn't a very pleasant tale."

"Tell me about Crissie instead."

Hilary hesitated, her expression softening. "Crissie was special. To others she seemed very self-centered. But I understood her. She understood me."

"I know."

"I've never been as close to anyone as I was to Crissie."

Phila nodded.

"You know it all, don't you?" Hilary asked tightly.

"That you and she were lovers? Yes. I did some careful thinking last night, and finally put together what I'd learned about the families with some things Crissie had said about you all. Crissie was discreet and she never would have told me outright about her affair with you. But as I got to know all of you, it wasn't too hard to figure it out."

Hilary watched her. "You're not jealous, are you?"

"Crissie and I were best friends, but we were never lovers. She knew, even before I did, that we never would be." Phila took a sip of coffee. "She disliked men intensely. She thought they were all fools, although she occasionally found them useful. She used to say I was hopelessly trapped in my heterosexuality and that it was a damn shame." *A shame because I wasn't even enjoying it.* Crissie would be genuinely glad to know that Nick had definitely changed that much, at least.

Hilary's mouth curved grimly. "I did not realize why I could not respond to Nick or any other man until I met Crissie. I put Nick off until our wedding night because I was afraid he'd realize he wouldn't ever get the kind of response he wanted. I sensed he would be a physically demanding man, a passionate man. But when I met Crissie, I finally understood. I stopped fighting myself."

"But you married Reed."

"Only because of the baby. Reed has never touched me."

"You're both living rather lonely lives, aren't you?"

"I have my goals. I'm satisfied with them." Hilary's eyes were intent but no longer fierce. "If you know Crissie and I were lovers then you must know she intended to give me those shares or at least back me at the annual meeting. She knew how important they were to me."

"But she didn't give them to you, Hilary. Nor did she will them to you. She left them to me, and they didn't come with instructions."

"Crissie was full of life. She had no way of knowing she would die before the August meeting. It never occurred to her to change her will. She was too young to think about things like that. Neither of us even considered the possibility of her death."

"I don't believe she would have altered her will, even if she had thought about it. I've told you, Crissie and I were best friends."

*"But I was her lover."*

"She'd had other lovers, Hilary. She did not mention them in her will."

"Damn you, I know she intended for me to have those shares. She told me she did. You have no right to them. Are you so blinded by your infatuation with Nick that you're going to let him tell you what to do with those shares?"

Phila thought about that. "I'm not backing him because I'm infatuated with him."

"You think you're in love with him?" Hilary softened. "You think he'll marry you?"

Phila shook her head. "It's got nothing to do with any of that. It's a business decision."

"A *business* decision. You mean he's offering you so much money you can't resist? Did he finally find your price?"

"No." Phila said. "He was too smart to try. He knew I'd just get spitting mad if he tried to buy me off."

"What's his secret?" Hilary demanded.

"I trust him to do what's best for the families."

"You trust him? You're crazy. After what I just told you about what he did to me?"

"You didn't say it was Nick who raped you."

"Well, it was, you little fool."

"Was it?" Phila realized her coffee was getting cold.

"Yes, yes, *yes!*" Hilary leaped to her feet, the cup and saucer clattering as she half-dropped them on the small table. "He hurt me very badly. So very badly."

Phila looked down at her coffee. "I don't believe you, Hilary. In fact, I don't believe you were raped by anyone."

"Then you're a bigger fool than I thought." Hilary rushed for the door and then halted abruptly, not looking back. "Just tell me one thing, if you can. I have to know."

"What do you have to know, Hilary?"

"Why you? Why did Crissie love you so much? You weren't even her lover."

Phila felt the tears well up in her eyes and begin to course down her cheeks. "Don't you see?" she whispered. "Don't you understand? I was the one person with whom she could lower her guard and take the risk of being kind. I was the one person who wanted nothing from her except friendship, the one person who didn't try to use her."

"I never tried to use her."

"Sure you did. Everyone did. Except me. With me she felt safe. But she was wrong, wasn't she? In the end I couldn't protect her, could I?"

There was silence for a long moment before Hilary said very distantly, "We both loved her, but I don't think either of us could have protected her. She was her own worst enemy. How do you save someone from herself?"

Phila blinked back more tears. "I don't know. Oh, God. I just don't know."

The door squeaked on its hinges as Hilary opened it. "One more thing, Phila. Don't go near Eleanor again, do you hear me? I don't want you upsetting her. She's got enough to deal with."

The door slammed behind her.

Phila waited until her legs felt strong enough to support her, and then she got to her feet and went into the kitchen. Her tears mixed with the cold coffee as she poured it down the drain.

There was nothing like the laughter of a child to jerk you out of morbid thoughts, Phila decided later that afternoon as she walked along the path in front of the Lightfoot and Castleton front gate.

Jordan's screeches of excitement echoed across the lawn. She looked through the wrought-iron bars and saw that he was having a great time rolling down a small hill. As soon as he reached the bottom, he picked himself up and ran back to the top to start the process all over again. Cupcake and Fifi were charging up and down the grassy slope beside him, thoroughly enjoying themselves.

Phila stood for a minute, her fingers locked around the bars of the gate. She was aware of a strangely wistful feeling. Before she could properly identify the odd sensation, Jordan spotted her and waved enthusiastically. Then he came racing toward her. The rottweilers trotted after him.

"Hi, Phila. Hi, Phila. Hi, Phila." Jordan sang his litany of greeting as he barreled toward her.

"Hi, yourself. What are you doing?" She patted the dogs in an effort to fend them off.

"Gettin' dizzy." Jordan grinned proudly.

"Is that a lot of fun?"

He nodded vigorously. "Wanna try?"

"Not today, thanks. I'm already dizzy. Where's your mother?" Phila glanced automatically toward the Castleton beach cottage as Jordan pointed. She saw Victoria rise from the porch swing and start down toward the gate. "Oh, there she is." Phila straightened, trying to give the dogs a farewell pat. She was not in a good mood to deal with any adult Castletons or Lightfoots at the moment. "Tell her hello for me."

"Where you going?"

"I'm just taking a walk."

"Phila." Victoria was almost at the gate.

Phila groaned. "Hello, Vicky. Jordan and I were having a chat. I'm out for a walk."

"Jordan and I will go with you."

"Yes, yes, yes," Jordan said, clapping his hands.

Phila wished she had never turned left when she walked away from the cottage. She should have headed straight for the solitude of the beach. "Sure. Why not?"

"Where's Nick?" Victoria let herself and her son through the gate and fell into step beside Phila. Jordan scampered on ahead with the dogs.

"Playing golf with Reed."

Victoria looked startled. "He is?"

"Yes."

"They haven't played together in years."

"It's about time they did, then, don't you think?"

Victoria's eyes narrowed. "Hilary went down to the Gilmarten place to see you this morning. I saw her leave."

"Uh huh."

"What did she want?"

"The usual."

"She tried to get you to give her the shares?"

Phila watched the dogs investigating interesting odors at the side of the road. "That's about the only reason a Castleton or a Lightfoot would bother to seek me out, isn't it?"

"Can you blame us?"

"Nope. Vicky, I want to tell you something. I know your biggest concern is about Jordan's future inheritance. Rest assured that I won't do anything to jeopardize it."

"If you back Nick instead of Hilary at the annual meeting, you'll jeopardize my husband's future and, therefore, my son's."

"I think Nick has the best interests of Castleton & Lightfoot at heart."

"So does Hilary. She might not give a damn about anything or anyone else, but Eleanor's right. There's no doubt she's devoted to the firm."

"You don't like Hilary very much, do you?"

Victoria bit her lip and called out to her son. "Jordan, come back here. Stop running with that stick."

"Why don't you like her?" Phila persisted quietly.

"That's not really any of your business, is it?"

Phila thought for a moment. "I'll bet you think the baby was Darren's, don't you?"

Victoria came to a halt and whirled to face her. "You little bitch."

Phila closed her eyes and then opened them narrowly. "A lot of people seem to think of me in those terms lately. Your husband called me the same thing."

"He was right."

"Well, you're wrong. About him, at any rate. Hilary claims she was raped. Darren wouldn't have done such a thing."

"Any man might resort to rape if he's pushed far enough, just as any man might resort to murder," Victoria said tightly.

"Hilary didn't push him. Why should she?"

"Who knows how she thinks? She likes to control everyone and everything. She might have thought she could control Darren with sex. She certainly had Nick blinded for a while when they were engaged."

"Vicky, be reasonable. There's no traumatic secret past shared by your husband and Hilary."

"How do you know?" Victoria's gaze was locked on Phila's face.

"I'd sense it if there were. I'm good at that kind of thing. Darren is a little wary of her and probably with good reason. She's shrewd, and he knows it. He even admires her abilities to some extent. He's willing to deal with her because she's in a position to give him what he wants and she is, after all, family. But that's the extent of his interest in her. Believe me."

"You weren't here three years ago. You don't know what went on. Darren and I were having problems. We were on the brink of divorce. I suppose it would have been only natural for him to turn to Hilary."

"If that's what you've been telling yourself for three years, don't bother. That's not what happened. I'd know if something had gone on between those two. It would show when they're together. Hilary hates the man who got her pregnant, whoever he is. She would never be able to deal with him as serenely as she deals with Darren. I can't imagine why you thought the baby might have been your husband's."

Victoria's hands clenched at her sides. "I was never certain. But I sometimes wondered. Darren's father was, well, I'm sure you've heard."

"A man who made a career of chasing women. Yes, I've figured that much out."

"I used to lie awake at night and wonder if that kind of thing was hereditary." Victoria smiled grimly. "But mostly I managed to put the whole matter out of my mind. Then Crissie arrived on the scene a year ago. She picked up on the situation immediately. She used to go around saying '*like father, like son.*' "

"And manage to revive a lot of your secret fears?"

"Yes." Victoria's face was stark. "I guess she did."

"Burke must have been a real bastard."

"Please don't ever say that in front of Eleanor."

"It's too late. I said it yesterday."

Victoria's mouth twisted. "So that was what upset her so much. That was cruel of you, Phila."

"I know. I'm sorry. I was trying to defend Crissie, as usual."

"What a mess."

"Yes," agreed Phila, "it is. I intend to get out of it as soon as the August meeting is over. Unlike Crissie and contrary to popular opinion, I don't see any real advantage to being a Castleton or a Lightfoot. I don't intend to hang around."

Victoria glanced at her assessingly. "What's going to happen at the annual meeting?"

"I'm scheduled to back Nick in whatever he plans to do. Then I'll give the shares back to Darren."

"But that will be too late," Victoria said. "We need Hilary reelected CEO at that meeting."

"Sorry," Phila said. "But I trust Nick more than I trust Hilary. Speaking of trust . . ."

"What about it?"

"You might try telling your husband you trust him."

"Why should I bother? He doesn't really trust me."

Phila's eyes widened. "He thinks you're fooling around?"

Victoria waved that aside impatiently. "No. He thinks I accepted a bribe from Burke three years ago to drop divorce proceedings."

"Did you?"

"No. I stayed because I wanted to try to make the marriage work. I love him."

"Heck of a situation, isn't it? Each of you suspects the other of having done something unforgivable, and neither of you can ever prove your innocence to the other. An interesting problem."

"With no solution?" Victoria asked, her eyes shadowed.

"I didn't say that."

"What are you going to do, Miss Fox? Wave a magic wand and make it all better?"

"No, you and Darren have to do that. But the next time the two of you discuss the matter, consider the sources of your information. You might also consider the fact that in spite of your suspicions, neither of you has gone ahead and broken up the marriage, even though you're both proud people. There must be some love and trust left to work with in your relationship."

"Darren thinks I've stuck with him because I want to be a politician's wife. He's stuck with me because he wants his son."

"Maybe."

"It's the truth, damn you."

"Only if you want it to be."

# 15

❧

"No," Phila said, absolutely adamant. "Definitely not. I will not be dragged to that fund-raiser in Seattle."

Nick was patient. "It won't be that bad. You might even enjoy yourself."

"No."

"I have to go, and I want you to come with me. You wouldn't make me go alone, would you?"

"You won't be alone. You'll have all your friends and relatives with you. Everyone wants to get Darren off to a flying start in politics."

"Except you."

"I don't care what Darren does with his career. I wish him the best of luck, even if he does have the misfortune to be a Republican. But he certainly doesn't need me at the fancy fund-raiser, and his mother would just as soon I wasn't there, believe me. My presence would probably lower the tone of the whole event."

"Bigot."

"You bet."

Phila shoved her key into the lock of the Gilmarten door. It had been a hard day, what with dealing with Hilary and then Vicky.

Phila and Nick had just walked back from an after-dinner coffee-and-brandy hour arranged by Victoria. The invitation had come as a surprise late that afternoon, and Phila still was not quite certain why it had been issued.

The event had been reasonably civil, although Phila strongly suspected Eleanor of trying to use the opportunity to once more demonstrate the inappropriateness of Phila's presence in the household. Phila had ignored her for the most part, and so had everyone else.

Reed had not been able to avoid baiting Phila, of course, and Nick had appeared to enjoy the fun. But she felt she had held her own and at times had even enjoyed the arguments.

Even Victoria had gotten into the fracas over increasing financial aid and job-training assistance to single women on welfare. She had surprised everyone else by agreeing with Phila that more tax dollars should be spent in that area.

"I'm a mother," Victoria had said calmly when they'd all looked at her in blank astonishment. "This is basically a children's issue. What side do you expect me to take?"

But the argument over Phila's attendance at the fund-raiser had begun after the small gathering had concluded. It had developed on the way back to the Gilmarten place and had been conducted only between Nick and Phila. Nick had blithely assumed she would go with him to Darren's first major political bash. Nick assumed a lot lately, Phila told herself resentfully.

"Phila, why are you making such a big deal out of this? You're not nervous about meeting that crowd, are you?"

"There's no point in my going." She tugged off her lightweight jacket and hung it in the closet. "I'm not a member of either family."

Nick scowled as he sat down to unlace his shoes. "You're a part of the company."

"Not for long. Not after that August meeting."

Nick sat up and leaned back into the corner of the sofa, watching her broodingly. "What if I asked you to come with me for my sake?"

"Why should you care if I'm there or not?"

"I want you there."

"Forget it."

"You're supposed to be showing support for me, remember? That was our deal. A united front and all that."

"My going to the fund-raiser won't influence our so-called united front one way or the other. I don't want to go, Nick, and that's final."

He held up a palm in surrender. "All right. If you feel that strongly about it."

"I do." Why was he pushing her on this? she wondered. The fund-raiser did not affect his goal of saving Castleton & Lightfoot, as far as she could tell.

"I accept your decision."

"You're too damn gracious." She didn't believe him for a minute.

"How did your golf game go with Reed today?" she asked as she sat down in the chair.

"You heard him bragging this evening about how he beat me."

"Did you let him?"

"Hell, no. He's always been a strong player, and he's had a lot of practice lately since he abdicated the job of running Castleton & Lightfoot. He won fair and square. Cost me ten bucks and a beer."

"Did you talk to him?"

"Yeah, I talked to him. Hard to play eighteen holes of golf with someone without talking to him at some point."

"That's not what I meant, and you know it."

Nick's smile was wry. "I know what you meant. Let's just say I tip-toed around the subject of the baby and let it go at that, okay?"

"Oh." Phila was disappointed.

"It's a little hard to talk about, Phila."

"Yes, I guess it would be. After all, if I'm right the two of you are going to have to admit to some massive errors in judgment, aren't you?"

"And if you're wrong, bringing up the subject will just lead to more trouble and hostility and I don't need that right now. I've got bigger problems."

"Saving Castleton & Lightfoot?"

He gave her an odd look. "That's one of them. I did take a major risk today with Dad. I told him what I had found out about Hilary's plans to sell off a chunk of C&L."

"You did?" Phila was surprised. "That *was* a risk. What made you take it now?"

"You."

Phila sat forward in the chair eagerly. "Well? How did your father respond?"

"Said he'd think about it."

"Is that all? He'll think about it?"

"Yeah."

"But what if he talks to Hilary?"

"She'll deny everything, and I won't be able to prove a damn thing. But he didn't say he was going to talk to Hilary. He just said he was going to think about what I'd told him."

Phila examined the problem closely. "One thing in your favor is that he doesn't talk to Hilary very much at all. As far as I can tell, they're living like strangers in that big house."

"Yeah," Nick said again. "That was sort of the way it looked to me, too."

"So you decided to take the risk of telling Reed everything. Interesting."

"I'm glad you find it so fascinating since you're the one who nagged me into laying my cards on the table with Dad."

"I did not nag. I never nag."

"That's a matter of opinion. You ready to sweep me off to bed?"

"Honestly, Nick, sometimes you have a one-track mind."

"I know. It's really disgusting, isn't it? But, then," he added, brightening, "you don't love me for my mind, do you?"

She caught her breath and glowered to hide the emotions she was afraid might appear in her eyes. "Don't be crude."

"You love it; you're the earthy type at heart."

Phila wished he would stop using the word *love*. It definitely was not a subject she could joke about these days. It made her nervous. She got to her feet. "I'm tired. I don't know about you, but I've had a very wearing day."

Nick got up off the sofa in a smooth motion, smiling in sensual anticipation. "I'm pretty exhausted myself. Can't wait to get to bed."

"You're in an awfully good mood for someone who may have just made a major tactical error today."

"All because of you." He caught her hand and started swinging it as he walked into the bedroom with her.

"Sure."

He stopped and pulled her close. "Kiss me, baby," he growled. "I'm hot, and you're the only one who knows how to put out the flames."

She leaned against him, her arms stealing around his neck. "You're impossible."

"No, just hot, as I said." He kissed the side of her throat. "Make love to me until I go crazy, okay?"

"I thought you said you were exhausted."

Nick moved away from her, sat down on the bed and flopped back against the pillows, his arms open wide. "I am, but I know my duty. I'm all yours."

"Stop acting so noble. You're just horny."

"That, too."

Phila tried to restrain herself, but, as usual, she could not resist him. She stepped out of her clothes, aware of his attention on her every inch of the way. The look in his eyes was more than enough to get her excited.

"Baby, you are one beautiful, sexy lady," Nick muttered, his voice roughening as the last of her clothing dropped to the floor.

With a small, enthusiastic exclamation of delight and anticipation, Phila dove on top of him.

Nick was ready and waiting for her, silent laughter in his eyes.

A long time later, when she was feeling pleasantly drowsy, her head resting on Nick's shoulder, her leg sprawled across his heavy thigh, he spoke.

"Tell me," he said, circling her nipple with one finger, "the real reason why you don't want to go to Darren's fund-raiser?"

"You'll laugh."

"No, I won't."

"Promise?"

"I swear I won't even chuckle."

Phila took a deep breath. "I haven't got anything to wear."

Nick roared with laughter. Phila punched him in the ribs, but that didn't stop him.

"Shut up," she ordered. "I'm serious."

"I know. That's what makes it so damn funny. Philadelphia Fox, President of the Left-Wing-Left-Out-Cause-of-the-Month Club is too proud to go to a political party where she might actually meet a few of the people who finance the Right-Wing Causes of the Month because she hasn't got a fancy dress. I can't believe it. I should think you'd want to go in jeans just to make a statement."

"I'm not into statements. I'm too practical for that. And I will not humiliate myself deliberately by showing up underdressed for a black-tie affair, and that's that."

"I understand completely," Nick said, soothing her with a movement of his big hand. "We'll go back to Seattle a couple of days early and find you a dress."

"Nick, I cannot afford that sort of dress. In case it has escaped your notice, I am currently unemployed." *The man is dense,* she thought angrily.

"You happen to own a fortune in C&L stock. I'll float you a loan."

"The hell you will."

"Ah, my fine, proud lady. All right, then, I'll buy the dress for you, how's that?"

"Absolutely not."

"I owe you, Phila," he said, turning serious without any warning. "I'll buy the dress."

She looked at him for a moment, wondering how to interpret that statement. The last thing she wanted was to have him feel a sense of obligation toward her. "Never mind the dress," she finally said. "I don't want to talk about it."

"You can be a very stubborn, hard-headed little fox at times." Nick's hand slipped down over her gently curved stomach. His fingers slid between her thighs. "Lucky for you I'm so patient and understanding."

"I never knew you felt that strongly about child-welfare legislation," Darren said as he came out of the bathroom.

"You never asked." Victoria continued to leaf through her magazine, staring unseeingly at an advertisement for fine crystal sculpture.

Darren sat down on the edge of the bed. His bare back gleamed in the lamplight. "You and Phila would make a fine pair if you ever combined forces." He sounded amused. "You'd have Reed, Nick, Mother and me running for cover."

"Phila's not a member of either family, so she's not likely to be around once the issue of the shares is settled."

"I'm not so sure about that. I don't see Nick turning her loose really quickly even after he's got the shares."

"She may turn him loose." Victoria closed the magazine slowly. "Darren, Phila told me today she won't do anything to hurt Jordan's inheritance. She says she'll give the shares back after the August meeting. Said she had to back Nick until then."

"Did she?" Darren looked thoughtful. "So he is planning something, and he needs a little help."

"You know what he's planning. He hasn't spelled it out, but it's obvious he wants to take control of the company away from Hilary."

"Why now? Why wait three years and then come storming back like this?"

"Maybe when Eleanor called him about Phila he simply saw his chance and took it."

"Or maybe Nick knows something the rest of us don't know."

"What could he possibly know that we don't? He's been out of touch for three years."

Darren shook his head. "I'm not so sure about that." He looked over his shoulder at Victoria, his eyes searching her face.

"Whatever it is, I suppose we don't have any real choice. We'll have to back Hilary for the sake of your career."

Darren studied her a moment. "Tell me something, Vicky. Why do you hate her so much?"

Victoria flushed. She had known deep down where this conversation might lead. She had practically set herself up. She had been both nervous and determined, and now that the moment was upon her she was frightened. She hedged.

"We don't have a lot in common," Victoria mumbled.

"Bullshit. You've got a great deal in common. Same kind of family background, same kind of schools and you both married into the same kind of families."

Victoria tensed. "At least I didn't have to marry you for your money."

Darren went still. "No, that's true. Why did you marry me, Vicky?"

"You know the answer to that."

Darren examined his long, shapely fingers. "Tell me again. It's been a long time."

Victoria blinked back the tears. "I married you because I loved you." Her voice was so thick she could hardly understand her own words.

"What changed your mind?"

Something in Victoria snapped. *"Nothing changed my mind.* I still love you, damn it. I wouldn't have stayed with you after what happened three years ago if I didn't love you more than I love my own pride. Are you so stupid you don't even realize that?" She burst into tears, no longer caring if she humiliated herself. She felt as if she had been in a pressure cooker during all the hours since she had spoken to Phila.

Darren stared at her, his expression totally confused. "After what happened three years ago? You mean after Dad offered you cash to stay with me?"

"Oh, shut up." Victoria wiped her eyes with a quick, angry movement. "I knew there was no point trying to ask you. I knew it would just end up like this. I wish I'd had the sense to keep my mouth shut. Damn Phila."

"Phila? What's Phila got to do with any of this?" Darren was getting angry. "What the hell did you want to ask me? I don't remember any question."

"Because I've been afraid to ask it for three years," Victoria blazed. "I didn't know if I could trust you to tell me the truth, and I would have to leave if the answer was yes. Don't you see? I would have no choice. As long as I didn't ask, I could pretend most of the time that everything was all right, that the answer was no."

"Damn it, Vicky. What did you want to ask me?"

Victoria looked at him through her tears. "Was the baby yours?"

"Baby? *What* baby?" Then he caught on. Darren's eyes widened in amazement. "Oh, for God's sake. You don't mean Hilary's, do you? You can't believe the baby was mine?"

"Why not?" Victoria retorted. "For three years you've believed the only reason I stayed with you was because your father offered to make it worth my while."

"My father told me about that damned bribe," Darren said, his face taut and furious. "I know he offered to pay you off."

"But I didn't accept," Victoria raged. "I never said I'd take his money. But I could never prove it to you. You chose to believe him. Now he's dead, and I'll never have a chance to prove I'm innocent."

"What about me? How am I suppose to prove I'm innocent?"

"Are you?" Victoria held her breath.

"Hell, yes. I wouldn't go near Hilary Lightfoot in a bed even if I happened to be wearing a full suit of armor. I'm not blind. I saw what she did to Nick during the first year of their marriage. What's more, Hilary has absolutely no interest in me or any other man as far as I can tell. She's all wrapped up in herself and the company. What in God's name made you think the baby was mine?"

Victoria could hardly breathe. "I wasn't certain. I didn't want to believe it. For three years I've tried not to believe it. But you know how it was back then, Darren. We were having so many problems. And Nick and Hilary had just split up, and I was so afraid Hilary was turning to you for . . . for consolation."

"*Consolation.*"

"I knew she was terrified of no longer being married to a Lightfoot and I was afraid she'd decided to marry a Castleton, instead. Darren, you know as well as I do that the two of you spent a lot of time together during that period."

Darren's handsome face suffused with a dark tint. "She was upset," he agreed. "She did talk to me a few times."

"She's very beautiful."

"I know." He sighed heavily. "And she was scared. For a while I felt sorry for her."

"That's what I was afraid of." Victoria looked at the foot of the bed.

"You and I were always arguing back then. Sometimes I got damn sick and tired of it. Dad was always telling me you were probably going to walk out and take his grandson with you. He kept telling you thought you'd married beneath yourself. He said he knew the signs. He'd seen them in Mom when she married him. He said I'd better learn how to control you. Then he told me I probably wasn't man enough to do it."

"Oh, Darren."

"So, yes, I guess there were times when it was comforting to listen to Hilary's problems. At least I knew I wasn't alone. But I never slept with her, Vicky, Christ, even if I'd wanted to, I wouldn't have done it. Hell, the divorce wasn't even final at that point, remember? She was still married to Nick, as far as I was concerned."

"And you wouldn't have gone to bed with Nick's wife any more than he would have gone to bed with yours," Victoria concluded slowly. A vast sense of relief washed over her.

Darren nodded. "That's about the size of it. Nick and I were raised together. We're practically brothers. We wouldn't mess around with each other's wives any more than Dad and Reed would have swapped Mom and Nora. But there's no way I could ever prove it to you."

"I can never prove I didn't stay with you because of your father's promise to give me an extra helping in the will. Where does that leave us, Darren?"

He sat silently for a moment and then he touched her hand fleetingly. "We're still together, aren't we? We managed to stay together for the past three years, even though we both had a lot of doubts."

Victoria tried a small, misty smile. "Yes, we did, didn't we? Phila said there must be something solid underneath or we wouldn't have made it this far together."

Darren got into bed beside her. "Tell me again why you married me."

"If you bring up the subject of the dress one more time, I will strangle you," Phila announced the next morning as she hopped out of the way of the foaming surf. She was barefoot, her jeans rolled up to midcalf. The sea was in a frisky mood.

"I can't believe you're going to be so stubborn about this." Nick had taken off his shoes, too. He also had his jeans rolled up a couple of inches above his ankles.

"I can be stubborn about anything I want." Phila was about to continue on that theme when Jordan's voice shrilled across the expanse of beach.

"Hi, Phila. Hi, Nick. Hi, Phila. Hi, Nick. Hi, Phila."

"Kid's got a problem with his soundtrack," Nick observed as he waved at Darren, Victoria and their son, who were walking toward them.

"For Pete's sake. They brought the dogs." Phila braced herself as Cupcake and Fifi came charging toward her, their tongues lolling. At the last instant she realized they had already been swimming in the surf. They were soaking wet. "No, wait a minute, you brutes. Don't you dare shake. Stop it."

But it was too late. Nick prudently stepped aside while the rottweilers sprayed Phila. "Hi, Jordan," he said, hoisting the boy up into the air for a quick greeting. "What are you doing today?"

"Gonna find some good seaweed."

"Sounds like a great plan." Nick set Jordan on his feet. The boy immediately headed toward Phila, who was still trying to escape from Cupcake and Fifi.

Darren grinned at Nick. "His seaweed collection has a problem. The stuff self-destructs after it's been in his room for a while, and Mrs. Atkins throws it out."

"Maybe he should collect shells," Nick suggested.

Phila chuckled. "They're not slimy enough. Jordan's a connoisseur, aren't you, Jordan? He wants nice, slimy seaweed."

"Yes." Jordan nodded happily and went off to investigate a possible addition to his collection.

"Ah, now I get the picture," Nick said. " 'Morning, Vicky. You're just the person I wanted to see. I'm trying to convince Phila to go to Darren's fund-raiser with me. She says she doesn't have anything to wear. Maybe you can reassure her."

"Then you will be attending, Nick? I wasn't certain." Victoria studied him with faint anxiety in her eyes.

Nick smiled coolly. "It's a family event, isn't it? I was under the impression Eleanor thinks we should present a united front. I'll be there."

Darren looked at him and nodded brusquely. "Thanks. I appreciate that. The more arm-twisters there, the better. Vicky and I are still a little new at this, but my staff tells me we'd better get used to it."

Victoria watched her son playing near the edge of the water. "It takes money to run for office. Everyone knows that. Money and time. Campaigning is a full-time job, you know."

"I can see where it would be," Nick commented calmly.

Victoria seemed to come to some inner decision. She glanced at Phila. "Don't worry about having an expensive dress. Something simple in black will be just fine. Black goes anywhere."

Phila cleared her throat. "I don't have a single black item in my entire wardrobe."

Victoria surveyed the coral-striped top Phila was wearing with her green jeans. She smiled slowly. "Somehow, I'm not surprised."

"We'll find something for her to wear," Nick said. He caught Phila's hand. "Come on, let's finish this walk you insisted we take. I want to get in another session at the range before lunch."

"I'm getting tired of practicing with that gun, Nick. I don't think I was cut out to be Annie Oakley."

"I'll settle for Matt Dillon. Let's go." He nodded to Darren and Victoria as he tugged on Phila's wrist. "See you two later."

"Right." Darren took his wife's hand and they headed off in pursuit of their son.

Phila glanced back as the little boy yelled in happy excitement and raced toward another strand of seaweed. "Mrs. Atkins is going to have another specimen to deal with this afternoon."

"She won't mind," Nick said. "She loves Jordan."

"Everybody does. Jordan is a very lucky little boy. There are a lot of kids in this world who aren't that lucky."

Nick's hand tightened around hers. "Speaking of kids, how are we doing?"

Phila yanked her gaze back from Jordan. "What are you talking about?"

"I just wondered if you were getting set to come after me with a gun."

Phila's throat felt suddenly tight, her stomach turned queasy. "I won't know for a while yet. A few more days."

"You will let me know as soon as you find out, one way or the other, won't you?"

"Worried?"

"Not particularly. Are you?"

Phila set her teeth together and did not answer.

"Phila?" Nick pulled on her hand. "I asked if you were worried."

"Of course I'm worried. Any woman in my situation would be worried. The odds are that I'm not pregnant, though."

"It only takes one time."

"Thanks for the reassurance. You don't have to remind me," she retorted. "I've seen it happen often enough in my line of work. Ex-line of work."

"Do you ever think of having a family?" Nick asked after a moment.

"The subject has crossed my mind a few times lately," she muttered. "Hard not to think about it when you're worried you might be pregnant."

"I mean, in general, have you given the matter much thought?"

"No."

"Why not?"

Phila let out a long breath. "I'm afraid, I suppose. Families are so fragile. So much can go wrong, even when everyone's intentions are good. People get divorced so easily these days. They put themselves and their precious freedom ahead of their children and then lie to themselves and tell everyone the kids are better off because at least the adults aren't arguing over the dinner table every night."

"Statistically, you've got a point, I guess. The divorce rate is sky-high. The kind of work you used to do and your personal background probably haven't added to your faith in the stability of the American family, either."

"No."

"You've been exposed to the worst-possible-case situations, haven't you? First you lived it, and then you went into the business of dealing with children of families that were having major problems. Stands to reason you'd be a bit skittish on the topic."

"That's me. Skittish on the topic."

"It's kind of ironic, isn't it? You've made a career out of trying to salvage families and children, and yet you're afraid to have a family yourself."

"We've all got our personal hang-ups," she said.

"True." Nick was quiet for a moment, apparently lost in his own thoughts. "Did Vicky and Darren seem a little different to you this morning?"

"Maybe they finally got around to talking to each other."

"About what?"

"This and that," said Phila.

Hilary went cold when she walked into the study and saw Reed sitting at the desk. He hadn't sat in that chair for over two years. The niggling sense that she was losing control of everything made her stomach tighten.

"Hello, Reed. Was there something you wanted?"

Reed looked up from the thick document he was studying and smiled absently at her. He took off his horn-rimmed reading glasses and put them down on the stack of papers he had been going through. "I just wandered in here and happened to see the Hewett papers sitting on the desk. I remember you mentioned something about it last month. How is the deal going? Did you get old Hewett to stop belly-aching about the delivery dates?"

"I think we finally reached a compromise. I talked to Leighton in Purchasing and Contracts and he said Hewett was calming down." Hilary moved over to the desk and glanced at the papers under Reed's glasses. They were just the Hewett papers, she saw with relief.

Reed nodded. "Old Henry Hewett has been with us from the beginning. He took a chance on us back when C&L couldn't even guarantee to pay its light bill. I'd hate to see us stop doing business with him now."

"We won't." Hilary smiled reassuringly. "I didn't realize you were interested in the outcome of the contract negotiations. The last time I mentioned it you didn't want to be bothered with those kinds of details."

"I know." Reed got to his feet and shoved his hands into his pockets. He wandered toward the window and stood looking out over the sweep of lawn. "But things change sometimes. I've been letting you carry most of the load around here for a long time. I'm sorry, Hilary. I shouldn't have pushed it all off on you. For a while I thought Burke was taking care of things."

"He was."

"But after he died, I should have stepped back in and taken the responsibility."

Hilary propped one hip on the edge of the desk, her lizard-skin-shod foot swinging gently. "I wanted the responsibility. I needed it. We both know it saved my sanity. I would have been a basket case three years ago if I hadn't had the Lightfoot portion of the company to manage. C&L means everything to me, Reed."

He nodded, not looking around. "You've worked goddamned hard."

"I've given it everything I've got." Her voice was tight with feeling. She tried to relax.

Reed nodded again, and this time he did turn around. "You're an amazing woman, Hilary. I have nothing but respect for you."

"Thank you."

"You're welcome." Reed walked out of the room.

Hilary closed her eyes and took several deep breaths. Then she got up and went around to her chair. When she reached for the telephone, her fingers were trembling. She dialed the familiar number with great care. She should have thought of this sooner. Much sooner.

"Hello, Mrs. Gilford. Please put me through to Mr. Vellacott."

"I'm sorry, Mrs. Lightfoot. Mr. Vellacott is out of the office."

The fool was probably playing tennis. He always ducked out to play tennis in the afternoons when he thought she wouldn't notice. She should have replaced Vellacott a year ago. But he had been useful precisely because he paid so little attention to details. Hilary stifled her impatience. "Tell him I want him to call me as soon as he gets in, will you?"

"Of course, Mrs. Lightfoot. How is your vacation going?"

"Fine, thank you."

"We were all so pleased to see Mr. Lightfoot in the office the other day. It's been such a long time."

The cold feeling in Hilary's stomach got worse. "Yes, it has, hasn't it? How long was he there, Mrs. Gilford?"

"Not long. Half an hour or less. Seemed anxious to get back to Port Claxton."

"Thank you, Mrs. Gilford. Don't forget I want to speak to Mr. Vellacott as soon as he gets into the office."

"Of course."

Hilary hung up the phone and forced herself to think clearly. Half an hour was not long enough for Nick to have gotten a locksmith in to open the safe. Even if he had, he could not have known what to look for in the first place. If he had gotten the safe open and found the Traynor file it would be meaningless to him. Just another file on another potential supplier. She was not stupid enough to leave anything incriminating lying around.

Hilary started to drum her long, peach-tinted fingernails on the polished surface of the desk and then caught herself. She stilled her hand.

It could not fall apart now, not when she was so close, she thought fearfully. All she had to do was keep it together until the August meeting.

But she was losing total control of the situation, and she sensed it. She probably did not have to worry too much about Darren and Vicky. Eleanor could keep them from wavering. But Reed was a different matter. She had been so sure he was not going to be a problem, but now she was no longer certain.

Reed hadn't shown any real interest in the company for so long she had convinced herself he would never again get involved. But, then, she had been certain Nick would never come back, either. She had been wrong on both counts.

It was not right. She deserved justice. She deserved vengeance. She would not allow herself to be defeated at this stage.

"Crissie," she whispered softly, "if only you were still here. I need you. I need someone to talk to. Why couldn't Phila have been more like you?"

Something was happening to the whole plan; Hilary could feel it. Her instincts warned her that she had to control Reed. He was the biggest risk at the moment.

Hilary decided she had better have a talk with Eleanor.

# 16

*❦*

"I always felt this room turned out the finest of all the rooms in both beach cottages." Eleanor gazed around Reed's library, remembering the hours of planning and work she had put into this particular room. It had been very important to her that Reed's library be right.

"You did a goddamn good . . . I mean, you did a terrific job with it, Eleanor. Nora always said you had great taste." Reed moved over to the butler's tray. "Can I get you something?"

Eleanor glanced at the clock. "Why not? It is after five, isn't it?"

"It's definitely after five. In fact, I think it's getting a little late all the way around." Reed poured two brandies and carried one back to her.

"What makes you say that?"

"Nothing. Just an idle comment."

She took the glass from him and watched him seat himself in the wingback easy chair. She had chosen that chair with great care, wanting it to be comfortable for him. He was a big man; he needed a strong, solid chair.

"Why did you want to talk to me today, Eleanor?" Reed asked after a moment.

"I think you know the answer to that."

"No, I don't. But I am curious."

Eleanor gripped her glass. Reed was notorious about coming directly to a point. "The August meeting."

"Ah."

She looked at him. "Tell me the truth, Reed. Is Nick going to try to take over control of Castleton & Lightfoot at that meeting?"

"I think it's safe to assume he's going to attempt it."

"The only way he can do it is with your help. Are you going to help him?" She could be as blunt as any Lightfoot, Eleanor told herself.

"What makes you think I'm the only hope he's got? Darren could back him or you could. With either of you on his side plus his own shares and Phila's, Nick could do just about anything he damn well pleased."

"The Castletons, all of us, will back Hilary."

Reed nodded. "You'll have to vote as you see fit."

Eleanor leaned toward him. "We need her running things, Reed. The only other person we could even consider is you."

Reed shook his head. "No. I'm not going to step back into that job. Not for all the tea in China. It was good while it lasted, but it's time to turn it over to someone younger. Life is so goddamned short, Eleanor. I don't want to spend the rest of mine behind a desk."

"You want to spend it playing golf? Is that all you can think of these days?"

"No. Sometimes I think about grandkids." Reed sipped his brandy. "I envy you, Eleanor. You have your son and you have little Jordan. That's more than I've had for quite a while now."

"For better or worse, your son appears to have returned. The question is why and for how long?"

"I know. Interesting questions. I ask myself the same ones every day."

"Reed, if he regains control of the company, you know what he'll do with it. He'll start moving away from the government contracts. He'll start pushing again for a broader consumer market. There's no telling how far he'll go with his changes this time. You and Burke won't be there to stop him. He'll have C&L designing home-entertainment centers, for heaven's sake. That's not the kind of business this company was founded upon. Ten years ago you and Burke would have refused even to consider going in that direction."

"That was ten years ago and Burke is dead. I may be dead myself, one of these days." Reed smiled.

"Don't talk like that." The brandy glass trembled in her hand.

He frowned at her obvious alarm. "Hey, just kidding. I'm only trying to point out that what Burke and I wanted for the company ten, twenty or thirty years ago may not be what the next generation wants. And it's their company, Eleanor. The important thing is that C&L survive and that it stay in the families. Beyond that, Nick and Darren are welcome to do any damn thing they want with it as far as I'm concerned."

"What about Hilary?" Eleanor asked, feeling desperate. "Where does she fit into all this? She has some rights, too."

"Yes." Reed took another swallow of brandy. "She has some rights. I'm not denying that."

"She's given everything she has to C&L over the past three years."

"I realize that."

"Yet you're seriously thinking of backing Nick at the August meeting, aren't you?"

"I'm thinking about it, yes. That's all I'm doing at this point, Eleanor. Thinking about it."

Eleanor forced herself to remain calm. "You'd do that, Reed? You'd back Nick? Knowing what he did to all of us three years ago?"

"Lately I've begun to wonder if we all might have misinterpreted what happened three years ago. In fact, I'm beginning to think we may have been fools three years ago."

"It's all that woman's fault." Eleanor whispered. "She started all of this."

"Crissie Masters?"

Eleanor could barely bring herself to nod once in confirmation. She hoped she would not break down in front of Reed. It would be so terribly embarrassing. "Now we have Philadelphia Fox dropping into our lives, interfering with things that should never have concerned her in the first place."

"I think that when all is said and done, I'm going to owe Philadelphia Fox," Reed mused.

Eleanor looked up sharply. "Why do you say that?"

"No matter how you slice it, she's the one responsible for giving me back my son."

"Don't give her too much credit. You don't have Nick back. Not really. Keep in mind, too, that a woman with her sort of background is only looking out for her own self-interest. What else could you expect from her type?"

"Nora used to say that you had a thing about people's backgrounds," Reed commented. "I know yours is pretty fancy, but you've got to remember that mine isn't. Neither is my son's, when you get right down to it. We're just plain folks, Eleanor, even though you've done your best over the years. Plain folks can't look back too much. Nothing there to see. People like us tend to look to the future, not the past."

Eleanor did not think she could take any more. She put down the brandy glass and got to her feet. "Please think very carefully about what you'll be doing to all of us if you back Nick."

"Darren will do all right, even if Nick does take charge," Reed said gently. "Don't you worry about that son of yours."

That comment stopped her abruptly halfway to the door. "How do you know that?" Eleanor whispered.

"I've known him for as long as I've known my own son, remember?

Darren's a lot tougher than Burke ever realized. Or maybe Burke did realize it and was afraid to admit his son would go farther than he had. I don't know the answer to that one, but I do know that if Darren really wants to be governor, he'll get the job, one way or the other. He's got all of Burke's strengths but none of his worst weaknesses, thank God. He's also got a lot of you in him. The part that toughs it out to the end, no matter what the price."

Eleanor felt a curious warmth steal through her. "Burke never thought Darren would make it in politics or anything else," she pointed out, knowing that what she was really asking for was more reassurance.

"Don't mean to speak ill of the dead. God knows Burke was my best friend and partner for over forty years. But I gotta be truthful with you, Eleanor. In some ways he was a horse's ass."

Eleanor flinched. "Yes, he was, wasn't he?" she heard herself say just before her hand touched the doorknob. "Thank you, Reed. Thank you for believing in my son."

"Eleanor?"

"I'm glad you like this room, Reed," she said quickly, before he could continue. "I worked very hard on it for you."

"I know." Reed got to his feet and stood looking at her across the width of the beautiful room. "I've always been comfortable in here."

"Good."

"Why did you spend so much time on my library, Eleanor?"

"Isn't it obvious? I designed these rooms, let's see, when was it? Thirty years ago?"

"Thirty-one years ago."

"Yes. Well, no matter. I knew by then I'd married the wrong man, you see. I knew I was trapped and that I'd never have the man I loved. He was already very happy with someone else. But I wanted to do something for him. I wanted him to be comfortable in some small way and to know that I had been responsible for that comfort. I wanted him to think of me, if only for a second or two, each time he sat in that wing-back chair."

She let herself out the door.

"Are you sure I look all right?" Phila stood in front of the mirrored wall of Nick's bedroom and examined her image for the hundredth time. "I feel weird in black. Like I'm supposed to be going to a funeral or something." The dress was close fitting, accenting Phila's small waist. It was cut in an exquisitely simple style.

Nick stood behind her, tying his bow tie with practiced ease. "I'll admit it's not your best color."

"I *do* look terrible," Phila wailed, her worst fears confirmed. "I knew it. I tried to tell Vicky, but she insisted I buy it."

Nick grinned at her in the mirror. "I'm just teasing. You look terrific. Vicky was right. The dress is very sophisticated. I'm going to be proud as hell to walk into that room tonight with you on my arm."

"What's the bottom line here?" Phila demanded suspiciously.

"The bottom line is that I'm used to seeing you in shocking pink or Day-Glo orange, and somehow black just looks a little quiet on you, that's all."

"Meaning I'm not the sophisticated type?"

"You really are looking for trouble tonight, aren't you?"

"I told you I didn't want to go with you to this thing." She turned away from the mirror, knowing she was fussing too much. She should just accept the inevitable. She was going to go to Darren's fund-raiser because Nick had insisted she be there.

Phila was learning that when Nicodemus Lightfoot put his foot down about something, that foot was anything but light.

She collected the tiny black-and-silver purse Victoria had decreed was appropriate for the dress and stepped into the black evening pumps.

She had her reasons for being irritable and out of sorts tonight, and when the fund-raiser was over she would share the news with Nick. He would, no doubt, be vastly relieved. In the meantime, she had all she could do to deal with it herself.

"Ready?" Nick picked up his black tuxedo jacket.

"As ready as I'll ever be." She turned around and found herself staring at him. "Very impressive," she said at last.

The formal black-and-white evening clothes accentuated his powerful shoulders and the solidly built lines of his body. It made him appear deliciously dangerous, she thought.

"You look like you're seeing a whole new side of me," Nick murmured.

Phila grinned. "Actually, you look like a gangster. All you need is a red rose in your lapel and a bulge under your arm where your shoulder holster is supposed to be."

"And you look like a sexy little vamp." Nick tilted her chin with his forefinger and kissed the tip of her nose. "Let's go before I change my mind and decide to let you jump me."

"I didn't even know you were weighing a decision in that regard. I thought we had to go to this thing."

"Stop whining. We do have to go to this thing." Nick turned off the bedroom lights. "We'll save the jumping for later."

Phila grumbled and then automatically inhaled the magnificent view as they walked through the living room. The late-summer sun was disappearing slowly, bathing Elliott Bay and the islands in a warm, yellow glow.

"Heck of a view," Phila said. "You must have missed this place while you were living in California."

"I did miss it. I don't think I realized just how much until now."

"This is certainly a fancy condominium. Great location, great view, all the amenities. First-class urban design. I wonder how many low-income housing units were demolished so the developers could build this sucker."

Nick chuckled. "Save your energy. I'm not going to let you make me feel guilty about living here. I earned every square inch of this place. Just for your information, however, the building that used to be on this site was an old, abandoned warehouse. A real eyesore. Does that make you feel better?"

"Much." She took one last look around at the refined collection of polished antique furniture. "Have the Lightfoots and Castletons always gone for the Early Constitution look?"

"You don't like the interior design of this place?"

Phila shrugged. "Kind of dark. Needs some color."

Nick glanced around as he turned off the lights. He smiled. "I wondered about that myself."

By the time Nick and Phila arrived, a well-heeled, well-dressed crowd had already gathered in the large reception room at the top of the sleek downtown high-rise. Phila looked around warily as she walked through the door on Nick's arm. The room was full, she noted. Darren must be pleased. The lively hum of voices was interrupted here and there by an occasional laugh and the clink of ice in glasses.

A formally dressed trio of musicians played Mozart in one corner, and waiters carrying trays of hors d'oeuvres and drinks circulated through the crowd. The panorama of Seattle and its bay was spread out far below, magnificently showcased through huge windows. The last gleam of sunlight glanced off the Olympics.

But the view, the food, the drinks and Mozart all took second place to the main attraction of the evening. There was no doubt about it, Darren Castleton was the primary focus of attention. Lean, elegant, dynamic, he held center stage wherever he moved in the crowd. He did so easily, naturally, as if it were second nature to him. He came alive in a crowd like this the way a brilliant actor came alive on the screen. Beside him, Victoria looked just as beautifully at ease, just as much in control. The ideal American couple.

"Charisma," Phila murmured, snagging a glass of champagne off a passing tray.

Nick crunched an oyster wrapped in bacon. "Yeah, he's got it in spades, doesn't he? You sort of have to see him working a crowd like this to realize the effect he has on people."

"It's a rare form of power," Phila said slowly.

"Uh huh. I always knew Darren had something going for him, something I couldn't quite define, but as long as Burke was alive, it was subdued. As if whatever it was hadn't had a chance really to blossom. Now it's starting to shine. Jesus. The man really might be the next governor of this state."

"I think you're right," Phila said softly. "And look at Vicky. She'd make a perfect governor's lady. Heck, she'd make a perfect president's lady. She's so poised and charming and lovely."

"And when they bring out little Jordan for the photographers, they're going to get the front page in tomorrow's *Seattle Times*," Nick concluded.

"Be interesting to see if Jordan tries to display his self-destructing seaweed collection for the photographers." Phila glanced around and saw Eleanor moving toward them.

"There you are," Eleanor said grandly as she stopped in front of them. Her face was aglow with maternal pride. "Thank you for coming tonight, Nick."

"I said we'd be here." Nick took a glass from a passing tray. "Looks like everything's going well. Where's Dad?"

"Over there with Hilary, talking to some business friends." Eleanor glanced at Phila. "I see you decided to attend after all?"

"I couldn't get out of it." Phila smiled brilliantly. "I'll try not to embarrass the families."

"That would be much appreciated." Eleanor moved away with a nod to Nick.

"In our baiting mode tonight, are we?" Nick observed quietly, his eyes on the crowd.

"She started it."

"Eleanor didn't start anything. You're just edgy this evening. Why?"

"I am not edgy. It's Eleanor who's edgy, not me. If you want to calm her down, tell her you've decided to give full support to Darren in his bid for the governor's job."

"I'm here tonight, aren't I? Doesn't that show support?"

"It's a step in the right direction, but Darren requires more than that and you know it. He needs your help behind the scenes, not just at public functions like this."

"Philadelphia Fox, the political mastermind."

"That's me." Phila realized she was still feeling irritable and a little depressed. She reached for another glass of champagne.

"Has it escaped your notice that Darren is hardly a liberal Democrat?"

"No, but I have hopes for him."

"You think he'll convert?"

Phila smiled ruefully. "I don't have that much hope for him, but I think he can be made to see reason, which puts him several notches above the average Republican. He's educable."

"I'm sure he'll be delighted to hear that."

Phila grinned briefly. "I already told him." She glanced around again and spotted a familiar figure. "Hilary certainly looks gorgeous tonight."

"Hilary always looks gorgeous." Nick did not seem particularly interested. "Come on, we'd better mingle. This is business."

"Think of it as Family Unity night. The Castletons and the Lightfoots—just one big happy family."

Nick started into the crowd, towing Phila behind him. He nodded at several people, stopped to talk briefly with others and finally halted near a man and a woman who were standing near the windows. The woman, an attractive brunette in her early forties, glanced up and then smiled warmly.

"Nick! Good to see you again. It's been awhile. Are you just visiting, or are you home to stay?"

"I plan to stay this time. Phila, this is Barbara Appleton and her husband, Norm. They're old friends. Barbara, Norm, this is Philadelphia Fox."

"How do you do?" Phila said politely. "Don't I know your name from somewhere, Mrs. Appleton?"

"I make the papers once in a while, when there's nothing else of great importance occurring in the world." Barbara laughed.

Phila thought quickly, made the connection and brightened immediately. "Now I remember. You're one of the people working to get funding for day-care facilities for the children of homeless people. We've heard about your efforts all the way over in eastern Washington. I'm thrilled to meet you."

Barbara Appleton smiled, looking faintly bemused. "Most people run the other way when they're introduced to me. They're afraid I'll ask for money. Do you have an interest in the matter of day care for homeless kids?"

"I am—was—a social worker. Until recently I've been working with the foster-home program. I'm very aware of the homeless problem here in Seattle."

"The parents are under such stress, and the children suffer so. They desperately need a structured, safe environment. You can't raise children in cars and buses and shelters."

"If you're a parent, you can't very well hunt for a job or get training or deal with the bureaucracy of the welfare system if you've got a couple of kids in your arms. I think the day-care idea for those kids is great. How's the project going?"

"We're supporting two centers now and hope to get a third started this fall."

"Have you talked to Darren and Vicky about this?" Phila asked.

Barbara's eyes narrowed thoughtfully. "No, as a matter of fact, I haven't. I assumed Darren would not be particularly supportive."

Phila tossed that assumption aside with a flick of her hand. "Oh, don't worry about Darren, he's not a reactionary, ultraconservative, right-wing turkey like the rest of the Castletons and Lightfoots. He's much more flexible, much more open to information. What's more, he's married to a woman who is very interested in children's issues."

"Is that right?" Barbara's gaze drifted toward the center of the room, where Darren and Vicky stood talking to a circle of people. "I hadn't realized that. Perhaps I'll just have a word or two with Victoria Castleton. Norm, go ahead and get out the checkbook. It looks as though we may be making a contribution tonight, after all. Nice to have met you, Phila. Good to see you again, Nick. Let's get together for dinner soon."

"Yeah, we'll do that," said Nick, his eyes amused as he nodded at the other two. When the Appletons were out of earshot, he looked down at Phila. "Congratulations. You just got money out of the tightest checkbook in the room."

Phila was astonished. "Why are they here, if they're not strong supporters?"

"According to Vicky, you don't dare not invite Barbara and Norm to an affair like this. They wield a lot of clout in this town. But no one actually expected to get their financial support tonight. Barbara's notorious about only backing a few selected pols. When she does back them, however, they generally do well. She can bring money out of the woodwork. Lots of it. Let's hope you didn't oversell Darren's support for children's issues."

"I didn't. Darren will listen to children's advocates. I know he will. If he doesn't, Vicky will make him listen." Phila was sure of herself. She looked thoughtfully around the room. "You know, a person could do a lot with a roomful of money like this."

"That's the whole idea." Nick's voice was bland. "What's that funny expression on your face? You thinking of getting into politics?"

"Who, me?"

"Don't look so damned innocent."

"Heavens, I'd make a lousy politician."

"That's true. You're too mouthy. You'd be much better at the fund-raising end of things."

"You think so?"

"Sure. You're the type who'd be happy to beat up on people until they forked over a contribution. It takes nerve to be an arm-twister at an event like this."

Phila looked around. "This could be fun. Let's go practice."

Nick groaned. "Give the woman a taste of power and she goes wild."

Phila spent the rest of the evening listening, observing and asking questions. It took her mind off her other problems. Reed gravitated toward her at one point, a drink in his hand, and asked how she was getting along.

"Well, no one's tried to throw me out yet."

Reed nodded, pleased. "A good sign. You must be keeping your mouth under control."

"I'm getting sick and tired of comments on my mouthiness. Where's Hilary?"

"Talking to some business acquaintances. Where's Nick?"

"Over there with that heavyset man in the corner."

Reed glanced in that direction and nodded. "That's Graveston. Owns a couple of restaurants here in town."

Eleanor spotted them and left a small group of women to come over to Reed.

"There you are, Reed, I've been looking for you. Have you seen the Brands yet?"

"Over near the buffet table," Reed said. "Why?"

"I want to make sure they meet Darren and Vicky. Everything is going very well, don't you think?"

"It's going great," Phila said, even though she hadn't been asked. "Darren's a natural, isn't he?"

Eleanor looked at her. "Yes, he is."

"Nick and I were talking earlier about how this political business definitely seems to be Darren's proper niche. Be a shame to waste all that charisma. Lord knows we need more decent men in office."

Eleanor's gaze sharpened. "You and Nick were discussing this?"

Phila nodded, sipping at her champagne. "Nick's seen the light, you know, Eleanor."

"What light have I seen?" Nick asked from directly behind Phila.

Phila jumped in surprise and then smiled meaningfully. "The light about Darren's future in politics. I was just telling Eleanor that you've decided it's the right thing for him."

Nick looked at his father. "With her around, I don't even need to open my own mouth. She's starting to do all my talking for me."

Reed's grin came and went. "I've noticed."

Eleanor was staring at Nick. "Do you mean it?"

"Ask Phila. She seems to be doing all my thinking for me tonight." Nick glanced across the top of Eleanor's head. "There goes Howard Compton. I'd better say hello." He started to excuse himself and then spotted the full glass in Phila's hand. "How much champagne have you had already?"

"This is only my second glass. I think. Maybe it's my third. I'm not sure. Don't be such a grouch."

"Keep an eye on her," Nick said to Reed. "She's a bit testy this evening. In this mood she gets into trouble easily."

"I don't know what you expect me to do with her. Want some more food, Phila?"

"Yes, please." She smiled widely at Reed. "Don't pay any attention to Nick. He never wants me to have any fun."

Half an hour later Phila found herself standing alone conveniently near the hall that led to the rest rooms. She decided she'd better take advantage of the opportunity. She went down the carpeted hallway and pushed open the appropriate door.

She stood staring in amazement at the plush facilities. The room had been done in soft turquoise and rose and featured a couple of graceful velvet sofas, a wall of mirrors lit with makeup lights and marble trim on all the stalls.

But it was the view from the window in each stall that captivated Phila. The scenic panorama would have graced any upscale condominium, and here it was wasted on a rest room. Real class. Phila started opening stall doors to see which cubicle had the best view.

She was watching the lights of the city from the middle stall when she heard the outer door of the lounge open and close. Phila hurried out to wash her hands, embarrassed that someone might discover her enthralled with the view from a rest-room stall.

She stopped short, her insides twisting with sudden, sick tension as she saw Hilary standing by the long row of marble sinks. Phila's pleasantly lightheaded feeling died when she saw the anger twisting the other woman's beautiful face. It was obvious Hilary had psyched herself up for a confrontation.

She looked like a savage queen, Phila thought, awed by the threat of the uncontrolled emotion in Hilary's eyes.

"Hello, Hilary," Phila said cautiously.

"God, you have a talent for looking innocent, you little bitch."

Phila sucked in her breath as a cold, anguished chill shot through her. "I know how you must be feeling—"

"You know nothing of how I feel. *Nothing*. You really think you're going to win, don't you?" Hilary asked. "Oh, I've seen the way they're starting to pay attention to you—believe in you, listen to you. And because of you, they're all starting to believe in Nick again. An interesting process. But you won't win, Phila. I can't let you. I've put too much time, too much of myself into this game, to lose it all now."

Phila mentally fought the onslaught of Hilary's fury. "Nick told me all about Traynor and your plans to ruin the company. But I can't let you do that to the families. They don't deserve it."

The lounge door opened again, and Nick strolled into the room with as much aplomb as if he were walking into a boardroom. He stood there, raw and masculine-looking, amid the luxurious, ultrafeminine surroundings. He looked at Phila.

"I saw you head for the ladies' room and I saw Hilary follow. Something told me I'd like to be included in a high-level meeting like this. What don't we deserve, Phila?" he asked.

"She wants to punish all of you for what happened three years ago," Phila said softly, her eyes on Hilary's rigid features. "But it isn't fair. You're all innocent. Except Burke, of course."

"You're right, you know." Hilary folded her arms under her breasts and watched Phila. "I intend to take C&L apart bit by bit and make a fortune for myself in the process." Hilary turned her eyes on Nick. "I'm going to destroy everything any of you care about."

"It's taken you nearly three years to set it up but you're about ready to pull it off, aren't you?" Nick asked mildly.

"Yes," Hilary said proudly, "and I will pull it off. When I'm finished I'll have everything I want, everything I need, and the Castletons and Lightfoots will just have to watch their precious family firm go into the hands of strangers."

"There was no rape, was there, Hilary?" Phila asked. "It was a seduction. You seduced Burke out of desperation when you realized Nick was going to leave the firm and go through with the divorce if you refused to follow him. You knew you had no chance of seducing Reed. He would never have touched you. Neither would Darren. But Burke was a different breed of cat."

"You're wrong. There was a rape. It was a rape in almost every sense of the word except the physical as far as I was concerned. Everything I had been promised was taken from me. I had made a bargain with the Lightfoots. I had married one of them, and in return I was supposed to get what I wanted."

Phila nodded slowly as the rest of the puzzle fell into place at last. "But when you realized you were going to lose all of it, you turned to Burke, didn't you? It had to have been Burke. He was the weak one. You knew he was the only one left you could use."

"He wanted me so badly he could taste it. He had wanted me ever since I'd walked in the front door as Nick's wife."

"Probably because you fell into the category of forbidden fruit," Phila said. "You played on that, didn't you? You thought if you controlled Burke he would support you after you lost your status as a Lightfoot wife. You were terrified of losing that status. It was all you cared about. It was the reason you had married Nick in the first place."

"True." Hilary smiled. "You think you know me so well, don't you? Because of Crissie, I suppose?"

"That's part of it. You were right, Hilary. You did have a lot in common with Crissie. You need an enormous amount of financial security the same way Crissie needed it. You're pathological about it. It's the single most important thing in the world to you."

"A woman has to take care of herself in this world."

"With your marriage falling apart and with no possibility of getting your hooks into Reed or Darren, Burke was your only chance of hanging on to some security. How far did your fantasies take you, Hilary? Did you actually think he might divorce Eleanor and marry you?"

"It was always a possibility," Hilary agreed. "But there was no need to go that route after I accidentally got pregnant. I hadn't even thought of that approach. But when I realized I was going to have the baby, I suddenly saw how much simpler everything would be if I said the baby was Nick's. As the mother of a Lightfoot baby, my status would be inviolate for the rest of my life."

"But why set out to take apart the company, Hilary?" Nick asked softly. "Why not just be satisfied with taking control of it?"

Hilary slid a cold glance in his direction. "Because after I lost Burke's baby, I realized I was in constant jeopardy. I knew that, sooner or later, you would probably come back like a king returning to claim the throne. You always considered C&L your birthright."

"But you were Reed's wife. You were safe," Phila pointed out.

"Just how long do you think I would have remained Reed's wife if everyone discovered the truth? I couldn't take the chance. I saw my opportunity to take over when Reed began losing interest in the company. I realized that if I handled things right, I could gradually acquire enough power to sell off the company and make myself safe and secure for the rest of my life. I wouldn't need Lightfoots or Castletons at all. I would be free. *And that's exactly what's going to happen."*

"It isn't going to go down that way, Hilary," Nick said. "I'm back."

Hilary smiled. "You came back too late, Nick. Or perhaps too soon. Either way you don't have the power to take over now. Even with Crissie's shares, you can't get enough family backing by August to pull it off. I'll still be CEO after the annual meeting."

"Don't count on it."

"You think the families will believe any of this? You can shout yourself hoarse trying to tell them what's going on. They won't buy it. I've had three years to work on all of them. By now they all have reasons for wanting me to stay in charge. You're the renegade as far as they're concerned, not me."

"I know."

Hilary's beautiful face became tight with sudden fury. "None of it had to happen this way. It's all your fault, damn you. We had a business deal, you and I. You violated our agreement."

"It was supposed to be a marriage, not a business arrangement. I wanted a wife, not a business partner."

"A wife? You wanted a fool of a woman who would follow you barefoot through the burning sand anywhere you chose to lead." Hilary's lovely mouth twisted with sarcasm. "What kind of an idiot did you think I was? I married you because you were the heir apparent to C&L. Not for any other reason. What other reason could there have been?"

"Good question. Certainly not because you loved me?"

"You bastard. Love had nothing to do with it. It was business on both sides. You wanted me for what I could bring to the family: beauty, background and breeding."

"You wanted me because your family fortunes were on the skids. You wanted to marry money."

"It's the way it's done in our world, Nick. Remember? I was brought up to understand these things, just as Eleanor understood them forty years ago."

"You don't have a glimmer of understanding, Hilary." Nick propped one shoulder against the wall.

"That's not true. I was prepared to hold up my end of the deal. I would have made you a good wife as long as you were head of C&L. But within eighteen months of our wedding you were getting ready to walk away from the firm just because Reed and Burke wouldn't let you do what you wanted with the company. *And you expected me to go with you."*

"Yeah. Real dumb on my part. Somewhere along the line I got the idea that a wife is supposed to stick with her husband regardless of what kind of job he holds."

"That's an outdated, chauvinistic, stupid thing to say."

"Depends on the wife," Nick said. "My mother would have followed my father into a swamp."

Hilary gave a sharp exclamation of disgust and turned back to Phila. "Crissie understood. She knew what I wanted, what I needed. She would have helped me."

"She understood, but she didn't turn the shares over to you and she never bothered to change her will, did she?" Phila shook her head. "Some part of her could never have let you destroy C&L, Hilary."

"You're wrong. She would have backed me all the way."

"No, I don't think so. The thing is, Hilary, no matter what happened, no matter how much she sympathized with you, she could never have allowed you to hurt the Castletons that badly. You see, in the end, when the chips were down, Crissie considered herself family."

# 17

❧

"I need a drink." Phila walked through the door of Nick's condominium and headed straight for the kitchen.

"You've already had enough champagne to float a tanker. It's a wonder you can still stand up. What is it with you tonight? I've never seen you like this." Nick shot the bolt on the door and followed her.

Along the way, he managed to leave behind his bow tie, black jacket and gold cuff links. By the time he reached the kitchen he looked thoroughly disreputable and dangerously sexy as far as Phila was concerned. She decided it wasn't fair.

"I'm celebrating." Phila jerked open the cupboard and removed the half-empty bottle of scotch. She had a little trouble getting a glass off the next shelf. It almost slipped out of her grasp.

"What are you celebrating?" Nick reached out casually and took the bottle from her hand. Then he reached for the glass.

Phila ignored the question and sighed softly. "It was very sad, wasn't it, Nick?" She looked at him as he splashed a minuscule amount of scotch into her glass and handed it to her.

"What was sad? That little scene with Hilary in the women's room? It wasn't sad. It was inevitable. She's beginning to feel the pressure. Tonight she realized she's losing."

"How did you happen to walk in when you did?"

"I've learned that it's best to keep an eye on you. You do have a way of getting into trouble."

"Totally untrue. I resent that." She tasted the scotch and realized she really didn't want any more to drink after all. She put the glass down on the counter.

"When did you realize the baby was Burke's?" Nick asked quietly.

"It all came together tonight when Hilary started talking about how she had been cheated. It's obvious when you stop and think about it, though. Everyone should have realized it a long time ago. After all, there's no way you could have done it and then walked out. You're just not the type. And Darren is a little too wary of Hilary to be comfortable going to bed with her. Besides, he loves Vicky. But the real clue was the way Eleanor acted."

"Eleanor? How did she act?"

Phila shrugged. "She was always so protective, so adamant about supporting and defending Hilary. After a while it became obvious she suspected the truth or at least part of it. She still believed there had been a rape. But deep down I think she believed it was Burke who had raped Hilary, not you. Hilary probably planted that fear herself, and played on it to her own advantage."

"Christ."

"Whatever the reason, Eleanor felt she had a responsibility toward Hilary. After all, she was the one who had brought Hilary into the families. Then, too, she feels a kind of kinship with her because they both married into the families for similar reasons."

"Kinship or not, the last thing she would want is for the truth to come out. That would tarnish old Burke's image as well as the image of family unity beyond repair."

"Right. In this case, poor Eleanor was forced to choose which family to protect. She stuck with the Castletons, naturally, although she could never really turn completely on your family, either. She's very fond of you and Reed. So she tried to ignore everything, as usual, and did her best to keep the image intact. She's an expert on living the image."

"For the past three years she was the one who kept me posted on what was happening in the families. Why did she bother?"

"She felt guilty about the way you had been forced to take the rap. But there had to be a bad guy, and you were the logical choice for the job. She could not admit it was Burke."

"And there was my father, conveniently offering marriage to atone for my behavior."

"And as a means of keeping his grandchild. Don't forget that part. He really did believe the baby was yours."

Nick frowned. "Why was Hilary so certain Crissie would have backed her with the shares? How did those two get to be so close?"

"Crissie and Hilary were lovers."

"They were *what?*" Nick stared at her, dumbfounded.

"You heard me."

"Hilary prefers women?"

"Yes. So did Crissie. Don't look so shocked, Nick. Fact of life, you know. Some women do."

He looked a little dazed. "I know. I realize that. But I never thought Hilary might be like that. It just never occurred to me. Damn. It explains a lot. Maybe that's why we . . . she and I . . . Maybe that's why I could never get her to . . ."

"Could be," Phila agreed.

"And Crissie?"

"Uh-huh. She hated men because she had been badly abused by a couple of her mother's live-in boyfriends. Knowing her father had deserted her before she was even born didn't help matters, either."

Nick's expression was stark. "What about you and Crissie?"

Phila shook her head, a small smile playing around the corners of her mouth. "No. We were friends, Crissie and I, but not lovers. Frankly, I wasn't sure I was cut out for sex of any persuasion until I met you."

Nick grinned slowly, his eyes revealing his satisfaction. "Aw, shucks, ma'am, t'weren't nothin'. Just glad to be able to help out."

"Sometimes the redneck in your soul is not far below the surface."

"I told you in the beginning I come from a long line of shitkickers."

"So you did."

Nick paused and then said gently, "You didn't tell me what you were celebrating."

She looked at him. "I just found out today I'm not pregnant."

"I see." He watched her with one of his inscrutable expressions.

Phila was annoyed by his lack of reaction. "Well? Aren't you relieved?"

"Not particularly. What about you? Are you relieved?"

"Of course I'm relieved. Why shouldn't I be relieved?" She began to pace the kitchen, "This makes everything much simpler all the way around."

"You think so?"

"Don't be dense. It certainly does."

"I guess I don't have to worry about you coming after me with a gun," Nick observed thoughtfully. "But I can't help thinking that a miniature Philadelphia would have been sort of cute."

"It's not a joking matter, Nick."

"No, ma'am."

"This way we both have all our options open."

"Right. Nothing like having options."

"Are you going to take this seriously or not?" she raged, swinging to a halt in front of him.

"That depends."

"On what?"

"On the answer to my next question." Nick braced his hands on the counter and leaned back. He studied Phila carefully. "Do you think," he said, "that it's just barely possible you might be a little in love with me?"

The room spun around Phila. She reached out and grasped two fistfuls of Nick's pleated white shirt and scowled fiercely up at him. "Are you making fun of me?"

"Absolutely not."

"You're laughing."

"No. It's just a nervous reaction, I think."

"You are never nervous. You're always cool as a glacier. Besides, what have you got to be nervous about?" She tightened her hold on his shirtfront.

"Well, I'm in love with you, and it stands to reason I'm a tad anxious in case you might not be in love with me."

"*Nick.*" She released his shirt to clamp her hands behind his head. Then she stood on tiptoe and pulled his face down to hers. Her mouth crushed his until she felt his teeth grind against hers.

"Does this mean yes?" Nick lifted his head and grinned down at her.

She clung to him, burying her nose against his pristine white shirt. "I love you. I've been falling in love with you for ages. I was so disappointed at first today when I discovered I wasn't pregnant. Then I told myself it was for the best. It *is* for the best. Only it would have given me a good excuse to hang around you and I did want to hang around. Oh, Nick, I was so scared you wouldn't be able to love me back."

He propped up her chin with his finger, his eyes gleaming behind the lenses of his glasses. "To tell you the truth, I was sort of hoping you'd gotten knocked up that first time. I realized it the next morning when you threatened to come after me with the gun. I found myself thinking that wouldn't be such a bad fate."

"Knocked up? Is that any way to talk? Show some respect, Lightfoot."

He looked down at her with eyes full of laughter. "I'll try. But I think I could do a much better job of it in bed."

A rush of excitement went through her, and then she remembered exactly why she was celebrating. Phila sighed and leaned her head back against his chest. "Soon," she promised.

"Yeah, like two minutes from now. Let's go, honey. I can't wait for you to start ripping off my clothes."

"Nick, for heaven's sake, weren't you listening? I said I was celebrating the fact that I wasn't pregnant, remember?"

"How could I forget?"

Phila grew exasperated. "Well, how do you think I first realized I wasn't knocked up, as you so delicately put it, you big idiot?"

"Uh, the usual way, I guess?"

"Yes, the usual way. Now do you get the point?"

"About not going to bed? I fail to see the problem."

"Nick, for pete's sake, can't you demonstrate a modicum of sensitivity here?"

"I get it. You're embarrassed at the idea of throwing yourself at me during this particular time of the month. How's that for sensitivity?"

Phila collapsed against his chest. "Good lord, what brain power. Must be all of two watts. Hard to believe they let you run a zillion-dollar-a-year corporation."

He nuzzled the place behind her ear and wrapped his hands around her waist. "I've got news for you, sweetheart, a good executive never lets petty details get in the way."

"But, Nick . . ."

"I don't mind, if you don't."

"Well, I certainly do mind. It doesn't sound like a respectable idea at all."

"Are you uncomfortable? Got cramps?"

"No." Her voice was muffled against his shirt. "This is getting embarrassing."

"Are you flowing very heavily?"

"No. Just spotting. I told you, I barely started today, but . . ."

"Then let's go fool around, huh?"

"Nick, I can't. I'm too embarrassed by the whole idea, and that's that." She pushed herself away from him and started to stalk out of the kitchen. Nick caught up with her at the door.

"Take it easy, love," he said with a smile and scooped her up into his arms. He started down the hall to the bedroom.

"Where are we going? What are you doing?"

"You are obviously too embarrassed to make your usual assertive moves on me tonight, so maybe the time has come to try it another way."

"What other way?"

"Trust me."

"Hah. Why are you carrying me?"

"Because I feel like it. Do you mind?"

She thought about it carefully. "No, I guess not."

"Good, because it's too late to argue."

He strode into the bedroom and stood her carefully on her feet while he turned back the covers on the bed. Then he smiled at her as he removed his glasses and set them on the bedside table. There was love and laughter and a rapidly kindling desire in his normally cool eyes.

"Okay," he said. "Sit down."

Phila sat down abruptly on the edge of the bed. She watched with more curiosity than anything else as Nick went down on one knee in front of her and began removing her high-heeled evening shoes. "What are you doing now?"

"What does it look like I'm doing? I'm undressing you."

"You're doing a good job of it."

"I've been learning from you," he said. He eased her out of the black gown and then went to work on her pantyhose and bra. She closed her eyes, savoring the feel of his hands.

"Go take care of things in the bathroom, honey. When you come out, I'll be ready."

Phila nodded agreeably and opened her eyes just far enough to find the bathroom door. When she emerged a few minutes later she saw Nick waiting for her. He was naked and fully aroused. She stood staring at him, thinking about how magnificent he looked.

"Hi," she said.

"Hi, yourself."

"I used to think you were too big, you know," she said.

"Did you?"

"I don't like big men."

"Maybe I'll shrink with time."

"I doubt it." Then she giggled as her eyes went lower to his heavy, thrusting manhood. "On second thought, maybe parts of you will shrink from time to time."

"But probably not for long. Not with you around." He came forward and took her hand to draw her over to the bed.

Phila sank down onto the sheets with a vast sense of relief. "Do you really love me, Nick?" She gazed up at him with dreamy eyes.

"I really love you."

"I've never been in love before. Not really. It's nice, isn't it?" she asked.

"Very nice. And for the record, I haven't ever really been in love before, either. Not like this. Nothing has ever felt the way it does with you."

He ran his fingers slowly along the inside of her thigh. She squirmed a little beneath the sensual stroking and somehow his palm slid over her, cupping her intimately. A familiar liquid heat began to build between her legs.

"Nick?"

"Hmm?"

"You're going to do this your way tonight, aren't you?"

"Yes." He kissed her breast and then raised his head to look down at her. His eyes were intent. "I want you to learn to trust me in every way there is."

"Yes."

"Will that be so hard for you?" he asked gently.

"No." It was the truth, Phila thought in growing wonder. She was floating. His hands felt good—strong and sure and safe. His mouth drifted lightly, lazily over her whole body. He tasted her as if she were a rare delicacy, sampling the curve of her shoulder, the underside of her breasts, the insides of her ankles and every place in between.

It had never been quite like this before, she reflected in a fleeting moment of rationality. She had never just lain flat on her back and given herself up to the erotic sensations. Always before she had been too busy exploring him, learning her own power, delighting in the thrill of being able to make him explode beneath her touch. Too busy feeling safe and in command of everything.

For the first time since she had met him their lovemaking position was reversed. She waited for the familiar sense of panic. But nothing happened. Everything was happening so slowly and she was feeling so relaxed that she could not manage to work up any real alarm.

This was Nick, and with Nick she would always be safe.

His hands continued their infinitely patient movements. Time ceased to have any meaning for Phila. She felt heavy and warm, filled with a languid sensuality that made her begin to twist and turn on the sheets. Her legs parted.

When Nick's finger strayed into the crisp strands of silk at the apex of her thighs Phila moaned and pulled a pillow over her mouth. His finger stroked lower, separating the soft folds and circling her gently.

"Nick, Nick." Phila tossed aside the pillow but did not open her eyes. She lifted herself against his hand and he slid a second finger into her moist heat. "Oh, my God, *Nick.*"

"Does that feel good, sweetheart?"

"Yes, yes, yes."

"How about this?"

She trembled and clutched at the pillow again as he flicked the small, swelling nub of sensation between her thighs. Simultaneously he plunged his fingers back into her and Phila was suddenly flying into a million sparkling pieces.

*"Come here."* Instinctively she released the pillow and grabbed at him. In that moment it didn't matter who was on top and who was on the bottom. She just wanted to feel all of him. She had to have him close to her.

Nick allowed her to pull him down on top of her. He entered her heavily as the last tremors of her release began to fade. He plunged quickly, withdrew himself almost completely and then, when she cried out in frustration, drove forward again.

Nick was the focus of her whole world. He was over her, in her, enfolding her, confining her within the sensual prison of his arms. Phila was aware of his weight along every inch of her body. She was also aware of feeling safe and cherished as she never had before in her life.

She felt as if she had finally come home.

Before Phila could grasp the fact that her first climax was nearly over, another one was upon her. This one was slow, deep and seemed to last forever. She called Nick's name and held him closer, wrapping her legs around his hips.

"Sweetheart. Oh, *Phila.* Love me, Love me."

"I love you, Nick."

Nick went rigid in her arms, arching over her, filling her, crushing her beneath him as he lost himself in her warmth. Phila was dimly aware of his shuddering release and she held on to him more tightly than she had ever held on to anything or anyone in her life.

When it was over he collapsed along the length of her, his legs pinning hers, his hands holding her wrists gently captive. His solid weight pressed her deep into the bedding.

Phila came slowly back to her senses. The first thing she was fully aware of was the musky, sexy scent of the man lying on top of her. The next thing she focused on was the fact that she was trapped beneath Nick's full weight. She waited again for the panic, but it did not come.

When the old fear did not materialize, she began drawing an interesting pattern on Nick's strongly contoured back.

"You all right?" He shifted drowsily, lifting himself up on his elbows. His eyes glittered with the age-old expression of the fully satiated male, but there was a tenderness in his gaze that made Phila catch her breath.

"I think so." She smiled up at him. "You're on top."

"I told you I decided it was time to experiment with a new position."

She grinned. "I think the basic missionary position is considered a classic."

"You've got to admit that, for us, it's definitely a change of pace."

"True. Very wicked."

He waited a few seconds and then made an observation. "I can't help noticing that you're not clawing and kicking and trying to push me off onto the floor."

"No." She moved one leg experimentally. Nick let her slide it out from under his. She curved her foot and drew it up along the back of his calf. The hair on his leg tickled the sole of her foot, and she smiled.

"Do you like it better this way?" Phila asked softly, searching his face.

"I like it any way I can get it with you." He kissed her throat. "Believe me, there's nothing on this earth like the feel of you throwing yourself on top of me. But I've been wondering when you'd trust me enough to let me return the favor."

Phila narrowed her eyes. "It was a matter of trust, in a way, wasn't it?"

Nick nodded, his gaze serious. "I sensed that much right from the beginning. I figured the day you could let me make love to you like this would be the day I'd know for sure we were making real progress in this relationship."

"Typical of a man to look for progress in terms of a physical relationship," she said with mocking scorn.

"Yeah." He kissed her thoroughly and moved reluctantly off to the side. "Not, you understand, that I ever want you to give up your patented flying assault tactics." He yawned.

"You're a greedy man." She punched him lightly on the shoulder and slid out of bed. "Be right back." She headed for the bathroom.

When she returned a few minutes later she thought he had gone to sleep. But his arm curved around her as she crawled back into bed beside him.

"I've been thinking," Nick said.

"What about?"

"Getting married."

Phila froze. "Married! Who? Us? You and me?"

"You've got to admit there's a certain logic to it."

Phila sat up, holding the sheet to her breasts. "Good grief, Nick, we can't possibly get married." She swallowed nervously. "But thank you very much for asking," she added lamely.

He didn't move, but his eyes pinned her in the shadows. "You've got a problem with the idea of marrying me?"

She took a steadying breath. "Be reasonable, Nick. Anyone who marries a Lightfoot or a Castleton marries into a lot of family. It would be miserable for everyone concerned if you married someone the other members of the families didn't like. Let's be honest here. If there's one thing we can say with absolute certainty, it's that I'm not Miss Popularity as far as the rest of the Lightfoots and Castletons are concerned."

"Phila, I'm asking you to marry *me*, not the other people in the families."

"They could never accept me, Nick, and you know it."

"I don't give a damn if they accept you. I'm the one you're marrying. We don't have to deal with any of the rest of them except at the annual meetings."

"And Fourth of July celebrations and Christmas and summer holidays and Darren's political functions and Eleanor's dinner parties and a hundred other events during the year."

"You're exaggerating. We won't go to any of those things if you're uncomfortable."

"I told you I would be uncomfortable at that fund-raiser tonight, and you insisted on dragging me to it."

"That was different," he bit out.

"Was it? I don't think so."

"I thought you'd find it interesting once you got there, and I was right. Just as I was right about you enjoying a new position in bed tonight."

"Don't try to draw any parallels between going to a political fund-raiser and going to bed, for heaven's sake."

"Hell, if you feel that strongly about family events, we'll avoid them. I've skipped them for the past three years, haven't I?"

"Use your head, Nick. You can't possibly run the company and avoid socializing with the families. Besides, look at it from my point of view. Do you think I want to be the reason you don't take part in all the family traditions? I'd always feel guilty about coming between you and the rest of them."

"That's a damn fool notion."

"Is it?" Phila used the back of her hand to brush away the dampness that had gathered behind her eyelids. "Nick, I don't want to be another Crissie."

"Shit." He reached up and pulled her down beside him, folding her close. "So that's what this is all about."

"I know what that rejection did to her. I'm not sure I could take it day after day. You don't know what that kind of thing does to someone, Nick."

"Don't I?" His voice was soft and harsh. "I spent three years living with it."

Phila was silent as the reality of his words sank in. "Yes, you did, didn't you?"

"Phila, no one is going to say one word out of line to you. If anyone tries it, he or she will answer to me. That will be understood right from the beginning."

"I don't think it will work, Nick."

"Trust me."

"It's not a question of trust. It's a question of emotional reality. The

Castletons and Lightfoots do not like me or approve of me. I've been able to handle that because right now I'm in an adversarial position with them. We all know I'm on the opposite side of the fence. We're natural enemies, and we can all deal together on that basis. But if I marry you, I'll become family and that will create a real mess, believe me."

"You're overanalyzing the situation. Probably comes from your training as a social worker."

"This is not funny, Nick."

"I know. I'm just trying to get you to see the situation from a different perspective. You're looking at it from your usual antiestablishment point of view. Things will work out if you'll just settle down and give everyone a chance."

"That's a totally unrealistic approach to a complex, highly charged situation. Leave it to a man to think things will be that simple."

Nick propped himself on his elbow and leaned over her menacingly. "I don't care what label you put on it, it happens to be my approach, and I will damn well guarantee you it will work."

Phila heard the implacability in his words and heaved a small sigh. "I don't think so, Nick. I'll tell you what, we'll compromise."

"I am not in the mood for any wimpy compromises. Lightfoots don't do that kind of thing."

"Stop acting like the king of the jungle and listen to me, will you?" She looked at him, pleading with him to understand. "Let's just go on as we have been for a while. We'll try living together. I'll attend a few more family functions. We'll see if any of the rest of them get to the point where they can accept me. Maybe in a few months or a year or so things will be different. Then, if you're still interested, we can talk about marriage."

"We'll talk about it now, damn it."

Phila bit her lip. "Don't be too quick to assume that marriage is what you want."

"Why should I change my mind?" he asked. "I never change my mind. That's another thing Lightfoots don't do very often."

"Is that right? Well, you may change your mind about marrying me when I tell you I'm going to give my C&L shares back to Darren tomorrow."

Nick was stunned into silence. When he finally spoke, his voice was cold and brutally soft.

"Like hell you are," he said.

# 18

Nick shoved back the covers with a violent motion, climbed out of bed and stalked to the window. He stood looking out at the darkened waters of Elliott Bay. "I need those shares."

"No you don't."

"You're an ex-social worker, not an MBA. What the hell do you know about it?" he asked savagely.

"I may not know business, but I know people. This is a golden chance for the families to unite behind you. Darren will back you. Your father, too. I think."

"You think?" Nick darted a furious look at her over his shoulder. "What do you mean, you *think* they'll back me? I'm not playing games with C&L's future based on your emotional assessment of the situation, lady. There's too much at stake to take that kind of risk. I want to know your shares are in my corner, and I want everyone else to know it, too. I've explained all that. My best chance of getting one of the others to back me is for everyone to know you're backing me."

"Yes, I know, but it would be better all the way around if I gave them back to Darren and let him vote them," Phila said quietly.

"Better for whom? For what?"

"Family unity."

"Don't give me that crap about family unity. What do you care about the family unity of the Castletons or the Lightfoots?"

It was a good question, but Phila could not think of a way to answer it. She was following her instincts, and her instincts told her that she was doing the right thing. She gathered her legs close to her chest and hugged them. With her chin propped on her knees she watched Nick with the wary attention any intelligent being gives to a predator that has finally been aroused. She tried to speak calmly.

"It will be better for everyone, including you, if you take control of the company with the consent of as many of the members of the families as you can get," she said. "I'm fairly certain your father will back you, and I think Darren will. If Darren does, that means you've got Vicky's vote, too. With any luck Eleanor will fall into line if she sees the others backing you. You'll have a united front. The only nonparticipant will be Hilary."

"You know nothing about running a company. We're not playing psychological games here."

"Yes we are. You've been playing them all along. You just pin a different label on it. What do you call using me to convince the others it's safe to back you, if not a mind game?"

Nick paced back to the bed. He leaned over her, and she inched back onto the pillows. He planted his hands on either side of her head, caging her. "Listen to me, my smart-mouthed, troublemaking little do-gooder. I'm walking a very tricky line trying to save Castleton & Lightfoot. I won't have you jeopardizing everything at this point. The whole idea was for you to hang on to those shares until after the annual meeting. Once I have C&L back from Hilary, you can do what you damn well please."

"Nick, I really think it would be better if I got out of the picture."

"It's too late for you to get out of the picture. You've been in it since I found you in Holloway, and you're going to stay in it until I say otherwise."

She was getting nervous. He wasn't touching her, but she was starting to feel some of the panic she had once felt when he used his physical size to pin her to the bed. Phila tried to ease herself farther back against the headboard. "Nick, please listen to me. I know what I'm doing."

"No, you don't."

"It will be better this way. I'm sure of it. I have a feeling about it. You need to know the families are behind you. They need to feel they picked you freely as their next CEO. This is a family matter, and I'm an outsider."

"You've been happy enough to get involved up until this point."

"That was different. That was because of Crissie and then, later, because you asked me to stay involved. But now I want out. Besides, I'm tired of being used and manipulated."

"Is that what you think has been happening?"

"Of course. You've been doing it from the beginning. I love you and I think you love me, but I'm not completely blind. You used me to get back into the family nest, and now you're trying to use me to get back the company itself. Swell. Go right ahead and take back the company. I agree with you; it's for the best. But do it without me."

"Damn it, Phila." Nick straightened, plowing his fingers impatiently through his hair. "What's happening here? You won't marry me; you won't back me with those shares. You expect me to believe you really love me?"

"I do love you, Nick." She pushed aside the sheet and stood up slowly. "I'm doing this for your own good."

"Don't give me that crap."

"Trust me." Her smile was wobbly. "Wasn't that what you were saying to me a little while ago when you made love to me?"

He scowled. "It's not exactly the same thing."

"You don't think I'm having to go on trust, too? After the way you've used me right from the beginning? You don't think falling in love with you after everything that's happened requires a major chunk of trust?"

"Stop saying I've used you."

"Why? It's the truth, isn't it?"

"I can't believe I'm standing here arguing with you like this. It wasn't more than twenty minutes ago that you were going wild under me."

She touched his arm. "It will be better this way. Believe me. The families need to settle family business together. They need to know they're not being pushed around by an outsider. I'm not family, Nick. I don't have any right to interfere."

"You already have interfered, damn it."

Her mouth tightened. "That's true, isn't it? But I'm getting out now. You don't need me any longer. I'm almost sure you'll get what you want at the annual meeting. Everything's changed since you came back. You'll see."

"I'm not so sure about that. The risk is just too great, Phila. Everything is too delicately balanced. If everyone knows you're out of the picture I'm not sure what will happen."

"They'll back you. The thing is, Nick, they all want to back you. All except Hilary, of course. But deep down they all want to believe in you again and they sense that you're the one who should be running things. I can tell."

"You going to give me a written guarantee?"

Phila shook her head. "You don't need one."

"You're a hundred percent sure of your analysis?" he asked, eyes scathing.

"Well, no. There's no way to be a hundred percent sure. Not when you're dealing with human beings."

"That's the whole point. That's why I want your shares in my corner."

"I have to do what I think is best."

Nick dropped down onto the bed and lay looking up at her with a grim, watchful expression. "You're right, you know."

"About the families backing you?"

"No. About my having used you."

Phila didn't say anything. She just looked at him.

"It all came together when I found you. I knew right away that with you I had the missing piece I needed to get back into the game. But you weren't what I expected. I wasn't always sure *how* to use you."

"Thanks a lot."

"Half the time you surprised me by going off on a totally different tangent than the one I had anticipated. Like the first morning you played golf with my father."

Phila reached for her robe and drew it around herself. "What about it?"

"I thought it would be interesting to throw the two of you together. I thought Dad would get a kick out of arguing with you and you might be able to draw him out of his shell, maybe get him to take more of an interest in what was going on around him and with the company. I thought I could work with that. I didn't realize you were going to start out by lecturing him on my terrific sense of responsibility."

"Oh."

"I was more astonished than he was. During the past three years I'd forgotten what it was like to have someone believe in me without any hard evidence."

"People rarely get hard evidence to believe in, not when it comes to judging other human beings. You almost always have to go on instinct and trust."

"Yeah. Well, the way you handled my father wasn't the only thing that threw me. There was the totally unexpected way you got Vicky and Darren to take another look at their own pasts and what Burke had done to them. You also realized what was motivating Hilary before I did. You even understand Eleanor and her compulsive need to protect the family image. Every time I turn around lately, you're dabbling in family business."

"I'm through dabbling."

"No, you're not, but we'll go into that later. I've got enough to deal with at the moment."

"I'm not going to change my mind, Nick. Tomorrow I'm phoning Darren and I'm going to tell him the shares are his to do with as he pleases."

"Yeah. I believe you." He didn't take his eyes off her. "Screw the shares. There's a part of you that still doesn't trust me, isn't there?"

She frowned. "This has nothing to do with trust. I'm doing what I think is right."

"I'm not talking about your decision to give the shares back to Darren. I'm talking about us—you and me. You don't trust me completely."

"Should I? After you've just admitted you used me?"

"That worked both ways. You were using me, too."

"Yes."

"Tell me, Phila," he said, his voice growing rough and low and beguiling.

"Tell you what?"

"Whatever it is you need to tell me."

"I don't know what you're talking about."

He exhaled slowly. "You're lying."

"So?" Phila challenged. "What are you going to do about it?"

"The only thing I can do." He caught her hand and tumbled her down on top of him. "Make wild, passionate love to me, sweetheart."

"I thought you were angry at me."

"I'm definitely pissed. As usual, you're not following the rules. But I don't want to argue about it right now."

"You think if we make love again I'll become sweet and compliant and change my mind about the shares?"

"I think if we make love again I'll become a lot less pissed. Isn't that a worthy goal in and of itself?"

Phila smiled very brilliantly. "It certainly is."

Victoria stood with her tennis racket in one hand, watching anxiously as Darren hung up the court phone. "Did I hear that correctly? She's giving the shares back to you? Just like that?"

"Just like that." Darren absently tossed a tennis ball into the air, caught it and tossed it again.

"What about Nick?"

"What about him?"

"Well, what did he have to say about all this?" Victoria frowned impatiently. "Is he going along with the idea?"

"It didn't sound to me as if he had much choice. Phila made her decision all by herself. She says she's answered her personal questions about what went on around here while Crissie was in our lives, and now she's taking herself out of the picture."

Victoria twirled her racket slowly between her fingers. "She acts as if she just dropped in, asked a few questions and decided to leave. So casual. The truth is, she changed everything. She put doubts in everyone's minds about things we've all assumed were true for three years. She shook up both families pretty thoroughly. Now she's just going to walk away?"

Darren scratched his jaw. "So she says. I don't see Nick letting it happen that way, though."

"All right, maybe she won't be able to walk away from him, but she's apparently walking away from her slice of C&L." Victoria paused. "*Our* slice."

"Apparently."

"You think there's something more involved?"

"Not exactly. She acts as if she no longer cares what happens to C&L, but I don't believe that. As long as Nick is involved with the company, she'll care about it."

"She's in love with him." It was a statement. Victoria was sure of herself on that score.

"But she's not going to back him at the annual meeting even though that's what he probably intended her to do all along."

"Which means that Nick will need your help and his father's if he wants to assume control of C&L." Victoria thought for a minute. "What are you going to do, Darren?"

"I'm going to give the entire matter my closest attention." He grinned. "That's what politicians are supposed to say when they get caught flat-footed by a surprising turn of events, isn't it?"

"Eleanor will back Hilary all the way."

"Probably. But I no longer even know that for certain. Everything seems to have become slightly bent out of shape since Phila and Nick landed."

"You've always voted with your mother."

"I generally voted the way my father voted, too. But not out of blind loyalty to him. It was because all of us usually wanted the same things for the company."

"Burke always wanted what was best for the company. I'll give him credit for that much. It was all he really cared about." A slight morning breeze ruffled the hem of Victoria's short white skirt as she stood momentarily lost in thought. "Crissie used to say things about the two of you."

"What kind of things?"

"The wrong things. They're not important any longer." She stood on tiptoe and kissed him. "You're not at all like your father, thank God. A part of me knew that all along, and that's the real reason I didn't go through with the divorce three years ago when the future looked darkest."

Darren reached out and pulled her into his arms. His eyes were very clear and serious. "The world of politics can get rough, Vicky. There may come a time when I'll get sick and tired of it and want to walk away from it."

"It doesn't matter. I'll walk away from it with you if that's what you want. All I care about is you and me and Jordan."

He nodded, stroking her hair. "You and Jordan are the most important things in my world."

Victoria smiled tremulously and stepped back. Her eyes were shining. "That's settled. Your serve, I believe."


"She gave the shares back to Darren today." Eleanor finished pouring tea from the silver Crossley pot and busied herself with the spoons. She did not look at Hilary. "Such an odd, unpredictable girl."

"Perhaps she's decided she's caused enough trouble." Hilary sipped her tea with an outer calm she did not feel. Frantically she tried to assess the new information. This was the last move she had expected from Phila after their confrontation. Maybe it was all going to work out, after all. "I'm surprised Nick allowed her to do it."

"Darren thinks she made the decision on her own and that Nick probably is not at all happy with it."

Hilary considered that, cautious of her feeling of vast relief. Perhaps Phila's loyalty to Crissie and therefore to Crissie's lover had won out. She might not have felt right about turning the shares over to Hilary directly, but she would know that giving them back to Darren was almost the same thing.

Hilary wondered if Nick would get rid of Phila now that she was no longer of use to him. It seemed likely. He was a businessman, after all. He knew when to cut his losses.

"I imagine that will be the end of the relationship between Phila and Nick," Hilary observed aloud. "Nick is too smart to keep a liability around for long."

Eleanor nodded slowly. "She's certainly not his type."

"It would have been a bit awkward having her in the families."

"Extremely awkward. But I don't suppose there was ever any real possibility that he would have actually married her. There was no need, unless that was the only way he could have gotten hold of the shares."

"Well, this certainly simplifies things," Hilary said, hoping she was right. "You and Darren will be able to make your own decisions now."

"Yes, of course, dear. Darren and I only want what is best for C&L."

"And for Darren's career," Hilary added pointedly.

"Naturally." Eleanor smiled with vague satisfaction. "The fund-raiser went off rather well the other night, didn't it?"

"It was definitely a success." Hilary recalled the scene in the women's rest room and wanted to throw the bone china teacup against the wall.

"I heard that even Barbara Appleton and her husband wrote out a sizable check." Eleanor frowned. "Strange, isn't it? I've always found Barbara so distressingly liberal in her views. I'm surprised she was interested in contributing to a Republican campaign. Vicky said it had something to do with her interest in child-welfare issues."

"A contribution is a contribution. It doesn't matter where it comes from, does it?"

"Very true, dear. Perhaps Barbara has seen the light at last. After all, my son is going to make a real change in this state, and everyone wants to back a winner. Who knows how far Darren will rise in public office or what he'll accomplish in the future?"

"Provided he has family backing and family money behind him."

"That goes without saying, dear. More tea?"

"Goddamn it, what the hell does that mouthy little gal think she's doing now?" Reed's voice was so loud that Nick had to hold the phone five inches away from his ear.

"Disobeying my explicit instructions, for one thing." Nick munched a cracker with some cheese on it. Phila had just returned from her daily trek to the Pike Place Market. Every time she went she discovered a new and more exotic cheese. He didn't know the name of this particular specimen, but it held strong overtones of goat.

"Well, what in hell are you going to do at the annual meeting if you can't control her shares?"

"Same thing I've been planning to do all along. I'm going to try to get myself elected chief executive officer of C&L."

"Christ almighty, she's a real little maverick, isn't she?"

"Only in some things." Nick looked up as Phila came into the room carrying two glasses of wine. "In other ways she's quite predictable."

"She's going to run you ragged."

"Yeah, I know. It's probably my karma." Nick took a glass from Phila's hand. She sat down beside him and curled her legs under herself. He smiled at her magenta top and turquoise pants.

"What are you going to do if you don't beat Hilary at the meeting?" Reed asked in a more subdued voice.

"I've still got another job to go back to, remember?"

"I remember. What about Phila? Will she be going back to that other job with you?"

"Definitely. That's not open to debate the way the future of Castleton & Lightfoot is. Got to go now, Dad. I'll see you at the meeting. If you've got half the brains I've always assumed you have, you'll vote for me." Nick hung up the phone before his father could respond.

"The wine," Phila announced, "is supposed to complement the cheese perfectly. Brings out all the subtle nuances."

"Is that what they told you at the wine shop?"

"Yep."

"I've got news for you, Phila. There is nothing subtle about goat. You don't want to draw out the nuances, you want to drown them. This wimpy Riesling isn't going to do the trick. It would take a gallon jug of dollar-ninety-eight red to get the job done."

She smiled serenely. "I'm still learning the fine points of trendy cuisine."

"I've noticed." He crunched another cracker with cheese on it. "You do realize the families are in chaos?"

"Are they?"

"Hilary must be going nuts trying to figure out what you're up to now."

"What about you?"

"Me? I've given up trying to figure you out. I'm just going to ride the roller coaster to the end of the line."

"And if it doesn't stop where it should?"

"Then you and I leave for California the day after the annual meeting," Nick said without any hesitation.

Phila eyed him cautiously. "Are you sure you'll still want me around if what I'm doing keeps you from saving C&L?"

Nick smiled deliberately. "Yeah, Phila, I'll definitely want you around if you cause me to lose the company. I'll want to work out all my frustrations on your sweet ass."

"That sounds like fun."

Much later, in bed that night, Nick lay awake thinking about his own words. After having come this far, it was more than a little disconcerting to lie there seriously contemplating losing C&L at this stage.

But it wouldn't be so bad, he realized. It would be a damned shame if C&L got broken up into bits and pieces and run by outsiders, but sometimes that was the way things went. Everyone would survive.

As long as he had Phila, Nick decided, losing C&L wouldn't be the end of the world. She talked blithely about this being a golden chance for the families to reunite but the truth was, she was his golden chance in more ways than one. But damned if he was going to tell her that at this juncture. He knew that deep inside she was worried she might be wrong about the outcome of the annual meeting and that was just fine with him.

If he was going to sweat it out, she might as well sweat, too.

Reed looked up from his evening paper as Tec mixed martinis at the small bar. "Mariners won."

Tec dropped a toothpick loaded with giant green olives into a glass. "Yes, sir, I heard. That's the kinda thing that can make a man contemplate returning to his religious roots, ain't it?" He carried the drink over to Reed.

"I suppose you also heard the shares are back in Darren's hands?"

"Yes, sir. That little Phila is just one big surprise after another, ain't she?"

"Goddamn right." Reed munched an olive and went to stand in front of the window to watch a sleek yacht glide through the waters of Puget Sound. The Bainbridge Island homes had been built with an expansive view of the water, just as the summer cottages in Port Claxton had. "I wonder what that son of mine thinks he's going to do now?"

"Anybody's guess, sir. Nick always did play 'em close to the chest."

"I'll say one thing. I was dead wrong three years ago when I told him he didn't have any guts. He's got 'em, all right."

"Beggin' your pardon, sir, but it takes more'n guts to walk back in here after what happened three years ago and try to take over the company. Takes a pair of stainless-steel balls." Tec broke off as Hilary appeared in the doorway. "Evenin' ma'am. Can I fix you a martini?"

"Yes, please, Tec." Hilary smiled wearily as she walked into the room. She sat down gracefully in the green silk damask-upholstered Chippendale chair. "Hello, Reed. How was your day?"

"Fine. Played eighteen holes with Sweeney over in Bellevue. Won twenty bucks."

"Congratulations." Hilary took the drink from Tec. "Thank you, Tec. That will be all for now." She dismissed him with a nod and waited until he had left the room before she spoke again. "Well, it will all be over one way or the other tomorrow, won't it?"

Reed didn't turn away from the view. "You make it sound like Judgment Day."

"Probably because that's the way I see it. The families will be sitting in judgment on me and on everything I've done for Castleton & Lightfoot during the past three years." Hilary smiled again, briefly. "I hope I'm not found wanting."

"You've done a hell of a job with the company, Hilary."

"Thank you, Reed. Your approval means a great deal to me. C&L is more important to me than anything else in the world. It's my life. I wonder if you and the others will remember that when it comes time to vote for the next CEO."

"Hard thing to forget." He ate another olive.

"A lot of things can be forgotten when the prodigal son returns home. That's understandable."

"It's been three years, Hilary."

"Yes, but has anything really changed? Once before, Nick walked out on all of us, not just me and the baby, but the company, too. What is there to say he wouldn't do it again if he regained control of C&L?" She got up and moved over to stand beside her husband. "The thing we all have to ask ourselves is, what does Nick really want?"

"What do you think he wants?"

Hilary took a deep breath. "Revenge. I think he wants control of C&L so that he can turn around and destroy it. He's never forgiven any of us for what happened three years ago. He was the heir apparent, the man with the golden touch. He saw C&L as his future personal kingdom. When you and Burke refused to let him take the company in the direction he wanted, he lost his temper. He took out his rage on me first, and then on all the rest of you. I don't think he'll be satisfied until he's destroyed the company."

Reed stirred his martini with the spear that had held the olives.

Hilary waited a moment longer before she said, "There's only one thing I really regret."

"What's that?"

"I'm sorry I lost the baby. I would have liked to have given you the grandchild you've always wanted, Reed."

Of course the baby had not been Nick's, Reed thought. He wondered how he could have been so blind three years ago. Phila was right. Nick was his son, and no son of his would walk out on his child.

# 19

Nick walked into the plain, unpretentious office that C&L had used as a boardroom since before he was born. This was the room in which all the major decisions regarding C&L's future had been made. Today it would witness the one that would determine the company's survival.

Tradition. C&L had long since reached the point where its annual meetings could have been held in plush, modern, corporate-style surroundings complete with paneled walls and thick carpets, but it clung to tradition. Even Hilary had not dared mess with this particular ritual, Nick thought as he examined the familiar surroundings.

"There you are, Nick." Reed, dressed in a pair of golfing slacks and a polo shirt, was sitting at the round table in the center of the room. "We're all ready and waitin'. Let's get on with it. Got a one o'clock starting time at the course."

"Wouldn't want to delay you," Nick said.

Eleanor, Darren and Vicky were already seated at the table. Hilary, looking serene and elegant in a white silk suit, was just drawing up her own chair. She arranged a stack of folders neatly in front of her and glanced up without speaking as Nick sat down beside his father. The others murmured their greetings.

"Coffee," Tec announced, carrying a pot into the room.

"Thank you, Tec. You may go now," Hilary said.

"Yes, ma'am."

Hilary looked around the table. "I believe we're ready to begin."

Phila, loaded down with two huge bags full of fruit, vegetables, cheese, pesto and wine made her way up First Avenue from the

Market and hoped she had not made a very serious mistake.

Perhaps she should have hung on to those shares. She might have been wrong about Nick already having all the support he needed within the families. What if Hilary had done some major damage during the past few days?

Phila tried to tell herself that Darren was not a fool and neither was Reed. They could see for themselves that they had all misjudged Nick three years ago. She did not expect Eleanor to shift allegiance because the older woman had her own reasons for backing Hilary. But Darren was an independent thinker. He would not be swayed by his mother's vote. And Vicky would vote with Darren.

Phila tried to add up the various components of the situation in a variety of ways, but there was no getting around the fact that without her, Nick needed the support of at least two others on the board.

But he needed to take control of the company with as much family support as he could get, Phila reminded herself as she leaned a shoulder against the glass doors of the condominium lobby. It would be so much better for everyone concerned if the outsider stayed out. The Lightfoots and Castletons needed to settle the future fate of the firm among themselves.

Phila freed one finger to punch the elevator button and glanced at her watch. By now the meeting was in full swing. She wondered how long an annual C&L stockholders meeting lasted. She was going to go nuts waiting for Nick to walk back through the door this afternoon.

The elevator doors slid open on the top floor, and Phila stepped out into the carpeted hall. She struggled with her keys and packages as she approached Nick's apartment.

She was wondering if she and Nick would be on their way to California in the morning as she opened the front door. She used her foot to nudge one grocery bag into the slate-tiled foyer. Holding the other bag in one arm, she closed the door behind her.

She was halfway to the kitchen when she realized she was not alone in the condominium. She opened her mouth, but the scream was trapped in her throat as a huge hand clamped over her lips.

"Did you think you could escape me, you lying little bitch?" Elijah Spalding hissed in her ear. The cold metal of a gun barrel pressed against her throat.

"Before we call for the vote," Hilary said calmly, "I would ask that all of you think very carefully about what each of you wants for Castleton & Lightfoot. You've asked Nick what he envisions for the future of the company, and he's told you he will take it in a new and unproven direction. Are you willing to turn your back on the successful track record C&L has established in the field of military instrumentation?"

"Don't overstate the case, Hilary." Nick looked expressionlessly at his ex-wife and wondered how he could ever have wanted to marry her. She wasn't his type at all. "I'm not going to make the transition all at once. We won't dump the government contracts until we have things working profitably in the commercial area."

Darren frowned. "What about your plans to expand the Pacific Rim markets? That's easier said than done, Nick. Those are tough markets to crack."

"I've spent the past three years developing contacts in those markets. When C&L is ready to move into them, the markets will be ready for us."

Reed poured himself a third cup of coffee. "C&L has done just fine working for the government all these years."

"Times change, Dad. There are other ways to grow and expand. C&L hasn't changed its basic mode of operation in nearly forty years. It needs some fresh conquests and some new direction. Nothing stays the same forever. The company is getting calcified."

"We just finished an excellent second quarter and things look fine for the third," Hilary interjected. "How can you say the company is calcified?"

"There are other factors besides the quarterly bottom line that have to be considered," Nick said quietly.

"Such as?" Hilary challenged.

"Such as management foresight. We should be planning for the next century, not just a year or three years from now."

"Government contracts aren't going anywhere. There'll always be a need for our kind of product," Reed said.

"We've always done so well in the past," Eleanor said. "I'd hate to see us change too quickly."

Nick looked at her. "It won't happen overnight, Eleanor. I'll make sure we keep everything balanced before we make commitments in any direction." This wasn't going to be easy. When it was all over, he was going to know he'd been in a fight. Castletons and Lightfoots were stubborn, hard-headed and opinionated. He wished he had Phila sitting beside him. He could have used a little moral support.

"You lied and they all believed you, didn't they? Did that give you a feeling of power, bitch? To have that whole courtroom believing your lies? Well, I hope you got a thrill out of it then, because I'm going to make you sorry you ever opened your mouth. I warned you I would punish you for the lies you told. I warned you, didn't I? Didn't I?"

He smelled. His huge body stank. Phila breathed quickly through her nose, feeling as if she were about to suffocate. She could not stand his hand over her mouth much longer. She was getting sick to her stomach. He was dragging her back out of the kitchen. In desperation, she let herself go limp.

When she sagged against him, Spalding released her mouth so that he could grab her more securely. The muzzle of the gun scraped her arm. "Lying bitch. Lying little tramp. You had no right to take those children away from me. They were mine. I was gonna raise 'em right. Teach 'em discipline and obedience."

"The way you did little Andy?" Phila asked, forcing herself to keep her voice low so that he wouldn't panic and put his hand back over her mouth.

Spalding's frightening blue eyes blazed. "Andy refused to obey me. And I made it real clear to all the children that they had to obey me. I had to make an example of him. I had no choice." He shook Phila so hard her head snapped back. "No *choice*. He was mine to do with as I wanted."

"Did you make the others watch? Is that why they were all so frightened the next day when I tried to talk to them?"

"I told you, I had to teach 'em discipline. They had to know what would happen if they didn't obey me. Discipline is the key. And a kid learns discipline best when he's scared shitless. That's the way I learned it from my Pa."

"I don't want to hear your crazy reasoning or your excuses. There are no excuses for what you've become and, deep inside, you know it. You're a murderer, Elijah Spalding. You're nothing but a child abuser and a child killer. The scum of the earth. Beating those children and killing poor little Andy wasn't all you did either, was it? You used some of them in other ways, too, didn't you? You raped some of them."

Spalding's heavy face turned red with his fury. "Those kids were given to me to do with as I saw fit. I was supposed to raise 'em. I had the responsibility to do it right. They were *mine*. I had a right to do whatever I wanted to them. I had to enforce discipline. I had to let them know I was in total control."

Nick looked around the circle of faces as Reed seconded the motion for a vote. In that moment he knew Phila had been right. Win or lose, it was better this way. This was family business. If he did win, he needed to know the families backed him. If he lost, the hell with it. California and Phila were waiting.

"All those in favor of appointing Nick CEO, say aye."

"Aye," said Reed.

A curious relief went through Nick. If nothing else, he now knew for certain that his father believed in him again.

"Aye," said Darren.

"Aye." Victoria looked at Nick and smiled faintly.

Eleanor hesitated, glancing once at Hilary, and then she nodded brusquely, "Aye."

Hilary put down the silver pen she had been toying with for the past few minutes. Her smile was as serene as ever, but her eyes were bottomless pools of bitterness. "That seems to settle the matter, doesn't it? Congratulations, Nick. You've won."

A taut silence followed that observation. It was broken by Reed, who reached out to slap Nick on the shoulder. His eyes were gleaming with satisfaction. "Better call Phila and tell her the news. She'll be on pins and needles, if I know her."

Nick's brows rose. "You think so?"

"Yep. Give her a call. That little gal will be a nervous wreck by now wondering what happened." He reached for the phone and shoved it over in front of Nick.

Nick picked up the receiver and dialed, aware of the others watching him. It was as if they all wanted Phila to be a part of this morning's decision, he suddenly realized. They were treating her like family.

In the condominium the phone rang for the third time. "That will be Nick," Phila said patiently. "He knows I'm here. If I don't answer, he'll be suspicious."

The phone rang a fourth time.

"All right, answer it, damn it, but don't say anything to make him think I'm here or so help me, I'll wait for him after I've finished with you and I'll kill him, too. I swear to God, I will."

With trembling fingers, Phila picked up the phone, trying to think clearly. She knew it would be Nick on the other end of the line. He was her only hope.

The phone rang four times before she answered. Nick knew instantly that something was wrong. Her voice was thin and breathless.

"Phila?"

"Oh, Nick. Nick I'm so glad you called." The false cheerfulness burned Nick's ears. "Everything's fine here, but do you know, after you left this morning I realized I had forgotten to thank you for that gift that you and Darren and Reed and Tec gave me. You remember the present I'm talking about?"

"What the hell *are* you talking about?" Nick demanded, hunching over the phone.

"Yes, that's it. That's the one. Well, I just want you to know I'm going to get a lot of use out of it starting right now. Can't wait to use it, in fact. I . . . Oh, dear. I've got to run. I'll talk to you later, Nick. *Hurry home.*"

Nick slammed down the receiver and surged to his feet. Everyone else at the table stared at him in astonishment.

"Something wrong?" Reed asked.

"I'm not sure, but I think so." Nick was already moving around the table, heading for the door.

Darren stood up. "What the hell's the matter, Nick?"

Nick paused briefly at the door. "What's the only thing any of us ever gave Phila?"

"We taught her how to use a gun," Darren responded instantly.

"Exactly. She just told me she had an immediate use for our gift. And she asked me to hurry home."

"Goddamn it," Reed breathed. "You think it's the guy she put in jail?"

"I don't know. I'm not taking any chances. Eleanor, call nine-one-one. Tell them we've got a suspicious situation and we'd appreciate having it checked out right away. If you don't get the feeling we're going to get help in a hurry, call the manager of my condominium building and ask him to go upstairs and check on Phila. Tell him I'm on my way."

Eleanor reached out immediately to pick up the phone. "Of course, Nick."

Nick went through the door. "Thanks," he called back over his shoulder.

"Hold on, a second," Reed announced, shoving back his chair. "I believe I'll go along for the ride. Tec will want to come, too, just in case."

"Count me in," Darren said, rising swiftly to his feet.

Victoria was out of her chair. "I'm going with the rest of you."

Thirty seconds later Hilary and Eleanor sat alone at the table. Hilary watched Eleanor punch out 911 and begin speaking in the imperious tones the older woman always used when she wanted instant results from the people she employed.

Just like Eleanor to think of the cops as her personal employees, Hilary thought fleetingly as she quietly gathered up her files.

Eleanor had finished speaking just as Hilary reached the door. She put down the receiver. "They're on their way," she announced.

Hilary nodded. "That doesn't surprise me. It's rather amusing, isn't it? The Lightfoots and Castletons are rushing to Philadelphia's rescue."

"Perhaps it's only simple justice, Hilary. She seems to have done her best recently to rush to C&L's rescue."

"That's one way of looking at it."

"Where will you go now, Hilary?" Eleanor asked. "What are you going to do?"

"Does it matter?"

"Yes, it matters. You're family, Hilary."

"No. Not any longer. I don't think I ever was. Not in any real sense. Not in the way Phila is going to be."

Hilary let herself out the door and closed it very quietly behind her.

Phila could have wept and she knew she probably would have if she hadn't been too scared and too busy trying to think clearly. Spalding still had her pinned against his bulk. He started to drag her toward the bedroom. She marshaled her thoughts. Once before she had manipulated this man. She knew how to push his buttons. She must do it again.

"You'd better leave me alone and get out of here while you can. The authorities will be looking for you."

"By the time they figure out where I've gone, I'll be out of here."

"How did you find me?"

"I made Ruth keep track of you. She went and hired somebody to find you and tell her where you were all the time."

Phila closed her eyes in silent anguish. She had never been safe, not even during the time she had spent in Port Claxton. Someone had been watching her. The realization was almost as horrifying as her present situation.

"What are you going to do, Elijah?" she asked, fighting to keep her voice calm.

"First, I have to punish you for the way you ruined everything. I'm going to hurt you for what you did. Hurt you bad, the way we used to hurt the women prisoners when I was workin' as a merc. And when you're crying and beggin' for mercy, I'm going to kill you."

"You're a fool. What will you do? Where will you run? You'll have to hide for the rest of your life because everyone will know for certain this time that you're a murderer. The man I'm living with will hunt you to the ends of the earth. He's a powerful man, Spalding. A lot more powerful than you are."

"You're only his whore, not his wife. Why should he care about you when you're gone? I'll be safe."

"Nothing will protect you from Nick Lightfoot. You'll be looking over your shoulder as long as you live."

"Shut your mouth, bitch. I can take care of myself."

"Not a chance, Spalding. I want you to know what you're risking by killing me. I put you in jail once before, remember? You'll be going back there because of me."

"I said *shut your mouth,* you bitch. You don't know what you're talking about." He dragged her as far as the bedroom door and then through it. He released her, took a step back and gave her such a violent slap with the back of his hand that Phila fell onto the bed.

Phila tasted blood from her cut lip. When she opened her eyes Spalding was towering over her with maniacal lust in every line of his face. She had seen that look on a man's face once before, the afternoon she had been attacked in the foster home. But this time there was no Crissie to save her. She watched in horror as Spalding began unzipping his dirty trousers.

*"No."* She remembered the other time, remembered the lamp Crissie had used.

Without stopping to think she lashed out and caught the base of the bedside lamp. It flew from the table and crashed against Spalding's side.

"Bitch." Spalding leaped back in an instinctive movement as glass shattered. He raised his gun hand to shield his face from the fragments of the exploding light bulb.

Phila rolled to the side of the bed, yanking open the bedside table drawer. Her fingers closed around the familiar grip of the .38. *Just aim it and pull the trigger.*

Lying half on and half off the bed, she jerked the gun out of the drawer, whipped it around toward Spalding whose hands were just falling away from his eyes. She fired.

The roar of the revolver deafened her. Spalding shrieked, staggered back against the wall and then went down with a thud. Blood welled from his shoulder, staining his shirt and trousers. His hand twitched but he did not move.

Phila's ears were still ringing a few seconds later when Nick, followed by a lot of familiar faces, came through the bedroom door.

"Holy shit," said Tec Sherman.

Spalding groaned.

"He's alive," Reed observed. "She must still be rushing her shots."

"I'm working on the problem," Nick said as he gathered a trembling Phila into his arms and held her close.

"I'm glad he didn't die. He deserved it for what he did to those children, but I'm glad I don't have to live with the knowledge that I killed someone." Phila shuddered as she sat drinking brandy a long while later. The police interviews had been exhausting. The aftermath of a shooting, even one done in self-defense, was extensive, she had discovered.

But Castletons and Lightfoots had been everywhere, fixing tea for her, buffering her from the endless police questioning, dealing with the lab technicians, ushering the medical people in and out of the condominium. They had all hovered protectively over Phila during the long process, and Nick had never left her side.

"Might have been a goddamn sight simpler if you had punched his ticket for a one-way trip," Reed said. "The way the bleeding-heart liberal laws are in the country these days, the bastard'll probably be able to turn around and sue you from jail when he recovers."

"We can handle any lawsuit Spalding throws at us," Nick said as he poured another shot of brandy into Phila's glass. "After all, we can afford better lawyers than Spalding will ever be able to buy. And you know how it works, the one with the most expensive lawyer wins."

"Very reassuring." Phila smiled weakly as she looked around at the circle of faces in Nick's living room. Everyone was there except Hilary. Even Eleanor had grabbed a cab after making her phone call to the police.

Tec Sherman smiled contentedly. "Shot was a little wide on account of you rushed it, but under the circumstances you did damn good, ma'am. The creep'll live, but you made your mark, that's for dang sure."

"How are you feeling?" Victoria asked as she handed out cups and saucers. "Heart still pounding?"

"I think it's slowly returning to normal, thanks to all of you. I honestly don't know what I would have done if you hadn't been here. I could hardly think straight when the police arrived."

"The detective told me privately that the whole case looked real clean. For starters, Spalding is an escaped prisoner. The deck is stacked against him from the get-go," Reed said. "Shooting him was a clear case of self-defense."

"Speaking of which," Phila said softly, "I owe you gentlemen my thanks. I would not have known how to defend myself if you all hadn't nagged me into learning how to shoot that horrid gun."

"Always nice to be appreciated," Nick murmured. "Drink your brandy, Phila. It will help you sleep."

"I doubt it. I'm not going to sleep a wink tonight."

"You will," he promised.

But contrary to Nick's prediction, Phila was still lying wide awake at one o'clock in the morning. A variety of emotions were clamoring for attention in her mind. Her mood seemed to be very fragile. She ricocheted between peaks and valleys. For a while a sense of euphoric relief would prevail; a moment later she would find herself on the verge of tears.

"Take it easy, honey. It's going to be all right. You'll be fine after you've had some sleep. It's just nerves." Nick's voice was deep and soothing. He pulled her into his arms, cradling her carefully against him. "You're going to be okay."

"I hope so."

"Is it any worse this time than it was last time?"

She froze. "What are you talking about?"

"I'm talking about the last time you had to deal with Spalding on your own."

"Oh."

His fingers worked slowly through her hair in a gentling movement. "When are you going to trust me enough to tell me the full story about what happened that time, Phila?"

"I did tell you the full story. You even checked up on it yourself. I saw that copy of the newspaper article you got hold of while you were here in Seattle. Besides, why should I want to talk about the trial? It's the shooting that's upset me." Phila couldn't seem to marshal her thoughts in a straight line the way she always had to when she discussed the Spalding trial.

"Maybe you're trying to keep too much inside. You don't have to bottle it all up, you know. Not any more. You're not alone now. You've got me. I love you, Phila."

"I love you, too, Nick."

"So tell me the truth and get it out of your system."

She held herself very still in his arms. "It's not fair to put the burden on anyone else."

"It won't be a burden for me. I've got no problem handling a few perjuries committed in the name of putting away a guy like Spalding. I'm no bleeding-heart liberal, remember? I'm a Lightfoot."

Her eyes widened. "How did you know?"

"Know what? That there was more to that whole incident with Spalding than you had told me?" He shrugged. "Just had a hunch. It had something to do with the drug charges against him, didn't it?"

Phila nodded her head against his chest. "I planted the heroin on him during the struggle in the restaurant parking lot. I set him up for that arrest, Nick. I arranged everything. I couldn't think of anything else to do. He'd already killed one child. I was so afraid he would kill another. He was hurting all of them. Raping them. I had to stop him."

"I know."

The words rushed out of her in a torrent now. "I knew the cops took their morning coffee break every day at that restaurant. In a small town like Holloway, you get to know the routine. There were always a couple of patrol cars parked in front of the restaurant at ten-fifteen in the morning. People used to joke that if they ever decided to pull a bank robbery, they'd be sure to do it around ten-fifteen."

"So you knew the cops' schedule and timed everything accordingly?"

"I knew what time they would be pulling in, and I knew I could make Spalding explode. It was easy enough to goad him into a violent response. But I didn't think a simple assault charge would do the job. I needed a felony count. Something that would get him put in jail."

"So that he wouldn't be eligible to go on running a foster home?"

"Yes."

"Where did you get the heroin?" Nick asked.

"Good grief, Nick. You know as well as I do that it's easy enough to buy drugs these days. As a social worker I had all kinds of contacts and information, including information about people who could get me the heroin. When it was over, all I had to do was let the law take its natural course. All I had to do was lie on the stand and make damn sure I stuck with that lie. The fact that Spalding had been a mercenary who had worked in Southeast Asia and South America was in my favor."

"The jury was willing to believe he might have started using drugs in those places and had been continuing to use them here in the States," Nick concluded for her.

"Yes." Phila fell silent, aware that she was waiting for his response.

"Damn it to hell, Phila."

She tensed. "I'm sorry, Nick. It was a terrible thing to do, but I couldn't think of anything else. I had to stop him. I had to get the kids away from him."

"*Sorry.* For God's sake, don't apologize. The only thing to be sorry about is that we don't have a foolproof way to offer kids protection from creeps like Elijah Spalding. You should never have been forced into a situation where you had to take such an incredible risk to save those children."

She let out the breath she had been holding. "I didn't want to tell anyone, ever. I figured I had made the decision to do it in the first place and I would have to live with what I had done. I couldn't ask anyone else to help bear the burden of the truth."

"But you quit your job."

"I had to quit. I knew I couldn't go on working as a caseworker. This time I hadn't just bent a few rules. I'd gone past all the boundaries. Taken the law into my own hands. I was no longer a professional, I was a vigilante."

"You don't feel guilty, do you? Because you sure as hell shouldn't."

"No. It isn't guilt I feel. I'd do it again, if I had to. But it was hard, Nick. Hard to do. Hard to live with afterward. Just like the shooting today."

"Keep in mind that you're not living with it alone any longer." He kissed her, his eyes gleaming in the shadows. "I love you."

"What really made you think there was more to the story than I had told you?"

"There seemed to be a lot of convenient coincidences in the account. Coincidences that sounded like a lot of luck or some very clever planning. I knew how badly you had wanted to shut down the Spalding foster home. I also knew you well enough to know you'd do whatever you had to do if you thought it was right. Then there was that bit about Ruth Spalding adamantly claiming her husband had to be innocent of the dope charges. She was so convinced you'd lied. It all added up to a question mark."

Phila was awed. "Sometimes you're a little too smart, Nick. Too clever and too slick. It scares me."

"But sometimes I'm just an ordinary dumb macho male." He grinned. "As you have pointed out on numerous occasions."

Phila began to relax for the first time all day. "True. I'll try to comfort myself with that thought. Good heavens, I almost forgot. What happened at the annual meeting? Who's the new CEO of Castleton & Lightfoot?"

"Guess."

"They voted for you? All of them?"

"All except Hilary."

"Oh, Nick, that's wonderful. I knew you'd win." She threw her arms around him. "I just knew it."

Nick rolled over onto his back and looked up at her with laughing eyes. "I've got news for you, honey. I won before I even walked into that meeting this morning."

"What's that supposed to mean?"

"I had you, didn't I?"

"That would have been enough? Even without C&L?"

"More than enough."

She kissed him thoroughly. "Congratulations, Mr. Chief Executive Officer."

"Just call me boss."

"Never."

"Then," he said smoothly, "you can call me husband."

Phila raised her head to look down at him. "You still want to marry me?"

"Phila, we are definitely going to get married. There was never any doubt about that. I decided this morning that I was willing to give you a little time to get comfortable with the idea of marrying into the families."

"Oh, gee, thanks."

"I knew you weren't sure how they felt about you," Nick continued, unperturbed. "But after the way they all rushed over here to save you today and stayed to protect you from the cops and the reporters, you can't doubt any longer that they're on your side. Face it, honey. You're family now, whether you like it or not."

# 20

T he voluminous white satin skirts of Phila's wedding gown
drifted down in gleaming, rippling waves from the railing where
she had her ankles propped up on the boards of the Gilmarten
porch. She sat in a comfortably decrepit wicker chair, a glass of
champagne in one hand. Her veil was draped over the railing beside
her crossed ankles. A light late-evening breeze ruffled the gossamer
netting.

Her new husband was sitting beside her, his chair tipped back on
two legs, his ankles propped up next to Phila's. Nick was still wearing
his formal black-and-white wedding attire, but he had long since removed his jacket. His shirt was unbuttoned at the collar, and his tie
hung loosely around his neck. He had a glass of scotch in his hand.

The wedding had been a traditional Castleton and Lightfoot affair,
according to Victoria. It had taken place on the lush green lawn in
front of the Lightfoot beach house with most of the populace of Port
Claxton in attendance.

The families, it seemed, liked weddings and made the most of
them. Phila told herself she should be grateful somebody hadn't
brought out fireworks. It had been bad enough having to fend off
Cupcake and Fifi at the buffet table.

The last of the guests had, with obvious reluctance, finally left less
than a half hour earlier. Nick had wasted no time whisking Phila away
from the beach cottages to the privacy of the Gilmarten place. There he
had poured himself a scotch and filled Phila's champagne glass. Then
they had both gone out onto the porch to watch the evening close in
around them.

"I've been thinking," Phila announced, feeling more content and happy than she could ever remember being before.

"I'm going to hate myself for asking this. What have you been thinking about?"

"Hilary."

"Of all the damn fool things to be thinking about at a time like this. Phila, this is our wedding day. The last thing you should be thinking about is my ex-wife." Nick swore under his breath. "Make that my father's ex-wife."

"Hilary's and Reed's divorce isn't final yet."

"It will be soon enough. There's sure as hell no need for you to be thinking about it right now."

"But I've come up with a really terrific idea, Nick."

"Yeah?" He eyed her suspiciously. "Like what?"

"Like why don't you sell Lightfoot Consulting Services to her?"

Nick's feet came down off the railing and hit the porch with a thud. "Sell her Lightfoot Consulting? Are you out of your mind? Why in hell would I want to do a thing like that?"

"Now, Nick, be reasonable. You said yourself just the other day that you won't be able to continue running Lightfoot Consulting as well as Castleton & Lightfoot. You can't spread yourself that thin."

"Yeah, but I sure as hell never meant to turn my company over to Hilary, of all people."

"I didn't say turn it over to her. I said sell it to her in exchange for her shares in C&L."

"The families will get those shares back after the divorce. It's in the prenuptial contract Hilary signed."

Phila was dumbfounded. "There was a contract?"

"Sure. It was decided years ago that anyone marrying into the families would get a block of shares to vote but that those shares would revert back to the rest of us in the event of a divorce. All Castleton and Lightfoot brides sign wedding contracts. If we ever get any grooms from outside the families, they'll sign them, too. It's a tradition."

"I didn't sign anything!"

Nick grinned and sipped his scotch. "I know."

"Well? Why wasn't I asked to sign a contract?" Phila demanded.

"I decided to break with tradition in your case. Besides, I know damn good and well you're not going anywhere. You're stuck with me for life." Nick repropped his feet up on the railing alongside Phila's. His chair tilted back on its two back legs once again.

"Is that so?"

"Damn right. Where else are you going to find a man who will let you attack him every night with your special Patented Flying Assault?"

"Oh, Nick." She didn't know quite what to say. Then she smiled. "You're right, you know. I was extremely lucky to find you. There's probably not another male on the face of the earth like you."

"If there is and if he ever gets close to you, I'll personally remove him from the face of the earth."

Phila heard the cool certainty beneath the bantering tone. She slid a quick glance in his direction and saw the implacable expression on his face. She decided it would be best to go back to the original subject.

"About Hilary."

"Do we have to talk about this now?"

"Stop whining, Nick. I'm serious. Sell her Lightfoot Consulting. She'll thrive on the challenge of expanding that company. And it will be all hers."

"This," Nick announced, "is the dippiest idea you've come up with yet. Give me one good reason why I should sell Lightfoot Consulting to Hilary."

Phila smiled. "I could give you plenty of logical, practical, intelligent reasons but there's really only one that counts."

"Which is?"

"She's family."

Nick groaned and swallowed more scotch. "I knew you were going to be trouble the day I met you."

"The feeling was mutual," Phila said cheerfully.

A cool, soft darkness had enveloped the porch.

"I'll think about it," Nick finally muttered. "But not tonight."

"All right," Phila agreed. "Not tonight."

Nick glanced at his watch. "It's about that time."

"What time?"

"Time," he explained patiently, "for you to drag me off to bed."

Phila felt a warm, tingling sensation move through her, stirring all her nerve endings the way a summer breeze stirred leaves. She sighed happily. "I guess it is about that time."

She put her champagne glass down on the railing and leaned over to kiss Nick. The wicker chair tipped precariously and started to collapse. Phila tried to steady herself by clutching at the back of Nick's chair. As it was already balanced delicately on two legs, Phila's weight was more than sufficient to send it toppling over onto its back.

Nick grabbed Phila and flung out one arm to break their fall. They both landed harmlessly on the edge of an old sofa and rolled off onto the porch. When they came to rest they were entangled in the skirts of Phila's wedding gown.

Nick pushed aside a wave of satin and grinned up at his wife. "A new technique?"

"I'm not used to wearing long dresses," Phila explained, turning pink.

"Maybe it would be easier if I carried you off to bed this time. After all, it is our wedding night. Would you mind very much if we did this the traditional way tonight?"

She smiled down at him, her love in her eyes. "Not at all," she said graciously. "I know how big you Lightfoots are on tradition."

"Yeah. Something to be said for tradition." Nick got to his feet and helped Phila to hers. Then he picked her up, her long skirts falling in a snowy wave over his arm, and carried her inside the old beach house.

"I think," said Phila a short while later as she lay naked and gently crushed beneath her husband's weight, "that I could get to like it this way."

Several months later Nick and Reed took advantage of a rare sunny morning in winter to get in a round of golf on a private course that bordered Lake Washington.

"How come Phila was in such a prickly mood this morning?" Reed asked, shading his eyes with one hand as he watched Nick's fairway shot.

"You know Phila. She's often prickly in the mornings." Nick shoved the iron back in his golf bag.

"Not like she was this morning. You two been arguing?"

Nick swore. "A small disagreement, that's all."

"Goddamn it, Nick, don't you know any better than to argue with a pregnant lady?"

"I hate to disillusion you, Dad, but your precious Phila is not above using her delicate condition to get what she wants."

"So give her what she wants."

Nick smiled fleetingly. "You don't know what you're saying."

"Well?" Reed demanded as he climbed back into the golf cart. "What does she want?"

"More money from Castleton & Lightfoot for Barbara Appleton's day-care centers. This is the third time she's hit me up for cash for that project in the past six months."

"Big deal. She's worked hard with Barbara to keep those centers running. You coughed up the money the other two times with barely a whimper. Why dig in your heels now?"

"Because Phila doesn't show any signs of ever being satisfied," Nick said grimly. "Left to her own devices she's going to run amok giving away C&L money."

Reed chuckled. "Nick, I'm going to level with you. I'll be the first to admit you're doing a hell of a job with Castleton & Lightfoot, even if I don't agree with every move you've made since you've been in charge. But you've still got a lot to learn when it comes to handling women."

"Oh, yeah? You're an expert?"

"Let's just say I've had a little more experience dealing with Phila's type. Way I see it, you got no choice but to do what I finally did with Nora."

Nick glanced thoughtfully at his father. "You convinced everyone to let Mom handle most of the charitable contributions for Castleton & Lightfoot."

"Worked out just fine."

"The hell it did. You were always arguing with her over where the money was going."

"So do it more formally than I did. Set up a Castleton & Lightfoot Foundation. Put Phila in charge, and give her a budget. Make her stick to it."

Nick climbed out of the cart and stood in the middle of the fairway, staring at his father. "Have you gone soft in the head? Put Phila in charge of a foundation designed to give away C&L money?"

"Think of the tax write-offs."

Nick began to grin. The grin turned into a roar of laughter.

"What's so funny?" Reed demanded.

"All right, I'll do it. I'll let Phila set up a foundation and I'll put her in charge. But don't come squawking to me when she presents her list of worthy charities and institutions at the annual meeting."

Reed grinned, slightly abashed. "You think a few of the old stand-bys are going to get dropped?"

"Not only will some of your favorites get dropped, but I can personally guarantee you the first thing Phila will do is demand an increase in her foundation's budget. Don't look now, Dad, but C&L has acquired a conscience and her name is Philadelphia Fox Lightfoot."

"I reckon I can live with a conscience as long as I get my grandkid."

"Don't worry. You'll get your grandchild. Hell, you're going to get a whole bunch of grandchildren."

"Think you can talk Phila into having more than one?" Reed looked pleased at the prospect.

"Yeah," said Nick, already anticipating the way Phila would give herself to him in bed that night even though she had argued with him that morning. She would be all over him, hot, fiery and full of a boundless love. "I'm working on the problem."

# SILVER LININGS

*To Claire Zion and baby Rose*
*and the future* . . .

# 1

The only thing she really knew about Paul Cormier was that he was dying.

The blood from the wound in his chest had soaked through his white silk shirt and white linen suit and was running in small rivulets over the white marble tile.

The old man opened his eyes as Mattie Sharpe crouched helplessly beside him, grasping his hand in hers. He peered up at her, as if he were trying to see through a thick fog.

"Christine? Is that you, Christine?" Even in a croaked whisper, his accent was elegant and vaguely European.

"Yes, Paul." Lying was the only thing she could do for him. Mattie held his hand tightly. "It's Christine."

"Missed you, girl. Missed you so much."

"I'm here now."

Cormier's pale blue gaze focused on her for a few seconds. "No," he said. "You're not here. But I'm almost there, aren't I?" He made a sound that might have started out as a chuckle but turned into a ghastly, gurgling cough.

"Yes. You're almost here."

"Be good to see you again."

"Yes." A hot, torpid island breeze wafted through the front hall of the Cormier mansion. The silence from the surrounding jungle was unnatural and oppressive. "It's going to be all right, Paul. Everything will be fine." Lies. More lies.

Cormier squinted up at her, his gaze startlingly lucid for an instant. "Get out of here. Hurry."

"I'll go," Mattie promised.

Cormier's eyes closed again. "Someone will come. An old friend. When he does, tell him . . . tell him." Another terrible gasping sound drained more of the little strength he had left.

"What do you want me to tell him?"

"Reign . . ." Cormier choked on his own blood. "In hell."

Mattie didn't pause to make sense out of what she thought she'd heard him say. Automatically she reassured him. "I'll tell him."

The hand that had been clutching hers slackened its grip. "Christine?"

"I'm here, Paul."

But Cormier did not hear her this time. He was gone.

The horror of her situation washed over Mattie again. She struggled to her feet, feeling light-headed. Without thinking, she glanced at the black and gold watch on her wrist as if she were late to a business appointment.

With a shock she realized she had been in the white mansion overlooking the ocean for less than five minutes. She would have been here two hours earlier if she hadn't gotten lost on a winding island road that had dead-ended in the mountains. At the time the delay had made her tense and anxious. It occurred to Mattie now that if she had arrived on time, she probably would have walked straight into the same gun that had killed Paul Cormier.

The toe of her Italian leather shoe struck something on the floor. It skittered away across the tile.

Mattie jumped at the loud sound in the eerily silent hall. Then she glanced down and saw the gun.

Cormier's, probably, she told herself. He must have tried to fight off the intruder. Dazed, Mattie took a step toward the weapon. Perhaps she should take it with her.

Even as the words formed in her mind she shuddered. The last gun she had handled had been a little plastic model that had come in a box labeled, "Annie Oakley's Sharpshooter Special. For ages five and up." A friend had given it to her on the occasion of her sixth birthday. Mattie had practiced her fast draw for hours, whipping the toy gun out of its pink fringed, imitation leather holster over and over again until her concerned parents had taken it from her and replaced it with a box of watercolors. Mattie had dutifully played with the paints for approximately ten minutes and succeeded in producing a cheerful yellow horse for Annie Oakley to ride. The picture had been cute, but was not deemed good enough to hang on the refrigerator next to her sister Ariel's latest rendition of a bouquet of flowers.

Her training in handguns thus halted at such an early stage, Mattie realized now that she had absolutely no idea of how to use the lethal-looking monster lying at her feet on the white floor.

On the other hand, how complicated could it be? she asked herself as she stooped to pick up the heavy weapon. Every punk on every city street back in the States owned and operated one. It was a sure bet most of them were too illiterate to read the manuals. Besides, it was easy to see which end to point away from herself.

Oh, God. She was getting hysterical. It was a sure sign of losing control. She had to get a grip on herself. She could panic later if necessary.

Mattie took several deep breaths while she fumbled the gun into her elegant black and tan leather shoulder bag. She paused as she noticed the bloodstains on the strap. Cormier's blood. It had come from her hands.

She had to move quickly. A man was dead and among his last words had been the advice to get out of the mansion in a hurry.

She did not doubt that the danger was still hovering. Mattie could sense it as if it were a palpable presence. She took one last look at the body of the silver-haired old man. She had a fleeting vision of white—white linen suit, white buck shoes, white silk shirt, white marble tile, white walls, white furniture. White, endless, pure, unadulterated white. Except for the red blood.

Mattie felt her stomach heave. She could not be sick now. She had to get out of here. She stumbled for the open front door, her heels clattering loudly on the marble. Her only thought was to reach the battered old rental car that she had picked up at the tiny island airport two hours earlier.

She was nearly out the door when she remembered the sword.

Halting, she glanced back into the room of white death. She knew she could not go back. *Valor,* the fourteenth-century sword she had been sent to collect, was valuable but not worth the trip back into that room. Nothing was worth going back into that room. Aunt Charlotte would understand.

What was it Aunt Charlotte had told her about the ancient weapon? Something about there being a curse on it. *Death to all who dare claim this blade until it shall be taken up by the avenger and cleansed in the blood of the betrayer.*

The terrible prophecy had apparently been fulfilled in Cormier's case, Mattie thought. Not that she believed in such things. Still, Cormier had claimed the blade and now he was dead. Mattie suddenly had no interest whatsoever in locating the medieval sword and taking it back to Seattle.

She whirled around again and ran through the open door, scrabbling in her purse for the key to the rental car. Perhaps that was why she didn't see the man who stood on the veranda to one side of the open door.

Nor did she notice the booted foot he stuck out in front of her until she tripped over it and went flying. She sprawled on the white planking of the veranda, the wind knocked out of her. Before she could get back enough breath to scream, she felt something cold and metallic against the nape of her neck.

Mattie wondered with an odd, clinical detachment if there would be any small warning sound before the trigger was pulled.

"Hell, it's you, Mattie," said a deep male voice Mattie had not heard in nearly a year. The gun was no longer pressed against her nape but Mattie was still frozen with fear and shock. "You almost got yourself killed. I didn't know who was going to come running out that door. You all right, babe?"

Mattie managed to nod, still fighting for breath. She opened her eyes and realized the wooden planks she was staring down at were less than three inches away. She could not seem to gather her thoughts. It was all too much. *Stress.*

A big hand closed around her shoulder. "Mattie?" The dark, rough-edged voice crackled with impatience.

"I'm okay." A strange relief washed through her at the thought. Then came another chill. "Cormier."

"What about him?"

"He's in there."

"Dead?"

She closed her eyes. "Yes. Oh, God, yes."

"Get up."

"I don't think I can."

"Yes, you damn well can. Move it, Mattie. We can't lie around here chatting." Strong fingers locked around her waist and hauled her to her feet.

"You never did listen to me, did you, Hugh?" Mattie brushed aside the tendrils of tawny brown hair that had come free of the neat coil at the nape of her neck. She looked up into gray eyes that were so light they could have been chips off a glacier. "What are you doing here?"

"That's supposed to be my line. You were due into St. Gabe at nine this morning. What the hell are you doing here on Purgatory?" But he wasn't paying attention to her, not really. He was eyeing the driveway behind her. "Come on."

"I'm not going back into that house."

Predictably enough, he ignored her. "Get inside the hall, Mattie.

You're a sitting duck standing in the doorway." Without waiting for a response he yanked her back through the wide opening.

Mattie stumbled after him, keeping her eyes averted from the sight of Cormier's body. She clutched at the strap of her shoulder bag in a vain effort to keep her fingers from trembling.

"Don't move," Hugh said.

"Don't worry, I won't." She hoped she would not be sick all over the marble floor.

He released her and strode quickly over to the body in the white linen suit. He stood looking down for a few seconds, taking in the absoluteness of death in one glance. The expression on his face was difficult to read. It was not shock or surprise or fear or horror—just a remote, implacable sort of fierceness.

Mattie watched him, aware she should be grateful he had appeared at this particular moment in her life. No one else she knew was better qualified to get her out of this sticky situation than Hugh Abbott.

Too bad the mere sight of him enraged her. Too bad that after that humiliating debacle last year she had never wanted to see him again as long as she lived. Too bad that the one man she needed right now was the same one who had devastated her after she had surrendered to him, body and soul.

He had not changed much in the past year, she realized. Same thick, dark pelt of hair with maybe a bit more silver in it. Same lean, whipcord-tough body that still didn't show any hint of softening, despite his forty years. Same rough-featured, heavily carved face. Same beautiful, incredibly sexy mouth. Same primitive masculine grace.

Same lamentable taste in clothing, too, Mattie noted with a disdaining glance. Scarred boots, unpressed khaki shirt unbuttoned far enough to show a lot of crisp, curling chest hair, a well-worn leather belt and faded jeans that emphasized his flat belly and strong thighs.

Hugh glanced at her. "I'll be right back. I'm just going to get some stuff from the kitchen." He was already moving past the body. He held the gun in his hand so naturally it seemed an extension of his arm.

"*The kitchen.* For God's sake, Hugh. This is no time to grab a cold beer. What if he's still here? The man who shot poor Mr. Cormier?"

"Don't worry. There's no one else here. If there were, you would be as dead as Cormier by now."

Mattie swallowed as he left the room. "No, wait, please don't leave me here with—" Mattie bit off the rest of the frantic plea. She, of all people, ought to know better than to plead with Hugh Abbott to stay. "Damn you," she whispered.

Mattie stood listening to the ring of Hugh's boots on the marble tiles. She heard him move down a hall into another room, and then there was nothing but the awful silence and the hot breeze.

Glancing nervously out the door, she toyed with the keys of the rental car. Nothing said she had to stand around and wait for Hugh. She could drive herself back to the airport. Right now she wanted nothing more than to get on a plane and leave this dreadful island.

But she was feeling very lost and uncertain. Practicing a quick draw with the Annie Oakley special had been one of her few forays into the world of adventure. Her artistically oriented family had emphasized more civilized and sophisticated pursuits.

Hugh Abbott, on the other hand, understood situations involving violence and danger all too well. As chief troubleshooter and free-lance security consultant for Aunt Charlotte's multinational company, Vailcourt Industries, he was on intimate terms with this sort of thing.

Mattie had privately thought of Hugh as her aunt's pet wolf long before she had met him last year. Nothing she had learned about him since had given her any cause to change her mind.

She heard his boot heels on the tile again. Hugh reappeared carrying two large French market-style string bags that bulged with an assortment of unidentifiable items.

"All right. We've spent enough time fooling around here. Let's go." Hugh glided around Cormier's body, not looking down. He saw the keys in Mattie's fingers. "Forget that junker you rented. You're not going anywhere in it."

"What do you mean? Are we going to take your car? Where is it, anyway?"

"A few hundred yards up the road. Hopefully out of sight—but who knows for how long?" Hugh strode toward her. "Here, take one of these. I want to keep a hand free." He thrust one of the string bags into her fingers as he glanced out the door and up at the leaden sky. "It's going to start pouring any minute. That should help."

Mattie ignored the comment about the impending rain. She was too busy trying to juggle the heavy string bag and her purse. "What are these sacks for? We don't need this stuff. I just want to get to the airport."

"The airport is closed."

Mattie stared at him in shock. "Closed? It can't be closed."

"It is. I barely made it in myself. There are armed men on the road, and every plane that didn't get off the island as of forty minutes ago is probably in flames by now. Including mine, goddamn it. Charlotte's going to have to reimburse me for that Cherokee. It was a real sweet little crate."

"Dear heaven. Hugh, what's going on? What is this all about?"

"With your usual fine sense of timing, you walked straight into the middle of what looks like a two-bit military coup here on Purgatory. At the moment I have no way of knowing who's winning. In the meantime the only way off the island is by boat. We're going to try for Cormier's cruiser."

"I don't believe this."

"Believe it. Come on, let's go."

"Go where?" she demanded.

"First to the bathroom." Hugh started down the hall.

"For God's sake, Hugh, I assure you I don't have to use the bathroom. At least, not right at the moment. Hugh, wait. Please stop. I don't understand this."

He turned in the doorway, his eyes cold. "Mattie, I don't want to hear another word out of you. Come here. Now."

Deciding she was too stressed out to think clearly, Mattie trailed after him. She closed her eyes as she stepped around Cormier's body and found herself following Hugh down a white hallway into a luxurious bedroom suite done in silver and white.

"Mr. Cormier certainly didn't like colors very much," Mattie muttered.

"Yeah. He used to say he'd worked in the shadows long enough. When he retired he wanted to live in the sun." Hugh opened a door off the bedroom suite.

"What did he mean by that?"

"Never mind. It doesn't matter now. Here we go." Hugh strode into the bathroom.

Mattie followed uneasily. "Hugh, I really don't understand." She frowned as she watched him step into the huge white tub and push at a section of wall behind the taps. "What in the world—?"

"Cormier built a lot of ways out of this place. He was a born strategist."

"I see. He was expecting trouble, then?"

"Not specifically. Not here on Purgatory." Hugh watched as the wall panel slid aside to reveal a dark corridor. "But like I say, he was always prepared."

"Oh, my goodness." Mattie shivered as she stared into the darkness. The old uneasiness she always felt in confined places stirred in the pit of her stomach. "Uh, Hugh, maybe I should warn you, I'm not very good in—"

"Not now, Mattie." His tone was impatient as he stepped into the black corridor and turned around to reach for her hand.

"Do we have to go this way?" Mattie asked helplessly.

"Stop whining, babe. I don't have time to listen to it."

Thoroughly humiliated now, Mattie found the strength to step into the corridor. Hugh pushed a button and the panel slid shut behind her. She held her breath but discovered she did not have to stand long in the darkness. Hugh switched on a flashlight he'd taken from one of the string bags.

"Thank God you found a flashlight," Mattie said.

"No problem. Cormier kept a couple in every room of the house. I picked this one up in the kitchen, but there's probably one in here, too. Electricity is always a little erratic on an island like this. Come on, babe."

The hallway was narrow but mercifully short. With the assistance of the light and several deep breaths, Mattie was able to control her claustrophobia just as she did in elevators. Hugh was pushing another button and opening an exit in the side of the house before her own personal walls had begun to close in to any great extent.

Mattie stepped outside with a sense of relief and found herself in the middle of a leafy green jungle bower that grew right up to the side of the mansion. She batted at a huge, broad leaf that was directly in front of her. "Well, that wasn't so bad, but I really don't see why we had to leave that way. It seems to me it would have been simpler to walk straight to the car."

Hugh was moving forward into what looked to Mattie like a wall of thick foliage. Once again he ignored her comment. "Stay close, Mattie. I don't want to lose you in the jungle."

"I'm not going into any jungle."

"Yes, you are. You and I are going to do the only smart thing we can do under these circumstances. We're going to stay out of sight until we can get hold of transportation."

"Hugh, this is crazy. I'm not traipsing off into that jungle. In fact, I'm not going anywhere at all until I've had a chance to think."

"You can think later. Right now you're just going to move." He was already vanishing into the greenery.

Aunt Charlotte's pet wolf was apparently accustomed to giving orders and having them followed. He had been known to give orders to Charlotte, herself.

Mattie stood irresolute near the wall of the mansion, the string bag dangling from her fingers. Common sense told her she should be running after Hugh. He was, after all, the expert on this kind of thing. But a sickening combination of disbelief, shock, and an old irrational anger held her frozen for an instant.

Hugh glanced back over his shoulder, eyes narrowing. "Get moving, Mattie. Now."

He did not raise his voice, but the words were a whiplash that broke through Mattie's uncertainty. She hurried forward, fighting with her purse and the string bag.

Two steps past the barrier of broad leaves, Mattie found herself completely enveloped in an eerie green world. Her senses were overwhelmed by the rich, humid scent. The ground beneath her shoes was soft and springy and nearly black in color; a giant compost pile that had been simmering for eons. It sucked at her two-hundred-dollar Italian shoes as if it were a living thing that feasted on fancy leather.

Massive ferns that would have won first place in any garden show back in Seattle hovered in Mattie's path like plump green ghosts. Long, meandering vines studded with exotic orchids billowed around her. It was like swimming beneath the surface of a primeval sea. A couple of fat raindrops landed on her head.

"Hugh, where are we going? We'll get lost in here."

"We're not going far. And we won't get lost. All we have to do is keep the house to our backs and the sound of the ocean to our left. Cormier was a wily old fox. He always made certain he had a bolt hole, and he kept the escape plans simple."

"If he was so clever, why is he dead back there inside that mansion?"

"Even smart old foxes eventually slow down and make mistakes." Hugh pushed past a bank of massive leaves that blocked the way.

The leaves promptly sprang back into position. A mass of beautiful white lilies slapped Mattie right in the face. "Ariel was right," she muttered under her breath at Hugh's disappearing back, "you really aren't much of a gentleman, are you?" She pushed at the lilies, the string bag and her purse banging wildly about her sides.

"Watch out for these leaves," Hugh advised over his shoulder. "They're real springy."

"I noticed." Mattie ducked to avoid the next swinging mass of greenery. She was grateful for the aerobic exercise program she had begun nearly a year ago on her thirty-first birthday. She had taken it up as one of many antidotes to the stress that seemed to press down on her from all directions these days. Without that regular exercise, she never would have had the physical stamina to keep up with Hugh Abbott as they raced through a jungle.

Not that it was ever easy for a woman such as herself to keep up with Hugh under the best of circumstances. As he had once made very clear, she was not his type. Mattie winced at the memory of that old humiliation.

"Not much farther now. How you doing, babe?" Hugh vaulted lightly over a fallen log and reached back to give Mattie a hand.

"I'm still here, aren't I?" Mattie asked between her teeth. The rain was getting heavier. The canopy of green overhead began to drip like a leaky ceiling. Mattie heard something tear as she scrambled over the log. She thought at first it was the seat of her beautifully tailored olive green trousers but realized it was the sleeve of her cream-colored silk shirt instead. It had gotten caught on a vine.

"Damn." Mattie glanced down at the rip and sighed. "Why would Cormier show you his escape route?" she asked, raising her eyes to Hugh's back. "I didn't know you even knew him."

He didn't turn or even slow his pace as he answered. "You'd have found out I knew him if you'd stuck to your original schedule and been on the plane to St. Gabe this morning the way you were supposed to be. Didn't Charlotte's travel department make the reservations for you?"

"They made them. I altered my plans at the last minute when I saw the itinerary. I recognized St. Gabriel Island and realized I was being set up. I decided I didn't need you for a tour guide."

"Even though you were going straight into Purgatory?" he asked dryly. "Come on, now, Mattie. You know what they say. Better the devil you know. Look what happened when you decided to go your own way."

"I suppose you would have realized instantly that there was a military coup going on here?"

"Long before you did, babe. As soon as I contacted the tower, I knew something was wrong. If you'd been with me, we wouldn't have even touched down. I'd have turned and headed for Hades or Brimstone and tried to contact Cormier by phone to see what was happening."

"Hugh, please. I realize that you are ever vigilant and always prepared when it comes to this sort of thing and I'm not. But I really don't need any of your lectures right now."

To Mattie's astonishment, his voice gentled. "I know, babe, I know. I'm still a little shook, myself, that's all."

She stared at his broad-shouldered back, not believing her ears. "You? Shook?"

"Hell, yes. I was afraid I was going to walk in and find you dead in that hall along with Cormier."

"Oh."

"Is that all you can say?" The gentleness had already vanished from his rough voice.

"Well, I can see where it would have been a bit awkward explaining things to Aunt Charlotte."

"Christ. There is that, isn't there? She'd have had my head." Hugh came to an abrupt halt. He was looking at a small, fern-choked stream flowing past his boots. "Okay, here we go."

Mattie peered at the twisting ribbon of water. "Now what?"

"We turn left and follow this stream." Hugh glanced back the way they had come. "I think we've got the place to ourselves. Everybody's busy with the revolution. Let's go."

The rain was coming down harder now, battering at the leaves so violently that it created a dull roar. Mattie followed Hugh in silence, her whole attention focused on keeping up with him while she juggled the string bag and her purse.

The black earth was turning to mud. Her shoes were caked with it. Her hair had long since come free of its neat coil and hung in limp tendrils around her shoulders. Her silk shirt was soaked. The rain had cooled things down a little, but not much. The whole jungle seemed to be steaming like a thick, green stew.

Mattie eyed the ground, watching each step she took so that she did not stumble in the tangle of mud and vines. She took a closer look at the vines when she caught her toe on one.

"Hugh," she asked wearily, "what about snakes?"

"What about 'em?"

"Do they come out in the rain?"

"Not if they've got any sense."

"Damn it, Hugh."

He chuckled. "Forget about snakes. There aren't any on these islands."

"Are you sure?"

"I'm sure."

"I hope you're right." She dragged the string bag over another fallen log. Something small and green came alive under the hand she had used to brace herself. *"Hugh."*

He glanced back. "Just a little lizard. He's more scared than you are."

"That's a matter of opinion." Mattie forced herself to take several deep breaths as the small creature scuttled quickly out of sight. "Hugh, this really isn't my kind of thing, you know?"

"I know it's a little outside your field of expertise, babe, but you'll get the hang of it. Your problem is you've spent too much of your time with those namby-pamby art collectors whose idea of living dangerously is investing in an unknown artist."

Mattie bristled at this echo of their old argument. "You're quite right, of course."

He didn't seem to notice her sarcastic tone. "Sure, I'm right. You ought to get out of Seattle more often. Go places. Do things. Charlotte says this is your first vacation in two years. When was the last time you did something really exciting?"

Mattie shoved wet hair out of her eyes and set her back teeth. "About a year ago when I seduced you and asked you to marry me and take me back to St. Gabriel with you. You may recall the occasion. And we both know where that bit of excitement got me."

Hugh was silent for an embarrassing amount of time before he said, "Yeah, well, that wasn't quite what I meant."

"Really?" Mattie smiled grimly to herself and pulled a shoe out of the mud. "I assure you, that was adventurous enough for me. I've been thoroughly enjoying the quiet life ever since. Until now, that is."

"Babe, about last year—"

"I don't want to discuss it."

"Well, we're going to discuss it." Hugh slashed at an orchid-covered vine with his hand. "Damn it, Mattie, I've been trying to talk to you about that for months. If you hadn't been avoiding me, we could have had it all worked out by now."

"There is nothing to work out. You were quite right when you told me I was not your type." She pushed wearily at more vines. "Believe me, I couldn't agree with you more."

"You're just a little upset," he said soothingly.

"You could say that."

"We'll talk about it later." Hugh came to an abrupt halt.

Mattie promptly collided with him.

"Ooooph." She staggered backward a step and caught her balance. It was like running into a rock wall, she thought resentfully. No give in the man at all.

"Here we go," Hugh said, apparently oblivious to the collision. He was looking up.

Mattie followed his gaze, aware that the roar of water had grown considerably louder during the past few minutes. She realized why when she peered around Hugh's broad shoulders and saw twin waterfalls cascading out of the old lava cliffs in front of her.

The two torrents plunged fifty feet or more into a fern-shrouded grotto. The pool at the base of the falls was nearly hidden by masses of huge, exotic blooms and the twisted rock formations typical of long-cooled lava.

Mattie frowned. "This is Cormier's escape route?"

"The escape route is behind the falls. There's a network of old lava caves in this mountain. One of the tunnels leads to a cavern that opens in the middle of a sheer rock cliff that faces the sea. The cavern is partially flooded. Cormier always kept a boat in there."

"Caves?" The sense of uneasiness that had been bothering Mattie since they had entered the dense jungle crowded closer. "We have to go through a bunch of caves?"

"Yeah. Don't worry. Nothing tricky. Cormier marked the route so we won't get lost. Ready?"

"I don't think so, Hugh." Her voice was high and thin.

Hugh shot her an impatient glance as he started toward the grotto. "Don't dawdle, babe. I want you off this damned island as soon as possible."

He was right, of course. They could hardly hang around here. There was too much chance of running into the same people Paul Cormier had recently encountered. *But oh, God, caves.* Her worst nightmare made real.

Mattie was already damp from the rain and her own perspiration. Now she felt icy sweat trickle down her sides and between her breasts. She took a few deep breaths and chanted the mantra she had learned when she had taken lessons in stress-relieving meditation techniques.

Hugh was already moving along a rocky ledge that vanished into inky darkness behind one of the falls. He balanced easily on the slippery, moss-covered boulders, his movements unconsciously graceful. He looked back once more to make certain Mattie was following, and then he disappeared behind a thundering cascade of water.

Mattie took one more deep breath and prepared to follow. She reminded herself grimly that she had once vowed to follow this man anywhere.

What a fool she had been.

The mist off the falls looked like smoke as she passed through it. If she had not already been soaked by the rain and her own sweat, she would have been drenched by the spray. As it was, she barely noticed the additional moisture.

But her Italian leather shoes had not been designed to undergo this sort of abuse. Mattie clung to her purse and string bag and struggled desperately to balance on the uneven surface. She felt her left foot slide across a slick patch of moss, and everything started to tilt.

"Oh, no. Oh, *no.*" Wide-eyed and helpless to save herself, she started to topple backward into the pool at the base of the falls.

"Watch your step, babe." Hugh's hand shot out of the darkness and clamped around her wrist to steady her. With effortless ease he yanked her to safety behind the falls.

"There you go, babe. No sweat."

"Tell me something, Hugh," she asked acidly. "Were you always this fast on your feet? You move like a cat."

"Hell, no. I used to be a lot faster. I'm forty now, you know. I've slowed down some. Happens to everyone, I guess."

"Amazing." Her voice was drier than ever, but Hugh didn't seem to notice.

He was busy rummaging around in the string bag. "And I'll tell you something else, babe," he added, "No matter how fast you are, there's always someone faster. That's one of the reasons I finally got smart and took that nice cushy job with your aunt."

"I see." His answer surprised her. It also made her curious. She really did not know all that much about Hugh Abbott. "Have you ever actually met someone faster than yourself?"

Hugh was silent for a heartbeat. "Yeah."

"What happened to him?"

"He's dead."

"So he wasn't quite fast enough."

"I guess not."

But their conversation couldn't distract Mattie from the horrible darkness that loomed ahead. *A cave.* She would never be able to handle this, she thought. Never in a million years. This was far worse than any elevator or dark hall or jungle. This was the real thing, straight out of one of her childhood nightmares.

Mattie's stomach twisted.

She started to tell Hugh she could not go another step when something went crunch under the toe of her expensive, ruined shoe. Automatically Mattie looked down and saw the flattened body of the biggest cockroach she had ever seen in her life.

"That does it," Mattie announced. "You'd better get out of the way, Hugh. I'm going to be very sick."

# 2

❧

"Y ou are not going to be sick," Hugh said with implacable certainty. "Not here, at any rate. Not now. We don't have time for that kind of nonsense. Put down those bags and come here."

Automatically she obeyed, dropping the string bag and her purse to the ground. Her stomach churned. The memory of the blood in the white room mingled with the image of the dead insect at her feet. The gloom of the cavern threatened to swallow her alive.

"Damn it, Mattie, get a hold of yourself."

She felt Hugh's hand close around her arm. She was vaguely aware that he was leading her back toward the entrance of the cavern. But she was totally unprepared for the shock of having her head thrust under one of the waterfalls.

"Hugh, for heaven's sake, I'm going to drown!" But the water was refreshingly cool. Her nausea receded. Mattie started to struggle, and Hugh dragged her back into the cavern. She turned to confront him, sputtering. She felt like a drowned rat and knew she probably looked like one.

"Better?" Hugh asked, not unkindly.

"Yes, thank you," she whispered, her tone very formal. She stared straight ahead and realized she could see nothing. "Hugh, I'm not very good in confined spaces."

"Don't worry, babe, you'll do just fine." He went back to rummaging around in his string bag. "Only takes a few minutes to get through these tunnels. Now, where did I put that flashlight?"

"Please do not call me babe."

He acted as if he didn't hear her. "Ah, here we go. I knew I'd stuck it in here somewhere." He pulled the flashlight out of the bag, switched it on, and played it across the cavern walls. "Like I said, no problem. We'll be through here in no time. We just follow Cormier's markings. There's the first of them."

Mattie picked up her burdens and stared bleakly at the small white mark on the damp wall of the cavern. She would never have noticed it if Hugh had not pointed it out. "Couldn't we walk through the jungle to the other side of this mountain and approach Cormier's secret dock from that direction?"

"Nope. That's the beauty of his hiding place. No access from the sea side except by boat, and you'd have to know about the flooded cavern or you'd never notice the opening in the rock face. The only other route in is through these caves, and if someone didn't know the way, he'd get hopelessly lost in minutes."

"I see. How very reassuring," Mattie said weakly.

"I told you Cormier was one sly old fox. Ready?" Hugh was already moving forward with characteristic self-confidence, clearly expecting her to follow without question.

He did everything with that supremely arrogant, blunt, no-nonsense style, Mattie reflected angrily. Literally everything, including making love, as she knew to her cost. She doubted Hugh would have even known how to spell *finesse* or *tact* or *subtlety* if asked to do so. The words were simply not in his vocabulary.

How could she have ever thought herself in love with this man? she wondered in disgust as she trailed after Hugh. She had nothing at all in common with him. He was obviously not even the least bit claustrophobic, for instance. It would have been nice to know he had some small, civilized neurosis, some endearing little weakness, some modern anxiety problem.

She, of course, had plenty of all three.

It took everything she had to follow Hugh through the dark maze of twisting caves. With every step the walls narrowed, trying to close in on her. Just as they used to do in those old, frantic dreams of her childhood, dreams in which there had been no way out.

She'd had enough psychology in college to understand those dreams. They had been manifestations of the anxiety and pressure she had felt during her childhood to find an acceptable niche in a family that considered lack of artistic talent a severe handicap.

The dreams of being caught in an endless tunnel had become less frequent after she had gone off to college. She rarely had them at all these days, but they had left their legacy in the form of her claustrophobia.

Mattie followed Hugh past several dark, gaping mouths that led into other twisting corridors. Her skin crawled as waves of fear moved over her, but Hugh never hesitated, never seemed uncertain. He just kept moving forward like a wolf at home in the shadows. Every so often he paused only to check for a small mark on the cavern wall.

Mattie concentrated on the circle of light cast by the flashlight and tried to picture the view of Elliott Bay she enjoyed from the window of her apartment in Seattle. During meditation training she had learned to summon up such serene pictures in order to quiet her mind.

The walk through the winding lava corridors was the longest walk of her life. Once or twice she felt large, wriggling things go crunch underfoot, and she wanted to be sick again. Every ten steps she nearly gave in to the urge to scream and run blindly back the way she had come. Every eleven steps she took more deep breaths, repeated her mantra, and forced herself to focus on the moving beam of light and the strong back of the man who was leading her through the caves of Purgatory.

She resented Hugh with the deep passion a woman can only feel for a man who has rejected her, but she also knew that she could trust him with her life. If anyone could get her out of here, he could.

"Mattie?"

"What?"

"Still with me, babe?"

"Please don't call me babe."

"We're almost there. Smell the sea?"

With a start Mattie realized she was inhaling brine-scented fresh air. "Yes," she whispered. "I do smell it."

She concentrated on that reassuring rush of fresh air as she followed Hugh around another bend in the corridor. Not long now, she told herself. Hugh would lead her through this. He would get her out of here. He was a bastard, but he was very good at what he did and one of the things he did best was survive. Aunt Charlotte had always said so. But, then, Aunt Charlotte was biased. She had always liked Hugh.

Mattie bit back another scream as the corridor briefly narrowed even further. Her pulse pounded, but the scent of the sea grew stronger. The corridor widened once more, and she inhaled sharply again.

"Here we go. Paul always knew what he was doing." Hugh quickened his own pace.

Mattie remembered Paul Cormier lying on the white marble floor. "Almost always."

"Yeah. Almost always."

"Did you know him well, Hugh?"

"Cormier and I went back a long way."

"I'm sorry."

"So am I." Hugh came to a halt as the passageway abruptly ended in a wide, high-ceilinged cavern.

Relief washed over Mattie as she realized she could see daylight at the far end of the huge cavern. She was safe. Hugh had led her out of the terrible dream.

She dropped her purse and the string bag and hurled herself into his arms.

"Oh, God, Hugh."

"Hey, what's this all about?" Hugh chuckled softly as he let his sack drop to the floor. His arms closed around Mattie with a warm fierceness. "Not that I'm complaining."

"I wasn't sure I could stand it," she whispered into his khaki shirt. She could feel the gun in his belt pressing into her side and smell the masculine scent of his body. There was something very reassuring about both. "Halfway through that awful tunnel I was sure I would go crazy."

"Hell, you're claustrophobic, aren't you?" His hands moved in her wet hair.

"A bit." She kept her face buried against his shoulder. He felt solid and strong and she wanted to cry. She had only been held this close to him once before, but her body remembered the heat and power in him as if it had been yesterday.

"More than a bit. Jesus, I'm sorry, babe. Didn't realize it was going to be that bad for you. You should have said something."

"I did. You said there wasn't any choice."

He groaned, his hand tightening around the nape of her neck. He dropped a kiss into her hair. "There wasn't."

He framed her face with his big palms, lifted her chin, and brought his mouth down roughly on hers.

Hugh's kiss was everything Mattie remembered, disconcertingly intense, just like the man himself.

No subtlety, no finesse, but dear heaven, it felt wonderful. For a moment Mattie surrendered to Hugh's kiss, losing herself in it. But as the lingering terror was pushed aside by this kindling passion, reality crept stealthily back between the cracks.

Mattie tore her mouth free. She was trembling again, but not from the memory of old anxiety dreams this time.

"You okay now, babe?" Hugh massaged her shoulders with strong, reassuring movements. His gray eyes were full of concern.

"Yes. Yes, I'm okay." Mattie was furious with herself for the loss of control. She pulled away from Hugh and turned to gaze around the large cavern as if she had found some extremely interesting modern art sketched on the walls. "What a wretched place."

Hugh released her reluctantly, his narrowed eyes automatically following her gaze. He played the flashlight over the scene. "Well, shit."

"What's wrong?" Mattie glanced around anxiously, following the beam of light.

"The boat's gone."

Mattie very nearly did scream then. She realized just how much she had been counting on the reality of Cormier's escape boat. She fought back the urge with every ounce of willpower at her command.

The beam of light in Hugh's hand told the story. There was a large, natural pool in the middle of the cavern. It was filled with black seawater that lapped against the rocky ledge. At the far end of the pool was a narrow opening that revealed a passageway in the cliff wall that was just large enough for a small boat. A narrow ledge ran along the mouth of the opening like a lip. The rain-spangled sea lay beyond.

"Now what?" She was amazed at the cool tone of her voice. Perhaps she was beyond anxiety now and was well into a state of numbed terror. Except that she was not truly terrified, she realized vaguely. Not with Hugh standing beside her looking so thoroughly annoyed.

Hugh glanced at her, his eyes narrowed consideringly. "We'll figure out something. Don't go hysterical on me now."

"Don't worry, I won't. A good case of hysterics takes energy, and frankly, I'm exhausted. Are you going to tell me we have to turn around and go back out through those awful corridors? Because if so, I think you had better knock me unconscious first. I'm not up to a return trip."

"Relax, babe. This cavern is as good a place to hide as any until we can liberate another boat. There are plenty around. On an island like this nearly everyone has a boat of some kind."

"I don't think I can manage a night in this place," Mattie said honestly.

"It's a big place, Mattie, with fresh air coming in from the sea. When the storm is over we might even get some moonlight in through that opening."

Mattie sighed. "I suppose there's no real alternative, is there?"

"Nope." He reached out and ruffled her wet hair in a bracingly affectionate fashion. "Come on, babe, cheer up. We'll camp over there near the boat entrance. You'll be able to see out. It will be just like looking at Elliott Bay through your apartment window."

Mattie remembered the night he had stood with her in her apartment and looked out at the bay, and how, when morning had come, she had been standing alone in front of that window. She shuddered. "What about the, uh, sanitary facilities?"

He grinned briefly. "Just walk out along that ledge that borders the entrance. Outside there's a few square yards of jungle growing on a sort of natural veranda on either side of the opening. You can use that."

"What about the tide? Is this cavern going to fill up with more sea-water later on?"

"No. This is high tide now. Cormier said the water never gets above that mark on the wall over there. I expect it can get a little exciting in here during a major storm, but other than that, no problem."

"I see. What do you think happened to Cormier's boat?"

"Beats me," Hugh said philosophically.

"Perhaps someone already found this cavern and took the boat. Maybe this isn't such a safe place after all," Mattie said nervously.

"I don't think anyone else knows about this place. But even if some-one does, we're staying put."

"Why?"

Hugh was unlacing one of the string bags. "Out in the open jungle we'd be too vulnerable, especially with you clomping around making a lot of racket. No offense."

"None taken," she retorted.

"This cavern, on the other hand, is relatively easy to defend. If someone did come in by boat, we could always retreat into the tunnels if necessary. Any fight in that network of caves behind us would be one-on-one. And we'd have the advantage because we know how to interpret Cormier's wall markings."

"I see." Mattie's stomach clenched at the casual way he talked about a shoot-out in the cavern. She stood still for a moment staring out through the opening in the rocky wall. The fresh air wafting into the big cavern was reassuring. And the cavern itself seemed large enough. It was gloomy, but she did not sense the walls closing in on her the way she had back in the corridors they had just come through.

"Mattie?"

"I won't sleep a wink, of course, but I don't think I'll go bonkers on you," she said.

"Attagirl, babe."

"Do me a favor, Hugh. Try not to be too condescending, okay? I'm really not in the mood for it."

"Sure, babe. How about something to eat? Bet you're starving by now." Hugh pulled a small tin of liver pâté out of one of the string bags and held it aloft for her inspection.

Mattie shuddered. "I gave up meat a couple years ago. It's not very good for you, especially in that form. Pâtés are full of fat and choles-terol and who knows what else."

Hugh eyed the tin with a considering gaze. "Yeah, I'm not real fond of pâté, myself. Give me a good juicy steak any day. But beggars can't be choosers, right?"

"They can be as choosy as they want until they're a lot hungrier than I am right now." Mattie sat down on the nearest rock and cast a withering glance at the liver pâté, the caves that had terrified her, and the man who had humiliated her. She wondered what the instructor in last month's antistress class would have advised to do now.

A few hours later Hugh shifted slightly against the rough wall of the cave and watched the wedge of silver moonlight creep slowly toward Mattie's still, silent shape. She was curled up in a semireclining position, her head pillowed on her leather purse. He knew she was not asleep.

Earlier she had managed to eat some of the water crackers he had taken from Cormier's cupboard, but she had not touched any of the other food he had brought along.

Hugh thought about the ashen look on her face when she had emerged from the narrow cavern passages, and his mouth tightened. The lady had guts. He knew what it was like to keep moving ahead when your whole body was bathed in the sweat of fear and your insides felt loose and out of control. He had nothing but respect for anyone else who could manage the trick.

Hugh watched the dark water lapping against rock. He would have given a great deal to know what had happened to the boat that Cormier had always kept at the ready here in this cavern. It was not like his friend to be taken off guard.

Cormier had always been a planner, a careful strategist who had prided himself on being prepared for all contingencies. Now he was dead. And the escape boat was not where it should have been.

There were several logical explanations for the missing boat. It might simply have been sent to a local yard for repairs or a new paint job. Cormier always took care of his equipment.

But there were not many good explanations for how Paul Cormier had allowed himself to be taken unawares by a killer.

On the other hand, Cormier had been an old man, a man who had thought himself safe here in the paradise called Purgatory. The past was behind him now and there had been no reason to fear the future.

Hugh told himself he would worry about what had happened to Cormier later. There was a time and a place for vengeance. He had other things to worry about at the moment.

He watched the moonlight touch Mattie's bare feet. Right now the first priority was to get her safely off the island. Cormier would have been the first to agree with that. The old man had been old-fashioned when it came to dealing with women.

*"A man must always protect the ladies, Hugh. Even when they bare their little claws and assure us they can defend themselves. If we cannot take care of our women, we are not of much use to them, are we? And we would not want to have them conclude we are totally useless. Where would we men be then? A man who is not willing to defend a woman with his life is not much of a man."*

Hugh studied Mattie. Her trousered legs were now bathed in pale silver. He recalled the shock on her face a few hours ago when she had emerged from Cormier's mansion. The memory would send a finger of anguish down his spine for years to come. She should not have had to witness that kind of violence. She was a sheltered city creature. She had always been protected from the brutal side of life.

It had been almost a year since Hugh had last seen her. Not that he had not tried. He'd deliberately arranged three separate excuses during the past eight months to report to Charlotte Vailcourt in person at Vailcourt headquarters in Seattle. Charlotte had conspired willingly enough with the pretenses. Acting was easy for her. Before she had abandoned her career to marry George Vailcourt, she had been a critically acclaimed legend of the silver screen.

He and Charlotte had thought their plans to surprise Mattie in Seattle were flawless, but on each occasion Hugh had arrived in town only to find Mattie gone.

The first time she had been off on a buying trip in Santa Fe. The second time she had been visiting an artist's colony in Northern California.

After that Hugh had begun to suspect her absences were not a coincidence.

On the third occasion Hugh had ordered Charlotte not to say a word to anyone about his impending visit. But somehow Mattie had discovered his plans the day before he hit town. She had left that same day to attend a series of gallery showings in New York.

Hugh had been furious and he'd made no secret of it. He had snarled at his boss, told himself no female was worth this kind of aggravation, and taken the next plane back to St. Gabriel.

But a thousand miles out over the Pacific and two whiskeys later, he had forgotten his own advice to forget Mattie Sharpe. He had spent the remainder of the long flight concocting an infallible scheme to force Mattie to meet him on his turf. He'd had it with chasing after her. She would come to him.

Out here on his own territory he would have the advantage. Hell, once her plane touched down on St. Gabriel, she would not even be able to get back off the island without his knowing about it well in advance.

What he'd needed was a reason for her to come out to the islands.

The memory of Paul Cormier's collection of antique weapons had been an inspiration. Hugh had only met one other person who collected such gruesome stuff. That person was Charlotte Vailcourt, who had taken a keen interest in her husband's collection after his death.

Sixty years old, wealthy, shrewd, and delightfully eccentric, the former star turned business wizard had a passion for old implements of violence. She claimed they nicely complemented her executive personality. There were times when Hugh was inclined to agree.

Charlotte had been thrilled with the scheme to strand Mattie on St. Gabriel. Long convinced that Mattie desperately needed a vacation, she had talked her niece into taking one at a plush resort just a bit beyond the Hawaiian Islands. And as long as she was going that far, Charlotte had said casually, she might as well hop over to Purgatory and pick up a valuable medieval sword from a collector named Paul Cormier.

Nobody had mentioned that the route to Cormier's island was via St. Gabriel.

"Hugh?"

"Yeah?"

"Who is Christine?"

Hugh frowned. "Christine Cormier? Paul's wife. She died a couple years ago. Why?"

"He thought I was her there at the end."

Hugh shut his eyes and rubbed the back of his neck. "Damn. Paul was still alive when you got there?"

"Only for about three or four minutes. No more. He told me there was no point calling for help."

"Christ." Hugh leaned his head back against the wall. He remembered the great red wound in his friend's chest and the blood that had stained the floor and Mattie's clothing. "Was that the first time you've ever had to, uh . . ."

"Watch someone die? No. I was with my grandmother at the end. But that was so different. She was in a hospital and the whole family was there." There was a long pause. "She was a famous ballerina, you know."

"I know."

"I still remember her last words," Mattie said.

"What were they?"

" 'Pity the younger girl never showed any signs of talent.' "

Hugh winced. "She was talking about you?"

"Uh-huh. Aunt Charlotte said Grandmother might have been one of the finest prima ballerinas who had ever lived, but that didn't change the fact that she had all the sensitivity of a bull elephant. Even on her deathbed."

Hugh was silent for a moment. He'd seen enough of her multitalented family to guess that Mattie, the only one without any artistic bent, had probably always felt like a second-class citizen. Her decision to forge a career as an art gallery owner had been viewed by the other members of the clan as a final admission that she had not inherited any of the family's brilliant genes. Only Charlotte had understood and sympathized.

"I'm sorry you had to walk in on Cormier like that," Hugh finally said.

"I felt so damned helpless."

Hugh smiled to himself in the darkness. "Paul was probably terribly embarrassed."

"It's hardly a joking matter, for God's sake."

"No, I didn't mean it as a joke." Hugh tried to think of how to explain. "You had to know Paul. He was a gentleman to his fingertips. Took pride in it. He would never have dreamed of inconveniencing a lady. When I saw him a couple of months ago, he gave me a long lecture on how to deal with women. Said my techniques were lousy."

"Did he really? Mr. Cormier was obviously a very perceptive man."

"That's my Mattie. Sounds like you're pulling out of the shock. What did you say when Paul called you Christine?"

Mattie shrugged as she stared at the moonlight crawling slowly up her rumpled silk shirt. "I did what people always do in a situation like that. I held his hand and let him think I was Christine."

Hugh studied her intently. "What makes you think everyone does things like that?"

"I don't know. Instinct, I suppose. There's so little you can do to comfort a dying man." She moved around a little, obviously trying to get more comfortable. "He wasn't hallucinating all the time, though. At one point he warned me to get out of there. Then he said someone would come. Maybe he meant you. And then he made a little joke. It was amazing. Imagine someone being able to joke about his own death."

"What did he say?"

"He said something about intending to reign in hell, I think. You know that famous quote from *Paradise Lost?* 'Better to reign in hell than serve in heaven'?"

"I know it." Hugh smiled to himself with grim satisfaction. "Sounds like Cormier. He probably figured his chances of getting into heaven were slight. But he'll do all right if he goes down instead of up. I'd back him in a contest with the devil any day. Paul may have had the manners of an angel, but I've seen him—" Hugh stopped himself abruptly. No sense bringing up Paul's past. It might lead to questions about his own, and Hugh definitely did not want that.

"Well, he thought he saw Christine again right at the very end, waiting for him, so maybe he went the other way after all."

"Maybe. He loved her very much." Hugh was silent for a moment, thinking. *I should have been there with you, Paul. After all these years together, I should have been there at the end. I'm sorry, my friend.*

"Thanks, Mattie."

"For what?"

"For staying with him for those last few minutes. You probably shouldn't have hung around. You probably should have run like hell. But Paul was a good friend of mine. I'm glad he didn't die alone."

Mattie was silent. "I'm sorry you lost a friend."

"I just wish you hadn't had to go through that," Hugh continued, his voice roughening.

"It was something of a shock," she admitted.

"Why in hell didn't you do as you were told and follow the original flight schedule?" As soon as the words were out of his mouth, Hugh wished he had bitten his tongue.

Mattie sighed. "Please, Hugh. No lectures. Not tonight. I know it will be very difficult for you to resist, but I would very much appreciate it if you would try."

"But, why, Mattie? Was the thought of seeing me again all that terrible? You've been deliberately avoiding me for months. Nearly a whole damned year."

She said nothing.

Hugh eyed her, feeling a deep anger tinged with guilt. He brushed aside the guilt and concentrated on the anger. It was an easier emotion to deal with. "You nearly got yourself killed today because of your stupid determination to avoid me at all costs." He swore under his breath, thinking about what it had felt like to walk up the steps of Cormier's too-silent mansion and see that ominously open door.

There was no response from the still figure on the cavern floor.

"Mattie?" He heard the edge in his own voice and frowned.

She continued to stare silently out into the night.

Hugh swore again, knowing he should not have brought the subject up so soon. But he was not, by nature, a patient man. In fact, Hugh thought he'd exercised more patience with Mattie Sharpe during the past year than he had with every other person in his whole life combined.

The entire, convoluted mess was his own fault, of course, as Cormier had taken pains to point out a few months ago.

*"Hell hath no fury like a woman scorned, Hugh. You're old enough to know that. You have only yourself to blame for the situation in which you find yourself. Now you're going to have to work very, very hard to get her back. I rather think the exercise will be good for you."*

Hugh, as Cormier had carefully explained, had made the fatal blunder of rejecting Mattie's heart and soul a year ago. But he had compounded his error by taking her body, which she had offered along with the rest.

The lady apparently held a mean grudge. Cormier had warned him that women were inclined to do that.

There had been only one night with Mattie because Hugh had been booked on a plane back to St. Gabe the next morning. His stormy engagement to Mattie's brilliant, dazzling sister, Ariel, had at last ended in a hurricane of tears and recriminations. Ariel never did anything without a lot of melodrama, Hugh had discovered to his disgust. He was only grateful he'd found it out before the wedding. In the end he had wanted nothing more than to escape to his island and lick his wounds.

The last thing he'd intended doing that final night in Seattle was spend it with the quiet, restrained, obviously repressed, business-obsessed Mattie.

Mattie, whom he'd barely noticed while he struggled to deal with the fire and lightning that was Ariel.

Mattie, who had been waiting quietly in the wings all along, knowing that the engagement to Ariel could not last.

Mattie, who had nervously called him that last night in Seattle and asked if he would come to dinner.

To this day Hugh was still not quite certain why he had accepted the invitation. He knew he had not been fit company for anyone, let alone someone as quiet and unassuming and nervous as Mattie. He had been consumed with rage, both at Ariel and at himself. All his fine plans to head back to St. Gabe with a wife in hand had gone up in smoke. Hugh, as Charlotte Vailcourt had frequently noted, was not accustomed to having anyone mess up his plans.

There were a lot of reasons Hugh had not gotten to know Mattie well by the time his engagement to Ariel had ended. For one thing, he simply had not spent much time with her. He had been too busy quarreling with Ariel over her unexpected refusal to move out to St. Gabriel. Ariel had somehow gotten the impression that Hugh had been planning to move to Seattle. The battle, once joined, had taken up every spare minute of Hugh's time.

But another reason why a man tended not to notice Mattie right off was that she was very different from Ariel. Mattie was a quiet, warm rain where Ariel had been a full-blown storm.

Everything about Mattie was more muted and less obvious than her sister.

Ariel's eyes were a fascinating, witchy green. Mattie's almost green gaze was softened with gold into a shade that was closer to hazel. Ariel's hair, cut in a dramatic wedge, was jet black; Mattie's, worn in a prim coil, was a warm honey brown.

Both women were slender, but Mattie's figure, which was nearly always encased in a severe, conservative business suit, seemed flat and uninteresting. Ariel, on the other hand, always appeared willowy and dramatic in the one-of-a-kind clothes she favored.

But that last night in Seattle something about Mattie had tugged at Hugh's senses. She had looked like a calm port in which to rest for a while after the storm. He had been lured gently into her web by an oddly old-fashioned womanly charm that was entirely new to him. The home-cooked meal of pasta and vegetables and the quiet conversation had been both soothing and simultaneously arousing. Her anxiousness to please had been balm to Hugh's lacerated ego. Her shy, rather hesitant sexual overtures had made him feel powerful and desired.

He knew she was not his type, but when the time had come he had taken Mattie to bed and lost himself in her warmth. He had been deeply aware of a sense of gratitude toward her.

The next morning Hugh had awakened with a hangover and the gnawing certainty that he had made a really stupid mistake.

The last person he had wanted to get involved with at that point was another Sharpe sister. He'd had it with the women of the clan. In fact, he'd had it with women and city life in general. He just longed to go home and devote himself to his fledgling charter business.

As he had packed his bag and phoned for a cab to the airport to catch his six o'clock flight, Hugh had tried to ease his way out the door by thanking Mattie for her hospitality. That was when she had made her plea, a plea that had echoed in his ears nearly every night since that last one in Seattle.

*"Take me with you, Hugh. I love you so much. Please take me with you. I'll follow you anywhere. I'll make you a good wife. I swear it. Please, Hugh."*

Hugh had fled after first making a further mess of the matter by trying to explain to Mattie that she was not really his type.

He had not been gone more than a couple of months before he had finally admitted to himself that he had picked the wrong sister the first time around. Trying to rectify his error was proving far more complicated than he would have initially believed possible.

"Had Cormier lived here on Purgatory for a long time?" Mattie asked after a long silence.

"He settled here a few years ago. I think he liked the irony of the name."

"Purgatory? Why is it called that?"

"It's part of the Brimstone Chain. A few of the islands in the group have active volcanos. Guess they made the original settlers think of fire and brimstone. Purgatory's the biggest one in the string. It's been independent since right after World War Two. None of the bigger countries wanted to own it."

"Why not?"

"No commercial or military value. Not even any tourism to speak of."

"Apparently someone's willing to fight for it."

Hugh thought about that. "Yeah. Funny that Paul didn't pick up on that. He usually had an instinct for trouble. He always claimed Purgatory was paradise simply because it wasn't worth fighting over." Paul had long ago grown weary of battle. Just as Hugh had. "Why don't you try to get some sleep, Mattie?"

"I couldn't possibly sleep tonight." There was a shudder in her voice.

Hugh made a decision. He got up, walked over, and sat down right next to her, aware of the tension radiating from her. Deliberately he put an arm around her shoulders. She tried to pull away. He ignored the small, ineffectual movement and gently pushed her head onto his shoulder. Her body was taut and warm alongside his.

"Close your eyes, Mattie."

"I told you, I can't." She stiffened. "Hugh, I wish you wouldn't do this."

"Close your eyes and imagine you're dozing off in front of your living room window."

She said nothing more but she did not try to pull away from his grasp. Hugh waited, absently rubbing her shoulder.

Fifteen minutes later he realized she was asleep.

For a long time Hugh sat there enjoying the feel of holding Mattie at long last after all these months. He wondered what Cormier would have advised at this juncture.

*"Patience, Hugh. You've already pissed in your chili once, as our dear friend Mr. Taggert is fond of saying. Don't screw up again."*

The problem, Hugh thought, was that he'd already been patient for months. He was not sure how much patience he had left. He was forty and he was alone.

And over the past year he had gotten very tired of being alone.

\* \* \*

Mattie awoke the next morning to the scent of flowers. Exotic flowers. Rich, lush, vibrant flowers. Their perfume was a heavenly cloud that seemed to envelop her.

She opened her eyes and saw the massive bouquet lying on the floor of the cave directly in front of her face. It was a huge collection of vividly colored blossoms. There were dozens and dozens of flowers— orange, pink, and white lilies, spectacular bird of paradise, red torch ginger, heliconia, and myriad orchids. They were heaped in beautiful disarray. A veritable mountain of gorgeous blooms. Mattie knew that a mass of orchids and other exotics such as this would have cost two or three hundred dollars back in the States.

She smiled and reached out to touch a crimson petal. It was like velvet under her fingertips. Hugh must have gone out very early to collect such a wealth of flora.

*Hugh.* Of course this tower of flowers was his doing.

Mattie snatched her fingers back quickly and scowled at the huge assortment. It was really quite ludicrous. There were far too many flowers. A single perfect orchid or one golden yellow hibiscus bloom would have been far more tasteful than this colorful, confused heap.

It was no surprise that Hugh was as heavy-handed in presenting flowers as he was in everything else he did. As she had observed before, the man did not have a subtle bone in his body.

That thought brought back unwelcome memories of the one night she had spent in bed with Hugh Abbott. No, *subtle* was not a word that came to mind. What came to mind was the old phrase *slam, bam, thank you, ma'am.*

No wonder Ariel had broken off the engagement shortly after returning from Italy with Hugh in tow last year. She had explained to Mattie that Hugh had obviously been merely a phase she had been going through. He represented the Elemental period in her evolving artistic style. It was one of her shorter-lived periods.

Mattie sat up stiffly, stretching her limbs cautiously to see how much damage a night on the stone floor had done. She had to bite back a groan. Then she realized that Paul Cormier would not be waking up at all this morning and she sighed.

She got to her feet, aware that she was alone in the cavern. When she glanced at the level of seawater in the small, natural boat basin, she realized the tide must be out.

There was no sign of Hugh. She assumed he was out scouting around or doing whatever men like him did in situations such as this.

When she walked over to the ledge near the cave's entrance and peered out, Mattie could see the small patch of green foliage clinging tenaciously to a rocky overhang that jutted out above the sea.

Above and below the natural veranda there was nothing but sheer cliff. The facilities were definitely primitive, but there was not much choice.

A few minutes later she returned to the cavern and washed her hands in seawater. Then she turned her attention to the contents in the string bags.

Hugh's trip to Cormier's kitchen had been brief, but he had managed to make quite a haul. Mattie found several more small tins of fancy pâtés, marinated oysters, a jar of brine-cured olives, some homemade tapanade, sun-dried tomatoes, bottled spring water, and a wedge of hazelnut torte. There was also a bit of brie and a chunk of Stilton and some day-old French bread. Hugh had even swiped a white linen kitchen towel.

Mattie surveyed the lot and decided the only thing that vaguely resembled breakfast was the brie. She tore off chunks of the bread and began to spread it with the cheese.

When a boot scraped on the rocky floor behind her, Mattie started nervously and leapt to her feet. She whirled around, clutching the knife she had been using to spread the cheese.

"Hugh." She inhaled deeply. "Don't ever sneak up on me like that again. I'm very jumpy these days."

"Sorry. Didn't know if you'd be awake yet."

He switched off the flashlight he was carrying and sauntered into the main cavern from the tunnel they had used yesterday. He was looking disgustingly refreshed and energetic, Mattie thought in annoyance. An occasional night spent on a gritty stone floor apparently did not bother him in the slightest.

His jeans and khaki shirt were a little stained but basically did not look much different than they had yesterday. Other than a day's growth of beard Hugh appeared none the worse for wear. He looked like Mr. Macho Adventurer, always at home in primitive jungles, barren deserts, or other perilous locales.

Mattie, who had been congratulating herself on surviving the night, suddenly felt weak and puny.

"Want some brie and French bread?" She did not look at him as she held some food for him.

"Thanks. Paul always said living at the edge of the world was no excuse for sacrificing the good things in life."

"So I gathered. Mr. Cormier was obviously a gourmet."

Hugh grinned around a large bite of bread and brie. "Hey, stick with me, babe, and it'll be nothing but the best all the way."

Mattie winced. "Nothing but the best and plenty of it?" She nodded toward the huge pile of flowers.

Hugh looked pleased as he followed her glance. "Nice, huh? I found 'em right outside the front door this morning when I went out to take a . . . Uh, when I went outside."

"For your morning ablutions?" Mattie smiled sweetly.

"Yeah, right. Did you go out?"

"Yes, thank you." She glanced back toward the bright heap. "And thank you for the flowers," she added politely.

Hugh's expectant expression hardened. "Don't fall all over me or anything on account of a few flowers."

"Don't worry, I won't."

"Ouch." He took another bite of cheese and bread. "You're certainly back in fighting form this morning, aren't you?"

"Believe me, the last thing I want to do this morning is fight." She frowned at the tunnel entrance behind him. "What were you doing in there?"

"I left a little before dawn. I was going to bury Cormier."

Mattie bit her lip. "Oh, Hugh. I should have gone with you."

He shook his head. "Wouldn't have done any good. Somebody had already taken him away."

She was startled. "His family, perhaps?"

"Cormier had no family. He was alone after his wife died. Whoever took his body cleaned the place out; the sword, the rest of his medieval collection, and everything else that wasn't nailed down."

"Good heavens, I forgot all about the damn sword. Do you think it's possible someone killed him for his collection? Aunt Charlotte said it was extremely valuable."

"Possible. But it's more likely somebody he trusted, maybe a member of his household staff, was overcome with revolutionary fervor," Hugh said.

"You shouldn't have gone back there," Mattie declared. "You might have run into whoever came for Cormier's body."

"I'm not entirely stupid, you know. I took a few precautions. The cars are gone, too."

Mattie looked up, startled. "Oh, my God. My suitcase was in that car. All my clothes. And my vitamins."

Hugh cocked a brow. "Your vitamins?"

"I always take vitamins first thing in the morning."

"Why? Don't you eat properly?"

She scowled at him. "My diet is a very healthy one, thank you. But

I supplement it with vitamins to counteract the effects of stress and tension."

"I always thought sex was supposed to be good for that."

Mattie looked at him with narrowed eyes. "Well, I don't get a lot of sex, so I have to use other techniques to combat stress."

"Easy, babe." Hugh's eyes gleamed. "I can take care of the shortage of sex in your life for you. Like I said, nothing but the best if you stick with me."

"Oh, shut up. What do you think happened to the cars?"

"Someone must have hot-wired 'em. They got lifted along with just about everything else."

"Looters." Mattie wrinkled her nose in disgust.

"Yeah."

Mattie's fingers clenched around the slice of French bread. She looked directly at Hugh. "So what, exactly, are we going to do next, O great, exalted leader?"

"Keep an extremely low profile, as Charlotte would say. We'll stay out of sight today. With any luck the situation, whatever it is, will cool off a little. Tonight I'll go out and see if I can find us a boat."

"We're just going to sit in here all day?" Mattie was alarmed.

"Afraid so. What's the matter? You worried about having to make conversation? Just think of all the stuff we have to talk about. We haven't seen each other in nearly a year."

"We did not have a great deal to say to each other a year ago. I doubt that anything's changed." She began rewrapping the brie. The plastic wrap crackled under her fingers.

"Look, Mattie," Hugh said with exaggerated patience, "you're stuck with me for the next few days. It's not going to kill you to relax and treat me like an old friend of the family or something."

"You're hardly a friend."

"Are you kidding? I'm the best one you've got at the moment. Who else is going to get you out of Purgatory in one piece?"

"That's blackmail. You want me to be nice and friendly to you because you're doing me a favor? Just how friendly am I supposed to be, Hugh? What will you do if I can't work up any warm feelings for you? Will you get mad and leave me behind when you find a boat?"

He moved so quickly she never had a chance to get out of range. One second he was half-sprawled on an outcropping of stone beside her; the next he had his long, strong fingers wrapped around her wrist in a grip of steel.

"Hugh."

His gray eyes were dangerously cold. "Another crack like that and I'll do something very drastic. Understand?"

"For heaven's sake, Hugh. Let me go." She wriggled her hand in his grasp.

"Damn it, Mattie, I've spent eight months trying to see you again, and you've done nothing but evade me."

"What was I supposed to do? You made it clear you didn't want me." The old rage and hurt welled up out of nowhere. She wanted to lash out at him, hurt him the way he had once hurt her. "As it happens, I spent the past year coming to the conclusion that you were right."

"About what?"

"You told me I was not your type, remember? I agree with you now." Her chin came up proudly. "More important, you're not my type. I should have seen that from the beginning."

"How do we know we're not each other's type? We haven't given ourselves a chance."

"I gave you a chance," she reminded him in a scathing voice. "I offered to follow you to the ends of the earth, remember? And you turned me down flat."

"I've told you before, you've got lousy timing. And last year your timing was all wrong."

She was incensed. "Oh, sure. Blame it all on me."

"Why not? I'm tired of having you blame everything on me. And your timing is bad, babe. Look at the way you're starting this stupid fight while we're trapped in this goddamned cave in the middle of an island that's undergoing an armed revolt. Talk about lousy timing."

"You started this, Hugh Abbott."

"Is that so? Then I might as well finish it."

He used the grip on her wrist to yank her into his arms. And then his mouth came down on hers with enough force to swamp her senses.

# 3

Mattie clutched at Hugh's shoulders as he released his grip on her wrist to encircle her with his arms. He pulled her tightly to him and leaned back against the rocky outcropping. She was lying on top of him, her breasts crushed against his chest, her legs tangled with his. Her emotions were in chaos. She wanted to scream. She wanted to swear. She wanted to slap Hugh Abbott as hard as she could.

But most of all she wanted to let herself savor the heat of him and the fierce, hot, masculine passion she had known so briefly all those months ago.

"You feel like you've been waiting in cold storage for me, babe," Hugh muttered. "There hasn't been anyone else this past year, has there?"

"No, damn you, *no.*"

"Yeah. Good. I told Charlotte to let me know right away if she saw any man moving in on you. Mattie . . . Mattie, babe, you've been driving me crazy." His mouth shifted heavily on hers and his fingers kneaded her back with hungry impatience. He kissed her throat and then his teeth closed lightly around her earlobe. The small nip was wildly sensual. "Lord, you feel good."

Mattie shut her eyes, inhaling the scent of him. His clothing smelled of sweat but his skin smelled of the sea. The stubble of his beard was like sandpaper against her cheek. She was vibrantly aware of the swift arousal of his body under hers.

"Kiss me, Mattie. Kiss me the way you did yesterday afternoon when you were grateful to me for getting you through those damn caves." He lifted her chin and captured her mouth once more.

Mattie surrendered to the excitement this man seemed able to elicit so easily in her. With a soft little moan of passion she opened her mouth and let him inside.

He accepted the invitation instantly, his tongue plunging hungrily between her lips, his hands sliding down to her breasts. She felt his fingers on the buttons of her silk shirt and then he was inside, un-hooking her bra, touching her.

There was a certain rough care in the way he cupped her breasts, as though he was almost in awe of her feminine softness. He touched her the way he would have touched a kitten, his big hands moving a little awkwardly, but cautiously on her. Mattie sighed as his callused thumbs glided over her nipples.

"It's been so long," he breathed. His voice was husky with desire. "Too long. Why the hell did you keep ducking me this past year? We could have had all these months."

His big, warm palms slid down her stomach to the fastening of her trousers. When Mattie heard the metallic hiss of the zipper she finally came to her senses.

The thing you had to keep in mind about Hugh Abbott was that he always moved fast. If a woman was going to say no, she had to say it quickly.

"*No*," Mattie gasped, levering herself up and back. "No, damn it. What in the world do you think you're doing?" She wriggled farther away from him, sitting back on her heels. "Pay attention, Hugh Abbott. And get this clear. I'm not about to have another one-night stand with you."

"For God's sake, Mattie." He reached for her, his gaze still gleaming and intent with desire.

But Mattie was already scrambling to her feet, her trembling fingers refastening her clothing. "Good grief, I can't believe I let you do this to me. Of all the stupid, asinine . . ."

Hugh swore and gave up the attempt to pull her back into his arms. He collapsed back against the rock and watched her through nar-rowed, brooding eyes. "You wanted it. You wanted it as much as I did. Don't lie to me, Mattie. Not about that."

"I expect it's the stress," she said with forced calm. "It has odd and unpredictable effects on people."

"Stress? Don't give me that. Do you city people blame everything on stress these days? Even a little old-fashioned lust?"

"I suppose you never suffer from stress?" she muttered, moving several feet away from him. She sat down again, pulled her knees up under her chin, and wrapped her arms around her legs.

"I don't know. I don't think too much about it."

"But lust, on the other hand, is something you do understand, right?"

Hugh started to answer with what looked like an automatic yes and then paused, obviously sensing a trap. "Babe, let's not argue over this," he said with surprising gentleness. "I can see you're kind of on edge. I didn't mean to rush you. If you want to talk a little first, that's all right with me. I mean, I know women like to talk about things; to *communicate*. Paul always said . . . Never mind. It's been a long time since we've seen each other. You probably just feel a little shy, that's all."

"No kidding." Her voice dripped sarcasm.

"Hey, it's okay, babe. We've got all day. We can't go anywhere until tonight. Why don't we just sit here and sort of get comfortable with each other again?"

"Oh, my God." Mattie nearly choked. Hugh Abbott trying to be modern and sensitive was too much to take. "Ariel was right. You're hopeless."

"Ariel? What the hell has she got to do with this?" Hugh demanded, clearly annoyed.

"You remember my sister, Ariel, don't you, Hugh? You were engaged to her for a couple of months last year. Don't tell me it's slipped your mind. You met her in Italy when she went there to tour the galleries. You two ate pasta, drank cheap red wine, and did kinky things in famous fountains at three in the morning. Then you returned to Seattle with her. The two of you told everyone you were engaged. Does any of that sound vaguely familiar?"

Hugh groaned. "Ariel was a mistake."

"I'm aware of that. I believe I mentioned the fact to you a year ago."

"Yeah, you did."

"She's married again, you know. Her second husband is a man named Flynn Grafton. He's very nice. An artist."

"Charlotte said something about it," Hugh muttered, not showing any great interest in the matter. "Look, Mattie, I don't want to talk about Ariel."

"I do," Mattie said with sudden violence. "I want to know why you fell in love with her and planned to marry her when it was obvious she was all wrong for you. I want to know why you didn't notice me until I threw myself at you, and even then you didn't bother to catch me."

"Forget Ariel. That was a year ago and I've already told you it was a mistake."

"And I was another mistake, wasn't I, Hugh? Do you make mistakes like those a lot?"

"Not often enough to be convenient," he shot back. "Damn it, you aren't the only one who's had a hard year. I haven't been with another woman since you, Mattie."

"You expect me to believe that?"

"Believe what you damn well want to believe. You're really spoiling for a fight, aren't you?" Hugh leaned his head back against the stone and stared out at the sea. "Want to tell my why?"

She bit her lip, horrified to realize how close she was to losing her self-control. It was so unlike her; so alien to her personality. She never made scenes; never screamed at a man; never embarrassed herself with outrageous behavior. A woman like Ariel could get away with that sort of thing. Mattie did not even want to try.

Mattie had been the calm, controlled one in the family for as long as she could remember. The only time she had ever lost her common sense and abandoned herself was a year ago with Hugh Abbott, and she had regretted it ever since. She made it a point not to repeat mistakes.

"Forget it," she said brusquely. "I'm sorry I brought the subject up. I know we're trapped here together until we can get off this island. There's no sense quarreling."

"Why?"

She scowled at him. "I told you why. Because we're stuck in this cave, and we have to work together until we can get out of here."

"I'm not talking about that. Don't worry, I'll get you off the island. I'm talking about why you want to bring up Ariel and the past and fling them both in my face."

At that point Mattie did something she never did. She lost her temper. "Maybe because I want to make certain I don't make a fool of myself a second time!" she shouted.

In the deep silence that followed her words seemed to echo endlessly off the cavern walls. But all Mattie heard was *fool, fool, fool.*

She was appalled. "Oh, God. There. Does that satisfy you, Hugh?" she whispered. "Please. Just let it alone, all right?"

He studied her in silence for a moment. "I can't let it alone, Mattie. I want you."

She shuddered and averted her eyes. "You don't want me."

"Come here and I'll show you." His voice was coaxing now, like velvet.

Mattie rolled her eyes in exasperation. "You wanted Ariel, first, remember? What is it with you? Now that you've gotten over your irritation with her, you're willing to consider another Sharpe sister? If you can't have one of Charlotte Vailcourt's nieces, you'll take the other?"

"Oh, hell."

Mattie hugged her knees more tightly to her chest. "I know Aunt

Charlotte wants you in the family. She makes no secret of it. Thinks you have good genes. Says you're a throwback. Says you're not a soft, neurotic wimp like so many modern men."

"Nice to be appreciated for one's finer qualities," Hugh growled.

"She asked you to look up Ariel in Italy because she figured my sister was her best shot at getting you into her little breeding program. Men have always been attracted to Ariel. They can't help themselves. And you were no different, were you? Aunt Charlotte was thrilled when the two of you came back engaged. But since that didn't work out, she's trying to pair you off with me. I told her you'd turned me down flat last year, but she says it was just bad timing."

"It was. I told you that."

"Well, I've got news for both of you. One chance is all you get, Hugh Abbott, and you've used up yours. I don't care what kind of high-level promotion or how big a cash bonus Aunt Charlotte is offering you to marry me."

The second the words were out of her mouth, Mattie knew she had gone too far. One look at the expression in Hugh's icy eyes told her that. There was an instant of shocking silence, and then she prudently leapt to her feet. She did not know where she intended to run, but she knew she had better get going.

She never stood a chance. Moving with the fluid strength that characterized all his actions, Hugh came to his feet and reached for her. A year of aerobic training was no match for that kind of masculine power. Mattie was helpless. Hugh's hands clamped around her upper arms and he held her motionless in front of him.

"You will apologize for that crack," he said, his tone verging on the lethal. "You will tell me you are very, very sorry you said that. You will say you know it's not true. And you will say it now."

Mattie looked pointedly down at his hands on her arms. "Sure, Hugh. I'll say anything you want me to say. You're a lot bigger and stronger than I am and I'm trapped here with you, so you just tell me what you want to hear and I'll say it."

He stared down at her in a kind of awed wonder. "You're really determined to push your luck, aren't you?"

"What luck? I've had nothing but bad luck since I hit Purgatory. Please let me go, Hugh."

"Not until you apologize, by God. We'll stand here like this all day if that's what it takes."

She believed him. "All right, I'm sorry I implied Aunt Charlotte was trying to buy you. There. Satisfied?"

For a few seconds it did not look as if he was satisfied in the least.

Then, with a short, explicit oath, Hugh released her abruptly. He jammed his fingers through his hair. "You really know how to get to me, don't you? You know all the right buttons to push."

Mattie stood tensely, watching him. "Hugh, this is crazy. We have got to stop arguing. Who knows how long we're going to be together in this mess?"

He slid her a long glance. "Doesn't it mean a damn thing to you that I've spent the last eight months trying to make up for the stupid mistake I made a year ago?"

She clasped her hands together. "That's just it. You didn't make a mistake last year. You were right to reject my utterly ridiculous offer. We're all wrong for each other, Hugh. I realize that now. What I can't figure out is why you've changed your mind."

"Well, it sure as hell isn't because Charlotte Vailcourt promised to promote me or give me a fat bonus if I marry you," he retorted.

Mattie chewed her lower lip. "I know. I'm sorry. It's just that I was so angry. Dear heaven. I never lose my temper. I don't know what got into me."

Hugh was quiet for a long while. The only sound in the cavern was the hollow echo of water slapping at rock. Then his mouth curved faintly at one corner. "Well, I'll be damned."

Mattie eyed him suspiciously. "What's so funny?"

"Nothing. I was just thinking that maybe it's a good sign you're trying to stick pins in me whenever you get the chance."

She blinked. "A good sign?"

"Yeah. Think about it." His smile broadened into a satisfied grin. "You wouldn't be so prickly about our relationship if you'd really lost interest in me, would you? You wouldn't have gone out of your way to avoid me this past year if you didn't give a damn any longer. You're nervous around me because you're still attracted to me and you're afraid of being hurt again. That's what this jumpy behavior on your part is all about. I'll lay odds on it."

Mattie's brows rose. This was a whole new side to the man. "Since when did you become an authority on interpersonal relationships?"

"You like to think I'm some sort of Neanderthal in the sensitivity department, don't you, Mattie? Why is that? Because it makes you feel superior?"

"It isn't just my opinion, you know," she murmured.

"We're talking about Ariel again, I take it? Hell, I already know she thinks I'm something out of the Stone Age. That's why she got interested in me in the first place. She was using me as inspiration for her damned painting. Don't you think I eventually figured that out?"

Mattie flushed and coughed slightly to clear her throat. "I, uh, hadn't realized you were aware of it precisely, no. When the two of you came back from Italy together and announced your engagement, you looked so damned pleased with yourself, Hugh."

He rubbed the back of his neck. "I was pleased. Ariel's a beautiful woman and the timing was perfect. I was getting set to quit doing odd jobs for Charlotte and start working full time at my own business on St. Gabe. I was looking for a wife to take out to the islands with me, and Charlotte set it up for me to meet her niece while I was on assignment in Italy. Said she thought we'd suit."

"I see."

"Hell, there I was looking for a wife and Ariel was just sort of conveniently dropped into my lap. It all seemed to go together into a nice, neat package."

"I know, I know. Let's just forget about it, Hugh."

"I'm willing to forget Ariel," Hugh said. "But not you. I want another chance, Mattie."

"Why? Because you're still looking for a wife, and you think I'll be more amenable to moving out to the edge of the world than Ariel was?"

He frowned. "A year ago you said you'd follow me anywhere."

"That," said Mattie with a bright little smile, "was a year ago. Now, let's stop rehashing the past and start discussing our immediate future. How, exactly, do you plan to find us a boat, and where will we go if we get hold of one?"

Hugh considered her bright smile for a long while. Then he shrugged and smiled back. "Finding the boat is my problem. Don't worry about it. As to where we'll go, that depends on what kind of boat I find and how much fuel I can steal. Don't you worry your pretty little head about such petty details, Miss Mattie."

She folded her arms beneath her breasts and glowered at him. "Wonderful. I'll leave it all up to you."

"You do that. Us Neanderthals have our uses."

Mattie realized he was not going to be forthcoming on the subject of the impending plans for engaging in boat theft. She sighed and looked bleakly around the cavern. Then she glanced down at the bloodstains on her silk shirt and trousers.

"I'd give anything for a hot shower and a change of clothes," she muttered.

"No hot showers, but you're welcome to take a bath. You can use one of those dish towels I found in Cormier's kitchen. Won't take long to dry off in this heat." Hugh strolled over to the opening in the rock wall and pulled the gun from his belt. He idly checked the cartridge.

"You mean take a bath here in the cavern?" Mattie eyed the saltwater lapping at the edges of the natural basin.

"Why not? I took one this morning. Felt good. You'll be a little sticky afterward because of the salt, but it wears off."

Mattie looked down into the water. "I can't see the bottom."

"So don't go diving for pearls." He thrust the gun back into his belt and pulled a couple of metal packs out of his pocket. "Whoever collected Cormier's body must have picked up that fancy little Beretta he always carried. I found some spare clips but not the pistol. He would have died with that thing in his hand."

Mattie remembered the gun in her purse. "A big ugly pistol? Kind of a yucky blue color?"

Hugh turned his head, one brow cocked. "Ugly is in the eye of the beholder. Paul loved that gun. You saw it?"

Mattie nodded and went over to where her shoulder bag lay. "I picked it up. I didn't know who or what I might run into on the way back to the airport." She picked up the purse, opened it, and removed the heavy blue metal gun. "Here. Is this what you're looking for?"

Hugh came toward her and took the weapon from her fingers. "Well, I'll be damned." He looked genuinely approving. "Nice going, babe. You've just doubled our firepower."

Mattie gritted her teeth. "That does it. I've had it. Never, under any circumstances, call me *babe* again. Understand?"

"You really are touchy today, aren't you, babe? I imagine all the recent stress has made you a little high strung."

"Damn it, Hugh."

"Going to take that swim?"

"I'm thinking about it." She glanced at the dark water, torn between wanting to wash off yesterday's blood and sweat and a fear of swimming in that bottomless pool. "Where will you go while I do it?"

"Nowhere." He shoved a fresh clip into Cormier's pistol. "I'll just sit right here and watch."

She shot him a disgusted glance. "Then I guess I'll forget the swim."

Hugh grinned. "Hey, I'm just teasing you. I'll turn my back and stare politely out to sea, if that's what you want. But it's not like I haven't already seen you in the buff."

"You were too drunk that night to remember anything you saw."

"Not quite," he assured her, still grinning and totally unrepentant. "If I'd been that drunk I wouldn't have been able to get it up, and I don't recall any problems in that department. And I remember everything I saw. And touched. Believe me, I've thought about it a lot during the past year, and I don't believe I've forgotten a single thing. You were very tight and very wild. A real surprise, I got to tell you. Looking at you dressed for work, no one would have believed it."

"Must you be so crude?"

"It's fun to watch you turn that nice bright shade of pink."

"Well, enjoy it because that's all you're going to see today. I can stand being hot, dirty, and sweaty another day, if you can."

"Oh, I can stand it. In fact, at the risk of sounding even cruder, there's something real sexy about you the way you are now. I think I like you best when you're not all neat and pressed and ready to sell expensive art to all those suckers you call clients."

"No wonder Ariel got fed up with you."

"Ah, ah, ah. We agreed not to talk about the past, remember? Ariel's not here. It's just you and me, babe."

*"Don't call me babe."*

"Oh, right. I forgot. Slipped my mind."

"How could it slip your mind?" Mattie raged, skating once more on the ragged edge of her self-control. "I don't think you even have one."

"In that case," he said with grave logic, "I don't see how you can hold me responsible for a few slips of the tongue."

Mattie bit off a muttered oath, vaguely aware that for some odd reason she felt better now than she had since she had walked into Cormier's mansion yesterday. Yelling at Hugh was apparently therapeutic. And she really did want a bath.

"Look, I'll make a deal with you," Mattie said, her hands on her hips.

"Sounds interesting." He was examining the Beretta. "What kind of deal?"

"Promise me you'll go sit by the entrance and keep your back turned while I take a short swim, and I'll give you my word that I won't mention our unfortunate, extremely embarrassing one-night stand last year again. Okay?"

Hugh appeared to turn the terms over in his mind. Then he gave a decisive nod. He never took long to make up his mind about anything. "Deal."

Mattie did not trust the too-innocent expression in his eyes. "Go sit out there on the ledge and watch sea gulls or something." Her fingers went to the buttons of her silk blouse.

"Right. Sea gulls." Hugh obediently ambled toward the cavern entrance and sat down on the rock ledge that lined the opening. He lounged there, one booted foot drawn up, his back to Mattie. "Yell when you're done."

Mattie kept her eye on him as she quickly slipped out of the sadly wrinkled shirt and trousers. When she was down to her bra and panties she hesitated again, making certain Hugh wasn't going to spin around.

She stepped over to the edge of the cavern pool and dipped a toe into the dark water. It felt comfortably cool and inviting. She sat down on the edge and dangled her feet in the seawater. Then she unhooked her prim little bra and slipped it off.

Once into the water she bobbed for a moment, sliding the wet scrap of her modest cotton briefs down over her hips. She lifted them out of the water, squeezed them tightly and placed them on the rocky edge to dry. They would be damp when she put them back on but would no doubt dry quickly against her skin.

She stroked hesitantly toward the far end of the dark pool, letting herself get accustomed to the feel of endless black depths beneath her. It certainly was not as pleasant as swimming in a sunny cove where one could see the white sand below the waves, but it did feel good. The exercise, itself, was soothing, of course. Exercise was very good for stress.

Mattie swam almost to the entrance where Hugh was still sitting with his back to her, turned around, and swam back. It felt so invigorating, she did several more laps.

And then something lightly brushed her leg under the surface.

"Hugh!" Mattie's scream bounced off the cavern ceiling.

Hugh uncoiled from the ledge and was at the edge of the pool nearest her before Mattie, splashing furiously, reached the side. He bent down, holding out his large, strong hands, and Mattie instinctively reached up to grasp his fingers. He lifted her straight up and out of the water in one swift, easy motion. She came out of the sea with a whoosh, naked, wet, and glistening.

"Something . . . something in the water." Shivering, Mattie pushed her dripping hair out of her face and stared wildly at the evil-looking pool. "I felt it. It touched my leg."

"Probably just a bit of seaweed. Or maybe a school of little fish."

"It could have been a shark or something. Damn, I hate swimming in places where you can't see the bottom." Mattie trembled again and hugged herself. Belatedly she realized she was standing stark naked on the rock. Her head came up abruptly and she realized Hugh was staring down at her with open admiration. There was a sexy glint in his eye.

"I doubt if it was a shark, babe," he said gently. "Don't get nightmares over it. Up there at the front of the cave the sunlight is bright enough to show the bottom of the pool. I'd have seen something as big as a shark swimming around down there."

"Turn around," she ordered through her teeth.

"Why? The damage is done. Besides, I was going to peek anyway. I was just waiting until you climbed out."

"You," Mattie announced as she stalked quickly over to where she had put the linen dish towel, "are a low-down, sneaky, lying, two-faced, yellow-bellied snake."

"I know," Hugh said sadly. "But I mean well. Most of the time."

"Where did Aunt Charlotte find you, anyway?" Mattie yanked on her trousers and shirt as quickly as possible, aware that he was watching every move with a regretful, hungry look.

"Under a rock."

She frowned at the casual way he said that. She looked back over her shoulder. "What on earth do you mean by that?"

Hugh shrugged. "Where else would you find a low-down, sneaky, lying, two-faced, yellow-bellied snake?"

"Good question." She was not going to apologize. She glared at him as she finally finished dressing. "Thank you for pulling me out of the water so quickly."

He grinned. "That's one of the things I like about you, babe. You always remember your manners, no matter how pissed off you are. And for the record, you look even better naked now than you did a year ago. Stronger in the shoulders and a nice tight, high little ass. Not that it wasn't real cute a year ago, mind you. But it's definitely firmer now. You must be working out or something, huh?"

"Go to hell, Hugh."

He waved a hand to include the entire island of Purgatory. "Haven't you noticed, babe? We're already there. You and me together."

It was still a couple hours before dawn when Hugh materialized in the cavern. Mattie, who had been waiting anxiously for his return from the scouting foray, tried to read his expression in the backglow of the flashlight. He looked cold and savage, she thought uneasily. Back to normal. All the sexy, teasing humor that had lit his eyes earlier the day before was long gone. Hugh Abbott was working now.

Aunt Charlotte had once said that no one worked quite like Hugh Abbott.

"Did you find a boat?" Mattie asked.

"I found one." He crouched beside the string bags, checking to see that they were securely packed. "Good, sturdy, fast-looking cruiser. Full tanks. She'll get us out of here, but we're only going to get one crack at her." He glanced up. "You understand what I'm saying? You do exactly what I tell you and you don't make a sound."

"Yes. I understand." Mattie felt her fingers trembling on the flash-light she was holding. Hugh was telling her this was going to be a dangerous piece of work.

"Right." He stood up and hoisted one of the string bags. He handed her the other one. "First sign of trouble, we drop these. They might come in useful once we're off the island, but we can survive without sun-dried tomatoes and brie if we have to. Ready?"

She glanced at the pistols he was carrying. One was stuck in his belt. the other was in his hand. Aunt Charlotte's pet wolf was ready for the hunt.

"Yes," Mattie said, her pulse thudding in her veins. "I'm ready."

"You going to be okay in the tunnels?"

"I think so. If we hurry."

"We'll hurry," he promised her. "Come on, babe. Stick close to me."

Mattie closed her eyes briefly as they stepped back into the tortured passageways. It was not going to be any easier this time than it had been the first time, she realized instantly. She bit her lip and concentrated on Hugh's moving form ahead of her. She struggled desperately not to think about old dreams, old failures, and old fears.

There was only Hugh and right now he was the sole point of focus in her narrow, confined world.

Hugh glanced back once or twice during the endless journey, but he said nothing. Mattie was grateful. It was difficult enough dealing with the feeling of being trapped inside the mountain. She did not think she could have handled sympathy from Hugh on top of it.

She was bathed in sweat by the time they reached the twin water-falls that marked the entrance to the maze of caves. But she had managed to refrain from screaming, she thought, not without pride.

Hugh edged out from behind the waterfalls and plunged into the jungle.

It seemed to Mattie that they walked for hours through the dense, alien green world, but in reality it probably was not more than forty minutes before they emerged into a wide, sandy, picture-perfect cove.

A shaft of moonlight revealed a handsome, powerful-looking boat bobbing languidly beside an old run-down wooden dock.

Hugh stopped at the edge of the jungle, surveying the cove and its surroundings. He leaned down to whisper into Mattie's ear. "Straight to the boat. Get on board. Lie down on the bottom and stay there. Got it?"

"Got it."

And she did have it, Mattie thought as she obediently started forward out into the open. In fact, she was doing just fine until Hugh whirled around, grabbed her, and yanked her back into the dense undergrowth.

"Shit," he muttered.

The next thing she knew she was being shoved face down into the warm, humid earth.

In that same instant gunfire crackled across the beautiful moonlit cove.

# 4

Silence.

Unnatural, terrifying silence.

Too much silence.

Mattie lay motionless, unable to breathe, her face buried in a pile of decayed vegetation. She was crushed under Hugh's weight as he sprawled on top of her, gun in hand. She could feel the battle-ready tension in him.

"Don't move." His voice was a mere thread of sound in her ear.

Mattie shook her head quickly to indicate she understood. She struggled to breathe. There did not seem to be much point in mentioning the obvious fact that she could not have moved, even if she had wanted to do so. The man weighed a ton.

The ominous silence that hung over the cove continued. It seemed to Mattie it went on for months, weeks, years, eons. She finally began to wonder what would happen next. After the initial terror wore off, the suspense became somewhat boring.

Finally, just when she had begun to think she was going to have a permanent reduction in the size of her already small bustline, she felt Hugh move.

There was no sound, but Mattie discovered the grip of the Beretta being pushed into her hand. Her finger was guided to a small mechanism.

"Safety. You take it off before you pull the trigger. Got it?" Again, Hugh's voice was a whisper of breath directly in her ear.

Mattie wondered if she should explain about her extremely limited experience with the Annie Oakley Special. She decided this was not the time to tell Hugh she had never fired a real gun in her life. Weakly she nodded her head again, knowing he would sense the movement.

"Stay put. Be right back. And for God's sake, take a good look before you pull that trigger. I don't want to end up like Cormier."

Visions of the horrible red mess in Paul Cormier's chest rose up to temporarily blind Mattie. She clutched the gun and fought a scream of protest.

Then she realized the weight that had been pressing her into the earth was gone. Hugh had risen soundlessly and disappeared into the undergrowth.

Mattie lay where she was and strained to hear some hint of his passage through the greenery. She could hear nothing.

Somehow, the utter lack of noise from Hugh was almost as terrifying as the too-silent cove. It spoke volumes about his unconventional lifestyle. How could she possibly have ever considered marrying the man, she wondered bleakly. Definitely not her type. Absolutely nothing in common.

The answer, of course, was ludicrously simple: She had been certain she was in love with him; certain that they shared some deep, common bond; certain that she understood him as no other woman would ever understand him; certain that he was lonely and needed her just as she needed him.

The only certainty about the entire situation was that she had been an idiot.

There was a crackling sound off to her right. Mattie instinctively froze like a deer caught on the road in a set of headlights.

The sound came a second time, louder. She thought she could hear heavy breathing.

Not Hugh, then. He would not be making so much noise.

She was slowly turning her head, her fingers clenching the gun, when another shot roared out over the lovely cove. She went totally still once more.

The crackling noises stopped.

Silence.

More eons of silence.

And then the crackling sounds came again. Closer this time.

With a sinking heart Mattie realized that the noises were headed straight for her hiding place. She sat up very carefully and braced her back against the trunk of a vine-covered tree. The vines shifted silently behind her like a nest of writhing snakes. Mattie stifled the impulse to leap away from the tree.

She gripped the Beretta in both hands and pointed it in the general direction of the soft crackling sounds.

From the far side of the cove came a rush of crashing, breaking, and splintering. A man's startled screech started to climb into the dawn sky but was abruptly choked off.

Mattie did not move. She was fairly sure the scream had not been Hugh's, but that was all she could tell. She kept the gun in her hand pointed into the mass of leaves and vines in front of her.

The crackling sounds escalated abruptly, as if someone who had previously been creeping through the undergrowth was now racing forward toward the sandy beach.

And then the reality of what was happening hit Mattie full force. Someone else was headed for the escape boat.

The thought of another trip back through the caves and another day spent in the cavern while Hugh hunted up a second boat was all the impetus Mattie needed. Her fingers tightened on the Beretta.

A large man burst through the wall of green leaves less than two feet away. He did not look down as he dashed toward the beach.

"You can't have it." Mattie pointed the gun straight up at him. "It's ours."

There was enough dawn light to see the startled expression on the man's unpleasant face. He slammed to an abrupt halt and looked down at where Mattie was sitting with the gun clutched in her hands.

"What the fuck?" The man blinked, first in astonishment and then in growing outrage. "Give me that gun, you little bitch." The voice was a soft hiss.

He stretched out a beefy hand, intending to take the weapon from her as if she were a child.

Mattie fumbled for a second and then found the safety. She slid it off without a word. The soft snick was very loud in the small space between herself and the man.

"Fucking bitch." The huge hand retreated instantly.

"Don't move." Mattie sat very still, holding the gun trained on the man's midsection. "Not one inch."

"That boat ain't yours."

"It is as of now," she told him. It was amazing how quickly the principles of a lifetime could collapse under the pressure of the need to survive, Mattie reflected. Stress, no doubt. She had never stolen anything in her entire life, and now she was planning to participate in grand theft.

"Look, lady, we can do a deal," the man said urgently.

He was interrupted by sounds out on the beach. He turned quickly to look at the boat.

Mattie risked a quick glance and saw Hugh appear from the jungle on the far side of the clearing. He was holding his gun trained on a short, wiry little man.

"Mattie?" Hugh spoke quietly as he neared her hiding place. "It's okay. You can come out now. Hurry, babe. We've got to get moving."

"Uh, Hugh, we have a problem here."

"What the hell?" And then Hugh was close enough to see the still-life scene of woman-seated-on-jungle-floor with-gun-pointed-at-very-large-man.

But it was the short, wiry man who burst into a stream of abuse which he promptly hurled at the huge man Mattie was holding at gunpoint.

"Goddamn your sorry ass, Gibbs. I knew you were gonna try for my boat. I damn well knew it." The small man spat viciously into the sand. "You always was a slimy son of a bitch."

"That boat is just as much mine as yours, Rosey," the big man retorted sullenly. "I knew you'd be plannin' to sneak off in it this mornin'. Some pal you turned out to be. All that garbage about how we was gonna get out of here together today. It was all bull. Well, you ain't goin' nowhere without me, you hear me?"

"Gentlemen, please," Hugh said, "restrain yourselves. This is neither the time nor the place for an argument."

"Oh, yeah? Says who?" The small man named Rosey glared up at him. "You ain't any better than Gibbs, here. Worse. You're plannin' to steal my boat, too, ain't ya?"

"Yes, as a matter of fact, I am." Hugh looked at Mattie, who was still sitting on the ground. "Come on, babe. I'll keep an eye on Mutt and Jeff here. Take the bags down to the boat and get in. I'll be right with you."

"Now, see here, mister, you can't just take off and leave us here." Rosey's voice started to rise into a wail. "That boat's ours. We need it to get off this island until things cool down. No tellin' what's happenin' here on Purgatory. It's a goddamned revolution or somethin'. We'll get our throats slit if we hang around."

"Keep your voice down or I'll slit your throats myself and save the revolutionaries the work."

The new and strangely terrifying lack of emotion in Hugh's voice rather than the threat itself had an electrifying effect not only on Mattie but on Gibbs and Rosey. The two men stared open-mouthed at Hugh. It was clear they believed every word.

Hugh flicked an impatient glance at Mattie, who was getting unsteadily to her feet. "I said move, babe."

Very conscious of the heavy weight of the gun in her hand, Mattie edged around the massive Gibbs and started toward the beach. As she passed Hugh she glanced uneasily up at his set face. She thought again about what they were about to do. She started to speak, found she could not, cleared her throat, and tried again.

"Uh, Hugh, this is their boat."

"Jesus, Mattie. Not now, okay? We'll discuss the ethics of the situation later. When we're ten miles out at sea. *Move.*"

"I just meant maybe we should take Mr. Gibbs and Mr. Rosey with us. After all, they probably want off this island as badly as we do. And it is their boat."

Rosey and Gibbs turned their heads instantly to stare at her. They looked startled at first, and then a gleam appeared in the short man's eyes.

"I can see that you're a real lady, ma'am. Lord knows why you're hangin' around with this scum," Rosey said, nodding in Hugh's direction. "But I want you to know I sincerely appreciate your thinkin' of us in our moment o' crisis. Poor old Gibbs and me will probably be gutted like a couple of fish by the locals, but I want you to know our last thoughts will be of you. We surely do thank you, ma'am."

"Hell," said Hugh. "Mattie, will you do as you're told before the idiots who are running this two-bit coup decide to come down here to take a morning swim and find us all standing around chatting?"

"Like Rosey said, it's real sweet o' you to think of us, ma'am," Gibbs whispered forlornly. "When they're slicin' us up for fish bait or hangin' us in front o' the post office, you can bet your sweet little, uh, backside, we'll sure be thinkin' o' your kindness. Like an angel, you are, ma'am. Just like a pure little angel."

"Move, damn it," Hugh snapped.

Mattie bit her lip. "I don't see why we couldn't take them with us, Hugh. After all, it is their boat and it's quite large. There's plenty of room. If we leave these two men here, they might very well be killed."

"No great loss, I promise you."

"Hugh, please, I'll never be able to sleep at night if we just abandon them to their fates. It's not right."

"Lord love us," Rosey said piously, "you was right, Gibbs. She is a pure little angel. And real good-lookin' to boot."

"Hugh, I really think we should . . ."

Hugh groaned. "Mattie, listen to me, it would be downright stupid to take these two with us. They're a couple of professional lowlifes. Trust me on this. We'd have to keep an eye on them every inch of the way. Don't you understand?"

"We could tie them up in the boat or something," she said eagerly, sensing she was making headway.

"No, damn it," Hugh vowed, "I am not going to go against my better judgment just to please a woman who doesn't know what the devil she's dealing with here."

"Please, Hugh. It's just not right. And it's not as if we don't have the room."

Gibbs and Rosey waited with hopeful expressions.

"Shit," said Hugh. "I know I'm going to regret this."

Half an hour later, comfortably ensconced under the canopy of Rosey's swift cruiser, Mattie watched the Pacific dawn explode across the sky. For the first time since she had walked into Cormier's beautiful white mansion, she was able to take a relaxed breath.

Purgatory was no longer in sight. The boat's wake was churning merrily as it made rapid headway toward Brimstone. All seemed right with the world again.

The large man, Gibbs, was sitting across from Mattie, his hands tied behind his back. Rosey was at the wheel. Hugh was sprawled in the seat next to Rosey, his gun still held casually at the ready. He was the only one of the group who did not look cheerful.

"What in the world was happening back there on Purgatory?" Mattie asked to break the ice that had settled over the crew the instant the boat had been untied from the dock.

"Fuckin' idiots, you should pardon my language, ma'am," Gibbs said, pitching his voice over the dull roar of the engines. "Don't have the sense to leave a good thing well enough alone. Ain't that right, Rosey?"

Rosey's small, wiry shoulders lifted in a philosophical shrug. "Right enough. Everyone on Purgatory was happy the way things was. Had ourselves a right nice little government that didn't believe in taxes and committees and paperwork. Kept things simple, ya' know? Didn't interfere in a man's business so long as he kept his nose clean while he was on the island. Worked real well for everyone."

"Fuckin' right," Gibbs volunteered with a sad shake of his massive head. "Worked real well. Can't imagine why some fool would want to mess things up."

"Apparently someone wanted to modernize things," Hugh muttered.

"I guess," Rosey said.

"Had there been an active opposition party on Purgatory?" Mattie asked with a thoughtful frown. "Some group that had been agitating for reforms?"

"Nah. Weren't nothin' to reform," Gibbs told her.

Rosey scowled. "The whole thing just kind o' blew up outa nowhere, ya' know? No warnin' or nothin'. All of a sudden the airport's closed, everyone's told to stay in their homes, and there's armed men in fatigues all over the damned place. No one was ready for that kind of takeover."

"What happened to the president or whoever was in charge on Purgatory?" Mattie inquired.

"Don't rightly know, ma'am," Rosey said. "If he had any sense, which he did, the old pirate, he got hisself off the island right quick like. Either that or he's probably occupyin' the one jail cell we got on Purgatory."

"Or else he's dead," Gibbs said gloomily. "I'll kind o' miss old Findley. Me and him was drinkin' buddies. Man played a mean game o' pool."

"It's incredible," Mattie said, shaking her head.

"It happens," Hugh said, sounding bored.

She shot him a quizzical glance. "What do you mean by that?"

Hugh shrugged. "Just what I said. These things happen. There's always some idiot around who wants to run things."

Gibbs and Rosey nodded in worldly understanding.

"Yep," Gibbs said. "Always some joker around who figures he can line his pockets a little better if he's in charge."

"It usually comes down to money," Hugh explained. "Money and power. They always go together."

"Put the two together and you get politicians," Rosey said in disgust. "There's always a few of 'em, even on a nice peaceful island like Purgatory. Can't trust 'em as far as you can throw 'em. Nothin' but trouble."

There was a profound silence as everyone considered that unalterable fact of life.

"Will you go back to Purgatory?" Mattie asked Rosey.

"Maybe. Maybe not. Depends on what happens."

"Yeah," said Gibbs. "Depends. Had a good setup on Purgatory, but I reckon we can find another patch o' ground, huh, Rosey?"

"Yep. Always a good deal out there somewhere if you got the brains to look for it."

They arrived at Brimstone late in the day. Mattie gazed around with interest as she stepped off the boat. The village looked a lot like other backwater Pacific island communities with its pretty little harbor and a waterfront filled with taverns and small shops. The jungle rose behind the small town, looming over it like a giant green monster that threatened to absorb the small cluster of buildings in one gulp.

Mattie realized she'd had enough of jungles.

"Now what?" she asked, turning to Hugh, who was untying Gibbs. Rosey was securing the boat, his eyes already scanning the waterfront for the nearest tavern.

"Now we say a fond farewell to our two cheerful guides. Then we hunt up a place to spend the night."

"We're going to be stuck here overnight?" Mattie looked askance at the buildings along the waterfront. There was nothing resembling a world-class luxury resort in sight.

"Probably. Brimstone only has one flight out a day. Next one isn't until tomorrow sometime. No charter operation based here. Yet." Hugh finished releasing Gibbs from his bonds and vaulted out onto the dock. "So long, gentlemen. Good luck and thanks for the use of the boat."

"Sure. See ya' around," Rosey said cheerfully. He grinned at Mattie, his eyes crinkling. "Nice to have met you, ma'am, and we sure do thank you for convincing your man to take us off Purgatory with you."

"Fuckin' right," Gibbs said with a toothless smile. "Thanks, ma'am. You all take care now, you hear?"

"Come on, Mattie." Hugh took her arm and propelled her forcefully along the dock.

"Good-bye," Mattie called over her shoulder. "And thanks."

"I'm glad to see the last of those two," Hugh said as he tugged Mattie up the steps to the paved road that fronted the harbor.

"What an odd pair. They seem like the best of friends, yet Gibbs was apparently planning to steal Rosey's boat and Rosey was waiting with a gun to stop him. What on earth do you suppose they'll do now?"

"I don't know and I don't particularly care. But let's get one thing straight, babe. Next time we're in a situation like that, I don't want you trying to call the shots. You do as you're told and you don't stand around arguing with me. Clear?"

"I knew you were just waiting until we were alone to start lecturing me." She lifted her chin. "But I don't have to stand here and let you chew me out, Hugh Abbott. We are now back in civilization. Sort of. I can book my own flight off Brimstone and be back in Seattle in a day or two. And that's exactly what I'm going to do."

Hugh came to a halt and stood glowering down at her. "What the hell are you talking about? You think that now the excitement's over you can just casually go home?"

"I don't see why not."

"You're supposed to be on vacation, damn it."

"I've got news for you, Hugh. I find life in Seattle far more restful and relaxing than life out here in the islands. Do you know that in all the years I've lived in a city I have never once walked into a house and found a man who had been shot to death? I have never had to crawl through horrid caves or spend a night in a cavern or steal a boat or point a gun at someone?"

Hugh's expression softened in the warm sunlight. "Babe, about that bit with the gun back on Purgatory. You did a fine job of dealing with Gibbs. I was proud of you. I know you haven't had much experience with that sort of thing, but you were terrific. I mean, really terrific. And I also know what it was like for you to have to go through those caves, not once but twice. And I know stealing a boat was kind of a novelty for you."

"Kind of."

"Like I said, I was real proud of you, babe."

"You don't know what that means to me, Hugh." She mocked him with a sugary smile.

"Oh, hell, Mattie. You can't go home now. You've got to give me some time." Hugh stabbed his fingers through his hair. "That's what this whole thing was all about."

Mattie could not bear the expression of chagrin and disappointment in his eyes. She glanced across the street, staring blindly at what appeared to be a small inn. "I'm sorry, Hugh. I really am. But there's no point in trying to pursue this relationship. We both know that."

"No, we both sure as hell do not know that." He clamped a hand around her upper arm and hauled her across the street toward the inn. "We'll talk about it later, though. I've got to see about getting us off this island, and you probably want to do some shopping. You've been wearing those same clothes for a couple of days. And you'll probably want to take a bath, I bet."

Momentarily distracted by the mention of clean clothes and a bath, Mattie allowed herself to be led across the narrow street and into the tiny inn lobby. She glanced around with resignation at the nonfunctioning fan overhead, the single worn chair, and the aging copies of *Playboy* on the small wicker table. There was no one behind the desk.

"Is this the best Brimstone has to offer? I've got my bank card. I don't mind staking us to something better," Mattie whispered to Hugh.

"Sorry, this is it. Brimstone hasn't exactly been discovered by tourists yet. Don't worry, it's clean. I've stayed here a couple of times myself." Hugh leaned over the counter and hit the bell.

A few minutes later a thin old man with a leathery face stuck his head around the corner. "What you want?"

"A room for the night," Hugh said.

"Two rooms," Mattie hissed.

He ignored her, digging into his wallet for several bills. "The best one you've got."

"I know you. Yer name is Monk or Bishop or something, ain't it? You was here once or twice before." The old man eyed the cash and came forward reluctantly. He was working a wad of chewing tobacco with great energy.

"Abbott. Hugh Abbott. The lady wants a room with a bath. Got one?"

"Yep. One. Yer in luck." The old man made the cash disappear from the countertop. He grinned at Mattie. "Take all the baths you want, ma'am. Be stayin' long?"

"Just overnight," Hugh informed him as he reached for the battered-looking register. "We're leaving tomorrow morning on the first flight out of here. Hank Milton still operating out at the strip?"

"No. Hank went back to the States six months ago. Got a new guy comin' in once a day in the afternoons now. Leaves at eight in the mornings. Goes to Honolulu but he'll stop off anywhere in between if you pay him enough. Name's Grover. You better look him up this afternoon if you wanna be on his milk run. That plane o' his is small and usually goes out full."

"What this island needs is more frequent and reliable air charter service," Hugh said as he scrawled something in the register.

"That it do." The old man nodded agreeably. "That it do. We're all startin' to get civilized out here."

Hugh smiled with satisfaction as he picked up the key. "Come on, babe," he said to Mattie, tossing the key into the air and catching it easily. "Let's get you upstairs. You can take your bath while I look up Grover."

Mattie eyed the single key in his hand. "What about a second room for yourself?"

"I'll take care of it later," he assured her as he hustled her up the stairs.

"Hugh, I'm serious about this. I do not intend to share a room with you."

"I hear you." He halted at the landing, glanced at the number on the key, and turned to the left. "I won't say I'm not a little hurt, however. After all, you didn't seem to have a problem sharing a room with me last night, did you? But I won't push it."

"Thank you," she said dryly. Then a twinge of guilt overrode her better judgment. She touched his arm and looked up at him. "Hugh, I'm not trying to be difficult about this. I just feel it would be better for both of us if we don't start something. I really don't think I could stand to go through a second time what I went through the last time you and I got involved."

"This is different, babe." He bent down and kissed the tip of her nose as he stuck the key in the lock.

"You keep saying that, but it's not."

"Take your bath," Hugh said as he pushed open the door. "I'll be back in an hour or so. Besides booking that morning flight, I want to get a shave. We'll have dinner at a little place I know down the street. Great burgers."

Mattie winced. "What about the food in those string bags? There's still some cheese left. Gibbs and Rosey didn't eat all of it on the boat."

"I don't care if I never see another can of pâté or jar of stuffed olives again. What I want right now is some red meat. See you later, babe."

Mattie was too weary to argue anymore about anything. She would deal with it later, she told herself as she stood surveying the hot, horrid little inn room.

The bed looked lumpy. The small rug beside it had once been shocking pink but was now gray with grime. The single bulb in the overhead fixture was probably all of twenty watts.

Hugh had called this a nice, clean place, she remembered. Obviously his idea of decent accommodations was somewhat different from her own. He had not even blinked when he'd opened the door and revealed the sleazy interior of the room.

It made Mattie wonder just what sort of accommodations he was accustomed to. She knew that he brushed up against luxury once in a while simply because he had to in the course of working for Charlotte Vailcourt. Furthermore, he had recognized brie and sun-dried tomatoes when he saw them. But it was equally clear he was totally at home in depressing surroundings such as this.

It occurred to Mattie again that she knew next to nothing about Hugh Abbott's past. In fact, now that she thought about it, neither did Charlotte. Mattie remembered asking her aunt about her pet wolf's background on one occasion and Charlotte had simply shrugged. *"Who knows? Who cares? The man's good at what he does and that's the important thing."*

She put her purse down on the tattered, grimy chenille bedspread. At least no one was pointing a gun at her and there was no blood on the floor. What was more, she could see the ocean from the small window, and the view was spectacular.

Things were definitely looking up.

Downstairs in the narrow lobby Hugh paused to lean over the front desk and bang the little bell.

"What you want now?" the old man asked, not unpleasantly. He was still chewing briskly.

Hugh tugged his wallet out of his jeans pocket and removed a couple of bills. "This is for you."

"For a second room?" The man's brows climbed derisively.

"No. For saying I am booked into another room in the event any-one, including the lady, inquires. Do we understand each other?"

"We understand each other just fine." The clerk pocketed the bills without missing a single chew. "Say, you just come from Purgatory?"

"Yeah."

"What the heck's goin' on over there, anyhow?"

"Don't know yet. Some kind of military coup. Heard anything?"

"Nah. Had a few people like yourself passin' through on their way to what you might call more pleasant locales, but no one seems to know what's goin' on back on Purgatory. They just figured they'd best get out while the gettin' was good."

"Smart. I had a friend who didn't make it out."

The clerk sucked on his wad of tobacco for a while. "Sorry to hear that."

"Uh-huh. Do me a favor, will you?"

"What kind of favor?"

"Keep an eye on the lady. If she goes out shopping, make sure no one follows her back up the stairs to her room, okay?"

"Sure. I'll keep an eye on her. But it might be kind of hard tellin' the difference between her visitors and the ones who come to visit the other lady we got stayin' here. The other one, she works out of here, if you know what I mean."

Hugh's mouth went grim. "No one follows my lady upstairs except me, got it?"

"Sure, sure. Whatever you say."

Hugh went out the door and stepped into the hot afternoon sun-light. It struck him that tonight would be the first time he had ever taken Mattie out to a real restaurant meal. He grinned as he started down the street in search of Grover the pilot. It would be a real date. Their first. You couldn't really count that night a year ago at her apart-ment. At least, Mattie wouldn't want to count it.

Maybe he'd see if he could find a bottle of brandy or rum to take back to the room after dinner, Hugh told himself. Mattie needed to loosen up a bit and relax. She'd been through a hell of a lot lately.

Definitely too much stress.

# 5

❖

"Well, well, well. Hello there. Didn't realize I had competition moving in next door. Welcome aboard, honey. The more the merrier, I always say. The name's Evangeline Dangerfield. What's yours?"

Mattie, who had been standing in the hallway outside her room, struggling with the rusty key in the aging lock, glanced up in surprise. Another woman was lounging in the open doorway of the room next door. Mattie, who would have been the first to admit she had led a somewhat sheltered life until quite recently, had never seen anything quite like her. Not close up, at any rate.

Evangeline Dangerfield appeared to be a few years older than Mattie, although it was difficult to tell precisely how much older because of the thick makeup. Her light brown eyes were heavily outlined in black, and the silver eyeshadow that went all the way up to her brows glittered iridescently. Her full, pouty lips were scarlet, and there was a slash of dark pink beneath her cheekbones. An unbelievably thick mane of improbably blond hair was pulled up high on her head and cascaded down her back in a million curls. The mass was anchored with rhinestone clips that shone in the weak hall light.

The rest of Evangeline Dangerfield was equally exceptional. She was an obviously well-endowed woman who showcased her two main assets in a startling low-cut sarong-style dress. The dress, a flower-splashed creation of red, violet, and yellow, was a size too small for Evangeline's shapely derriere, and the hem was well above the knees. Red heels with three-inch spikes and an assortment of rhinestone jewelry completed the ensemble. Her fingers were tipped with long scarlet nails that obviously required an enormous amount of time and effort.

"How do you do?" Mattie, on her way out to try to find something to replace her much-abused silk blouse and olive slacks, felt rather dowdy. It was a familiar feeling, one she frequently experienced around her sister Ariel. "My name's Mattie. Mattie Sharpe."

"Mattie Sharpe, huh? Nice to meet you, Mattie. Been a while since I talked to another working woman. When did you hit the island?"

"An hour ago. Just got in from Purgatory."

"Oh, yeah. I hear all hell is breaking loose over there. Some kind of revolution or something, huh? Don't blame you for leaving. That kind of thing is hard on business. So how long you here for?"

"Well, I don't know for certain. Hopefully, just a day or so." Mattie looked down at her stained clothing. "I had to leave all my things behind. I was on my way out just now to buy some fresh clothes."

Evangeline was instantly sympathetic as she gave Mattie a swift head-to-toe once-over. "You poor kid. You look like hell. No offense. It must have been real rough over there on Purgatory. I guess you probably need to make a few quick bucks here on Brimstone before you can move on, right?"

"Well . . ."

"No problem, honey. There's plenty to go around tonight. Navy ship in the harbor. We'll both have all the trade we can handle and I don't mind sharing."

It dawned on Mattie that she was talking to a professional call girl and that Evangeline assumed that Mattie was in the same business. "That's very generous of you."

"Hey, sisters got to stick together, right?" Evangeline smiled brilliantly. "Look, you aren't going to find any good working clothes in the shops around here. Believe me, I know. Brimstone is the backwater to end all backwaters. I have to make my own things or order them from a catalog. Why don't you borrow some of my clothes for tonight?"

Mattie was fast becoming fascinated. "Do you think they'd fit?"

Evangeline eyed Mattie's slender figure with a critical eye. "You're a little small on top, but we can work around that. I'm pretty handy with a needle. Why don't you come in? We won't be going to work for another few hours. The boys always like to get a few drinks under their belt first, don't they? Plenty of time to run something up for you."

This was rather like falling down the rabbit hole. Mattie wondered what Ariel would say if she knew her prim, conservative sister was being mistaken for a prostitute. Then she wondered what Hugh would say.

And suddenly she could not wait to find out.

"That's very kind of you, Evangeline." Mattie stepped forward. "I can pay you for the clothes."

"Forget it. It's worth it just to have another woman to talk to." Evangeline moved aside to allow Mattie through the door. "That's the thing I miss most out here, you know. Intelligent conversation with another woman. Most of the people I talk to are men, and their conversation tends to be somewhat limited. How about a drink? I make a mean rum punch."

"Thank you." Mattie smiled gratefully as she took in the gaudy room. Everything appeared to have been done in red. Red and gold wallpaper, red velvet curtains, red plush bedspread, red rugs. There were mirrors on the ceiling over the bed and along one wall. "Your room is certainly a lot fancier than mine."

"No thanks to the management of this joint." Evangeline laughed, a rich, throaty sound, as she went over to a small lacquered cabinet and picked up a bottle of rum. "I had to do all the upgrades myself. Took months to get the fabric for the curtains and the spread. This liquor cabinet was a real steal. Got it from a guy who came through on his way to Honolulu with a boatload of stuff he was importing from Singapore."

"It's beautiful. You must have spent a fortune on all this decorating."

Evangeline shrugged. "I figure it's an investment, you know? You got to put some of the profits back into the business if you want to see an increased return. That's my theory."

Mattie nodded, feeling very much on familiar territory all of a sudden. "That's certainly true, isn't it? During my first couple of years I plowed almost my entire income back into my business. I still have to put a lot into it."

"Ain't it the truth?" Evangeline opened the door of a tiny refrigerator and removed some ice cubes. They clinked as she tossed them into the two drinks she had just finished mixing. "Here you go. Have a seat while I see what I've got in the closet."

Mattie accepted the drink and sat down in a red velvet chair. It was rather like finding oneself in the middle of a play, she thought as she took a cautious swallow of the potent rum-and-fruit-juice mixture. "How long have you been working here on Brimstone?"

"About four years now. I was in Hawaii for a while and it was okay, but I decided to find myself someplace where the competition wasn't so fierce. Here on Brimstone I'm the only working woman on the island." Evangeline opened a closet door and stood, one hand on a gracefully cocked hip, and perused the contents. "Let's see what we've got. Ah, here we go. This should suit you just fine."

Mattie blinked at the tiny little handful of red lace and satin

Evangeline was holding out for inspection. "Is that the slip?" she asked weakly.

"Hell, no. It's one of my best outfits. I never wear slips, not unless I get some john who's got a thing for underwear. Takes long enough to get in and out of my clothes as it is. Let's see how this looks on you."

Mattie took a long swallow of her drink before she rose cautiously to her feet and began unbuttoning her blouse.

Evangeline made more sympathetic noises when she spotted Mattie's prim little bra and briefs. "You poor kid. You didn't get out of that mess on Purgatory with much, did you?"

Mattie was embarrassed by her discreet underwear. She thought of the suitcase full of tasteful traveling clothes she had left in the car on Purgatory. "I had to leave all my good things behind," she explained apologetically.

"Yeah, I can see that. What a shame. Hope things cool down over there so you can go back and collect your stuff. In our line of work a good wardrobe is essential, isn't it?" Evangeline held out the scrap of shiny red satin. "I made this a month ago and it's hardly been worn. Been saving it for a special occasion. Let's get it on and see what needs to be done. You'd better take off that bra. This dress isn't made to be worn with one."

Mattie took another swallow from the glass of rum punch and then did as instructed. No worse than undressing in the ladies' locker room at the health club back home, she told herself. She pulled the red dress down over her head.

There was no problem getting it as far as her waist, but she had to work a bit to get the sarong-style skirt down over her hips. She turned toward the wall of mirrors and stared at herself in amazement.

The dress was not much bigger than a bathing suit. It was cut daringly low in front, and the skirt revealed an incredible length of thigh. There was virtually no back to it at all.

"Not bad," Evangeline said with a critical nod of satisfaction. "A little loose in front, but we knew that would need some work. And I'll have to take it in a bit around the hips but other than that, it's perfect. You look good in red, Mattie. I'll bet you wear a lot of it."

"Actually, I don't," Mattie said honestly. She recalled her closet full of expensive but exceedingly dull clothes. The colors in her wardrobe tended toward gray, beige, and navy blue. "But I may start wearing more of it. I think I like red."

She realized she had never felt quite this way in a dress before. She felt a little wild. Maybe it was just a reaction to all the recent stress she had been under.

"Red definitely does something for you. Kind of brightens you up."

Evangeline began pinning the dress, causing the already low neckline to go even lower. "Are those shoes the only ones you've got?"

"I'm afraid so. I left the others behind with my clothes."

"Shame. Shoes are so damn expensive. What size do you wear?"

"Seven and a half."

"No problem," Evangeline said. "So do I. I'll loan you the ones I've got on. They're perfect for that dress. Okay, I've finished pinning. Take it off and I'll make the adjustments."

"This is certainly very nice of you," Mattie said as she slipped the red dress off and handed it over to Evangeline.

"My pleasure. Like I said, it's been a while since I had a nice chat with an intelligent person." She went over to the closet and wheeled out a small table that held a sewing machine. "How was business on Purgatory before things turned sour?"

"Not bad." Mattie finished dressing in her trousers and silk shirt and sat down again. She picked up her drink. "But I don't think I'll go back."

"Yeah? Where will you head next?" The sewing machine hummed energetically as Evangeline went to work.

"Seattle."

"Been there before?"

"Yes. In fact, I lived there before I, uh, went to Purgatory."

"No kidding? I've always wanted to go to Seattle. Maybe next time I take a vacation I'll go there."

"If you do, be sure and look me up," Mattie said with a rush of good will toward this woman who was going out of her way to be kind. "I'll leave my name and address."

"It's a deal. I make it a practice to take a vacation at least twice a year. A woman needs a break, you know? All work and no play isn't good for you."

"I know. Stress definitely takes a toll."

"That's a fact." Evangeline expertly trimmed the seam of the sarong's skirt. "And we've sure got our share of stress in our line of work, don't we? The business isn't what it used to be, what with these new diseases and all. Which reminds me, you need any rubbers for tonight?"

Mattie choked on a sip of rum and juice. "I didn't bring any with me," she said carefully.

"Figured you might have had to leave those behind along with your clothes. Check that cabinet over there by the bed. I keep a bunch handy. Help yourself."

Mattie stared at the red wicker cabinet for a moment and then slowly got up and went over to open it. Inside was a large basket filled with little foil packages. She took a handful and dropped them into her purse. "Thank you."

"Can't be too careful these days. Doesn't pay to take chances. By the way, who's your broker?"

"My broker?"

"Yeah, your stockbroker." Evangeline looked up with a quizzical glance and took a pull on her drink. "Or are you into CDs and money market accounts?"

"Oh. I see what you mean." Mattie frowned consideringly as she sat down again. "Yes, I tend to favor certificates of deposit and money market accounts. The stock market is just too volatile for my taste. Not a good place for the small investor anymore."

"I know what you mean. I keep telling myself I should get out, but a part of me likes the thrill, you know? Of course, I don't put everything into the market. Just what I can afford to lose. The rest goes right into T-bills and stuff. I'm no fool. I've seen too many women in this business wind up with nothing after years of hard work. I'm not going to be one of them."

"You're absolutely right. Nobody's going to give us a pension. Self-employed people have to look after themselves."

"Ain't it the truth?" Evangeline nodded as she went to work on the bodice of the little red dress. "How about another drink?"

"Sounds great. Tell me, Evangeline, what are you going to do when you retire?"

"Funny you should mention that." Evangeline looked down at the red dress she was altering. "I've been thinking about retirement a lot lately. It's time to get out of the business. Like I said, it isn't what it used to be. Don't laugh, but I'd like to open up a small dress shop somewhere out here on the islands, you know? Design my own things for tourists. I think I'd be good at it. What do you think?"

Mattie looked at the beautiful workmanship on the red dress. She knew art when she saw it. "I think you'd be terrific at it."

Hugh was smiling with anticipation as he bounded up the inn stairs an hour later. He had a bottle of rum in a paper bag under one arm, and he'd splurged on a new shirt at the little general store on the waterfront. He was ready for the big date with Mattie.

"We're going to party tonight, babe," he announced as he opened the door of the small room. "Got it all planned. A real date. First we'll hit that little place that serves the great burgers, have a couple of drinks and some food, and then I figure later we can come back here and— Holy shit."

Hugh came to a dead halt just inside the door and stared at the exotic creature sitting on the side of the bed.

"Hello, Hugh. As a matter of fact, I am rather hungry." Mattie smiled at him.

"Mattie?" Hugh slowly closed the door behind him without taking his eyes off her. He could not believe what he was seeing.

She was wearing a minuscule red dress that almost revealed her nipples. It clung to her hips like a lover and rode halfway up her thigh. She had her legs crossed, her feet daintily arched in impossibly high, spiky red heels. Her tawny-brown hair danced around her shoulders, soft and loose and inviting. Her green-and-gold eyes were brilliantly outlined and accented with glittering turquoise eyeshadow. Her mouth was a dark red flower. Rhinestones glittered on her fingers and wrists and in the small cleavage revealed by the dress.

"What do you think, Hugh? Is it me?" She grinned at him, her eyes full of an unfamiliar mischief.

"What the hell happened to you?" Dazed, Hugh moved slowly over to a table and set down his packages.

"I met the nicest lady down the hall. A working woman. Just like me. When she realized I had nothing suitable for tonight, she loaned me some of her things." Mattie got up and pirouetted.

Hugh's mouth went dry. His gaze traveled down the length of her spine to where the red dress curved tightly over her hips. "There's no back to that dress."

"I know. Good thing it's warm here on Brimstone, hmmm?"

Hugh took a step closer, eyes narrowing as she turned back to face him. He had never seen that particular expression in her eyes. "Mattie, have you been drinking?"

"Just a couple of rum punches." She waved her hand in an airy gesture, and the rings on her fingers glittered like diamonds. "Don't worry, I'm in complete control. My friend Evangeline says you can't work drunk. Men tend to take advantage of you if they think you're tipsy. Men are like that, you know. Always trying to take advantage of a woman."

"This Evangeline person. What exactly does she do for a living, or should I ask?"

"I told you. She's a working woman." Mattie laughed up at him. "And she thinks I'm one, too. She took pity on me because I had to flee Purgatory without the tools of my trade." Mattie tossed a handful of little foil packages into the air. They rained down over the bed. "Evangeline is a very nice person, Hugh."

"I don't believe this."

"I know." Mattie giggled. "And neither would anyone else back home in Seattle. I wish I had a camera so you could take a picture of me. Evangeline says I look terrific in red."

"You do," Hugh admitted. "But you need a little more of it."

"Now, Hugh, don't be a prude. Are you ready to go out to dinner?"

"Yeah, but I'm not taking you anywhere dressed like that."

"Then I'll go out by myself."

She was at the door and through it before Hugh realized she meant business. He swung around and went after her. "Now, just one damn minute, Mattie."

"You can't come along if you're going to lecture me," she informed him from the top of the stairs. "I'm sick and tired of your lectures. I intend to have fun tonight."

"Mattie, hold on a second. Damn it, come back here." Hugh started down the hall with long, determined strides.

But Mattie had already scampered down to the lobby and was waving at the clerk as she went past the front door.

Hugh was right behind her.

"Got a navy ship in the harbor," the old desk clerk said as Hugh went past. "You'd better hang on to her or yer not gonna see her till morning."

"Damn," said Hugh.

He caught up with Mattie outside on the street. A beautiful scarlet butterfly flitting through the tropical night, she was already attracting too much attention. A young man in a white Navy uniform leered and let out a loud wolf whistle. Hugh glowered at him and reached for Mattie's arm.

"What the devil do you think you're up to, Mattie?" he demanded as he pinned her to his side.

"Just going out for a bite to eat." She smiled at a man who was tying up a sailboat. The man's mouth fell open and he stopped work to stare. "Isn't this amazing, Hugh? Evangeline is right. Red is definitely my color."

"Babe, the way that dress is cut, it wouldn't matter what color it was." He realized she was enjoying herself. "Look, I don't want to rain on your parade, but it's not exactly safe for you to be running around in that outfit."

She looked up at him with innocently widened eyes. "Why ever not, Hugh? After all, I've got you along to protect me, don't I?"

He exhaled on a low groan. Then he decided two could play at that game. "Who's going to protect you from me, babe?"

"No problem. You've seen me in less and you weren't exactly overwhelmed, were you?"

"If you misjudge other men as badly as you misjudge me, you're going to be in a lot of trouble."

"Nonsense." She patted his arm with condescending affection. "We both know you'll behave yourself. What would Aunt Charlotte say if I told her you'd gotten out of line?"

He tightened his grip on her arm. "You ought to know better than to wave a threat at me, babe," he warned softly. "I only answer to Charlotte when it comes to business. She doesn't have anything to do with the rest of my life."

"Tough talk." Mattie gave a gurgle of husky laughter. "But I don't believe a word of it. What would you do if you didn't get all those nice, lucrative assignments to clean up little messes around the world for Vailcourt?"

"I'd spend more time on my own business." Hugh abruptly decided against dragging her back to the room. A sexy, teasing Mattie was a wonderful thing. He had never seen her in quite this mood, and he realized he did not really want to squelch it. She was having too much fun and—if he played his cards right—so could he.

He steered her toward the open-air tavern at the end of the street. There was no absolutely safe place to take her tonight. Brimstone was full of sailors, and even at their best, the local taverns and bars tended to be rough. He would just have to make certain everyone realized she was private property.

"And just what is this mysterious business of yours, Hugh? It's got something to do with airplanes, doesn't it?" Mattie clung to his arm, practically draped over it as she gazed up at him with wide, inquiring eyes.

"I told you, I'm building up a charter business on St. Gabe." He eased her through the tavern's entrance and was immediately aware of the sensation Mattie caused. Catcalls and whistles echoed from one end of the long bar to the other. Hugh wondered if he was going to get through the evening without a fight. "This is really stupid," he muttered as he aimed Mattie toward a booth near the railing.

"It's fun." Mattie slid across the vinyl seat, exposing another three inches of thigh. "I feel good tonight. I think it's a new me. I'll have a rum punch, please."

"You'll have dinner," Hugh informed her.

"What a grouch. Very well. Dinner first. And then a rum punch."

"We'll drink it back in the room," Hugh decided, giving the man at the end of the bar his coldest glance. The man, who had been staring intently at Mattie, heaved an obvious sigh of regret and turned back to his drink.

"A beer for me," Hugh told the middle-aged waitress. "And a cola for the lady. Then a couple of hamburgers. Big ones. Make mine a double."

Mattie smiled past his shoulder up at the waitress. "I'd like to make a couple of changes in my order, please. I'll have fruit juice instead of cola. And put some rum in it, will you, please? And instead of a hamburger, I'll have a salad. And, um, let's see, what else have you got that doesn't have meat in it?"

"No meat? You want fish instead?" the woman asked.

"No pieces of dead animal of any kind," Mattie stipulated. "I don't eat dead meat. And neither should he," she added, patting Hugh's arm. "One of these days I'll cure him of the habit."

The waitress looked bemused. She glanced at Hugh for guidance. When he simply shrugged in resignation, she looked at Mattie again. "We've got French fries. You want some of those?"

"All right," Mattie agreed. She turned back to Hugh as the waitress disappeared. "So tell me more about this charter business," she said in a deliberately provocative tone. "I want to hear every little detail about it. I'm just fascinated by that sort of thing. I'll bet you're a big honcho in the air charter business out here in the islands, aren't you?"

"This lady who put you in that dress give you lessons in how to talk to a client or something?"

"How can you say that?" Mattie looked hurt. "I'm serious, Hugh. I want to know everything. I've just realized there is a great deal I don't know about you."

The beer arrived. Hugh hadn't really wanted one, but he knew the bottle would be useful if things turned rowdy before dinner was over. He looked speculatively down at Mattie. "Are you trying to flirt with me?"

"What if I am?" She hunched her shoulders and the neckline of the red dress dipped so low for a second or two that it revealed the dusky curve surrounding one nipple.

Hugh realized he was staring. Already half aroused, he could feel himself getting very hard, very fast. He took a quick swallow of beer. "I'm not complaining. I just want to be sure you know what you're doing."

"I'm just trying to learn a little more about you, Hugh Abbott. Do you realize I know almost nothing of your past?"

With great effort he managed to lift his gaze back to her eyes. "You're not missing much. Sit up straight, will you?" She really was flirting with him. *Damn.* He just wished they didn't have an audience. Every man in the room must be aware of the look she was giving him.

He was torn between his own roaring desire and a need to protect his newfound treasure from the lustful gazes of other males.

"What did you do before you went to work for my aunt?"

"This and that. Odd jobs. Mattie, you'd better sit a little straighter. I mean it. That dress is about to fall off."

"Evangeline designed it to look that way. She's very talented when it comes to dress design. I think she may have missed her calling."

"Yeah. Maybe." Hugh moved slightly, trying to ease the tightness of his jeans. "What did you say her name was?"

"Evangeline Dangerfield."

"Hell of a name. Wonder where she picked that up."

"She says it's not her original name. It's sort of a *nom de mattress*, I believe. She suggested I think of something a little more interesting than Mattie Sharpe, myself. What do you think?"

Hugh's mouth curved briefly. "I think Mattie Sharpe is just fine."

She frowned slightly. "But do you think it's sexy enough? Does it have romantic allure? Does it promise passion and excitement and fulfillment?"

"Yeah," said Hugh. "It does."

"Advertising and image are so important, you know."

"I'll keep that in mind as I build up Abbott Charters."

Mattie leaned closer, her eyes smoky. "Tell me more about Abbott Charters."

And then, to his own astonishment, Hugh found himself doing just that. He could not resist. She was hanging on every word as if nothing in the world were more important than his hopes and plans and dreams for the future.

Nobody had ever listened to him with such intensity, he realized vaguely at one point. He rambled on about his goal for getting some contracts with the United States government and some with local businesses. He talked about the difficulties of getting aircraft serviced out here in the islands. He explained how St. Gabe was starting to become more popular with tourists and how he planned to encourage them to use Abbott Charters. He talked about organizing scuba diving tours at nearby islands. On and on he talked.

Mattie was obviously enthralled. She prompted him with questions now and again, but mostly Hugh just talked.

And talked.

The food arrived and Hugh kept talking as he ate. He described his plans to become the most reliable charter operator in that section of the Pacific. He detailed his goal to provide a first-class professional operation that would supply everything from fishing boats for tourists to freight service for business.

"I'm thinking about a franchise operation eventually," he said. "For example, the guy who's going to take us off the island in the morning is running a shoestring operation with one plane. If he bought an Abbott Charter franchise he'd instantly look bigger and more successful than he is. He'd get more business, and I'd have another base of operations."

Hugh discovered he was still talking about his schemes and ambitions half an hour later when they left the tavern and started back down the street. He was a little surprised to have gotten through the meal without having to bash a few heads, but he wasn't complaining. Obviously everyone had figured out right away that Mattie was not available, he thought proudly. Probably had something to do with the way she was focusing so completely on him.

"I'll pour you a drink now," Hugh said magnanimously when they reached the privacy of Mattie's room. "Sit down."

Sitting down meant sitting on the bed. There were no chairs in the room. Mattie obediently kicked off her red heels, leaned her delightfully bare back against the old wicker headboard, and stretched her legs out in front of her. "When will you tell Aunt Charlotte you won't be accepting any more free-lance jobs for Vailcourt?"

"The way things are going, I'll be in a position to do that in another six months or a year," Hugh said as he poured a shot of rum into two glasses. "It's going to be good out here, Mattie. You'll see. Abbott Charters is going to work. A year from now I'm going to start work on a house. I've already picked out a chunk of property that overlooks the prettiest little cove you've ever seen."

Footsteps sounded outside in the hall. They went past the door and stopped at the next room. Evangeline Dangerfield's door opened. There was a murmur of voices and then silence. Hugh sat down beside Mattie on the bed and went on talking about his dream house. Mattie sipped at her rum.

A short time later the unmistakable squeak of bedsprings could be heard through the thin walls. Hugh ignored the sound as he described the veranda he was going to build around his spectacular dream house. Mattie took another sip of rum.

A man's guttural shout of sexual release rumbled through the walls. Mattie bit her lip as her eyes met Hugh's and then slid away. She giggled.

Hugh pretended to ignore the second set of footsteps in the hall while he explained that his beautiful dream house would be open to the island breezes on three sides.

When the third set of footsteps went past the door on the way to

Evangeline's room, Mattie wriggled a little on the bed. "Hard way to make a living," she observed, yawning.

"Yeah." Hugh was finally beginning to have a problem concentrating on what he was talking about. The rhythmic squeak of bedsprings and the noisy sounds of masculine climax kept interfering with his train of thought. Mattie's yawn had done interesting things to the top of the little red dress.

"I guess I'd better stick to running an art gallery," she said, easing herself down onto the pillows. She put her glass on the table beside the bed. "I don't think I'd have the energy for Evangeline's kind of work. Do you know, Hugh, I am absolutely exhausted all of a sudden."

"You've been through a lot today," he started to say sympathetically. Then he realized her eyes were closing. "Hey, Mattie?"

"Good night, Hugh. Be sure and turn off the light and lock the door when you leave." With a soft little murmur, she went to sleep.

Hugh sat watching her for a long time while he finished his drink. He hadn't gotten around to telling her about the bedroom in his dream home, he realized. It was going to be a big room with a big bed and a view of the sea. He was sure she was going to like it.

The bedsprings next door began to squeak again.

Hugh put down his glass, stood up, and slowly undressed down to his briefs. Then he pulled down the bedspread and eased Mattie under the sheet. He thought about undressing her but finally decided the red slip of a dress was a perfect nightie.

He went over to his shopping bag and found his revolver. Then he turned out the light and slid under the sheet beside Mattie. He put the revolver under the pillow.

Hugh folded his arms behind his head and listened to the endless parade of footsteps in the hall. He began to wonder if he was going to stay in this painfully aroused condition all night long.

When one particular set of footsteps stopped outside Mattie's door instead of going on to Evangeline Dangerfield's room, Hugh was still awake.

He sighed and quietly reached under the pillow for the gun.

# 6

Hugh felt Mattie move beside him as the door opened. She turned in her sleep, her leg sliding along his, her hand settling on his bare chest. He could feel his body's instantaneous response all the way down to his toes. The lady always did have lousy timing. One of these days he hoped she would get it right.

He forced himself to keep his eyes on the widening crack of light in the doorway. First things first.

A familiar figure was revealed briefly in the weak light that entered the room from the hall. The figure crept stealthily into the room, easing the door shut behind him.

Hugh pulled the hammer back on the revolver. The soft, deadly click was as loud as a cannon in the small room. The figure near the door froze, obviously recognizing that particular sound at once. A man of the world.

Mattie's hand shifted slightly on Hugh's chest at that moment, her fingertip grazing his flat nipple. Hugh stifled a groan and watched his quarry.

"I knew I was going to regret taking you off Purgatory, Rosey." Hugh kept his voice to the level of the softest of whispers, but he knew Rosey heard him.

"What the hell . . . ?" Rosey's muttered exclamation was nearly as soft as Hugh's words had been.

Mattie murmured in her sleep and her fingers began to slip gently through Hugh's chest hair to his belly, which went taut at the caress. He held himself as still as Rosey.

"Wake her up and I'll be real pissed, Rosey."

"I thought you was sleepin' down the hall. Desk clerk said so." Rosey sounded peevish, but he obediently kept his voice low.

"You thought wrong."

Mattie's foot came into contact with Hugh's leg. He could feel her toes nibbling at him like tiny little fish. The delicate, unconscious caress sent a ripple of electricity through him.

"Look, no hard feelings or anything, okay? It was all a mistake, see." Rosey started to edge backward to the door.

"A big mistake. What were you after?"

"Just a few bucks. I know she's got a wad in that fancy purse of hers. You can always tell by the purse and the shoes, y'know? Real leather. High-quality stuff."

Hugh relaxed slightly, aware of the ring of truth in Rosey's whining voice. His initial annoyance had been generated by the certainty that Rosey must have seen Mattie in the red sarong earlier this evening and had come to her room with something more reprehensible in mind than simple motel theft. "You're lucky I'm feeling in a good mood tonight, Rosey. I'm not going to blow your head off. At least not right at the moment."

"You wouldn't do it anyway," Rosey declared with rash insight. "*She* wouldn't like it. Just like she didn't approve of you threatenin' to cut me and Gibbs' throats on Purgatory. Like she wouldn't let you leave us behind."

"She might not approve, but she couldn't stop me. Get me mad enough, Rosey, and I won't give a damn what she thinks. Keep that in mind and we'll get along just fine."

Mattie sighed softly and her hand moved lower, her fingers sliding inside the opening of Hugh's briefs and tangling lightly in the thick, curling hair there. A distinct bulge appeared in the sheet that covered his thighs. Hugh stifled another groan and through monumental willpower managed to keep most of his attention on Rosey.

The wiry little man had sidled back to the door and was starting to open it.

"Hold it," Hugh ordered quietly just as Mattie's thumb gently trailed across the base of his heavy erection. He realized his manhood had come free of the briefs. His muscles were all violently taut, and the hand that held the gun trembled faintly.

With great care, Hugh uncocked the revolver. No sense accidentally spraying Rosey's few brains against the wall in a moment of uncontrollable passion. "I want to talk to you for a second, Rosey."

"Look, I told you, it was all a mistake. I wasn't gonna hurt her. Just needed a few bucks. Me and Gibbs didn't have much with us when you stole our boat, y'know. We're kinda short."

"Something tells me it wasn't the first time you've had to leave town in a hurry. Rosey, before you go, I want to make certain we have an understanding. First, come anywhere near Miss Sharpe again and I'll be very, very annoyed. Clear?"

"Yeah, yeah. Clear. Now, don't get up or nothin'. I'll see myself out."

"One more thing."

"Sheesh. Don't you ever stop givin' orders?"

"Not until I get what I want."

Rosey hovered near the door. "What the hell do you want?"

"A name. A friend of mine died on Purgatory."

"Yeah? Who?" Rosey sounded vaguely interested now.

"Paul Cormier."

There was a small pause. "I knew Cormier. He was okay, him and his white shoes and all. Made me a couple of loans when I needed 'em bad to pay off some folks. Bought the farm, huh? I'm sorry to hear that."

"Somebody shot him and left him to die. If you ever hear a name, Rosey, I want it. I want it very badly."

"I don't know who killed him," Rosey said hastily.

"There's money in it, Rosey. A lot of money. Come up with a name and the money's all yours. Contact me or a guy named Silk Taggert over on St. Gabe. Got that?"

"Yeah, sure. I got it. I'm leavin' now, if that's okay with you. Got things to do, people to see, places to go. Say good-bye to the little lady for me."

"I'll do that." Hugh sucked in another deep breath as Mattie's fingers slipped between his thighs. "And lock the door behind you."

"Anything you say." The wedge of pale light from the hall widened briefly once more as Rosey hurried out of the room, and then there was darkness again. Hugh waited until he heard the lock click.

Mattie's leg slid over his thigh and she stirred gently, nestling closer.

Hugh shoved the revolver under the bed where it would be within easy reach. Then he reached beneath the sheet and found Mattie's hand. It was resting alongside his upthrust shaft, her fingertips just touching the full globes underneath.

"Oh, Christ."

He thought he would lose it all right then and there.

Holding his breath, Hugh pushed his briefs down over his hips and fumbled free of them. Every inch of the way he feared he would wake Mattie and bring his own dream to an abrupt end. But she just wiggled a bit and snuggled closer.

When he had stripped off the underwear, Hugh carefully folded Mattie's fingers around himself. He moved experimentally, lifting his hips slightly. Her hand tightened briefly.

"Damn." Hugh squeezed his eyes shut and inhaled deeply.

For a moment or two Hugh seriously considered torturing himself to death in that position until morning. But he did not think he had the stamina for it. He was already too close to exploding.

Mattie stirred again and her lips brushed against his shoulder. He looked down and in the pale light from the window he saw that one soft, sweetly rounded breast had escaped the bodice of the red dress.

Fascinated, Hugh touched Mattie's nipple with his thumb and felt it grow as hard as a berry. The soft fingers clinging delicately to his manhood tightened again for an excruciating instant.

Hugh caught hold of the top of the red sarong and eased it down so that Mattie's other breast came free. For a long moment he simply lay there feasting on the beautiful sight spread out in front of him.

Then, deciding to push his luck, he moved one hand down to her thigh and slid his palm up under the short red skirt of the sarong.

Mattie released him and rolled onto her back, her eyes still closed. Her legs shifted restlessly.

Hugh edged his fingers higher under the red satin. The warmth and softness of the inside of her thigh almost sent him over the edge. When her legs parted slightly of their own accord, he stifled another muffled groan.

His questing fingers found the scrap of cotton that shielded the moist, feminine flower he sought. For a moment or two he contented himself with stroking her through the fabric, but when he felt the cotton grow damp he knew he was not going to be able to stop there.

Mattie moved again, arching her hips slightly against his touch. She mumbled something in her sleep, something that sounded like an impatient demand. Hugh slid his fingers inside the leg opening of the cotton panties.

Mattie inhaled quickly and her lashes fluttered. Through sensually narrowed lids, her eyes met his in the shadows. Hugh did not dare move. He realized he was holding his breath.

Then, without a word, she reached up for him, twining her arms around his neck and pulling him down to her. Her eyes closed again.

*She wanted him.* Hugh thought he would go out of his mind then. He groped roughly at the satin skirt, shoving it quickly up over Mattie's hips to her small waist. Then he yanked the cotton panties downward.

She was ready for him, moist and welcoming. Hugh came down on top of her, probing hungrily. He buried his lips against her warm throat and simultaneously thrust deeply.

Mattie cried out, her whole body stiffening.

"Oh, babe. *Oh, babe. Mattie.*" Hugh's voice was hoarse with his desire. She was tight and hot and wet, just as he had remembered. Months of shattering dreams had finally crystallized into a glittering reality. *She wanted him.* He pounded into her, a year's pent-up need fueling his passion.

He heard the soft little gasps, felt her arching herself beneath him, and he reached down to find the little nub hidden in the thick, soft curls at the apex of her thighs. When he touched it, she went off like a rocket. She convulsed beneath him. She went wild. She clawed at his back. She clung to him as if he were the only man left on earth.

He hastily covered her mouth, drinking in the gentle, feminine sounds of release. And then he was going up in flames himself, his entire body uncoiling like a powerfully compressed spring that had been under tension far too long. The sensations ripped through him, seeming to last forever.

When it was over at last, Hugh was covered in sweat as if he had just completed a long-distance run. He raised his head to look down at the woman in his arms and realized she had gone back to sleep.

Hugh exhaled heavily. He really did not feel like talking now anyway. He felt too good, too replete, too content. Why mess up the perfection of the moment with a lot of idle chitchat? Slowly, reluctantly, he eased himself out of Mattie's clinging warmth. Then he rolled onto his back and gathered her against him.

"Babe, we're going to be damn good together," he whispered. "Just like you told me a year ago. Damn good." For a long time he lay looking up at the ceiling of the shabby little room and listened to the sounds of footsteps in the hall.

It occurred to him that this waterfront fleabag of an inn was probably not at all the sort of place Mattie usually chose to stay in when she traveled.

Mattie's first thought when she awoke the next morning was that the mattress must have been even lumpier than it had looked yesterday. She felt stiff for some reason.

And a little sticky between her thighs.

And uncomfortable. The red sarong was bunched awkwardly around her waist.

Then she opened her eyes and the all-too-vivid dream she'd had during the night flooded back.

It had not been a dream, of course.

Mattie groaned, turned onto her stomach, and buried her face in the pillow.

*Idiot. Fool. Dolt. Dunderhead. Half-wit. Dunce.*

She was trying to think of other suitable terms of endearment for herself when she heard boot heels in the hall and a cheerful masculine whistle. A few seconds later the door of the room opened.

"Hey, babe, you awake yet? Time to rise and shine. Got a plane to catch. I brought you some coffee and a roll. The roll is a little stale, but it's edible."

"Oh, my God," Mattie said into the pillow. Hugh's voice held the unmistakable tone of a man who is very certain he's in control of his woman and his world.

"Up and at 'em, babe." Hugh put something down on the dresser and stepped over to the bed to give Mattie an affectionate swat on her rear. "Believe me, I know how you feel. Nothing I'd like better than to crawl back into that bed with you, but we've got to get moving. Plenty of time for fooling around later."

Mattie turned her head on the pillow and opened her eyes with a strong sense of foreboding. Hugh was grinning down at her, gray eyes gleaming with sexy satisfaction. He looked his usual vital self dressed in his jeans, boots, and khaki shirt. His hair was still damp from a recent shower. She looked past him, gauging the distance to the tiny bath.

It was worth a shot.

"Excuse me," Mattie said very politely as she slowly sat up, tugging the sheet around herself. "I'm not at my best in the mornings."

"Have some coffee. Got it next door at a little hole in the wall joint. Stuff tastes like a cross between burned tires and battery acid. It'll wake you up." Hugh thrust the cup of steaming brew into Mattie's fingers.

Clutching the sheet, Mattie looked down at the thick, black liquid. It looked and smelled stronger than the espresso all her friends drank back in Seattle. "I prefer herbal tea in the mornings."

"You look like you need something powerful to get you going this morning, babe. Drink up."

She did not have the fortitude to argue. She sipped obediently. The dark coffee sent a severe jolt through her entire system. "Yes, that certainly will wake me up."

"Told you so. Off you go to the showers, babe."

Exerting heroic effort, Mattie stood. She headed straight for the bathroom, the sheet trailing behind her like the train of a somewhat tattered and stained wedding gown.

She would be home soon, she told herself over and over again. In a day or two she would be back in comfortable, familiar surroundings where she did not have to worry about waking up in sleazy waterfront inns with strange men.

*Damn. How could she have been such a fool?*

Mattie shut the bathroom door quite forcefully and turned to gaze at her reflection in the cracked mirror over the sink. She looked like a walking disaster, she decided critically. Her hair was a wild, tousled mess, there were shadows in the hollows of her cheeks and under her wide, dazed eyes. She wondered if this was how Evangeline looked after a hard night.

Slowly Mattie let the sheet slide to the floor. The red sarong dress that had seemed so sexy and daring last night looked cheap and tacky this morning as it bunched around her waist. Mattie stepped out of it, turned, and entered the small tin-walled shower. She stood under the weak rush of cool water for a very long time, trying to think of how to handle the situation she had created for herself.

One thing was for certain. Hugh was going to be impossible to deal with now. Mattie strongly suspected that as far as he was concerned, last night had settled everything. Hugh was a very linear thinker, a straightforward, insensitive sort of man when it came to most things. She knew that he would assume his "relationship" with Mattie was back on track after last night.

The bathroom door opened. "Here you go, babe. Your fancy shirt and trousers. They're looking a little beat up, but don't worry, we'll get you some new things on St. Gabe."

The door closed once more. Mattie decided that one of the hardest things to deal with this morning was Hugh's cheeriness. It was intolerable.

Her spirits began to revive as she finished showering and got dressed. The brilliant sunlight pouring in through the window and the sight of the turquoise sea did wonders to help dispel the sense of doom that had been hanging over her when she first awakened.

She could handle Hugh Abbott.

She *must* handle Hugh Abbott.

She would be cool and casual and ever so sophisticated and blasé about the whole thing.

She would not give him so much as an inkling of how much the entire event had upset her.

"When do we leave?" Mattie forced herself to ask calmly as she emerged from the bathroom.

Hugh looked at her, his eyes warm and possessive. "In about twenty minutes. We'll be on St. Gabe by noon."

"Great. I can't wait to get out of here." Mattie's gaze flickered around the dingy little room. She knew she would never forget it as long as she lived.

Hugh followed her glance. "Not exactly the honeymoon suite at the Ritz, is it?"

"Not exactly."

"Things on St. Gabe aren't a whole lot fancier, but I've got plans, babe. You'll see. I just need a little time."

"Right. Time cures all, doesn't it?" Mattie picked up her purse and slung it over her shoulder. "I want to say good-bye to Evangeline before we leave."

"Doubt if she's up yet. A woman in her line of work tends to sleep days."

Mattie smiled coolly. "You're an authority?"

Hugh's brows rose in silent warning. "Now, don't go implying anything, babe. I told you, I've been keeping myself pure and chaste for you. And after last night I've got to admit it was worth the wait."

Mattie felt herself turning pink under the intent gleam in his eyes. She busied herself removing a business card from her purse and scrawling a note on the back. "I'll just leave this under her door."

"Tell her thanks from me for the red dress," Hugh murmured as Mattie picked up the scrap of red satin and the red heels and stepped past him.

She ignored him as she went down the hall to Evangeline's room and knelt to push the business card and the red dress under the door.

"What the hell . . . ?" Evangeline sounded sleepy and disgruntled as she abruptly opened the room door. "Oh, it's you, honey. Have a good night?"

Mattie got quickly to her feet. She blinked at Evangeline's attire, a see-through black nylon peignoir trimmed in fluffy fake fur at the hem and neckline. She had taken time to put on a pair of fake-fur-trimmed matching black high heels.

"I was just leaving," Mattie said. "I wanted to say good-bye. And to remind you that if you ever get to Seattle to be sure and look me up. My number is on that card."

"You bet." Evangeline smiled through a yawn and gave Mattie a quick hug. "Good luck, honey." Then she glanced past Mattie. "You leavin' the island with him?"

Mattie glanced over her shoulder and saw Hugh leaning negligently against the upstairs railing, arms folded across his chest. "Uh, yes. We're flying out in a few minutes."

"Watch out for the kind that like to do favors for you," Evangeline warned. "Sooner or later they get the idea that they own you."

"I'll remember. Good-bye, Evangeline. Take care of yourself."

"Bye, honey. Hey. Keep the dress, why don't you? It looks terrific on you, and I don't feel like letting it out again."

Mattie looked at the red dress thinking she never wanted to see it again. "Oh, I couldn't possibly—"

"No, no, I mean it. A present, you know? One working woman to another. Like I said, we got to stick together."

"Thank you." Mattie knew there was no polite way to turn down the gift. She stuffed the red sarong into her shoulder bag and smiled weakly. "Well, good-bye."

"See ya." Evangeline yawned sleepily and closed the door.

Mattie turned to find Hugh still watching silently from the railing. She stood there looking at him, unable to think of anything clever to say.

"Ready?" He came away from the railing.

"Yes."

The small chartered plane landed on St. Gabriel's single runway five minutes before the rain squall hit. By the time the pilot had taxied up to the main terminal, a building that was not much more than a large shack of corrugated aluminum, the rain was coming down in buckets.

Mattie was surprised to find herself invigorated by the wild downpour. She actually laughed as she jumped down onto the tarmac and raced toward the metal shack.

"Don't worry, it'll be over in a few minutes," Hugh assured her as he grabbed her wrist and tugged her into the shelter of the terminal building.

Mattie shook the rain from her hair and listened to the roar on the roof as she glanced around curiously. Several figures were lounging around inside the terminal. They greeted Hugh with easy familiarity, their eyes going straight to Mattie.

"Hey, Abbott. What's that you brought back with you? A little souvenir?" one of the men asked.

"Meet my *fiancée*, Mattie Sharpe."

Mattie winced. This was going to be more awkward than she had thought. Things were even more settled in Hugh's mind than she'd feared.

"Pleased to meet ya, Mattie."

"'Good luck to ya, ma'am. Abbott here could use a woman around to polish up his manners."

"When's the wedding?"

Hugh was grinning as he led Mattie through the small terminal. "Don't worry, boys. You'll all be invited to the party."

Mattie found herself back outside and being stuffed into a Jeep. The rain was already moving on, leaving a steaming green landscape in its wake. In spite of her forebodings, a new sense of excitement gripped her. This was Hugh's island; his home. This was the place she had been willing to move to sight unseen a year ago. She could not help wondering what her life would have been like if Hugh had taken her up on her offer to follow him out here.

"You're going to love it here, Mattie," Hugh announced as he slid behind the wheel.

Mattie said nothing.

"First thing we'll do this afternoon is get you some clothes. That red thing is cute as hell, but you can't wear it all the time, can you?"

"Probably not."

"We'll stop in town before I take you on out to the house. You can do some shopping while I check in at the office."

The road into the tiny town of St. Gabriel followed the cliffs above the sea. Thick jungle vegetation hugged it on one side, and down below on the other side Mattie could see pristine white beaches and foaming breakers. There was a gray Navy ship and a big, sleek white cruise ship anchored just off shore.

"Navy puts in here regularly. Has for years. But now we're starting to get a little more tourist trade," Hugh explained above the noise of the wind rushing past the open Jeep windows. "Cruise ship comes in once a week. One of the big hotel chains is talking about putting in a first-class resort. Lot of divers are starting to come here. St. Gabe is on the way, babe. You and me are going to be part of it."

Hugh drove the twisting, narrow road with the casually efficient competence that characterized everything he did. Mattie found her gaze straying to his strong hands as they curved around the wheel. Memories of those hands on her body during the night flooded her mind.

Hugh's lovemaking could hardly have been described as artful, but there was a raw power and an elemental passion in it that had been as overwhelming this time as it had been the first time, a year ago. Mattie shivered as she recalled her own uncontrollable response. Last night, when she had awakened to find him looming over her, nothing in the world had mattered except having him become a part of her.

*Fool. Idiot.*

The small town hugging the waterfront of a beautiful, natural harbor looked faded and worn. It was obvious no one went out of the way yet to attract the trickle of tourists Hugh claimed were starting to come to St. Gabriel.

"We're still not used to tourists here yet," Hugh explained as he parked the Jeep in front of a building that had *Abbott Charters* painted on the front. "But one of these days St. Gabe is going to start waking up to the fact that we're all going to get rich. When it does you'll see some civic action downtown. Come on, babe, I'll introduce you to a couple of the guys who work for me."

Curious in spite of her mixed emotions regarding Hugh, Mattie followed him into the interior of Abbott Charters. It was a warehouse-style building with a small office in one corner. On the walls there were a couple of pinup calendars featuring overly endowed females in clothes that resembled Mattie's red sarong.

"Mattie, this is Ray and Derek. They fly for me," Hugh announced as two men, one young, one middle-aged, took their feet down off a desk and stood up.

Mattie smiled and shook hands. The two men had the look of bush pilots the world over: a sort of easy machismo and an aura of bravura. They gave Mattie the once-over with raffish eyes, but they seemed to acknowledge that Hugh's presence beside her made her private property.

"You get that government shipment over to St. Julian?" Hugh asked as he stopped beside a battered metal desk and picked up a sheaf of papers.

"Took it over yesterday, boss," Ray, the younger of the two pilots, said laconically. "What have you been up to? Heard there was some trouble on Purgatory. Get caught in it?"

"Mattie did. I found her in time, but Cormier's dead."

"Damn. Who got him?"

"Don't know yet," Hugh said, tossing aside the papers. "But sooner or later I'll find out."

Mattie heard the cold certainty in Hugh's voice, and she turned to glance at him in surprise. She had not realized he intended to try to track down Cormier's killer. "Hugh? What do you mean, you're going to find out? How can you do that?"

"Never mind, babe." He smiled at her and turned to the older pilot. "You finish the inspection on that Cessna?"

"Yeah, boss. No major problems."

"Check out that fuel line on the Beech?"

"It's fixed."

"Keep an eye out for corrosion?"

"Sure, boss. Like always." Derek winked at Mattie and added conspiratorially, "The man's a damn tyrant when it comes to maintenance."

"You want to get caught out over the water with corroded equipment, that's your privilege," Hugh said. "But do it in someone else's plane. Not one of mine. I can always find more pilots but good, reliable aircraft are hard to come by."

Ray grinned widely at Mattie. "Don't worry, his bark is worse than his bite. Most of the time, that is."

Mattie smiled back. "I'll keep that in mind."

Hugh looked at her. "I'll bet you're ready to do some shopping, aren't you, babe? There's a couple of stores farther down the street. Why don't you go have a look while I finish checking up on things here? I'll be along in a few minutes."

"Fine." Mildly irritated at being sent off as though she were a child who was too young to hear an adult conversation, Mattie turned on her heel and strode toward the door.

"I think she's mad, boss," Derek observed.

"She's been under a lot of stress lately," Hugh explained.

Two doors down from Abbott Charters Mattie saw a window display that included jeans and short-sleeved shirts. She went inside and made her selections quickly. There was not much choice.

When she reemerged a few minutes later she walked across the street to take a closer look at the wide variety of boats bobbing in the harbor. There were several sailboats, a few fishing boats, and one large cruiser that had *Abbott Charters* printed neatly on the bow. Apparently, Hugh was in the boat as well as air charter business. An astute businessman covering all the bases.

She strolled along the waterfront for a short distance, taking in the picturesque setting with a weird sense of déjà vu. *This would have been her home if she had come here a year ago.* Somehow it all looked exactly as it should, as it had in her dreams and fantasies.

She leaned over the concrete balustrade and found herself staring into the uncovered stern section of one of the boats. For a second she could not believe her eyes.

She was looking straight down at a half-finished painting. It was sitting on an easel that had been set up in the aging boat amid a welter of brushes, paints, coiled ropes, and fishing gear.

The painting was incomplete, but it was stunning.

The artist had obviously taken the lazy, sun-drenched scene of the main street of St. Gabriel as his starting point. But the painting had gone far beyond a mere reproduction of the quay, bars, and faded storefronts that lined the waterfront. This was no tranquil scene of a picture-postcard island paradise. It was a primitive, incredibly sensual image of savage beauty.

In the half-finished painting the jungle behind the town throbbed with both unseen menace and a sense of life in its rawest form. The beautiful waters of the harbor threatened the tiny outpost of civilization yet somehow held promise for the future.

The painting was at once a universal statement on the human condition and a compelling landscape scene. It was a work of art on several levels, totally accessible to a wide variety of viewers.

And Mattie knew immediately that she could sell it for a small fortune back in Seattle. Perhaps for a very large fortune if she shrouded the painter in enough mystery.

All of her instincts as a businesswoman snapped to full, quivering attention. Like a hound on the scent, she hurried down the dock steps and peered through the windows of the boat's cabin. She had to locate the artist, and she hoped like hell he was not already represented by another dealer.

She leaned down to call into the cabin. "Anybody home?"

There was no response.

She waited impatiently for a moment or so. When there was still no sign of life, she glanced at the name painted on the hull of the old boat and tried again.

"Excuse me. Is anyone home on board the *Griffin?*"

"Don't go holdin' yer breath waitin' for an answer from ol' Silk, lady. He's already up at the Hellfire. Won't be back till Bernard rolls him out the door sometime after midnight."

Mattie glanced down the dock and saw a grizzled old man crouched over a coil of rope. His skin looked like leather and his eyes had a permanent, sun-induced squint. He was wearing a pair of old pants that hung precariously on his scrawny frame and a cap that looked as if it might once have been decorated with a military insignia.

"Hello," Mattie said politely. "I'm looking for whoever painted that picture."

"That'd be Silk, all right. He's always fiddlin' around with those paints o' his. 'Cept when he's busy workin' or drinkin', o' course."

"Of course. And I take it he is now drinking?"

"Yup. Take a look at the time. Dang near four o'clock. Silk always heads for the Hellfire at three sharp on Wednesdays. Real regular in his habits, Silk is."

"Thank you for the information," said Mattie, turning. "I'll try the Hellfire. Is it up there on the waterfront?"

"Yup. But I don't reckon you want to be goin' in there, ma'am." The old man eyed her skeptically. "Silk can get a might difficult to manage once he's had a few. Specially when it comes to females. Silk likes females and he don't get a shot at very many around here. Just an occasional tourist." The man spit a wad of chewing tobacco into the harbor. "None of us gets much shot at females. Not many females get this far. They usually stop in Hawaii. Worse 'n livin' in a dang monastery."

"Really? If that's the way you feel, then why do you choose to live way out here?"

"Used to it, I reckon. What you want with Silk?"

"I just want to do a little business with Mr. Silk."

"Yeah? Funny. Wouldn't have pegged you right off for the type. Kinda thin for that sort o' work, ain't ya? But if that's your aim, I'd get the money up front if'n I was you. Silk don't like payin' for it after the fact, if you know what I mean."

"I'll keep your advice in mind," Mattie said as she started toward the steps that led up to the street.

The novelty of being mistaken for a professional prostitute had begun to wear thin, she reflected. Definitely time to go home.

*Just as soon as she had acquired some paintings from this Silk person.*

She did not want to have to label her Pacific trip a complete disaster, which, until now, was what it definitely had been.

# 7

The Hellfire bar was another classic island dive. Mattie decided she was in a position to judge now, after having spent most of yesterday evening in one. This tavern was open to the breezes, just as the one last night had been. It had a sluggish ceiling fan and a long, long backbar filled with the basics: beer, whiskey, rum, vodka, and gin. There was no white wine as far as Mattie could see.

The crowd was light and appeared to consist entirely of men who looked as if they had spent their lives working around docks and fishing boats. In one corner sat a handful of sailors who were presumably off the Navy ship that Mattie had seen at anchor in the harbor.

In another corner near the rail that separated the interior of the Hellfire from the street sat a mountain of a man. He had an overgrown beard and a shock of hair that had obviously been bright red at one time. He was dressed in a flower print shirt that hung unbuttoned to the waist and revealed a great expanse of massive, tanned chest. He also had on a pair of shorts and a pair of thongs. There was a glass of what looked like whiskey on the rattan table in front of him.

The splotches of paint on the shorts were all the clue Mattie needed. Smiling her best gallery-owner smile, she started across the room, deliberately ignoring the wolf whistles and moist sucking sounds that came from the group of sailors.

"Mr. Silk? I'm Mattie Sharpe from Seattle. I just saw the painting you're working on down on the *Griffin,* and I think it's absolutely wonderful. I'd like to talk to you about representation."

The big man turned his head very slowly to stare at her with slightly bloodshot blue eyes. His leonine face went well with the rest of him, Mattie decided. He was truly huge all over, but everything about him appeared to be very, very solid.

The blue eyes lit up as they settled on her. She continued to smile back, feeling quite hopeful. She had never met an artist who was not more than anxious to sell his work.

"Well, well, well." The voice fit the man, a deep, booming, Southern drawl. "Who the hell did you say you were?"

"Mattie Sharpe. I own a gallery back in Seattle called Sharpe Reaction, and if the painting I saw on board your boat is a sample of the body of your work, I would love to represent you."

The man's grin was slow and magnificent and revealed two gold teeth. "The body of my work, eh? Sit down, Mattie Sharpe, and let me buy you a drink. We can have us a real nice discussion on the subject of my body."

Mattie sat down. "Thank you. Is Silk the name you prefer or would you rather I use your first name?"

"Honeypot, you can call me anything your little heart desires. But if you can't think of something better, Silk'll do just fine." Silk turned and called out to the bartender. "Bernard, my lad, bring the lady whatever she wants."

"What's she want, Silk?" the bartender called back.

Silk turned to Mattie. "What'll it be, Mattie Sharpe?"

"Iced tea would be nice."

"Hey, Bernard, you got any iced tea for the lady?"

"I think I got some tea and I know I got ice. I guess I can put the two together. Take me a few minutes, though."

Silk nodded in ponderous satisfaction. "No rush, Bernard. No rush at all. Me and the lady are going to just sit right here and get to know each other. Ain't that right, Mattie Sharpe?"

It occurred to Mattie that the man called Silk might be a little farther gone than he had originally appeared. "About your painting, Silk."

"Forget my painting. We can talk about that later. Much later. Tell me about yourself, Mattie Sharpe. Tell me what you like to eat, what your favorite color is, and how you like for a man to ball you. Tell me all the little details. I always aim to please."

Mattie stared at him, uncertain whether she had heard him correctly. Surely he had not actually said what she thought he had said. "My gallery is quite successful, Silk," she began earnestly. "I feel certain your work would do very well there. It has the timeless appeal of landscape art and the immediate impact of a powerful, passionate statement."

Silk's grin got bigger. "That's me, Mattie Sharpe. I ain't nothin' if not passionate."

"All good artists are passionate about their work. Look, I'm only going to be here on St. Gabriel for a very short time. But if we can work out a suitable contract, I would like to take some of your paintings back with me."

Silk put one elbow on the table and rested his broad chin on his hand. "Do you like it slow and easy or hard and fast?" he asked. "I can go either way, but they don't call me Silk for nothin'. I'm at my best when I'm going slow and easy. Maybe with you on top, huh? You're kind of a little thing, and I wouldn't want to accidentally squash you. Yeah, I think slow and easy would be best."

Mattie groaned and reluctantly got to her feet. "I think we had better have this conversation at some other time, Silk."

"Nonsense. We're doing just fine, Mattie Sharpe. Sit down and keep talking." Silk's big hand snaked out with an astonishingly quick, flashing movement, locking around her wrist. There was enormous strength in his fingers.

Mattie gasped as she was jerked back down onto her seat. She stared at the huge paw wrapped around her wrist. Artists were notoriously difficult at times, but this was getting out of hand.

"Let go of me," Mattie said very firmly.

"Now, now, don't be in such a rush, honeypot. Bernard'll be here with your iced tea in a minute or two, and you can drink it while we talk. Then we'll just wander down to the *Griffin* and fuck each other's brains out. How does that sound?"

"I said, let go of me."

"Now, honeypot, don't go getting impatient. I told you, slow and easy. All in good time." Silk leered happily at her. "I'll be at my best after another couple of drinks. Smooth as Silk, like they say."

"I have no intention of seeing you at your best." Mattie snatched up his half-finished whiskey with her free hand and hurled the contents straight in Silk's face. The big man yelped and his grip slackened slightly on her wrist. She yanked her hand free and stepped quickly back out of reach.

"Hey, man, what do you think you're doing?" one of the sailors bellowed, getting to his feet. "Let the lady alone."

"Yeah, let the little gal alone!" yelled another man at the same table. "She'd much rather have some civilized company, I'll bet. Wouldn't ya, lady?" The second sailor stood up also, staggering slightly as he found his balance.

The rest of the men at the table quickly got to their feet, exhibiting varying degrees of stability.

Instantly chair legs scraped on the scarred wooden floor of the

Hellfire as everyone else in the room scrambled to his feet. Enthusiastic shouts rose to a clamor.

Silk lost interest in Mattie at once. His whole face glowed with a beatific expression as he rose majestically. "Well, now, lads, looks like we have us a slight difference of opinion here. What say we settle the matter like the gentlemen we all are?"

"Any time, Silk. We'll back you against these sweet little Navy pussies any time. You just say the word."

Silk glanced over his shoulder at Mattie. "Don't go nowhere now, Mattie Sharpe. I'll be through here in just a minute or two, and we can carry on right where we left off."

With a roar, Silk launched himself toward the group of sailors. The regular patrons of the Hellfire followed suit.

Mattie was stunned by the speed with which the brawl erupted. With one hand instinctively going to her throat, she sidestepped to avoid a flying chair. Then she backed hurriedly toward the door.

A man who had apparently abandoned shaving and deodorant upon moving to St. Gabriel made a grab for her arm. "What d'ya say we just kind o' slide on outa here, sweetheart? Nobody's gonna miss us."

Mattie rammed her elbow into the man's ribs and extricated herself from his grasp when he bent double. She fumbled with the catch of her shoulder bag.

"Can you hear me, Silk?" she called out above the din.

"I can hear you just fine, Mattie Sharpe. Be right with you." Silk smashed a beefy fist into a hapless face and turned to show Mattie a wide grin.

Mattie plucked one of her business cards out of her purse and waved it in the air. "I'm going to leave my card here on the bar. I'll look you up tomorrow morning when you're, uh, recovered. I really feel we can do business together, and I— Oh!"

Mattie's voice rose on a yelp of alarm as her business card was snapped out of her fingers. A familiar male hand closed around her arm with a force that was just short of bruising.

"Damn," said Hugh. "I should have known. Can't leave you alone for a minute, can I?"

"*Hugh.*" Mattie breathed a sigh of relief. "Thank heavens it's you. I don't mind telling you, I was getting a little nervous. Artists are usually somewhat eccentric, but I've never had anything like this happen before when I've approached one."

Hugh wrapped a hand around the nape of her neck and hauled her toward the door. "I suppose you started this?"

Mattie was outraged. "Me? What a nasty thing to say. I had nothing to do with this stupid brawl. I was just trying to conduct a little business."

"Uh-huh."

"Yep. She started it all right, Abbott," Bernard the bartender announced. "Walked right in and sat right down at Silk's table. Silk being Silk, you know what happened next. And we both know Miles is going to expect someone to pay for it."

"Send the bill to Silk," Hugh suggested.

"Can't do that. He'll try to pay for it with another painting. We already got enough of his pictures stashed away in the back room. Don't need another one."

"All right, all right. Bill me for whatever you can't get out of the Navy."

"You got it." The bartender went back to polishing glasses as the bar fight raged across the floor of the Hellfire.

"Now, hold on just one hot minute," Mattie said. "You shouldn't pay for any of the damage being done in here. It's not your fault, Hugh."

"We all know whose fault it is." Hugh yanked her toward the door. "But don't worry. I intend to get reimbursed. I'll just take it out of your soft little hide."

"Don't you dare talk like that," Mattie retorted indignantly. "I am a totally innocent victim."

Before Hugh could respond to that statement, a familiar voice boomed out across the sounds of thudding fists and flying chairs.

"Now, just a dadblamed minute, Abbott. What d'ya think you're doing? You can't go running off with that little gal. I already got dibs on her. You just leave her be. I'll be through here right quick."

Hugh halted and turned around to confront Silk, who had emerged from the center of the brawl to reclaim his departing victim.

"Sorry, Silk. A slight misunderstanding here. Mattie belongs to me. Brought her with me from Purgatory."

Silk's eyes widened in outrage as he glared at Mattie. "The hell you say."

"Afraid so. Now, if you'll excuse us, we're out of here."

"Now, see here, this just ain't fair, Abbott."

"I know, Silk, but that's the way it goes. Finders keepers."

Mattie was incensed. "Will you two kindly stop discussing me as if I were a side of beef?" A glass whizzed past her head and she ducked instinctively. A split second later it shattered against the wall behind her.

Silk's massive hand closed around Mattie's free wrist. "Don't you worry none, Mattie Sharpe. I'll be glad to teach Abbott here some manners. He gets kinda uppity at times."

"Oh, my God," Mattie said.

"Let her go, Silk. You've got business to attend to." Hugh side-stepped a chair as it went skidding past his booted foot.

"But the whole point of this here business is so me and Mattie Sharpe can go screw . . . umph."

Silk lost his balance and toppled to the floor like a felled oak as Hugh did something very fast and very efficient with his foot and one hand.

"I said, let her go, Silk." Hugh spoke with surprising gentleness. "You know I always mean what I say."

Silk propped himself up on his elbows and eyed Mattie through slitted eyes. "You said you brought her with you from Purgatory?"

"Yeah. I'm going to marry her as soon as I can get things arranged."

Silk looked up at him in open astonishment. "No fooling? Hey, can I come to the party? I haven't been to a real live wedding party in years."

Mattie sighed.

"Sure," Hugh said easily. "You can come to the party."

Silk staggered to his feet, dusted himself off, and gave Mattie a huge grin. "Don't you worry none, Mattie Sharpe. I'll make sure it's a real wingding of a party. It'll be a party to remember, that's for sure. We'll invite the whole damn island."

He turned and waded back into the fray.

"Let's just hope he doesn't do any damage to his hands," Mattie said as Hugh hauled her out the door and into the street.

"Damn it to hell." Hugh shoved her into the passenger seat of the Jeep and got in beside her. "Is that all you can think about?"

"Talent is where you find it. I'd hate to see his artistic career ruined because his hands got injured in a barroom brawl."

"Silk hasn't got an artistic career. He works for me when he works at all, and the rest of the time he just sits around in his boat painting or else he sits in the Hellfire drinking." Hugh sent the Jeep roaring out of town. "Once in a while he gets real lucky when some stray lady tourist wanders in and decides he's picturesque."

"I see."

Hugh slid her a dangerous sidelong glance. "Can't really blame the guy for thinking he'd gotten lucky this afternoon, can I? The way you behaved, it's no wonder."

"For heaven's sake. You make it sound like I went in there to pick him up," Mattie said tightly.

"Well, didn't you?"

"No, I did not. I went in there to do business with the man."

"What the hell did you think you were doing wandering into a waterfront bar all by yourself and sitting down at the table of a complete stranger?" Hugh snapped. "Where's your common sense, Mattie?"

"Stop acting as if what happened back there was all my fault."

"It was your fault. I told you that."

"Hugh, I don't want to hear another word about it, understand? I've told you before, I don't like listening to your little lectures. And while we're on the subject, there's something else I'd better mention. I'd rather you stopped telling everyone we're going to get married."

"Why? It's the truth."

"It is not the truth. We have no plans for marriage. You're only going to embarrass yourself if you go around telling everyone you're about to become a groom."

He took his attention off the narrow road just long enough to shoot her a searing look. "What the hell do you mean, we're not getting married? We got that all settled last night, damn it."

"We did not settle anything last night!" Mattie yelled back. "All we did last night was have sex together. If you will recall, we did that once before and it didn't end in marriage."

"Christ, woman, are you going to throw that in my face again?"

"Yes, I am. You deserve it." She braced herself on the window frame of the Jeep as Hugh slammed the vehicle to a halt. "Why are we stopping?"

"Because we're in the middle of an argument and I want to give it my full attention." Hugh swung around in the seat to confront her, one arm draped over the wheel, the other lying along the back of the seat. "Mattie, what's gotten into you? You knew I figured everything was okay between us this morning."

"I knew you were probably making some assumptions, but who am I to try to set you straight? You never listen to me."

"Give me a chance. Talk to me. Tell me why you won't marry me," he said roughly.

"Try it the other way, Hugh. Why should I marry you?"

"Because you love me."

"Is that right?" She faced him with fury and passion now. "How do you know that for certain?"

"I've always known it." He looked exasperated and helpless in the way only a man can when caught in the middle of a dreaded *relationship* discussion. "Since that night we spent together a year ago. Before that, if you want to know the truth. I wasn't completely blind to the way you acted around me. You were always sort of anxious and uneasy."

"Stress."

"Don't give me the stress excuses. If I wasn't sure how you felt about me back then, I got a damn good idea during the past eight months when you deliberately avoided me every chance you got. You were afraid to see me because you knew the effect I'd have on you."

"Bull."

"And if there was any doubt left, you cleared it up last night. You wanted me, Mattie. Admit it, damn it. You wanted me."

"I don't know what came over me last night. I went a little crazy. It was the stress. It must have been."

"It was not the goddamned stress. You wanted me. You can't hide a thing like that."

"Wanting is not necessarily loving. You're old enough to know that."

"It is with you."

"You don't know that, damn you!" she shouted.

"Mattie, babe, you're getting upset."

"Of course I'm upset. You're trying to tear my world apart again. I won't let you do it a second time, Hugh. It took me long enough to put myself back together last time. Do you hear me? I won't let you do it to me."

"Babe, listen to me. I've told you I'm sorry. I didn't know what the hell I was doing last time. I made a mistake. I've been regretting it ever since. But this time around things are going to be different."

"Are they?" she asked, almost viciously.

"Damn right."

"*Prove it.*"

That stopped him for an instant. He looked blank. "What do you mean, prove it? How am I supposed to do that?"

"Are you sure you really want to marry me?"

He began to look wary now. "Hell, yes. Why else would I be going through this kind of nonsense?"

"Because you've got your one-track brain set on getting yourself a wife. Because I'm convenient. Because I once volunteered to move out here to the edge of the world, so you figure I won't give you a hard time about it the way my sister did. Because you think you can handle me."

Hugh rammed his fingers through his hair. "You're trying to make it sound like a business deal or something."

"I think it is, in a way. You want a wife and I appear to be available. You don't have a lot of opportunity for finding suitable wives out here on this backwater island, do you? Some man down at the docks said living on St. Gabriel was rather like living in a monastery."

"Now, Mattie, babe—"

"It's pretty clear why you fixated on me after Ariel opted out of the engagement. I'm a known quantity and I must have looked like I'd be a great deal easier to manage than Ariel. After all, I don't make scenes. I don't quarrel in public. I'm not melodramatic."

"Come on, babe, you're being ridiculous."

"No," Mattie said tightly. "I don't think I am. I'm being realistic. What you don't seem to realize is that I'm not the same woman I was a year ago. I made some decisions that morning after I humiliated myself."

"What decisions?"

"I told myself that never again would I settle for playing second fiddle to my sister. I had enough of that while I was growing up. Enough of watching her get the dates while I prayed the phone would ring just once for me. Enough of having her cast-off boyfriends come to me for sympathy and comfort. Enough of watching her win all the prizes and get all the applause."

"For crying out loud, Mattie."

But Mattie was too wound up to stop this time. "It was humiliating always being second best. It was miserable having people chalk up her tantrums to a budding artistic temperament while I always got a lecture on self-control. I hated being sent to counselor after counselor to find out if I was an underachiever or if I was just a hopeless case."

"Spare me a dissertation on your early childhood traumas, okay? I'll tell you something, babe, you don't know what real trauma is," Hugh said through clenched teeth. "You with your fancy private schools and your art lessons and your rich aunt Charlotte."

"Is that right?" she raged back.

"Damn right. You know what trauma is? It's having your old man run off when you're six years old and you're glad to see him go because it means the beatings will stop. It's having your mother give you up to foster care because she can't figure out how to deal with you and her own miserable, screwed-up life at the same time. It's having people tell you you're bound to wind up in jail sooner or later because you come from bad stock."

Mattie stared at him, aghast. Then her eyes narrowed. "Oh, no you don't, Hugh Abbott. You're not going to pull that old trick on me."

"What old trick?" he roared.

"You're not going to belittle my feelings by making me feel sorry for you. All my life my feelings have been less important than anyone else's. Everyone else got to be temperamental, but not me. I was expected to be *nice.*"

"Oh, yeah? Well, I've got news for you. You're not being very *nice* at the moment, babe. You're yelling louder than a damned fishwife."

"You know something? It feels good. Right now I have a right to feel used, damn it. You are trying to use me. You're accustomed to giving orders, accustomed to having things go the way you want them to go. Ariel gave you a setback last year, but that didn't stop you, did it? You've regrouped and decided to attack a weaker target this year. Well, I won't stand in for her. Not this time. Do you hear me?"

"Mattie, that is not the way it is." Hugh clearly had himself under control again.

"Isn't it? You're picking me this time because you think I'll be so damn grateful to marry you I'll get down on my knees and thank you. Well, that's not how it's going to be."

"Babe," Hugh said soothingly, "take it easy."

"I will not take it easy. We're going to settle this here and now. If you really want me, you can damn well prove it."

"I'm going to marry you. What the hell more do you want?"

"I'll tell you what I want." She was feeling goaded now—dangerous, reckless, and up against a wall. "You can stop expecting me to give up my career and my friends and everything else back in Seattle to move out here to the edge of the world to make a home for you."

"But, babe—"

"*Stop calling me babe!* If you really want me, Hugh Abbott, then you can give up your business and your lifestyle and your friends and move to Seattle."

Hugh's mouth fell open as he stared at her in stunned amazement.

Mattie realized with a sense of shocking satisfaction that it was the first time she had ever seen Hugh Abbott caught completely by surprise. She sat back in her seat, folding her arms protectively under her breasts, and studied him through cool, narrowed eyes.

"Are you nuts, Mattie? Me leave St. Gabe? With everything I've got going here?"

"Yes, that does put a different slant on the subject, doesn't it?" she noted sweetly. "Rather like asking me to leave Seattle."

Hugh closed his mouth. His big hand tightened ferociously around the steering wheel. "Is this some kind of game, Mattie? Because I don't like games."

"It's no game. I told you, I'm tired of being second best. Just once, *just once*, mind you, I want to know I'm first. I want to be wanted for myself, not as a fill-in for Ariel. Just once I want to finish in front. And if I can't be first, I don't want to even enter the damned race this time."

Hugh was silent for a long time, his hooded eyes never leaving her set face. "I don't believe this," he finally said.

"Believe it, Hugh."

"You want me to give up Abbott Charters? Forget the house I was going to build for us? Live in a damned city and go to gallery openings and drink espresso?"

She smiled grimly. "It is a lot to ask, isn't it? Just as much as you're asking of me."

"But I've got a business to run."

"So do I."

"How the hell am I supposed to get Abbott Charters on its feet from Seattle?"

"How the hell am I supposed to run Sharpe Reaction from St. Gabriel?"

"It's not the same thing," Hugh shot back. "Damn it, Mattie, when you move out here, I'll take care of you."

"If you come to Seattle, I'll take care of you. I make enough to support both of us."

"I'm not going to let you make me into some goddamned kept man," he said through gritted teeth.

"Well, I don't want to be a kept woman."

"Babe, be reasonable. You were willing enough to move out here a year ago. You begged me to take you with me when I left Seattle."

"That," said Mattie, beginning to feel like a broken record, "was last year."

"Shit." Hugh sat back in his seat and wrenched the key in the Jeep's ignition. The engine started with a roar.

Mattie closed her eyes tightly, but she could not stop the tears from trickling down her cheeks. Angrily she brushed at them with the back of her hand.

"Mattie? Are you crying?"

"No. I won't let you make me cry a second time, Hugh. I will never let you make me cry again."

There was silence from the other side of the Jeep. And then Hugh said quietly, "All right. We'll try it."

She blinked away more moisture. "Try what?"

"I'll try proving to you that you're first. I'll go back to Seattle with you. I can go on working for Charlotte, so you won't be supporting me. We'll see how it goes."

Mattie jerked her head around to stare at his hard profile. "You don't mean that."

He shrugged. "I never say things I don't mean."

"You can't come with me to Seattle. You'd hate living there."

"I've lived a lot of places that were a lot worse."

"Hugh, this is crazy."

"Yeah. I agree. But I can't think of any other way to prove I want you more than I wanted Ariel. And that's what this is really all about, isn't it? Proof? You'll get your proof, Mattie."

She heard the grim determination in his rough-edged voice and she shuddered. "I don't believe you'll really pack up and come back to Seattle with me."

"You sure don't trust me very much, do you, babe?"

"Frankly, no. You're hatching some kind of scheme. I can tell."

"I'm going back to Seattle with you. Let's leave it at that, okay?"

"No," Mattie said defiantly. "I won't leave it at that. While we're on the subject, I think I should tell you that there will be no repeat of last night's little incident."

"I agree. I don't want you wearing that little red job out in public, anyway."

"I'm not talking about the dress," she yelled, "I'm talking about us! Sleeping together. Sex. You and me in a bed. No more of it. At least not until I figure out what you're up to."

"Shit," Hugh said.

"I am beginning to realize you have an extremely limited vocabulary, Hugh Abbott."

"It's the stress. When I get under a lot of stress, I always say *shit*."

# 8

❧

"Are you out of your tiny little mind?" Silk Taggert shoved a bottle of beer into Hugh's hand. "Go to Seattle? And stay there for who knows how long? After you're just getting the business going here? Why in hell would you want to do that? It's damn stupid, Abbott. You're a lot of things, but stupid you normally ain't."

"It's a relationship thing, Silk. Hard to explain." Hugh took a long pull on the beer and leaned back against the bulkhead. He was sitting in the stern of the *Griffin* waiting for Mattie to finish picking up the ingredients for dinner from one of the local shops down the street. "Hell, I don't know if I understand it myself."

"You tried this relationship stuff once before, remember? It didn't work out then. What makes you think it'll work this time?"

"Mattie's different."

"Don't sound like it. Sounds just like the other one. Leads you on and gets a proposal out of you and then refuses to move out here and set up housekeeping." Silk sat down in front of the easel and picked up a brush.

"I made a mistake last year," Hugh said. "I'm paying for it."

"How long you going to go on paying?" Silk dabbled the brush in water and then in blue paint.

"Don't know." Hugh took another swallow of beer and thought gloomy thoughts. "Until I can convince her of something, I guess."

"What's she want to be convinced of?" Silk studied the blank white canvas and then put in a wash of blue that came close to the color of the afternoon sky over St. Gabriel.

"That she's more important to me than her sister was, I guess."

"Well, shoot." Silk studied the blue wash with slitted eyes. "You could spend a lifetime trying to convince a woman she's the most important thing in your life. Women are never satisfied."

"Mattie will be. Eventually. She just needs a little time to get used to the idea that I mean what I say."

"What are you gonna do with the charter business while you're busy convincing Mattie she's Number One?"

"That, my good man, is where you come in."

"Oh, no, you don't. I ain't running it for you. I don't mind making a few flights when you're short of pilots, or doing some maintenance for you, but I don't want to play boss. You know I can't stand paperwork."

"I need you, Silk. You're the only one I can trust to handle Abbott Charters while I'm in Seattle."

"Forget it."

"It'll only be for a few weeks or so at the most." Hugh leaned forward, resting his elbows on his thighs and cradling the beer bottle between his palms. "I just need some time in Seattle."

"She know you're only planning to spend a few weeks convincing her?"

Hugh scowled. "No, and if you open your big mouth, I will personally close it for you."

"You're gonna keep working for Vailcourt, aren't you?"

"Might as well. The money's good. Work's easy. Charlotte Vailcourt thinks handling Vailcourt security is hard and dangerous, but she doesn't know the meaning of the words *hard* and *dangerous*. Don't see why I should be the one to set her straight. Not as long as she's willing to pay me a fortune to consult."

"Yeah, you got it cushy working for Vailcourt, all right." Silk added a lemon tinge to the blue sky. "You ever tell this Mattie Sharpe what you used to do for a living?"

"Hell, no." Hugh gave his friend a cold stare.

"Don't worry. I'll keep my mouth shut," Silk said quietly. He deepened the yellow. "But you don't know women. If they think there's some mystery in your past, they won't stop digging until they uncover it."

"I can handle Mattie."

Silk snorted. "Sure. That's why you're leaving everything behind here on St. Gabe and traipsing off with her to Seattle. Who's handling who, boss?"

"Look, let's just forget this whole subject, all right?"

Silk heaved a massive shrug. "Whatever you say, boss. But take it from me, you're wasting your time. Things ain't what they used to be in the old days when a good woman would follow a man to the other side of the world and stick with him come hell or high water.

Nowadays we got this new liberated female who wants her own career and a fancy condo and what you call a sophisticated lifestyle. What's more, she wants to marry a man who works for a corporation, drinks white wine, and drives a BMW."

"So now you're an expert on the modern woman?"

"A wise man learns by observation," Silk informed him loftily. "I watched you screw up last year. I ain't looking forward to watching you shoot yourself in the foot again. It's embarrassing."

"Mattie's different," Hugh insisted stubbornly. "Once she's sure of me, she'll stop fussing about where she lives."

"Sure."

"Hey, you want to come over to dinner tonight?"

Silk's bushy brows climbed. "You making another batch of that godawful chili?"

"No. Mattie's going to be doing the cooking." Hugh could not help feeling smug. It was curiously pleasant to be able to extend an invitation for a home-cooked dinner to a friend. He liked the idea of entertaining in his own home. Just like a real married man. "She's a great cook. I told her to pick up some nice thick steaks and stuff for a salad. Maybe dessert. What do you say?"

Silk considered that. "Sounds good. I haven't had a real homecooked meal since that little blond tourist lady made me scrambled eggs when she stayed overnight on the *Griffin.*"

"That was damn near a year ago."

"Yeah. I'm drooling already. Don't mind telling you. But I doubt if Miss Mattie Sharpe will want me coming to dinner. I didn't exactly get off on my best foot with her yesterday."

"I explained all that," Hugh said.

Silk put a dark blue wash in over the area that would be the sea. "Well, if you're sure she won't poison me, I'd be mighty pleased to join you."

"Good. Six o'clock." Hugh glanced up and saw Mattie approaching along the quay. She was wearing the new jeans she had bought yesterday and a flower-splashed top. She had complained that the jeans were too tight and that the bright, short-sleeved camp shirt was rather garish, but he thought she looked terrific. Which only went to show how low-class his tastes were, Hugh supposed. He got to his feet. "One more thing," he said to Silk. "Don't stop off at the Hellfire first."

Silk contrived to look offended. "I got manners when I need 'em, Abbott. Don't worry, I won't embarrass you by showing up three sheets to the wind. You hear anything yet from Purgatory?"

"No. It might take a little time. But the word is out. Bound to hear something sooner or later." Hugh vaulted onto the dock. "We'll get whoever did it."

"I get first crack at the bastard who blew Cormier away when we do find him," Silk muttered.

"You're going to have to get in line. I'm first. Whoever it was came too close to getting Mattie, too, remember?"

Silk frowned thoughtfully at Mattie, who was making her way down the harbor steps, two large sacks of groceries in her arms. "You know, I still say she's going to lead you around like a bull with a ring through its nose and then dump you, but I got to admit she's got some sass and spirit. Handled me real good yesterday when I got out of line. Threw a glass of whiskey right in my face. Saw her punch out another guy who tried to grab her on the way out of the bar."

Hugh grinned with expansive pride as he recalled Mattie holding a gun on Gibbs. "Yeah. She's definitely my kind of woman. Now all I've got to do is convince her of that."

"I think it's going to be a little tougher than that, boss. What you got to do is convince her you're her kind of man. Again."

As far as Hugh was concerned, dinner was a roaring success. This was part of what a real home was all about, he decided in deep satisfaction. This was the way it was supposed to be, a man and a woman creating a warm and happy little world where friends were welcome. It had never been this way for Hugh in the past, but he was determined that it would be in the future.

He admitted to himself he'd had a few qualms when Mattie had calmly announced she had not bought the steaks as instructed but was going to make a fancy pasta dish instead.

Hugh had not been at all certain of how Silk would react to trendy health food. But after the first bite, he knew he need not have worried. After one curious glance, Silk had immediately begun putting away the pasta by the truckload.

Taggert had appeared a bit anxious when Hugh opened the door of the small, wooden framed beach cottage earlier. But once Mattie broke the ice by asking questions about his paintings, he'd mellowed instantly.

"So you and my old buddy Hugh, here, are going to tie the knot, huh?" Silk reached for a third helping of salad and bread.

"Right," said Hugh.

"We're thinking about it," Mattie demurred.

Hugh scowled at her, but she appeared oblivious. He reached for another bottle of beer, started to drink straight from the bottle, and then remembered his manners and poured it into a glass.

"More pasta, Silk?" Mattie smiled and held out the bowl.

"You bet." Silk reached for the bowl. "This is the fanciest spaghetti I've ever had, although I got to admit I've come across some pretty interesting noodle things in places like Malaysia and Indonesia. I remember one dish of rice noodles and peanuts and hot peppers that—"

Hugh kicked his friend under the table. Silk gave him a reproachful glance. The problem with Silk was that he usually meant well, but he did not always know when to keep his mouth shut. As far as Hugh was concerned, the less said about Indonesia and other exotic locales from their shared pasts, the better.

"I think I know the dish you're talking about," Mattie was saying. "It uses lemon grass and coconut milk, doesn't it?"

"Uh, yeah," Silk said, eyeing Hugh with a sidelong glance. "Something like that."

"I've made it myself, once or twice. Tell me, how many paintings do you have completed and ready for purchase?" she asked.

Silk shrugged. "Who knows? Probably a couple dozen or so. I can get some back from Miles at the Hellfire if you want 'em. You really serious about taking 'em back to Seattle?"

"Deadly serious," Mattie said.

"Dang. What makes you think you can sell 'em there? I can't hardly give 'em away around here."

"Probably because the general level of artistic taste here on St. Gabriel is pathetically low," Mattie said dryly. "Most of the art I've come across so far has been the sort one finds on the girlie calendars hanging in the offices of Abbott Charters."

"Now, hold on," Hugh interrupted. "I didn't hang those up. Ray and Derek did that."

Mattie gave him a skeptical look and turned back to Silk. "Don't worry, Silk. I can sell your work. Guaranteed."

"What makes you think folks back in Seattle will think my work is worth a lot of money?"

"They'll think it is worth a great deal of money because I will tell them it is worth a great deal of money," Mattie explained very gently.

Silk's eyes widened appreciatively. Then he gave a great shout of laughter. "I like your style, Mattie Sharpe. Something tells me you and me were born to do business together."

Hugh was about to comment on the unlikely friendship budding before his eyes when the phone rang. He got up reluctantly to answer it. The only calls he ever got were business calls, and he really didn't want to take one right now. The only problem was, he could hardly afford to ignore one.

"Abbott Charters," he said automatically, his eyes on Mattie and Silk, who were engaged in an animated discussion on the subject of art gallery contracts.

"Abbott? That you?" The voice was low, rasping, and familiar.

Hugh was suddenly paying full attention to his caller. "This is Abbott."

"It's me. Rosey. Remember me?"

"Yeah, Rosey, I remember you."

"Remember what you said? About being willing to pay big bucks for some info?"

"The offer's still open."

"Good." There was gloating satisfaction in Rosey's rasping voice. "I'm here and I got what you want. I think. But it'll cost you, pal. This is dangerous stuff."

"You're here? On St. Gabe?"

"Yeah. Got in this afternoon. I been lyin' low, waiting to see if I was followed. But it looks like I'm in the clear. I've done some checkin' around. Know that old, abandoned warehouse just north of town? Right near the beach?"

"I know it. Lily Cove." Hugh realized that the conversation at the table had ceased. He looked across the small room and saw that Mattie and Silk were both watching him intently.

"Meet me there in half an hour."

"All right."

"And Abbott?"

"Yeah, Rosey?"

"Bring cash. A thousand big ones."

"Christ, Rosey, I'm buying information, not a bridge."

"This information is worth it. If you don't want it, I can sell it somewheres else."

"Come on, Rosey. We both know you're bluffing. Who else would want this kind of information?"

"I don't know yet, but I got a feeling there's more than one guy who'd pay for what I've got."

"But you're in a hurry, right, Rosey? You need the money tonight. You can't afford to sit around and wait for another buyer."

"Goddamn it, Abbott," Rosey said, his voice taking on the characteristic whine, "if you want the name you're after, be at that warehouse in half an hour. With the thousand."

"Five hundred and that's it, Rosey."

"Sheesh. Okay, okay. Like you say, I can't hang around. Five hundred."

The receiver on the other end was slammed down in Hugh's ear. He gently replaced the phone and looked at Silk and Mattie.

"That was Rosey?" Mattie asked.

"Yeah." He met Silk's steady blue gaze. "He's got a name. Wants five hundred in cash for it."

Silk shook his head. "Poor guy's got delusions of grandeur."

"What name?" Mattie demanded, starting to look anxious.

"The name of the guy who shot Paul Cormier. Or so he says. Who knows with a rodent like our friend Rosey." Hugh walked over to the tiny kitchen and opened a chipped metal cabinet. He found his revolver behind the sack of pinto beans he kept for making chili.

"You're going to see Rosey? Tonight? Hugh, what is this all about?" Mattie got to her feet clutching the spoon she had been using to serve the pasta. "Why are you taking your gun?"

"Yes, I'm going to talk to Rosey, and I'm taking the gun because when one is dealing with the Roseys of this world, one feels more secure when one is armed." He shoved the revolver into his belt and went over to the table. He felt ridiculously pleased by her unnecessary concern. "Now, don't worry. I won't be gone long."

"I don't like this," Mattie stated emphatically. "I don't like it at all."

"I'll be back before you know it." He bent his head and kissed the tip of her nose. "Silk will stay here with you until I get back. Won't you, Silk?" He met the big man's knowing eyes.

"Sure," Silk said. "If that's what you want."

Hugh nodded. "That's what I want."

Silk shrugged. "You're the boss. You going to give him the five hundred?"

"Probably. If the information is good."

"Where you going to get that kind of money at this time of night?"

"I'll stop off at the office on the way. There should be a couple of grand in the safe. Derek and Ray got paid in cash for delivering those medical supplies to St. Julian."

Mattie followed as Hugh went toward the door. "You will be careful, won't you?"

"I'll be careful."

"How will you know if Rosey is telling you the truth? Maybe he'll just give you a name, take your money, and run."

"He wouldn't get far," Hugh said. "And I think he's just barely smart enough to know that." He kissed her again and firmly closed the door in her anxious face. He went out to where the Jeep was parked in the drive.

It was starting to rain again. Another squall was about to sweep over the island. The palms rustled in the breeze and the night scents of the jungle were strong.

He was going to miss St. Gabriel for however long he had to stay in Seattle, Hugh thought as he started the Jeep and drove toward the main road. It was odd how the island had become home during the past couple of years. It was the first real home he could remember. He couldn't wait to start building his dream house overlooking the sea. He just knew Mattie was going to love it.

But first he had to survive Seattle.

He drove into town, past the loud taverns and bars, and parked in front of Abbott Charters. He let himself in the front door and walked through the darkened interior to the small office, where he kept a big old-fashioned safe. He switched on the light.

There was nearly five thousand in the safe. Hugh reminded himself to get it to the bank in the morning, and then he counted out five hundred in large bills, folded it up, and stuffed it into his pocket. He'd put it down on the books as petty cash.

On the way out of the office Hugh automatically glanced around with a proud, possessive eye. Abbott Charters was starting to thrive. Another year or two and he would be ready for serious expansion. He considered the business his first and only real accomplishment in life other than keeping himself alive. It was the one positive thing he had ever created from scratch. It was his dream, his future, his hope for a different sort of life than the one he had been living for the past forty years.

He wondered if that was how Mattie felt about her art gallery. The thought was unsettling and he pushed it aside. Mattie would be okay out here. He would see to that.

On the way out the door Hugh ripped the nearest girlie calendar down from the wall and tossed it into the trash can.

Ten minutes later Hugh pulled the Jeep off the road and parked it a discreet distance from the abandoned warehouse on Lily Cove. He walked silently through the jungle to the edge of the clearing, where the sagging structure crouched like a dinosaur carcass in the pale moonlight.

Trust Rosey to pick a suitably picturesque spot for the deal. Hugh frowned as he scanned the clearing for signs of life. Something like this was better handled in the loud, noisy, well-populated environment of the Hellfire. But Rosey obviously preferred scuttling around in the shadows. Once a rat, always a rat.

There was one vehicle parked near the precariously tilted loading dock, a small, rusty compact Rosey had probably picked up at the airport.

The gaping dark opening above the loading dock was the obvious way into the building. Hugh considered it briefly and then decided to enter the warehouse through a side door that hung on its hinges.

There was no sound from the black interior. Outside the rain was starting to fall more heavily. It swept into the building through the wide-open loading dock entrance.

Hugh eased the revolver out of his belt and edged through the doorway and into the shadows. Knowing how swiftly aging wood rotted in this climate, he slid one booted foot along the floor.

The toe of his boot found thin air. Hugh yanked his leg back and glanced down. He could see almost nothing in the shadows but he knew his suspicions were correct. The floorboards had rotted away in sections. He would have to move carefully or risk breaking a leg.

"Rosey?"

There was no response. Hugh kept his shoulder in contact with one wall as he worked his way silently around the building to the loading dock entrance. The rain was thrumming on the roof now, hiding any small sounds that he or anyone else might make.

Something was wrong and Hugh knew it. If all had been well, Rosey would have made his presence known by now and demanded his money.

The figure lying in the rain on the loading dock looked like a heap of old clothing at first. Hugh crouched in the shadows, gun in hand, and stared at the too-still bundle. He swore silently.

*Rosey, you damned fool. Why didn't you meet me in town? Why play games?*

He waited another minute or two, but his senses told him the warehouse was empty except for himself and Rosey. Hugh straightened and went reluctantly over to the rain-soaked body.

Very gently he reached down and turned the bundle over. In the weak light Hugh could see the dark, wet stain that soaked the front of Rosey's shirt. Hugh checked for a pulse.

Rosey groaned softly.

Startled, Hugh hunkered down beside him.

"Rosey?"

"That you, Abbott?" Rosey's eyes fluttered.

"Yeah, Rosey, it's me."

"Son of a bitch got me. Thought I was being so careful. Tell Gibbs, will ya, if you see him. He'll wonder."

"I will. Rosey, who did this?"

"Rain . . ." There was a curious, wondering tone in Rosey's voice before the single word ended in a choking, bloody gargle.

"I know it's raining, Rosey. I'll get you out of it. Who was it, man?"

But Rosey was gone.

Hugh got slowly to his feet and looked down at the little man who had died in the pouring rain.

Two deaths in less than a week. *Damn*, Hugh thought in disgust. Life had been going so well lately, too. And now this.

Just like old times.

Mattie poured another cup of green tea for Silk and watched as he polished off the last of the sweet potato pie she had made for dessert. He had eaten nearly the entire pan.

"So how long have you lived here on St. Gabriel?" Mattie asked.

"Couple of years," Silk said around a mouthful of pie.

"About as long as Hugh, then?"

"Right. Me and him moved out here together."

"Really? Where were you before you arrived here?"

"Here and there." Silk grinned. "No fixed address, I guess you'd say. Hugh was doing odd jobs for Vailcourt, and I just sort of drifted around with him, helping out sometimes."

"Fascinating. Did my aunt know you were on the payroll?"

"Nah. Hugh figured why bother her with the details. She's an executive type. Folks like that only care about the bottom line. He just put me down under petty expenses when he sent his bills into Vailcourt Accounting."

"I see." Mattie hid a smile. "I take it you've known Hugh for a long time?"

"Sure. We been working together for years."

"Where did you meet him?"

Silk scowled, looking thoughtful. "As best as I can remember, I think it was a bar somewhere along the coast of Mexico. I forget the name of the town. Neither of us stayed there long. Had a little trouble."

"You were working in the area?"

"Abbot and I was flying charter for a guy who was running a little operation there. Pretty cushy job but it didn't last long."

Mattie propped her elbows on the table and rested her chin on her folded hands. "You said that job did not last long. What did the two of you do after that?"

Silk grinned. "You plying me with sweet potato pie and tea in order to get me to talk?"

"Just idle curiosity," Mattie explained airily as she got up to clear the table.

"Yeah, well better exercise your idle curiosity on the boss. He'll nail my hide to the wall if I get too chatty."

"Why?" Mattie inquired innocently.

"He doesn't like to talk too much about the past."

"Any particular reason?"

Silk leaned back in his chair, replete. "He pretty much likes to forget his past for the most part. Not the sort who looks back, you know? Abbott's got his eye on the future these days."

"Was Paul Cormier a big part of Hugh's past?"

Silk's engaging grin belied the shrewd intelligence in his big blue eyes. "Cormier? You could say he was an old friend. Hugh's real loyal to old friends. Probably because he hasn't got too many of 'em."

"Anyone else besides you now?"

"Well," said Silk very smoothly, "I reckon there's you, too."

Mattie shot him a quick glance as she filled the cracked sink with hot water. "Hugh and I have not really known each other very long," she murmured. "This is the first time I've seen him in nearly a year."

"I know. He told me you'd been ducking him. He didn't like that." Silk shook his head. "Never seen a female who could make Abbott run around in circles the way he's been doing these past few months. And now you're dragging him all the way off to Seattle. He's gonna hate Seattle."

"Yes," said Mattie. "I know. Don't worry, Silk. He won't be there long."

Silk's eyes narrowed abruptly. "What the hell's that supposed to mean?"

"Just that I'm certain Hugh will soon get tired of Seattle and bored with me when he realizes I have no intention of moving here to St. Gabriel. He'll give up on his big plans to marry me, and he'll be back here before you know it." She smiled bleakly. "After all, he's got a business to run."

Silk looked baffled. "You mean you're taking him back with you even though you know he won't be staying long?"

"I'm not taking him back with me. He's insisting on accompanying me on the return trip."

"Yeah, but that's so's he can convince you that he likes you better than your nitwit sister. He told me all about it."

The sound of the Jeep in the drive halted Mattie's reply. Relief poured through her. "He's back."

"Sure. What did you think he was going to do? Spend the rest of the night drinking at the Hellfire or something? Hugh ain't the type."

"No, I was afraid he was walking into trouble. That Rosey he went to see is not a very nice little man." Mattie quickly dried her hands on the ragged towel and went toward the door.

It opened and Hugh strode into the small hall, shaking the rain from his hair.

"Hugh, I've been so worried. Thank heavens you're all right." Mattie raced forward and threw herself into his arms.

"Well, well, well," Silk said from the other side of the room. He surveyed the couple with a beatific smile. "Ain't that a picture. Maybe this little trip to Seattle is going to turn out all right after all. I left you a slice of pie, boss."

"Thanks," Hugh said over the top of Mattie's head. His eyes met Silk's.

"Trouble?" Silk asked.

"Yeah."

"Mattie had a hunch there would be," Silk said with a sigh.

"I still can't believe that Rosey's dead," Mattie said two hours later as she paced the floor of Hugh's small beach house. "Whoever killed him could have killed you, too. I knew that meeting was going to be dangerous. I just had a feeling."

"Well, it wasn't. Not for me, at any rate." Hugh opened the refrigerator and reached inside for a beer. "Just for Rosey."

"So now you and Silk are back to square one as far as finding Cormier's murderer goes." Mattie rubbed her palms up and down her bare arms. Silk had left an hour ago after Hugh had gone through all the details of his late-night meeting at the warehouse. The big man had not seemed particularly shocked by Rosey's death. It was almost as if he was accustomed to that kind of news.

"We'll find him."

"How are you going to do that in Seattle?" Mattie asked.

"Silk will be in touch if anything turns up. Seattle's not the end of the world."

"Aren't there police or federal agencies who should be handling this kind of thing?"

"Not on Purgatory. They're in the middle of a coup over there, remember?" Hugh went across the room and opened a cupboard.

Mattie watched him pull out a well-worn khaki green duffel bag that looked as though it had been hauled around the world several times. She sank down onto a wicker chair and watched as Hugh carried numerous changes of underwear and shirts out of the bedroom and dumped them into the duffel bag.

"Why the rush? Why do we have to leave tomorrow?" she asked. The sense of urgency had been hovering in the air ever since Hugh had walked back in the door.

"No sense hanging around here. Silk's going to look after Abbott Charters for me. We might as well head to Seattle."

"There's more to it than that, isn't there? You're more worried about this second murder than you want to admit. You're afraid there might be some danger here for me, aren't you? Hugh, if finding Cormier's killer is so important to you, why don't you stay here on St. Gabriel and I'll go home by myself?"

"Sure. And start ducking me again every time I try to call or see you? Not a chance, babe. I'm not letting you out of my sight this time. You want proof I'm serious about marrying you. You're going to get it."

"Damn it, Hugh, I know you're serious about marrying me. That's not the point. It's the *reason* you want to marry me that I don't trust."

He stopped packing the duffel bag and stood, feet braced, hands on hips, and regarded her with grim intent. "Now, you listen and listen good, babe. I want to marry you for all the normal reasons. I want a wife and a home, a real home. I want to have someone to talk to in the evenings, someone to warm my bed, someone to eat with, someone who gives a damn if I come home late. What's not to trust about that?"

She stared at him, her hands twisting together in her lap. "There are a lot of women who would be glad to do all that for you."

"I don't want a lot of women. I want you." He took two long strides over to where she was sitting and lifted her to her feet. "And I do not want to hear another word about my staying here on St. Gabe while you flit back to Seattle. Understood?"

Mattie looked up at him sadly. "I don't think it's going to work, Hugh."

"Leave it to me, babe. I always get the job done."

# 9

❧

Three days later Mattie picked up a canapé from a passing tray and surveyed the throng of well-dressed people milling around a prestigious Seattle gallery.

Plastic champagne glasses were everywhere. They were in people's hands, overflowing the wastebaskets, and standing around on every available empty surface. There were also a lot of little paper napkins, bits and pieces of canapés, and discarded programs. Most of the people in the room seemed more interested in being seen themselves than in looking at the art that hung on the walls.

Not that the art on the walls was not good. It was. The gallery was showing some of the best avant-garde stuff ever done on the West Coast. The show was, after all, a retrospective display of the works of Ariel Sharpe.

The canvases had been grouped according to the artist's four clearly recognized periods: her Early Dark period, her Exploratory period, her short-lived Elemental period, and the latest, which had been dubbed her Early Mature period.

Mattie caught a few of the snippets of conversation going on around her. *"The emotion is incredible, right from the first . . . such brilliant use of color, even in the Early Dark period, when she was using only black and brown . . . a sense of cataclysmic inevitability . . . a surprisingly shocking use of line, but she was getting divorced from Blackwell at the time, and that kind of thing always has an impact with her. She's so emotional . . . a bit rough and crude,* Art Brut, *if you will, but it is from her Elemental period, after all. . . ."*

Mattie had no trouble recognizing the talent in her sister's work. The strong sense of line and color added an emotional sophistication and a visually compelling quality to the abstract designs which took them far beyond the ordinary and into the realm of the brilliant.

And the expensive.

Mattie nibbled her canapé and unconsciously began tapping the toe of her black leather pump. She glanced at the black and gold watch on her wrist.

Hugh was due a half hour ago. He had promised to show up at the opening right after his meeting with Charlotte Vailcourt. The meeting had been scheduled for four o'clock and it was now nearly six.

She knew he had not been looking forward to tonight's event, but Mattie had insisted he attend. Going to openings was part of her world, and if he was determined to fit into that world, he could darn well make an effort to learn something about it.

Mattie glanced impatiently at her watch again. She was beginning to suspect that Hugh was deliberately stringing out the meeting with her aunt in order to avoid the gallery show. She was wondering if she should phone Charlotte's office when a voice hailed her from halfway across the crowded room.

"Mattie, you're back from paradise. I thought you'd be gone another week or so. It was supposed to be a vacation, wasn't it?"

Mattie turned her head to smile at the tall, blond Viking god making his way toward her through the throng. "Hello, Flynn. I got back early. Paradise is not all it's cracked up to be. Things didn't go according to schedule, but I guess that's what happens when you take the budget tour package."

"Well, glad you're back safe and sound. And glad you could make it here tonight." Flynn Grafton was a striking man by any standards. His mane of pale hair was pulled back in a ponytail at the base of his neck, a dramatic contrast to his all-black attire, which consisted of black multipleated pants, a black shirt with wide, flowing sleeves, and black boots polished to a high gloss. The only ornament was a silver Egyptian ankh he wore around his throat.

"Looks like another successful show for Ariel," Mattie observed.

Flynn nodded proudly. "It turned out well, didn't it? Elizabeth Kenyon always does a great job. Good crowd. The usual number of moochers who always float from one opening to another for the free munchies, naturally, but what the heck. They add color."

Mattie chuckled. "I thought I saw Shock Value Frederickson and a couple of her friends nibbling her way through the hors d'oeuvres."

"Starving artists, one and all. But there are some genuine buyers here. It's going well. Ariel will be pleased."

"Speaking of Ariel, where is she? I've been here over half an hour, and I haven't seen her yet."

Flynn's noble brow contracted in a brief frown of concern. "I don't know. She was due fifteen minutes ago. She was planning on making her usual entrance after everyone had arrived. I called home, but there was no answer."

"She must have gotten held up in traffic."

"Probably." Flynn's expression of concern relaxed slightly. "She's been sort of tense lately. To tell you the truth, I'm a little worried about her."

"Ariel's high strung, Flynn. You know that."

He shook his head and munched a canapé. "This is different."

"Any idea why she's more tense than usual?"

"Sure. I've been pointing out that her biological clock is ticking. She's three years older than you, Mattie. Thirty-five. If we're going to have a kid, we'd better get moving. The whole notion has her panicked."

Mattie gave him a startled look. "I can imagine. I thought Ariel had decided not to have children years ago. I distinctly remember her telling me that the day she married you. Said it would interfere with her art."

Flynn smiled complacently. "She's just scared because of her track record in love and marriage. After all, she's already been divorced once and lord only knows how many engagements got broken along the way."

"Ariel? Scared? That's a crock. Believe me, Flynn, my sister has more pure, unadulterated self-confidence than anyone else I know except possibly a certain party she was once engaged to last year."

"You may be her sister, Mattie. But you don't really understand her the way I do. Never mind. I'm glad she's running late and I'm glad you're here. Gives us a chance to talk. I've been thinking it over, and I want do some stuff for your gallery. Were you serious about taking a look at some of my work?"

"Any time, Flynn. But you know as well as I do the kind of thing I hang. I'm very commercially oriented. That means I can't use your experimental work."

"I know, I know. But I've got a series in mind that would be perfect for Sharpe Reaction clients."

"Ariel will have a fit," Mattie warned gently. "She'll probably try to strangle us both. You know what she thinks about the kind of stuff I sell."

Flynn smiled wryly. "Yeah. Commercial schlock. Don't worry about Ariel. I'll handle her. This is between you and me."

"If you say so. Flynn, you know I'll be glad to look at anything you bring me. You really have a great talent. Ariel's quite right about that. You're just undiscovered, that's all. Unlike her."

"I'll tell you something, Mattie. Undiscovered talent is about as useful as feathers on a hog. Look, why don't I bring some canvases by in a few days?" He broke off and glanced toward the door. "Ah, there she is. About time she got here. Who's that with her?"

Mattie turned her head to follow his glance. Her stomach clenched with a sick feeling that could only be jealousy. She fought to control it. "That," she told Flynn, "is Hugh Abbott. Ariel was once engaged to him."

"Oh, yeah. The guy from her Elemental period, right?"

"Right."

"That was really a dead-end direction for her," Flynn said, dismissing Hugh with ease.

"Yes, I thought the same thing at the time." Mattie watched her sister descend like a queen on the gathering.

Ariel was especially striking tonight. But, then, her sister always looked dramatic. Her lustrous black hair, translucent white skin, and exotic green eyes lent themselves quite naturally to drama of all kinds.

Ariel applied the same intuitive sense of design to her clothes as she did to her art. She had favored black for years, ever since her Early Dark period. It still suited her, although her painting had become much more colorful. Tonight she was riveting in a totally black strapless gown and black high-heeled sandals.

Her jewelry consisted of only a pair of jet earrings that dangled to her shoulders. Her sleek black hair was parted in the middle and worn in a shining wedge that gave her finely chiseled features the air of an Egyptian princess.

The only touches of color on Ariel were her scarlet mouth and her startling green eyes.

Mattie thought wistfully of the little red satin sarong she had brought back with her from the islands. It would have made quite a splash here tonight. But, of course, it would have been totally inappropriate, she told herself firmly. The conservative gray business suit and pastel silk blouse she had on was what she always wore to this sort of function. Only the artist was supposed to look exotic or outrageous.

She saw Hugh scanning the room with an impatient glance. He was wearing the one jacket he owned, a rather battered-looking navy blue blazer over a white shirt and his usual pair of jeans. He also had on his boots. There was no tie.

His eyes met hers, and she smiled wryly. He started toward her, leaving Ariel amid a circle of admirers.

"How well do you know this guy?" Flynn asked, helping himself to another canapé.

"Why do you ask?"

"Because he looks annoyed."

"That's his usual expression." Mattie locked her smile in place as Hugh came to a halt in front of her and glanced pointedly at Flynn.

"Hello, Hugh," Mattie said. "I don't believe you've met Flynn Grafton. A wonderful artist. He married Ariel about six months ago."

Hugh nodded brusquely and shook the hand Flynn offered. "Congratulations," he said crisply.

"Thanks. I hear you're the guy from Ariel's Elemental period."

Hugh's expression got darker. "That's not exactly how I think of it."

"Hey, don't be embarrassed. I can see why you wouldn't want to be associated with that particular time frame in her work. I mean, we all know it was a useless digression when taken in the total context of her art, but the stuff she did during that period is very collectible. People are paying a fortune for it simply because it was such an odd detour, professionally speaking."

"Is that right?" Hugh muttered.

"Personally, I've always kind of liked some of the stuff from that period. There's a certain rough-edged, primitive quality to it. Rather like early Ashton or Clyde Harding."

Hugh's mouth was a humorless line. "Look, do you mind if I talk to Mattie for a few minutes? In private?"

"No, no, take your time," Flynn said. "I'll see how Ariel's doing. Talk to you later, Mattie."

"Fine." Mattie took a sip of her champagne and watched Flynn saunter away through the crowd.

"All right, spit it out." Hugh grabbed a plastic glass from a passing tray.

"Spit what out?" Mattie asked politely.

"You want to know why I'm late and why I arrived with Ariel." Hugh swallowed most of the contents of the glass in one gulp.

"I do?"

"The answers are that, A, the meeting with Charlotte ran late and, B, Ariel was just getting out of a cab in front of this joint when I arrived. I couldn't avoid walking in with her."

"I see."

"Good." Apparently considering the subject closed, Hugh glowered down at her. "Now, what's with you and Grafton?"

Mattie glanced up in astonishment. "What on earth are you talking about?"

"He was looking at you the way a dog looks at a bone. Real intense."

Mattie shrugged. "He's an artist. Artists are always intense in one way or another. He wants me to look at some of his work. I said I would. That's all there was to it. What did you and Charlotte decide?"

Hugh frowned, looking as if he wanted to pursue the topic of Flynn Grafton. But he reluctantly altered course. "Everything's swell, just like I told you. She's happy to keep me on the payroll and says I can work here at the home office for as long as I want. Won't have to travel."

"What are you going to do here at headquarters?"

"She wants a new security plan worked up that can be implemented at all the Vailcourt offices around the world. I told her no problem."

"And how long will you be happy doing that, Hugh? I see you as a field man, not an office type."

"The experience will be good for me," he told her. "The more I learn about the business end of running a corporation, the better."

"Because you plan to go back to St. Gabriel to run Abbott Charters eventually, don't you? Admit it. You see this Seattle jaunt as just a short hiatus you have to tolerate until I come to my senses and see the light, right?"

"Forget Abbott Charters and forget St. Gabe. I don't feel like arguing right now. Who's this heading our way?"

Mattie looked across the room and heaved a small sigh. "It never rains but it pours."

"What's that mean?"

"Just that there's quite a crowd of Ariel's exes here tonight. That's Ariel's first husband, Emery Blackwell. From her Early Dark and Exploratory periods. They were married five years."

"He looks drunk as a skunk."

"He probably is." Mattie bit her lip in concern.

Emery hid his problem fairly well. He was in his late fifties, but he had the craggy, slightly dissipated good looks that suited authors whose status had once been near-mythical in high-level literary circles. He was aging well, in spite of his increasing fondness for the bottle. It was true his jaw was getting a bit thick and there was evidence of a certain softness around his midsection, but he paid attention to his clothes, and they, in turn, hid a multitude of sins. His shock of silver-gray hair was as stunning as ever, and his pale eyes brimmed with intelligence, even when they were slightly bloodshot.

Mattie had always liked Emery, and he had always treated her with an avuncular affection.

"He's been under a lot of stress in the past few years," Mattie confided softly to Hugh as Emery approached. "His career has been in the doldrums for ages, although he still gets tapped for lectures and readings occasionally."

"More stress, huh? Is that the cause of everybody's problems back here in the States these days?"

"A large portion of them, yes." Mattie smiled at Emery as he came to a halt in front of her and inclined his head with regal grace.

"Mattie, my love, you look positively splendid, as always. How would you like to join me on Whidbey for a few days? I could use a muse. Bring something comfortable to change into, dear. We'll drink cognac and talk about poetry."

"You know I never really got the hang of poetry, Emery. And you look pretty splendid yourself, tonight." Mattie went on tiptoe to give him a small peck on the cheek. "But, then, you always do."

"It's called style, my dear. Some of us have it—" Emery broke off to give Hugh an amused head-to-toe glance. "And some of us don't. Pray introduce me to your rustic friend, Mattie. He is a friend, I assume, and not a hired thug?"

"Hugh Abbott," Hugh announced coldly. "I'm going to marry Mattie."

"Good lord, Mattie." Emery turned back to her with an expression of stagy astonishment. "I told you that you should have invited me to go along when you went on vacation. Send you out to the wilds of the Pacific alone and look what happens. You come back with a really tacky souvenir."

"I may be tacky, but Mattie thinks I'm cute." Hugh shoved an entire canapé between his teeth and bit down hard.

"Mattie's tastes have always been a little plebeian, to say the least. That's why she's been so successful with her gallery. And it may explain her problem with men."

Mattie scowled at both males. "That's enough out of both of you. If you want to squabble, go outside in the alley."

"Much too physical. I wouldn't lower myself to that sort of activity, my dear," Emery demurred.

"I would." Hugh stuck another entire round of cheese-and-pimiento-decorated cracker into his mouth and chewed vigorously, showing his teeth. "Any time, Blackwell."

"Dear, dear. Where ever did you find him, Mattie?"

"I didn't. Aunt Charlotte did. He works for her."

"That explains it, of course." Emery smiled benignly at Hugh. "Charlotte Vailcourt is a noted eccentric."

"Pay's good, too," Hugh said.

Mattie lifted her eyes toward heaven in a silent plea that was answered almost immediately when a handsome, rather hard-eyed woman in her late forties joined the small group. She was an imposing female built along statuesque lines, who favored southwestern turquoise and silver jewelry.

"Hello, everyone," Elizabeth Kenyon said cheerfully. "I do hope you're enjoying yourselves." Her hazel eyes were bright with the glow of success.

Elizabeth Kenyon's gallery was one of the most important on the West Coast, and everyone knew it. She catered to wealthy collectors whose only goal was to be considered at the vanguard of the contemporary art movement.

Elizabeth, herself, was important both socially and in the art world. She could make or break an artist, and she had done both frequently. She had a reputation for being able to cow clients into buying anything she told them was collectible, and she had broken the creative spirits of artists whose works she deemed retrograde.

Mattie admired Elizabeth Kenyon enormously. Although Mattie, herself, had a different taste in art and knew she was much too soft-hearted for her own good when it came to dealing with artists and clients, she respected Elizabeth's success. Someday, Mattie sincerely hoped, Sharpe Reaction would be in the same league as Elizabeth Kenyon's gallery.

"Good evening, Elizabeth," Emery said with another gracious inclination of his head. "Fantastic bash, as always."

"Thank you, Emery. You know how thrilled I am that you were able to attend. Your presence is always an asset at this sort of thing." She turned to Mattie. "Who is your friend, Matilda, my dear?"

"Hugh Abbott," Mattie said.

"Mattie's fiancé," Hugh drawled, sliding Mattie a mildly disgusted glance as he completed the introduction. The warning gleam in his eyes made it clear he was getting tired of having to explain his status in Mattie's life.

"Abbott. Abbott. Abbott. Now, where have I . . . ? Oh, yes." Elizabeth's eyes brightened. "Weren't you the one from Ariel's Elemental period?"

"Excuse me," Emery Blackwell said, drawing himself up and reaching for another glass of champagne. "I believe this is where I came in. I think I shall go mingle. See you later, Mattie. Elizabeth." He ignored Hugh, who, in turn, ignored him.

"Later, Emery," Mattie said, raising her glass in a small farewell.

Elizabeth frowned at Emery's retreating back. "I'm afraid dear Emery has not only become rather passé, but he doesn't handle his liquor as well these days as he used to. I rather wish he had not bothered to attend tonight. But I suppose he couldn't resist. In spite of the divorce, he still feels a sort of paternal interest in Ariel's success."

"Well, he was a major influence on her early work," Mattie said, feeling obliged to defend Emery. "And he introduced her to all the right people back at the beginning. That certainly didn't hurt."

"Nonsense. She already knew most of the right people through her own family connections." Elizabeth smiled at Hugh. "How long will you be staying in Seattle, Hugh?"

Hugh caught Mattie's eye. "As long as it takes."

"I see." Elizabeth looked momentarily blank at the oblique answer. Then she nodded to both of them and moved off through the crowd.

"Matilda, dear, how are you?" said a new voice at Mattie's elbow. "I just spoke to your sister a few minutes ago. She tells me your parents couldn't be here tonight."

"Hello, Mrs. Eberly. Good to see you again. Ariel's right. Mom and Dad are both busy. Mom's teaching in an artists-in-residence program at a private college back East this spring, and Dad went with her. He wants to finish his book on the Modern-Postmodern continuum and thought this would be a good opportunity to do it. Do you know Hugh Abbott?"

The elderly woman turned to Hugh. "Abbott. No, I don't believe I do." Her bright eyes widened. "Unless, of course, you're the one from Ariel's—"

"Don't say it," Hugh advised with a wry smile. "If I hear about Ariel's Elemental period one more time tonight, I think I'm going to be sick all over a tray of canapés."

"Well, it wasn't one of her best periods, was it?" Mrs. Eberly said, patting his hand consolingly. "But that's not to say you should feel personally responsible for it, my boy. After all, some good did come out of it."

"Yeah. She broke off the engagement. I've been feeling grateful for months."

"That wasn't quite what I meant," Mrs. Eberly murmured. "What is this rumor I hear about you and Matilda, here, being engaged?"

"It's a fact," Hugh said roughly. "Not a rumor."

"Where did you hear that, Mrs. Eberly?" Mattie asked.

"Gossip, my dear. You know how it is. I pride myself on being something of a sponge when it comes to gossip. I soak it up wherever I go. Can't imagine you married to someone who wears boots and jeans, but, then, they always say opposites attract."

"Mattie and I actually have quite a bit in common," Hugh said.

Mattie smiled brilliantly up at him. "Such as?"

"You want a list?" he asked with soft menace.

"That would be fascinating." Mattie deliberately turned back to

Mrs. Eberly, who was watching the scene with a fascinated gleam in her shrewd brown eyes. "By the way, Mrs. Eberly, I've got another one of Lingart's red pieces in the gallery, if you're interested."

"Thank you, Matilda. Hold on to it for me, will you? I do believe he's starting to move into his yellow period. There won't be too many more reds, I'm afraid. And I do so want to corner the market."

"It's yours," Mattie promised. "But if you think the Lingart painting is good, just wait until you see what I brought back with me from the islands."

"You mean besides this fine specimen of machismo?" Mrs. Eberly gave Hugh a smiling glance.

"Much more collectible, I assure you," Mattie said. "The artist's name is Taggert. Silk Taggert. I'm planning an opening for his work a week from Friday."

"Count on me, dear. I love everything you've ever sold me." She swept the art that was hanging around Elizabeth Kenyon's gallery with a single raking glance. "I realize this sort of thing is very avant-garde and quite the in thing. Quite formidable in its own way. But the sad truth is, I really don't want it hanging in my home, if you know what I mean. I don't *enjoy* looking at it. When I buy something for my own home, I want to just love looking at it every time I walk into the room."

"You're in good company, Mrs. Eberly. The Medicis and the Borgias and a few other notable art collectors from the past had the same idea about art collecting."

Hugh frowned and started to make a comment, but at that particular moment the crowd parted to reveal Ariel sweeping down on them. Her exotic emerald eyes were on her sister.

"Mattie, I can't believe this thing about you and Hugh." Ariel gave her sister a delicate hug of greeting while she narrowed her eyes at Hugh. "What in the world do you think you're doing?"

"Well, I—"

"Never mind," Ariel said briskly, stepping back, "we'll discuss it later. This isn't the time or the place. I understand you've been talking to Flynn. I want to discuss that little matter with you, also. I'll drop by the gallery tomorrow sometime."

"Fine," Mattie said quietly.

A group of moneyed-looking people moved up to commandeer Ariel's attention. She turned to them at once and moved off toward one of the paintings from her Exploratory period.

Elizabeth Kenyon materialized beside Mattie again. "Mattie, dear, would you do me an enormous favor?" she whispered.

"What's that?"

"Get Blackwell into a cab or something. He's becoming a bit obnoxious. I don't want him upsetting any of the clients. I swear, I'll be forever in your debt if you'll get him out of here for me."

Mattie groaned, glancing across the crowded room to where Emery Blackwell was in serious danger of dumping the contents of his glass into the cleavage of a Wagnerian lady of middling years. "All right, Liz. But, remember, you owe me."

"Thank you, dear." She smiled as she turned away, her hard eyes straying once more toward Hugh. "You always did have a way of picking up the bits and pieces Ariel leaves behind in her wake, didn't you, Mattie?"

Mattie gritted her teeth and went toward Emery. She was vaguely aware that Hugh was following her through the throng.

"There you are, Emery," she said when she reached his side. "I've been looking for you." Mattie deftly removed the glass from his hand. "There's someone just dying to meet you." She flashed the large woman a placating smile. "Will you excuse us? Emery is always in such demand."

"Of course," the woman said, looking vaguely disappointed.

"Mattie, my love, you arrived just in the nick of time," Emery murmured as she led him away. "I do believe I was about to make a descent down an extremely treacherous precipice without benefit of proper climbing apparatus. Haven't seen a woman built along those lines in a good ten or fifteen years." Emery cast a last, wistful glance at the massive bosom he was forsaking. "They just don't make them like that anymore."

"Oh, I don't know about that," Hugh said easily. "I've got some calendars back in my office that have pictures of females built like that."

"You would," Emery agreed.

Mattie sighed. "Emery, you're getting drunk and you always get obnoxious when you drink."

"Kind of you to notice. I do try. Where are we going?"

"You're going home in a cab," Mattie said as she steered him toward the door.

"I've got a better idea. Why don't we go get a bite to eat? Just you and me, of course. Leave the Elemental creature behind."

Hugh crowded close as he followed the pair out the door. "Forget it, Blackwell. Mattie and I already have plans."

"Pity," Emery said.

"Hey, Mattie," Flynn called, hurrying toward the three, who were halfway through the door. "Leaving already?"

"Afraid so," Mattie said.

"Don't think it hasn't been fun," Hugh growled.

"Look, I'll get those canvases to you as soon as possible, Mattie." Flynn followed them all out onto the sidewalk and stood waiting with them until a cruising cab pulled into the passenger loading zone.

"That'll be great, Flynn. But, like I said, Ariel is not going to approve."

"Don't worry about it." Flynn opened the cab door and ushered Blackwell inside.

Mattie slid in beside Emery.

"Where the hell are you going?" Hugh demanded as he watched Mattie get into the cab.

"Home. I think I've had enough champagne and soggy canapés tonight. Want to come along? We're on Emery's way."

Hugh glared at her in frustration and then got into the backseat of the cab beside her.

"You three have a nice evening," Flynn said casually, bending down to say good-bye.

"Shit," said Hugh.

"My sentiments exactly," Emery Blackwell intoned as the cab pulled away from the curb.

"You shouldn't have been there tonight, Emery," Mattie admonished. "You promised me you would stay up at your place on Whidbey Island until you got the second book of the Byron St. Cyr series completed."

"Now, don't scold, Mattie, my love. I deserve a break. I swear on my honor as an aging scholar who has sold his soul to the devil of commercial fiction, I will head straight back to Whidbey tomorrow. I just couldn't resist attending that opening tonight." He looked across Mattie at Hugh, who was filling up a large chunk of the cab. "What about you, Abbott?"

"What about me?"

"Don't you feel a certain perverse pleasure in seeing your influence in Ariel's work? A little claim to artistic immortality, eh?"

"Bull."

"Succinctly put. A man of few words. Well, as for myself, all I can say is, I'll take my moments of fame when and where I can. All glory is fleeting. Do you know I actually had to explain to a couple of people in that gallery just who I was, Mattie? A humbling experience."

"Don't worry, there will be a whole new level of fame waiting for you when you emerge as the mysterious author of the best-selling Byron St. Cyr series," Mattie said gently. "Stop feeling sorry for yourself and start looking forward to the day you get to sign autographs at the mall."

"Dear Lord," Emery moaned. "What a fate. Autographs at the mall. I have truly made a devil's bargain, Mattie Sharpe. And it's all your doing."

"Your first book will be out in the stores in a couple of weeks, Emery, and you're going to feel much different when you see it selling like hotcakes. Trust me."

"My future is in your hands, Mattie, love."

Ten minutes later the cab pulled up in front of the restored early-nineteenth-century building in Pioneer Square that housed Mattie's large loft apartment. Mattie and Hugh climbed out, and after a bit of quiet nudging, Hugh reluctantly paid the fare, including enough to cover the cost of getting Emery Blackwell to his Capitol Hill residence.

The cab departed with Emery sitting regally in the backseat. Mattie dug out her keys and opened the security door of her building.

"What an evening," Hugh muttered as he punched the elevator call in the hallway.

"A little different from the Hellfire on a Saturday night, isn't it?" Mattie observed.

"Give me the Hellfire anytime."

"You'd better get used to evenings like this one, Hugh," Mattie told him sweetly. "I go to several openings a month and hold a lot myself during the year for my own artists. I'm sure you'll want to accompany me to each and every one. After all, you intend to be a part of my life here in Seattle, don't you?"

"For as long as it takes," Hugh said grimly.

# 10

⁂

That night it occurred to Hugh for the first time that things were not going to go as smoothly or as easily as he had anticipated.

He sprawled on Mattie's black leather couch amid a tangle of sheets, his hands folded behind his head. It was nearly two in the morning, but the view through the high, curving windows that lined Mattie's huge studio was neon-bright. The glow of city lights at night always irritated Hugh. He preferred the velvet, flower-scented darkness of an island night. If he closed his eyes, he could conjure up a mental image of pale moonlight falling like cream on the sea.

Seeing Mattie in her world tonight had been more of a shock than it should have been. After all, he knew what she did for a living; knew her sister and something about the family. Why had it been surprising to see Mattie looking so at home amid that crowd at the gallery? he wondered.

A part of him knew the answer. He had not wanted to admit that she was a part of that world. For the past several months he had been remembering the night of passion followed by her soft plea to take her with him back to the islands. *Take me with you, Hugh. I love you so much. Please take me with you.* And for the past week he'd had her out there on his territory, where he made the rules and where he felt comfortable.

When he had arrived here in Seattle with her three days ago and moved into her glossy apartment, he had been confident of his ability to convince her to move to St. Gabriel within a matter of days. He had been so certain that all he needed was a little time to overcome the feminine pique she felt because of his past engagement to Ariel.

Now things were looking a lot more complicated than they had appeared from St. Gabe. A new sense of uncertainty was gnawing at his insides.

And after two nights he was already damn tired of sleeping on the couch.

Hugh tossed aside the covers of his makeshift bed and got to his feet. He crossed the red and gray carpet that designated what he thought of as the living room area of the huge studio and padded over the gleaming wooden floors to the windows. He stood there for a long while watching a late-night ferry crossing Elliott Bay.

Still restless, he wandered over to the kitchen area and rummaged around in the shadows until he found the sack of oat bran muffins Mattie had bought for breakfast. He pulled one out and took a bite. He didn't think he was ever going to become a big fan of oat bran, but he'd eaten worse things in his life. Paul Cormier's sun-dried tomatoes, for instance.

That recollection brought back a lot of other memories, some of them unpleasant. But most of all it brought back the image of the gaping red hole in Cormier's chest.

Hugh had never had a lot of friends. Cormier had been one of the few. Truth was, for a while there, Cormier had been more than a friend. He'd been almost a father in some ways back in the early years, when Hugh had still been searching for himself and a way to test his own young manhood. From Paul he had learned a lot of the important things, like how to have pride in himself, how to live by a code of honor. And how to survive.

Hugh was suddenly, acutely aware of his deep loneliness. The sensation came more and more frequently of late. The only time it was ever really banished was when he was making love to Mattie.

A soft sound from above made him turn and look up at the open loft-style bedroom that jutted out over the living area. The loft had a shiny red metal railing around it. Mattie's bed was lost in the shadows behind the railing.

Mattie was the one who could banish the loneliness.

Hugh came to a decision. He put down the half-finished oat bran muffin and walked over to the narrow spiral staircase. Silently he climbed up the wrought-iron steps to Mattie's bedroom aerie.

Tonight at the gallery he had experienced genuine uneasiness as he had watched Flynn Grafton and Emery Blackwell hover around Mattie as if they had a prior claim on her.

This was not a sure thing he had going with Mattie, after all. He could lose her, Hugh thought, and he knew of only one way to reassert his own claim on her. He needed some reassurance. He had to know she still wanted him physically, even if she was trying to talk herself out of wanting him as a husband.

He had to know that on some level, at least, she was still his, the way she had been since their first night together all those months ago.

Mattie was still wide awake when she sensed Hugh's presence near the bed. She had been unable to sleep since she had climbed the stairs to her little fortress in the sky two hours ago.

Some part of her had known this would happen, if not tonight, then tomorrow night or the next. Soon. The inevitable could not be postponed for long. The attraction between herself and Hugh ran too deep, and the fear that she might still be in love with him was too strong to ignore. She turned slowly to see him standing beside the bed, wearing only his briefs.

"Hugh?"

"Tell me you want me, Mattie. At least give me that much."

"I want you. You know that. That isn't the point."

"It is tonight." He leaned down, lifted the covers, and crawled in beside her. "If you don't want me to touch you, I won't. But I can't take any more nights alone down there on your couch." He reached out and caressed the curve of her shoulder. "I've spent too damn many nights alone, babe."

Mattie searched his face for a long moment and then, with a small sigh of surrender, she raised herself up on her elbow and kissed his sensual mouth. Her lips grazed fleetingly across his. Her fingers glided over his hard chest like butterflies.

"*Mattie.*" Hugh's groan of relief came from deep within him. He half lifted himself and pushed her eagerly back onto the pillows. Then he came down on top of her like a ton of bricks.

Mattie lay crushed beneath Hugh's weight, her mouth open to him. She was aware of his big hands moving hungrily on her, sliding down over her breasts to her stomach and lower. He wedged his leg between her thighs, prying them apart, and then his hand was on her in an intimate caress.

Mattie gasped, feeling herself growing warm and moist almost instantly. His tongue filled her mouth. She arched her hips, straining against him, and her head tilted back over his arm.

"That's it, babe. God, yes. So hot. So wet. So good." He settled himself quickly between her legs and reached down to wrap her thighs around his hips. "Squeeze me tight, babe. Take me inside and hold me."

Mattie felt the heat and excitement flood her senses. She wanted to tell him to slow down, but she could not find the words. It was all so hard and fast and overwhelming with Hugh. Making love with him was as primitive an experience as swimming in the sea or running through a jungle. There seemed to be no slow, delicate, civilized way to do it.

She could feel his manhood prodding at her now, feel his fingers parting the soft petals, guiding himself into her.

"Tight," he said in husky wonder as he flexed his hips to drive himself deep inside. "Babe, you feel so damn good."

And then he was in all the way, filling her, stretching her, setting off five-alarm fires at each of her nerve endings. His mouth covered hers again, and his possession of it was as deep and damp and complete as his possession of the slick, tight, sensitive sheath between her legs.

Mattie closed her eyes and let go of whatever strings still bound her to earth. She put her arms around Hugh and clung to him with all her strength.

It was a wild, glorious run through the night with a giant wolf. She was free at last and with her true mate. There was nothing soft or gentle about the trip, but when it all ended in a shower of tiny, delicious convulsions that rippled through her, Mattie was exultant.

She turned her face into the pillow and took long, deep breaths.

"Mattie?"

"Yes?"

"From now on I sleep up here with you. Do we agree on that much, at least?"

"Yes."

"You see?" Hugh chuckled in the darkness as he rolled onto his back. "We do have a lot in common."

"Sex isn't everything, Hugh."

"No, but it's a start." He sounded lazy and satisfied. "A damn good start. And it isn't all we've got going for us," he added around a huge yawn. "I told you that earlier tonight."

"So just what do we have in common?" She was curious in spite of herself. Mattie propped herself up on her elbows and looked down at him. "Go on, Hugh. Name one thing."

The intensity in his silvery-gray eyes was clear even in the shadows. "Don't you understand? We're both misfits, babe. Changelings. Round pegs in square holes for most of our lives."

Mattie blinked, startled. Then she frowned. "That's not true."

"It's true. I think you recognized it first. That's probably why you begged me to take you with me a year ago. You understood it instinctively then, but after I left you behind you were too angry to give me a second chance. Now you're making up excuses, telling yourself I only want you because I didn't get Ariel. You're bent on trying to convince me our lifestyles are too different to allow us to get together."

"Our lifestyles *are* too different. There's no compromise possible for us, Hugh. And you did want Ariel at first. You can't deny it. You still wanted her, even after you made love to me that first time."

"No."

"Yes, it's true, damn it. You said I wasn't your type, remember? 'Thank you very much for the roll in the hay, but I've got a plane to the islands to catch.' "

"You're running scared, Mattie," he said gently. "Why don't you admit it? I know it took everything you had to make your big offer a year ago, and I was a fool for turning it down. But you've got plenty of guts, babe. I know that for sure now after watching you handle yourself out in the islands. Why not give our relationship another chance? A real chance?"

She sucked in her breath on a fierce exclamation. "I don't have to make my offer again, remember? You've already made yours. You chose to follow me to Seattle. You're here now, so I don't have to go back there, do I?"

They were silent for a long time while they gazed at each other through the shadows. It was a contest of wills. Mattie could feel Hugh's determination beating at her, looking for weak spots. She held herself very still, the way a rabbit did when confronted by a wolf.

And then the wolf grinned. "Relax, babe. It's going to work out. You'll see. You just need a little time to learn to trust me. Now, go to sleep. We've both got to go to work tomorrow."

"Hugh," Mattie said on a wave of genuine anxiety, "do you like working at Vailcourt headquarters?"

"I've worked in worse places."

"You don't like it. You hate it, don't you? You're not an urban person, Hugh. We both know that."

"Don't worry about it. Like I said, I've worked in worse places."

"But, Hugh—"

"Hush, babe. Go to sleep." He pulled her against his side, cradling her close to his hard, lean strength, and put one muscled leg over her slender calf.

Mattie sensed him slipping into sleep within minutes. But she lay awake for a long time.

Mattie lounged back in her chair behind the tiny desk in her office and studied the bizarre-looking creature in front of her.

Shock Value Frederickson, as she was calling herself this month, was about twenty-five years old. She was thin to the point of being scrawny and had a lot of chartreuse hair that stood out in a stiff, gelled halo around her head. She was wearing a couple of dozen clanking metal bracelets on each arm and four rings in each ear. She also had a ring in her nose, a delicate steel one. Her light hazel eyes were outlined in black and gold, and her clothes were a hodgepodge of Salvation Army rejects held together by a heavy metal belt.

"So what do you think, Mattie?" Shock Value indicated her latest metal sculpture, which was sitting on the floor beside her chair. "Will you handle it for me?"

Mattie sighed. "You're obviously still in your End-of-the-World period, Shock. It's interesting, but we both know it's not going to appeal to my clients. Maybe Christine Ferguson's gallery can handle it."

Shock Value squirmed uneasily in her chair. Metal jangled on her wrists and ears. "She didn't want it, either. Neither did anyone else I tried. Mattie, I'm in kind of a bad spot at the moment. I spent my last ten bucks on supplies, and I haven't sold anything in months."

"I thought you were getting by with that restaurant job I lined up for you."

"I was. And it was really great of you to get me that job, Mattie, but they just didn't understand me there." Shock Value leaned forward earnestly. "You know what? They actually canned me just because I came in late a few times. Can you believe it? I told them I'd been working all night in my studio and time had sort of gotten away from me, but the manager wouldn't listen."

"I see."

"Mattie, please. I'm working on some really strong stuff. I just need a little time and a little cash to carry me for a few weeks until I can finish it."

"More stuff like *Dead Hole?*" Mattie nodded toward the piece on the floor.

Shock Value shook her chartreuse-fringed head impatiently. "No, no, that's all gone. I've worked through that period. I mean, it was useful and everything because it got me focused, you know? But now I'm working toward the important stuff. But I need to be able to *work.*"

"You should have spent your last ten bucks on food instead of supplies, Shock. You're getting too thin."

"I don't care about food. I've got to be able to buy my materials. You know how expensive metal-working supplies are."

"The whole point of getting you that job in the restaurant was so you wouldn't starve yourself for your art. That place allows the employees one free meal a day."

"I know. But I usually missed it."

Mattie groaned. "Have you looked into food stamps? Welfare?"

"Mattie, the government wants you to prove you're looking for work. I can't do that. I'm already working. My art is my work. I swear I'll go back to being a waitress just as soon as I finish the piece I'm designing now. I just need a few more weeks of freedom. I've got to get some cash. Fast. If you can't sell *Dead Hole,* could you at least make me a small loan?"

Mattie surveyed the piece Shock Value had brought with her. *Dead Hole* was one of several creations the young artist had done lately using wire, rusted iron, and used Styrofoam cups.

There was no doubt but that Shock Value's work was uniquely robust and filled with energy. Mattie had seen the possibilities in it right from the start. But the art was not quite ready to be born. Mattie knew that no matter how energetic it was, *Dead Hole* was never going to sell in her gallery. It had a power all its own, but it was the power generated by ugliness.

Still, one of these days Shock Value Frederickson was going to be brilliant, and in the meantime the woman had to eat.

"Will a hundred hold you for a while?" Mattie finally asked.

Shock Value nodded quickly. "Anything. You can keep *Dead Hole* as collateral."

Mattie reached for her purse in the bottom drawer of her desk and took out the five twenties she had just picked up at the bank. "Here you go. You can take *Dead Hole* with you, but I want you to swear on your life that you'll let me have first crack at whatever it is you're working on now. Deal?"

"You got it." Shock Value beamed in relief as she scooped up her metal sculpture and plucked the twenties from Mattie's fingers. "You won't regret this, Mattie, I promise. Thanks."

Shock Value whirled and headed for the door of the small office with her usual frenzied energy. She nearly collided with Ariel, who was just about to enter.

" 'Scuse me," Shock Value mumbled, rushing past with *Dead Hole* clutched in her hands.

Ariel looked at Mattie. "How much did you give her?"

"A hundred."

"You'll never see it again." Ariel walked in and sat down in the chair Shock Value had just vacated.

Mattie put her purse back in the drawer. "I don't know about that. Shock's going to be very good one of these days. Maybe even commercial once she gets control of her talent. Her work has an edgy, vibrant quality that might translate very well into the sort of thing I can sell here at Sharpe Reaction."

"You mean if she makes her work *pretty* enough to appeal to your middlebrow businessmen, shopkeepers, and computer-nerd clients?"

Mattie grimaced. "I know you don't have a high opinion of the sort of people who buy the work in my gallery, Ariel, but I could do without another lecture on the subject. Face it, I'm one of those hopeless cases who really does believe there's such a thing as good art for the masses. Like Mrs. Eberly says, why hang something in your living room that nauseates you whenever you look at it?"

Ariel's smile was bitter. "Yes, we both know your own tastes, don't we? But that's not really what I want to talk about."

"What do you want to talk about?"

"Tell me, sister dear, do you like playing Earth Mother to my Castrating Bitch role? Personally, I'm getting a little tired of it. I'd appreciate it if you'd leave my men alone."

"Oh, hell," Mattie said. "It's going to be one of those unpleasant big sister versus little sister chats, isn't it? You know how I hate those. You always win." Mattie leaned precariously back in her chair and checked to see that there was water in the small hot pot sitting on the floor behind her. When she saw it was full, she switched it on.

"Mattie, this has gone too far."

"You want some herbal tea and some oat bran muffins? I have a couple left over from breakfast."

"For God's sake, Mattie, no, I do not want an oat bran muffin. How can you think about health food at a time like this? But that's you right to the core. I can't stand it. I have never been able to stand it. No one in the family can stand it. The rest of us vent our emotions in a normal, healthy way, but not you, you always try to change the subject."

"You know I'm not very good at confrontations," Mattie reminded her humbly. She eyed the oat bran muffin and decided she wasn't hungry. "They make me tense."

It was true. When it came to arguing with anyone in her temperamental, high-spirited, high-strung clan, she was always at a disadvantage for the simple reason that she was the only one in her family who truly dreaded scenes. They made her physically sick. Everyone else thrived on them. What's more they were very good at them. On the rare occasion Mattie had tried to stage a major scene, she had always felt outclassed, outgunned, and outacted.

Except when she had staged one with Hugh, she realized. She had actually lost her temper with Hugh more than once, and she had not felt nauseated at all.

"Maybe you don't handle scenes well because you're such a wimp, Mattie. If you'd just fight back once in a while, you wouldn't get so tense."

Mattie sighed. "I don't have the personality for the kind of dramatics you and Mom and Dad and everyone else in the family enjoy so much. That kind of thing just puts me under a lot of stress. You know I try to avoid stress these days."

"You don't know what stress is," Ariel shot back. "I'll tell you what real stress is. Last night was real stress for me."

"Last night?" Mattie glanced up in surprise. "What was so stressful about last night? The retrospective of your work was a great success."

"Oh, sure. You think it was my work everyone was talking about after you left? Well, it wasn't. The main topic of conversation was that cozy little scene of you and Flynn and Emery and Hugh all huddled together out on the sidewalk talking like the great friends you obviously are. And then you, my dear sister, had the gall to get into a cab with my ex-husband and my ex-fiancé and drive off into the night. How do you think that made me feel?"

"I didn't think anyone noticed," Mattie said weakly.

"Bullshit. You like doing things like that, don't you? You like making me look like the Wicked Witch while you play Snow White." Ariel sprang to her feet and took a turn around the room.

"That's not how it is, Ariel." Mattie watched her sister warily. Ariel was working herself up into one of her full-scale storms. She was capable of generating real thunder and lightning when she got going.

"Don't tell me how it is. I know how it is. It's always been like that. Everyone thinks I'm some sort of Amazon goddess in a cast-iron bra who gets her kicks from destroying men. But it's not true." She spun around and glared at Mattie. "The divorce from Emery was not my fault, you know."

"I know, Ariel."

"No, you don't know, damn you. How could you know? You've never been married. Why should you bother? You're having too much fun comforting the men who get bruised and battered by me, aren't you?"

"Now, hold on, Ariel . . ."

"Too much fun letting everyone think you're the only one with any real sensitivity; too much fun compensating for your lack of artistic talent by demonstrating the depths of your womanly empathy and understanding. You've already hooked Emery and Hugh, but you're not satisfied. Now you've finally got your claws into Flynn, too."

"That's not true." Mattie sat stunned in her chair. It had never occurred to her that Ariel might actually be jealous of Flynn. Ariel always seemed so self-assured when it came to men, as assured as she was about her talent.

"It is true. You want to add Flynn to your collection of scalps, don't you? You want to prove you can make him turn to you for a comforting bosom to cry on just like the others do. Do you know what Emery once said about you? He said you were such a sweet, old-fashioned sort of woman. Very gentle on a man's ego. The kind who was born to be waiting faithfully back at the castle when the warrior came home from battle."

Mattie put her head in her hands. "God, that does sound awful, doesn't it? Especially when everyone knows that in real life men are bored to tears by that kind of woman."

"I won't let you do it, Mattie."

"Do what?" Mattie looked up again.

"You can have Emery and you can have Hugh, if you really want them, although Lord knows why you would. *But you cannot have Flynn.*"

"I don't want Flynn, damn it." Mattie shot to her feet as the stress of the moment finally galvanized her into action. "I didn't want Emery, either. We've never been anything more than friends and that's the gospel truth. The only one I ever wanted was Hugh, and he wasn't particularly interested when I offered myself on a silver platter last year. So stop making it sound like I'm some kind of Jezebel who specializes in your cast-off men. I don't want your leftovers, Ariel. I never did."

Ariel was staring at her. "What do you mean, you offered yourself to Hugh on a silver platter last year?"

"Oh, damn, why did I let you drag me into this stupid argument. Forget it. Forget everything." The rare and unfamiliar passion of rage died as quickly as it had arisen. Mattie sank back wearily into her chair, surprised to discover that although she felt drained, she didn't feel sick to her stomach. She was getting better at anger. Maybe it was from all the practice she was getting with Hugh.

"Tell me what you mean about that silver-platter crack," Ariel insisted, planting her hands on Mattie's desk.

"There's nothing to tell. I made a fool of myself last year after you dumped Hugh. That's all. Believe me, I learned my lesson." The water was boiling in the hot pot. Mattie reached down to flick the switch and noticed her fingers were trembling. *Stress,* she thought. She was shaking from the stress. She must be sure to get to her lunch-hour aerobics class today. The exercise would help deal with the anxiety.

"How did you make a fool of yourself? What happened between

the two of you? Were you seeing him while I was engaged to him?" Ariel yelled in fury.

"No, of course not. Your men never notice me until after you've finished with them. You ought to know that. They're all much too dazzled by you."

"What happened? How did you make a fool of yourself?"

"Let it go, will you, Ariel?"

"No, I will not let it go. I want to know. Tell me what happened."

Mattie exhaled heavily. "This is so embarrassing. The night before Hugh was scheduled to fly back to St. Gabriel, I called him. Told him he could spend the night at my apartment. Made some idiotic excuse about my place being cheaper than an airport hotel, which is where he was planning to stay."

"Oh, Mattie."

"I know. It sounded just as lame then as it does now. But he showed up on my doorstep around dinnertime. He was not in a good mood. He was angry and restless, like a caged wolf. He'd already had a couple of drinks. I made the mistake of giving him a couple more along with dinner."

"My God. You were playing with fire."

"Umm, yes. It was a new experience for me," Mattie admitted dryly. "I'm sure you can imagine the outcome of the evening. Hugh downed a good deal of very expensive after-dinner brandy and then he more or less fell into bed with me. I confess I gave him a small shove."

"What did you think you were going to accomplish?" Ariel demanded tightly. "Were you trying to prove you could seduce him?"

"No. Not exactly." Mattie fiddled with a pen on her desk. "I wanted him to take me with him when he left town on the flight to St. Gabriel the next morning."

Ariel stared at her sister in amazement. "You wanted to run off to the islands with him? You? I can't believe it."

"What can I say? I went a little crazy. Believe me, it won't happen again."

"But he claims he's engaged to you. He's staying with you at your apartment."

"He's the one talking about marriage. I'm thinking of our present arrangement as an affair." Mattie smiled bleakly. "Don't worry, Ariel, it won't last. One of these days Hugh will get on another flight back to St. Gabriel."

"Poor Hugh."

Mattie scowled. "Poor Hugh?"

But Ariel had already made one of her lightning-swift mood

swings. "And poor Emery. You know, lately, I've begun to wonder why I always seem to attract losers. It's awkward, you know, because people think I'm the one who ruined them, but the truth is that they carry the seeds of their own destruction within them. I'm like a catalyst or something that speeds up the process."

"For Pete's sake, Ariel."

"I'm not responsible for Emery and Hugh ruining their lives."

"Of course you aren't. And their lives aren't exactly ruined. They've both got plenty of big plans for the future, I promise you."

But Ariel was off on a new dramatic tangent. "Last night I felt so guilty when I saw you with the three of them out there on the sidewalk."

"There's absolutely no need for you to feel guilty." Mattie was used to this role, too. She had spent years soothing Ariel and everyone else in the household.

"Maybe it is my fault, somehow. Maybe I do something to destroy them."

"Ariel, stop it. That's not true and you know it." Mattie was getting alarmed now. Ariel's emotions could be unpredictable. "For heaven's sake, don't start wallowing in a lot of unearned guilt. It's not your style and it will take days for you to get back out of it so that you can paint."

"It doesn't matter. I haven't painted in weeks. I'm too frightened by what's happening between me and Flynn."

"Afraid of what?"

"That I'll do to him whatever I did to Emery and Hugh." With a sob, Ariel fled to the door.

# 11

Mattie got off the elevator on the twenty-sixth floor of the downtown highrise and walked along a wide, carpeted hallway. She took several deep breaths to force back the familiar tension and realized she had a death grip on the paper bag she was holding as well as on her purse strap. It had been a long ride up and the elevator had been very crowded.

Memories of the caves of Purgatory had started to nibble around the edges of her thoughts by the twelfth floor, when five more large specimens of corporate humanity had gotten on board. Real anxiety had set in by the twentieth, when the doors had stuck shut for a moment. She had literally leaped off the elevator when it had finally arrived at the twenty-sixth floor.

She always had some problem in elevators, but this last experience had been especially difficult. The fact was, she was having more trouble than usual handling the normal stresses in her life these days. Perhaps that was because she was experiencing more than the usual amount, she reminded herself grimly. Living with Hugh Abbott under the same roof was not exactly conducive to serenity. It was like having a large beast underfoot, one who was just waiting for the day when he would go back to the wild. Dragging her with him, of course. She knew that was always in the back of his mind, no matter how often he reassured her that he was willing to stay in Seattle indefinitely.

*Indefinitely, hah.* She knew Hugh Abbott better than that. The man was extremely low on patience.

Perhaps she should start doubling up on her vitamin B and niacin tablets in the mornings, Mattie thought. They were good for stress.

There were several excellent paintings hanging on the walls of the twenty-sixth floor of the Vailcourt building. It was one of the three management floors. Mattie had chosen the art for the offices at her aunt's request, and she was pleased to see that it still looked as good now as it had the day the pictures were hung. Some art did not wear well, even though it looked terrific when it first went up. It was a fact of life in the business. Only the truly good stuff looked terrific five, ten, or a hundred years later.

Mattie halted at the open door of one of the offices and glanced inside. Two people were seated at two large desks, a young man and a woman of about fifty. There was a desktop computer on each desk. Around the room was an array of state-of-the-art office equipment: Fax machines, exotic telephones, laser printers, and assorted computer peripherals. There was also a lot of paper stacked up on various surfaces. Modern machines seemed to generate more paper than the old ones.

The attractive, well-groomed young man at the first desk looked up and saw Mattie standing in the doorway.

"May I help you?" he inquired in plumy accents.

"I just dropped by to see Hugh, that is, uh, Mr. Abbott, if he's in," Mattie said, moving slowly into the office. She felt oddly ill at ease and realized it was because it was very difficult to imagine Hugh working in such sophisticated surroundings. It just wasn't *him*, somehow.

"Mr. Abbott is very busy," the young man said smoothly. "Did you have an appointment?"

"No, no, that's all right," Mattie said quickly. "If he's busy, don't bother him. I happened to be in the building, and I thought I'd say hello while I was here."

"I'll be glad to give him your name and see if he can find time for you," the young man offered.

"Mattie Sharpe. But, really, it's okay. Don't worry about it. I'll just run along. Here, you can give him this, if you will." She held out the paper bag she was holding in one hand. "He forgot it this morning. On purpose, I suspect."

"Miss Sharpe." The name obviously clicked immediately. The young man, who had been reaching out to take the paper bag, dropped his hand and smiled. "One moment please." The secretary pressed the intercom button on his desk and started to speak into it.

At that moment the door of the inner office was yanked open, and Hugh stuck his head out. "Gary or Jenny, one of you bring me that report on the Rome office, will you? And make it quick, I haven't got all day."

"I've got it right here, Mr. Abbott," the woman said calmly, reaching for a thick folder on her desk.

"Great. Thanks." Hugh held out his hand as the secretary got to her feet.

"Excuse me, Mr. Abbott," Gary said. "You have a visitor."

"Not now, Gary, I'm busy." Hugh started to flip through the folder. "I told you I don't have time to see anyone until this afternoon." He looked up and spotted Mattie standing near the secretary's desk. "Hey, it's you, babe. Didn't see you there."

"Probably because my suit is the same color as the carpeting," Mattie grumbled, glancing down at her beigy-brown attire.

"Well, I'll admit you do stand out better in red," Hugh said with a grin. "Come on in." His easy smile changed abruptly to a scowl as he examined her more closely. "What happened to you, anyway? You look like hell."

"Thank you. The suit isn't that bad, is it?"

"Forget the damned suit. You're white as a sheet." Hugh closed the door behind her and waved her to a chair near the floor-to-ceiling windows. "You look the way you did when we went through those caves on Purgatory."

"The elevator was a bit crowded," Mattie explained as she sat down. She gazed around at the plush surroundings, taking in the polished wooden desk, the thick carpeting, and the designer chairs. "Nice office. Not a girlie calendar in sight."

"Don't worry. I've ordered a few to put up around the room to make myself feel more at home. What are you doing here?"

"A royal summons. My aunt phoned me up this morning and said she wanted to see me. Said she could fit me in around ten o'clock."

"This is Thursday. She always has a massage at ten o'clock downstairs in the health club on Thursdays." Hugh sprawled in the big, elegant executive chair and put his booted feet up on the gleaming surface of the desk.

"Right. She's invited me to join her. She says we can talk while we're getting massaged."

"What are you two going to talk about?" Hugh asked with narrowed eyes.

"You, probably. That's what most people seem to want to discuss with me lately. I just stopped off here to give you this." Mattie opened her brown paper bag and drew out a container of thick, brightly colored juice. "You ran off and left it behind this morning."

Hugh looked shocked. "My bug juice? After all that special effort you went to this morning to mix it up for me in the blender? I accidentally left it in the refrigerator? I can't believe I'd do a thing like that. I'm getting forgetful lately, aren't I?"

"Stress, no doubt."

Hugh chuckled. "So what is it this morning?"

"A combination of lime, papaya, banana, and wheat grass with some bran added for texture. I told you when I was making it this morning that it's great for supplying you with plenty of midday energy. Lots of vitamins and special enzymes."

"Gary makes a pretty good cup of coffee," Hugh said, looking hopeful. "Lots of energy in coffee."

"But no real nutrition," Mattie said with an admonishing frown.

"Right. No real nutrition. Okay, stick the bug juice in that little refrigerator over there, and I'll drink it later. When are you supposed to meet Charlotte?"

"I should go on up there now," Mattie said, opening the section of bookshelving that was humming softly on the other side of the room. "This is impressive, Hugh. Your own refrigerator. All the comforts of home."

"Not quite," he drawled. "I could use a couch."

"Why would you want a couch?" she asked as she straightened, and then her eyes met his faintly mocking, very sexy gaze. She blushed. "Oh. You have a one-track mind, Hugh Abbott."

"I'd just like to be better prepared for visits from you," Hugh said as he took his feet down off the desk. He cast a thoughtful glance at the polished wooden surface. "Of course, there is the desk, isn't there?"

"Forget it," she said firmly, memories of the night flooding her veins with heat. "I'm due upstairs. Got to run."

"Some other time, maybe. Come on, I'll escort you up to Charlotte's palace."

"That's not necessary. I know you're busy."

"Not that busy."

He took hold of her arm and guided her out through the office and into the hall. There was a crowd of people waiting to board the elevator that had just opened.

"Excuse me, folks," Hugh said in a cool, commanding tone as he tugged Mattie past the small group and into the empty elevator. "Emergency security check. Next elevator will be along in a minute."

The doors closed on a row of startled expressions, leaving Mattie and Hugh alone in the elevator. Hugh punched the button for the presidential floor.

"What was that all about?" Mattie demanded.

"Figured you'd had enough of crowded elevators today." Hugh folded his arms and propped his shoulder against the wall. He smiled.

"So you kicked everyone off this one just so I wouldn't have to ride in a packed elevator?" Mattie began to giggle. "Honestly, Hugh."

"What's so funny?"

"Watching you throw your weight around. You're very good at it, you know. It must come naturally."

"You don't get what you want in this world unless you go after it." He reached for her, pulling her close and kissing her fiercely just as the elevator doors opened. "I learned that a long time ago, babe."

"This feels incredible, Aunt Charlotte. Absolutely incredible." Mattie was lying facedown on the massage table while a white-jacketed woman with amazingly strong hands worked on her bare back. She was being kneaded, punched and pounded, and it felt wonderful. "You say you do this once a week?"

"At least," Charlotte Vailcourt said from the next table. "Sometimes more frequently if I'm under an unusual amount of stress."

Another woman in white was working earnestly on Charlotte. Mattie opened her eyes and glanced over at her aunt. Charlotte Vailcourt had always been a beautiful woman. She was nearly sixty now, but she still managed to draw every eye whenever she walked into a room. It was not just a case of physical beauty, although she had plenty of that left thanks to a fine bone structure and a great deal of money; it was also a matter of grace and style.

Charlotte Vailcourt was loaded with grace and style. Those qualities had been the hallmark of her career as an actress, and they had carried her safely through the deep, dangerous waters of the international business world after she had taken control of Vailcourt Industries upon the death of her husband. It was Charlotte who had expanded the firm into the international realm of operations. The business had thrived under her leadership.

"I'm going to have to try this on a routine basis myself," Mattie said languidly as she felt tension dissolve throughout her body. "So relaxing."

"I had a hunch you'd enjoy it. You've been under an unusually high level of stress yourself, lately. Hugh gave me a full report on what you went through on Purgatory. I was absolutely shocked. Poor Mr. Cormier."

"I have to tell you, it certainly made me wonder if there wasn't some truth to the old legend surrounding that sword, Aunt Charlotte."

"You mean that bit about 'Death to all who dare claim the blade until it's been taken up by the avenger and cleansed in the blood of the betrayer'? Typical medieval nonsense. All first-class ancient swords like *Valor* have legends and curses attached to them. Part of what makes them interesting. No, I'm afraid Mr. Cormier's problem was a combination of the usual, bad luck and bad timing."

"It was bad, all right," Mattie agreed with a small shiver of memory.

"You needn't have stumbled into the middle of it, you know. Why on earth didn't you stop at St. Gabriel, the way you were supposed to? You could have avoided that nasty little scene on Purgatory altogether. Hugh would never have walked into that sort of thing with you. He has an instinct for trouble."

"You know why I changed my reservations."

Charlotte sighed. "So much for my attempt at playing matchmaker. Still, on the whole, I didn't do too badly, did I? Hugh tells me you're engaged."

"Don't look so satisfied, Aunt Charlotte. I don't think I'd go quite so far as to call our present arrangement an engagement."

"That's what Hugh's calling it, so that's what I'll call it."

"I see. You two took a vote and I've been outvoted, is that it?"

"Now, don't go getting tense again, Mattie. You'll undo all the good work these nice women are accomplishing. When do you think you'll move out to St. Gabriel?"

Mattie stiffened and her masseuse responded by digging her thumbs into a pressure point. "Ouch. I'm not moving out to St. Gabriel. Didn't Hugh explain that part? He's decided to move to Seattle."

"Not permanently."

Mattie smiled grimly. "Then you'll have to ask him when he's leaving."

"Mattie, you know you can't keep him here long. Hugh Abbott will never be happy in the city. He's like a wild animal. He'll never become completely civilized, no matter how much sushi and white wine he consumes. All his hopes and dreams are waiting for him back on his island."

"I know. I'm waiting for him to admit that and go back to St. Gabriel."

"He won't go back without you."

"Then he'll wait until hell freezes over."

"You're tensing up again, ma'am," the masseuse said, sounding annoyed.

"Sorry," Mattie mumbled.

"The thing is," Charlotte said gently, "you're part of his hopes and dreams now. He won't leave you behind."

"He did once before."

"Are you going to hold that against him for the rest of his life?"

Mattie thought about it. "Maybe. At least until I can be sure I'm not a stand-in for Ariel."

"I don't believe it. That's not like you, Mattie. Hugh made a mistake a year ago, but that's because he was mad as hell and didn't know his own mind. For heaven's sake, dear, he's a man. Men aren't very good at analyzing themselves, you know."

"I know. But I'm tired of analyzing him, too. I thought I had him figured out a year ago. I thought I understood him and that once he was free from Ariel's spell he'd see the light. But he didn't, Aunt Charlotte."

"It only took him a couple of months to come to his senses. Be reasonable, Mattie." Charlotte sighed. "He was really thrown for a loss when Ariel broke off the engagement. He needed time to get his act together again. Poor Hugh, he thought he'd wrapped everything up in a nice, neat package for himself. All his plans were in order, and he's very accustomed to making things work out according to his own plans, you know. Even if he has to sort of hammer them into place."

"You can say that again."

"I blame myself, in part. I should never have arranged for Hugh and Ariel to meet."

"Why did you?" Mattie asked tightly. "You've made no secret that you'd like him in the family, but why choose Ariel for him the first time around? Why didn't you toss me into his lap?"

"Oh, dear. I had a feeling you might be harboring some resentment on that score."

"Forget it, Aunt Charlotte. I'm used to Ariel getting picked first. I've always been her understudy."

"Really, dear, must you sink back into that old self-pity routine? I thought you'd outgrown that years ago."

Mattie winced as the masseuse crushed her shoulders. "Sorry. Old habits are hard to break."

"Well, it's not as if you don't have cause in this instance, I suppose. In this case I did consciously choose Ariel for Hugh. And I admit it was a big mistake. All I can say is that at first glance they somehow seemed very suited to each other. They're both very vibrant, colorful, dramatic people. I thought they would strike sparks off each other."

"They did. More than sparks. Explosions."

"But they didn't set any long-term fires, Mattie. You and Hugh did."

"It's another mismatch, Aunt Charlotte. Trust me."

"Well, one way or another, you'd better be prepared for real fireworks if you insist on tying Hugh to Seattle. Because he can't stay here indefinitely, and he won't leave without you."

"Is that right?" Mattie retorted, feeling pressured again. "What about me? Why should I pull up stakes and move to his godforsaken little island? What about my career? What about my sushi and white wine? I'm happy here, Aunt Charlotte. Finally. After all these years I'm actually happy."

"Are you, dear?" Charlotte asked softly.

"I think I'm getting tense again," Mattie declared.

"Just relax, dear."

"Aunt Charlotte?"

"Yes, dear?"

"What do you know about Hugh's past?"

"His past? Well, he's worked for Vailcourt on a free-lance consulting basis for nearly four years."

"I mean, before he went to work for you."

"I'm afraid I can't tell you much."

"Because it's confidential? Personnel policies don't permit telling me?"

Charlotte smiled. "It's not so much a matter of personnel policy as it is the plain and simple fact that I don't know exactly what Hugh was doing before he came to work for me."

Mattie frowned. "I find it hard to believe you'd hire someone you knew absolutely nothing about, Aunt Charlotte."

"Something about his style rather appealed to me," Charlotte said thoughtfully. "He just walked into my office one day without an appointment and told me I needed him. Said one of the South American field offices of Vailcourt Mining was in jeopardy because a group of rebels was about to destroy it in order to make a political statement. Hugh told me that for ten thousand dollars he would deal with the situation."

"And he did."

"Oh, yes, dear. He certainly did. The rest, as they say, is history."

Hugh sprawled in his executive chair, heels stacked on the desk, and eyed the magnificent view of Elliott Bay through the office windows. When he got back to St. Gabriel, he'd have to see about ordering up a chair like the one he was presently occupying. But he already knew he had a better view back in the islands. There was something about having to look at the expanse of the bay through solid glass windows that could not be opened that bothered him.

But, then, there were a lot of things about city life that irritated him. The sooner he got Mattie out of here, the better.

"Where the hell have you been, Silk?" Hugh said when Taggert eventually rumbled inquiringly into the phone. He could hear the sounds of the Hellfire evening crowd in the background. "I've been trying to reach you for two days."

"I was off island," Silk said, sounding stone-cold sober. "Took a little trip to Hades to see if I could pick up any leads."

"Any luck?"

"Word is that things have settled down on Purgatory. The revolution or whatever you want to call it is over, and it's business as usual over there, apparently."

"Who's in charge?"

"Good question, boss. A lot of the old crowd, believe it or not, including Findley, the pool-shooting president. The official word is that the coup failed and things are back to normal. But the rumor is there's a new man in charge behind the scenes and that the important government officials now answer to him."

"In other words, the coup worked but the new strongman has enough sense to stay out of the spotlight."

"Sounds like it. And whoever it is, he's also smart enough to use money, not guns, to buy the loyalty of the local officials."

"Money always did talk over on Purgatory," Hugh observed. "That's one of the things Cormier liked about it."

"As Cormier pointed out, money talks everywhere. It's just a bit more obvious on a small island like Purgatory. Don't forget, in the old days, that island was a pirate stronghold. It hasn't changed all that much."

"Yeah. Interesting." Hugh was silent for a moment, running possibilities through his head. "You ever find Gibbs? The guy who was Rosey's partner?"

"Nope. No trace. Looks like he's skipped."

"Probably for good reason. Must have found out what happened to his friend. Sounds like the next step is to try to track down some of Cormier's former house staff. See if we can get one of them to talk. Find out if they saw anything the day Cormier was killed."

"My guess is that they're all going to be suffering from amnesia. Assuming we can even find one or two of 'em."

"If we can find one, we can make him talk. Keep working on it, Silk. I'm going to try something from this end."

"Like what?"

"Ever heard of computers? Information networks? Worldwide data bases?"

"Where the hell are you going to get hold of a computer with enough information to help us find out something about Cormier's killer?"

"I'm sitting on top of one of the most sophisticated computer networks in the world, Silk. Call me when you get a handle on something."

"Right."

"By the way," Hugh said, "Mattie's scheduled your opening for tomorrow evening. There's going to be champagne and all kinds of free eats. They do that kind of thing up big around here."

"Damn. Wish I could be there. Sounds like my kind of party." There was a pause on the other end of the line. "She really think my stuff is going to sell?"

Hugh was amazed at the degree of uncertainty in Silk's voice. It wasn't like the big man to be uncertain of anything. "She says you're going to make her rich."

"Damn," Silk said again in tones of great wonder. "When I think of how I had to ram those canvases down Miles's throat in order to cover my tab here at the Hellfire, I could just spit. He'll have to beg for 'em now, by God."

"Revenge is sweet."

"Ain't it just?"

Hugh hung up the phone and took his boots down off the desk. He got to his feet, went over to the small refrigerator, and removed the bottle of juice Mattie had brought with her that morning.

The two secretaries that had been assigned to Hugh looked up inquiringly as he strode through the outer office on the way to the elevators.

"See ya," said Hugh.

"What shall we say concerning your estimated time of return to the office, Mr. Abbott?" Gary asked just as Hugh reached the door.

"Tell 'em I'll be back in a while." Hugh went out into the corridor and punched the elevator call button. Secretaries who tried to set schedules and run a man's life were a nuisance. He knew the two he had were among the best in the business, but they annoyed him as often as not.

Hugh was doing his best to learn how to manage a staff, however, because he figured that sooner or later he would be hiring office help for Abbott Charters. He sure as hell did not want to keep doing all the filing himself, and he could not trust Derek or Ray or Silk to do it. Their idea of file management was to toss everything that wasn't edible or spendable into the nearest wastebasket.

"What in the world have you got in that bottle?" Charlotte Vailcourt asked when Hugh sauntered through her office door a few minutes later.

"Bug juice. Mattie made it." Hugh set the bottle on Charlotte's vast slate desk. "Want some?"

"Another one of her high-energy, antistress concoctions, I presume?" Charlotte eyed the juice warily.

"Yeah. I haven't tried this particular formula yet, but if it's like the others I've tasted, we'll be lucky to survive." Hugh went over to the black lacquer wet bar across the room and found a couple of glasses in the cupboard.

"Why do you keep drinking her 'bug juice,' as you call it, if you can't stand the stuff? Why not just toss it into the nearest flowerpot?"

Hugh shrugged as he came back across the room and poured two small glasses full of the juice. "It's not that bad. I've had worse things to drink." He swallowed the entire contents of his glass in one long gulp and grimaced. "But I can't recall just when."

Charlotte grinned as she sipped tentatively at hers. "I suppose the fact that she goes to so much trouble to elevate your health consciousness is a sign of how much she cares about you."

"That's what I tell myself when I'm eating pasta and veggies instead of a nice bloody steak." Hugh sank down into a black leather and chrome chair.

His gaze went briefly to the large glass cabinet that held several of Charlotte's most interesting specimens of old armor. The lighted case displayed a row of swords with unusual hilts, some gilded, some studded with semiprecious stones, and an arrangement of daggers of various sizes.

"Is that rapier new?" Hugh asked idly. "I don't remember seeing it in there last time."

"Yes. It arrived yesterday. Seventeenth century. Rather nice, don't you think?"

"If you like that kind of thing." Hugh brought his gaze back to his boss. "Charlotte, I need a favor."

"I thought you might. You don't normally come up here just to visit. What sort of favor?"

"I want to borrow some of your computer people. I need a little research done."

"On what?"

"On what might have happened on Purgatory."

"According to the one short article I saw in the newspaper the other day, the coup was crushed almost immediately."

"That's the official version, but a friend of mine says there's a rumor that someone else is in charge now. Someone working behind the scenes. I figured if I could do a little fishing in some of your data banks, I might be able to come up with a name."

"My data banks or someone else's?" Charlotte asked with arched brows. "Never mind. I don't think I want to know the answer to that. Go ahead and talk to Johnson down in Systems. He can use our computers to talk to just about any major data bank in the world. Just don't give me too many details, all right? And tell Johnson I don't want any tracks left that could lead back to Vailcourt."

Hugh grinned. "Appreciate it."

"Consider it a wedding present."

"I'll do that." Hugh stood up. "You want the rest of that bug juice?"

"No, thank you. I'm afraid you're going to have to finish it all by yourself."

"I was afraid of that." Hugh reached for the bottle and headed for the door.

"By the way, Hugh," Charlotte said behind him.

"Yeah?" He turned, one hand on the doorknob.

"How is Vailcourt's master security plan coming along?"

"Be finished with it in another couple of weeks or so at the outside."

"And then what?"

"Then, with any luck, I'll be on my way to St. Gabe with Mattie."

"I'm afraid you've still got some convincing to do in that department."

"It'll work out."

Charlotte absently tapped a gold pen on the desk. "I hope so. I honestly think she would be happy with you if she lets herself."

"Damn right," Hugh said forcefully. "I'll make her happy, Charlotte. I swear it."

"None of us can actually make someone else happy, not really. We each have to find our own happiness within ourselves. We have to work at it. It takes courage."

"She's got guts," Hugh said. "She'll be all right. She just needs a little time to get used to the idea of being with me on a permanent basis."

"I hope you're willing to give her the time, Hugh," Charlotte said with a meaningful look. "I hope you won't try to push her too fast. You do tend to operate rather quickly, you know."

"Well, I can't hang around here forever. I've got a business to run and a house to build. And I'm not getting any younger."

"You really think she's just going to toss it all away for you, don't you? Her business, her lifestyle, her friends. Isn't that somewhat arrogant on your part, Hugh?"

He scowled. "I'll take care of her."

"She doesn't need to be taken care of. She's perfectly capable of taking care of herself. Lord knows, she's had to do it for years. No one in the family knew how to take care of her. She wasn't like the rest of them. Her needs were different. Her talents were different. No one knew quite what to do with her when they found out she wasn't going to fall into the same mold as the rest of them."

"You seem to understand her."

Charlotte smiled. "Probably because I left the artistic world many years ago and went into the business world. When I found myself at the reins of Vailcourt, I learned a great deal about an area of life I had previously ignored. The experience has taught me to recognize and respect people such as you and Mattie. You're both entrepreneurs at heart. You both are inclined to take risks."

"You think Mattie is a risk taker?"

"Certainly, although she doesn't think of herself that way. She takes risks frequently. She took a major one when she started Sharpe Reaction. Ariel and the rest of the family had a fit because she went for the commercial market. They didn't support her at all, and believe me, in the beginning it would have helped a great deal if she had been allowed to hang some of her mother's work or a few of Ariel's paintings."

"They didn't want her to succeed."

"No, not because they didn't love her. They simply didn't approve of what she was doing. The Sharpe clan is very elitist when it comes to art."

"Except for you."

Charlotte smiled. "As I said, running Vailcourt has broadened my horizons. But my point about Mattie is that she is quite capable of taking risks. Heaven knows she does it every time she discovers a previously unknown artist and features his work in her gallery. Her reputation rides on the quality of the artists she hangs, you know. She can't afford to make many mistakes. And like any good businesswoman she makes it a practice to learn from her mistakes."

Hugh got the point. He felt himself turning a dull red. "She didn't make a mistake with me. It was just a case of bad timing. Sooner or later she'll get that through her head."

Charlotte considered that. "I suppose it's a good sign that she's starting to get very curious about your past. We talked about it while we had our massage this morning, you know. She had a lot of questions."

"Shit." Hugh felt his insides tighten. "My past has nothing to do with my present or my future. I've told Mattie that. She doesn't need to know anything more than she already does."

"Women, especially women who have learned from experience to be prudent when it comes to men, sometimes take a slightly different view."

"Shit," Hugh said again as he went through the door and slammed it behind himself.

"Enjoy your bug juice," Charlotte called after him.

# 12

⚜

"What do you think about putting the lagoon series on the right-hand wall and the paintings of the town itself on the left-hand wall?" Mattie stood in the center of her gallery, studying the blank white walls. She'd been puzzling over Silk Taggert's work all afternoon. She had deliberately waited until after closing time to hang the paintings in order to create an air of expectation and curiosity in the local art community. She wanted to surprise everyone. She had all the placements carefully planned out and all she had to do was hang the work in its prepared locations. But time was getting short and she was in a hurry.

It was proving difficult to concentrate on the design of the display, however, because her sister was pacing furiously up and down the room. Ariel's fluttering black skirts and voluminous black silk top made her look like an exotic black butterfly as she flitted from one end of the gallery to the other.

Mattie automatically glanced down at the tailored little navy blue suit, white blouse, gold chain necklace, and black pumps she, herself, was wearing and felt like a moth rather than a butterfly. She wished the suit were red instead of navy blue. Thoughts of the daring little red sarong that she had brought back with her from the islands danced in her head. It was neatly tucked away in the darkest corner of her closet.

"Will you stop blathering on and on about those paintings? I'm trying to talk to you about something important." Ariel waved her hands in a graceful gesture of total frustration, whirled, and strode back the other way.

"These paintings are important. Right now they're more important than anything you've got to say to me, Ariel. You know I've got an opening scheduled for tonight." Mattie bent over the stack of pictures leaning against the wall. She had just finished uncrating them and was anxious to see how they would look on the walls of her gallery.

"Another opening for another one of your boring artists who paints pretty little pictures for people who like *nice* art?"

Mattie was incensed on Silk's behalf. "There is nothing boring about Silk Taggert or his pictures." She picked two at random out of the stack and put them up on the wall. "Take a look at these, Ariel. Take a good look, damn it, and tell me they're boring."

Ariel heaved a dramatic sigh and swept the pictures with a single cursory glance. One was an oddly disturbing harbor scene, the other a painting of the jungle that caught both a sense of primitive menace and the feeling of abundant life.

"Island landscapes? Give me a break, Mattie. That's the sort of thing hotel chains hang in the rooms. You can buy them by the dozen anywhere. They all look alike. I'm sure *your* clients will love them, of course. They're only one step beyond putting posters on their walls, anyway. This stuff will probably look like great art to them."

"Ariel, you are elitist and self-centered and you've got a really bad case of tunnel vision when it comes to art. What is it with you? You think the only good art is the kind that does nothing more than express the artist's personal neurosis? I've got news for you, you and your kind wouldn't have survived in business for more than five minutes during the Renaissance."

Ariel, not surprisingly, looked taken aback at the unexpected attack. It was axiomatic in the Sharpe family that Mattie did not disagree on matters of artistic taste with the other members of her clan. It was understood she did not have a proper grasp of the subject.

"For heaven's sake, Mattie, there's no need to get all worked up about it. Besides, I want to talk to you about something else entirely."

But Mattie was all worked up. It felt good to be arguing with Ariel. Odd how she found herself doing it more and more frequently of late. Ever since she had come back from the islands, in fact.

"You know something?" Mattie snapped. "Back in the good old days people understood what art was supposed to do. It was supposed to appeal to them. It was supposed to speak to them, not just to the artist. It was supposed to mean something important, something universal. It was supposed to be beautiful. And it was supposed to represent certain ideals and values and hopes and dreams."

"Really, Mattie, I think this has gone far enough."

"Back then people knew good art when they saw it, and that's what they bought. Artists created work to please the customer, and you can't deny that some of the greatest art in the world was produced under those conditions. Nowadays you elitist insiders in the art world are trying to tell the customer what he's supposed to like, and you've managed to cow a lot of them into buying what you tell them is good art. But my customers are different. They're buying what they really want to buy, stuff they enjoy hanging in their homes."

"Mattie, this is crazy. I don't want to discuss the art establishment with you."

*"Take a close look at Silk Taggert's paintings and tell me they're bad art!"* Mattie yelled.

"Mattie, for heaven's sake, keep your voice down," Ariel hissed.

"Why should I? It feels good to yell at you. I think I'm releasing a great deal of stress this way. Years of it, in fact. Look at Silk's pictures, damn it."

"All right, all right, I'm looking at them. Get a grip on yourself, will you? It's not like you to be so . . . so emotional." Ariel turned to study the paintings. She peered at them for two or three long minutes. Her eyes narrowed thoughtfully.

"Well?" Mattie challenged. "Are you going to call them boring?"

"No," Ariel admitted reluctantly. "They're not boring. This guy has talent, I'll grant you that."

"A lot of talent."

"Okay, okay. A lot of talent. Too bad he's wasting it on pretty seascapes and landscapes."

"The fact that he's using familiar subjects is what makes his work so accessible. Can't you understand that? It makes the pictures work on several different levels. The appeal ranges from the physically attractive to the mentally stimulating. People, real people, like art that does all that. And I'll tell you something else, Ariel. This is just the sort of appeal Flynn would have if he tried doing more realistic art."

Ariel whirled on her, raw fury in her eyes. "Don't you dare try to seduce Flynn into doing this kind of thing for you. Do you hear me? Don't you dare."

Mattie groaned, her anger evaporating. "Forget it. Look, Ariel, I've really got a lot of work to do here before the show. If you don't mind, I'd like to get to it."

Ariel hesitated. "Here, I'll give you a hand. I think you're right about grouping the pictures by subject. I'll handle the jungle scenes."

Mattie stared at her in astonishment. "Thank you."

"Don't look so amazed. I'm not a bitch goddess all the time, you know. I told you I want to talk to you, and this looks like the only way I'm going to be able to do it."

"I was afraid there was an ulterior motive." Mattie centered a painting of the harbor and stepped back to eye it. "Let's get on with it. What do you want to lecture me about?"

"I want to know what you think you're doing getting engaged to Hugh Abbott." Ariel hung a jungle scene. "How did it happen, Mattie?"

"It's a bit difficult to explain. I'm not quite certain how it happened, myself. And I'm not sure I'm engaged. That's Hugh's interpretation of the situation, not mine. I haven't made up my mind yet."

"Oh, Mattie, be honest. The man's living with you. He's telling everyone he's going to marry you. Did you have to go this far just to prove you can have what I once had?"

"I didn't do it to prove anything."

"Yes, you did. You've always envied me. My talent, my success, my men, my looks. Everything."

"That's not true. Oh, sure, maybe when we were kids. But that was a long time ago. People grow up, Ariel."

"Is that right? Then how come the one man you finally decide to get serious about is one of my exes? An ex-fiancé, in this case. Don't you think that's too much of a coincidence? Why choose that particular male? Tell me, Mattie. Go on and admit the truth."

"I didn't choose him. At least, not this time around. He chose me." Mattie stalked back into her office to look for some tools.

Ariel followed, sweeping through the doorway behind her. "He chose you? What's that supposed to mean?"

"Ask Hugh. He's the one who insisted on getting engaged. I've been deliberately avoiding him for a year. He set things up for us to meet out on Purgatory, not me. Whatever happens doesn't concern you."

"Doesn't concern me? He's my ex-fiancé, damn it."

"So what?" Mattie snapped. "You threw him back, remember? You didn't want him."

"And neither should you. Mattie, listen to me. I'm saying this for your own good. He's all wrong for you. Trust me. I know him. If you must have one of my men, take Emery. At least he's genuinely fond of you."

"Thanks a lot."

"Okay, so he's much too old for you and his career is on the skids, but he knows your world and the people in it. You can talk to him about things like art and wine and books. He'll respect your career. He won't try to drag you off to some godforsaken island and expect you to sit around under a palm tree and shell coconuts."

"I'm not interested in marrying Emery, thank you very much. And I don't plan to sit around twiddling my thumbs under any palm trees."

"What else can you do out there in the middle of nowhere? Or do you have some illusion about changing Hugh? If so, you're in for a rude awakening. I should know. I thought I could civilize him, too. But I was wrong. And if he wouldn't change to please me, what makes you think he'll change to suit you?"

Mattie sorted through a toolbox until she found a screwdriver. Clutching it tightly she turned back to face her sister. "Excuse me, Ariel. I still have a lot of paintings to hang."

Ariel's face softened. "Oh, Mattie, I'm sorry if I hurt your feelings. I'm doing this for your own good, I swear it. I am speaking to you now as your older sister. For a while I was sure I could convince Hugh to see reason and move back to the States. But I soon found out the truth. He won't leave that damned island of his for any woman."

"Get out of my way, Ariel. I've got work to do."

"Mattie, you don't want to marry him. The man is a throwback. He belongs in the Middle Ages or something. His attitude toward women and marriage is several hundred years out of date. Oh, I know the macho approach in bed is kind of interesting at first, but you'll get tired of it, believe me."

Mattie felt herself turning a fiery shade of red. "You may be my sister, Ariel, but I don't have to discuss my love life with you."

"Why not?" Ariel snapped, exasperated. "Just think of the sisterly confidences we can share now that we've both slept with the same man. Let's be blunt about this. I know for a fact he's not that good."

"Shut up, Ariel." The anger was rising once more.

"It's true. Mattie, I'm warning you, that slam-bam-thank-you-ma'am approach gets old real fast."

"*I said, shut up, Ariel.* I don't want to hear another word."

"Hugh is not the man for you. He wasn't the man for me. As far as I can tell, he's not the right man for any modern woman. He's an outdated, inconsiderate, insensitive clod, Mattie. Listen to me. We're talking about your whole future here."

"All right. You want me to say it? That I'm scared? That I'm not real sure what I'm doing? Okay, I'm scared. I'll admit it. I don't know what—"

The small, crackling sound of a paper bag being opened drew Mattie's startled attention to the doorway behind her sister. Hugh lounged there, one shoulder propped against the frame. He was fiddling with a sack from the Thai take-out restaurant around the corner. He looked up from a perusal of the contents of the bag as a sudden silence fell on the office.

"Hey, don't let me interrupt," he said calmly, withdrawing a small carton from the sack. "I just stopped by with some dinner for Mattie.

Figured she needed something to fortify her energies before the big opening."

"My God," Ariel breathed. "Look at you. So damned cool. So disgustingly sure of yourself. How could you be such a complete and utter bastard, Hugh Abbott? How could you?"

"Well," Hugh began, looking thoughtful, "it's not easy, I can tell you that."

"Oh, shut up." Ariel brushed past him, black silks streaming behind her.

A moment later the outer door opened and closed with a reverberating slam.

Silence descended again on the small office.

Hugh eyed the viselike grip Mattie had on the screwdriver. "Tell you what. If you put that down slowly and carefully on the desk, I'll serve dinner."

Mattie realized she was trembling. She dropped the screwdriver onto the desk, went around to the back, and sank abruptly into her chair. Her knees felt weak.

In numb silence she watched Hugh lay out a meal that featured noodles and vegetables in a spicy peanut sauce.

"Eat up," Hugh said as he spread a napkin across her lap and pushed a paper plate full of noodles in front of her. "When we're finished I'll help you hang the rest of Silk's pictures."

"Thank you." Mattie stared blindly down at the noodles.

"Think nothing of it. Even us outdated, inconsiderate, insensitive clods have our uses."

Mattie continued to stare at the noodles.

Hugh started to eat his. He munched in silence for a full minute, and then he arched a single, inquiring brow. "Slam-bam-thank-you-ma'am?"

Mattie blinked and at last picked up her chopsticks. "It's not that bad."

"Thank you," Hugh said with great humility. "I do try, you know. And I'm willing to study hard and learn. I'm a fast learner."

And suddenly Mattie couldn't help herself. She thought of his intense, highly erotic, incredibly sexy brand of lovemaking, and she started to giggle. The giggle mushroomed into laughter, and a moment later she was convulsed with it. Hugh watched in quiet amusement, looking obliquely satisfied.

It was only later that she realized that the laughter had been as effective at reducing her stress level as venting her anger had been earlier.

And it was Hugh who had somehow given her the gift of both kinds of freedom.

\* \* \*

The Silk Taggert show was a huge success. Hugh spent most of it leaning negligently against one wall, a glass of champagne in his hand, and wishing his friend could see what was happening. Silk would have gotten a kick out of all these sophisticated, trendy people going crazy over his work. Hugh made a note to try to remember as many of the comments he had overheard this evening as possible.

" . . . *It leaves me with the strangest sense of longing . . . I can't wait to get that lagoon scene on my wall . . . Such spectacular colors, real colors . . . What a change from all the gray and brown and black you see so much of in Seattle galleries these days . . . So bold and vibrant . . . A nice change. I get so tired of subtlety . . . That jungle feels alive . . . Dangerous but beautiful . . . Captures the power of nature . . .*"

Mattie was everywhere, looking very businesslike in a proper little suit, her hair neatly coiled at the nape of her neck. She was mingling with the crowd, chatting with potential buyers, and turning a blind eye to the serious inroads a few apparently starving artists were making at the buffet table. She had told Hugh earlier she considered the free food eaten by artistic moochers at these events as a contribution to the arts.

"This stuff isn't bad," a young woman with chartreuse hair and a lot of metal hanging from her clothing announced to Hugh.

He looked at her. "You mean the art?"

"Nah. The food. The art's good, but the food is really terrific, isn't it? Mattie always puts on a first-class feast. She's not stingy like some of the gallery owners." The young woman squinted up at Hugh. "Who are you? The artist?"

"No. A friend of his. He couldn't be here."

"Too bad. It must be nice to watch people going nuts over your work. I'd give anything to have them go apeshit like this over my stuff."

"What sort of stuff do you do?"

"Metal sculpture. The name's Shock Value. Shock Value Frederickson. But I'm thinking of changing it. It doesn't go with my new direction, you know?"

"Yeah?"

"My work is getting more refined," Shock Value explained patiently. "Things are just flowing for me now, thanks to Mattie, and the flow is changing everything."

"Mattie? How the hell is she involved?"

"She's sort of like one of those old-fashioned patrons, you know? She's keeping me in groceries while I work on my latest project. One of these days I'll pay her back."

"Uh-huh. How much has she loaned you?"

"I don't remember exactly," Shock Value said carelessly. "Wow, there's a friend of mine. Haven't seen him since he broke his ankle doing some performance art in the park last month. Nice talking to you, whatever your name is. See you around."

A long time later Hugh watched Mattie carefully lock the door of Sharpe Reaction. She looked quietly elated.

"Went well, huh?" Hugh took her arm to walk down the sidewalk to her apartment.

"Very well. I sold everything I had. I hope Silk will be pleased."

"Yeah. He'll be as excited as a little kid at Christmas. He's never had any real success before. Not in anything. I can't wait to tell him." Hugh was silent for a while, thinking. "You're really good at that kind of thing, aren't you?"

"What kind of thing?"

"Handling that crowd of potential buyers tonight. Showing Silk's work. Running your gallery. The whole bit."

"It's what I do for a living," she said quietly.

"Yeah."

"What's wrong, Hugh?"

"Nothing."

"Are you sure?"

"Watching you this evening just made me think about some things, that's all," he muttered, wishing he'd never opened his mouth.

"Like what?"

"Never mind." But the truth was, he was definitely beginning to worry. Mattie was very much at home in this world. She was successful in it. She had friends here. She was a part of the art community.

Tonight he had seen just how well she moved in this environment, and the realization haunted him. Until now he had been telling himself that she would adapt easily enough to St. Gabe when the time came, but now he was beginning to wonder if the time would ever come.

He had been so blithely certain that once he had convinced Mattie she was not just a stand-in for Ariel that she would give up everything to move to St. Gabriel.

Now he was beginning to wonder if that would be the case. Viewed objectively, what did he really have to offer her compared to the life she had created for herself here in Seattle?

Only himself.

Silk was right. These weren't the good old days when a man could expect a woman to pull up stakes and follow him anywhere. Maybe Charlotte had a point when she called him arrogant.

"Hugh? Is something wrong?" Mattie was looking up at him with worried eyes as they came to a halt in front of the door of her apartment building.

"Nothing's wrong. Forget it, Mattie." He opened the security door, walked Mattie down the hall, and punched the elevator button in silence. Mattie continued to throw small, anxious glances in his direction, but he ignored them. He was thinking.

In fact, Hugh was concentrating so hard on the host of new worries that had arisen to confront him this evening that he almost failed to notice that the bolt on the front door of Mattie's apartment was not in position.

He, himself, had locked it earlier. He never made that kind of mistake.

Someone had opened the door tonight and failed to set the dead bolt again. Whoever it was might still be inside.

Hugh stepped back and clamped a hand over Mattie's startled mouth to prevent her from saying anything. She went very still, her eyes widening in silent question.

"Someone inside," he breathed into her ear. He took his hand away from her lips when she nodded her understanding of the situation.

Mattie mouthed a single word. "Police."

He shook his head and pulled her quietly along the corridor to the door that opened onto a utility room. He opened it, reached inside, and found the switch that operated the hall lights. When he flipped it, the hall outside Mattie's apartment was immediately plunged into darkness except for the pale glow of the emergency sign at the end of the corridor.

"Hugh?" Mattie's faint whisper was now laced with anxiety.

"Wait right here."

"What are you going to do? There might be a burglar inside. You're not supposed to confront them. You're supposed to go use a neighbor's phone and call the police."

"Give me two minutes. If I haven't got the situation under control, go ahead and call the cops."

"I'd rather you didn't—"

"Hush, babe. I'll be right back."

It was the thought that it might not be a simple thief at all that was making him do this the hard way. After all the excitement on Purgatory followed by the death of Rosey and the disappearance of Gibbs, a man had to wonder if there might, just possibly, be something besides an everyday, garden-variety burglary in process inside the apartment.

And if there was, Hugh wanted some answers. The opportunity was simply too good to miss.

His eyes were adjusted to the shadows now. Hugh pushed the door open and went in fast and low. He was counting on the darkness behind him to give him the cover he needed.

A picture of the layout of the big studio firmly etched in his mind, he dived behind the leather sofa and flattened himself. He glanced up at the bedroom loft first. There was no one up there. He could tell that much from the glow coming in through the high windows.

The entire room was shrouded in darkness. Whoever had invaded it earlier had turned off the light that Hugh had deliberately left on in the kitchen alcove.

Hugh was processing that piece of information when he heard someone shift on the sofa cushions. Leather squeaked softly.

Hugh rolled to his feet, vaulted over the back of the sofa, and slammed into the body on the cushions.

A man yelped in startled surprise as the wind was knocked out of him. Gasping, the intruder thrashed about like a fish on a line. His wild gyrations succeeded in causing both Hugh and his victim to slide off the sofa and onto the carpet with a dull thud.

Hugh pinned the man to the floor and then wrinkled his nose as the unmistakable odor of brandy fumes assailed his nostrils.

Whoever he was, the guy had been into Mattie's small supply of liquor.

"Hey," the intruder managed in strangled tones. "Take it easy, damn it. Let go, will you?"

The lights went on. "I've called the police," Mattie said forcefully from the open doorway. "They'll be here any minute. Hugh, are you all right?"

Hugh looked down at the man he had trapped beneath him. "Shit. You'd better cancel that call to the cops."

"Well, actually, I didn't call them," Mattie explained, moving into the room. "I haven't had a chance. I just said that in case whoever was in here got any ideas of shooting his way out. I thought he might think twice if he knew the police were on their way." She stopped abruptly, her eyes widening in shock. "Good grief. What are you doing, Hugh? That's not a burglar."

"Hi, Mattie." Flynn Grafton looked up at her from his prone position on the floor. His blond hair was spread out in a pale fan around his head and his gaze looked distinctly red and watery. "Sorry about this."

# 13

❦

"Good grief, it's Flynn." Mattie hurried forward, deep concern in her eyes. "For heaven's sake, let him up, Hugh. Did you hurt him? Flynn, are you okay?"

"He's fine." Hugh got to his feet, annoyed with the speed with which Mattie's concern had shifted from him to Ariel's husband.

"I think I'm okay." Flynn shook his head slightly as if to clear it. He sat up slowly and blinked in the light as Mattie crouched beside him. "Christ. You landed on me like a tank, Abbott. Who did you think I was? Jack the Ripper?"

"It was a possibility. What the hell are you doing here, Grafton? How did you get inside?"

"Ariel has a key. I borrowed it." Flynn's words were slightly blurred.

"Why?" Hugh demanded roughly.

Mattie scowled at him. "Stop badgering Flynn. Can't you see he's still trying to recover from your assault? I hope there's no serious damage. That sort of trauma can cause all kinds of stress-related injuries from back problems to headaches. You definitely overreacted, Hugh."

"I overreacted?" Hugh stared at her in disbelief. "The guy sneaks into your apartment, drinks your booze, and sacks out on your couch waiting for you to come home, leaves all the earmarks of a burglary in progress, and you call it an overreaction when I jump him?"

"Thank heavens you weren't carrying your gun. This is exactly how accidental shootings occur."

Hugh looked up toward the ceiling for inspiration and patience. "Give me a break. I've never accidentally shot anyone in my life. That kind of thing I tend to do on purpose."

"Calm down, Hugh," Mattie said, her voice soothing. "I realize you're still a little wired from the adrenaline, but there's no need to get short-tempered."

"Wired? Short-tempered? You haven't seen anything yet, babe."

She smiled brightly. "Why don't you make us all a nice pot of herbal tea? I have some chamomile in the kitchen. That will settle everyone's nerves."

"My nerves are just fine, thanks. I'm not real happy, but my nerves are in great shape."

"Well, perhaps Flynn would like some herbal tea," Mattie said, glancing down at the artist who was struggling to his knees.

"No," Flynn whispered, holding up a pleading hand and looking seasick. "No herbal tea. To tell you the truth, I'm feeling a little rocky at the moment. Don't want to puke all over your nice rug."

"Don't even think of getting sick in here," Hugh warned.

Mattie frowned. "Don't sound so menacing, Hugh. You're just going to make him more tense."

"This may come as a serious shock to you, Mattie, but I really don't give a damn about Grafton's stress level." He turned to Flynn, who was pulling himself up onto the couch. "Stop playing the wounded innocent and tell me what you're doing here before I really get stressed out to the max and take you over to that window, open it, and drop you onto the street."

"*Hugh.*" Mattie sent him a reproachful glance.

Hugh ignored it, his eyes on Flynn. "Let's have the explanation, Grafton."

Flynn made it to the couch and sank wearily down onto the cushions. He put his head in his hands. "I came to ask Mattie if I could spend the night."

"The hell you did. That settles it. I am going to drop you out the window. But first I'm going to do a neo-impressionistic job on that pretty face of yours." Hugh started forward.

"No, Hugh, stop. Stop this at once." Mattie threw herself into his path, holding up an imperious palm. "This isn't Purgatory or St. Gabriel, damn it. You're back in civilization now, and you will behave in a civilized fashion, do you hear me?"

"Out of my way, Mattie."

"No, I will not get out of your way. This is my home and I run things here. Now, you are not going to beat up Flynn. Is that clear? I'm sure he didn't mean what you thought he meant when he said he wanted to spend the night."

"He meant to spend the night with you. You heard him. He said so himself," Hugh snarled. "Get out of my way, Mattie."

"He just wanted to sleep on my couch, didn't you, Flynn?" Mattie turned to her uninvited guest for confirmation.

Flynn raised his head, looking baffled by the commotion. "Sure. Just wanted to sleep on the couch. Ariel and I had an argument. Came over here to see if you'd put me up, Mattie. What's the problem?"

"I don't believe this." Hugh pinned Mattie with his coldest gaze. "Does he spend the night on your couch regularly?"

"Of course not." Mattie looked anxiously at Flynn. "This is the first time he's ever asked to stay here. I take it the argument was pretty bad, Flynn?"

"Bad enough." Flynn collapsed back against the cushions, closing his eyes wearily. "I keep telling myself she's entering her Early Mature period, but I'm not so sure anymore. I know she's temperamental by nature, but lately it's been downright crazy. Her moods are all over the place."

Mattie patted him gently on the shoulder. "What did you fight about?"

"Same old thing. My painting. But this time she really went bonkers."

"Why?"

"Because I told her my mind was made up. I've got some stuff ready to show you, Mattie. I want you to tell me if you think you can sell it to your crowd of upwardly mobile Borgias and Medicis."

Mattie sank down onto the couch beside Flynn. "No wonder Ariel blew up. She's been fighting you every step of the way on this project."

"Yeah. But I've made up my mind to do it, Mattie. I can't live on her money any longer. Besides, truth is, I'm damned tired of doing art for art's sake. Hell, maybe I just want to prove my old man wrong after all these years. Maybe I want to show him that I can make a living at my art. I don't know. All I know is that I want to try putting some stuff into your gallery."

"I understand," Mattie said, still patting his shoulder.

"Look, I'm sure this is all very touching," Hugh interrupted sarcastically. "And believe me, I'm well aware of how temperamental Ariel can be. But that's no excuse for you to come here looking for a place to bed down for the night, Grafton. Nobody is spending the night in Mattie's apartment except me. Clear?"

"Now, Hugh," Mattie said, her tone soothing once more, "there's no need to run around beating your chest and defending your territory. Look at the time. It's much too late for Flynn to find somewhere else to stay. There's absolutely no reason he can't spend the night here on my couch."

"He's history," Hugh stated. "Get out of here, Grafton. Now."

Flynn nodded, his eyes bleak. "I'll call a cab."

"There's no need for that, Flynn," Mattie said firmly. She shot Hugh a defiant glance and turned back to Flynn. "Where would you go at this hour, Flynn? A hotel? It would cost a fortune, and you don't have any money, remember?"

"I've got Ariel's credit cards."

"Great idea," Hugh muttered. "Use one of your wife's credit cards to pay for a fancy suite in some big downtown hotel while you hide out from her. There's a certain poetic justice in that."

"No, I guess that wouldn't be right, would it?" Flynn straightened, looking very noble and stoic. "I'll think of something, Mattie. Don't worry about me. I'll find somewhere to spend the night. It's too late to get into any of the missions, but I can always find a doorway or something."

Mattie was aghast. "But, Flynn, you can't possibly sleep on the streets. I won't allow it."

Hugh eyed the pathetic little scene while he dug his wallet out of his jeans. "Tell you what. I'll make this even easier. I'll stake you to a night in a hotel, Grafton. It's worth it just to get you out of here."

Mattie sprang up from the couch and came toward Hugh with a determination in her gaze that made him immediately uneasy.

"Will you stop behaving like a jealous Tarzan? There is no reason Flynn can't stay here. It's past midnight. I am not sending him out at this hour."

"Then let him go home and sleep in his own bed."

"This is my apartment, he is my brother-in-law, and I say he can sleep here."

Hugh sensed defeat in the making, but he braced himself, planted his fists on his hips, and tried his most intimidating glare. "I say he goes."

"You don't have any right to make demands around here."

"Is that a fact? In case it has escaped your notice, we happen to be engaged. That gives me a few goddamned rights."

She eyed him for an icy moment and then switched tactics with dazzling speed. "Hugh, I don't want to quarrel over this. Flynn's had too much to drink, he's very depressed and under a lot of stress, and he has no money of his own. It won't hurt you to let him sleep on the couch just this once. Please?"

"Damn it, Mattie." It was not fair that a woman's pleas could break through a man's defenses so easily, Hugh told himself as he started to weaken.

A gentle snore interrupted the low-voiced argument. Hugh glanced toward the couch and saw that the man he was trying to evict had gone back to sleep. Hugh knew a strategically indefensible position when he saw one. Sometimes the only good option was a carefully orchestrated retreat.

And revenge, of course. There definitely remained the pleasures to be had in exacting vengeance.

Half an hour later Hugh stretched out beside Mattie in the loft bed and pulled her into his arms. He had waited patiently while she had found a blanket to throw over Grafton, brushed her teeth, taken her evening ration of vitamins, and changed into her prim little flannel nightgown.

"Hugh, I want to thank you for backing down on this little matter of letting Flynn sleep on my couch," Mattie whispered earnestly as she snuggled close. "I know you were annoyed to find him here, and I realize that under the circumstances you had every right to react as you did. It won't happen again, I promise."

"You're right. It won't happen again." He kissed her throat, inhaling the sweet, feminine scent of her body. He was already hard with sexual anticipation, he realized. He let his hand glide down her arm.

"Hugh?"

"Yeah, babe?" He slowly pushed her proper little nightgown up over her knees and then edged it higher.

"Hugh, we can't. Not tonight." She batted ineffectually at his roving hands. "Flynn might wake up and hear us. It would be horribly embarrassing."

"Then you'll just have to try real hard to be very, very quiet, won't you?" He gently pried apart her tightly closed thighs. She was so soft, he thought. Her skin was like velvet. He smiled to himself when he felt the first small, delicious shiver go through her. He loved it when she trembled like that.

"Stop it," Mattie hissed. "You're doing this to get even with me, aren't you?"

"No way, babe. I'm doing this on account of I'm such a sweet, sensitive guy who happens to be hornier than hell." He tugged the nightgown off impatiently and tossed it over the loft railing.

Mattie gasped in horror as the gown fluttered downward. "For heaven's sake, Hugh. What will Flynn think when he sees that nightgown down there in the morning?"

"He'll think what he's supposed to think. That I'm staking out my territory."

"Well, I suppose I should be grateful you don't do it in the usual manner of wolves and other wild animals," she retorted tartly. "Really, Hugh, there's no need to be quite so primitive about all this. *Oh.*" She clapped a hand over her own mouth as she realized she had moaned aloud.

"Hush, babe, or he'll hear you. Think of the embarrassment." Hugh slid down between her legs, moving lower and lower along the delightfully curving length of her until he could taste her essence.

"Ummph, no. I said no, *oh.*" Mattie held the pillow over her face. She used one hand to hold it in place and clenched her other fist quite painfully in Hugh's hair.

He used his thumbs to part her carefully, and then he used his tongue.

"*Mmmmph.*" Mattie yanked the pillow away from her face. "Oh, my God, Hugh." She slapped the pillow back in place. "*Mmmmph.* No. Oh, Hugh."

Hugh waited until she was arching frantically, her muffled moans threatening to turn into the now-familiar cries of delight that he had gotten addicted to hearing during the past several days.

When he decided Mattie was too far gone to remember to use the pillow to muffle her breathless little moans, he moved heavily back up along her soft body, spread her thighs more widely apart, and thrust himself slowly, deeply, into her wet heat.

When he yanked the pillow away from her face, she looked up at him with huge, luminous eyes. He saw her teeth were clamped on her lower lip in an effort to keep from crying out.

"Slam-bam-thank-you-ma'am?" Hugh murmured on a soft, husky laugh.

"Like I said, it's not so bad."

He grinned and covered her mouth with his own. A moment later he swallowed her soft shriek of ecstasy as she contracted tightly beneath him.

Then he quickly released her lips and buried his own face in the pillow to stifle his groan as he poured himself into her.

His own muffled shout of triumphant release made the bed vibrate.

The angry shrill of the telephone brought Mattie out of a sound sleep with a start. She flailed around in the rumpled bed until she managed to silence the offending instrument by the simple expedient of lifting the receiver in the general direction of her ear.

She regretted the action immediately. A tearful Ariel was screaming more loudly than the phone had been ringing.

"He's there with you, Mattie, isn't he? I know he is. He went to you just like all the others did. Put him on the line right now. I want to tell Flynn Grafton to his face that he will never be able to crawl back into my bed. I don't care how hard he begs."

"Good morning to you, too, Ariel. Nice of you to call." Mattie opened her eyes and gazed at the ceiling. She was alone in the bed. Down below she heard the low rumble of men's voices and the clink of a pot. The aroma of strongly brewed coffee wafted upward.

"I hope you're satisfied, Mattie," Ariel sniffed. "After all these years I hope you're finally satisfied. You've done it, haven't you? You've gotten your sneaky little claws into the only man I ever really wanted."

"Ariel, contrary to popular opinion around here, Flynn and I are not having an affair."

There was a click followed by the hollow sound on the telephone line that indicated someone had picked up the downstairs receiver.

"Oh, God, an affair," Ariel whispered, apparently unaware of the other presence on the line. "An *affair*. I knew it. I was praying that it was just a one-night stand. Something done in the heat of the moment like that stupid fling you had with Hugh last year. Something you might have at least had the decency to regret the way you regretted that. But, no. No, you're bragging about it, aren't you?"

"Ariel, you're not listening. I just told you, I am not sleeping with your husband. I have never slept with your husband. I have no desire to sleep with your husband. And he has no desire to sleep with me. He loves you."

"He went to you last night. He didn't come back home. He went straight to you. Did you comfort him, Mattie, the way you did the others? Offer him herbal tea and sympathy? Tell him you understood all the stress he was under? Damn you."

"For Christ's sake, give it a break, Ariel," Hugh ordered brusquely. "Grafton's here, all right. He slept on the couch. I should know. I'm the one who spent the night in Mattie's bed. I would have noticed a third party in the sheets, believe me. I'm fussy that way."

"Hugh? You're there, too?" Ariel's sobs halted with dramatic swiftness.

"I'm here, all right."

"You were there all night?"

"Where the hell else would I be? I'm engaged to Mattie, remember?"

"Thank God," Ariel said, switching instantly from pathetic victim to vengeful shrew. "Put Flynn on the line at once."

"My pleasure," Hugh said.

There was a brief, fumbling sound and then Flynn's voice spoke very coolly into the phone. "Ariel?"

"Flynn, how could you do this to me? I was so frightened when I woke up this morning and realized you'd never come home. Do you have any idea of what I've been through? Do you know what it was like having to call my own sister to find you? How dare you do such a thing?"

"You're the one who told me to get out and stay out, remember?" Flynn sounded vaguely preoccupied. He also sounded as if he were munching on something.

Mattie dropped the receiver back into the cradle, got out of bed, and reached for her robe. She went to the edge of the loft and looked down over the waist-high red metal railing.

The first thing she noticed was her modest nightgown. It had been tossed rather negligently, Mattie thought, over the back of the chair Hugh was occupying.

Hugh himself looked arrogantly at ease, quite the master in his own home, as he sprawled in the chair. He had a mug of coffee in his hand, and there was a plate of bran muffins on the low table in front of the couch. He had not bothered to put on anything except a pair of jeans, Mattie realized. His bare feet were propped on the coffee table, and his bare shoulders gleamed in the morning sunlight.

Flynn, rumpled from a night in his clothes, was eating one of the bran muffins as he listened to Ariel's tirade.

"I hear you, Ariel," he said calmly. "Ease up, honey. You've made your point."

Flynn took another bite of muffin and wrinkled his nose while he listened to Ariel's response.

"What was I supposed to do after you locked the door? Stand out in the hall and beg?" he finally asked.

More munching while Flynn listened.

"No," he finally said during a pause. "Nothing's changed. I know you don't like it, but I've done a lot of thinking about this and my mind is made up. I'm going to ask Mattie to hang my more commercial stuff and that's final." Flynn finished the muffin and picked up his mug of coffee. "Ariel, I may be the greatest undiscovered artist who ever lived, but I'm also your husband. With any luck, one of these days I'll be a father. I've got some pride, okay? I want to carry my own weight in this family. Maybe I'd better talk to you later when you're feeling calmer."

Flynn hung up the phone quite gently and sat hunched over his coffee. "The lady is very unhappy," he said to Hugh.

"I got that feeling," Hugh replied. "Wish I could help you out with a few tips on handling her, but the truth is, I never did understand Ariel. She and I were like oil and water. Or gasoline on a fire. Whatever."

"Yeah, I know. It's not that I can't deal with her usual moods. I understand those. They're part of what makes her a great artist. She's very sensitive and she needs to be handled delicately. But last night I just lost it, you know? Told her I was tired of feeling like a kept man. Tired of feeling like I'm standing in her shadow, making no contribution to the relationship. We really got into it. Sorry I turned up here. That was a mistake."

"I guess one time isn't going to be a problem," Hugh allowed magnanimously.

"It won't happen again," Flynn promised.

"Right." Hugh sounded satisfied.

"It's just that this was the first place I thought of when I found myself locked out. The thing is, Mattie always seems so quiet and calm and levelheaded. So sensible and unemotional. Sort of soothing."

"She has her moments," Hugh said dryly. "But she sure is a hell of a lot different than Ariel, I'll give you that. I could never get a handle on Ariel during our engagement. She was either moping around in some tragic state of depression or else she was exploding. It was a real roller-coaster ride, and it didn't help matters any that I had no patience for any of it after a couple of weeks."

Flynn nodded wisely. "Like I said, Ariel needs to be handled delicately."

"I'm not the kid-glove type."

"No. I can see why you two never made it. I take it you don't seem to have the same problem dealing with Mattie?"

"No sweat," Hugh assured him. "Sure, sometimes she gets a little feisty. You've got to watch out for that streak of pride she has. But I understand pride. I can deal with it. Given a little time I can always find a way to settle Mattie down when she occasionally gets a little temperamental."

Mattie looked around for something convenient to drop over the loft railing. She considered the tall, heavy black vase but discarded it as overkill. She picked up the glass of water she kept beside the bed instead.

"The thing about women like Mattie," Hugh was saying down below, "is that you've got to make them understand . . ."

"For the record, Hugh Abbott," Mattie called as she leaned out over the railing and tipped the full glass of water, "no lady worth her salt likes to hear first thing in the morning that she is so dreadfully dull a man can handle her with 'no sweat.' But, then, I've always said you have a lousy way with compliments. No finesse at all."

Hugh yelped very nicely and scrambled up out of the chair with amazing speed as the water splashed down over his head and bare shoulders.

Flynn looked on, amused.

"Like I said," Hugh muttered, using a napkin to wipe water off his shoulder, "she has her moments."

"I can see that." Flynn picked up another bran muffin and eyed it critically. "You really like these things?"

"You get used to them," Hugh said. "It's the herbal tea and the bug juice that are a little hard to swallow."

Mattie sat in her office chair later that morning, her hands folded on the desk, and watched her sister storm back and forth across the room. Ariel had been alternating between tears of rage and tears of self-pity for the past fifteen minutes. It was getting hard to tell the difference. But in either mood she managed to look her usual exotic self in flowing black trousers and a black blouse with billowing sleeves.

Mattie was again painfully aware of the bland, businesslike look of her coffee-colored suit and beige blouse. Maybe it was the string of pearls that really elevated the outfit to the level of total forgettableness, she decided critically. Or perhaps it was the low-heeled pumps. She really was going to have to go shopping one of these days. The desire for a red business suit was becoming irresistible.

And maybe, if she got very adventurous, she would invest in a pair of three-inch red spike heels, just like the ones Evangeline Dangerfield had loaned her for that wild night on Brimstone.

"I'm sorry I blew up at you on the phone this morning," Ariel said, sniffing delicately into a tissue. "I can't believe I did that. Lately, it's almost like after all these years our roles have been reversed or something. For the first time I've actually been jealous of you. It's so ludicrous."

"Simply ludicrous."

"It's irrational."

"Right. Totally irrational."

"Especially when I know there is absolutely no real reason for it," Ariel concluded.

"True," Mattie agreed.

Ariel swung around and looked at her with eyes that brimmed with sincerity. "I want you to know that I really do realize there is no basis for my irrational jealousy, Mattie. I don't understand it, but I just don't seem to be completely sane on the subject of Flynn. I've never felt this way before about any man."

"Maybe that's because you've never been afraid of losing any of your previous men. After all, none of the others have been terribly important to you."

Ariel nodded. "I guess that must be it. I really do love Flynn. What I feel for him is so different than what I felt for any of the others. He's the only one who's ever understood me. Well, that's not entirely true. Emery understood me, but it was sort of the way a mentor understands his protégée, you know? Toward the end of our relationship, he just could not handle my success at all."

"Did you understand him? What he was going through as he saw himself slipping slowly into obscurity?"

"It was hardly my fault he couldn't write anymore," Ariel retorted.

"I know, I know. Forget I said that."

Ariel nodded willingly enough. "Hugh, of course, never did understand me. Not at all. He was really just a sort of wild fling for me. I don't know how on earth I managed to get myself engaged to him."

"Probably the same way I did," Mattie observed. "By fiat. Hugh has a way of taking command."

"Yes, I know. It's very annoying, isn't it? However do you tolerate it, Mattie?"

"Sometimes I don't," Mattie said, thinking with a sense of pride of how she had won the battle over Flynn's sleeping arrangements last night. And she *had* won it, by God. She had actually made Hugh Abbott back down. Even better, she had dumped cold water on him this morning. She was definitely showing signs of genuine spirit, Mattie decided.

"Well, you're certainly welcome to him, although I still think you're making a big mistake."

"Thank you," Mattie murmured.

"Damn. I've gone and offended you again, haven't I? And the truth is, I came here to apologize, Mattie. I made an absolute fool out of myself this morning on the phone, and I want to tell you how sorry I am for screaming at you."

Mattie felt her brows climb. Apologies for an outburst from Ariel or any other member of the family were rarer than hen's teeth. In the Sharpe clan temperamental explosions were considered normal. Nobody except Mattie ever got upset over one.

"Don't worry about it, Ariel," she said gently. "It was perfectly understandable. I'd have made the same kind of fool out of myself if I'd quarreled with Hugh and then discovered he'd spent the night at your place."

"Thank you, Mattie. That's very generous of you."

"All right, you've apologized and I've told you to forget it. You knew I would. So what do you really want from me this morning, Ariel?"

Ariel sniffed into the tissue again. "You think you know me so well, don't you?"

"Well, I have known you all my life," Mattie reminded her, smiling.

"You've really had to put up with a lot from me over the years, haven't you?"

"It wasn't that bad," Mattie said, feeling a little wary now.

"Sometimes when we were growing up I'd feel guilty about it, even though I knew I had no reason to feel that way, of course. I mean, it wasn't my fault I inherited talent and you didn't, was it?"

"Of course not."

"I used to wish you'd find something you could really excel at so I wouldn't have to feel so damned sorry for you. You worked so hard trying to prove yourself at so many things, and they were all disasters. Remember the year you determined to become a ballerina like Grandmother?"

"Don't remind me. I limped around for weeks from all that work at the barre."

Ariel smiled. "And then there was the time you were so sure you could become a great artist like Mother. You used to sit up until three in the morning practicing your drawing. You never could do a proper nude, could you?"

"Never got much past fruit," Mattie admitted. "And then there was that year in college when I was certain I was going to write, just like Dad. You don't have to remind me of that, either. Ariel, what's the point of all this?"

Ariel heaved a dramatic sigh. "It's hard to put into words. It's just that, maybe because you tried so many things and failed before you started this gallery, you learned something the rest of us never had to learn."

Mattie studied her, remembering all the depressing years of failure. "Just what is it you think I learned?"

"I don't know." Ariel waved the hand with the damp tissue in it. "How to cope with normal life or something. How to take risks, maybe. How to try and fail and then be able to accept the failure and go on to something else. None of the rest of us ever had to do that, you see. We always knew we had talent. It might have made us a bit neurotic at times; we might have had to struggle to master it or sell it, but we always knew deep down we had it. You've never had that kind of inner certainty."

"Well, I definitely floundered around for years getting my act together, I'll admit that much."

Ariel blew into the tissue. "But all that floundering made you more adaptable or something. More understanding of other people. More accepting of their little foibles and weaknesses. More approachable."

"So I'm an easy touch. What do you want from me now?"

Ariel raised her head, her eyes tragic. "I want some advice, damn it."

"Advice? You're asking me for advice?"

"Please, Mattie. Don't make me grovel. Help me. I don't know where else to turn. You seem to understand men so much better than I do. They feel comfortable around you. I've never worried about making a man feel comfortable. I've never needed to worry about it. But now I want you to give me some pointers on handling Flynn. I don't want to lose him, Mattie. I'm scared. And I'm pregnant."

# 14

❦

"You're pregnant?" For a long moment Mattie could think of nothing else to say. "Does Flynn know?" she finally asked.

Ariel shook her head. "No. I've only just realized it myself. I haven't told him yet."

Mattie considered the matter. "Is there a problem here? Do you want a baby?"

"Yes, but Mattie, I'm scared. I told you, I'm not like you. I can't take things in my stride the way you do. I don't cope well. I stopped taking precautions because Flynn kept talking about having children and how my biological clock was running out. But now that the inevitable has happened, I don't know what to do next. I'm starting to do stupid things like fight with Flynn and accuse you of sleeping with him. I can't paint. I feel like I'm floundering. It's just awful."

"When are you going to tell Flynn?"

"Don't you understand? I'm scared to tell him. I'm scared to death that when he finds out he's going to be a father, he'll be more determined than ever to get into the commercial mainstream with his painting. I don't want him giving up his art for me, Mattie. I can't let him make that kind of sacrifice."

"Because you know deep down inside that if the situation were reversed, you wouldn't do it for him?" Mattie suggested quietly.

Ariel froze, an expression of shock on her face. "Oh, Lord, you're right of course. You're absolutely right."

Mattie examined her fingernails for a long moment. They were blunt, neatly curved nails with no polish on them. "You want advice? I'll give it to you for what it's worth. From what I know about Flynn, I would say that underneath that trendy facade, he's really a decent, old-fashioned guy who needs to feel he's doing the right thing as a man. So let him do it. Tell him about the baby. Encourage him to go ahead with his more commercial style of painting. Let him know you respect him as a man, not just as an artist, and that you need him. Let him feel he's holding up his end of the marriage."

"I'm afraid he'll be seduced by success," Ariel whispered.

"What's wrong with that? What's wrong with finding out he can do stuff that will sell like hotcakes? I think it's what he really wants, Ariel, so stop trying to force him into a different mold."

"But, Mattie—"

"These days a lot of artists are beginning to be a lot more personally ambitious again. They want success in their lifetimes, not posthumously. It hasn't been fashionable to be artistically ambitious for the past hundred years or so, but things are changing. Very soon it's going to be just like the old days, the way it was before somebody got the notion that the only good art was art nobody understood."

A sound in the doorway made Mattie glance up. Shock Value Frederickson stood there, her hair tinted silver and black. She was holding a large metal object in her arms that was very nearly as large as she was.

Mattie smiled slowly. "Speaking of great art. Lord love us, Shock Value, what have you got there?"

Shock Value glanced diffidently at Ariel. "Am I interrupting anything? Suzanne out front said you weren't busy in here."

Mattie was already out of her chair, circling the desk for a better look at the metal sculpture Shock Value was holding. "You can interrupt me anytime as long as you've got something like this in your hot little hands. This is fantastic, Shock. Absolutely fantastic."

Shock Value grinned, looking enormously relieved. "I'm calling it *On the Brink.* You really like it?"

"I love it. I always knew you had talent, Shock, but this is unbelievable. Take a look at this, Ariel." Mattie took the soaring, powerfully worked metal from the artist's hands and placed it on the floor in front of her desk.

Ariel studied the piece thoughtfully. "You're right, Mattie. It's really something. Very strong stuff. You're going to display it here in Sharpe Reaction?"

"You bet I am, so that Shock gets the public exposure. But it's not for sale. As of this moment this piece is mine, all mine. Let's make a deal, Shock."

Shock Value smiled. "Mattie, you can have it for free. I owe you. A lot, I think. I don't even remember how much."

"You don't owe me this much," Mattie assured her. "If you won't put a price tag on it, I will. Sit down while I write up a bill of sale."

Shock Value took a seat. "I'm really sort of relieved that it's okay. I wasn't sure what I was doing. You know, I think it would be a good idea for me to get away from the city for a while. Too many distractions, you know? I think I need a change of environment. I need to go somewhere and refresh myself while I work out this new direction in my style."

Mattie glanced up from the paperwork. "You really think so?"

Shock Value nodded quickly. "I turned a corner when I started working on *Brink*. I could feel it. I need to focus this new energy. I don't want to work in isolation, but I really think I have to get away from the city. Someplace quiet and sort of inspirational, if you know what I mean."

"Someplace where they don't sell colored hair gel and metal-studded leather pants?" Ariel asked with a little smile.

"I guess," Shock Value admitted. "But a nice place."

"Some place like a tropical island, perhaps?" Mattie said slowly.

"Man, that'd be perfect," Shock Value said with a grin.

"You've got to come with me, Mattie. I simply don't have the guts to do this alone. Lord knows, I'm no Hemingway." Emery Blackwell slumped dejectedly in the chair in Mattie's office. "You got me into this, and you simply cannot abandon me now in my hour of need."

"Of course I'll come with you," Mattie assured him. "I can't wait to see it. Just give me a minute to finish off this paperwork. I'm right in the middle of something. Would you like a cup of herbal tea or something to calm your nerves?"

"A shot of whiskey, maybe, not tea."

The door of Mattie's office opened, and Hugh took one step into the room before he spotted Emery. He scowled. "Why is it I can't go anywhere these days without tripping over you or Grafton, Blackwell? The two of you are getting to be damned nuisances."

Emery looked up with lofty disdain. "If my presence offends you, Abbott, feel free to take yourself off elsewhere. You're not needed around here at the moment, as it happens. Mattie and I have an appointment in a few minutes."

"The hell you do." But Hugh's voice contained more resignation than heat.

He sauntered over to the desk, tipped Mattie's face up, and kissed her ruthlessly. It was a kiss of possession, rather than passion. The kind of kiss a man uses when he's drawing lines and issuing challenges in front of another man. The woman's response was not particularly important. It was the impact on the other male that counted.

Mattie smiled frostily. "You've made your point."

"Dear me," Emery murmured. "However do you tolerate all that dreadful machismo, Mattie? Ariel could only put up with it for a few weeks."

"Most of the time it can be ignored," Mattie explained cheerfully.

Hugh growled with mock menace. He lounged against Mattie's desk and folded his arms across his chest. "All right, let's have it. What are you two up to this afternoon?"

"We are proposing to walk all of two blocks down the street to the bookstore," Emery informed him. "I do hope that doesn't offend your hopelessly antiquated sense of male territoriality."

"Heck, no," Hugh said. "I'll go with you, sport that I am."

"Shouldn't you be working?" Emery suggested pointedly.

"Took the afternoon off. I get to do that, you know. I have this really important, fancy, executive-level job that lets me do that."

"How odd," Emery murmured.

Mattie leaned back in her chair. "There's no need to go with us, Hugh. Emery and I will only be gone a few minutes."

"No sweat, babe. I've got nothing better planned. And I wouldn't mind hitting a good bookstore."

"Oh, do you read?" Emery asked.

"Without even moving my lips on my good days," Hugh assured him.

"Congratulations. Quite an accomplishment for a man of your rather peculiar abilities."

"Gentlemen," Mattie interrupted forcefully, "I would appreciate it if you would do your sniping outside of this office and away from me. If you cannot be civil to each other, please leave. Otherwise, you will both shut up while I finish this paperwork and then we will all go together to the bookstore."

"Sure," said Hugh. "By the way, just why are we making this trek as one big, happy family, anyway?"

"We are going to look at the first book in Emery's new mystery series. It arrived in the shop yesterday, and they got it out on the shelves this morning."

"How do you know?"

"I called," Emery said coldly. "Anonymously, of course."

Hugh grinned. "Of course. I'll bet you've been calling anonymously for the past couple of weeks, right?"

Emery sighed. "Really, Mattie. What do you see in him?"

"It's kind of hard to explain sometimes," Mattie admitted.

"Don't start," Hugh warned.

"She tells me you're claiming this is a more or less permanent move to Seattle," Emery murmured, crossing his legs and adjusting the crease in his trousers. "Personally, I think you're lying through your teeth."

"Is that right?"

Mattie looked up uneasily as she heard Hugh's voice go cold.

"Yes," Emery said, "that's right. You're just playing games, aren't you, Abbott? I'll wager you're just biding your time, secretly planning to sweep Mattie off to that godforsaken little hellhole of an island you call home."

"What if I am?" Hugh drawled. "Would you have any objections?"

"As a matter of fact, I would. Mattie's a civilized woman and deserves civilized surroundings. She will make her own decisions, naturally, but let me make something perfectly clear, Abbott."

"And what would that be?" Hugh asked, voice dropping another ten degrees below zero.

"Mattie is a friend of mine. If it should come to my attention that you are not treating her well or if you fail to make her happy, you will hear from me. Is that understood?"

"What'll it be, Blackwell? Pistols at dawn?"

Mattie got to her feet, outraged. "Stop it, both of you. Stop it at once, do you hear me?"

Emery rose majestically. "Just watch your step, Abbott. You may be a few years younger than I, but that only means I've had that much longer to get meaner and craftier." He turned to Mattie. "Are you ready to go, my dear?"

"Well, I'm not sure." Mattie eyed both men consideringly. "This is a totally new experience for me, you realize. I've never had two men fighting over me. I'm having so much fun listening to the two of you snarl and growl and snap that I hate to see the entertainment end."

"Don't worry," Hugh said as he took her arm and started toward the door. "It's not likely to stop just because we're out in public."

"Actually," Mattie said, "that's what I'm afraid of. I do have a reputation in this neighborhood, you know. I'm the quiet Sharpe. I don't take part in public scenes."

Emery smiled grandly. "I assure you, Mattie, I, for one, will not embarrass you. I cannot speak for your hellhound here, however. I leave it to you to control him."

"Relax, babe," Hugh said. "I promise not to rip Emery's head off his shoulders while we're inside the bookstore."

"I suppose I'll have to be satisfied with that much. Let's go." Mattie led the way out the door and through the gallery. She waved casually to her assistant as the trio went past the front desk. "We'll be back in a few minutes, Suzanne."

"Sure thing, boss," Suzanne answered with a wave.

*St. Cyr's Axiom* was sitting face out on the new-books shelf in the mystery section of the large bookstore. Right where it was supposed to be. It even had a neatly lettered sign under it advising browsers that this was a work by a local author.

Mattie took one look at the evocative cover with its subtle, sexy, menacing appeal and hugged Emery.

"It's gorgeous!" she exclaimed. She released Emery and stood back to admire the book from all angles. "Absolutely beautiful. It's going to sell like crazy."

"Why should it? Nobody's ever heard of the author." Emery examined his pseudonym on the book and shook his head. "Just one more new mystery in an already overcrowded genre."

"The cover will sell it," Mattie assured him. "And once the average browser reads the first page, he'll be hooked. Here, I'll show you. We'll run a little experiment." She plucked a copy of *St. Cyr's Axiom* from the stack and handed it to Hugh.

"What am I supposed to do with this?" Hugh demanded, examining the cover.

"You get to volunteer as our average bookstore browser for this on-the-spot consumer test. Read the first page."

"Without moving your lips," Emery added.

Hugh looked at Mattie. "Do I have to do this?"

"Yes, you do. Get busy."

With a great show of reluctance, Hugh opened the book and scanned the first paragraph of *St. Cyr's Axiom*. Then he went on to the second and third paragraphs.

Mattie grinned as he started to turn the page. "That's far enough. It proves my point." She snatched the book out of Hugh's hand. "See what I mean, Emery? If even Hugh couldn't resist turning the page, nobody will be able to resist."

Emery turned a most unusual shade of red. "I am deeply flattered, Abbott."

"No big deal," Hugh muttered. "I was just going to finish the sentence, that's all."

"Buy a copy of your own if you want to finish it." Mattie put the book back on the stack. "Well, I've got to get back to work. Emery, your new career is launched. Congratulations."

"St. Cyr is never going to win any Pulitzers," Emery said.

"Who cares? It's going to sell, and that's even better than winning prizes."

Emery finally permitted himself a small, rueful smile. "How can you be so damn sure of yourself when it comes to second-guessing the marketplace, Mattie, my love?"

"It's a knack," Mattie told him. "Hugh, stop trying to sneak a peek at the second page of Emery's book. Buy it and be done with it. I'll bet Emery will autograph it for you if you ask him nicely, won't you, Emery?"

"Certainly," Emery said.

Hugh took the copy of St. Cyr's Axiom over to the counter. "Forget the autograph."

Emery sighed. "Mattie, love, it does worry me so to see you engaged to a man of such astonishingly limited social polish. You really do deserve better, my dear."

"I know, but at my age a woman can't afford to be too picky," Mattie said with a daring grin. It occurred to her that teasing Hugh could be rather amusing at times.

Hugh ignored them both as he paid for the book.

The trio returned to Sharpe Reaction in thoughtful silence. At the door of the gallery Emery came to a halt and looked down at Mattie with deep affection.

"Mattie, my love, I owe you more than I can say, and I am only just beginning to realize it. Do you know, I must confess it really was something of a thrill to see all those copies of St. Cyr's Axiom stacked up in that bookstore. Much better distribution than I ever got with any of my important literary stuff."

"Just wait until the paperback edition comes out and you see it sitting on a rack at a supermarket checkout stand right next to the tabloids and flashlight batteries," she advised with a chuckle. "Then you'll know you've really arrived."

Emery laughed and kissed her forehead. "Who would have guessed? Life takes odd turns now and again, doesn't it?"

"It certainly does."

"Well, I suppose that's what keeps it interesting." He arched a laconic brow at Hugh, who was watching the little scene with an irritated expression. "I wish you the best of luck with your odd turn, Mattie. But watch him closely. I wouldn't trust him any farther than I could throw him, if I were you. He has plans to carry you off, my dear. Mark my words."

There was a short, charged silence between Mattie and Hugh as they watched Emery walk away down the sidewalk.

"Do you?" Mattie finally asked quietly.

"Do I what?" Hugh's narrowed gaze was still on Emery's back.

"Have plans to carry me off, or are you really going to settle down here permanently in Seattle?"

"You still don't trust me, do you, babe?"

"Hugh, I'd trust you with my life. In fact, I have on a couple of recent occasions."

"But not with your heart?"

"I'm thinking about it."

"You do that, babe," he said as he pulled her close and kissed her full on the mouth. "You think about it real hard. Because one way or another this is going to work."

Hugh removed a massive pile of computer printouts from the one visitor's chair in Johnson's office and sat down. The intense young man in horn-rimmed glasses, running shoes, polyester slacks, and an unpressed white shirt looked up warily.

"I told you I'd call if I got anything, Mr. Abbott."

"I happened to be going by your office, so I thought I'd just drop in and check on the progress," Hugh lied. The Vailcourt computer facilities were located several floors below management and were definitely not on his way to anywhere. "You told me yesterday you'd verified that there's a new presence on the political scene on Purgatory. I wanted to see if you'd come up with a name or some background yet."

Johnson sighed, took off his glasses, and rubbed the bridge of his nose. "Nothing yet. I told you I'd call. Scout's honor, Mr. Abbott. I know this is important to you."

"Real important."

"I get the picture. Look, all I can tell you at this time is that the situation has changed slightly on Purgatory, but no one really knows how yet. Nor does anyone seem to care. I've given you everything I've been able to dig out of two or three fairly good intelligence data bases. There just isn't much available. Mostly because the situation on that dipshit little island is not of great interest to anyone."

"Except me."

"Yes. You." Johnson picked up a pen and tapped it impatiently on the desk. "I'll call when I get something."

"Any time. Night or day." Hugh got to his feet.

"Right. Night or day," Johnson agreed wearily.

Hugh paused at the door. "You actually went into two or three government data bases? *Intelligence* data bases? Just like that?"

"Just like that. It's my job, Mr. Abbott."

Hugh nodded, impressed. "You know, I could have used you in the old days. You and that computer of yours would have been worth your weight in gold."

"Really? What sort of work did you do in the old days?"

"Nothing very important. Call me. Soon."

Johnson called at five-thirty that afternoon, just as Hugh was getting ready to walk out the door of his office. The two secretaries had already left, so Hugh reached for the phone himself when it rang.

"Mr. Abbott? This is Johnson down in Systems. I think I may have a little more information for you. Some of it's just coming in now, and there may be more later. It's not much, but it could be something."

"I'll be right down." Hugh hung up and dialed Mattie's gallery. She answered on the third ring. "It's me, babe. Listen, I'm going to be a little late getting home. There's some info on Purgatory coming in on one of the computers downstairs."

"All right. How late will you be?" she asked, sounding distracted. He heard voices in the background and realized she was probably with clients.

"Don't know. Be there when I get there."

"Be careful on the way home," she said automatically. "It'll be dark. First Avenue can be rough in the evenings."

Hugh allowed himself to wallow briefly in the luxury of having someone worry about him. "Sure, babe. I'll be careful. See you later." He tossed the phone back into its cradle and headed for the elevators.

Mattie could feel the walls closing in.

"Knees up high and *kick*. And *kick*. And *kick*."

The heavy throb of rock music combined with the thundering herd of aerobic dancers to make the wooden gym floor shudder. Mattie kicked out as hard as she could, skipped, turned, and joined the herd as it pounded to the far end of the room.

Her grandmother the ballerina would be turning over in her

grave. Mattie sent up a silent apology as she always did during aerobics class and then kicked out even more wildly, skipped, turned, and thundered back down to the other end of the room. Technique and grace were not big factors in this kind of thing. Grandmother had always been a fanatic about technique and grace. Mattie could still hear her lecturing the little girl at the barre during that period when Mattie had determined to follow in grandmother's footsteps.

What a mistake that had been. Another wrong direction.

Electric guitars screaming in her ears, Mattie whipped around in a frenzied movement. She had her heart rate up good and high now. The sweat was dampening the thin, supple fabric of her leotard.

The decision to go to the after-work aerobics class at her health club had been an impulse that had struck right after Hugh had announced he would be late getting back to the apartment. Mattie had missed her regular noon-hour class, and she always did some form of aerobics three or four days a week. She could practically feel the stress levels sink after thirty or forty minutes of strenuous dancing.

"Grapevine!" the instructor yelled out over the pounding music. "And kick . . . two, three, four, and grapevine, two . . . three . . . four . . ."

Mattie kicked vigorously, aware that she had a great deal of stress to work off. The tension was building daily. The sense of pressure had been mounting. She could feel it, a palpable field of energy pressing on her as surely as claustrophobia.

She knew that sooner or later she was going to have to make a decision. Emery and Ariel and Aunt Charlotte were all probably right about Hugh. He wasn't planning to stay in Seattle permanently. He was playing a waiting game, and he was not a patient man.

One of these days he would come home from work and announce that he had given her enough time to get used to the idea of trusting him. He would tell her he was leaving for St. Gabriel on the six o'clock plane the next morning.

And she would have to make her decision.

The walls were definitely closing in on her.

"And up and out and up and out and up . . ."

She was not ready to take the risk a second time. She would not be a stand-in for Ariel.

"Reach and pull. Reach and pull. Move it, people. Reach and pull . . ."

Hugh had claimed he would stay here in Seattle as long as necessary. But Mattie knew better. She could feel him getting restless. The last three mornings she had awakened to find him already awake beside her, gazing out at the dawn. She had known instinctively that he was thinking about his island and Abbott Charters and his dream home.

"Slide and skip, two . . . three . . . four. Slide and skip, two . . . three . . . four . . ."

Aunt Charlotte was right. Hugh was not meant to live in the city. He had started to build a dream for himself out in the islands, and now, half-finished, it called to him. Mattie tried to tell herself that her dreams were right here in Seattle, but a part of her denied it.

" . . . And two, three, four, and slide, turn, kick . . . and two, three . . ."

A part of her knew that her dreams were forever linked to Hugh's.

So she would have to make a decision.

Mattie wondered how much time she had left.

The walls were definitely closing in.

Half an hour later, showered and changed back into the well-tailored pin-striped suit she had worn to the office that day, Mattie left the health club and started the five-block walk to her apartment. It was dark and a light rain was beginning to fall. Hugh was going to get wet on the way home tonight. He never remembered to take an umbrella with him to the office.

Mattie had just unfurled the umbrella she always carried with her in her briefcase when she heard the footsteps behind her.

Footsteps on a city street were hardly unusual, but there was something about the pace of these particular footsteps that sent a flicker of anxiety down her spine. A woman who lived alone in the city soon developed a certain degree of street savvy. There were footsteps and there were *footsteps*.

The sidewalk was uncrowded at this hour. The rain and the cold had driven most people indoors. The few people who were still out were hurrying toward the shelter of bus stops, restaurants, or parking garages. She listened for a change in the pace of the person walking behind her.

But the footsteps behind Mattie did not quicken or slow. They beat a steady tempo that matched her own brisk stride.

She was getting paranoid, Mattie told herself. There was no cause for alarm. If worse came to worse, she could always run out into the middle of the street and scream bloody murder.

Unless whoever was following her jumped her suddenly and dragged her into a dark alley.

She clung more tightly to her purse and briefcase and hugged the outer edge of the sidewalk. She remembered reading somewhere that it was safer to walk near the curb.

The sense of being followed was sending chills down her spine now. At the corner Mattie swung around abruptly and looked back in the direction she had just come.

Two men were on the sidewalk behind her. One had his keys out and was heading toward a car parked at the curb. The other was staring into a shop window. He was wearing a cap and had the collar of a khaki-green trenchcoat pulled up high around his neck. But Mattie caught a glimpse of his face and realized he was a young man, probably in his early twenties. He didn't look like a street thug; he looked more like a soldier, especially in that military-style trenchcoat.

She *was* getting paranoid. Maybe she'd lived a little too long in the city. Mattie crossed the street and hurried down the next block. Midway she whirled around and saw that the man who had been looking into the window was still behind her. An aura of menace hung in the air.

Mattie gave up trying to fight the anxiety. She was probably going to regret this, but there was only one appealing option available. She turned and stepped into the first warmly lit doorway she saw.

And found herself in a sleazy, smoke-filled tavern. Music blared from tinny loudspeakers. The smell of alcohol fumes, burning tobacco, and old cooking grease were thick in the air. A couple of men at the bar swiveled around on their stools and eyed her with lecherous interest.

Mattie ignored them as she clutched her purse more tightly than ever. A waitress paused and looked her up and down.

"Help you?" the woman asked without much real interest.

"I'd like to use the pay phone, please."

"Back near the rest rooms."

Mattie kept her gaze averted from the crowd at the bar as she walked the gauntlet of staring eyes toward the phone.

It seemed ridiculous to call a cab for a two-block ride. The driver would probably be furious at the cheap fare. She would try the apartment first.

Hugh answered the phone on the first ring. "Where the hell are you, Mattie? It sounds like a bar, for God's sake."

"Smells like one, too." She wrinkled her nose at the unpleasant odors emanating from the bathrooms. "I'm only two blocks away from the apartment, Hugh. Look, I hate to ask this, but could you come get me? There's someone outside on the sidewalk. I think he might have been following me."

"Which bar?" Hugh's voice now had that familiar cold edge.

Mattie gave him the address.

"Stay put near the front door. Don't move until I get there. Understand?"

"I understand." Mattie hung up and made the endless trip back past the crowd seated at the bar. She could handle anything this lot might try, she told herself. After all, she had survived a barroom brawl on St. Gabriel. The thought gave her confidence.

Nevertheless, when Hugh came through the front door five minutes later looking lethal, she didn't hesitate for an instant.

She went straight into his arms.

# 15

"Whaat the hell did you think you were doing walking home alone in the middle of the night?" Hugh raged as he stood towering over Mattie.

"It wasn't the middle of the night, Hugh. It was only seven o'clock." Seated with her legs curled under her on the couch, Mattie sipped a reviving cup of herbal tea. "I knew I shouldn't have called you. I knew you'd only start yelling."

"I've got a right to yell. You had no business out there at this hour."

"I've never had trouble coming back from the after-work class before."

"It only takes once. Damn it, a city is not a safe place for a woman alone."

"I can tell you right now, you'll never get me to move out into the 'burbs. It's a jungle out there."

"This isn't a joke, Mattie." Hugh leaned over her menacingly and flattened his hands on the back of the couch on either side of where she was sitting. "City streets are dangerous and you can't deny it. You're the one who warned *me* to be careful on the way home tonight, remember?"

It was hard to argue that one. "Well, yes. But that's because you're not used to Seattle. You haven't lived here long enough to develop street smarts. You kind of have to get the hang of living downtown."

"Is that right? And you've got the hang of it, I suppose?"

"Oh, yes," she said easily. "The sort of thing that happened tonight really isn't typical. I handled it, didn't I?"

"Hell. This is a really stupid argument. I'm right and you're wrong and that's all there is to it. You'd be a lot safer living out in the islands than you are here in Seattle. I can guarantee it."

"May I remind you that I encountered more violence out in your neck of the woods than I have ever encountered in my whole life?"

Hugh ran his fingers through his hair. "That was an unusual situation."

"So was tonight."

"Damn it, Mattie . . ."

"The thing is," Mattie said slowly, "I'm not used to having someone chew me out like this just because I had a little trouble on the way home."

"Get used to it. And while you're at it, get used to not coming home alone at night, period," Hugh advised forcefully.

"I'm not sure I like it."

"Not sure you like what? Having me tell you that you can't come home alone at night? Let me tell you, you ain't seen nothin' yet, babe. There are going to be all kinds of rules after we get married."

"I've been doing just fine without any of your rules for thirty-two years, Hugh. Damn. I should never have called you. It wasn't any big deal."

He glared at her. "No big deal? You get followed by some creep who might have intended anything from grabbing your purse to slitting your throat or rape? You don't call that a big deal?"

"I probably overreacted. Maybe no one was following me. Maybe that man on the street behind me was innocently walking home, too."

"Hah. You say that now because you're all safe and sound and cozy and warm again. But that's not what you were saying twenty minutes ago when I found you in that damn bar. And while we're on the subject, why the hell did you have to pick that joint? It was a real dive. Every jerk in there was leering at you."

"It was the first place I saw when I decided to get off the street. Hugh, are you going to keep yelling like this or can we get something to eat? I'm hungry."

"I've got a right to be concerned here, Mattie."

"I know. But as I said, I'm just not used to it," she explained softly.

He eyed her for a long, thoughtful moment. "No, I guess you're not, are you? You're too accustomed to taking care of yourself."

She tried a tentative smile. "Just like you."

"Yeah. Sort of. Come on, let's eat. I'll finish chewing you out later."

Mattie started to get up off the couch. "I've got some buckwheat noodles and vegetables I can fix."

"Forget it. After all the excitement, I need something more substantial." Hugh was already reaching for the phone. "I'm going to order in a pizza."

Mattie was horrified. "A *pizza*."

"I've had a hard day, Mattie. I need real nourishment. I'll tell you something. This business of being able to order up a pizza in the middle of the night and have it delivered is about the only really good thing about city living I've discovered yet. While we're waiting for it to get here, we'll have a drink. I think we both need one."

Forty-five minutes later Mattie had to admit the aroma of a fresh pizza was far more captivating than it ought to have been. She decided to forget about a well-balanced meal that evening and decided to enjoy herself. She deserved a break.

"So how did it go with the guy in the computer lab at Vailcourt?" she asked around a dripping bite.

"He didn't have a whole lot. Just a possible name to pin on whoever it is that seems to be running things behind the scenes on Purgatory."

"What name?"

"McCormick. John McCormick. It doesn't mean anything. He seems to have come out of nowhere. There's no paper on him, no background, no history at all. Which means the name's an alias. Johnson is going to try to check deeper, but he says he probably won't find much. I called Silk and told him what I had. The name may mean more out there by now."

Mattie nodded. "Any sign of Gibbs yet?"

"No. He definitely lit out for safer country. I'd sure as hell like to know what spooked him and who killed Rosey."

"This McCormick person?"

"Looks like it, but why? Apparently, he's safely in power there on Purgatory. Why should he care if a couple of bit players learned his name? Hell, the name is showing up in the computers now. He can't hope to keep it a secret."

"But you said it doesn't mean anything," Mattie said slowly. "Maybe Gibbs and Rosey found out it does mean something. Maybe they found out who he really is, and McCormick didn't like it."

"Or maybe they saw something they shouldn't have seen," Hugh said thoughtfully. "A couple of bozos like those two could easily have stumbled into the wrong place at the wrong time."

"Or Rosey's death might have nothing at all to do with this McCormick person," Mattie pointed out. "It might all be a remarkable coincidence."

Hugh gave her a wry look. "Yeah. Remarkable."

"Coincidences do happen, you know."

"Not where I come from."

Mattie studied the three acrylic paintings Flynn had propped up in front of her desk. Ariel was hovering near the door in an uncharacteristically reticent fashion.

The silence in the small room was laced with the peculiar tension that always exists at such moments between artist and dealer.

Mattie smiled slowly. "I love them," she said, enthralled. "I absolutely love them."

"You sure?" Flynn asked, breathless with relief.

Mattie felt the delicious thrill of discovery. The paintings were vivid, evocative images that tapped Flynn's undeniably powerful inner vision. But they were not the dark, grotesque, unidentifiable scenes that had formerly characterized his work.

These pictures were filled with color and light and energy. Mattie knew they would sell in a red-hot minute.

"They're perfect," she told him, unable to look away from one particular painting, a shimmering image of a woman standing at a window that looked out on a jarringly primitive landscape. "Absolutely wonderful. I'll hang all three immediately. Deal?"

Flynn's eyes lit with elation. "Deal." He watched her go around behind her desk to pull out a blank contract.

"They're really good, aren't they, Mattie?" Ariel moved forward, radiating a more familiar self-confidence now that judgment had been passed. "I don't know why I gave Flynn such a hard time about trying something for you. It was stupid of me to worry that he might be prostituting his talent. How can you prostitute talent, anyway? It's either there or it isn't."

"That's been my guiding philosophy since the day I set up Sharpe Reaction," Mattie admitted.

"And Flynn is loaded with talent, isn't he?"

"Yup. Loaded. And now he's found a way to make that talent accessible to other people. People who have enough money to pay for it."

Out of the corner of her eye Mattie saw Flynn turning red under the unstinting praise. He deserved it, she thought. It was more amusing to witness Ariel's dramatic about-face. There was nothing quite like the fervor of the newly converted.

"What does it matter if Flynn caters to mainstream tastes for a while?" Ariel demanded passionately. "All the great artists of the past did it. Just think, Raphael, Michelangelo, Rubens, all of them. They all had to please their patrons. Art has always had to walk the fine line between pursuing individual vision and making that vision compelling to the public."

Mattie slanted Flynn an amused glance as she opened a drawer and pulled out the paperwork she needed. "I agree. But, then, I sell commercial schlock for a living, so I'm somewhat biased."

"Don't say that, Mattie," Ariel instructed fiercely. "It's hardly as if you're pushing pictures of matadors painted on black velvet, you know. You're developing the next generation of important collectors, making them aware of great artists such as Flynn and thereby expanding their consciousness of art in general."

"My God," Mattie murmured. "My sister has turned into a raving supporter of art for the masses. I don't know if I can handle the shock."

"You're teasing me," Ariel complained.

"I know. Sorry."

"It's all right. I deserve it."

Mattie looked at a smiling Flynn. "She's really appalling when she's in her noble repentant role, isn't she?"

"Appalling, all right. Fortunately, that's one of her least favorite acts." Flynn grinned at his wife.

Ariel stuck her tongue out at both of them and then chuckled happily. "I told Flynn about the baby, Mattie."

"And that settled the matter of what I'm going to paint for a while," Flynn stated firmly. "Pretty exciting, isn't it? Imagine me being a daddy. I went out and bought a set of watercolors and brushes for the kid this morning."

"You're going to be a terrific father," Mattie told him. For the first time she allowed herself to wonder just what sort of father Hugh would be. Probably an overprotective one, she decided. But definitely a committed one. A man like Hugh took his responsibilities very seriously.

She remembered what he had once said about his own childhood in the heat of an argument. She knew instinctively that he was the kind of man who did not repeat the past, but rather learned from it and thereby changed the future.

Men like Hugh were very rare in the modern world. Perhaps they always had been.

The walls threatened to close in again. Mattie took a grip on herself and several deep breaths. She had some time. She did not have to make any decisions right now at this very moment.

The office door opened and Hugh sauntered in carrying an open bottle of Mattie's favorite mineral water.

"This place is sure crowded a lot lately," he announced. "Every time I come in here I trip over a past, present, or future member of the family."

"Speaking of family," Ariel said coolly, "on behalf of Flynn and my-

self, I'm warning you that you'd damn well better take good care of
Mattie. I don't know what she sees in you, but as long as she sees
something she wants, you'd better behave. Make her cry a second
time, Abbott, and you'll regret it."

Hugh glowered at Mattie. "Promise me you won't cry under any
circumstances," he ordered. "I can't stand the idea of having to explain
myself to these two and Emery Blackwell and Charlotte Vailcourt and
your parents and God knows who else happens to think you need protection from me."

Mattie grinned wickedly, feeling suddenly lighthearted. "Looks
like you'll have to watch your step, won't you, Abbott?"

"The stress is definitely beginning to take its toll on my good nature." He drank the remainder of the mineral water in one gulp and
made a face. "Christ, this stuff is awful."

"Why drink it?" Flynn asked curiously.

"Mattie thinks it's better for me than soda pop."

"What you need is a good cup of espresso," Flynn said. "Come on,
I'll buy you one. I'm celebrating."

He had been joking back in Mattie's office, Hugh told himself later
as he stood watching her choose fresh broccoli at a stall in the Pike
Place Market. But the truth was, he was getting a bit stressed out.

Maybe *stressed out* was not quite the right phrase. Maybe what he
was feeling was a little old-fashioned guilt.

Hugh did not like guilt. For most of his life it had been an alien emotion. Usually he was sure enough of himself and of his own personal
code of honor that he did not experience guilt. Regrets, yes, but not guilt.

He knew his present uneasiness had not been caused by the rash of
folks, such as Emery Blackwell and Ariel, who had felt compelled to
warn him to treat Mattie well. Hugh already knew he was going to
treat her well. Hell, he would protect her with his life, if necessary, and
he would see to it she never went without. When it came to the basics,
he was sure he would make a good husband for her in the old-fashioned sense.

The problem was that while parts of Mattie were delightfully old-
fashioned, there were other parts of her that were very modern. Very
sophisticated. Very New Woman.

Hugh wondered again, as he did more and more frequently these
days, if his long-range goal of dragging Mattie away to the islands was
really the right thing to do. She looked so at home here in Seattle, he
thought as he watched her move from the broccoli to the piles of red,
orange, yellow, and purple peppers.

Damn it, she was happy here. He could hardly deny it. She was also financially established here. And independent. She had friends, family, a career, and a lifestyle. She mingled with artists, writers, and businesspeople, all of whom accorded her a lot of professional respect.

Compared to all that, Hugh knew he did not have a lot to offer out on St. Gabriel. Silk was right. The days of dragging intelligent, accomplished women off to the frontiers were over.

It had all been a lot easier in the old days. Hell, it would have been a lot easier last year if he'd had the sense to take Mattie up on her offer the first time around.

"Wait until you taste these peppers sautéed in a little olive oil and with some olives and capers," Mattie said in a confidential tone as she paid the produce dealer. "Fantastic. It'll be great served with focaccia or this great potato and cabbage soup I make."

"Mattie?" Hugh took the sack of broccoli and peppers from her as they started toward another stall.

*"Hmmm?"* Her attention was clearly on dinner.

He did not know what to ask or how to ask it. He had been so sure of himself until now. So sure she would come with him when the time arrived. He smiled crookedly. "I should have taken you out to the islands with me last year."

"Who knows?" she said quietly. "Maybe things turned out for the best after all."

"No," he stated categorically. "They did not. We wasted one goddamned entire year."

She did not respond to that.

Mattie sensed that something had changed in Hugh's attitude toward her. She could not put her finger on it, but it made her uneasy. She wondered if his limited patience was finally at an end. He was probably getting ready to give her an ultimatum, she thought as she watched him pour her a glass of wine.

"How's the job going?" she asked as she sliced the multihued peppers in lacy circles.

"It's okay." Hugh sat on a stool at the counter hunched over his glass of wine and watched her prepare dinner.

"You don't sound exactly fired up with enthusiasm."

"Like I said. It's okay."

"How much longer will it take you to get a security plan worked up for Aunt Charlotte?" She was fishing for an answer to the question of how much time she had left, Mattie realized. But she was afraid to ask Hugh directly.

Hugh turned the glass of wine between his palms. "It depends."

"On what?"

"Lots of things. You want me to do anything?"

Mattie sighed. She wasn't going to get any answers tonight. "You can rinse the broccoli."

"Sure."

The phone rang just as Hugh dumped the broccoli into a colander, and Mattie went across the room to answer it. The sultry voice on the other end of the line took her by surprise.

"Evangeline? Is that you? I can't believe it. Where are you?"

"Right where I was when you left Brimstone. Look, Mattie, this isn't exactly what you'd call a social call."

"Is something wrong?" Mattie glanced over at the kitchen and saw that Hugh was watching her curiously from the sink.

"No, not exactly. At least I don't think so. But I'm not real sure. Does the name Rainbird mean anything to you?"

"No." Mattie frowned. "Nothing at all. Why?"

" 'Cause I had a trick last night who was stoned out of his gourd, and he kept talking about this guy named Rainbird. Said he was looking for someone who had slipped off Purgatory during the coup. A man. Said it was worth a lot of money to find him. I remembered that man you had with you."

Mattie's eyes widened in shock. "Good grief."

"You sure the name doesn't ring any bells?"

"No. But I'll ask Hugh."

"He's still around, then?"

"Well, yes, as a matter of fact, I still see a lot of him."

"I was afraid of that. Look, I know it's none of my business, but isn't that kind of risky, honey? I mean, you know how it is. Get close to a John, and the first thing you know, he wants a cut of the profits. Then he starts telling you that you need him for protection. Then he starts giving orders. Next thing you know, you've got a lousy pimp."

"I'll keep that in mind," Mattie promised.

"You do that. Besides, if this jerk Rainbird is after him, you don't want to be standing nearby. Innocent bystanders have a way of getting hurt, if you know what I mean. What do you want with a man, anyway?"

"Well . . ."

"Face it, honey. Men aren't any good for women like us. We're too independent by nature. Look, I've got to run. I can hear someone coming down the hall. Probably a customer. You take care of yourself, now, you hear? And watch out for this guy named Rainbird."

"I will. Oh, and Evangeline?"

"Yeah, honey?"

"Thanks for calling. It was good to talk to you again." Mattie slowly replaced the phone and looked thoughtfully at Hugh.

"Evangeline Dangerfield? What the hell did she want?"

"For one thing, she was rather alarmed that I'm still seeing you. She says men aren't any good for a working woman such as myself."

Hugh swore. "This is why a man has to keep tabs on his woman's friends. You start hanging out with females like Evangeline, and you pick up idiotic notions. That the only reason she was calling?"

"No. Hugh, does the name Rainbird mean anything to you?"

"*Shit.*" Hugh dropped the pan of broccoli into the sink as if it had suddenly become red hot. "Rainbird? Did you say *Rainbird?*"

"I think that was the name." Mattie was alarmed by Hugh's reaction.

Hugh came around the edge of the counter. He was across the room in a matter of seconds, reaching for her. His eyes had gone the color of cold crystal.

Mattie instinctively tried to take a step backward, but she was too late. He seized her and held her still in front of him.

"Where did you get that name?" Hugh demanded.

"Evangeline." Mattie swallowed.

"Jesus Christ."

"She said one of her customers had gotten drunk and talked about a man named Rainbird looking for someone who had slipped off Purgatory during the coup. Do you think it was Rosey? Or Gibbs?"

Hugh ignored that question. "Why did Evangeline call you?"

"Because she knew I had just come off Purgatory with you, and she wondered if you were the person this Rainbird was after. But that's impossible, isn't it? Hugh, what is this all about? Why are you acting like this?"

"Rainbird. So that's what Rosey was trying to say."

"Hugh?"

"I asked him who had attacked him." His mouth was a grim line. "He opened his eyes for a second, looked up, and said *Rain.* I thought he was talking about the rain that night. But he was trying to say *Rainbird.* He never finished the word."

Mattie took a deep breath, remembering Paul Cormier's last words. "Reign in hell."

Hugh stared down at her. "*Rainbird* in hell. Paul was trying to leave a message for me that Rainbird was there on Purgatory. *Shit.*"

"Who is he?" The repressed violence in Hugh was making Mattie tense. She could feel his fingers clenching into the flesh of her upper arms. "What do you know about him?"

"He's supposed to be dead, for one thing." Hugh looked at the phone. "Damn, I should have talked to Dangerfield myself. Where was she calling from? Her room in that inn?"

"Yes. She said a customer was on his way down the hall."

"The customer can damn well keep his pants zipped for a while longer." Hugh dug out his wallet and fished through some bits and pieces of paper. "Here it is."

"What?"

"The receipt for our room. The phone number is on it." He was already punching out the number.

Mattie could feel Hugh's tension radiating from him in cold waves. It was a battle-ready sort of tension, a terrifyingly masculine thing that assaulted her on all fronts. She waited in silence while Hugh put through the call. A moment later he had the inn clerk on the line.

"She can't be gone," Hugh said into the receiver. "She just called us from there. She's with a customer and not answering the phone, that's all. Go upstairs and get her. *Do it now.*"

Mattie shivered a little at the savage tone in Hugh's voice. She looked around, thinking that the temperature in the apartment seemed to have dropped several degrees in the past few minutes. Hugh spoke again after a couple of minutes. "Goddamn it." He tossed down the phone.

"She's gone?"

He nodded brusquely. "Left right after she called you. Walked out the front door. With a suitcase."

"Alone? Or with whoever was coming down the hall to her room? Hugh, do you think she's in any danger?"

"I don't know." Hugh was already punching out numbers on the phone.

"Who are you calling now?"

"Silk."

There was another tense pause before Hugh gave up in frustration and dropped the receiver back into the cradle. "Shit," he said again. "Goddamn it to hell. Rainbird. After all these years."

Mattie sat down on the edge of the couch, her arms crossed under her breasts. "Don't you think you'd better tell me what this is all about?"

He looked at her as if surprised to see her still there. She could tell he was a million miles away in his mind. "No."

She stared at him, nonplussed. "No? Hugh, you can't just say no like that. You have to tell me what's going on here. I'm involved in this, too."

"No, you're not involved and you're not going to get involved. Silk and I will take care of Rainbird, and then it will all be over. For good this time."

"You can't shut me out like this."

"I'm not shutting you out. This has nothing to do with you."

"The hell it doesn't," Mattie said, gritting her teeth.

"Let it be, Mattie. I'll deal with it."

Something snapped inside Mattie. She jumped up in front of Hugh, clenching her small fists at her sides. "Now, you listen to me, Hugh Abbott. I've had about enough of taking orders from you, and I've had enough of your refusal to talk about your past. You've got some nerve, you know that? You won't tell me anything about yourself, but you expect me to give up everything and move out to that stupid island with you."

"Now, babe, I never said that."

"You didn't have to say it," she stormed. "It's been perfectly obvious from the beginning. Why do you think I've been so tense lately? I knew that sooner or later you'd pin me down and force me to make a decision. But how can I do that when you won't even tell me who you really are or where you've been most of your life? It's obvious your past has come back to haunt you. That means it affects our future. I demand to know the truth."

"My past does not affect you," he said, spacing each word out carefully, as if by stating the concept forcefully enough he could make it reality.

"Everything that affects you affects me." Mattie was near tears. "Don't you understand? I love you, Hugh. *I love you.* I have to know what's going on here."

He stared down at her for a long while. Then, without a word, he opened his arms and she stepped into them. He buried his lips in her hair and held her so tight Mattie thought her ribs might crack.

"Babe," he muttered, his voice husky. "I never wanted you to know. I didn't want you to find out about any of it. Not ever."

# 16

❧

"Once upon a time," Hugh said slowly, "I worked for Jack Rainbird." Hugh let his arms fall away from Mattie, and he moved over to the window to stare out through the rain-streaked glass. "It was not one of my more rewarding enterprises."

"What did you do for him?" Mattie's voice was soft and laced with deep concern.

Hugh wondered how long it would be before the concern turned to disgust. "A lot of things."

"Hugh, this is no time to be evasive. I have to know what's going on here."

He exhaled heavily. "Yeah, I guess you've got a right. Okay, here's how it went down. When I got out of the Army, I got a job with a fly-by-night air charter outfit that operated down in South America. The guy who ran it would take any cargo, fly in any weather, and not ask any questions. The pay wasn't bad. And I learned almost everything I know about running a charter service from the wild man who ran that one. That's where I met Silk, by the way."

"He was working for the same outfit?"

Hugh nodded. "Silk and I became a team. What one of us couldn't handle in the air or on the ground, the other usually could. Sometimes getting the plane back into the sky after making a delivery was a real challenge."

"Because the planes were not properly maintained?" Mattie asked.

He studied the reflection of her frowning face in the window. "No, the planes were kept in great shape. That was one of the boss's two rules. The planes got properly serviced even if everyone in the operation went hungry for a while."

"Then what was the problem?"

"The problem," Hugh said quietly, "was that sometimes the clients did not want witnesses who might have snooped around the cargo. Sometimes the clients had enemies who did not want the cargo transported in the first place."

"I see. It was dangerous."

Hugh shrugged. "Sometimes. On the whole it wasn't bad work. Silk and I, we sort of liked it. There was hardly any paperwork, no dress code, and like I said, the boss only had two rules. I told you the first one: take care of the planes."

"And the second?"

"Don't come back without one of the planes. Planes are expensive, you see. A lot more expensive than pilots."

"That sounds a little cold-blooded."

"Just good business."

"Planes are more expensive than pilots. I heard you say something like that to Ray and Derek." Mattie smiled faintly. "But you didn't really mean it. You were just emphasizing the importance of maintenance."

Hugh's brows climbed at her naive faith in his basic good nature. "Well, my boss meant it. Every word. At any rate, things went fairly well for me and Silk for quite a while. We made a little money, did a lot of flying, and got the planes back in one piece. And then one day we broke the rules."

"What happened?"

"We were flying a cargo into a very remote location in South America. It was supposed to be supplies for some fancy scientific research team, but Silk and I knew it was probably something else."

"Like what?"

"Like guns. But, as usual, we didn't ask any questions. We just tried to do the job and get out. But this time we almost didn't make it. The plane got shot up. I got it back in the air but not for long, and we went down in some bad country."

"My God," Mattie whispered.

Hugh smiled in spite of his mood. "Hey, don't look so horrified. Obviously we made it out."

"Obviously. But you lost the plane."

"And our jobs. Silk and I were not in the best of shape when we finally walked out of that damned jungle. The jungles in South America are different from the ones out on the islands. They're a lot more dangerous. A lot can go wrong. And it seemed like just about everything that could go wrong did go wrong, from Silk picking up a fever to us meeting up with some folks who wanted to use us for target practice. But the worst thing that went wrong was that we had no cash left by the time we paid Silk's medical bills."

"But you got another job?"

"Yeah. Working for Jack Rainbird."

Mattie chewed on her lower lip. Her expression as reflected in the window was very determined looking. "Doing what?" she finally asked.

"Rainbird was the head of a group of professional mercenaries," Hugh said bluntly. "He sold his team's services all over the world."

Her eyes widened in the glass. "You became a mercenary? A hired gun?"

"Yeah." Hugh braced himself against the shock and disbelief in her voice. He had expected both, but they still came as quick jabs in the gut. Perhaps that was because there were times when he had the same reaction to his own past.

*A hired gun. A man who signed on to fight somebody else's war, carry out somebody else's vendetta. For cold, hard cash, up front.*

People from Mattie's world, where the big battles were all verbal ones fought over weighty questions of artistic merit, could only be expected to recoil in horror from such a truth. In Mattie's world a man could be forgiven for showing up for a date with paint stains on his hands, but not old blood.

In Mattie's world a man did not make a living at warfare.

In Mattie's world a man was expected to have a civilized past.

In Mattie's world there would be no place for a man like the one Hugh had once been.

Hugh was aware of the old, familiar chill in his gut. He could hear it reflected in his voice. The cold sensation was automatic after all these years. It was a way of protecting himself when things were about to turn very bad. He could hardly feel anything at all when he went real cold like this.

Hugh kept his gaze fixed on Mattie's reflection, waiting impatiently now for the look in her eyes to change to one of shock and disgust; waiting for her to turn away from him.

He was waiting, as usual, for things to turn very, very bad, the way they had so often over the course of his life.

"Obviously not your sort of work," she said thoughtfully, her brows drawing together in a considering fashion. "It wouldn't really suit you at all."

"Not my sort of work?" Hugh stared at her, open-mouthed and momentarily speechless. "Uh . . . well . . ." There was no point telling her he'd been damn good at that kind of work, he decided. He was not especially proud of that fact. And she was right, the job hadn't suited him at all, even if he had been competent at it.

"Silk was also part of this team run by Jack Rainbird?" Mattie asked.

"Yeah. And Paul Cormier. Silk and I were in charge of logistics. We were responsible for figuring out how to get the team in and back out again once a job was done." Hugh spoke slowly, his mind still on Mattie's unexpected reaction to his grand confession. "Rainbird dealt with the client, took the money, and gave us our shares. It was run sort of like a corporation in that respect."

"Who were the clients?"

Hugh shrugged. "CIA as often as not. Or some front operation they were backing."

"A nasty lot."

"The work is steady. They pay well. And on time," Hugh told her, his voice harsh.

"Well, of course. They could hardly expect people to continue taking risks doing their disgusting little jobs all over the world for them if they didn't pay well and on time, could they?" Mattie asked practically. "What happened in the end? Why do you hate Rainbird so much?"

"He betrayed the team."

"Betrayed you?" For the first Mattie really did look shocked. "How did he do that?"

Hugh shrugged. "He took the client's money, as usual, but he also took money from the opposition. The opposition was paying better, I guess. Or maybe they had something more valuable to offer. Who knows? Maybe Rainbird just wanted out of the business and thought he'd take the opportunity to cash out big. But the net result was that he set all of us up on that last raid. The opposition knew when, where, and how we were going to be coming in, and they were waiting."

"Oh, my God, Hugh."

"Silk, Paul, and I and a couple of other guys made it out alive. But we lost most of the team."

"And Rainbird?"

"He vanished. Word was he'd been killed by the opposition after he'd pulled his little trick. That was a logical possibility. Silk and I and the others assumed it was probably true. After all, the guys who'd paid him off to betray the operation knew better than anyone else they couldn't trust him."

"I suppose that's true."

"The only thing a mercenary has to sell is his sword and his guarantee of loyalty. Both belong to the client for the duration of the contract. Once he gets a reputation for changing employers in midstream, business has a way of declining."

"Yes. I can understand that," Mattie said weakly. She sank down onto the couch. "So you all thought he was dead."

"He knew he had better be dead as far as we were concerned," Hugh said.

"I see. Because he knew that those of you who had survived his betrayal would hunt him down?"

Hugh's hand, which was braced against one of the window frames, bunched into a hard fist. "Yeah. He knew it."

Mattie looked up. "You said Paul Cormier was also part of this . . . team of professional mercenaries?"

Hugh nodded. "Cormier was the strategist for the team. He'd been in the business a long, long time. Long before Rainbird was on the scene. Paul worked with me and Silk to set up the Rainbird operations. Like I said, he was one of the few who got out of that last operation alive. Hell, one of the reasons we did get out was because of Cormier. He believed in contingency planning. He told me later Rainbird wasn't the first team boss he'd worked for who had turned sour."

"It's beginning to look like Cormier wasn't killed by some marauding rebel or houseboy who went crazy on Purgatory, isn't it?" Mattie noted quietly.

"It's a lot more likely Rainbird was behind the coup in the first place. He would have gotten to Cormier right at the start because Cormier would have recognized him."

"And Cormier would have come looking for you and Silk and the others so that you could all go after Rainbird."

"That's about the size of it. Looks like the Colonel decided to come back from the dead, and Cormier was in the way."

"Now what happens, Hugh?"

"Now Silk and I have to take care of some old business."

"I was afraid you were going to say that." Her hands twisted together in her lap. "I don't suppose it would do any good for me to ask you not to try to hunt him down?"

"No."

"I'm so afraid," she whispered. "There's only you and Silk. Rainbird apparently runs a whole island now."

"He won't have more than a few people around him. Five or six at the most. I know him. I know how he thinks. He never trusted anyone completely. Always said it was smart to keep the leader's inner circle down to a small number. The more people around, the more of a chance of betrayal. He ought to know."

"But how can he maintain control of the island with so few people?"

"There were probably more at the beginning until he'd established himself. But now, according to Silk's information and the stuff Johnson pulled out of the computer, the guy behind the scenes on Purgatory is keeping a low profile. That means he's cut some deals with the people in charge."

"You mean Rainbird's using money, not raw firepower, to run the show?" Mattie asked shrewdly. "Makes sense."

"Yeah. He's bought himself the perfect safe harbor out in the middle of nowhere. He can do just about anything he wants there, launder money, run drugs, organize mercenary teams, *anything*. And no one could touch him."

"Why did he pick Purgatory?"

Hugh shrugged. "Things are a little loose politically out in the Pacific, but even so, there aren't that many islands you can just take over without some larger power noticing or getting annoyed. Purgatory was one of the few that nobody gives a damn about. No military bases, no tourism, nothing."

"Damn. I don't like the idea of you and Silk taking him on yourselves. There must be some other way to stop Rainbird. Can't you tell the government or something? Let them handle it?"

"They have no interest in Rainbird or in Purgatory. Besides, as far as the government is concerned, there is no Rainbird. Just some joker named Jack McCormick, remember? A small-time strongman who may or may not be pulling the strings in a two-bit island government. Unless he gives them a problem somehow, he'll be ignored."

Mattie's eyes narrowed. "Besides, as far as you're concerned, this is personal, isn't it?"

"It's personal, all right."

"What is this Rainbird really like, Hugh?"

"Remember I once told you that no matter how fast a man was, there was always someone around who was faster?"

"I remember. You told me that on Purgatory."

"Well, Rainbird is the guy who is always faster."

Mattie's eyes widened. "What do you mean?"

Hugh shrugged. "Just what I said. He's damn good at what he does, Mattie. Fast, utterly ruthless, and smart. But most of all, fast. I've never seen reflexes like Jack Rainbird's. A natural fighting machine. Good with everything, his hands, a gun, a knife, a rock, you name it. He literally moved like greased lightning. Just like they used to say about those old western gunslingers. Jesus, could he move. You never knew he was behind you until you looked down and realized your throat was bleeding."

Mattie hugged herself, her eyes huge with horror. "How old is he?"

"My age. Maybe a year older."

"You said you'd slowed down a little. Maybe he has, too."

"Maybe." But Rainbird had always been faster, Hugh reminded himself. So even if he'd slowed down some, he was still going to be slick. Very, very slick.

"Is that all you know about him? That he had unusually swift reflexes and fighting abilities?"

"No, I know a few other things," Hugh admitted.

"Such as?"

"Women were drawn to him like moths to a flame. All kinds of women, young and old, rich and poor, single and married. One, a very beautiful, very rich wife of an American diplomat in Brazil, told me once that women knew he was dangerous, but that that was part of the thrill. She said there was something hypnotic about him. Something to do with his eyes, she said."

"The man sounds like a vampire," Mattie said with disgust.

"All I know is that he had something. Rainbird was never without a woman when he wanted one. And he got any woman he wanted. Cormier always claimed that a man who could have any woman never learned how to love one woman properly. But I never noticed Rainbird complaining."

"Of course not. He wouldn't even know he was missing something. A man like Rainbird is essentially incomplete emotionally and pretty much of a coward at heart."

Hugh blinked in astonishment. "A coward? Rainbird? You don't even know him."

"No, but I've met men who go from woman to woman and never seem to be able to bond permanently with one. Every woman has met a man like that at some time in her life. They can be very amusing because they've usually developed a lot of surface charm, but a smart woman doesn't do anything more than entertain herself for a while with one. Men like that are useless in the long run. Bad genetic material, as Aunt Charlotte would probably point out."

"The hell you say." Hugh was fascinated.

"It's true. It's hard to explain. It's just that, once you scratch the surface on a man like that, there's nothing underneath." Mattie's shoulders rose and fell in a small shrug. "They're empty shells. Something important is missing. When a woman says a man is literally no good, that's the kind of man she's talking about. He's no good to her in terms of bonding and survival because he has no guts or staying power. He can't be trusted to make a commitment and keep it. Like I said, he's simply no good."

"Do all women look at men in those terms?" Hugh asked, stunned.

"Smart ones do."

He stared at her, his mouth abruptly gone dry. He was afraid to ask the obvious question, but he could not resist. "Mattie, is that how you look at me? Is that why you didn't want to give me a second chance? Is that why you wouldn't move to St. Gabe? You think there's nothing under my surface?"

She shook her head, then went to him in a soft little rush and wrapped her arms around his waist. "Oh, no, Hugh. You aren't anything like that. You're as solid as a rock."

He grinned faintly in relief. "And just as dense?"

"Maybe. At times." She lifted her face, smiling at him with misty green-gold eyes. "But I suppose you've found me a little dense lately, too, haven't you?"

"Nothing I can't work around." His voice felt thick in his throat as he cradled her head in his hands. "Babe, I've got to go back out to the islands."

"I knew you were going to say that. I know I can't talk you out of it. But I want you to take me with you," she begged. "I can't stand the thought of waiting here, not knowing what you're doing or what kind of trouble you'll be facing. Let me come with you."

He was startled. "Hell, I can't do that, babe."

"At least let me come with you as far as St. Gabriel. I could wait there until you and Silk take care of this Rainbird person. Please, Hugh. You can't leave me behind. Not this time."

"Not this time? Mattie, what are you saying? This isn't like the last time. There's no connection at all. It simply isn't safe. Christ, babe, I can't take you with me."

Her eyes filled with tears. "That's what you said the last time."

"It's not the same thing. Mattie, don't cry. For God's sake, don't cry, okay?"

"I want to go with you," she said. "Please, Hugh. Take me with you. I'll be safe on St. Gabriel."

"No, damn it." He was beginning to get angry now. This was crazy. "No way. I don't want you anywhere near this. You're going to stay right here, safe and sound."

"You can't make me stay here this time."

"The hell I can't," he shot back. He clamped his hands around her shoulders and gave her a small shake. Then he looked down into her tear-filled eyes. "Listen to me, babe. You're going to stay here and that's all there is to it. That's an order."

"You're very good at giving orders, aren't you?" She sniffed and stepped back quickly away from him, dashing toward the little spiral staircase that led up to her sleeping loft.

Hugh watched her run up the metal steps and throw herself down onto the bed. Then she was out of his line of sight. But he could hear her sobbing into the pillow.

Not for the first time in his life, he felt like a real jerk. He went into the kitchen, tossed his unfinished wine down the sink, and poured himself a glass of whiskey.

Mattie was still sniffling up in the loft when he sat down near the phone and started thumbing through the yellow pages. Ten minutes later he had his flight booked to St. Gabriel. Another early morning departure.

Just like last time.

Hugh was sitting in the same chair, still working on the same glass of whiskey a half hour later when he heard muffled noises from the loft. He glanced up but still couldn't see Mattie. He went back to staring out the rain-lashed window and wished Rainbird were already in hell.

Mattie had been able to accept his past, Hugh realized. He was still dazed by that miraculous fact. But she seemed unable to forgive him for abandoning her a second time, even though it was for her own protection. He wished he could make her understand his own need to keep her safe.

She was not accustomed to being taken care of, he reminded himself. That was the crux of the problem. He had tried to tell her this wasn't like last time. He wanted to explain that for his own sanity he had to know she was thousands of miles away from Rainbird.

"Hugh?"

He heard the soft footsteps behind him, but he was reluctant to turn around and face her. He had handled a lot of things in his life, but he did not want to deal with the accusation he knew he would see in her eyes. "Yeah, babe?"

"When does your plane leave?" Mattie moved up behind him.

"Six."

"I should have known."

"Mattie, I'm sorry," he said roughly. "But this is the way it has to be."

There was a small silence. "You'll take care of yourself?"

"Word of honor."

"You'll come back to Seattle?"

"God, yes, babe. Count on it." He did turn around then, and the first thing he saw was that she was smiling slightly.

The second thing he saw was that she had changed into the little red sarong she had worn that night on Hades.

"Jesus, babe."

"I didn't want you to forget me," she whispered as her arms slid around his neck.

"Never. No matter what happens." He reached up and tumbled her down into his lap, kissing her with a hunger that he knew could only be temporarily assuaged, a hunger that would be with him all of his life. "I'll be back."

Mattie refused to cry the next morning when she drove him to the airport. She kept a determined smile pasted to her face the whole time, even when she waved good-bye at the gate.

She did not allow the tears to fall until the jet had backed slowly away from the loading ramp and was headed for the runway. Then she went into the nearest ladies' room and sobbed for a long while.

When the tears were finally finished, she bathed her face in cold water and went back out to the parking lot to find her car.

He would be back, she told herself. He would not do something really stupid like get himself hurt. He had survived this long. No one could take care of himself as well as Hugh. He was a survivor.

But so, apparently, was this mysterious Rainbird.

Mattie parked the car back in the garage beneath her building and changed into a neat little gray checked business suit. Then she coiled her hair into its familiar bundle at the nape of her neck and left for the gallery. The only way she would stay reasonably sane until Hugh returned was to keep herself so busy she would have no time to think.

She phoned Charlotte later in the day and told her what had happened. Her aunt commiserated with her but seemed convinced Hugh would be fine.

"He's taken care of himself for quite a while. I'm sure he'll handle this little problem in no time," Charlotte said. Then she hesitated. "So he finally told you about his mysterious past, did he?"

"I gather he lived a little rough," Mattie said carefully.

"Well, we guessed that much."

"He was a professional mercenary for a while, Aunt Charlotte."

"Yes, I wondered if that might not be the case. It accounts for many of his skills and a lot of his inside knowledge of certain matters, doesn't it? How did you take the news, Mattie? He worried excessively about that, you know."

"I told him it was obviously not a suitable line of work for him."

Charlotte laughed at that. "Did you really? How odd."

"Why do you say that?"

"Oh, no particular reason. Just that I would have imagined he'd have been rather good at that sort of thing."

"I don't care what he did in the past or how well he did it," Mattie said fiercely. "He's built a different life for himself now."

"He's going after this Colonel Rainbird," Aunt Charlotte pointed out gently.

"Old business," Mattie said quietly. She knew then she had accepted the inevitable. Hugh had to be free to live his new life, and he was the only one who could close the door on the past. "It has to be cleaned up. And it's not exactly something that can be turned over to the police, Aunt Charlotte, although I wish to God it were."

"It sounds as though you've come to terms with things. But it doesn't surprise me that you've got the inner fortitude to deal with this. You're a strong woman. Always have been. And Lord knows, Hugh needs a woman who is strong enough to handle his past as well as his present and future."

"Hugh may have lived a harsh life, but there is one thing I know for certain."

"And that is?" Charlotte prompted.

"He would never have lived a dishonorable life."

"Umm, yes, I'm inclined to agree with you. Now, why don't you have some of your famous bug juice, Mattie dear? Take a few anti-stress vitamins, go do your aerobics workout, and try not to worry about Hugh too much. He'll be back for you."

"That's what he said."

"The problem, of course," said Aunt Charlotte, "is what are you going to do when he does come back?"

She hung up the phone before Mattie could think of a response.

The next morning on the way to work Mattie spotted the figure huddled in the gallery doorway from halfway down the block. She sighed inwardly. It was not all that unusual to find a street person had spent the night sleeping in the minimal shelter provided by the shop entrance. Sad, but, unfortunately, not unusual.

She would wake him up and send him on his way with enough money for a cup of coffee.

She was fishing in her purse for a dollar when she realized it was no stranger who was crouched against the gallery window. The figure was wearing an outrageously fake fur coat and a pair of three-inch spike heels. She had a mass of unlikely blond curls boiling around her heavily made-up face.

"Evangeline!" Mattie shouted, breaking into a run. "What on earth are you doing here?"

"Hi, honey. Sorry about this. Got in this morning and came straight here. You said to look you up if I ever got to Seattle, and this was the address on that card you left me. When the cab let me off here, I thought there'd been a mistake." She glanced quizzically at the paintings in the window. "This gallery really belong to you?"

"All mine." Mattie thrust the key into the lock and opened the door. "Come on inside and warm up."

"Jeez. This is really something. It's an art gallery, isn't it?" Evangeline eyed the contents of the shop with astonishment as Mattie turned on the lights. "You're not really in the business, at all, are you?"

"You mean, your particular business? No. But I am in business. How about a cup of tea?"

"Yeah, anything. I've had nothing but lousy airline food for the past twenty-four hours." Evangeline followed her into the office and watched her plug in the little hot pot. "Got a bathroom?"

"Over there." Mattie nodded toward the small door.

"Thanks. Be right out."

When she returned, Evangeline had taken off the fake fur. She was wearing a skin-tight island-style sheath. She looked like an exotic flower that had been freshly plucked in the jungle and plunked down in Mattie's mundane little office.

"I suppose you wonder what the hell I'm doing here," she said, sniffing suspiciously at the herbal tea.

"The question did cross my mind. You're more than welcome, though. It's good to see you again. You look great. I love that dress."

"Just a little something I whipped up a couple of weeks ago. I had to leave a lot of really nice stuff behind, damn it."

"I take it you left Hades in a hurry? Hugh tried to call you back after you phoned the other night, and the desk clerk said you'd already left with a suitcase. I was worried. What happened, Evangeline?"

"Remember I told you some trick was coming down the hall to my room and I had to get off the phone?"

"Yes?"

"Well, it wasn't a john. It was some guy named Gibbs. He wanted to talk to me about a friend of his. Someone named Rosey."

"Rosey's dead. He was killed over on Purgatory."

"That right? Well, his friend Gibbs was afraid of that. Wanted to know if I knew what the hell was going on. Mentioned this Rainbird guy again and said he sounded like trouble. He told me about the way your friend Abbott had stolen his boat to get off Purgatory and how Abbott had offered money for information on whoever might have shot a man named Cormier. When the name Rainbird came up again, I got real nervous. It occurred to me that I might already know a little too much. I've always trusted my instincts, you know?"

"So you decided to leave Brimstone?"

"Not just Brimstone. I decided to put a lot of distance between me and this Rainbird character until things cooled down. It occurred to me I needed a little vacation and it wouldn't hurt to come back to the States to check up on my investments. Brokers and accountants can get a little sloppy if you don't breathe down their necks once in a while, you know?"

"That's true," Mattie agreed. "I make it a point to check in with mine in person a couple of times a year."

"Right. So I figure I'll kill a couple of birds with one stone. Take care of business back here and wait for things to settle down out there."

"That may have been a very smart move. I don't know for certain what's going on, but there's real trouble brewing. Hugh left yesterday morning."

"Yeah? What's he going to do?"

"I wish I knew," Mattie said sadly. "Look, if you don't mind sleeping on a big couch, you're welcome to stay with me for a while until you decide what you want to do."

Evangeline looked startled at first and than strangely grateful. "That's real nice of you, honey. Sure you don't mind?"

"Not in the least. I think I'll rather enjoy having company."

Evangeline grinned. "I'll take you out to dinner. My treat."

"Sounds great. We can talk business investments."

They made a decidedly odd-looking pair that evening as they walked into the lounge of one of Seattle's best restaurants and sat down for a drink. Every eye in the place turned at least briefly toward Mattie's companion. And then, having assessed Evangeline and come to certain conclusions, those same eyes turned with great curiosity to Mattie.

Evangeline looked extremely dashing in another of her own creations, a flower-splashed, low-necked dress with long sleeves and a hem that ended mid-thigh. Mattie felt quite staid in the demure, heather-toned, high-necked dress that Evangeline had decided was the only wearable garment in Mattie's closet aside from the red sarong. Mattie had declined to wear the sarong out in downtown Seattle on the grounds that it was too cold. This wasn't the islands, after all.

"This is great, you know?" Evangeline glanced around at the ferns, polished wood, and dapper customers. "Usually when I'm in a bar, I'm working. Nice to be able to come in and just sit down and relax."

"I'm glad you're enjoying it. Evangeline, I'd like to ask a favor."

"Sure, honey."

"Would you go shopping with me tomorrow? I could use some advice."

Evangeline laughed and heads turned again. "You bet. Can't think of anything I'd rather do than go shopping." She leaned forward. "And confidentially, honey, you could use some help."

"I know."

"I didn't want to say too much, but the truth is, I was a little shocked by what you've got in that closet of yours. All the wrong colors. And you need a style that makes the most of your figure. You're a little thin, but that's okay. The right styles will make you look sleek. Those business suits just sort of cover you up, if you know what I mean."

"I had a feeling they weren't quite me." Mattie smiled. "At least, not any longer."

"So you and this Abbott are together full-time, huh?" Evangeline sipped her wine. "For real?"

Mattie nodded. "He says so."

"Is he planning on moving here to Seattle or are you going out there?"

"That's one of the things we're still working on," Mattie admitted.

"I'll bet you end up out there," Evangeline said thoughtfully. "I don't know Abbott very well. Just saw him with you that morning. But my guess is that he ain't the city type."

"No, I don't think he is."

"And men aren't very adaptable. Ever notice? They tend to get real set in their ways. Much more so than women."

"I expect that's one of the reasons why women have usually had to do the adapting," Mattie agreed with a sigh. "It's not fair, is it?"

"Nope. But that's life, I guess. So what will you do if you go out to St. Gabe with him? Lie around and get a tan?"

"Tanning is no longer considered a healthy leisure-time activity," Mattie said.

"I heard that. Sort of like sex. I'm thinking of going out of the business real soon."

"You're going to open that little dress boutique you talked about? Design your own clothes for tourists?"

Evangeline nodded. "I think I've got enough in certificates of deposit, T-bills, and stocks to do it now. First thing I've got to do is find a good location, though. Hawaii is too crowded. Commercial rents are sky high. I need a place that's just about to get discovered, you know? Some place where the tourists are just starting to head. Brimstone ain't it."

"Hugh says St. Gabe is on the way to being discovered," Mattie said almost to herself. "The tourists are starting to show up regularly."

"Yeah? Hey, maybe you and me could both go into business there. Wouldn't that be a kick?"

"I can't sew." Then Mattie smiled slowly. "But I can sell paintings. And if I can sell art, I can probably sell anything. Tourists always buy souvenirs, don't they?"

"You're serious, aren't you?"

"I've got to figure something out. And fast. The walls are starting to close in on me."

"I know the feeling. Been closing in on me for years. This Rainbird thing was the last straw."

Mattie was never quite certain what woke her that night. She had been sleeping fitfully anyway, so perhaps it was simply the change in the pattern of shadows on the ceiling when the door to the huge studio was stealthily opened.

Whatever it was, she knew that something was very wrong. For a few seconds she lay absolutely still, wishing desperately that Hugh were there beside her. Then she heard the tiny squeak that signaled the door being closed.

Mattie took several deep breaths, fighting to overcome the panic that gripped her. She could not just lie here like this while someone burglarized the apartment. Evangeline was asleep on the couch. Whoever had come into the studio would see her.

Mattie pushed back the covers and silently got out of the bed. She tiptoed to the railing and looked down.

There, silhouetted in the light coming in through the high windows, was the figure of a man. The faint neon glow glinted off the gun in his hand as he aimed it at Evangeline.

Without skipping a beat, Mattie's fear turned to fury. This was her apartment, her sanctuary. She would not allow anyone to invade it like this.

Mattie snatched up the heavy black vase by her bed and hurled it over the edge of the railing, straight at the intruder's bare head.

There was a horrendous crash. The man with the gun crumpled to the floor, his gun skittering across the wooden surface. The intruder groaned and tried to rise. Mattie grabbed the phone and yanked the plug out of the wall. She raced down the spiral staircase with some vague notion of using the phone as a club.

But she needn't have worried.

Evangeline screamed as she woke up and took in the situation at a glance. Obviously accustomed to emergencies such as this, she leaped up off the couch and began bashing the fallen man over the head with the nearest available object. It was Shock Value Frederickson's brilliantly executed metal sculpture, *On the Brink.*

The man groaned once more and fell back onto the floor.

# 17

❦

"Good grief, Evangeline, be careful with that sculpture. It's going to be worth a fortune in another five years." Mattie had just rounded the last turn in the staircase and leaped off the last step, phone raised on high. The hem of her flannel nightgown trailed behind her as she flew across the room. "Are you all right?"

"Yeah, thanks to you, honey. You're a great one for coming to the rescue, aren't you?" Evangeline, dressed in a skimpy black lace nightie decorated with not-so-discreetly placed black lace roses, lowered *On the Brink* and surveyed the man on the floor. "Anyone you know?"

"Why on earth would I know him? Must be a burglar or rapist or something." Mattie flipped on the nearest light switch and took a closer look at the young, dark-haired man on the floor. He was dressed in black jeans, black boots, and a black pullover sweater. He looked like a movie version of a cat burglar. Or an assassin. "Oh, my God."

"You do know him?"

"It's the man who was following me home in the rain the other night."

Evangeline looked up. "Who is he?"

"I don't know his name. I just saw him behind me the other evening. He was wearing a trenchcoat then, and I had a weird feeling he was watching me." Mattie put down the phone she had unplugged in the loft and reached for the downstairs extension. "I'll call nine-one-one."

She had gotten as far as punching out the number nine when the man on the floor stirred. She hesitated, glancing in his direction. "Do you think we should hit him again, Evangeline?"

Evangeline hovered over the sprawled figure with *On the Brink* held at the ready. "I'll handle it."

The man's lashes fluttered, and he looked first at Mattie and then at Evangeline with dazed eyes. "Bitches."

"Be ready to cream him if he so much as moves an inch, Evangeline."

"Too late," the man muttered. "Trap's already closing on Abbott and Taggert. Too late to save them."

Mattie froze. "Trap? What sort of trap? What are you talking about?"

The man's lips thinned in a vicious parody of a death's head grin. "Nothing you can do, bitch."

"What is this trap for Silk and Hugh?" Mattie snapped, her fingers trembling on the phone.

"Like lambs to the slaughter." The man's lashes fluttered weakly and he groaned. "Never know what hit 'em."

"When the police find out what you were up to, they'll take care of everything," Mattie said defiantly.

The man showed his teeth in another deadly grin. "Get real, bitch. As far as the cops are concerned, I followed a whore back to her apartment, and we had a little falling out, that's all. Happens all the time."

"Not in my apartment," Mattie said.

The intruder slid back into unconsciousness.

Evangeline and Mattie traded glances, and then Mattie went ahead and punched out the number of the emergency code.

Silence fell on the room while they waited for the police.

"I guess we should get ready for the cops," Mattie said after a minute.

"Yeah. Look, Mattie, you want me to disappear or something?"

"Of course not. You're staying right here. This is my apartment and you're a friend of mine," Mattie reminded her. "I assure you my reputation can withstand an investigation by the Forces of Moral Righteousness and the FBI combined. That's the beauty of having led a very dull life." She eyed Evangeline's black lace nightie. "Still, it might not hurt if we both put on a robe or something."

Evangeline grinned. "Yeah, wouldn't want 'em to get any ideas. I'll keep an eye on this turkey while you go find one. I've got something in the suitcase I can use."

Mattie went back up to the loft to pull on her brown chenille bath robe and a pair of fluffy bedroom slippers. She surveyed herself in the mirror and decided it would have been impossible to look any more dowdy if she had deliberately tried.

When she got back downstairs she saw that Evangeline had found a see-through black negligee in her suitcase and was shrugging into it.

Mattie cleared her throat delicately as she surveyed the negligee.

"I'm sure the Seattle police have seen just about everything, but there's no sense showing them more than necessary. After all, we do want them to keep their mind on business. Do you want to borrow a robe? I have a spare."

Evangeline looked skeptically at what Mattie had on. "Does it look anything like that one?"

"I'm afraid so." Mattie went to the closet and found the old faded bathrobe. "But we can replace both the one I'm wearing and this one when you take me shopping."

"Well, all right." Evangeline tugged on the old robe with a grimace of distaste. "Speaking of cops, just exactly what do you plan to tell them?"

"I don't know." Mattie sat down on the couch. "We could tell them everything, I suppose, but who's going to believe it? We can't prove a thing about Rainbird or the rest of it. Also, I'm not quite sure how much of his past Hugh wants dredged up. I think we need diplomatic advice."

"Who from?"

"From someone who knows about handling delicate situations like this. My aunt Charlotte." Mattie was already punching in Charlotte Vailcourt's private number, the one that reached her anywhere, day or night.

When Charlotte came on the line, Mattie explained the situation as rapidly as possible. Charlotte's response was immediate.

"Say nothing about the Rainbird connection for now," Charlotte advised. "You're right, we don't know how awkward any of this could be for Hugh or his friend. It's not up to us to start raking up their past, not after all the work they've done to conceal it. Also, he wouldn't want us calling attention to whatever he's planning to do on Purgatory."

"I agree. He said it was personal business. What about this creep on the floor? Just another ordinary, run-of-the-mill rapist-murderer foiled by two savvy young businesswomen?"

"Exactly. As far as you know, you are two innocent women who were followed home by a homicidal pervert. These days no one, especially a cop, will even blink at that explanation. Happens all the time. And he probably won't say much of anything at all to the police without a lawyer. It's in his own best interests to keep his mouth shut."

Mattie shuddered. Then she heard the sirens out in the street. "They're here, Aunt Charlotte. I'll call you later."

It all happened just as Charlotte Vailcourt had predicted. The gun was a particularly damaging piece of evidence against the intruder, and Mattie's pristine background as a law-abiding, taxpaying member of the business community was unassailable.

When the furor had died down and the police had taken their leave,

Mattie and Evangeline made tea. Evangeline toasted slices of whole-wheat sourdough bread while Mattie tried to call Hugh.

"No answer," Mattie said, replacing the receiver reluctantly. "I'll try Abbott Charters."

The phone in the office of Abbott Charters was answered on the third ring.

"Yeah?"

Mattie frowned at the chewing noises on the other end of the line. She was surprised how clearly she could hear them overseas. "Is this Derek?"

"Yeah," said Derek. "Who's this?"

"Mattie Sharpe. I'm calling for Hugh."

"I thought he was in Seattle."

"You haven't seen him?"

"Not since he left for his vacation."

Mattie decided not to mention the fact that Hugh's trip to Seattle was not supposed to have been a mere vacation. "What about Silk?"

"Didn't see Silk last night in the Hellfire, come to think of it. Hang on a second." Derek yelled across the room. "Ray, you seen Silk lately?"

"Not for a couple of days at least."

Mattie felt herself getting increasingly tense. "Derek, listen, this is important. If you see Silk or Hugh, please ask them to call me or Charlotte Vailcourt immediately."

"Right. I'll leave a message on Abbott's desk, and I'll take a note down to Silk's boat. I'll also let Bernard at the Hellfire know. That do?"

"Yes. Thank you." Mattie hung up the phone and looked at Evangeline. "That man who broke in here said Hugh and Silk were headed for a trap."

"Uh-huh." Evangeline spread marmalade on a slice of toast. "Sure did, honey. What are you going to do?"

"I don't know. I can't reach Hugh. No one's seen him, but he should have gotten to St. Gabriel yesterday."

"Could have had trouble with connections."

"Not this much trouble."

"No, guess not."

"I'm worried, Evangeline."

"Don't blame you. But I don't see what you can do except try to get word to Abbott that he might be walking into a setup of some kind."

Mattie jumped to her feet. "I'm going out there."

"St. Gabe?" Evangeline stared at her in amazement. "I don't know if that's such a good idea, honey."

But Mattie was already heading for the closet where she kept her suitcase. "Something's wrong. I can feel it. I told Hugh he should have taken me with him. Damn it, I *told* him. He never listens to me."

"So what else is new? Men never listen to women."

"I've got to go out there and find him. There's a flight at six. If I hurry, I can just make it." Mattie hauled the suitcase out and opened it on the floor. She went into the bathroom and started collecting her toiletries. "As it stands now, I know more than anyone else does about this whole mess, and I can't get the information to anyone who can help. So I'm going to go look for Hugh myself."

"You think he'll appreciate that?"

"Probably not, knowing him. But he isn't here, is he? So there's nothing he can say about it."

"You got a point." Evangeline looked around. "I'll check into a motel or something."

"You're more than welcome to stay here." Mattie looked up suddenly. "Unless, uh, you're planning to go back to work?"

Evangeline grinned. "Don't worry, honey. I never work when I'm in the States. Too risky what with the cops and diseases and pimps with guns and everything else you folks have back here. Relax. When you return, your snow-white reputation will still be intact."

Mattie grinned. "Pity."

It started to rain just as Mattie's jet touched down on the St. Gabriel runway. She made the mad dash across the tarmac to the small terminal along with the rest of the handful of passengers who had been on board.

Inside the terminal building she paused briefly to try another phone call to Hugh's house and the office of Abbott Charters, but there was no answer at either place. Hoisting her suitcase, she went over to see about renting a car.

"You're Abbott's lady, ain't ya?" the man behind the counter asked, peering at her intently. "What are you doin' back here without Abbott? He still in the States?"

Mattie frowned as she picked up a pen to sign the brief contract. "You haven't seen him? He was supposed to be back here ahead of me."

"Nope. Ain't seen hide nor hair of him. Course, he could've come through on the evening flight. I don't work evenings."

"Yes. Maybe that was it." She quickly signed her name and collected the keys.

It took her a few minutes to get the hang of the stick shift in the battered green Jeep, but Mattie eventually pulled out of the small parking lot and onto the main road into town.

In spite of her deep fears, she was amazed at how comfortingly familiar everything seemed. *It was like coming home,* she found herself thinking. But that made absolutely no sense. No sense at all.

She stopped briefly near the harbor to check Silk's boat for signs of occupancy. But there was no one on board the *Griffin.* Mattie hesitated and then stepped into the stern to check the paints and brushes that were sitting near the easel.

The brushes were not even damp. Silk had not been at work here recently.

On a hunch she went across the street to the Hellfire.

"Well, hello, Mattie," Bernard said in obvious surprise from behind the bar. "What are you doing here? Where's Abbott?"

"You haven't seen him?"

Bernard shook his head. "Sorry. Derek said I was to have him call you if I saw him, but he hasn't been here. I thought he was in the States with you. Supposed to be on a short vacation or something."

"He left three days ago. He should have been back here by now."

"Unless he stopped off in Hawaii or one of the other islands to pick up some supplies or see some business contacts. He does that, you know. He has a lot of clients scattered all around out here."

"I hadn't thought of that," Mattie admitted. "But what about Silk?"

"Like I told Derek, Silk hasn't been keeping to his usual routine for the past few days. But I sort of figured that's 'cause Abbott left him in charge of his business, and Silk knows there'll be hell to pay if he tries to run Abbott Charters and drink at the same time."

"Thanks, Bernard. If you see either of them, tell them I'm on the island. I'll be at Hugh's house."

"Sure. You're finally ready to move out here, huh? Abbott said it wouldn't take long."

Mattie wrinkled her nose but declined to respond. She got back into the Jeep. She fumbled with the gears again and headed along the island road toward Hugh's small beach cottage. She was not certain what to do next, but she told herself she felt a little better knowing she was on the scene and not sitting thousands of miles away in Seattle. For all the good it did.

She was beginning to suspect that Hugh and Silk had already left for Purgatory. Perhaps they had rendezvoused in Hades. A cold chill deep in the pit of her stomach made her insides clench. She had to face the fact that Rainbird's trap might already have closed.

The small driveway in front of the beach cottage was empty. There was no sign of life or recent habitation. Mattie switched off the Jeep's engine and sat for a moment behind the wheel. Her sense of uneasiness was very strong right now. Memories of the horror that had awaited her when she had walked into Paul Cormier's white mansion were vivid in her mind.

No, she told herself, it would be all right. She was not about to walk into another death scene.

But the gnawing anxiety was getting stronger. For a second she considered turning the key in the ignition and driving back into town. But she knew she had to look inside the cottage to reassure herself that Hugh or Silk was not lying dead on the floor within. *She had to know.*

Mattie forced herself to get out of the Jeep and walk to the front door. She had the spare key Hugh had given her in her hand, but the instant she slid it into the lock, she knew she didn't need it. The door was open.

Literally sick with anticipation, Mattie pushed open the door and stared into the empty front room.

She exhaled slowly when she realized there were no dead bodies on the floor. Of course, that still left the bedroom.

Mattie walked slowly through the eerily empty cottage. There was no evidence that Hugh had been here recently—no coffee cup in the sink, nothing in the refrigerator.

She was beginning to think that Hugh had never come back to St. Gabriel at all. That meant he had probably gone to Hades or even directly into Purgatory. And apparently Silk had joined him.

She was too late. Rainbird's trap had closed.

Mattie opened the bedroom door and found herself looking straight into the barrel of a gun.

"About time you got here, lady."

For an instant she could not breathe. She had been so grateful the house didn't contain any dead bodies that she had not even stopped to think it might contain a few live ones.

She went very still and looked up into the face of the young man holding the weapon. He was not very tall, but he was heavily built and had a cruel mouth and eyes that had probably never been innocent. He was dressed in military boots and khakis, and he held the gun as if he was very accustomed to it. As she stared at him he made a show of flicking the briefest of glances at his stainless-steel wristwatch.

"Who are you?" Mattie managed in a tight voice.

"You can call me Goody. I work for someone who wants to meet you, Miss Sharpe. That's all you need to know."

"What have you done with Hugh and Silk?"

"Me?" The thin brows rose. "Why, nothing. Yet. But they'll be taken care of soon enough. Let's go." He used the gun to motion her back down the hall. "Move it, lady. We've got a plane to catch."

"I'm not going anywhere with you."

The man grinned. "That's what you think. You got two choices, lady. Either you walk outside to the Jeep, or I knock you unconscious and carry you out. Take your pick."

"What if I don't like the options?"

"They're the only ones you've got."

Mattie looked at him and believed every word he was saying. She turned and walked slowly down the hall and outside to the Jeep. Goody stayed three steps behind her all the way.

"You drive," Goody said, glancing once more at his watch.

"How did you know I was coming here to the cottage?" Mattie asked as she struggled once more with the gears.

"We knew several hours ago that Mortinson had bungled the operation in Seattle. He didn't report in on time, so he's out of the picture. Christ, the man must have been a complete idiot not to be able to take out one whore and pick you up."

"That's what Mortinson was supposed to do? Kill my friend and kidnap me?"

The man scowled, looking as if he was afraid he'd said too much. "Forget it. Doesn't matter now. You're here, just like we figured you'd be when we found out you'd left Seattle. We knew we couldn't grab you in the St. Gabe airport terminal or near it. Abbott's got too many friends on the island, and they all know you belong to him. Someone would have noticed."

"Yes." Mattie's mouth was dry.

"I figured you'd check his house sooner or later, so that's where I waited for you. Now, let's move this bucket a little faster. I'm in kind of a hurry."

"Don't you think someone at the airport might notice the gun?" Mattie struggled with the gears and backed slowly out of the drive.

"No one will be close enough to see us. When you get to the airport, drive straight out onto the service road that parallels the runway. The plane will be waiting."

It was.

Everything went just as Goody had told her it would. The Cessna was at the end of the runway. No one appeared to notice the two people who parked the Jeep on the service road and walked out to board the plane.

That was one of the problems with the casual way things were run out here in the islands, Mattie thought bitterly. This sort of thing would never have happened back home in Seattle. Unauthorized vehicles were simply not allowed out on airport runways back in the States.

The young pilot glanced only briefly at his unwilling passenger. He nodded once at Goody as the gunman latched the door.

"What took you so long?"

"She took her own sweet time. Christ, let's just get this thing off the ground. The Colonel will be getting impatient."

Mattie fastened her seat belt, closed her eyes, and wondered where Hugh was.

They reached Purgatory an hour later. Mattie was once again marched across an active runway and thrust into a waiting vehicle. No one said a word. She was surrounded by three armed men now, Goody, the pilot, and the driver of the car. All wore military-style clothing and all were surprisingly young. Mattie estimated their ages at between nineteen and twenty-three or twenty-four at the most.

Her stress level, already sky high, went up another couple of notches when she recognized their destination. Paul Cormier's white island mansion looked as beautiful this time as it had when she had first seen it.

Mattie got out of the car at the point of a gun and walked up the steps to the wide veranda. The door was opened by a young man who looked as if he ordered his clothes from *Soldier of Fortune* magazine. He had a gun strapped to his thigh.

"This way, Miss Sharpe."

The first thing she noticed was that someone had cleaned Paul Cormier's blood off the white marble. For some reason that made her angry. It was as though some part of her felt the evidence of murder should not be erased until justice was done.

The anger gave her strength. She walked swiftly down the white marble hall to the wide white room that fronted the house. The view of the sapphire-blue ocean through the bank of open French windows was dazzling. She concentrated on it rather than on the man who was rising from a white leather couch to greet her.

"Miss Sharpe. Allow me to introduce myself. I am known now as Colonel McCormick, but I believe you are no doubt aware by now of my previous name, Jack Rainbird."

Mattie turned slowly to look at him, as if she found him a nuisance when all she really wanted to do was admire the view. She let her glance slide critically over him from head to foot.

Jack Rainbird was an astonishingly handsome man by any standards. He appeared to be in his early forties, as Hugh had said, but he had the strong, bird-of-prey features that would not even begin to soften for many years. His eyes were a clear, light, honest blue. His blond hair, graying at the temples, had been precision cut with a razor to lie close to his head. His body was trim and there was a crisp military set to his head and shoulders. He was wearing perfectly pressed khakis. His belt buckle shone and his boots had been polished to a high gloss.

All in all, Mattie thought, Rainbird had the classic heroic look historically associated with a leader of men. That was, of course, undoubtedly one of the many things that made him so dangerous. The other thing was his undeniable sexual charm. Hugh had been right. The man had it in spades. He exuded it like an aura.

Mattie felt the first uneasy twinge of a throat-closing claustrophobia.

"This is Paul Cormier's house," she said boldly, more to counteract her own tension than anything else. "You have no business here."

A smile flickered briefly around Rainbird's finely crafted mouth. "What can I say? Best accommodations on the island, and I like having the best. Besides, our friend Mr. Cormier no longer has any need of his lovely island home."

"You killed him."

"Do you always jump to conclusions, Miss Sharpe? That is generally considered a dangerous thing to do."

"You killed him. Or had him killed."

"Obviously your mind is already made up. I imagine I owe that to Abbott. He, naturally, would have a somewhat biased view of events."

"Why?"

Rainbird gave her a look that was half amused, half surprised. "Why, because he hates my guts, of course." He walked across the beautiful room to a white liquor cabinet. "May I offer you a drink, Miss Sharpe?"

"No, thank you."

"I was afraid you might be difficult about all this." Rainbird splashed whiskey into a crystal glass. "You've been hanging around with Abbott for too long. The man has poisoned your mind against me."

Mattie took a deep breath and asked aloud the question that was screaming in her mind. "Just where is Hugh and his friend Silk?"

Rainbird smiled at her over the rim of his glass. "Now, that, Miss Sharpe, is what I am hoping you will tell me."

She stared at him, open-mouthed. "You mean you don't know, either?"

"I'm afraid not. And the whole thing is getting to be something of a problem. I never did like having Abbott running around loose. The man's too damn unpredictable. Always does things his way instead of the military way. That was one of the reasons I had to . . ." Rainbird smiled again. "Never mind. That's ancient history."

"Well, you've gone to a lot of trouble for nothing, Colonel Rainbird. Because I have no idea where Hugh is. And I wouldn't tell you if I did."

"Then we shall just have to put out the word that you are here with me and wait for him to come and collect you, won't we?" Rainbird's blue eyes glinted. "Howard will show you to your room now. You may change for dinner."

Mattie's chin lifted. "I should warn you I don't eat meat."

"Excellent," Rainbird said with a smile. "Neither do I. Gave it up some time ago along with cigarettes. Do you know, I believe we are going to discover a great many things in common, Miss Sharpe. It has been a long while since I have had the pleasure of entertaining an intelligent, attractive woman. And knowing you are Hugh Abbott's will make it all the more interesting."

# 18

It was too much to hope that she would be shown to the master bedroom suite. Mattie thought of the secret panel behind the elegant bathtub and sighed. Hugh had said there was more than one emergency exit in this house. She surveyed the room that had been assigned to her.

It was as lovely as every other room in the gracious white mansion. The windows all opened onto the veranda and a view of the ocean. The walls were strips of white marble interspersed with sparkling mirrors. Mattie tentatively pressed on a few of them to see if by chance Cormier had built one of his escape routes in this room. She had no luck, either in the main room or in the adjoining bath.

That meant her only hope for escape was to finagle a way into the master bath. Mattie's heart sank as she realized that was probably going to be a lot easier to do than she might have wished. She had seen the look in Rainbird's eyes and knew what he intended. Before the night was over, he was going to drag her into the bedroom suite, if only for the pleasure of raping Hugh Abbott's woman.

Mattie opened her suitcase slowly and examined the contents. Too bad she had not had a chance to go shopping with Evangeline before leaving Seattle. It looked like the blue and white striped silk camp shirt and prim little navy-blue skirt were going to have to serve as her seduction outfit.

She stood in front of the mirror for a minute before leaving the room and unbuttoned the silk shirt a little lower than she normally would have. Then she took her hair down and brushed it out so that it danced around her shoulders. It made a lot of difference, she realized.

She reached for her makeup kit, wishing Evangeline were there to give advice.

Dinner was served by Howard, who looked exactly the same as he had when he'd greeted Mattie at the door, except that he'd draped a white linen napkin over his arm. It didn't quite go with the gun on his hip, Mattie thought.

She was seated at the end of a long, thick glass table supported on four legs fashioned of carved white stone. Rainbird was seated at the opposite end. He was wearing a white dinner jacket and a black bow tie. Paul Cormier's beautiful crystal, silver, and china glittered on the table, reflecting the candlelight.

"No need to look uneasy, Miss Sharpe." Rainbird sounded amused. "I assure you, I am not planning to poison you. Enjoy your meal. Howard is an excellent chef. Cooking is one of his many areas of expertise. He is a very versatile young man."

Howard glowed under the praise and watched anxiously as Mattie sampled her rice pilaf. She looked up and saw him watching her.

"It's wonderful," she said honestly.

"Thank you, ma'am." Howard inclined his head.

Rainbird's mouth lifted slightly at the corner. "I'm sure you've made his day, Miss Sharpe. You may leave us now, Howard. I'll call you if we need anything."

"Yes, sir." Howard vanished into the kitchen.

Mattie looked down the table at Rainbird. His elegantly carved cheekbones were highlighted by the soft glow of candlelight, and he looked even more handsome than he had in daylight. "Are all your men as young as Howard and the others?"

"Now, yes. I learned the hard way some years ago that young males work out better in this sort of service. Not only are young men more attracted to the life of adventure I offer, they are more amenable to taking orders. The older we get, the more cynical we become, and the less inclined we are to put our trust in others."

"I see."

Rainbird chuckled indulgently. "Don't look at me like that. Young men are much easier to train and mold. It's a fact of life, Miss Sharpe. Why do you think that the draft age is always set as low as possible? The military has always preferred eighteen- and nineteen-year-olds."

"Because they're more impressionable."

"Exactly."

"Are you always so calculating, Colonel Rainbird?"

"Always." He forked up a bite of vegetable curry and chewed meditatively. "It is the primary reason I've lived this long."

"Is there a secondary reason?"

His charming grin came and went. "I have been blessed with excellent reflexes. They have come in handy on occasion. And not just when I'm fighting with someone."

Mattie blushed and quickly changed the subject. "Do you mind if I ask why you are here on Purgatory?"

He smiled, pouring more wine. "Purgatory, my dear Miss Sharpe, is the perfect home for one such as myself. The government, what there is of it, is most accommodating."

"Because it takes orders from you?"

"Let's just say we all get along very well together here. A live-and-let-live philosophy."

"That didn't apply to Paul Cormier, did it?" Mattie asked softly.

"You may not believe this, but I am truly sorry about Paul."

Mattie held his clear blue gaze. "Did you kill him, Colonel Rainbird?"

A trace of sorrow flickered in the depths of the beautiful sky-blue eyes. "No. I give you my word of honor as an officer and a gentleman, Miss Sharpe. I did not kill Paul. He and I had gone our separate ways over the years, but we were former comrades in arms and I had nothing but the utmost respect for him. I still considered him a friend. I intended for us to be neighbors here on Purgatory."

"Then who killed him?" Mattie blurted out, confused and frustrated by Rainbird's obvious sincerity and undeniable charm.

"I assure you, I made it my immediate business to find out. The culprit was a house servant who decided to kill and rob his employer under cover of the military activity that was taking place on the island. He is presently in the village jail awaiting trial. Justice will be done, Miss Sharpe. Have no fear. I am a man who believes in justice."

She looked straight into his eyes and knew with terrifying clarity that he was lying. "Is that right? Then why did you lead a coup on a perfectly peaceful island?"

"All was not as it seemed on the surface here on Purgatory, Miss Sharpe. May I call you Mattie?" Rainbird did not pause for a response. "The small local government had no military arm, and it found itself threatened by a group of local renegades—hoodlums, really—who had obtained a cache of automatic weapons. I came ashore with my men at the request of the president. It is not an uncommon sort of action, Mattie. Small, ineffectual governments such as Purgatory's frequently need the assistance of men such as myself."

"And now you've decided to stay?"

Rainbird nodded. "I see in Purgatory exactly what my friend Paul saw. A lovely, relatively peaceful place where a man who has grown weary of battle may live out his life on his own terms."

Mattie narrowed her eyes consideringly. "What about that man you had following me in Seattle?"

"That man was your bodyguard, Mattie. I assigned him to keep an eye on you while you were involved with Hugh Abbott. Abbott has killed innocent bystanders before and will probably kill again. I didn't want you to be one of the victims. I realize you are not yet prepared to believe me when I tell you Abbott is dangerous, but sooner or later you will see the truth."

It was then Mattie realized for certain what she had suspected earlier. Rainbird did not know she had seen the man break into her apartment and attempt to kill Evangeline. Apparently the Colonel had not yet communicated with his assassin. He would know there had been a failure in his plans, but he did not yet know at what point things had gone wrong.

Perhaps the intruder had not regained consciousness, or maybe he had awakened with convenient short-term amnesia. Mattie had heard that was common in cases of blows to the head, and the man who had invaded her apartment had certainly endured a number of those.

"Forgive me, Mattie," Rainbird was saying, "but may I ask you how you came to be involved with Paul Cormier?"

Mattie considered her words carefully. "He was selling an item from his collection of ancient armor to someone I know. As I was going on vacation in the Pacific at the time, I was asked to pick up the item and take it back to Seattle."

"Ah, yes, now it makes some sense. Perhaps you would like to see the collection? I removed it temporarily while the house was being cleaned, but it is now back in place, and it is very impressive. Do you know anything about antique armory?"

"No." Mattie decided not to mention her aunt's collection. The less Rainbird knew, the better.

"Paul acquired some remarkable pieces. I shall be delighted to show them to you."

Mattie's nerves were live wires of tension and fear by the time the meal drew to a close. Rainbird's charm was like a foul cloud reaching out to envelop her. *Vampire,* she thought nervously as she took a tiny sip of wine.

When the Colonel poured her a glass of brandy and led her down a wide hall to the library, she realized her fingers were trembling. Rainbird did not appear to notice.

"Impressive, isn't it?" Rainbird said as he led Mattie into a lovely room filled with books and glass cases of various sizes and shapes. "The cases are all individually sealed and climate-controlled, of course. Salt air is not good for old metal."

"No, I imagine it isn't." Mattie wandered from case to case, her brandy glass in hand, and tried to look interested in the daggers, swords, helmets, shields, and mail inside. She focused on her breathing, trying to calm herself. When the time came to act she simply could not afford to collapse from stress. She stopped in front of a case that held a single weapon, a sword.

"That is a particularly interesting specimen, isn't it?" Rainbird observed, moving softly to stand directly behind her.

"Yes. I think that may have been the sword I was sent to collect." Mattie felt the old, familiar sensation of walls closing in around her. It was, she realized vaguely, the first time she'd ever had another human being trigger her claustrophobia. Elevators, caves, stress, yes. But not another person.

"Fourteenth century, according to Paul's records," Rainbird mused. He was very close to her now. His knuckles gently brushed the line of Mattie's neck. "Finest Spanish steel." His breath was warm on the bare skin of her neck as he lifted her hair in his hand. "It has a name, you know. *Valor.* A good weapon deserves a name of its own."

"I've heard there's also a legend attached to it." Mattie could hardly breathe. She felt as if she were being suffocated by Rainbird's closeness.

"Ah, yes." Rainbird's fingertips touched her neck with infinite gentleness. "Something about the blade being dangerous for anyone to claim unless they're an avenger after a betrayer, no? Charming curse, isn't it? But the betrayer, whoever he was, has been dead for several hundred years. And so has the avenger who was meant to take up the blade."

"Do you think so?" A shiver of dread went straight down Mattie's spine as Rainbird's fingers trailed across her shoulder.

"Yes. The avenger and the betrayer are long gone. But the blade survives." Rainbird stroked her arm. "It is a beautiful sword, isn't it? A blade made for killing, not for ceremony. Note the clean lines of the pommel and hilt." His hand slid along the curve of her arm. "No useless ornamentation or expensive gemstones. The blade reminds me of you, Mattie. Clean and elegant. Cool on the outside. But forged in fire. Beautiful."

Mattie sucked in her breath in a startled gasp as Rainbird eased closer. His fingers were gliding just inside the collar of her shirt now. She felt his lips move softly, lightly on her nape. The claustrophobia was so strong she was almost sick with it.

"Mattie? You are really very lovely, you know. I have never met anyone quite like you."

She looked up at him, half-hypnotized and fully terrified by the utter clarity of Rainbird's gaze. Mattie realized then why he could look at her with such complete sincerity. It was because he had no concept of conscience or remorse. There was nothing there under the surface, just as she had tried to explain to Hugh. *Nothing there at all.*

This was a man who could commit any crime and feel nothing for the victim. He could look his next victim straight in the eye and smile.

*Not like Hugh,* she thought. She understood then that Hugh had never lied to her. Not once, not even a year ago.

With Hugh, a woman would always know where she stood—if she was paying attention and not letting the past get in the way.

When Hugh made love, there was no doubting the genuineness of his passion. When he chewed you out, you knew he was mad. When he laughed, you knew he was happy. When he made a commitment, you knew he would keep it.

And if he were about to kill you, Mattie realized, you would know it. He would not smile at you with seductive eyes when he pulled the trigger. All the hellish cold of impending death would be there in his wolf's gaze.

"I find you as fascinating in your own way as I do the sword in that case," Rainbird murmured. "But I suppose that is not so very strange. You are a creature fashioned for passion, and the blade is an object designed for clean, cold violence. Sex and violence are forever linked. Two sides of the same coin. Have you learned that yet, Mattie?"

"No," she said, her throat tight as the walls closed in. "No, and I don't believe you. They are not linked. One is life and one is death."

"Such an innocent." His mouth brushed across hers again. The blue eyes were smiling and intent. "I am willing to bet you have never been made love to properly, Mattie Sharpe. I can see the lack of knowledge in your eyes. You're nervous, aren't you?"

"Yes." That was putting it mildly, Mattie thought.

"I told you that good sex and good violence are linked, but that doesn't mean I like my sex to be violent. Quite the contrary, Mattie. I am a man who likes subtlety and nuance. I appreciate delicate things, and a woman such as yourself is a very delicate creature, indeed. You would find me a very gentle, very considerate, very careful lover. I would take my time with you. All the time in the world."

"Please . . . I . . . ."

He silenced her with another feather-light kiss. Then, with a small, endearing smile flickering again around the corners of his mouth, he took her hand and led her out of the library and along the veranda to the master bedroom suite. He did not turn on the lights as he urged her through the French doors. A sliver of silver from the moon angled across the room.

Mattie struggled for composure. The massive white bed in the center of the room loomed in the shadows. "What about Howard?"

"Howard will not bother us." Rainbird smiled his beautiful smile. "Don't be afraid, Mattie. I'm not going to rape you. I don't do things that way. There is a place for violence, but it is not in the bedroom."

"You prefer to exercise the power of seduction?" She tried a small, tentative smile of her own.

"As I said, I prefer subtlety." Rainbird's finger drifted along the vee of her shirt collar. "And I imagine any woman who has spent more than ten minutes with Hugh Abbott would hunger for a little civilized behavior. Especially someone as sensitive and lovely as you, Mattie."

She closed her eyes and took one step backward. She was feeling so nauseated now she was beginning to be afraid she would ruin everything by throwing up in the middle of Rainbird's big seduction scene. "Would you mind very much if I used the bathroom?"

"Not at all." He waved her gallantly toward the adjoining room.

He continued to watch her with an intent, vaguely amused expression as she edged toward the bath. His fingers went to the black tie around his throat.

Suddenly Mattie wondered if Rainbird already knew about the secret panel and had walled it up. Perhaps he was playing some horrible game with her. But she had no choice. She had to try it. It was her only hope of escape. The thought of going back out into that bedroom was enough to make her feel faint.

She closed the door of the beautiful bath, turned on the light, and took a quick glance around. Rainbird's personal items were there now, neatly placed along the white marble countertop: silver-backed combs, expensive after-shave and cologne, a single fresh hibiscus in a crystal vase.

Mattie's eyes glided over the mirror, and she almost failed to recognize the white-faced woman with the huge, frightened eyes who stared back at her.

A soft sound in the bedroom made her flinch. She had to make her move now. Mattie walked over to the sink and turned one of the handles of the silver faucet so that the water splashed merrily into the basin.

She started opening drawers quietly, remembering what Hugh had said about Cormier keeping a flashlight in every room of the house because of frequent power outages. Surely he would have kept one in this bathroom, since it had been planned as an escape room. Cormier was a strategist, Hugh had said. Rainbird would have had no reason to remove something like a flashlight.

She found what she was looking for in the bottom right drawer near the sink.

Picking up the flashlight, she stepped out of her shoes and went across the room to flush the toilet.

Water churned loudly in the fixtures.

It was all the cover she would get. Carrying her shoes, Mattie hurried to the marble bath, stepped into it and pushed on the wall panel as Hugh had before.

For a second nothing happened. Mattie thought the stress would overwhelm her. She simply could not go back out into that bedroom. She would become a screaming zombie here in the elegant bath if she did not escape *right now.*

The panel slid silently open. Mattie breathed a silent prayer of gratitude, hitched up her skirt, and stepped into the darkness. The sense of relief was enough to push aside the mounting sense of claustrophobia for a short time. She found the button on the other side of the panel and pushed it. The panel slid soundlessly back into place.

At that same instant there was a soft knock on the bathroom door.

"Mattie? Are you all right in there?"

Mattie switched on the flashlight, stepped into her shoes, and fled down the hidden hallway. She reached the door that opened onto the jungle and held her breath as she turned the handle.

Half expecting to meet up with one of the armed guards, she switched off the flashlight and stepped out into the night. She stood very still for a minute, waiting for her eyes to adjust. Then she darted into the jungle.

She had only the moon and the lights of the house to guide her. The soft, moist earth muffled her footsteps, but she knew she was making far too much noise in the undergrowth. At any moment one of the guards would surely hear her. She could only hope the crashing surf would give her some protection.

She went straight into the jungle, keeping the house lights at her back. They quickly began to fade, however, as the thick vegetation closed in around her. She had to concentrate on the sound of the ocean and the vague light of the moon to guide her. She did not dare turn on the flashlight.

*Ocean on the left. House to the rear. Straight on until you cross the stream.*

Rainbird's voice, sounding as if it were magnified through some sort of megaphone, blared out in the darkness.

"Mattie, come back. Don't run away. You won't come to any harm. You can't survive in that jungle, Mattie. There are too many things out there that can kill you. Especially at night. Things like snakes, Mattie. Do you want to find yourself in the coils of a giant snake?"

Hugh had said not to worry, Mattie recalled. There were no snakes in the jungles of Purgatory. Hugh had never lied to her. Rainbird could tell you he loved you while he slit your throat.

She plunged on. When the lights of the house disappeared entirely, she risked the flashlight in brief doses. At one point she scrambled over a fallen log and realized it was the one on which she had torn her silk blouse the first time she had come this way.

She was on the right track.

"Mattie, you're safe with me. You will die a horrible death out in that jungle. Trust me, Mattie. I mean you no harm." Rainbird's magnified voice was fading into the distance.

Hugh had said it would be virtually impossible to miss the stream. *Ocean on the left.*

Were those distant crashing sounds the footsteps of her pursuers?

She batted at the leaves, crawled over vines, pushed rare orchids out of the way as if they were so much noxious garbage in her path.

Mattie stumbled over a vine and went down on one knee. She put out her hand to steady herself and her fingers went straight into running water.

*The stream.*

Blindly she turned left. Now all she had to do was follow the rivulet of water to the waterfalls.

By now Rainbird would have sent his men out into the jungle on the theory that she would not go far. Perhaps he had assumed she would head for the sea in some primitive instinct to avoid the jungle.

She risked the flashlight again in short bursts of light. She quickly learned it was easier not to subject her eyes to the changes in shadows. Mattie continued her journey with the aid of the moon and wet feet. As long as her shoes stayed wet, she knew she was on the right path.

A familiar roaring sound told her she was approaching the waterfalls. Mattie picked up her pace, hoping she would not fall and twist her ankle. She still had all those caves to get through.

*God, the caves.*

And then what? she wondered bleakly. Assuming she survived the caves, she could not stay in Cormier's sanctuary forever. She would die of thirst and starvation. But she would worry about escape later. Right now the important thing was to get away from the blue-eyed vampire in the beautiful white mansion.

She would rather die of thirst and starvation in the cavern than lure Hugh to his death, and she knew that was what Rainbird intended.

Mattie burst through the last green barrier and came to an abrupt halt at the sight of the magnificent twin waterfalls bathed in silver moonlight. It was an eerie sight that touched some deep cord within her. There were things on this earth that were more powerful and would last eons longer than Jack Rainbird. And they could protect her from him now.

Mattie went forward and stepped up on the first of the wet, slippery rocks that outlined the foaming pool. She dared not fall tonight. Hugh was not here to catch her.

But this time she was not trying to juggle her purse and a French string bag full of pâté and bottles of sparkling water. This time it was a little easier. This time she was a little more determined.

Mattie did not slip. She leaped off the last rock, straight through a shower of water, and found herself in the black mouth of the cave. She flicked on the flashlight and scanned the walls for the marks Cormier had left behind.

Now came the hard part, she told herself ruefully. Now she had to walk through these twisting, turning tunnels of darkness all by herself.

It was worse than any crowded elevator but not quite as bad as having Jack Rainbird try to seduce her in a white and silver room. All things were relative, it seemed.

Twice she found herself turning down wrong corridors, but both times she was able to retrace her steps and find the small white marks on the walls. At several points along the way she wanted to close her eyes, but she did not dare. She might miss one of the white marks.

Her stomach was in knots. Her heart was pounding, and the flashlight threatened to fall from her damp palms. But she could not go back. The only direction was forward. Walking through the corridors was a lot like going through life without an obvious talent, Mattie told herself. You just kept moving forward until you found the right path.

She was getting close to the point of screaming, convinced she had made a wrong turn and was heading toward oblivion, when she caught a whiff of fresh sea air.

"Oh, my God." Mattie broke into a stumbling run.

The air became fresher and laden with the tang of salt. It was going to be all right, at least for a while. Rainbird and his men would never find her here.

Of course, neither would anyone else, she reminded herself grimly.

Obviously she would have to risk a trip back out sooner or later. But perhaps after a day or so Rainbird would not be looking so hard for her. Perhaps he would assume she had either escaped or drowned in the sea or died somewhere in the jungles.

She would worry about getting off Purgatory when she had recovered from this first, mad dash to freedom.

She was running full tilt when she reached the entrance to the massive cavern where she and Hugh had hoped to find Cormier's boat. The flashlight pierced the gloom in front of her, revealing the natural boat basin.

The first thing Mattie noticed was that this time there was a boat tied up at the dock. A swift, sleek, very powerful-looking cruiser.

Before she could comprehend the meaning of the boat in the cavern, a man's arm came out of the darkness and tightened like a steel noose about her throat.

Mattie tried to scream, but the sound was promptly choked off. She dropped the flashlight to struggle futilely with her assailant and felt the point of a knife graze her skin in warning.

"Well, shit," said Hugh, lowering the knife. "It's Mattie."

# 19

⁕

Mattie sat on a duffel bag next to Silk Taggert, who was calmly checking over a handgun, and watched Hugh pace the cavern with a restless wolfish tread. The forbidding expression on his hard face reminded her of the one he'd had the night she had called him to rescue her from the bar in Seattle. But this was a thousand times worse, Mattie decided. Hugh was a grenade waiting to be detonated, a sword waiting to be unsheathed.

"Are you sure he didn't hurt you?" Hugh demanded for the fifth or sixth time.

"He didn't hurt me. I told you, he admitted he was looking for you, then he fed me a lovely dinner. He told me he was a vegetarian, but I didn't believe him. Not for one minute."

Hugh gave her a strange glance. "Then what?"

"Then he took me to see Cormier's collection of old weapons." Mattie had already been through this recitation several times.

"And then he took you to the bedroom. Goddamn his soul."

"He didn't exactly drag me, Hugh," Mattie said patiently. "He assumed he was charming me. I let him think he was succeeding. The truth was I went with him because I remembered the panel in the bathroom. It was easy enough to duck in there for a minute or two. Having to use the bathroom is the greatest excuse in the world. And as far as Rainbird was concerned, it was safe to let me go in there. After all, there weren't any obvious exits except through the bedroom."

"Good thinking, Mattie," Silk said. He flicked a glance at Hugh. "Lighten up, boss. She did great and she's here, safe and sound. That's all that counts. Hell of a woman, if I may say so." He shoved a clip into the automatic. "Now you and I got work to do."

"I'll kill him."

"Yeah. I know. But first we got to get to him." Silk slanted a smile at Mattie. "Way I see it, we now got us some terrific inside information. A lot more than we had an hour ago."

"Oh, God," said Mattie, feeling drained. "I don't want you two involved in any more violence."

"A little late to worry about that," Silk said gently. "Don't you worry yourself into an ulcer over this, now. It'll be over before you know it. And then we can all get off this damn island. But it would sure speed things up if you could give us some details."

Mattie looked at him and then at Hugh and knew there was nothing she could do to stop either of them. The next best option was to try to help. "I'm afraid I wasn't paying a lot of attention to that sort of thing."

"Just think back and count all the faces you remember seeing and where they were."

"Well, I do remember thinking a couple of times that there weren't as many thugs around as I would have expected. Maybe half a dozen in all. I kept wondering where the army of occupation was."

Hugh stood at the edge of the basin of black water and stared down into it. "I told you. There is no army of occupation on Purgatory. No need for one. Rainbird is on the government's side, remember?"

"What there is of it," Silk added. "Never was much of a government here. That's one of the reasons Cormier liked it."

Hugh nodded. "What Rainbird did was classic. He made a brief show of force, handed out a few guns, and created a lot of confusion with a small group of trained men. There was no organized resistance on Purgatory. By the time the initial uproar was over, he had cut himself a deal with the folks who are officially in charge around here. Probably guaranteed to triple or quadruple the island's annual tax base with a corresponding increase in salary for the honchos and everyone else who cooperated. Money always speaks louder than guns in the long run."

"Yeah," Silk said. "You can get someone's attention with a gun, but you keep him on your side with money."

"But what does Rainbird get out of it?" Mattie asked.

"A safe harbor. He probably needs it in order to expand his business interests. God knows what he's into by now. Purgatory is perfect. A tiny, politically independent island of absolutely no strategic importance to anyone where he can relax, kick back, and run his empire."

"Probably had his eye on Purgatory for years after he realized Paul had moved here," Silk said. He turned to Mattie. "Anyhow, that's one of the reasons why you didn't see an entire army hanging around the place. But there's another reason for keeping the house guard down to half a dozen or less."

Mattie nodded. "Hugh explained Rainbird doesn't trust anyone and doesn't want too many people around him at any one time."

Hugh glanced back over his shoulder. "It's damn tough to find even five or six men you can trust with your life. Rainbird is pushing it by having that many around him, and he knows it. Probably intends to cut back as soon as he feels secure."

Mattie shivered and clasped her hands. "All right, give me a minute to think. There was Howard inside. He was the only one other than Rainbird who was actually in the house. He wears a gun strapped to his hip like some old western gunslinger. And then there was Goody, who was waiting for me at the beach cottage on St. Gabe."

"Shit," said Hugh. "I'll kill him, too."

Silk shot him a disgusted glance. "Shut up, boss. You ain't thinking straight yet. Let me and Mattie talk while you cool down. Go ahead, Mattie."

"Well, then there was the pilot . . ."

Mattie began to talk more quickly as she started to concentrate. It proved easier to recall details than she would have thought. All those years of art lessons and her work as a gallery owner were paying off. She really had developed an observant eye, she thought proudly as she concluded her report. She looked at Hugh expectantly, waiting for praise. She got a glare that under other circumstances would have frozen her socks off.

Silk tried to compensate. "Great job, Mattie." He gave her a slap on the back that nearly unseated her. "One of the best recon reports I've ever heard. This is going to make things a lot easier, ain't it, Hugh?"

"Shit," Hugh said again.

"Sometimes his vocabulary is what you might call limited," Silk confided to Mattie.

"I've noticed," Mattie said. "He told me once it was a sign of stress."

Silk grinned. "Is that right? Stress, huh? And here I thought all along it was just on account of he never learned his manners."

Hugh whipped around to face both of them and resumed his pacing across the cavern floor. "We can't move on Rainbird until we get Mattie out of here."

"It'll take two or three hours to get her to Hades. Another two or three to get back here. If we wait that long we'll lose a lot of the advantage we've got right now," Silk pointed out reasonably. "You know it, boss. Rainbird obviously doesn't realize we're on the island yet.

He's got his men scattered from here to breakfast looking for Mattie. That means he's as isolated as he's ever going to be."

"I know, I know," Hugh growled, shoving his hands into the rear pockets of his jeans. "But I don't like it. If something happens to us, Mattie is trapped here."

"She can take the boat."

"And do what with it?" Hugh stormed. "She's a city girl. What does she know about boats or navigation? How's she going to start the engine, let alone find her way back to Hades?"

"Excuse me," Mattie murmured, clearing her throat. "I would just like to point out that I may be a city girl, but the city I grew up in was Seattle. My father owned a boat all the years I was growing up. Ariel and I can both handle one. And I can read a chart. I wouldn't get lost between here and Hades if I had to find my own way."

"Well, I'll be damned," Silk said in deeply admiring tones.

Hugh gave Mattie a hooded glance. "Is that right?"

She nodded. "It's true. But I don't want to even think about leaving the two of you behind. Hugh, there's got to be a better way of dealing with Rainbird. I don't like the idea of the two of you going in alone against Rainbird and those half dozen overgrown boy scouts he's got around him. Those are not good odds."

"But we don't care about the boy scouts," Hugh explained quietly. His initial outrage was fading now, and a chilling, emotionless quality was entering his voice. "The only one we have to take out is Rainbird. When he's gone, the boy scouts will scatter fast enough. They're nothing without a leader."

"How will you get into the house?" Mattie asked, wishing she could find a way to talk them out of the whole project and knowing it was impossible.

"I told you Cormier built a lot of emergency exits from his house. They work just as well as secret entrances." Hugh ran a hand through his hair, frowning in thought. "We'll use the one in the kitchen this time."

"Sounds good to me," Silk said. "Get in, get out, and we're off the island before anyone even knows what happened. We'll be eating dinner on Hades."

"Wait," said Mattie, feeling desperate. "Are you sure there isn't some other way to do this? Couldn't you get more help?"

Silk grinned. "Hey, we've got you, Mattie Sharpe. So far you've been more use than a whole company of Marines."

Mattie groaned.

"Okay," Hugh said finally, his tone utterly cold now. "You're right, Silk. This is the best chance we're going to get. Let's go do it."

Mattie stood up. "Hugh?"

"Yeah, babe?" Hugh was crouched beside a pile of equipment, his back to her.

"Promise me you won't take any . . . any unnecessary chances." That sounded stupid. Of course he was going to take chances.

"Sure, babe. No unnecessary chances." He shoved a knife into his boot and checked his revolver.

"I love you," Mattie whispered.

Hugh thrust the revolver into his belt and stood up. "I love you, too, babe," he said absently. His attention was clearly on his preparations, not on the words he had so casually just spoken.

Mattie smiled mistily. He did not even realize that this was the first time he had actually said it aloud. The man could be so dense at times. "I know," she said softly. "I wasn't sure until recently. But now I know."

He glanced at her, briefly surprised. And then he scowled. "About time."

"Yes. Things have been a little confused lately," she murmured apologetically.

"Only because you were confused," he said bluntly.

"You may be right. Just be careful. You, too, Silk. You hear me? I don't want you to do anything that could cut short the brilliant artistic career you've got ahead of you."

He grinned and ruffled her hair with his huge paw as she walked over and hugged him tightly. "Hey, don't worry about me, Mattie Sharpe. You and I are going to get rich together. That's a promise."

"You two can talk about what you're going to do with all your ill-gotten gains some other time," Hugh said, heading for the tunnel that led to the waterfalls. "Let's get this business over with first."

"Right, boss."

Mattie watched as the two men vanished, silent as ghosts, in the caves of Purgatory.

And then she sat down to wait.

Hugh heard the voices in the cavern behind the twin waterfalls and knew that two of Rainbird's six-man bodyguard would have to be taken care of before he and Silk went on to the house. Mattie wasn't going to approve. Probably best not to mention the matter to her later.

He switched off the flashlight and waited for Silk to move up alongside.

"Two?" Silk asked.

"Yeah, I think so."

"Sounds like they're going to try to search these caves."

"Fools." Hugh thought a minute. "Might be easiest to just let them get lost."

"They're probably not that dumb. They'll use a rope or something."

"Rope, huh? Then let's hope they've got enough to hang themselves."

Hugh stepped into a side tunnel that branched off the main one, and Silk moved in beside him. Anyone who came this way would have to walk right past them.

A flashlight flickered in the main corridor. The first man in military fatigues moved past, a rope trailing out behind him.

"You see anything, Mark?" called a voice from the main cavern.

"Nothing. I can't tell if she came this way or not."

"She's probably got herself good and lost already. Rainbird's going to be pissed."

Mark halted and shouted down the corridor. "Miss Sharpe, call out if you can hear me. No need to be afraid. We'll get you out of here." His voice ricocheted off the cavern walls.

Hugh studied his quarry. Mattie was right. The kid was too damn young to be playing mercenary. But, then, Rainbird had always attracted bright-eyed young men who had dreams of being heroes.

Hugh remembered a few of his own youthful dreams as he stepped out into the corridor and brought the butt of his gun down on the hapless mercenary's head. Mark went down without a sound. Hugh dragged him into the side corridor.

"Mark?" The voice at the other end of the rope was not anxious yet. Just curious.

Silk reached past Hugh and tugged gently on the rope, as if Mark were still moving.

"See anything, Mark?" Another flashlight beam cut through the darkness of the main corridor. "Come on, Mark. What's going on? Where are you? You okay?"

Silk tugged on the rope again, drawing it farther into the main tunnel. The second young man followed it slowly, like a wary fish after a lure. When he went past the side tunnel, Hugh stepped out and used the butt of the revolver a second time.

"Got him." Hugh bent down and dragged the second man into the side tunnel.

Silk moved in and quickly used the rope to secure both unconscious men.

"Well, that eases the odds a bit," Silk observed as they made their way out past the waterfalls. "With any luck the rest of 'em will keep floundering around out here in the jungle for a while, and we won't have to cross their paths at all."

"There's always good old Howard the vegetarian gourmet chef."

The moon was almost gone by the time Hugh and Silk made their way over the waterfall pool rocks and found the stream. There was a familiar oppressive weight to the warm air. Hugh sensed the rain that was on its way.

They followed the stream until the sound of the ocean was clear, and then Hugh angled to the right. He and Silk pushed more or less blindly through the jungle, using what was left of the moon as a guide until the lights of the house came into view.

"No problem," Silk observed. "Plenty of cover right up to the house, itself."

"Let's go."

Hugh fumbled a bit trying to find the hidden entrance that opened inside the pantry. It had been a couple of years since Cormier had taken him on the grand tour of the white mansion. But he eventually found the panel in the side of the wall. It was shrouded in pale white lilies.

Inside the entrance a short flight of steps led up to the darkened pantry. Hugh risked the flashlight long enough to get a feel for the arrangement of canned goods, liquor bottles, and supplies that were stacked on the floor. Silk trailed silently behind him.

Hugh turned the flashlight onto the wall and found the circuit-breaker panel. He hit the switches, shutting off everything. Then he opened the pantry door onto darkness. He and Silk crawled out into the kitchen and waited.

"What the hell?" Rainbird's voice came from out on the veranda, sounding annoyed but not alarmed.

"The electricity has gone off, Colonel. I'll check the panel. Probably blown a fuse."

"Contact the men and tell them to get back to the house immediately," Rainbird snapped.

"But I'm sure it's just a problem with the fuses or maybe down at the generator. I'm pretty good with that kind of thing, Colonel . . ."

"I said call in the others. Do it now, Howard. And find some flashlights."

"Yes, sir. I think there's one in the kitchen."

Crouched in shadows behind a counter, Hugh listened to boot heels ring on marble. The redoubtable Howard was hastening to obey orders.

"Mine," said Silk in an almost soundless whisper.

Hugh nodded and Silk moved across the short distance to step back into the pantry.

Howard came around the edge of the counter, yanking open drawers and groping inside. Then his gaze fell on Hugh.

"Hi," Hugh said pleasantly.

Howard's mouth fell open, and he groped for his gun. Silk stepped out of the closet and coshed him. Howard slumped to the floor.

"You keep an eye on the main entrance," Hugh muttered. "If the rest of them come back, they'll probably come that way."

"Right. Give my regards to Rainbird. Tell him I'm sure sorry he didn't die six years ago."

"I'll do that."

Hugh moved quickly through the gloom of the living room and on down the hall. All of the main rooms opened onto the veranda, where Rainbird was standing. Hugh wanted the shortest approach to his quarry. From the sound of Rainbird's voice when he had given orders to Howard, the library would probably provide the ideal point from which to step out onto the veranda.

As soon as Hugh moved silently into the library, he saw he had calculated correctly. Through the open French windows he saw Rainbird standing with both hands planted on the veranda railing. He was peering into the darkness below him, obviously searching for the men who should have been returning on the double from the hunt for Mattie.

"Howard? Have you recalled them yet? Damn it, I said move, boy. I don't like this setup. Something's wrong. I want every available man back here right now." Rainbird paused when there was no immediate response. "Howard?"

"Howard's busy, Colonel. You know how it is. Always a lot to do in the kitchen." Hugh stepped out onto the veranda, his revolver in his hand.

"*Abbott.*" Rainbird swung around, clawing for a pistol that was stuck in his belt.

Hugh kicked out suddenly, aiming for the pistol. He caught it with the toe of his boot just as Rainbird started to aim. The weapon went flying over the railing.

"Still as fast as ever, aren't you?" Rainbird smiled thinly as he slowly lowered his hand.

"Not quite," Hugh said. "But fast enough to do this job."

"Do you think so? You were good, Abbott, but I was always a little quicker than you, remember? And unlike you, I've stayed in training for the past six years. Besides," Rainbird taunted softly, "we both know you aren't hard enough to pull that trigger on an unarmed man. That was always your biggest weakness, Abbott. That and the fact that you didn't take orders very well."

"You mean not well enough to walk into that trap you set in Los Rios? Why did you do it, Rainbird? That's the one thing we could never figure out. What was in it for you that made it worth trying to get the rest of us killed?"

"Money, of course. A great deal of money. And the timing couldn't have been better. You, Cormier, and Silk and the others were getting too difficult to control. You were asking too many questions about the jobs. Men who question their orders are useless to a good commander."

"So you decided to get rid of us. I guess that makes sense from your point of view." Hugh smiled bleakly. "You were smart to fake your own death when you realized that some of us hadn't died in that ambush. You knew we'd come looking if we thought you were still alive."

"Cormier thought he'd seen a ghost when I came through the door," Rainbird said with satisfaction. "You know, the old man was still surprisingly fast, too. He actually had his hands on that old Beretta of his when I shot him."

"I know."

Rainbird nodded. "So it was you who found him right afterward. I came back to clean up the place later after I'd secured the island. I realized someone else had been here. Footprints in the blood. Two rented vehicles parked nearby and no sign of anyone. And then I got word that you were looking for whoever had killed Cormier. Once you start something, you don't give up until you've finished, I'll say that much for you, Abbott. I knew I had to take you out along with Silk and the woman."

"And a poor jerk named Rosey."

Rainbird shrugged negligently. "He knew too much, and he was going to sell the info."

"You were right about one thing. I wouldn't have stopped looking until I figured out who killed Paul."

Rainbird smiled a gentle, vaguely regretful smile. "Yes. I understood that from the beginning."

"It was a mistake to kill Cormier. But it was an even bigger mistake to involve Mattie in this."

"Ah, yes. The very interesting Miss Sharpe. I congratulate you on her, Abbott. She is a woman after my own heart. She has spirit and intelligence. And a certain style. I like that. You'll forgive me if I say I'm rather surprised you had the brains to appreciate her. You were never the sort to understand or admire subtlety in a woman."

"I might be a slow learner, Rainbird, but I do, eventually, catch on."

"And have you learned to kill a man in cold blood?"

"I think that in your case I'll be able to handle it."

Rainbird grinned, looking genuinely amused. "No, Abbott, I don't think so. You'll lose your nerve at the last minute. We both know it."

In that instant a shot roared out through the jungle night, shattering the glass in the French window behind Hugh. Hugh fired over the edge of the railing and leaped for the cover of the darkened library.

Rainbird acted instantly, grabbing the knife out of his boot and launching himself after Hugh. Hugh spun around and raised the revolver. But he wasn't fast enough.

As always, Rainbird's incredible reflexes stood him in good stead. His weight crashed into Hugh, and both men went sprawling on the library floor.

Something sharp slashed at Hugh's arm. He felt the revolver fall from his hand, and then he was rolling swiftly away from Rainbird's knife.

Rainbird came after him, kicking out savagely. His boot caught Hugh on the arm. The pain was not the worst of it. The temporary loss of muscle control in his right arm was another problem altogether. It could get him killed.

Shots crackled from the far end of the house. Silk was returning fire to whoever was shooting from the jungle. Another shot into the library sent a shower of sharp glass hail down on Hugh and Rainbird.

Hugh saw the knife in Rainbird's hand glint briefly in the shadows. He jerked away again, groping frantically for his own boot knife.

But there was no time to grasp it. Rainbird was coming at him again, his killer's smile gleaming in the darkness.

Rainbird had always been faster. Faster and infinitely more ruthless because he took a strange delight in the act of bringing death to others.

Hugh scrambled backward, aware of sensation returning to his right arm. He barely dodged another swinging thrust of the knife as he got to his feet. He found himself up against a display case. Without looking at what was in the case, he smashed the glass lid with his bare hand and reached inside. The jagged edges of glass bit deep. Blood streamed down his arm.

His fingers closed around the hilt of a sword just as Rainbird leaped in for the kill.

Hugh yanked the sword out of the case. It was surprisingly heavy. But the weight and balance felt strangely comfortable, even familiar in his hand.

He brought the weapon around in front of himself and thrust the blade out and up just as Rainbird came hurtling through the air.

The sword sank into Rainbird's chest with sickening ease. A shattering scream rent the darkness and then there was an unholy silence.

For a few seconds Hugh just stood staring down at Rainbird's body. He looked up as Silk came pounding down the hall and into the library.

"He dead?" Silk asked, coming to a halt.

"Yeah. This time he's dead."

"About time." Silk squinted in the shadows. "You okay?"

Hugh nodded.

"Always knew you were faster than him. You just needed the right motivation is all. Come on, boss. We got to get out of here before the rest of those boy scouts get back. Mattie'll have our heads if we let anything delay us."

"I didn't plan to hang around." Hugh realized he was still grasping the sword. He looked down. It was the one he had arranged for Cormier to sell to Charlotte Vailcourt, the one called *Valor*.

*Death to all who dare claim this blade until it shall be taken up by the avenger and cleansed in the blood of the betrayer.*

"You going to take that sword with you?" Silk asked, already moving toward the door.

"Might as well. Charlotte will like having it in her collection. And I think Paul would have wanted her to have it."

There was no sense trying to explain to Silk that *Valor* felt clean now, Hugh decided as he followed his friend out into the hall. He could not even explain the feeling to himself.

Hugh paused briefly in the doorway and glanced back at the body of the betrayer. Rainbird lay in a widening pool of blood. Hugh suddenly remembered another ancient prophecy. *All they that take the sword shall perish with the sword.*

"You know, Silk, I'm sure glad you and me wised up a few years back and decided to get ourselves a couple of new professions," Hugh said. "Nobody stays fast enough forever."

# 20

Mattie stood on the beach in the moonlight and watched the glistening breakers as they rose and fell on the night-darkened water. The lights of Hugh's cottage gleamed in the shadows behind her, but she did not turn around. Hugh was busy on the phone inside the cottage, talking to Charlotte Vailcourt. Mattie had walked down to the beach to think.

Not that she had not already had ample opportunity to be alone with her own thoughts during the excruciating wait in the cavern on Purgatory. The short time that Hugh and Silk had been gone had seemed an eternity. When they had finally shown up with the blood-stained sword called *Valor,* she had known what had happened. She had not asked for explanations.

Without a word she had bandaged Hugh's bleeding arm while Silk readied the cruiser. They had been on their way within ten minutes. Nobody had said much on the long ride to Hades, where they spent what was left of the night with the local doctor, who treated Hugh's arm. All three of them had fallen asleep from sheer exhaustion, risen early, and been on their way back to St. Gabriel by dawn. And through it all Mattie had said nothing of her plans. She had been waiting for the right opening.

"Mattie?" Hugh's voice was soft in the shadows.

She turned and smiled at him. "Finally finish satisfying Aunt Charlotte's curiosity?"

"Yeah. Man, that woman can sure ask questions. But I think everything's under control at both ends now. The guy who broke into your place finally woke up. He's keeping his mouth shut, but the cops have him cold on three or four solid charges, including breaking and entering and assault with a deadly weapon. You and Evangeline sure did a number on him."

"Independent businesswomen have to be able to look after themselves."

His mouth crooked. "You're not exactly a soft little city girl, are you?"

"Tough as nails," she assured him.

Hugh grinned briefly. "Well, I wouldn't go that far. Parts of you are very, very soft. Come here, soft little city girl."

She walked into his arms, and they closed around her. "I'm so glad it's over, Hugh. The time I spent waiting for you in that cavern were the worst hours of my life."

"It's over, babe. It's finally over." His hold tightened. He turned her face up to his and kissed her with the old, familiar white-hot passion.

Mattie gloried in the sheer, overwhelming honesty of the embrace. Hugh loved her. She was certain of that now. All the tension that had set her nerves on edge for the past few weeks was finally gone, leaving behind a wondrous sureness and a sense of rightness that would last for the rest of her life.

Mattie's fingers went to the buttons of his shirt. She undid them slowly, letting her hands slip inside to feel the warmth and hardness of his chest.

"Babe," he whispered in an aching tone as her fingertips found the fastening of his jeans. "Babe, you don't know what you do to me."

"Tell me again that you love me, Hugh."

"Damn, but I love you. More than anything else on the planet." He was unbuttoning her shirt now. "Believe me?"

"I believe you. I should have understood months ago when you first started concocting schemes to see me."

"You can say that again. Wasted a lot of time, babe. But I'll let you make it up to me." He grinned, the wicked smile full of sensuality and loving promise.

"Wait, Hugh." Mattie trembled with desire as she felt his hand glide over her breast and down to her waist. "There's something I have to tell you."

"You're pregnant?" he asked eagerly.

Startled, she looked up at him. "Well, no. Not that I know of."

"Too bad. Maybe tonight, huh?" He pulled her down onto the sand and rolled over on top of her. He unzipped his jeans.

"Hugh, I am trying to talk to you about a serious matter."

He kissed her throat. "If it doesn't have anything to do with something really important like you getting pregnant, it can wait until later." His hand moved down to her hips and he tugged at her slacks.

Mattie abandoned the effort to talk to him. When Hugh Abbott made love, he gave it his full attention. She found herself crushed into the soft, warm sand, her clothes stripped from her in a few swift movements.

And then there was nothing of importance in the whole world except the weight and feel of the big man looming over her, blocking out the moonlight, covering her, sheathing himself in her, filling her completely.

*"Mattie."*

She clung to him as he carried her away on the wild, passionate ride into ecstasy. It would always be like this, Mattie thought fleetingly, a whirlwind of shattering excitement, a flashing, thundering, crashing, elemental explosion. A wild, free run with a wolf in the silver moonlight.

And she would never, ever tire of it.

A long time later Mattie felt water on her toes. She stirred beneath Hugh's heavy weight. "Hugh?"

"What's the matter, babe?" he asked in that tone of lazy satisfaction he always had after he'd made love to her.

"I think the tide's coming in."

"It's okay. I can swim."

She gave him a clout on his arm. "Smart ass."

"Ouch."

"Oh, my God, was that your wounded arm?"

"No, but it could have been."

She relaxed as she heard the laughter in his voice. "Hugh, I really do have to talk to you."

He groaned into her shoulder. "This is about Seattle, isn't it?"

"Well, yes, as a matter of fact. In a way it is."

"Babe, I really don't want to talk about it just now."

"We have to discuss this, Hugh. This is our future we're dealing with here."

"Our future is with each other. Everything else will work out. Eventually."

"You keep saying that."

He raised his head reluctantly and looked down into her eyes. His own gaze was shadowed and intense. "I mean it. I've been thinking about it, babe, and I realize there's only one way to handle the problem we've got."

"There is?"

He nodded. "I'm selling Abbott Charters to Silk. I'm moving to Seattle. For real. I just finished talking to Charlotte, and she says the job is full time if I want it. I told her I did."

Mattie looked up at him and knew he was telling her the truth. "Oh, Hugh." She framed his hard face with both hands and smiled gently. "That's very sweet of you, and I will never forget this as long as I live, but it's not the right answer."

He went very still. "You got a better one?" he demanded fiercely. "Because I'm not letting you go, Mattie. And that's a fact."

"Aunt Charlotte and everyone else is right when they say you belong out here, Hugh. This is the home you've made for yourself. You overcame enormous odds to build a new life out here, and I want to be part of that new life."

"Here?" He stared at her. "You're saying you want to move to St. Gabe?"

"I want to live in that beautiful house you're going to build, and I want to have your baby, and I want to start my own business here. And I want to do it all right now. So I am going to go back to Seattle on the first available plane and sell Sharpe Reaction. And then I will pack up all my belongings and move out here to St. Gabriel."

Hugh looked dazed. "But what kind of business are you going to build here?"

"I'm not precisely sure yet, but I think there's going to be plenty of opportunity for an ex-gallery owner with ties to the West Coast artistic community. I've got a few dreams I'd like to try. I'm going to look into the possibility of starting an artists' colony. A place where people like Shock Value Frederickson can come and get refreshed, maybe. For a price, of course."

"You're going to invite all your artsy-craftsy friends to come out here?" Hugh was clearly appalled.

"They'll spend money, Hugh. Lots of it. They'll love St. Gabriel. And they'll love the idea of a Pacific island art colony. And on the side I think I'll open a tourist-oriented boutique. I'll feature Silk's paintings for starters. And I think I can persuade Evangeline Dangerfield to move out here and set up a clothing design business. I can sell her creations alongside Silk's."

"The mind boggles."

"You've said yourself St. Gabriel is on the verge of getting discovered. I'll make a fortune selling stuff to the tourists while you clean up with Abbott Charters. Silk will made a bundle on his paintings, and Evangeline will be able to go into a whole new line of work. We'll all get rich, fat, and happy."

Hugh laughed softly, turned onto his back and pulled her down on top of him. "Life is never going to be dull with you, babe, I'll say that much."

"Hugh, the tide . . ."

"Like I said, I can swim and I'll take care of you. Trust me, babe."

She smiled and bent down to kiss him full on his beautiful, sexy mouth. "I do."

"About time."

Charlotte Vailcourt closed the folder on her desk, leaned back in her executive chair, and looked at Hugh, who was standing at the window watching the people on the street below. "An excellent proposal, Hugh. You have a talent for organization and planning. I imagine it will stand you in good stead as you build Abbott Charters."

"I learned a lot from you, Charlotte. I appreciate it."

"You have more than repaid me." She paused. "I would like to be able to call on you from time to time as we implement this security proposal. Are you going to be available for the occasional consultation?"

"As long as it's occasional, I think I can manage to fit you into my schedule."

"Thank you," Charlotte murmured with a smile. She glanced across the room to where *Valor* lay on black velvet in the display case. "And thank you for bringing back the sword. It is a fine blade, isn't it?"

"If you like that kind of thing."

Charlotte smiled in genuine amusement. "Well, I don't suppose I need to worry about the legend attached to it any longer, do I? One way or another, it seems to have been fulfilled." She gave Hugh an odd, speculative glance.

Hugh shrugged. He was no longer interested in *Valor*. It was a good fighting tool that had been available when he needed it. That was all that mattered.

"What's Mattie doing? Still packing?" Charlotte asked.

"Today she went shopping for her trousseau with Evangeline."

"This should be interesting. I can't wait to see what she's bought under Evangeline's guidance. Imagine going shopping with a professional call girl."

"Ex-professional. Evangeline is a real businesswoman now. Mattie says she's bought an industrial-grade sewing machine and about half a million spools of thread to take out to St. Gabe with her. She's planning to ask Silk to design some fabric for her. You know, I think Silk's going to go crazy when he meets Evangeline."

"You're going to have an interesting little group out there on St. Gabriel."

Hugh turned away from the window with a smile. "You'll have to come out and pay us a visit."

"I'll do that. You'll take good care of our Mattie, won't you?"

"Mattie is my life," Hugh said simply.

"All she's ever really wanted is you. Since the day she met you."

"All I ever wanted was her. It just took me a little time to realize it, that's all." An image of Rainbird dying on the point of a sword flickered in Hugh's mind. "You know, Charlotte, unlike some people I could name, I'm getting smarter as I get older."

"That's what makes you a survivor. You've got good genes, Hugh. So does Mattie. When are the two of you going to have a baby?"

"As soon as I can talk her into it."

"Think that will take long?"

Hugh laughed. "No, ma'am. Not long at all. She thinks I'll make a terrific father. Told me so herself," he added proudly. *A real home. The way it was supposed to be.*

"I think you will, too. The world needs more good men like you. Mattie saw your true potential the day she met you."

Hugh hid what he feared might be a telltale red in his cheeks by glancing at his watch. "I'd better get downstairs to my office. Time for another batch of bug juice. You know, I'm actually starting to like the stuff."

"You like it because you know Mattie spends an inordinate amount of time and energy concocting it just for you."

"That's how I knew for certain that she still loved me," Hugh admitted. "I figured she wouldn't go to all that trouble to feed me right if she didn't care about me. You'll be at the wedding?"

"Wouldn't miss it for the world. Evangeline is designing the bridal gown, I hear. Should be a sight to behold. I wonder if it will be in red."

Hugh was still laughing when he got off the elevator and walked into his office to pour himself a glass of bug juice.

Mattie paid for her cup of herbal tea and carried it over to the table where two extraordinarily good-looking men in their early thirties were waiting for her. Both men were wearing expensive Italian-cut linen jackets over their equally expensive designer shirts and trousers. Both had an air of casual, urbane elegance. Both also had physiques to die for. Mattie smiled to herself. It wasn't every day a woman got to sit down with a couple of hunks like this.

"Gentlemen," she announced as she put her tea down on the table and seated herself on a delicate wire-frame chair, "do I have a deal for you."

"We're listening," one of them said equably.

"You've got our full attention," the other murmured, sipping cappuccino with languid grace.

Mattie proceeded to lay out her plans in precise detail. She ran through the bulk of her proposal and then added a rider. "There's just one other thing."

"Anything for you, Mattie, you know that."

"I'd like a guarantee that for the next two years you will agree to show the works of Flynn Grafton."

"Don't be ridiculous," the first man drawled. "You don't have to ask us for a written guarantee. We would kill for Grafton's work. Saw it at the opening the other night. Fabulous. Absolutely fabulous."

Mattie nodded. "Good. I thought you'd agree. Then you like the overall arrangement?"

"You've got a deal, Mattie," the second man announced. He glanced at his friend. "Right?"

"A deal," the first man agreed, putting down his cup.

Mattie started to say something else but paused when the hair on the nape of her neck stirred. Instinctively she turned her head to see Hugh striding through the small espresso shop. His gray eyes simmered with a vaguely annoyed expression.

"Suzanne told me you were down the street having coffee with a couple of collectors," Hugh said, surveying the two exquisite young gods sitting on the other side of the table. "Just what do you two collect?"

"Anything Mattie says we should." The first man returned Hugh's gaze with interest. His eyes started low and traveled slowly upward to Hugh's broad shoulders. "She has absolutely fabulous taste, you know. We've never gone wrong when we've been guided by Mattie. Do feel free to join us."

"Thanks. I was going to do that," Hugh declared, sounding thoroughly disgruntled now. He dropped onto the seat beside Mattie and glowered at everyone.

Mattie grinned. "Hugh, I'd like you to meet Ryan Turner and Travis Preston. These two gentlemen are currently making a killing as stockbrokers. They have wisely decided to get out of the market while they're ahead and go into something with a little more class."

"Is that right?" Hugh cocked a brow. "Just what are they going to do now to keep themselves in those spiffy duds?"

"They're going to take over my gallery. Meet the new owners of Sharpe Reaction."

"A pleasure, I'm sure," said Travis, his gaze lingering on Hugh's shoulders again.

"Yes, indeed," Ryan murmured. "A great pleasure. Mattie, dear, you do have such wonderful taste."

"Well," Hugh said philosophically, "that's one less thing for me to worry about."

"What's that?" Mattie asked.

"When Suzanne told me I'd find you sitting here with a couple of real hunks, I'll admit I had a few brief qualms. It occurred to me I might find myself having to defend your virtue."

"Oh, God," Ryan said, "I really do love the machismo, don't you, Travis? So utterly primitive."

"Didn't you know?" Travis said to his friend in feigned surprise. "This is the one from Ariel Sharpe's Elemental period."

"That explains it, of course," Ryan said with a sigh.

Hugh looked at Mattie. "You know something? I think I've finally had enough of the wonders of life here in the sophisticated fast lane of the big city. It's time to go home."

"Yes," said Mattie. "I think it is."

Mattie woke before dawn on the morning she and Hugh were scheduled to leave for St. Gabriel. She stretched and slowly opened her eyes, aware of Hugh's heavy, masculine warmth beside her. She glanced at the clock and reached out to touch her husband's shoulder.

"Hugh?"

"I'm awake, babe." He curved his arm around her, drawing her down onto his bare chest. His gaze was sleepy and sexy and full of a very male contentment. "What time is it?"

"Four-thirty."

"Time to get up. We've got a plane to catch."

Mattie smiled and the fateful words she had spoken nearly a year ago came back to her. She said them again. "Take me with you, Hugh. I love you so much. Please take me with you."

His hands caught in her hair, and he dragged her mouth down to his. "Don't you know I couldn't leave without you, babe? You're my whole world."

This time they both caught the six o'clock flight to St. Gabriel and the future they would share together.